UNANIMOUS PRAISE FOR
Devil's Juggler

"For once the promotional literature . . . has it precisely right. Murray Smith's *DEVIL'S JUGGLER* actually *is* 'a blockbuster.'. . . Where has this guy been? . . . Smith's cool, detached writing will keep you plowing ahead with pleasure."

—*St. Louis Post-Dispatch*

"This effort by first-time novelist Murray Smith rates right up there with many of the novels by contemporary masters of the spy genre from the pens of the likes of John le Carré, Frederick Forsyth, or Bill Granger. . . . All three [story lines] are individually fascinating—with the professional and personal lives of the protagonists becoming so inextricably entwined—and then combine in a laser-beam intensity . . . high international intrigue and excitement."

—*Topeka Capital-Journal*

"A thriller that twists and turns to a chilling ending. . . ."

—*Des Moines Register*

"Exceptionally well written. . . . Smith has superb narrative skills. . . . the character of Jardine, an urbane, competent, and thoroughly ruthless man, is particularly well realized. . . . Thriller fans, take note."

—*Mystery News*

A BOOK-OF-THE-MONTH CLUB ALTERNATE SELECTION

DEVIL'S JUGGLER

MURRAY SMITH

POCKET STAR BOOKS
New York London Toronto Sydney Tokyo Singapore

Printed in the U.S.A.

This book is a work of fiction. Names, characters, places and incidents either are products of the author's imagination or are used fictitiously. Any resemblance to actual events or locales or persons, living or dead, is entirely coincidental.

A Pocket Star Book published by
POCKET BOOKS, a division of Simon & Schuster Inc.
1230 Avenue of the Americas, New York, NY 10020

Copyright © 1993 by Murray Smith

ISBN: 0-671-78468-4

First Pocket Books Paperback printing February 1994

10 9 8 7 6 5 4 3 2 1

POCKET STAR BOOKS and colophon are registered trademarks of Simon & Schuster Inc.

Cover art by Don Brautigam

Printed in the U.S.A.

For Jane

For Jane

The author wishes to thank the late Colonel Mario Castillo-Ruiz, formerly of the Colombian Policia Nacional, Tom Beattie, Sid Telford, formerly of the U.S. State Department, Sergeant of Detectives Ernie Favaro (the unwitting role model for all that's best in the NYPD), Lieutenant Ray Donelly, NYPD, and the several members of the U.S., British, Irish, and Colombian police, intelligence, and drug-enforcement communities who must remain nameless, for their vital assistance, their patience, and, more important, for their trust.

And special thanks to Christian and Kiaran, for their encouragement and irreverent comments throughout.

The author wishes to thank the late Colonel Ramiro Castillo Ruiz, formerly of the Colombian Police National; Thon Beattie, Sid Telford, formerly of the U.S. State Department, Sergeant of Detectives Ernie Fazio (the unwitting role model for all that's best in the NYPD), Lieutenant Ray Donahue, NYPD, and the several members of the U.S., British, Irish, and Colombian police, intelligence, and drug enforcement communities who must remain nameless, for their vital assistance, their patience and, more important, for their trust.

And special thanks to Christian and Harriet, for their encouragement and irreverent comments throughout.

corrida (ko-rē-*th*a) n [Sp., lit., act of running] A
bullfight.

———

The blood-dimmed tide is loosed, and
everywhere
The ceremony of innocence is drowned . . .

—W. B. YEATS 1865–1939

. . . And that's exactly how it ended. The one who had trusted him lying there in that tiny incense-wraithed chapel, tall candles on ancient five-foot-high holders. One candle at each corner of the casket. The male dog yelping and whining directly below, unable to accept that the cold, beloved thing in the box above was losing, hour by irredeemable hour, its familiar scent of sweat and tobacco and rum and gun oil.

It had been raining. October in Bogotá sees much rain. Streams of dung-colored water filled the gutters. The narrow street led down to the start of one of the *carreras* to the south of the city, leading through sprawling beggar- and cutpurse-ridden slums into the vibrant old quarter, the Candelaria, where white powder and flesh of all shades are traded for pennies. And the bars are packed and the music and laughter are imbibed with a quiet desperation that acknowledges this night might be one's last.

He found the car, an old Toyota with armor plates on

the doors and behind the backseat. Bulletproof windshield. Stiffened suspension and alloy cylinder head with straight-through twin exhausts. Courtesy of a young publisher who had branched out into the protected-car business. A profitable business to be in, in Colombia. For all the good it had done the man whose corpse lay in the chapel. The car started after a few turns of the ignition key, each one weaker than the one before. A tiny beggar child stared at him from the drying, steaming, potholed road. Round cheeks and Tartar eyes of the Indian natives. Old eyes. Past fear. Beyond pleading. The child held a metal ashtray at him. For a second the man thought he was being offered a gift, till he realized that was the receptacle he was supposed to put some coins in. He stared into the boy's liquid brown eyes, which were firmly fixed on the faded door of the Toyota. Then he gently touched the gas pedal, thinking anyone remotely sensible would have checked the car for some kind of bomb.

The bar in the *hostería* was medium busy. Three lithe and tranquil musicians in Spanish bullfighters' suits played a salsa version of "Honky Tonk Woman." Ramón, sitting moodily at the bar, glanced up as the man joined him.

"Arriba, hombre . . ." Ramón inclined his head at the bar girl, his eyes even more hooded than usual. The girl placed a tumbler of aquardiente in front of the new arrival, her open and warm smile a silent promise, then she moved away. Leaving him with Ramón and his hooded eyes.

He sipped the *anís*-based liquid, "liquid Colombia" that one had called it, the man lying up there in the hillside chapel, and he raised the tumbler to the mirror behind the bar, staring coldly at what he saw.

"You should leave Colombia now." Ramón shrugged

2

his shoulders as if he were putting on a coat, watching him in the mirror.

"I don't know . . ."

"Luís is waiting outside. There's an Avianca flight at ten. You can make it."

"Where to?"

"Does it matter?"

He gazed at the bar girl, lithe and coffee-colored, busy in conversation with a couple of small-time dealers from Cali, and beyond them, an English executive from one of those companies that insure you so if you get kidnapped they get you back, or try to. In the far corner, at the back near the bullfight band singing "Honky Tonk Woman," were two brothers who owned a ceramics factory on the road to Guatavita, with their wives, out for dinner in the old quarter. Behind him were three men, unknown, but he had heard them speaking German as he crossed to the bar. And in the other corner, beyond Ramón, to his right, at a table next to Ramón's two bodyguards, Mickey Small from the DEA and a colonel from the Colombian secret police, the DAS, whose name he should have known but right then couldn't remember. Maybe because he was appalled at the day's business. The gunfire had left him slightly deaf. And, truth to tell, slightly shaky. He drained the tumbler. Slid it, without looking at her, toward the bar girl, who was already reaching for the bottle, and he knew she was smiling that wonderful Colombian woman's smile.

"You have to go now." Ramón nodded to the girl, pointing down at his own glass.

"Yes. I know." Unconvinced.

"If you stay, the same thing will happen. This place gets under the skin. The country, the danger. Maybe it's the altitude. Who needs cocaine?"

"I don't know, Ramón. How about the band . . . ?" The man managed a wry grin.

Ramón met his gaze, unhooding his eyes a fraction. "I mean the same thing that happened to your . . . colleague. Have you ever read *Heart of Darkness?*"

"Yes, I have."

"Well, this time it happened the other way round."

The man from London, to whom Ramón, in his dealings, referred with his usual economy as *el Inglés*, stopped the tumbler in its rush to his mouth. Time for that on the plane. He didn't want this banana republican to think the firm's people could be fazed by a little thing like . . . homicide? Like murder.

He met Ramón's gaze reflected behind the bottles. "They'll maybe send someone to talk to you."

"They'll get nothing from me, *amigo.*"

El Inglés shoved his tumbler from hand to hand, a couple of inches apart, on the polished bar. Ramón affected indifference.

"So if I'm going to get that plane I'd better go."

The former deputy director of Colombia's secret service inclined his hooded-eyed head at the mirror and one bodyguard rose, straightening his coat over his holster. Then Ramón asked, almost offhandedly, "Do you mind if we use the Toyota? I can have the plates changed. A respray."

The man blinked, confused, like he had been when the beggar child offered his ashtray. Of course. Waste not, want not. "Sure. If you find anything belonging to him . . ."

"Send it to his wife?"

"Destroy it."

And that was how it ended. How the hell, he asked himself, as he rose and glanced at the bodyguard waiting by the door, how in the name of God could it have come to this?

1

JANE DOE
AT GRAND
CENTRAL

The crumpled plastic bag would be about three inches by two when it was straightened out and smoothed flat. Sergeant Eddie Lucco was not, to be a hundred percent honest, entirely sure at what stage of the forensic examination the crumpled scrap would be straightened, but he knew that when it was, when it was placed with tweezers into the transparent exhibit bag, it would measure about three inches by two. And the grains of white powder would by that time have been removed and analyzed and identified as coca powder cut and reduced maybe eight times from its pure state, mixed with chalk, baking powder—anything white of similar consistency and not too harmful—then mixed in equal quantities with baking soda and boiled in a pan of water until there was nothing left but the crystals that are called crack.

And the pale, wasted young hand, outstretched and fingers curled upward, it would probably be straightened too, at some juncture. Lucco realized that was a favorite phrase he used in his ruminations. At some juncture.

5

Judge Almeda used it, in New York District Court Number Five. A tough old bird. But self-educated. Took his law degree after eight years playing piano at the Algonquin, the nights nobody famous was there. Part of the American Dream.

Lucco stared down at the dead girl. Couldn't be more than eighteen. Tell her about the American Dream. And being a good cop with ingrained habits, he glanced at his wristwatch. It was ten before seven in the morning.

Back at the 14th Precinct, the big, black cop Benwell was locking up two kids aged about sixteen in the cage, his shoulders as broad as his bulky hips, made enormous with the beltload of regulation Smith & Wesson .38 revolver in its leather holster, nightstick, handcuffs, and a couple of pouches, one for the radio and one for the battery. Benwell glanced across the floor, past two detectives and a hooker who was making a formal protest to the desk sergeant about some omission of courtesy in her recent arrest. He nodded to Lucco, turning the key in the cage door, and ambled over to him.

"Sorta night . . . ?"

" 'Nuther bitch."

"Way it goes, man."

They met each other's glance, stone faces only just made human by friendship. Nothing fazed them. Eddie Lucco, the son of Neapolitans from Italy, slapped hands with Benwell as they passed. He was still thinking about that kid lying crumpled in the mortuary-clean rest room at Grand Central.

Eddie Lucco was a Homicide detective, rank of sergeant, working out of the 14th Precinct on nine separate killings and suspicious deaths that had happened in the last two months within the 14th's jurisdiction. Four drug pushers, two of them juveniles; two storekeepers, one black, female, aged forty-five, married, four children, one first-generation Polish, aged sixty-one, widowed, two married daughters; a taxi driver; a white male aged about thirty, height five-eleven, weight one sixty-four, missing third digit left hand; and a Hispanic vagrant aged between forty and fifty, height unknown because of the detail that his head was missing, those last two unidentified and known in the trade as John Does.

Lucco had not in fact been on duty when the kid was discovered. He had just seen off Nancy, his wife, who was taking the early-morning train from New York to Albany, where she was defending some realty fraudster. With luck the case would drag on the whole week, which would bring in more than he made in a couple of months.

The rest-room attendant, a black lady called Bessie Smith who had been there for about eighteen years and witnessed four homicides, a couple of dozen muggings, and two gang rapes, had come out onto the railroad-station concourse looking all het up and bothered. She had recognized Eddie Lucco as he passed, his mind half on his wife in the departed train, on her cooking and her legs and her rising legal career (in that order) and half on the murder by mini-Uzi machine pistol of the two juvenile crack pushers who had died the previous Friday in a deserted back lot less than eighty yards from the precinct station house.

"Sir, ain't you a cop? Mister, I remember you was down here last year an' took three of us back for a statement and gave us coffee an' got real mad whun we couldn't make an ID on Norman the crazy guy with the harelip."

Lucco had grinned and said he even remembered her name because not only was he a jazz enthusiast and for him Bessie Smith was the equal of Billie Holiday but he also had read the Edward Albee play, *The Death of Bessie Smith*.

"You mean there's two of us . . . ?" Bessie had heard all this before. Then she told him about the kid who had collapsed in the john and maybe she was dead but maybe there was a chance her young, too-thin body was capable of revival. Lucco had raced down the steps and even finding no pulse and a dreadful coldness to the limbs had gotten down on his knees and clamped the girl's jaw open, administering mouth-to-mouth resuscitation, oblivious to the flecks of vomit, oblivious to the smell of death. He was still on his knees, two fingers on the slender wrist, ascertaining the obvious, when the two Metro North uniformed cops arrived, and he remained there till the Patrol Supervisor sergeant arrived from the 14th Precinct, in which is located Grand Central Station. This officer, Eugene Wharton, on the last hour of his shift, thus became, according to the procedures of the NYPD, the Crime Scene Supervisor, which accounted for the look of genuine grief on his once-handsome Irish face.

By the time Eddie Lucco was back at work in Homicide, the corpse of the girl, as yet unidentified and therefore referred to informally as a Jane Doe, had been photographed, brusquely examined, and pronounced deceased by a middle-aged doctor with whiskey on his breath, and wheeled on a stretcher, face covered, past hurrying railroad travelers, ignored, unnoticed, and transported by ambulance to Bellevue Hospital on First Avenue at East Twenty-eighth Street, where Eugene Wharton would, without reluctance, hand over the cadaver to a Missing Persons detective who would fingerprint, photograph, and examine the corpse for any significant marks of potential identification. Then would come the autopsy.

Meanwhile, three thousand, one hundred and four miles to the east, it was two fifty-four P.M. and another legal process was occurring, this time in the Dublin Criminal Court, where sat Justice Eugene Pearson, aged forty-two and on his way up, headed for the very top. And politics, too, so the taproom gossip said, for wasn't the next *taoiseach* his former partner in Pearson and Pearson and still a mentor and close friend? And didn't the press love him? And even the English press and bar grudgingly admitted that since Justice Pearson had sat on extradition matters things had been, well, smoother. Less contentious. Less infuriating.

Justice Pearson knew that his half-moon glasses gave him the look of a caricature judge. But they helped him to see right to the back of the courtroom and read his notes and various items submitted at the same time. And he refused to pander to any considerations as to what he looked like to the rest of humanity. He gazed over his half-moon glasses at the man being considered for extradition. Dominic Mary MacMurrough. Dominic "Mad Dog" MacMurrough to the press. A slightly built, good-enough-looking fellow, with intelligent eyes and a relaxed, gently amused demeanor. Comfortable with himself.

The judge cleared his throat, holding MacMurrough's relaxed stare with his own, impersonal gaze.

"Mr. MacMurrough. Eight RUC police officers. Three British soldiers. A man strapped to the wheel of his van and forced to drive into a military checkpoint while his wife, seven months with child, and two infant children were held at gunpoint by your accomplices. This man forced to drive to certain death in the most callous and sadistic manner it's a wonder he didn't die of a heart attack first. Nine civilians killed or maimed by explosive devices planted by yourself or at your direction. I study my notes of this extradition hearing and nowhere do I find that you deny these charges which are laid against you by the British Crown Prosecution Service and for which you have been charged in England before your alleged escape from custody. Do you have anything to say to further your counsel's case that your alleged offenses did not occur within the jurisdiction of this court, that you do not recognize the authority of the United Kingdom's legal system for offenses allegedly committed in Northern Ireland, or the Six Counties, as you refer to them, that the alleged offenses were of a political nature and not therefore subject to the law of extradition within the constitution of the Republic of Ireland and that even if the foregoing were not proven in law, the judicial system in the United Kingdom, with regard to so-called Republican offenses, is such that you would not be guaranteed a fair trial and that your physical safety and perhaps your life would be in danger? Do you, before I make my decision, have anything else to say . . . ?"

Justice Pearson listened to the furious scribbling of reporters' pens in the silence that followed. Somebody coughed. He continued to gaze, imperturbable, at the prisoner, aware of the gazes of the relatives and sympathizers and worse on the public seats. If MacMurrough was wise, he would keep his mouth shut, just as if he were in Castlereagh, the dreaded Belfast interrogation center for the Royal Ulster Constabulary. But they seldom were that wise. After all, wasn't this the Republic? And wasn't this what the Republican Movement was fighting for? Provisional IRA or Republican Sinn Fein or Irish National Liberation Army or Saor Eirrin, whatever murderous differences they might have among themselves from time to time, this was Ireland and whatever the politicos and Church and legal establishment might huff and puff in public, down here they knew there was indulgence and reluctant admiration. For if they couldn't believe that, they couldn't justify their armed struggle. And as Justice Pearson knew with cold conviction, they could not have been more wrong.

But he was wrong about MacMurrough, for the slim terrorist did have the wisdom to keep his mouth shut. Except to murmur, "Nothing to say, your honor."

"Dominic MacMurrough. I know you are sustained by the belief that there is, here in the Irish nation, a sneaking indulgence, reluctant admiration perhaps, for you and your fellow Republicans, who do not deny involvement in the so-called Armed Struggle. And that the law will strain to keep you out of the hands of the legal process which obtains in the country where your alleged crimes were allegedly committed. Well, I know the law of Ireland and I am sworn to uphold it. So having examined the evidence sworn by the arresting officers of the Metropolitan Police Anti-Terrorist Branch and the RUC Special Branch, I have no alternative in law but to grant this application by the Crown Prosecution Service of Great Britain and Northern Ireland."

"Leave to appeal." Up jumped Peter Baker, the Provos' able and quite brilliant young counsel, who had refused a big-bucks job in Brussels, so it was said, to carry on the legal struggle.

"The framework of appeals has been exhausted, Mr. Baker. That's it. Take him into custody and I'll sign the papers and try not to lose him like the bobbies did. Court is adjourned, next case tomorrow morning."

The London television news was full of it. Hallelujah. At last the Irish bench was behaving like a civilized legal system, returning the animals of the Provisional IRA to face their just deserts. "No Hiding Place" trumpeted the *Daily Telegraph* the next morning, and even Charlie

Haughey, the *taoiseach*, was treated as marginally less than the womanizing fellow traveler of "the Boys," which was the British press's favored way of portraying him.

Mr. Justice Pearson was the toast of terror-weary Great Britain and parts of Northern Ireland, but by the time London was tuned in to the six o'clock news, the good judge was fishing a remote stretch of a small stream in the gentle hills above Bray, in County Wicklow. His companion was a bearded, pipe-smoking man from the north who had the same placid confidence as Dominic MacMurrough. As indeed did Justice Eugene Pearson. For they all had one thing in common, although the hapless Dominic never did find out.

The pipe-smoking man from the north tapped his pipe on his boot, gazing at the quiet-flowing waters of the stream, the moss and weed a few feet below, bending over the brown and blue-gray stones and pebbles, and he wondered at the clarity of the riverbed. Overhead, a blackbird whistled in the branch of a tall birch tree, and further afield, a curlew sounded. There was no evidence of the five trusted men in casual country-workers' clothes who rested in the woods, keeping an eye out for strangers.

"How's Mhairaid?" he asked, examining the bowl of his pipe.

"She's fine."

"And Siobhan . . . ?"

"Independent as ever."

Which dispensed with the pleasantries. The chief of staff of the Provisional IRA fished his tobacco pouch from the pocket of his comfortable old tweed jacket.

"Eugene, we're getting a bit short of the readies."

"How much are we talking about . . . ?"

"It depends. If we just want to motor on the way we have for the past twenty years, maybe a few hundred grand. If the council is to be persuaded to make the big push these next couple of years, we're talking maybe four mil."

Pearson knew that by the big push, the chief of staff meant taking bombings and killings not just to the mainland of Britain but to the European community and wherever British interests could be so savagely and continuously hurt, and so many lives taken, that the U.K. government would be forced to the conference table; the resulting agreement to withdraw from Northern Ireland would justify the previous twenty years of the Armed Struggle. Eugene Pearson was a sane and moral man, and he also considered himself to be a patriot, but he did not believe the IRA could keep going for another long haul. Public sentiment was evaporating by the month. Libya's Ghaddafi had provided tons of Semtex explosive, weapons, and ammo, all now safely buried in underground bunkers in the Republic and stashed in remote hides in the U.K. and on the continent. But much of it would rust and deteriorate unless funds could be raised to pay for deep-cover operators, safe houses, vehicles, and travel.

"A few million."

"Funds are drying up. Noraid isn't good for more than a couple of hundred grand. The collapse of the Eastern bloc has been a disaster. And with the Middle East, our Arab friends are running scared."

Pearson knew that. He watched the Belfast man light his pipe, wondering where all this was getting. It had to be serious, because meetings like this were kept to a minimum, for obvious reasons of security.

"Eugene, I'd like you to meet a man from Bogotá."

Pearson sighed. All roads, where vast, illegal finance is concerned, arrive eventually in Colombia. "We're not touching drug money." He watched a big brown trout hover in the stream, drifting down toward the bank, unmoved by the tempting fly being offered.

"Just see him, though. Would you do that . . . ? He has access to millions. Funds, not drugs. He knows how to keep his mouth shut and he's genuine. Our Miami man has checked him out."

"Bogotá to me means cocaine. The movement can't afford to be tainted and there I stand firm, Brendan, and that's the height and weight of it." For although the judge was a thoughtful and deeply committed, and most secret, asset of the Provisionals, he was—and it caused him no problems of conscience—at the same time a moral man and an able upholder of the law and its place in Irish society.

Brendan Casey sucked patiently on the match, allowing the aromatic tobacco smoke to wreath around him in the warm June air. As the flame reached his fingers, he flicked the match into the stream. "I've spoken to the four wise men. Be in the cocktail bar of the Georges Cinq Hotel in Paris, at seven o'clock. A week from Sunday. The fella will be called Señor Restrepo. Hear him out, Eugene. At least hear what he has to say . . ."

Nominally, Pearson was Casey's equal on the Army Council. But he did not have a history of participation in the armed part of the Armed Struggle. His value to them lay in his comprehensive understanding of just how far the terrorist movement could go without losing the sympathy and support it enjoyed in certain areas of national and world opinion. And in his intuition, which had proved canny and accurate. But Casey had come up from the ghetto, killing his first Brit soldier at the age of sixteen, commanding the Belfast Brigade at twenty, interned for three years, a member of the Provo delegation that had been flown to a smart house in Chelsea's Cheyne Walk for secret negotiations with the British government, then back to the military wing, then a place in the political hierarchy with Sinn Fein, his comfortable, confident, restless, burning-eyed personality suited to the media struggle—it was about then he adopted the pipe—until here he was now, the reasonable face of the Provisional IRA. And if push came to shove, Eugene Pearson was not under any illusion about who would survive. Perhaps quite literally.

———

A blackbird in Downing Street was a rare bird indeed, or was it? David Jardine was no expert on blackbirds, in fact it could be a nightingale, although he wasn't sure if nightingales sang at three in the afternoon. Actually, Jardine was not much of an expert on Number 10 Downing Street either. His field was offensive intelligence in what the Secret Intelligence Service euphemistically described as Denied Areas, i.e., where your operatives get killed when discovered, if they were lucky. Maybe it was a sparrow, did sparrows sing so beautifully? No, they chirruped, didn't they, any fool knew that. Jesus. The prime minister had just asked him a question. Seventh time in Number 10 in the two years since he was made controller South America and here he was daydreaming. He fixed the PM's inquiring gaze and stared politely back at the man, looking ruminative and very much in touch.

Silence.

Jardine was forty-eight. Tall, broad-shouldered, untidily assembled, he looked as if he had been through plenty and had kept his sense of humor. He was acutely aware of the glances of Steven McCrae, chief of SIS, and Giles Foley, the cabinet secretary.

God in your infinite mercy, he prayed (for he was a religious man), give me a bloody clue.

"Difficult? Or impossible. I think you're thinking impossible, Mr. Jardine." A straw. Clutch it with gratitude and praise the Lord.

15

Jardine uncrossed his long legs. Brushed his nose thoughtfully with his index finger. McCrae cleared his throat. A clock ticked discreetly on the mantelpiece.

"I believe . . . extremely difficult, Prime Minister. Impossible only if political parameters disqualify our, um, particular skills." Was it really true the man's father had been an acrobat? If so, he would surely recognize the verbal backflip that had launched Jardine across the void toward . . . ?

"I quite understand." An amused smile from the prime minister as he swung the metaphorical bar back to pluck Jardine away from blackbirds and into the tough, no-nonsense, smoke-free zone that was the hub of political power in England, the prime minister's office. "Giles?"

"The Foreign Office has indicated no objection, since HMG will be operating in support of the government and elected president of Colombia. They are fully behind your predecessor's decision to acquire spheres of influence in South America, where the United States have dropped the ball, so to speak."

"Excellent. Well, I don't need to know the details. But when President Gaviria and I meet, I would like to be able to assure him we are taking every step to help destroy the cocaine cartels in South America."

Steven McCrae cocked his head to one side, smiled politely. "Prime Minister, there is only one cartel, and it's based in Colombia."

"I know that, Steven. But perhaps if I broaden the scenario, the president will not be confronted with the fact that I have just told him we are running espionage operations inside his own sovereign state. Even to assist the Colombians, that seems a trifle . . . insensitive?"

Oh yes, an estimable acrobat. Jardine beamed magnanimously into the PM's gaze of steel and nodded his approval. So that's what they had been discussing. Piece of cake.

Nicola fastened her garter belt with practiced efficiency and bent to clip it to her stocking tops, flicking her tumbling hair, still lank from the shower, off her face. Jardine stood at the washbasin, sluicing the lather from his genitals with handfuls of water, the beating of his heart returned now to something near normal. For the hundredth time he marveled at what this sublime young woman could see in a middle-aged satyr like himself. Be fair, David, a bloody fit middle-aged satyr, with a good physique, if slightly chunkier than in youth, with tenderness and stamina and . . . imagination. God she's immaculate, this Nicola Watson-Hall, and just ever so slightly depraved. What a fortunate chap. From the street below, a van hooted impatiently. It had been even more congested before they made so many streets one-way in St. James's. Jardine angled his head to glance at his fake Rolex on the glass shelf above the basin. Twenty-five minutes to get back to Century and begin the always challenging process of finding, recruiting, training, and placing a team of agents to penetrate Denied Areas for the acquisition of secret intelligence. On this occasion inside the cocaine cartel of Colombia. In the mirror, he watched Nicola step into her shoes and glance around for her underwear. Quick glance at the Rolex . . . no, not really enough time. Damn. Still, time, as the Rolling Stones used to sing, is on my side.

"This must be the last time," said Nicola, stepping briskly into her slip. "You see, David, I'm pregnant. And I really do love Michael, so it's all got to stop."

"Pregnant. Oh Nicola, that's wonderful, you must be so happy, the pair of you, how nice." As if they were having a polite conversation at a drinks party or in Fortnum's tearoom.

"And before you ask, it's not yours, it happened in April when you were in Peru."

"My dear, I would never have dreamt of asking. And of course I respect your decision and if there's anything you need, either of you, you mustn't hesitate to ask."

She zipped up her skirt, tugged her Hermès jersey over her immaculate hips, smiled shyly, and avoided his gentle, mature, understanding gaze. "Look David, I don't regret it, it's been fun. I've got to dash now, Mummy's getting off the one-forty from Godalming. Take care."

And she was out of the bedroom, across the cramped lobby, and the door banged shut and she was gone. Two years of extramarital bliss. Damn.

Friday is called Poets Day in the British Foreign Service, of which David Jardine's independently financed organization was nominally a part. "Poets" is an acronym for Piss Off Early Tomorrow's Saturday. Whole sections were departing the office as David crossed under the concrete piles that held up part of the jaded, once-glittering glass-fronted multistory office block, some Fifties architect's attempt at idiosyncrasy. Under this overhang had once, believe it or not, been a small garage and filling station, whose few fitters and pump attendants and bookkeeper had been regularly followed and wooed by intelligence agents of several foreign powers in the mistaken belief that they must be part of the great glass-and-concrete box under which they toiled, like bears in a cave at the base of some dark, menacing, secret mountain.

Only in Britain, ruminated Jardine, in surprisingly good humor considering he had just lost overboard one of the more delightful aspects of his personal odyssey.

One of his little lifesavers, as he thought of the various treats, some carnal, some sybaritic, that he allowed himself for his continued sanity. Only in Britain could the most secret organ of government foreign policy tolerate an innocent private enterprise, a gas station, trading with the general populace at the physical and possibly literal cornerstone of its edifice. Although Jardine was no more an expert on architectural engineering than he was on blackbirds.

David Jardine's career had been fairly rough and untidy over the years in the field, as risking one's skin on clandestine operations was called, in the years before he became an executive. He had damaged his sacrum, his lower and upper back, and his neck in a catalog of traumas ranging from parachuting to street-fighting for his survival in some Berlin back alley. There was a pale scar running from beside his left eye to the corner of his mouth, and his ruffian's past made him something of a hero to his nonoperations staff and just about acceptable to the operators out there, in the field.

His office, his warren of offices, with its own secure tank, ops rooms, briefing room, and communications section, was entered only by those in possession of a particular piece of plastic and the knowledge of which particular combination of which keys to press, on which day and at which time of which day. Only then would the wood-veneered, steel-clad security door clunk open and even then, if your face was not familiar and accept-able to Mrs. Brownlow, whose office door was always open, you would find some polite young man or attrac-tive girl discreetly but firmly intercepting you and ascer-taining the who and the why of you and your presence. For this was a serious, deadly profession, and here in his real world, David Jardine was not ever to be caught with his brain in neutral and his trousers down.

At 3 P.M. in London, as Jardine sat behind his desk and quietly asked his demure Scottish secretary, Heather, to obtain the files on Pablo Envigado, Fabio Ochoa, and certain other alarmingly wealthy citizens of Colombia, it was 10 A.M. in New York City. The 14th Precinct, also known as Midtown South, was busy processing prisoners from last night and crimes from last night, last week, and last month, plus gearing up for the day ahead—its responses, investigations, arrests, court appearances, administration, and the continuing battle over who had and who had not paid up to date for the various pizzas and pastramis on rye sent in from Bergman's across the street. And coffee, much of which seemed to get spilled on transcripts of late-shift interviews.

Homicide Sergeant Eddie Lucco was getting a hard time from Detective Jimmy Garcia, who was the Missing Persons detective responsible for attempting to ID the dead teenager, the Jane Doe at Grand Central. Jimmy had sent out a Missing Persons Alarm to all police departments nationwide to determine if a woman, a girl, of Jane Doe's description was listed as missing. The depressing response was a common one. Some two hundred female postjuveniles answered the description from coast to coast. Some two hundred parents, most desperately anxious and heartbroken, others philosophic or with alcohol or emotional or drug-related problems of their own, would now be shown head and shoulder color photographs, five inches by four, of the dead girl, her hair combed by a considerate morgue attendant after the autopsy, the vomit cleaned from her disconcertingly beautiful face, at peace in death. This was an ordeal as much for the cops involved as for the parents, and it might or might not produce results.

The reason for Garcia's hostility was that he had a couple of dozen similar cases and here was this big wop from Homicide taking an interest in Jane Doe when he should be out solving the third Uzi grease-gun slaying in a week.

"Why are you asking me these questions, Sergeant? The autopsy? Are you assigned to Missing Persons all of a sudden?"

"Jimmy, we see a lot of shit around this precinct, right?"

"Sure thing, you ain't got no argument there." Garcia had a master's degree in law from working his way nights, like Judge Almeda, but he felt that for his image in the precinct he should talk like Mickey Spillane.

"So this kid got to me, that's all." Sergeant Lucco studied his coffee-stained plastic cup.

Garcia watched Lucco warily. The information Lucco wanted was whether the autopsy had revealed traces of crack plus evidence of poison, the presence of which could be explained by the cocaine base being cut with something white and not so harmless. In which case not only would Narcotics have to be notified but Homicide would then become involved because death by drug overdose had been complicated by impurities, which meant somebody had willfully contributed to the kid's death.

This happened all the time and Garcia did not feel guilty or even lazy about his reticence. It was just that there were so many goddam cases like this. If you followed the book every time you would never get out of the office because you would be typing reports and would anyone ever get arrested, or even interviewed? Gimme a break.

He continued to gaze at Lucco. He knew Lucco was considered a hard-assed bastard and a first-rate detective, with that Mafia-like Neopolitan's six-dimensional maze of grudges and favors. Detective Garcia sighed and let his shoulders sag in admission of the first round to Lucco. Lucco smiled. Except for his eyes.

"Okay," conceded Garcia, "but this is not formal, okay?"

"Whadda you mean, not formal?"

Jesus, Lucco's eyes were made of ice. Garcia thanked Mary he was not a murderer, or even a suspect, and sat more upright on the uncomfortable wooden chair. "If it's formal I can't tell you without Homicide getting involved. But that means I get it in the neck because I still, uh, haven't filed the goddam report to Narcotics. With a copy to Homicide Process."

Lucco nodded. "So you got a load of JD's and a load of OD'd JD's and the paperwork never catches up and you don't figure we'll ever get a make on the pusher so what's the point and like that. Okay, tell me, buddy. Off the record." And that cold smile again, and the stone face inclined in friendly fashion toward Garcia.

"You can guess, you found the cadaver. It musta been obvious."

"I never jump to conclusions. It's the wrong way for a detective to think."

Silence. Out in the comparative sanctuary of the precinct office, raucous laughter and the rattle of typewriters and the jingling of keys as some prisoner was let in or out of the cage.

"It was crack. Cut with talcum powder and chalk. She didn't OD according to the autopsy. She vomited because her stomach couldn't hold down the cup of coffee and half doughnut she had just eaten. Drunk. Swallowed."

"Meaning?"

"It's a moot point whether the crack or the doughnut killed that little junkie."

"Not to me." Lucco slowly rubbed the toe of one shoe against his trouser calf, to polish it.

"Whadda you mean?"

"To me impure cocaine is involved. That's a Section Forty-four offense and therefore a mandatory Homicide investigation. Send the Homicide copy here, Garcia, marked for my attention."

The slender Hispanic cop registered almost comical outrage. "But you said this was off the record!"

"I lied to you. Now get your butt outa here and do your fucking job, officer. I kissed that dead junkie when the vomit was warm on her kisser and I owe somebody for that. And so does she." He examined the toe cap of his left shoe. "You should go now."

"Sure thing."

2

THE WHORE
OF VENICE

Jardine blinked to refocus, reading diligently, for the eleventh time, page 43 (of 108) of File PDW8/5009—KEATS:

> He travels freely in parts of Antioquia, where it is no exaggeration to say the peasants regard him as an heroic figure. With the vast revenue, some US$ 24,000,000 per *week,* he can afford to make grand gestures and he has built schools, housing, hospitals, and, of course, football stadiums.
>
> Pablo Envigado is considered a blood-bolter'd thug and an upstart by the Cali and Bogotá families, who like to imagine they are descended from the conquistadores whose conquest of South America in the sixteenth and seventeenth centuries shaped the ethnic mix of Indians and Spanish adventurers whose descendants people the subcontinent today.

Thanks for the history lesson, Giles. Jardine smiled at the thought of Giles Abercrombie toiling out there in Quito, Ecuador, on the second floor of the British embassy's delightful old Spanish colonial building with its shutters and peeling stucco and revolving fans and polished wood floors. Giles was thirty-two and first spotted for the firm, aged sixteen, at one of those ancient English boarding schools that turn out estate agents and Lancers and languidly amusing copywriters along with occasional insurance salesmen and bookshop assistants. Very few doctors, mused Jardine. But Giles had a Classics teacher who, unknown to anyone at school, had been with the Outfit for eighteen years before the rubber truncheons and electrodes of KGB Latvia's interrogators had rendered him unsuitable for further service. And this gentleman had understood immediately that young Abercrombie would have been wasted as an estate agent or even a Lancer. Clock winds forward sixteen more years and here, after Manchester University and a spell with a famous Spanish shipping company, was Giles, working under diplomatic cover as First Secretary (Commercial) in Ecuador for the men in the glass building that used to have a gas station nestling cuckoo-like on its foundations.

"Sir." It was Heather.

Jardine pushed the file away and arched his aching back, pressing it a couple of times against the chair. He removed his reading glasses and glanced at the girl.

"What time is it?"

"Ten to eight." Heather had been recruited from Mar College, in Troon, Scotland. Jardine knew she harbored a desire to move up, by some feat of legerdemain, to executive grade, but unless personnel could be persuaded to send her to university, she didn't have a hope. Youth, however, is indomitable, and Heather, who was bright enough to know the score, believed that some magic wand would wave in this building so potent with power and magic and she would be taken aside, at some juncture, and promotion and admission to the world of Real Secrets would be hers. God, poor Heather, and yet . . . that's more or less what had happened to Giles Abercrombie.

"Christ, you have sent these people home, haven't you? How long have they been waiting?"

"Since six. I've passed them the less-sensitive material and asked them to familiarize themselves with it. Also some maps of Colombia and all the files of media coverage. So they think they're here this late on purpose."

Jardine stared at her with the merest hint of approval. "Nice work . . ."

"No problem, sir." And she turned and left the room with a slight flush of pride.

Jardine's group of offices included a communications room; two operations rooms subdivided into partitioned cubicles around the walls, each with its own array of maps and notebooks, pens and paperclips, that reminded him of the horse boxes in third-form classrooms at the Dorset public school where his son, Andrew, was a boarder; various offices; and a briefing room, which was used to receive and entertain visitors from the Foreign Office, the Ministry of Defense, the CIA, the Security Service, and the Cabinet Office. But not all at the same time, for that would be imprudent. Very few people ever got into Jardine's inner office—protected from surprise attack by Heather in her small outer room—other than fellow sphere and department directors, the deputy chief and, of course, the chief, although in the nature of things, David Jardine would normally be invited up to the Top Floor, as the floor second from the top (which housed the penthouse and more besides) was called, to see Steven McCrae. Sir Steven.

The briefing room also served as a sort of office club when not in use, and there was a comfortable atmosphere among the wall maps and projection screens and blackboards and video screens and tape decks. One filing cabinet held gin, Scotch, beer, and sherry. There were tumblers in a drawer below the Andes region relief-map table, along with some tea towels with "A Present from Bangor" in Gaelic lettering, brought back by Mrs. Brownlow from some summer excursion.

Three men and a woman, soberly dressed and with "this better be good" expressions on their faces, sat watching Jardine as he closed the door quietly behind him, walked lightly and deferentially past them as if afraid to disturb the daunting quiet, and slid open the filing-cabinet drawer to reveal a picnic-size vacuum cooler. He extracted a bottle of Dos Equis beer, deftly taking the cap off on a bent corner of the cabinet lid, and turned to face his audience.

"Let us pray." His voice was somber and commanding.

"Let us pray for a young man, who has the survival instinct of a fox, the cunning of Janice Chisolm in Operational Expenses, the mergibility of a chameleon, the memory of a mother-in-law, the intellect of a Medieval History don . . . and bilingual, totally, in South American Spanish."

He touched his chin with the top of the beer bottle, thoughtful, watching, taking in the various files on the tables where his assembled group sat, familiarizing himself with what each had been reading. There was Bill Jenkins, his Head of Operations, Kate Howard, from Personnel (Recruitment/Planning), Ronnie Szabodo, Special Projects, and Tony Lewis, Security Manager, West 8, which was the office's formal designation for South America.

Kate continued to read for a moment, her plastic-framed spectacles on the end of her nose. Kate had been in the Oxford University rowing crew, coxing it to victory through a choppy, blustery surface, and she looked similarly hunched and determined as she forced her way to the end of the file on "Contacts Between Extraditables and Colombian Authorities/Unofficial," seemingly oblivious to the presence, admittedly two hours late, of Controller South America. The others knew Kate used her degree in Behavioral Psychology like a black belt and they exchanged glances and waited patiently.

Jardine sniffed at the Mexican beer and tapped the top of the bottle against his chin as if he had made a private pact not to admit his thirst until Kate was ready. An interesting standoff.

Finally she looked up and pushed the spectacles back onto the bridge of her nose with the middle finger of her left hand, gazing at Jardine with an equal mixture of myopia and intellect. And mild interest, for she had heard stories about his private life.

Jardine rested his backside against the Andean relief-map table, cradling the bottle in both hands. "Subject is Keats, as Mrs. Brownlow has so quaintly code-named Pablo Envigado. Ochoa is Shelley. The others are Milton, Browning, and Wordsworth. And not a Coleridge among them . . ."

"Coleridge?" Tony Lewis looked puzzled, checking his notes.

"Joke," said Kate.

"Samuel Taylor Coleridge was an opium addict, you see," Szabodo volunteered, pushing his chair out from the table and stretching his legs. He linked his fingers and slowly thrust his arms straight, cracking the knuckles, which sounded like radio static.

"I knew that." Tony watched Jardine sip from his ice-

28

cold bottle. "I just don't see what opium has got to do with cocaine, or am I missing something?"

Jardine met Tony's gaze, dabbing his mouth with the back of his hand. "One other thing I should perhaps pray for is your joint forgiveness. It's Friday and you should all have been home hours ago." There were droplets of moisture on the bottle like in television commercials for Coke. The others watched him, using their studied patience to convey their annoyance.

"However, I was asked by the prime minister today to expedite, I believe that was the word he used, to increase our offensive penetration of the Colombian cartel."

"Increase . . . ?" Lewis frowned. "I'm sorry, David, am I being thicker than usual tonight? What's to increase?"

Kate took off her plastic spectacles and started to clean them on her cardigan tail.

Jardine smiled. "The chief was present. Also Giles Foley. One rather got the impression, and God knows Downing Street is not a place I frequent so I could be miles out, but one had the distinct impression the boss had indicated that this service was singing and dancing in the darkest heart of the Medellín mafia. In the *tavernas* and *hosterías*, cheek by jowl, and in receipt of trusted confidences from the chemists and shippers and lawyers and valets and mistresses and bodyguards and indeed the wives and kiddies of Pablo and Jorge and Fabio et al. The PM is scheduled to meet Colombian President Gaviria next Tuesday and he wants to be able to tell him we are, quote, conducting intelligence operations against the South American cartels. The results to be shared with such of those members of the Bogotá authorities as can be trusted, and as we know, there are indeed a few good and brave souls. For that has been the focus of our operation in that country until today."

"David, you said cartels, plural, but according to these files, there is only one cartel and it's in Colombia."

"Absolutely correct, Kate, and Steven did correct the Prime Minister. Now by Monday at . . . let us say eleven A.M., you will please produce, from your Unwitting file, the names of ten men who fit the bill. Bilingual South American Spanish. Age bracket twenty-six to thirty-two. Go over the list with Bill and Tony, who will assess them for one, operational suitability, and two, security status. I would like the three of you to reduce the short list to five. Bill and I will then whittle that down to three, then at ten o'clock Friday morning, one week from today, Ronnie will kindly present himself here with all available material on the three Joes along with a plan for recruiting them as contract operators."

"Or on secondment, if any of them are in the forces." Kate was peering angrily at her glasses, having made the lenses worse by rubbing them on her cardigan.

"Maybe. Maybe not." Jardine started to replenish the others' drinks. Always thoughtful. Always the mask of gentleness. "Cocaine is Colombia's principal economic resource. Or to be more accurate, trafficking in cocaine, refining it and smuggling it to the States and to Europe is Colombia's principal, its main, economic resource. Second? Coffee. Third? Emeralds. Fourth? Flowers."

"Are you saying everyone in Colombia is involved in some giant national conspiracy? From the president down?" This from Tony Lewis, who, being in Security, was always ready to believe the worst. He smiled his thanks as Jardine topped up his glass of Perrier water, lime flavor.

"No, Tony." Bill Jenkins straightened up on his seat, turning his earnest gray eyes on Lewis. "The Colombians are terrific people. They're good-natured, hard-working, personally honest, and deeply conscious of their honor. They love music and dancing. Marvelous cuisine, really mixed, superb terrain, from mountains to jungle to pampas to desert. To Caribbean beaches. Their women are . . . really something, great movers, flirtatious, welcoming. I tell you, if it wasn't for cocaine, Colombia would be the best bloody place in the world to live. Or for a vacation."

"If I didn't know you better, Bill, I would harbor grave suspicions you had defected to the Colombian Tourist Board. Thank you, David." Ronnie Szabodo accepted a bottle of Dos Equis from Jardine.

"But if it wasn't for cocaine," said Kate, "the country would not be able to support such thriving service industries and leisure-related factories and outlets." Kate, it was rumored, wanted out of Personnel and into Operations Management. "I'm reading all this stuff, this material, while we were waiting for you, David, and it seems to me that everyone in the country is touched either directly or indirectly by the stuff. Whether flying or renting aircraft, making ceramic tiles for the wonderful homes the players and their bribed offshoots keep refurbishing, driving them in taxis, healing them, or even burying them. The ripples reach everybody."

"The ripples do indeed." Jardine sat at the other side of her desk and pulled the seat around to face the others. "So infiltrating the cartel is going to be a long and delicate operation. Series of operations. We're all experienced people, we've done this in a dozen other environments. Hundreds of times. You mentioned secondment, but that might be unfair to a serviceman's career, if it runs into years. Plus, Pablo has access to very excellent intelligence and there's no point in making our operator, if he does turn out to be in the forces, a hostage to fortune. Therefore pristine contacts, I think, and Ronnie and I will just have to sell Joe the idea of resigning his commission, if that's the way the cards fall. If we choose a serviceman."

Silence. Jardine knew the others were weighing up with a degree of cynicism this demonstration of concern for a Joe, as free-lance operators, or short-term agents, were referred to, informally. And never in their hearing. In truth, David Jardine had always cared about his agents, and his reputation as an agent runner without equal was known to every serious intelligence service that needed to be aware of the British SIS.

"There's something unsaid here, which I need to get clear." Ronnie Szabodo produced a beat-up old pipe from his jacket pocket and stared at it in pleasant surprise, like a conjurer who didn't really believe that a dove would flutter from his sleeve. Ronnie affected the bored, laconic air of the typical English public-school Cambridge-educated SIS officer who was still in the majority when he was recruited in Hungary in 1957. His sturdy Hungarian accent, however, made his every utterance a delightful parody of the class into which he believed he had slipped quite effortlessly.

"It seems to me," he said, "your plan is to infiltrate a couple of operators in, working outside our established South American networks. And judging by your specification, David, you want virgins, in the sense that no one can track them to this outfit. And that's why I'm sitting here at eight of an evening, instead of propping up the bar in my local pub."

"Exactly so," replied Jardine. He had an instant picture of Szabodo, pint in hand, in too-new sports coat, tattersall-check shirt and cravat, probably with Royal Air Force colors. Ronnie had never been in the RAF but he wouldn't let that inhibit him.

"I just wanted it spelled out. To avoid confusion."

"Yes, Ronnie."

"Later on, I mean," insisted Szabodo. "We're talking black and expendable operators, correct?"

"Quite." Jardine gazed at Szabodo benignly, the way

he might, Kate reflected, look at a favorite gundog who refused to come to heel.

"So let's not beat around the bush," the Hungarian went on, oblivious to Jardine's beady stare.

"And during training and evaluation," said Jardine softly, "provided Security doesn't uncover some damning personal background horror, you and me, Ronnie, we'll choose the lucky one to infiltrate Pablo Envigado's Colombian operation."

Szabodo nodded, fumbling at his pockets for tobacco, with less fortunate results. "And if the poor bugger doesn't get his balls removed with a blunt saw, that'll be the blueprint for future operators, who in the meantime Kate and Bill will be lining up."

Jardine gently placed his empty beer bottle on the relief-map table, beside a mountain lake near Bogotá.

"Precisely."

Of Paris's three greatest hotels—the Ritz, the Georges V, and the Crillon—Ernest Hemingway favored the Ritz, particularly the bar, where he and his cronies would hold court. He invented a version of the daiquiri cocktail that is still in the bartenders' ancient black book. Justice Eugene Pearson had never been in any of the three but he would have preferred to have been in the cocktail bar at the Ritz because he had read *Death in the Afternoon*, *A Moveable Feast*, and *For Whom the Bell Tolls*.

But Eugene Pearson was not in the Ritz; he was sitting in the cocktail bar of the Georges V, on the avenue Georges-V in the Eighth Arrondissement of Paris, just across the river Seine from the Ministry of Foreign Affairs. A pianist played sophisticated numbers from *Porgy and Bess*, quietly and unobtrusively, with a degree of easy skill that Pearson appreciated, for he himself was a

fairly talented player of modern jazz, from Cole Porter to
Thelonius Monk. And his daughter was coming along
nicely. Siobhan, just turned eighteen, had such grace of
spirit and natural facility with the keyboard that he had
agreed readily to her changing her career plan from law
to music, and now she was at the conservatory and
though he and Mhairaid missed her terribly you have to
let them go sometime. And it wouldn't be long to the
summer vacation.

It wasn't half bad, this Georges V. Pearson sipped his
Perrier with ice and a slice of lemon, feeling quite
cosmopolitan and reflecting that if the Organization
could lay on a few more trips like this one, it would
make up for all the tedious Policy Committee meetings,
held secretly at regular intervals, to advise the Army
Council of the Provisional IRA on the effects of its Armed
Struggle and the likely effects of its planned actions.
Such meetings were held in dingy, cramped houses on
the Wolfe Tone Housing Estate on the outskirts of Dublin
or in the back rooms of one of the offices of the several
law firms secretly sympathetic to the cause. Nothing like
the class of the cocktail bar of the Georges V in Paris. It
seemed a shame to be drinking soda, but Justice Pearson knew there were times to keep a clear head, and
meeting a man from the Bogotá cartel was definitely one
of them.

There was a family sitting around one of the well-
spaced low tables. Father of about forty-five, elegant,
slender wife with short, corn-blond hair, two boys, hair
brushed neatly and wearing tweed jackets, aged maybe
fourteen and ten. Nice people, speaking French, which
was reasonable, considering this was Paris. There were
two deeply tanned smooth-skinned men, one with
slightly Tartar eyes, sitting separately, the one in the
camel-hair sport coat at the bar, the other, shorter,
thicker-set, in a corner, his gaze quietly alert, his news-

paper unread. Navy-blue blazer. Couple of wingers, as the Boys called unobtrusive bodyguards. Unless he was imagining it. Maybe they were just businessmen. The clandestine life was like night-vision sights: everything was seen in a different light. You could get paranoid. Then a broad-shouldered man entered, wearing an expensive, dark, worsted suit, of Savile Row cut. Light of step, slim build. An agile man. His clean, expensively cut hair longer than was at that time fashionable in Europe. Dark, watchful, amused eyes. Striking face, not handsome. But with . . . character. He gazed around the room and into the hotel area beyond, then walked lightly across to Pearson, smiling.

Pearson rose. He was aware of the man in the blue blazer rising without effort. Christ, what if this was a hit? The approaching man held out his hand as he reached Pearson. "Señor Ross . . . ?"

Pearson nodded. Gripped the man's hand. "Mr. Restrepo."

"I'm glad you could come. What are you going to drink? It might surprise you to know, but these sorts of meetings make me quite apprehensive. I think I'll have a large Scotch and soda." This last to the barman who had materialized like a genie as Restrepo and Pearson sat down. In the background, the shorter of the two bodyguards strolled away, going toward the dining room.

Pearson realized his heart was beating faster.

"Make that two."

Restrepo glanced around casually, ignoring the man at the bar. He waited until the waiter had withdrawn. Finally his gaze settled on Pearson. "How goes the struggle?"

Pearson held his gaze. Hell, this man was a mere attorney, and wasn't Eugene Pearson a judge of the Court of Appeal?

"I'm not sure what you mean. Life? Life is always a struggle."

"I understand you went on a fishing trip. One week last Friday."

"It's a most relaxing pastime."

"As a result of your conversation then, I have flown from a certain South American city to meet you."

"I don't believe in discussing business in public, señor. Perhaps after dinner."

"Dinner?"

"Well, I assumed . . ."

"What? Because I have access to millions we would be eating here? At the Georges Cinq?"

Pearson's face reddened. "Paris is a civilized place. It was a simple mistake, señor, to imagine our meeting would take place in a civilized environment."

"We have a saying in Colombia. 'To be civilized, it is necessary to enjoy life and respect it.' "

Pearson waited. There was silence as the waiter placed the drinks on the table. From across the room, the low, cultured tones of the French couple and the voices of their children made his clandestine rendez-vous seem tacky and irrelevant.

"Deux whiskey soda on the rocks, *messieurs."*

"Merci."

"C'est moi, monsieur." And the waiter moved away.

"So?"

"So I wonder if either of us qualifies."

The piano player was unobtrusively working his way through "Mood Indigo." It was one of the first pieces Siobhan had played that had startled Pearson with its effortless clarity, its indication of her potential as a musician. He met the Colombian's gaze. "Wars have to be fought. Are you saying soldiers can't be civilized?"

"Wars are fought on behalf of countries. Good health, Señor Ross."

"Slainthe." Perversely, after going to the trouble of entering the country under a British passport and checking in as a British businessman at the Hotel Cayre on the boulevard Raspail, Pearson used the Gaelic language, stung by this immaculately dressed Colombian gangster's lawyer.

"Or by revolutionaries fighting with the mandate of the people to usurp a tyrant." Restrepo's dark, intelligent eyes were inscrutable, but Pearson detected a hint of mockery.

"Or on behalf of a nation in chains," he replied.

"In recent weeks I've made something of a study of your twenty-year struggle in North Ireland," said the Colombian.

"I can't help noticing the, um, organization does not get many votes. Perhaps," asked Restrepo innocently, "they are rigged?"

"The people would give us an overwhelming mandate," Pearson replied, "if we were not engaged upon the Armed Struggle. The bloodshed has sickened many Republican sympathizers. The end maybe justifies the means, but some of the means have been self-defeating. Strapping men to the seats of cars containing bombs and threatening to kill their children unless the hapless victim drives to his certain death was an example. The murder of two British corporals on television sickened a lot of folk in the south. A six-month-old baby in Germany, machine-gunned by an activist with a history of psychopathic disorder. And many others. Over twenty years. Hardly vote catchers, but war is war."

"You take a remarkably mature view."

"We're not all stage Paddies suffused with hatred. I happen to be committed to getting the British out of Ireland. The niceties of democracy can take their course once that is accomplished."

"Also, perhaps, the Armed Struggle is necessary in

order to establish your organization's claim to a place in any serious planning for the future of the Six Counties. And their eventual return to the Republic."

"I'm impressed, Mr. Restrepo. You begin to understand. And yet, I sense something akin to disapproval."

Restrepo put down his glass, the drink hardly touched. Pearson's was empty, apart from three chunks of ice. Beyond Pearson, the blue-blazered bodyguard entered and gazed around, relaxed, as if looking for someone. Restrepo lifted a finger and caught the barman's eye, making the universal scribbling mime, requesting his check. "I think we should take a walk. The streets of Paris are made for sauntering, don't you think?"

Pearson watched him carefully, studying the lawyer for some clue, some hint of his weakness, his vulnerable spot.

Mr. Justice Pearson was feared among Ireland's attorneys and counsels, and by many defendants, for his unerring ability to sense and probe at the exposed nerve before slipping the stiletto of his sharp tongue in for the kill. But if this *consejero* of the cartel had a weak spot, he was not revealing it. Pearson gazed deep into his eyes. "That is probably why they coined the term *boulevardier.*"

Restrepo inclined his head and smiled. The barman lifted a small silver dish with the bill on it and moved toward them. But he was stopped by the Colombian in the camel-hair jacket, who checked the bill, counted out some folded notes from his pocket, and put them on the dish. The man in the blue blazer strolled out of the room ahead of Restrepo and Justice Pearson.

Warm lights of a floating restaurant reflected on the shimmering waters of the Seine, their varied yellows and ambers elongated, extending toward the Right Bank, beyond midstream. The bodyguard in the camel-hair jacket was halfway across the bridge to the quai Anatole-France, on the far side. Pearson and Restrepo strolled, hands in pockets, deep in conversation. The man in the blue blazer was some thirty paces behind them. A kid in jeans and leather jacket had also appeared, riding a Suzuki 125 trail bike, sometimes a short distance behind, sometimes in front. But never far away. There was a small, dark bundle, wrapped in canvas, fixed with rubber elastic bands to the metal rack over the back wheel. Pearson was under no illusion about what it might contain. The Colombians were known to favor the mini-Uzi 9mm submachine pistol, which could fire, under test-bench conditions, over 1,400 bullets per minute. So this fellow Restrepo was well protected, and discreetly. For the very best bodyguards, in low profile environments, were trained not to draw the slightest attention to their charges. And Pablo Envigado's family business had the very best bodyguards. Rumor had it they were trained by a team of men who had served in Britain's elite counterterrorist unit, the Special Air Service, led by an ex-SAS noncom called MacAteer. Rumor also had it that the SAS were currently engaged in secret operations in Colombia, to track down and destroy the cartel's leading members. He wondered where MacAteer really stood in that respect. A couple of renegade SAS men had made overtures to the Provos but the received wisdom (imparted by Mr. Justice Pearson in his clandestine role as Policy Advisor) was that nobody could ever be sure they were not planted by British Intelligence and so the bodies of each were dumped on quiet country roads, one in South Fermanagh and the other just outside Newtonards, a Prot stronghold. Neither murder was claimed by the Organization, but the message had been pretty clear.

". . . the Whore of Venice?"

"I'm sorry?"

Restrepo glanced sideways at Pearson as they walked over the bridge. Paris and the Seine behind them. "I said, have you ever heard mention of the Whore of Venice?"

"Can't say that I have. It sounds like a rather racy railway engine."

The kid on the Suzuki wheeled around at the far end of the bridge, the Left Bank, and rode slowly back. How could he see at night, wearing shades? Role-playing. That was the problem with those young men and women who lived on adrenaline and some role model acquired from the movies and a diet of TV videos.

"The Whore of Venice is the code name of an Italian millionaire. He owns several restaurants and boutiques in Venice. He is a secret transvestite. Also a magistrate and a leading light in the local commercial union."

"I haven't heard of him. We don't swap much European gossip in Dublin, we're all too busy pretending to enjoy our own theater and art. And gossip. Jesus, it would be difficult for a transvestite to keep it secret in Dublin. God knows a hair transplant keeps them going for weeks."

"The Whore of Venice is also the man who runs our cocaine-distribution business in Europe. The concession is worth twenty-seven million dollars to him personally."

"Profitable business," replied the judge, "living off other people's misery."

"It is not a concession he would part with, willingly."

"Mafia, is he?" asked Pearson.

"That is not an organization I've heard of." Restrepo's face was expressionless. The putter of the motorcycle was some way behind them.

"Señor Restrepo, I was asked to meet you. Here I am. What have you come all this way to say?"

A squat Simca car, in the dark-blue and white of the

gendarmerie, passed them, blue light flashing, and disappeared toward the boulevard St.-Germain-des-Prés.

The Eiffel Tower was visible, away to the right, beyond les Invalides.

Restrepo seemed preoccupied. Finally, he glanced at the Irish judge. "Cocaine does not necessarily contribute to people's misery. Any more than does Scotch whisky. Pardon me, or Irish. Alcohol is a recreational drug which is centuries old. And so is coca and its derivatives."

"Smooth words. You don't have to see the results dragged through the courts. Broken families. Vicious crime to feed the habit. Wasted lives. Early death."

"Gin. You're describing gin in nineteenth-century London."

"Whatever. It's a filthy business."

"And sending men to their deaths strapped to a carload of explosives—that's okay is it, Justice Pearson?"

"Our struggle to free Ireland has not been without its . . . embarrassments. There is an element among our . . . footsoldiery, which has become brutalized by familiarity with killing. It's been a hazard of military activity since . . . forever. However, we try to learn from our mistakes."

"Give laboratory animals unlimited access to cocaine, food, and water. They'll choose cocaine over and over again, until they die of malnutrition."

"That sounds to me like an admission. You have just proved my point."

"This isn't a debate around the bar of the Shelbourne in Dublin, Judge. It's a business proposition." Restrepo paused to gaze over the parapet at the Seine, the rooftops of Paris flanking the various quays, and the domes of the Sacré Coeur cathedral beyond. He seemed to be looking for something. "Concentrated cocaine, injected into the bloodstream or snorted into the mucous membranes of the nasal passage, has an instantaneous and unique effect on the brain and the central nervous system, engendering, at first, a dazzling clarity of thought and the most exquisite sensation of euphoria. It has been likened to the ultimate orgasm of the mind."

"And the poor sod spends the rest of his or her life trying to recapture the first time. Just like sex, really." Pearson felt that what to him was a racy remark might lessen the gulf he could feel growing between them.

"But much, much more addictive." Restrepo continued his stroll. "Anyone who tells you coke is not addictive is a cocaine virgin or a liar. When Don Fabio Ochoa started to take cocaine seriously as an export commodity, he was making between forty and fifty thousand dollars a kilo. His sons had gone to New York and Miami to arrange the forward shipments, difficult because there was a law against it and the U.S. Drug Enforcement Administration agents and Customs were shit hot. And what did they discover?"

"The fellows they were selling it to were selling it on for a hundred and thirty thousand a kilo. I too have done my homework, Mr. Restrepo."

"The Ochoa family are descended from the conquistadores, the original Spanish who colonized South America. They have known many successes and a few failures, but all the time, over four hundred years, they learned that to survive and prosper in the subcontinent, you need to have vision, imagination, muscle . . . and no pity."

"And you represent the Ochoas?"

"I work for Pablo. He in turn, is in touch with Don Fabio and the others. I have been asked to make you a proposition."

"Well, you know my feelings about cocaine. I can't

see any place for it in the Movement's policy, but I'll pay you the courtesy of listening."

The man in the camel-hair jacket had paused to light a cigarette. The Suzuki rasped slowly past, going on, over the bridge and turning left into the quai Anatole-France.

"Our information is that your funds are drying up." Restrepo seemed very slightly preoccupied, gazing ahead, over the curve of the bridge. "That you have nine tons of weapons and Semtex plastic explosive hidden in caches all over Ireland, England, and in Europe but lack the financial power to administer and fund the operations necessary to put that ordnance to good use. I also understand that support for the Armed Struggle is progressively diminishing and that your so-called doves on the Army Council and in the grass roots of Sinn Fein are losing interest in killing Brits because they can see it dragging on for another twenty years. By that time the IRA will be nothing but a small collection of jaded psychos hooked on bombs and terror as a way of life, with zero support from the community and the wasting, always denied, knowledge that they have been the principal factor in delaying the British government's obvious wish to arrange for the Six Counties in the north to be given their freedom."

"Your proposition . . . ."

"In the Provisional IRA, you have a highly skilled, professional, clandestine organization, stretching from the west coast of Ireland to eastern Germany and North Africa. You have twenty years' experience in evading the authorities and in keeping your secrets. I represent a clandestine organization stretching from the southernmost tip of South America to Alaska. Its sole business is the refining and distribution of cocaine, with profits that exceed Colombia's national debt. The European network, set up by the Whore of Venice, is imperfect. It is leaky. It has been penetrated by the DEA and European customs agencies. And the Whore has become greedy and therefore untrustworthy."

"If you're suggesting any form of collaboration, it's an insult to my organization. We have our morals and we are a highly disciplined movement." Eugene Pearson meant every word of this outburst. About forty yards ahead, a dark figure approached, strolling, almost sauntering. A heavily built middle-aged man, wearing a topcoat with a wide collar of astrakhan or some such fur, a long, dark scarf thrown loosely around his neck, and a black, broad-brimmed hat. Typical Paris, thought Pearson. Not at all unlike the Toulouse-Lautrec poster of that actor fellow he had pinned to his study wall when he was a law student at Trinity, about one million years ago. What was the actor's name? Braun, pronounced *"Brown,"* Aristide Braun. And a black wood cane, probably malacca, with a silver top.

Restrepo had been similarly preoccupied by the theatrical figure. The man in the camel-hair jacket, on the other hand, had scarcely given him a second glance. The Colombian lawyer affected not to have heard Pearson's complaint. "Use a few skilled men and women to set up a distribution network in Europe and I will ensure that two million dollars, each and every month, is paid to you wherever you want. Anywhere in the world, in any currency. Use it for your Movement or buy yourself a villa in the south of France. Frankly, that's of no consequence."

"Apart from the fact that your so-called proposition is outrageous and naive, what about the Whore of Venice?"

"Perhaps we should ask her. Here she comes. This is him now . . ."

Pearson stared at the approaching figure, a tall man, bulky, his long, astrakhan-collared topcoat flapping

around him, using the cane with some skill, its movements reminiscent of an eighteenth-century dancing-
master's stick. The face lines etched in dissipation but
with a certain style, long, high-bridged nose and pierc-
ing dark eyes, the impression being of a once-handsome
Punchinello, the very stuff of those Venetian masks for
the commedia dell' arte. And for the second time that
evening, the Dublin judge's heart started to beat more
rapidly. He was annoyed at having been suckered into
an encounter with the don, the *capo* responsible for
running all the Colombian cartel's cocaine into Europe.
In the name of Jesus, what if the drugs police or some
customs outfit were keeping tabs on the man? What
would become of the Justice's false identity then? Worse.
Holy Mary Mother of God, this Bogotá gangster's lawyer
had just offered Pearson the man's concession, worth
two million dollars a month.

"I don't really want to be seen with him."

"Nonsense, who's looking? The bridge is practically
deserted, my men have checked him for a tail; take it
from me, he's clean. His name, by the way, is Luigi
Montepalcino."

And the tall, bulky, theatrical figure paused, ex-
tended his hands and forearms, the rest of him perfectly
still. His voice was surprisingly deep, *"Amigo mío. Cómo
está?"*

Restrepo too had paused. He grinned broadly.
Stepped forward and gripped the Italian's hand, clapping
his left arm over Montepalcino's shoulder and embracing him. The two men were clearly pleased to see each
other. They muttered a machine-gun-quick salvo of Italian or Spanish greetings at each other. Pearson could
not be sure which language. Restrepo stepped back and,
smiling, beckoned to him, meeting Justice Pearson's
alarmed glance with a friendly gesture. "Señor Ross,

meet a very good friend of mine, I had no idea he was in Paris . . ."

Pearson gave Restrepo a startled look as if to say, Are you sure, is this really a coincidence? And we don't talk about *anything*, right? Then, because Montepalcino was waiting, a polite half-smile on his face, and Pearson saw no point in being rude, he approached the Italian. Was the man really a secret transvestite, my God, this was truly a long way from casting flies for trout in the hills of Wicklow. A helping thrust from Restrepo, who had gripped the reluctant Pearson's left elbow, propelled him into the arms of the bulky drug baron. No need for that, thought Pearson, and smiled, embarrassed, and started to move back, to make some space between them, "How do you do, Señor . . . ?"

"Montepalcino." The Italian smiled, revealing disconcertingly blubbery lips, and the top of his head lifted like a lid and his hair lifted as if in a wind and his right eye was replaced by a dark crimson jelly and the chainsaw rasp of the mini-Uzi filled Pearson's ears and to his horror, the murdered man stumbled forward as his knees gave out and clutched at Pearson, who instinctively fended him off, half frozen with fright, and the Uzi noise stopped abruptly, replaced immediately by the growl and roar of the Suzuki trail bike racing off toward the Right Bank and there was Mr. Justice Pearson, rooted to the bridge, his trouser legs wet with his own piss and his face flecked with blood, the Whore of Venice dead at his feet, one hand clutching the judge's left leg.

Flash!

A black Citroen hatchback had pulled up beside them. A swarthy young man lowered his camera and the car moved on.

A second car, a BMW, pulled up. The murder spot was getting like a taxi rank. Restrepo pulled Pearson away from the corpse and bundled him into the car, climbing in after him. With a screech of tires it made a U-turn and sped off toward St.-Germain-des-Prés. Shocked and shivering with adrenaline, breathing hard as if he had sprinted a hundred meters, Eugene Pearson noticed the boulevard Raspail drifting past and he even glimpsed his hotel, where he was booked in with a false British passport under the name of Ross, receding rapidly behind them.

"Take your time," said Restrepo, as relaxed as if he were on a drive home from the office. "The offer is open until Friday at noon."

...

3

THE CHANGELING

New York City is a lonely place, but no place in New
York is lonelier than the morgue at Bellevue Hospital.
Sergeant Eddie Lucco glanced at his wristwatch. It was
ten after two in the morning. He sipped from a plastic
cup of tepid brown liquid alleged to be coffee. The
electric clock on the pale green wall quietly clicked one
more minute off the night. He listened as the footsteps
of Dr. Henry Grace approached, echoing flatly on the
solid, rubberized floor, and turned the second page of
the pathetically brief autopsy result and forensic report.

"Sorry about that, Eddie, this is the time they start
coming in, on a Sunday night." Grace was a short, busy,
stocky man of about fifty. Thick, wiry gray hair and horn-
rim glasses.

"What do you have?" asked Lucco.

"Two fatal stabbings, one auto wreck, and an attempted suicide."

"Attempted? Sounds pretty damn successful to me."

"So you're wrong, pal." The pathologist glanced at

48

his clipboard of case forms, laid it on the desk. "Deceased slipped out of the fireman's rescue harness. I keep telling them those things are too goddamn loose. Three hours twenty minutes talking him off that ledge, poor bastard. You know his last words?"

"No."

" 'You're right, Officer, I got so much to live for.' "

"Jesus . . ." The detective shook his head.

"Life is a bitch."

"Amen."

"So this Jane Doe," the pathologist remarked. "How come you got it? You're such a big-shot Homicide cop."

"Luck of the draw."

"Bitch . . ."

"You said it."

Grace rummaged around in a drawer and produced a fresh plastic-wrapped bundle of latex gloves. He sat facing Lucco and rubbed his face with his hands. "So what can I do for you?"

"The kid. You say here, age between seventeen and nineteen. Why not sixteen? Or twenty?"

"You get to tell."

Slight pause.

"Okay." Lucco gazed at the remaining inch of coffee with something approaching antagonism. Nancy was into the third week of her case, commuting every Monday and Friday to and from Albany. It was paying for the new air-conditioning system and the decorating job on their apartment in Queens. Which meant they would get a good price when they sold up and moved to a better neighborhood, whatever that might mean. Last night he'd attended a double murder on Madison, in an apartment that must've had over a million dollars worth of art on the walls. And two corpses in the marble and antique-Italian-mirrored bathroom. A mother and father shot to death by their heroin-addict son while his girlfriend lay in an OD coma in his bedroom, a Yale pennant on the wall. "Okay. Harry, cast your mind back to this Jane D. You say you get to tell . . . ?"

"Sure. After a thousand autopsies I got a certain . . . nose."

"That's fine. I want you to help me, Harry."

"So ask."

"Just tell me all the instinctual things you did not write on the autopsy report. For instance, was she a hooker? Was she from a poor, illiterate background? Had she scrubbed floors? Was she a typist? Her dental work. Was it New York or Tennessee? Whadda you say? Let's go to work on this one, Harry, just for me."

And he reached into his coat pocket and produced a pint bottle of Jack Daniels, passing it across the table to the pathologist, whose hands had begun to tremble, almost unnoticeably, except to a detective.

———

"I've tried to come up with ten possibles." Kate Howard sat on the edge of Jardine's desk, laying a slim pink folder in front of him. She scratched her forehead with the tiny eraser on the end of her pencil. "And it's just not possible."

Jardine opened the folder and scanned the first page. There were six names on it, with potted biographies. Then six files, each with photographs of the subjects and detailed information, including psychological profiles, security-investigation results, and a form of assessment peculiar to SIS that was, in effect, a balance sheet of the individuals' human strengths and weaknesses. Weaknesses were not necessarily disqualifying factors unless they patently rendered the subject a bad risk or if they came remotely close to rivaling the strengths. A ratio of four to one was considered to be acceptable, in favor of strengths, in a potential contract operator's character. However, as in marriage, such theoretical assumptions generally proved to be quite inaccurate.

Jardine glanced at Kate's tweed-skirted hip on the edge of his desk and smiled to himself. Kate was so brainy and yet not really of this world. The secret toilers at Century were soon affected by the easy, intelligent, able, exclusive, unaffected, classless camaraderie of top secret business, with field operators and clandestine infiltration of Denied Areas, and radio ciphers flowing in and out round the clock, and work names and telephone taps and whole dummy enterprises up and running right around the globe. It all added up to the shared and exclusive and totally private knowledge of secret sexy clandestine magic . . . stuff.

And ruthless to a man.

And here was Kate, couldn't be more than thirty, sitting comfortably on the edge of a sphere controller's desk as if he were her tutor at Oxford or her favorite uncle.

"Why bring this to me? I thought you were going to work with Bill and Tony."

"Well, I will, David. I just need to know if six Joes, six potential Joes, are sufficient."

Jardine liked the use of the word sufficient, instead of enough. There was something terribly attractive about those young, carelessly well-bred and articulate girls the Firm still attracted. She was wearing something that smelled of carnations. Just a hint. Very fresh.

"To tell you the truth, I'm amazed you trawled six." He glanced up at her. Without glasses, he mused . . . "To tell you the truth, Kate. Six is bloody marvelous."

"Really?" She looked pleased. "I mean, we could have presented ten, I suppose. But they wouldn't have been right."

"That's fine. Be a good girl and put your head together with Bill and Tony. Whittle it down to three."

"I thought you might want a preview."

"Well, I don't. But thanks for offering."

"Does that mean I should run along now?"

"Kate, I love you dearly, but look at the pile of stuff I have to do. There's an awful lot more to South America than one Colombian drug syndicate. How'd you get in anyway?"

"I waited till Heather went for the coffee." Kate grinned, swung her legs off the desk, and left, holding the secret pink folder carelessly. That girl has style, thought Jardine, and sighed as he turned back to his mountain of work.

———

That afternoon, in the Court of Appeal in Dublin, two minor gunmen of the Irish National Liberation Army, a separate and even less discriminating group of fighters in the Armed Struggle than the Provos, were refused any further delaying tactics and returned to face trial in England for the murder of a courting couple who had parked quietly one evening just too close to an arms cache that the defendants required access to. The presiding judge was a somewhat subdued and thoughtful Justice Eugene Pearson, the memory of that disintegrating face lingering like the smell of Milltown cemetery after the rain. He wondered if there was some excuse he could dream up to put off the clandestine meeting scheduled for that evening, up there in the clean hills of Wicklow, with the chief of staff of the Provisional IRA. But of course no excuse was permitted when the Organization's funding was involved.

———

And three thousand, four hundred and sixty-one miles to the southeast, three Bedouin tribesmen watched as a column of eight T-62 tanks, ten BRDM six-wheeled armored personnel carriers, three Pat Hand track-mounted radar systems, and four ZSU 23/4 track-mounted antiaircraft vehicles sped south toward Kuwait's border with Saudi Arabia. The Iraqi markings on the tanks identified them as belonging to the 17th Motorized Infantry Brigade of the Republican Guard. The particular grouping of tanks, radar, and command vehicles identified the column as being the brigade headquarters unit. The brigade commander was one Colonel Talib Jafar al-Hadiffi, and his red-and-green pennant fluttered from the telltale command turret of his BRDM armored personnel carrier.

The Iraqis paid no attention to the three Bedou, with their four camels, sitting around a wispy, almost smokeless fire. Dust from the desert road swirled around the convoy, making a steady forty miles per hour, and hung over the road behind them as they receded toward the southern horizon.

One of the lean, bearded tribesmen reached into the folds of his djellaba and glanced at his two companions, who were scanning the desert around them. Then their eyes met his. They nodded. The tribesman lifted a satellite handset from the folds and spoke briefly into it. Then he pressed a couple of buttons on the transceiver on his lap.

Thirty-one seconds later, eleven thousand feet above the Saudi desert, two Harrier fighters of the U.S. Marines received a coded signal. Each was armed with laser-guided air-ground missiles, cluster bombs, and cannon. The leader checked his Head-Up Display and slid sideways into a shallow dive, followed by the second aircraft, streaking over the border into Iraqi-occupied Kuwait.

All that could be heard in each pilot's earphones

was the measured breathing of his buddy. The desert swooped up to meet them. At one hundred feet they leveled out, banking slightly to bring them streaking over the desert in a curve, until they were following the road taken by the convoy.

Colonel Talib al-Hadiffi and his brigade headquarters column was destroyed and left scattered in flames even before they were aware of the presence of the fighters. A second pass with smart bombs and cannon killed most of the survivors. The noise and the erupting sand and worn tarmac, coupled with multiple concussions and the searing heat, reduced in an instant the potent, steadily advancing convoy to a special piece of hell.

Then silence.

Then the groans of the wounded.

Then, twenty minutes later, the three Bedouins and their camels approached. They picked their way among the smoldering detritus until they reached the colonel's BRDM. The leader of the three dismounted and glanced to his companions, who were gazing around. They nodded. All clear.

Harry Ford lowered himself into the turret hatch, head first. The scene inside was grim. The impact of some missile had mutilated the men inside. Harry struggled to reach the canvas satchel still clutched in the hands of what had once been Colonel al-Hadiffi. Finally he prised it free and wriggled out of the still-hot, once six-wheeled coffin.

Without a word—for there were wounded and dying within earshot and if they heard Harry speak they would have to be killed, and that wasn't part of Harry's way—he climbed onto his camel, which he had, to the embarrassment of his troopers, called Daisy, and the three men rode sedately on, toward their rendezvous with a helicopter from Special Forces Group, Riyadh.

"We've whittled it down to three," said Jardine, waiting patiently as Ronnie Szabodo unraveled himself from his jacket, glancing around for someplace to lay it. As usual, he finished up by laying it on the floor, beside his chair. He carefully opened his spectacles case and put on his steel-rimmed reading glasses.

Szabodo looked up at Jardine and blinked politely. "Ready."

Jardine opened one of three folders and pushed it across the desk at Szabodo, turning it around to face the Hungarian.

"There's a lawyer, a navy pilot, and a soldier."

Szabodo opened the first folder, flipping through it rapidly, then starting at the beginning and reading carefully. Jardine became aware of the busy sound of a pneumatic drill, somewhere down in Lambeth, buzzing away, and the muted rumble of traffic. He found himself regretting, to his surprise, that he had given up smoking, albeit five years before. A lazy June day like this was just right for a luxurious drag of Turkish tobacco.

The clock ticked on the bookcase shelf behind him. The George III carriage clock that Dorothy had given him on their third wedding anniversary, with innards by Thomas Mudge, the inventor of the lever escapement mechanism, and face and casing by Christopher Pinchbeck the younger. A bastard timepiece but rare for that reason. Dorothy had purchased it on impulse, knowing nothing about horology except that David's grandfather had been a clockmaker and was his favorite relation. And she had bought it with her last two hundred pounds, with the same indomitability of youth that young Heather, his secretary, these days manifested so vulnerably.

"Jardine turned back toward Szabodo, who had just said, ". . . about them."

"Sorry, Ronnie. June afternoons like this I used to fall asleep in class."

"Eton, was it?" Jesus, Ronnie was such a snob he was delightful. Like a dog that couldn't keep its nose out of the rubbish can. It made him vulnerable. Like Heather's complete faith in her future with the Magic Office of Real Secrets. Jardine's instinctive recognition of others' vulnerable areas allowed him to feel a certain understanding of them. Natural leaders, his grandpa had taught him, should be keenly aware of their own failings. Sometimes, in his more private thoughts, David Jardine devoutly wished he could have the same confidence in his strengths.

"No, Ronnie, not Eton."

"Tell me about them. Those three. It's all very well the files saying they were each born in South America and have been talent-spotted, vetted, and all their little boxes have been ticked. Okay, they seem like able men, with good careers ahead of them. But I know you, David, and we would not be sitting here, you and me, unless you had done a hell of a lot more homework than is within these plain pink wrappers . . ."

Jardine gazed at Szabodo. "The lawyer doesn't know much about this business, although three years in the Crown Prosecution Service have brought him into contact with Special Branch and the Security Service. He's come into contact with this office twice. Once when he refused to whitewash a little nausea caused by an officer, who is no longer with us, who had broken into the home of a Belgian embassy commercial secretary and was caught burgling his safe. And then when someone, Bill's secretary it turned out to be, in Sovbloc leaked some classified docs to the *Sunday Times.*" Bill's secretary with the large bosom.

"We leaned on him?" asked the Hungarian.

"Not very hard. Legal Section had a quiet word,

damaging to the national interest et cetera. Malcolm wouldn't budge."

"Lefty?"

"As it happens," replied Jardine, "he's a member of the Labour Party but he's not particularly politically minded. Wrote a strong piece condemning militant and the loony left of Lambeth Council. Articulate man. Good brain."

"So he wouldn't play because . . ." Szabodo lazily turned over the pages of Malcolm Strong's file. "He is his own man."

"Seemed that way to us."

Szabodo stared at the file, maybe dissatisfied, certainly unimpressed. "Born in Crieff. Perthshire. Parents were visiting the father's family then returned to Argentina when baby Strong is two months."

"With a British birth certificate." Jardine glanced sharply at Heather as she opened the door, clutching an Urgent signal. She retreated. The door clicked shut.

"Dual nationality thereafter," continued Szabodo, reading from the file. "Scottish father, third-generation rancher. Argentinian mother. Educated Buenos Aires till age thirteen, then Edinburgh Academy and Kings College London. B.A., a good First. Frequent visits back to South America. Worked as Spanish interpreter during his first year of law, with a shipping firm in the city. Called to the bar . . . Crown Prosecution Service. Spotted by . . . Henrietta in Legal. Security NV okay . . . Highly thought of by colleagues, superiors believe destined for the very top . . . interest in him by the Treasury. Good listener . . . accurate reporter . . . reliable under pressure. Health very good. Unmarried. But living with an older woman . . . ." Szabodo peered at Jardine over the rim of glasses.

"A wine merchant. Her father's a solicitor in Salisbury."

"Thirty-four is the sort of age girls start wanting to have babies, isn't it?" Szabodo fumbled around the jacket on the floor, still looking at Jardine, searching for his pipe like a blind man.

"Let's leave out the various stations of the unmarried woman's cross, Ronnie. Can we do that?"

Szabodo shrugged. "You like the cut of his jib."

"Just so." Jardine had not moved during this exchange. He had legendary concentration. "Next?"

"Lieutenant William Guerolo, Royal Navy. A Harrier pilot. Joined during the Falklands war. At present on board RNAS Yeovil. I use the term on board correctly, David, even though Yeovil is a land base."

"He's flown on special duties," replied Jardine. "Behaved exceptionally well on an escape and evasion exercise, when he injured himself. Got captured and had the guts not to let on until he had completed the five-day interrogation. Two broken ribs and a dislocated wrist, with fractures."

"Bloody fool, he might have been unfit for flying." This from Ronnie, who had lobbed a Molotov cocktail down the barrel of a Russian tank. Budapest. 1956.

"Peruvian pride, you see. Mother Peruvian, wealthy banker, father from Leicester. Bloodstock breeder."

Szabodo looked less than impressed. "His Spanish is bilingual—are we sure?"

Jardine could feel the Hungarian's lack of enthusiasm, which worried him, for that would transmit itself to the as yet unsuspecting candidates. "Of course. Ronnie, your pipe has slipped out of the jacket. It's under the chair. . . . Back a bit. Left."

"Thank you David. And the third?" Szabodo put the files back on the desk in such a way that it was obvious they held little of interest to him.

"Henry Ford. He's with Special Forces out in the Gulf. Originally a Scots Guards officer. Tour with an undercover unit in Northern Ireland where he was mentioned in dispatches. Father from County Antrim, mother Scots/ Argentinian, daughter of Perón's foreign minister. Perfect South American Spanish, which explains why the army has sent him to Kuwait. Do you want a match?"

Ronnie caught the box of Swan Vestas and tamped down the tobacco in his pipe bowl, gazing at Jardine with his baleful Magyar stare. "You've been back in the office too long."

"What's eating you?"

"Listen, David, you don't have to sell this thing to me. It's my job. I indoctrinate new talent, help to recruit them, if my services are needed, and turn them into professional operators, thereby doing both them and us a favor."

"And . . . ?"

"So what are their bad points? Who are they screwing? How do they behave when they're pissed? Do they pay their debts—and I don't mean just money, I mean do they look after their friends? What do their worst enemies have to say about them? Are they greedy? Selfish? Thoughtless? Arrogant? What is their personal hygiene, for if they have BO they'll never get near Pablo Envigado, who has a fetish about cleanliness. Did you know that? I want the dirt, David, if I'm to help you at all. So please pick up the phone, get the nasty people onto this case, and we meet again when you have all the dirt on our three heroes." Szabodo scooped up his jacket and stood up, peeling off his steel-rimmed reading glasses with his left hand. He gazed down at Jardine and smiled. "I'm proud of you, David. I remember taking you in out of Wonderland and turning you into a spy. I'm too fond of you to allow you to turn into a civil bloody servant." The Hungarian paused at the door, his hand on the handle, and inclined his balding head slightly to one side. "I suppose that was insubordinate."

Somewhere out in Wonderland, as Ronnie Szabodo called the innocent, nonsecret world, an ambulance siren wailed and faded into the distance.

"It was timely. What the hell's happening to me, Ronnie? I wasn't taking this seriously." And one of those Joes is going to go out to Colombia and risk his balls.

Szabodo smiled. "Give me a shout when you've got the business on them. I'll be at home." And he left, leaving the door open so that Heather knew she could go in.

Jardine gazed at the empty doorway and smiled. Thank God for friends . . .

––––––

A pair of crows tugged at the entrails of a dead rabbit. The machine-gun tapping of a woodpecker sounded from the copse nearby. Justice Eugene Pearson sat on a boulder, gazing down the valley toward a low, white-washed, slate-roofed cottage. He watched the lean, bearded figure of the chief of staff climb easily up toward him, the old briar pipe clenched between his tobacco-stained teeth. This time, three of Casey's wingers could be seen, spread out across the area, two with shotguns, one with a big mongrel hound. One of earshot put on the lookout, as ever, for strangers.

Casey reached the judge and nodded, sitting on the turf and leaning his back against a rock. A fit man, and confident. Comfortable in himself.

"You met him, I hear."

"You knew, didn't you? You knew what was going to happen. You set me up to be an accomplice to . . . murder."

Casey frowned, as if concerned by Pearson's controlled anger. "I heard there was a shooting in Paris.

60

Some fella from Venice . . . Good God, Eugene. Was that Restrepo's work? And how were you involved?"

"As if you didn't know. They've got my photo. Standing there on some bridge with the Whore of Venice dead at my feet and his blood on my face."

"Well now, that sure is involved, all right. Eugene, as God is my judge, I never imagined that would happen. You poor aul sod. Tell us about it . . ." And he looked up, all innocent, gazing comfortably into Pearson's head with his killer's eye, behind gold-rimmed aviator glasses.

Eugene Pearson told him what had happened from the moment Restrepo had sat at his table. About Restrepo's pitch, about the Whore of Venice being the existing cocaine distributor for the cartel, his murder by the kid on the trail bike, the flash of the photographer's camera, and the drive through Paris until he was dropped off in Montparnasse, left to find his own way back to the Hotel Cayre, where he was sure the gendarmes would be waiting for him. But of course, mused Casey, they were not. The one thing the Provisional IRA knew was that you could murder a man in broad daylight and simply disappear without trace. Why, hadn't Casey himself done just that to two Brit soldiers as they had left a supermarket with their wives and toddlers? He could still see the pushchair and the plump, well-fed infant as he had pushed past the terrified Brit mothers and stridden off into the crowd of Saturday-morning shoppers, dropping the .45 Webley revolver into the pram of a couple of teenage girls on their seventh such job. It seemed like only yesterday but in fact that had been nineteen years ago, next month.

Brendan Casey glanced at Pearson as he finished his quietly outraged tale. "So what do you think, Eugene, is the man on the level? Because two million a month would sure bring things to a head."

Pearson stared at him. "Brendan, we can't link the

Armed Struggle to drug trafficking. Christ almighty, aren't we icing pushers in Dublin and Cork City? Think of the effect on Fianna, and the parents." Fianna was the youth organization of Provisional Sinn Fein, the organization's political wing.

Casey studied his pipe, which had gone out. The woodpecker had stopped. The three wingers had merged with the landscape and could no longer be seen. For a long moment, he didn't say a thing. Then he spoke, gazing at the cottage, way down the valley, "Eugene, I can rock the British government. I have enough weaponry to send London back to the Blitz. I have enough activists to slaughter soldiers and their whores throughout Europe and certain parts of the Gulf. This is a strategy you have had a hand in shaping, right?"

"You know I have."

"And you have a brother who is a Jesuit scholar . . ."

"Get to the point, Brendan."

"The point is," said the chief of staff, "I will sup with the devil, if it is going to help bring this thing to the boil."

"And when word gets around . . . ? The scandal will lose us support at the grass roots."

Casey sneered, his comfortable academic mask slipping. "The grass roots? Where would we be if we gave a shite about the grass roots? They're not good enough for the Ireland we're fashioning on this anvil, Eugene. On this anvil of lead and blood. Don't mention the grass bloody roots to me. If it was up to them there would be no Armed Struggle of any weight. Just a few bombs now and then, a few Brits shot in time for the six o'clock news. Just enough for them to get the occasional hard-on and nudge each other and wink and raise their glass of stout and say 'we did that.' Well there's no fuckin' 'we' involved. When the chips are down it's us. You and me and the forty-three other men and women who constitute the fighting arm of the Provisional IRA. Jesus, the Brits would wet themselves if they knew how few we really are."

Casey stood up and stared over the valley, not at the grass and trees but at Ireland's past and future. "Your task, Eugene, is threefold. Make sure we can do business with Restrepo. Work out a blueprint for an absolutely watertight unit to handle collection from the . . . importers and distribution. And make yourself responsible for seeing that the operation's kept at arm's length from the movement, so that if the shit does hit the fan, the Organization remains pure."

Somewhere in the copse, the woodpecker started again. Pearson was angry and afraid. Angry with himself for having been suckered into the dangerous position he found himself in, with some bunch of Colombians holding a photograph that could destroy him at any time. And angry with himself for being afraid of this semieducated Belfast hoodlum who had survived a dozen attempts to oust him by his even more bloodthirsty colleagues, who now ran the Provisionals from the uncivilized, brutal side of the border.

"I really cannot advise the council to have the remotest dealings with something so filthy as narcotics," he found himself saying. Obliged to say.

"There's a hotel in Florence," announced Casey, as if the judge had never spoken, "the Villa San Michele. It's an old monastery, with friezes so they say by Michelangelo. Book yourself in there for one night, between the sixth and the tenth of next month. I'll provide you with backup, from local friends in the Brigate Rosse. I'm annoyed with Restrepo for compromising you like that. We'll make sure it doesn't happen again."

Casey glanced back at Pearson. "Give my regards to Mharaid. And the girl." And he started off back down the hillside without looking back.

Pearson watched Casey go. Well, so be it, he would take the meeting in Florence. But without help from the Red Brigades; the fewer people involved the better. That he had to go, he didn't doubt, for Casey had set him up, the Machiavellian bastard, and in so doing had neutralized the principal voice of dissent on the Army Council. But sometime during the negotiation phase, Pearson knew he would find a way of spoiling Casey's dangerous, potentially disastrous, scheme. And he shuddered, involuntarily, unable to get that shattered face out of his mind. And the flash of the flashbulb. And the blood on his collar, on his jacket. He had burned them in his hotel room, torn into neat, small squares, with trembling hands. It had taken all night, and with the dawn, no peace had come.

There was a pub near the office called the Goose and Firkin. It was out of bounds to the toilers in the secret glass box but its ham rolls were thick and fresh and succulent, with crisp lettuce and tomatoes and tearjerking hot English mustard. And they brewed their own beer on the premises.

David Jardine—almost elegant in his light brown, double-breasted Prince of Wales check, colorful silk handkerchief tucked into his top pocket with a carelessness that Ronnie Szabodo spent fruitless hours in front of a mirror trying to achieve—moved carefully across the sawdust-covered floor, carrying two pints of beer past the students and Telecom workers and staff from the Eye Hospital, to the thick-set Hungarian, who sat at a table near the jazz piano player, so that no one could overhear their conversation.

Jardine had put the nasty people, as Szabodo had called Security Section, back onto the three possibles.

He had called Szabodo back in and now they knew all the things about Strong, Guerolo, and Ford that the young men would not like their mothers, wives, or bank managers to know. For instance, Guerolo had run up a debt with a bookmaker and paid it off with money borrowed from his bank for a "full-dress uniform." And Ford liked to give the impression he was part of the Ford dynasty, of Model-T fame. He was liked by his soldiers but considered by his brother officers to be too ambitious, to the point of ruthlessness. Strong had occasionally patronized seedy massage parlors when he was an undergraduate, a fact of which he was apparently now ashamed. Guerolo sometimes drank too much but knew how to keep his lip buttoned. Strong had a conviction for breach of the peace, which he had not declared when he applied for the Crown Prosecution Service and which, as he had clearly guessed, had not come to light, being eight years old and in another part of the country. And Ford had been sleeping with a girl corporal in the Royal Signals before he became engaged to the girl who was now his wife of eighteen months. For an officer to sleep with an enlisted rank was a court-martial offense, being a breach of military discipline. But Ford had not been found out, except by SIS's nasty people.

"Happier now?" asked Jardine as he sat down, placing one pint in front of the Hungarian.

"Getting there," replied Szabodo, lifting the pint glass to his lips and swallowing a good mouthful. He set the glass on the scrubbed wood table and met Jardine's gaze. "The lawyer is in front. At this stage."

"Many a slip, Ronnie. But I tend to agree with you."

"The flyer has possibilities. So does the soldier. But we've not had enormous luck with military types as operators unless we've caught them really young." Ronnie Szabodo gazed over his beer glass at Jardine. "Guerolo and Ford are just a bit too mature. More indoctrinated into the uniformed services way of thinking."

"Which is very different from ours?" Jardine could never be really sure what Szabodo was getting at. The Magyar brain sometimes seemed to transmit on a different frequency.

Szabodo grinned, the missing tooth beside his two front teeth a dark, piratical gap. The Hungarian only wore his uncomfortable denture plate in polite company, and he apparently did not consider David Jardine merited the effort.

"Immeasurably," he replied. "Time to tickle them up, don't you think?"

There was not really a set formula for recruiting a Joe, thought Jardine as his taxi made a right off the Mall, passing St. James's Place on the left. Take eagerness, for example. Eagerness was by and large regarded with deep suspicion by the office, the reason being that to the uninitiated, secret intelligence business is only familiar through spy fiction, earnest journalism, often hinting at skulduggery in the dark alleys of international affairs, exposés by disenfranchised former spooks, and "experts" who made up for ignorance with knowing references and cobbled innuendo. Plus supposition and fantasy. In fact, supposition and fantasy abounded, even among the worthiest of journalists and, contemplated Jardine wryly, as he paid the taxi driver in the lower part of Saint James's Street, civil servants, who should know better.

The meeting with the prime minister was a case in point. The PM himself was too practical to imagine all sorts of wild nonsense about the secret workings of SIS. But Giles Foley, the cabinet secretary, who had more contact with the outfit than most—even he, Jardine detected, was privately rather impressed with the secret, clandestine, slightly racy business of espionage.

And so of course was David Arbuthnot Jardine, but like the other alumni of the great glass box, he kept that fact most closely guarded. Those employed in the secret world pretended it was all terribly mundane. Even to each other.

Thus, eagerness was suspect. For it was bound to be based on penny thrillers and an overactive imagination and, worse, idealism. Idealism was the very worst. The only factors that might rescue a possible candidate from the curse of eagerness were either that the Joe lived under the thumb of a brutal oppressor and was enthusiastic about the opportunity to strike back or else the Joe had heard (wrongly) that the pay was quite good.

Nothing, on the other hand, would rescue the possible candidate from idealism.

Jardine strolled toward the club, not his club, which was in the same street and where he would never dream of acknowledging a potential agent, but the club of a respected acquaintance of long standing. Quite close to the safe house where Dmitri had been debriefed on the day of his defection. And just two blocks from the daily-rate apartment where he had trysted with Nicola. What a waste. And no cynics, he reminded himself. Never trust a man who believed in nothing. For then he could not believe in himself.

He mounted the few steps to the august building.

Was Strong a cynic? Jardine didn't know but he hoped soon to find out.

"Good evening, sir. Starting to rain?"

"Good evening. I am a guest of Mr. Goodwin." And David Jardine handed his dripping folding umbrella with something approaching insouciance to Paterson, the tall, pock-cheeked, cadaverous porter, of Pellings, one of London's oldest and most exclusive gentlemen's clubs.

Standing at the bar was Arnold Goodwin, QC, one of the ablest bankers in the country, deep in conversation with a stocky, well-fed young man with thinning hair and able, intelligent eyes. And fluent, bilingual Spanish.

"Why, David. How nice to see you. This is Malcolm Strong."

"How do you do?" David Jardine, DJ to his underlings, smiled his cobra smile. Nicola's pet name for him had been Cobra, for reasons that would be prurient to reveal. "I'm David Jardine."

"How do you do?" said Malcolm Strong, and he gripped Jardine's hand, thereby changing the course of his entire life.

4

DEAD END STREET

Eddie Lucco still enjoyed driving his Dodge sedan with the siren on and the red police light on his dashboard flashing. After two auto wrecks in the early seventies, he did not drive excessively fast. Steve McQueen and Gene Hackman must've been responsible for a plethora of dead and crippled detectives trying to duplicate their crazy car chases without the benefit of choreographed traffic, trick photography, and low loaders. The cop on duty at the scene of crime was Benwell's kid brother, Martin, and he lifted the yellow tape up to let the Dodge pass inside the cordoned area, its siren dying and the eyes of the small crowd that had gathered following its passage.

Lucco switched the engine off and put the gear to Park. He opened the door and climbed out, taking his time so that he could figure out which cops, which reporters, and whoever else were present. The sprawled legs of one of the victims protruded from under a uniformed cop's black cape. It looked to Lucco like

Batman in jeans had made a crash landing. He nodded to Danny Mulrooney, the big, as in large, Narcotics lieutenant, meeting the red-haired detective's small, piggy eyes with sparse ginger eyebrows above them.

"Bad news, Piggy. How'd it happen?"

In the background was the sound of another whooping siren, approaching through the five o'clock traffic. The Irishman peeled a stick of gum and fed it, ruminatively, into his mouth, as if Lucco had asked him a seriously difficult question. Finally he shrugged. "Motherfuckers heard his wire talking back to him. Fuckin' Tech. Department bastards, inefficient as shit. I want right now to take their fuckin' wires and shove them you know where. Kid was twenty-seven years of age, not a bad cop as cops go, and four fuckin' months of fuckin' work out the fuckin' window."

Fuckin' bad luck, agreed Lucco, as he glowered at Smarty Robson, the ratlike stringer for the *Evening News*, who had hovered, like a ghost, ever closer till he could eavesdrop on Pig Mulrooney's grief, which is what the big Irish detective had been expressing.

Robson twitched as Lucco's eyes bored into him. His shoulders sagged. He spread his hands, "Hey, gimme a break, Eddie. You know I ain't gonna quote that."

"Smarty, go play in the traffic." Lucco walked over to the corpse of Benjamin Ortega, the dead detective and lifted the cape, which was kind of sticky on the underside. Shot in the head so that one half of the face was still okay. Lucco wondered if the post-mortem photographer would have the grace to wipe the good part and straighten his hair. Like the Missing Persons photograph of Jane Doe, aged between seventeen and nineteen, lying cold and unclaimed in Bellevue morgue.

"I hear you got landed with a Jane Doe," observed Mulrooney.

Lucco studied the entry hole, about the diameter of

a ragged egg cup, just behind the left ear. Given the awful exit wound, the dead man had probably been shot with a mini-Uzi machine pistol. Favored weapon of the Colombians and the Yardies, the cocaine pushers from Jamaica. "Yeah, so I did. So here I figure we got a crack deal that went bad on you." The dead detective was black. "We're talking Yardies, right? So up here on Ninety-third, I figure it's gotta be Simba Patrice and one of his brothers. Let's see, Abdullah was in the deli on Broadway and Forty-fourth at one fifty. So we're talking PeeWee, that's my guess. And that big Cuban they use as a driver. Big Afro." PeeWee was the nickname the cops had for the youngest of the three Patrice brothers, all violent crack dealers, all known killers, the oldest being twenty-four.

"Eddie, you sure earn your pay." Mulrooney's pig eyes glanced around the scene as Lucco lowered the black plastic cape over the murdered undercover cop. "It was PeeWee greased Benjamin, and Roberto Ferdinand, the Cuban, was bagman. They ripped the fuckin' wire from off him, so the DA won't let me use the fuckin' tape in evidence. You wonder whose side they're on in that goddamn office."

Lucco learned that the other corpse was that of an innocent bystander, a wino who had got in the way, maybe mistaken for an undercover detective. He agreed that he would endeavor to arrest PeeWee Patrice and Roberto Ferdinand. Also he would haul in Simba Patrice, boss of the Blade Claw street gang and a point of contact with the Colombians who smuggled and distributed most of the cocaine that found its way into New York City from Antioquia via Medellín, Barranquilla, and New Orleans. He walked back toward his car, the big Irishman at his side. More police vehicles were arriving and a TV news team sat in their blue-and-white jeep talking to Benwell, trying to decide if the murder in broad daylight of a narcotics detective was worth getting their equipment out of the car for. Then they saw Mulrooney, who had something of a reputation as a dope buster, in close conversation with Lucco, who was known to be on the up in 14th Precinct Homicide. They exchanged glances, shrugged, and started, without much enthusiasm, to get out of the jeep.

"I figure you musta asked for it," observed Mulrooney as they reached Lucco's tan, unmarked Dodge.

"Asked for what?" asked Lucco, mystified.

"The Jane Doe. I mean, here you are. Coupla seconds on the scene here an' you know the who and the how and like that. You do Homicide standing on your head, but you know what?"

"What's that?"

"You were at Grand Central when the Jane was found, I heard that. Is that true?"

"Yeah."

"Well, sometimes they get to you. Some of them fuckin' cadavers." He shrugged, watching the reflection of his dead detective reflected on the driver's window of the Dodge as Lucco opened the door.

Lucco waited till Mulrooney met his gaze.

"I'll get PeeWee for you."

Mulrooney stared at him. He blinked, and a tear ran down his slab Celt cheek. He nodded. And turned away.

As Lucco climbed behind the wheel and started the engine, he heard Mulrooney's dulcet tones yelling at Smarty Robson and the TV crew to get their fuckin' feet out the fuckin' evidence. Eddie Lucco smiled and eased the car away as Benwell lifted the tape for him. Pull in PeeWee and the Cuban, he thought, and they might just recognize the photo of that kid. The Jane Doe.

Malcolm Strong was nothing like his file, which failed to surprise David Jardine. Neither the Personnel notes, the Security investigations, nor the psychological profile bore more than a passing resemblance to the mildly overweight, good-humored, competent man of medium height standing on the steps of Pellings beside Jardine, who squinted at the darkening sky, wondering if it was going to rain again.

"Do you have far to go?" asked the barrister.

Jardine mentioned Fulham but said he wanted to pop into Waitrose in the Kings Road first because he had run out of milk and one or two snacks for the deep freeze. He had already let Strong know that his wife was a television producer with the BBC and she was filming in Holland for a few days. Strong said he had his car and would be happy to give Jardine a ride.

"If it's not out of your way," Jardine said.

"Not at all. I live in Mallord Street," Strong replied. Jardine knew that. He knew the number, 64B, and he knew how many pints of milk Strong and Jean had delivered each week and about the daily copies of *The Independent* and the *Telegraph*, with *New Statesman* and *Yachting Monthly* at weekends. He also knew that Strong had his car with him because Ronnie and two of Kate's Recruitment/Planning section had communicated the fact to him before he had left the office and strolled down to Westminster Bridge, where he had caught a taxi. In Wonderland, as the Hungarian would have put it.

"Well, that would be very nice of you."

"It's just round the corner. You can sometimes get a parking space in St. James's Yard, it's so busy around here people don't usually bother to look." And Malcolm Strong strolled up the street and into the narrow lane called St. James's Yard, where his blue BMW 320, registration number G 121 RDH, was parked.

The initial, seemingly casual meeting had gone off

well. Arnold Goodwin and Strong knew each other not only as fellow members of Pellings but as keen followers of the turf. Strong was impressed by the banker, who had gone into the City from the bar, where he had specialized in company law, at the age of forty-two and had risen to the top in five years. Jardine guessed that was a career route that Strong had contemplated for himself.

Jardine had joined them in the smoking room, where one or two mutual friends had paused to take a drink and pass the time of day. Jardine was not a particularly clubbable person, and even though he was a member of one of the oldest and most prestigious gentlemen's clubs in town, he found he generally preferred the retainers, the porters and bar staff, to most of the members. He had mentioned this, confidentially, to Strong, and the young barrister had chuckled and appreciated Jardine's candor. There was nothing like honesty, he mused, to make a good impression on a decent man. Conversation had been fairly broad, but David Jardine had a natural charm that had got him out of many a difficult situation and into one or two almost unassailable bedrooms. He had trailed his coat with practiced ease, so that by the time Strong offered him a ride to King's Road, the circumstance had been so deftly manipulated that Jardine (and Ronnie Szabodo, who was not far away) would have been very surprised if the cards had fallen any other way.

Getting a potential recruit interested, long before the Joe was even remotely aware, was like any seduction, and like fly-fishing, there was no point in attempting it unless one really enjoyed the thrill of the chase. Jardine knew there was no chase involved in fly-fishing but he knew what he meant.

"Spanish," Malcolm Strong was saying, as he maneuvered the BMW into Hyde Park Corner. "Spanish and French. And a little Italian."

Jardine had asked him where he was going on holiday and when Strong had replied Madrid, he had inquired, seemingly making polite conversation, if the lawyer spoke any foreign languages.

"Italian?" Jardine said. "God, I'd love to be fluent in Italian. It would make my Puccini records make much more sense."

"What languages do you have, being a diplomat?" Strong inquired.

"Like you, Spanish. A little French. Some Russian. And German. Touch of Arabic."

"Je-sus." Strong laughed. "You must understand Italian." Then he glanced at Jardine and smiled. "But of course you said you'd love to be *fluent*."

"You're right, señor," replied Jardine, in correct and fluent northern Spanish, which is similar to South American Spanish. That is, without the Castilian lisp.

"*Arriba, hombre,*" said Strong. "You sound like you lived all your life in Vigo, or in Ecuador."

They carried on the conversation in Spanish, relaxing all the time. To Jardine's relief, Strong spoke totally fluent, unaccented Argentinian Spanish. When they pulled up outside Waitrose, in the King's Road in Chelsea, the first meet had gone so well that Jardine was almost tempted to suggest a beer in the nearby Phene pub, with its pleasant walled garden. But fifteen years of the delicate minuet that was agent recruiting quite properly got in the way, and Jardine hauled himself out and glanced up at the sky.

Big, thundery drops of rain were starting to fall. He leaned down and touched his forehead with his index finger. "*Muchas gracias, hombre. Buenas noches y vaya con fortuna.*"

Malcolm Strong smiled up at him, lowering his window the way we all have to do when somebody speaks to us from outside the car. "Great to meet you, David. Listen, if you're on your own tonight, why not pop round to our flat? We could nip out for a hamburger or something."

"Wouldn't dream of it, dear boy." Jardine grinned. He refrained from mentioning he knew what Malcolm and Jean, aged thirty-four, wine merchant, preferred to get up to after a hard day at their respective offices.

"Maybe lunch one day? It's so great to be able to speak in my native tongue, with someone who speaks the lingo."

"Your native tongue?" asked Jardine, looking genuinely surprised and all the time thinking to himself, you bloody great whore you. "How can that be?"

"I was brought up in Argentina. Listen, can I phone you? Do you have a card?"

"Just ring the Foreign Office, two-three-three three thousand. Ask for David Jardine in Protocol." The rain was landing like dead, wet, thunderbugs on his head and shoulders.

"Two-three-three three thousand. Protocol. I'll give you a ring, do you mind?"

"Not at all, dear boy. Welcome any chance to get away from the office."

"Are you in King Charles Street?" asked Strong, as he signaled he was pulling out and glanced in his mirror.

"General area. General area, Malcolm. You're all clear if you go now. Nice meeting you. Cheers."

And the BMW pulled away into the road, accelerating. Jardine gazed after it, satisfied. Ronnie Szabodo's gray Ford Escort was parked across the street. Jardine hunched his collar up against the rain and sprinted across King's Road to the Ford.

Inside the car, he pulled the door shut, rainwater dripping from his hair, down his forehead.

"How did it go?" asked the Hungarian.

"Like a bloody dream, Ronnie. Would to God I had the same luck with the ladies."

"I brought your overnight bag."

"Why?" Jardine was looking forward to a quiet whiskey with Ronnie, back at his Tite Street flat, and a plan of campaign to ensnare Guerolo and the young soldier, Henry Ford.

"Captain Ford is about to be promoted to acting major, to command B Squadron Twenty-two SAS. The way things are going in the Gulf, it'll be the chance of a lifetime for him. He's an ambitious young man, he's just been recommended for a Military Cross for work behind the lines dressed as Lawrence of Arabia or some such, and there's no way Harry Ford—he's called Harry, by the way, not Henry—there's no way, David old sport, he's going to turn that down to do a contract job with the firm. I mean, would you?"

Jardine slumped in the seat, his bounce evaporating. "Doubt it."

"So we strike him from the list?"

"Do we, hell. Sounds like the sort of guy I could use on Corrida."

"Corrida?"

"It's the code name for this job. Mrs. Brownlow swears Corrida just fell out from the computer, at random. No, we do not strike him from the list. Where is Johnny McAlpine right now?" Lieutenant Colonel J. C. D. McAlpine was the commanding officer of 22nd Special Air Service Regiment.

"Stirling Lines. Hereford."

"Okay, drive us down, I'll trade places if you get tired." Jardine lifted the car-phone handset from its cradle and punched out 192, for Directory Inquiries.

"What are you doing?" asked Szabodo.

"Book us in at the Dynador."

"It's done. That's why I brought your overnight bag."

"Might just change your name to Jeeves, Ronnie. Tell you what. I'll book us dinner in that smart little place run by the two poofs."

"I booked already," said the Hungarian, swinging the car right into Gunther Grove and heading north, for Oxford, Cheltenham, and the Bristol Suspension Bridge.

———

Round about the time when David Jardine and Szabodo were strolling through the streets of Hereford, after a decent enough meal of asparagus vinaigrette followed by poached salmon, with ornately sculptured pieces of courgette and tomato, plus a side order of new potatoes, washed down with a bottle and a half of Californian chardonnay, on their way back to the comfort of the Dynador Hotel and possibly a nightcap of malt whiskey, Harry Ford was inching his way, flat on his stomach, across the trough of a sand ripple toward a well-concealed bunker, under whose camouflage netting the pale, flickering green of electronic dials occasionally illuminated the faces of two Iraqi signals sergeants and a military intelligence major sitting on an upturned ammo box behind them. It was a moonless night. Overhead, the smooth thunder of American B-52 bombers passed relentlessly. The now familiar rumbling and concussion of carpet bombing and the noise, like calico tearing, of artillery rocket barrages were mercifully distant, for a change.

Harry wore the filthy, worn fatigues of an Iraqi corporal in the 43rd Security Company of the 17th Paratroop Brigade of the Republican Guard. His weapon was a silenced AKS assault rifle with folding stock, manufactured in the Soviet Union. Over one eye, held in position by a band around his head, was a night-vision device, which rendered everything within its field a clear picture in varying shades of green. Around his web belt were a variety of pouches and water bottles, along with a 9mm Makarov pistol, wire cutters, and a fighting knife. Only his feet gave him away, for neither Harry nor the sergeant and two corporals behind him would wear anything but the sand-proof, comfortable, lace-up desert boots, perfected over many years by the Research Wing at Hereford and made specially for their regiment by an old, established English shoe company.

Under the camouflage netting and the roof of sandbags over reinforced metal rods, Major Modhafar Nahji al-Salim listened intently to the coalition radio signals being intercepted by his two technicians. Modhafar was a graduate of Princeton University, where he had majored in political science. It had been his intention to settle in the USA and work in the media, possibly with some kind of teaching appointment on the side. He had returned to Baghdad in order to be at his mother's deathbed toward the end of the disastrous eight-year war with Iran. Modhafar had already served in the infantry for one year's obligatory service, but his family connections (his mother was in the diplomatic service) had secured his discharge and he had left Iraq for America and a new life.

Unfortunately for Modhafar, Iraq was short of experts on the American political system, and he was served with call-up papers for compulsory military service as he checked in at the airport for his flight back to the States. And here he was, five years later, a major in Intelligence (Interception and Battlefield Analysis) four weeks into another disastrous war. The measure of his success in his surprise military career was that the equipment his two sergeants were operating was Seconics B, a state-of-the-art electronic-interception facility manufactured by OmegaWerken GmBh of Munich and secretly transported to Iraq through Jordan by a South African arms dealer who was, as far as the Swiss/Belgian intermediary was concerned, the end user. Included in the eighteen-million-dollar deal was a course of instruction, and Modhafar and his team had been among twenty Iraqi intelligence and signals experts who had been trained in operating procedures during a secret four-week visit to the factory in Munich.

The job of the unit was to monitor signature emissions from coalition forces immediately south of their position in order to identify armored and infantry groupings preparatory to chemical delivery by FROG missile and artillery shelling.

The coalition forces immediately to the south were the 1st British Division, under Lieutenant General Sir Peter de la Billiere, a highly decorated soldier who had, on his way to the top, commanded the SAS Special Forces Group with skill and panache.

As Modhafar watched the various electronic dials and screens, listening in his earphones to reports from the two other Seconics B units in his Echelon 2 Battle Area, he noticed that enemy movement was changing from its usual pattern. With some interest, he plotted a forward prognosis and realized that the British were, for the first time, presenting worthwhile targets for a chemical strike. The FROGs were armed with a paralyzing nerve agent that caused agonizing and certain death within minutes of contact, either through the skin or by inhalation. Modhafar knew that such a risk by the enemy could only mean one thing—preparation for an imminent attack. And outside his bunker, Harry Ford and his team of three had just killed the last of the platoon of Republican Guards assigned to protect the Seconics B operators.

Silent killing is part of the Special Forces stock in trade. Harry and his team were seasoned professionals, who used Ibn trackers from Borneo and Mujahadeen Pathans from the Panshir Valley in Afghanistan to teach them and to test their skills in the deadly art of ghostlike infiltration and silent death.

Modhafar Nahji al-Salim was slightly annoyed when Sergeant Mukdad slumped over his dials and equipment. Still, thirty hours with no more than a few snatched minutes of sleep . . . Then followed cold alarm, stark terror in his groin, as the other sergeant, Ismail, jerked upright, half rising from his stool and vomiting blood, a great deal of it, all over the Seconics B monitors. Then a hard, dry, warm hand was clamped over his mouth, his elbows were pinioned to his side, his legs and feet were strapped in an instant by some kind of binding. His eyes, large and white, pivoted frantically as two shadowy figures attached small frame charges to the equipment, in precisely the correct places to destroy it forever.

Then one of the figures turned to lean close to his face. When the man spoke, it was in the language of Iraq, but the accent of Oman.

"Listen to me, Nahji al-Salim," the swarthy, mustached man breathed. To Modhafar's confusion, the men were dressed in Republican Guard paratroopers' uniforms. "You are a prisoner of war. You will be treated according to the Geneva Convention. We are taking you away from here. You can walk, or you can be left here dead with your men. I take it you prefer to come with us?"

The shame of powerful fear racked him from within, his heart thumped so that it seemed about to burst from his chest, his limbs trembled, and yet there was the hint of . . . kindness about his captor. He nodded. Harry Ford unwrapped the bindings around his legs and they helped Major al-Salim to his feet, hustling him out from the bunker and half dragging him rapidly from the position. He glimpsed the bodies of a dozen men lying on the dark sand, crumpled in death without having fired a shot. One of his captors hauled him upright as his legs collapsed.

"I think," whispered one soldier in English with a Scottish brogue, "he'd've preferred the bombing after all." And another of them chuckled.

———

"Harry Ford?" replied Johnny McAlpine, pouring tea from a silver teapot into three Delft china cups. "Delightful fellow. Great sense of humor . . ."

Jardine smiled and accepted the cup. He was in the living room of McAlpine's house, set in the country, not far from Hereford, where Johnny commanded 22 SAS Regiment. The two men were not strangers for, as Justice Pearson had correctly surmised, the Special Air Service was indeed operating in Colombia, helping to train protection, tracking, surveillance, and special-assault units of the Colombian DAS, its Secret Police, the National Police, and certain elite army companies. And in fact the relationship between the SAS and its Foreign Office client, the Secret Intelligence Service, reached back beyond Afghanistan, Argentina, Borneo, Oman, and Aden to the Second World War. Via many adventures in many countries, some hostile, some neutral, which would no doubt be horrified to learn of them. The regiment also operated in Northern Ireland, but that was for another client, the Security Service, known to the popular press as MI-5.

McAlpine sipped his tea and gazed out of his study window, across the back lawn to the farmland beyond, a few elm and birch trees dotting the somewhat bleak landscape. A flurry of crows settled on a far corner of the pasture, to the right of the wheat field. He wore a pair of comfortable cord trousers and a cotton shirt, with the sleeves fastened by gold cuff links. His necktie was of paisley pattern and his feet were clad in old, well-polished leather brogues. The colonel was not particularly tall, nor particularly aggressive-looking, considering his regiment's fearsome reputation. In fact, he looked more like a public-school teacher, history or classics, thought David Jardine, than a professional soldier. Only the lean figure and the eyes gave him away.

"How's Jerry?" asked McAlpine.

"He's fine." Jerry Kennedy, tipped to succeed Steven McCrae as chief of the intelligence service, had been the regiment's principal point of contact in the early days, bringing the SAS out of its backwater where potential rivals like the Parachute Regiment's independent companies and the Royal Marines' commando units had been jostling for involvement in special operations in the postwar cold-war world of the early 1960s. In the secret world, names of individuals were used like talismans, that indicated just how close, how up to date, how trusted, how close to the hub of things were the speakers. This was a world where much of the spoken word was oblique to the point of obscurancy. To the uninitiated, a conversation loaded with hints and confirmations, with trading of scraps of information and acknowledgment, would pass unnoticed, except perhaps for its banality. Thus mused Jardine as he watched McAlpine and sipped the tea, realizing even as the thought flitted by that he was being harsh on the soldier, who had long enough experience of the firm without the need to seem "in touch." Suspicion and elitism were soon acquired, working for the office. Jardine didn't know if he was too far divorced from Wonderland to shrug off such afflictions. He devoutly hoped not.

"It's good of you to see me at such short notice."

"I wasn't terribly surprised when you phoned." Johnny turned to face Jardine, leaning against the windowsill. "You stayed at the Dynador last night, rather than the mess, where you're always welcome, David. I couldn't think of many reasons for you people to be in Hereford other than us, but maybe that's big-headed. And you had with you that Hungarian who worked with the regiment on Codicil."

"Ronnie." Op Codicil had been to smuggle stranded agents out from East Germany when the Berlin Wall came down. "He's a card."

"Is he still with Exfiltration? I heard he had moved to Ops Training."

"Ronnie does a bit of everything, he's retired twice."

"Yes, but what else would he do . . . ?"

"Right now he's working for me in Covert Selection and Advances."

"Ah . . ." The colonel met Jardine's frank gaze. Not a man, thought Jardine, he would care to fall out with. "You can't have Harry Ford, David. I need him to take over B Squadron. We're in the middle of a war, you see." He smiled coldly.

Jardine realized the office was not alone in inspiring suspicion and elitism. It made him feel better. He told McAlpine that he had been required by the prime minister to find and recruit a handful of men with very particular qualifications to carry out a mission that was very close to the PM's heart. Jardine explained that he had been put in a difficult position because his boss, Steven McCrae, had, it seemed, given the impression the men were already recruited.

McAlpine's face had lost its relaxed and genial expression. "And one of my officers was mentioned in this context?"

"My dear Johnny, absolutely not. No no no. But there are very few candidates in the country who fit the bill. Your Harry Ford is one of only three. I'm sure you wouldn't want me to discuss the other two."

"What's so special about Harry?"

"His training. His aptitude. His reliability. And his . . . background."

"You know he's bilingual, is that it?"

"Bilingual. Yes, of course, it's on his file. Spanish, right?" Jardine's lack of expression conveyed that Ford's linguistic ability was known but was not of great importance.

"Spanish." Johnny gazed at him, preoccupied, listening.

Outside, the McAlpines' beat-up old Volvo passed the gray stone dike and turned into the yard, driven by Sheila, Johnny's wife, with a lean, swarthy man in sweater and leather zip-up beside her. A dusty, short wheel-based Land Rover pulled up on the road outside, blocking the gate. Two youngish men inside, hair long and untidy. Jardine noted with approval that the regiment looked after its commanding officer and his family. The lean man got out, then Sheila. Then a woman of about twenty-six, with silky, fair hair, cut on the long side, climbed out from the backseat. She was slightly above average height and said something that made Sheila and the bodyguard laugh. Her amused, intelligent eyes seemed to meet Jardine's as he watched from behind the living-room window. Jardine smiled at himself. The girl clearly had no idea he was there, or cared.

Johnny McAlpine moved away from the window and flopped into an old wing chair, neatly balancing his cup and saucer, revealing by his body language that he was relieved that Sheila had made it back one more time from the school run. Jardine reflected on what a bloody strain it must be to be one of the most targeted men in England from a variety of terrorist enemies. He knew that IRA had reconnoitered Hereford and its environs and that at least six conspiracies to murder Johnny or his brother officers had been foiled, two of them at the very last minute. To his surprise, David Jardine felt a strong twinge of emotion and sympathy. So much for cynicism. Thank God.

He laid his cup in its saucer on the desk. "Johnny, it's Colombia. I need to put a man inside the Medellín Cartel."

His sincerity, finally breaking through, communicated itself to McAlpine, who held his gaze.

"You know, David, there's a guy who sits in Century House, in a rather neglected office called ISML." ISML was the Intelligence Service Military Liaison section. The theory was that whenever the office wanted to work with the army—or borrow one or two of its specialists, or use a military unit in some far-off land where the army had a presence, as cover for a clandestine operation, or otherwise do business with the military—then ISML would be approached and wheels would turn, according to the procedures the system had laid down at that time.

David Jardine shuffled his feet slightly and contrived to look embarrassed, an emotion that was quite foreign to his instincts, then gave the well-worn reply to such a remark. "Problem is . . . Problem is, Johnny, this is a black operation. The fewer people who know the better. Even my own section, I swear, will not know the names of those three. Not their real names."

He hunched his shoulders until his neck had all but disappeared. The sight of Jardine trying to look discomfitted would have had Kate, the behavioral psychologist, reduced to tears of mirth.

"When?" asked the colonel, who was less than fooled by this performance. From the kitchen, the clink of cups and saucers. Muted sound of Sheila talking and laughing with the unknown girl with silken hair. Noise of a tap being run. A kettle being filled. Lovely, ordinary, routine sounds.

"Now. Ronnie is setting up a training course in Wales. We prepare three candidates. Select one for the job. The other two will probably go out there too, on other tasks."

Johnny McAlpine considered. For many moments, the only sounds were from the kitchen, from the clock ticking in the lobby outside the study, and a luxurious snoring from Hal, the old black Labrador stretched beside the long garden window, basking in the squares of sunlight that warmed the faded green carpet. Finally he glanced at Jardine.

"Thank you for being as honest as you can, David."

"He would, for his own safety, have to resign his commission. Naturally, he would be indoctrinated into my service, with full welfare benefits including pension."

"You don't want to borrow Harry, you want to steal him, don't you?"

"Only for the duration of the task. It might be as long as a year. The nature of the contract will be that he would be free to rejoin the army when that is done."

McAlpine shook his head slowly. "David, let me speak to you as a chum. It's a bloody expensive business spotting talent in the SAS, nursing them through command of a troop, selecting the guys to invite back. Watching them function as Squadron Two I/C, which is Harry's appointment as you know. Training them in languages, high-altitude free-fall, undercover work, sabotage, all our special skills . . . I don't really think you can walk in and poach them as soon as they come to the boil . . . What's wrong with your own outfit? Pluck somebody from the Foreign Office. Or the fucking navy."

"Harry Ford is the man of the moment. As far as my office is concerned." Jardine decided to bring his request into a more formal framework. The hint of leverage, if push came to shove.

But the CO of 22 SAS was able to cope with that. "I'm sorry, David. We've spent too long bringing Harry Ford up to this stage. I have a couple of excellent Spanish speakers, pass for natives, who are actually in Colombia right now. SIS is welcome to approach either of them. But no to Harry Ford." He smiled, his good humor returning. "Tell the prime minister I'm terribly sorry. A fresh cup of tea before you go? I'll have my adjutant fax up details of the two guys. They can be back in the U.K. within the week."

David Jardine shrugged. "Thanks for hearing me out. I would love that fresh cuppa."

So they moved through to the kitchen and sat with Sheila, drinking tea and eating her homemade scones, which were delicious. Jardine glanced around, but the girl who could make people laugh had disappeared.

"We hardly see you these days, David." Sheila smiled. "I suppose, like our boys, you're completely tied up with this ghastly man Hussein . . ."

Jardine agreed that was exactly right and with a sheepish grin to McAlpine thanked her for the tea, drove back into Hereford, and collected Ronnie Szabodo, who had been visiting one or two SAS senior noncoms who had worked with him on numerous unattributable acts of skulduggery around the world. Ronnie's background knowledge of Captain Harry Ford was now ten times what it had been before.

"He said no . . . ?" Szabodo guessed, seeing Jardine's expression.

"Don't blame him." Jardine watched as the Hungarian put the two overnight bags into the trunk of the Sierra and closed the lid.

"So what now? Pass and go for Guerolo?" Szabodo got into the passenger seat.

Jardine settled behind the wheel. "Ronnie, I think we ought to fly out to Riyadh. Let's have a word with Captain

Henry Ford." He reached for the car-phone handset and offered it to Szabodo.

Szabodo accepted the phone and looked at him with a frown. "When, David?"

"Does tomorrow cause problems for you?" asked Jardine, gently reminding Ronnie whom he was working for.

"Tomorrow's great," replied the Hungarian, nothing if not a survivor. He started to dial a number. "We could take off from RAF Lyneham at four tomorrow afternoon. We would need to be there four hours early to get issued with Noddy suits and gas respirators. Charlie Malone is our man in Riyadh. Word is he wanders around dressed up as a colonel on the General Staff."

"Charlie in drag," chuckled Jardine. "I love it . . ." He glanced at Szabodo. "You thought Johnny would say no, didn't you?"

"Well, so would I. If the operator's worth recruiting, he's going to be hard to acquire. Page three of the manual."

Jardine relaxed. His foot eased off the gas pedal. Dear old Ronnie, he never failed to put things in perspective. Szabodo glanced at him and smiled wryly. Someone answered at the other end of the phone. He started to make the necessary arrangements.

———

Eddie Lucco sat on the stool at the counter in the Manhattan Bar in Little Italy, New York. Framed black-and-white photographs of a number of more or less unknown jazz musicians filled the once-white walls of the small bar. Eddie Lucco gazed at the photograph of a sallow slim-jawed young man in his twenties, grinning from the seat at the upright piano that still blocked the way to the john, in the far corner. That young man was

Albert Almeda, who played nights while working his way through college. Judge Almeda. One of the detective's very few heroic figures. Now he was nearing sixty and the grin had faded with time. He ruled his courtroom at New York District Court Number Five like a tyrannical croupier, watching the game, sensing the stakes, nailing the cheats. Tapping sharply with his gavel to bring the court back to its senses, at some juncture.

Tonight, later, a girl would be playing an homage to George Gershwin, so a sparsely printed bill pasted to a wood panel behind the counter informed Lucco. Right now, a tape of Sonny Rollins live at Montreux was playing on the sound system. Steve, the barman, was an ex-marine sergeant. He held his back ramrod straight, even while he cleaned glasses and added up his accounts from a small machine. As the door opened behind Lucco, the barman moved smoothly to the far end of the counter.

Eddie casually flicked open the button of his 100 percent wool jacket. A present from Nancy, who was summing up tomorrow. Then it would be back to normal, no more junk food. No more beer with the guys and avoiding the scales with a guilty glance. The man who had come in was right beside him now. He sat himself on the stool next to Lucco's. He was about thirty. Fit. Below-average height. Thinning black hair. He wore a gray slub-silk suit that must've cost a thousand dollars, its expensive Italian cut spoiled by the shoulder holster. Eddie's right thumb tapped gently on the hammer of his own piece, which he kept stuck in his belt on his left side, under the real wool jacket. No chances should be taken where Minnie the Moocher was concerned.

"How ya doin'?" inquired Minnie solicitously.

"It's a bitch," replied Eddie.

"Yeah." Minnie caught Steve's eye and pointed at

Lucco's beer, then held up two fingers. Steve nodded, but did not look as if he was going to rush to comply.

Minnie sniffed. Minnie's sniffing, noted Lucco.

"So what's the heat?" The third-generation Sicilian New Yorker sniffed again.

Eddie Lucco ran the fingers of his left hand around the rim of his beer glass, thoughtfully. "I need PeeWee," he said.

"So who am I, the fuckin' Missing Persons Bureau?" Minnie flinched as Lucco's beer hit him in the kisser and gagged as the short barrel of the snub-nose .357 Magnum struck him hard just below his Adam's apple. Lucco followed through, carrying the hoodlum backward off his toppling stool, and his left hand grabbed Minnie's left wrist like a manacle as he manhandled the Moocher to the floor, flipping him onto his face, deftly removing the 9mm Colt from the shoulder holster and dropping one knee onto his spine. Suddenly Giuliano Mineovare found himself handcuffed, his wrists behind his back, his silk suit wet with beer and his immense self-respect seriously violated.

"You're dead, you wop pig." He spat at the floor, which was inches from his face.

"Carrying a concealed weapon is a five to ten, Minnie," Lucco said, hoisting the handcuffed man to his feet and dusting him down. Then, very quiet, confidential. "You must rate Mr. PeeWee Patrice real high to give up years of your life. Think of all that pussy just gone from your space . . ." Then he hustled Mineovare out of the bar and across the sidewalk into the back of his tan sedan with Detective Sam Vargos at the wheel.

The plastic upholstery squeaked and the springs creaked as Lucco pulled the door shut and Vargos drove away with a squeal of rubber.

Lucco sat relaxed in one corner, his necktie loose and the top button of his shirt undone. Nancy wouldn't go out with him like that she always said, but she always did, and secretly Eddie thought she quite liked the hard-nosed NYPD image.

The silence lasted for eight minutes, which is a long time with nobody saying anything. Sam Vargos was a good cop, and he and Lucco worked well together whenever they worked as a team. So nobody said a word as they cruised uptown past East Ninety-sixth and headed into Spanish Harlem.

"What precinct you guys taking me to? I want a goddamn lawyer."

Nobody replied. Outside, black hookers in blond wigs and miniskirts up to their fannies puffed cigarettes and leaned down, beckoning to the three turkeys in the Dodge.

"Tell you what, Sam . . ." said Lucco.

"What's that?" inquired Vargos.

"Let me just drop this wop piece a shit off here, but before we do, pass me that wad of hundreds and I'll tuck it in his top pocket."

"You bastard," said Mineovare.

"Then as we dump him we say, real loud and indis-creet like, 'Thanks for your help, Minnie.' Something like that. Whadda you say?"

"That would do it. Sure would . . ." Sam nodded gravely.

Mineovare turned his lazy, made-man's eyes on Lucco. "And if I find the Patrice kid for you?"

"You ain't got the idea, Minnie. Nearly there, but strike one is the call. When you leave this car, back in the nice part of town, I will know by then where to find him. Like now."

"Come on, Minnie," said Vargos. "The reason the sergeant is asking you is because we know you took ten grand in smack yesterday to give PeeWee bed and board." He grinned. "Till the heat's off."

They drove for a further three minutes in silence. Then Mineovare sighed. "If you break our trust," he said to Lucco in Sicilian dialect, "then you will never know the moment, but it will come."

"Whassat? Whaddid he say?" asked Vargos.

"It's okay, Minnie. We're cool." Lucco reached behind the gangster and unlocked the handcuffs, not removing his hard and unforgiving eyes from the prisoner's. "Where?"

Minnie the Moocher told him, mumbling the words. Vargos relayed the information by radio and they cruised around for fifty minutes until undercover detectives from the 14th Precinct confirmed that PeeWee had been spotted.

Vargos turned on the siren and made a left across outraged traffic, gunning the gas.

"Hey man, let me outa the goddamn car! I ain't coming with you, we got a deal . . ."

"Gimme a break," said Lucco, cuffing the hoodlum's right wrist to the grab bar. Then he flipped open the chamber of his revolver and reloaded with illegal but more practical ammunition.

The Dodge was out of sight, behind a big Michelob beer truck. One of the precinct detectives was baby-sitting Mineovare. Eddie Lucco and Detective Sam Vargos strolled toward the Pinball World games arcade, lit by garish neon and faded paint in what had once been bright colors. Black and white youths and their girls hung out, waiting for a fix or strutting their stuff. Some were up to fighter-pilot standard on the video games they spent all their spare quarters on. Among the young men and women in Pinball World at this particular time were nine undercover cops from Homicide and the 14th Precinct's Detective Squad.

Lucco and Vargos walked right in, knowing they looked like exactly what they were, two Homicide cops who meant business. They had been in radio contact with the undercover team, and the speed with which they homed in on the skinny black youth wearing gold-rim glasses and maintenance coveralls with "Pinball World" on the back was as impressive as a couple of laser-guided smart bombs.

PeeWee made two cardinal mistakes. One, he had turned his back and knelt beside an Indy 500 video game, pretending to fix it. Two, as the two cops got real close—and they were clearly looking for him—he turned and reached inside his coveralls for his piece. The noise of Vargos's Beretta wiped out all the babble of electronic amusement noise, and PeeWee was suddenly writhing on the floor, clutching his right arm just below the shoulder and juddering his legs like a break dancer.

Lucco stooped beside the prisoner and wrenched the mini-Uzi from inside the youth's coveralls. The nine other cops, who looked like a street gang in their variety of undercover garb, moved to cover the two arresting officers.

"Mo'fuck . . ." gasped PeeWee as Eddie Lucco hand-cuffed him and wrapped his necktie tight around the wounded arm.

Somebody was speaking on his personal radio, calling for an ambulance.

"You have the right to remain silent," Lucco said, annoyed at having to spoil a perfectly good necktie. "You have the right to an attorney, you worthless piece of shit . . ."

And so PeeWee Patrice was arrested for the murder of a twenty-seven-year-old Narcotics detective. But at the back of his mind, Lucco knew he had pulled in Patrice for one other reason: to find out if the pusher would recognize the photo of that kid, the Jane Doe who was lying on a slab at Bellevue morgue.

———

"The thing I like best about Eugene is in all the years I've known him he has not changed one jot." Padraic O'Shea, widely tipped to be the next *taoiseach,* or prime minister of Ireland, stretched his legs beneath the dinner table and pushed his chair gently backward. He was talking to Pearson's wife, Mhairaid, who sat on his right. O'Shea was at one end of the table and Pearson at the other. Between them were Tim Carson, a banker from Dublin; Desmond Browne, a bloodstock dealer with a stud on the Dingle Peninsula; and Cal Fitzgibbon, a neurosurgeon, originally from Dublin but now in New York, where he had an international reputation. And their respective wives. The occasion was a reunion of five past presidents of the Trinity College Saturday Club, which had been formed to have dinner and a lively debate on the last Friday of each term month, followed by a black-tie dance that lasted till breakfast, when the Saturday Club would then play rugby against invited rivals. Three of the men had met their wives as a result, one wife being Mhairaid, who had not been a student but had hung around with the varsity crowd, her father being a professor of Gaelic poetry.

Mhairaid smiled and said the thing she liked best about Eugene was the fact that he had changed a lot since she had first known him. This caused some appreciative laughter, then Tim asked in what way Eugene had changed.

"Well," said Mhairaid, "to begin with, in those days he was too damn rowdy and cocksure of himself."

"One of our senior judges rowdy?" remarked Desmond Browne, the bloodstock dealer. "Why, Eugene, I seem to remember you as a model of decorum . . ." And he raised his bushy eyebrows in disbelief at his own comment. The others laughed as the port was served and cigars lit.

"Jesus, you know I cannot for the life of me understand why the English send their ladies out at this stage of a party," said Carson, the banker, "just as it is getting into its swing."

"Tim, you're up early tomorrow, so don't be swinging too hard." Margaret, his wife, gazed in his direction with an expression that indicated she knew she was fighting a lost cause. The others chuckled. A relaxed group of successful Dubliners, all comfortable in each other's company.

"Permit me, ladies and gents, to propose a toast." Cal Fitzgibbon got to his feet. Desmond Browne hurried to refill his glass. Fitzgibbon raised his glass of port. "To the Republic . . ."

The others rose and, glasses high, intoned. "The Republic . . ." And drank. Then they all sat down.

Deborah Browne, plump and enjoying herself back in Dublin, turned to Mhairaid. "I heard Mollie O'Shaugnassy's eldest girl's pregnant again, you know that fellow she took up with at the Abbey Theatre, she—" Then Deborah made an "awful sorry" face and lapsed into silence as Tim Carson got to his feet with a serious expression on his face. Typical banker, she thought.

"One more toast, this time to the man who, I hear, will be leading us into the imminent election as head of the party. And if the polls are accurate and all the signs point in that direction, the man who will be next *taoiseach* of Ireland. Ladies and gentlemen, past presidents of the Saturday Club and their ladies . . . I give you, Dr. Padraic O'Shea, T.D., Ph.D."

The others got up and held their glasses pointed to

O'Shea, who sat there beaming shyly. "To Padraic," they intoned, sipped, and sat down.

"Come on, Padraic. Speech," Desmond said.

"Speech . . ." added the neurosurgeon.

Padraic O'Shea shuffled in his chair and, without getting to his feet, raised his third glass of port and inscribed a semicircle, embracing all the others, one by one. For this man was a politician con brio.

When he spoke, it was conversational, not hectoring. A confidence shared among friends.

"You know, I don't even know how you all vote," he said. "And that's the beauty of democracy. However, I am led to believe that Fine Gael will be in a clear majority, come the general election. It's true that I will be leading us into that election and, with God's good grace"—here Deborah crossed herself discreetly—"I will be *taoiseach*. Primus, as they say, inter pares."

There was a deeply satisfied murmur. It was always deeply satisfying to be in the know, to be trusted with confidences. To have the rumors of the serious press confirmed before the rest of the country became aware. To be sure, a secret had its own binding magic.

"But now, if I can count on your total discretion . . ." O'Shea spoke so quietly you could have heard a pin drop (oh yes, of course, Padraic, the others intoned, eager to be further admitted to the confidence of the next *taoiseach*). ". . . I would like to say that here at this table is another loyal supporter of my party, Eugene Pearson. And I am sure he will be as surprised as you when I ask him, here and now, as a member of that most secret and clandestine brotherhood . . ." (here Eugene Pearson almost swooned with alarm) "the Honourable Society of Saturday Clubbers . . ."—approving noises and more port being poured—"Eugene, I would ask you most seriously to consider becoming my attorney general in the next government."

Stunned silence. Then a buzz of approval and congratulations. Pearson sat stunned as Mhairaid stared across the table at him, tears of pride starting down her cheeks.

"Oh, Eugene," she said. "Oh, Padraic. How wonderful . . ."

And all Justice Eugene Pearson could see was the face of the Whore of Venice, scalp lifting. Left eye turning to bramble jam.

5

AGENTS OF INNOCENCE

Harry Ford quite liked the smell of gun oil. He had brought out several cans of Young's .303 rust preventative gun lubricant, purchased from James Purdey & Sons in London, whose shotguns were individually made for each client at a cost ranging from £50,000 to half a million the pair. Harry couldn't afford such extravagances, but he made a point of buying his bits and pieces of shooting equipment from Purdey's wood-paneled shop at the corner of Mount Street and South Audley Street, in Mayfair. The impeccably mannered staff there knew him as a polite and well-brought-up young man and he enjoyed the "good morning, Mr. Ford, how pleasant to see you again" courtesies whenever he visited Purdey's and the various other old-money establishments around town, like Lobb's the bootmakers, Huntsman the bespoke tailors, and the bar and restaurant at the Connaught Hotel.

Harry was a good soldier and an excellent leader. Even his detractors admitted the former Guards officer had a degree of style that harked back to a bygone age. As he sat cross-legged in his tent—or "basha," as the SAS called any temporary resting place in the field— planted in a deep hole in the sand and covered with camouflage netting, his silenced AKS assault rifle laid out in its component parts on a clean groundsheet, each piece glistening with gun oil, cleaning one of the four spare magazine clips, the Special Forces captain was quitely satisfied with life. He had just been to a briefing where the next phase of Operation Pomegranate, the SAS task of operating deep inside Iraqi territory, had been debated and finalized. Once again Harry's teams had been allocated high-risk operational responsibilities, and in a few hours they would be boarding two Chinook helicopters, which would fly over the Iraqi lines to drop them in darkness from a height of twelve thousand feet to free-fall for just over sixty seconds before opening their Ram-air wing parachutes and landing, silently and hopefully unseen, twenty minutes away from a Republican Guard operations control bunker, which had been identified that morning by a satellite listening station located near Canberra in Australia.

After the briefing, the senior SAS officer present, Major Desmond MacSweeney, had taken Harry aside and told him that although Johnny McAlpine had recommended him for a Military Cross for his several actions during recent operations behind the lines, the feeling at Special Forces Directorate in London was that, even with the diplomatic efforts being made to stop the conflict, a ground offensive was still on the cards. And the awarding of decorations for gallantry should be delayed until after the successful invasion and liberation of Kuwait, since each outfit would only be allowed so many Military Crosses, and even fewer Distinguished Service Orders. Queen's Gallantry Medal might be the answer. Certainly a second Mention in Dispatches. However, that decision did not signify a definite "no."

Harry Ford had been in the army for nearly seven years, and he was used to the impersonal thoughtlessness of the system. He had never been quite sure why he in particular had been recommended for the decoration and he simply shrugged and said thanks for telling me.

MacSweeney said the news was not all bad, and word was that if Harry kept his nose clean, he stood a fair chance of getting command of a squadron.

Henry Michael Alcazar Ford, therefore, had good enough reason to feel content with life. Was he apprehensive about the dangers of this constant combat? Not really, for even in peacetime life with his regiment was scarcely a highly insurable occupation. He had worked undercover in Northern Ireland and with the Mujahadeen in Afghanistan. He had also seen action in places the British government would prefer him to keep silent about.

The greatest satisfaction about this present war, Harry Ford thought, was that it was just that, a war. Where the enemy could be taken on and killed without the frustrating constraints of operating in the six counties of Northern Ireland, where known murderers strutted the streets, confident in the knowledge they were free from retribution because, contrary to press speculation and popular lore, the regiment was not permitted to act outside the civil law. A fact the Provos were well aware of. And since witnesses for the State had a life expectancy of days rather than weeks, few Republican or Loyalist bombers or torturers faced much worse than a few months inside for illegal possession of weapons, unless they were unlucky enough to be encountered or ambushed while committing an attack. In which case it was open season, but such lucky breaks were all too infrequent.

These were the thoughts idly flitting through Harry Ford's mind when Geordie, his squadron staff sergeant, poked his head around the open flap of the basha. Geordie was the drooping-mustached man who had been on the raid on the Seconics B site. He was a big, raw-boned Scot, and when he grinned, which was often, you could see a space between his two front teeth.

"Boss, there's a funny old bloke with a foreign accent here to see you. Some sort of spook. One of the lads remembers him from Op Spindrift."

"What does he want?"

"Dinna ask me, laddie. I only work here. He's with the Sloth and would you nip over and have a quick word . . ."

Ford sighed, glanced up at Geordie, and reassembled his AKS, slipping the silenced barrel on deftly. "Bloody spooks. That's all I need."

But like the cabinet secretary and others, he was quite pleased when the secret world touched him on the shoulder.

"Harry, this is Fred Estergomy from the Foreign and Commonwealth Office." Desmond MacSweeney, known throughout his regiment as the Sloth, indicated Ronnie Szabodo, who used, among several work names, the identity of Frederick Estergomy when traveling in Wonderland.

"Pleased to meet you." Harry Ford sized up the squat, smiling, slightly overweight man standing at the ops-room map, tamping tobacco into a well-worn pipe. Ronnie inclined—the merest movement, from the waist—in an infinitesimal bow. He wore a desert jacket

that was too big for him and camouflage trousers. A
satchel with his NBC suit and gas mask was by his feet.
The first thing Harry noticed was that the man was in
his early fifties. The second was his tobacco-stained and
irregular teeth. Then he became aware of two small,
round, indented scars on Estergomy's left forearm. Bullet wounds.

"Where did you get these?" he inquired, glancing at
the scars.

"Budapest. 1956. I understand congratulations are in
order."

"Really?"

"Military Cross, dear boy. Well done."

Harry grinned. Typical spy to be behind the times.
"You're a bit premature. They've changed their minds."

Which left an uncomfortable silence. Estergomy
glanced at the Sloth, who raised his heels off the floor-
ing.

"Well, then. I'll leave you two to it. Don't want to
rush you, but I've got the general at five. Harry, Fred has
authority from Special Forces Command Riyadh to explain to you what they want." And since neither Szabodo
nor Ford replied, MacSweeney picked up his gas mask
and NBC kit and left, maybe a trifle reluctant to abandon
his young captain to the company of this hoary old spy.

The Hungarian held a flame over his pipe and sucked
gently till the tobacco was well alight. He allowed great
puffs of smoke to envelop his head. The aroma reached
Harry, who recognized Dunhill's Standard Mixture, one
of the more exclusive tobaccos, mildly aromatic. He
bought it himself sometimes.

In the ensuing silence, Harry didn't say a word. He
let Ronnie eye him up and down like a trainer looking
over a horse. Well, this horse is a bloody thoroughbred,
chum. Harry willed the thought across the silent bunker,

politely watching Estergomy. He felt perfectly relaxed. Confident in himself.

Finally Szabodo smiled. "I'm sorry to intrude on your busy war, Captain. I suspect you're not going to like this, but I have authority from ComCen to borrow you for twenty-four hours."

Harry let this intelligence hang in the silence. His expression was neither hostile nor placatory. He just happened to be in this bunker because his boss had told him to present himself.

Szabodo, in those moments, had many of his reservations about Harry Ford dispelled. Ronnie Szabodo was a judge of men. He probably had no equal at his particular skill.

There had been occasions in the past when his life had depended on the right decision, sometimes with just seconds to make it. He could see that Ford had the demeanor of a loner. Of an able, intelligent, and battle-hardened professional fighter. He was also of a particular stratum of society, with natural self-confidence and a degree of style. The files had told Szabodo that Ford was an experienced horseman but those first moments in the unsuspecting candidate's presence brought the Hungarian a twinge of optimism. The boy had a quite un-English touch of . . . dash, élan, which might prove to be a positive asset should he pass the many hurdles of training and testing and be infiltrated as an Argentinian or Peruvian of good family into those particular circles in Bogotá or Medellín where he could, perhaps, be accepted at face value by the cartel.

Szabodo told Harry, without a blush, that his capture of the Iraqi Major Modhafar al-Salim was a major coup and that the interrogation of the unfortunate man was yielding valuable information. He said that his own boss had flown out from London to take charge of one aspect of the case and the Special Forces commander in Saudi had agreed that Harry should be helicoptered back to Riyadh to amplify his debriefing reports and give SIS firsthand information on the political situation behind Iraqi lines.

The local SAS commander had said that was okay, Szabodo went on, provided Harry could be back on duty within twenty-four hours.

"I don't actually see what help I can be," said Harry, scratching his shoulder. "Our own intelligence people extract the last juice of the lemon from a debrief."

Szabodo said there was another reason for his visit, which he had been asked not to discuss until they got back to Riyadh. He was courteous but quietly insistent. The sooner they left, he said, the sooner Harry could be back.

Harry Ford had acquired the irritating SAS habit of questioning just about any operational instruction on principle. He explained that he was just about to leave on a night drop into Iraq and that he would be gone for about eight days. He said that his current operational duties meant that, with great reluctance, he really could not comply with Ronnie Szabodo's request until his return.

Szabodo had smiled. "Your operational duties will go on right up to the capitulation of Baghdad, and that is probably weeks away. Major MacSweeney tells me your team can survive without you for twenty-four hours, and quite frankly, Captain, I work directly to the Cabinet Office and it's not really up to you to come on like a prima donna."

He noted, with professional detachment, that the young officer betrayed no loss of temper at this provocation.

"All the necessary documentation has been completed and your ops officer in Riyadh has kindly ordered your release till noon on Thursday. I'm sure we can have you back here long before that." He spread his arms, acknowledging Harry's frustration. "We're all fighting the same war, Captain Ford."

Harry nodded. Thoughtful. He had been looking forward to the job, a clandestine operation against the divisional HQ of the First-Chosen-of-God Republican Guard's Paratroop Division. But he also knew that the first phase of the operation—observing the site and making a battlefield appreciation of the chance of success—would probably be as far as the mission would go, for that particular headquarters, he suspected, was unusually difficult to infiltrate and professionally defended by experienced troops. So in a way, he was not missing anything that would specially further his military career. Particularly since it seemed battlefield medals were to be won by lottery and army politics rather than merit. And that was precisely the way Harry Ford approached his job. A study of military history would reveal that many successful generals were possessed of the same attitude.

"I'll require verbal confirmation of this from Major MacSweeney."

"Of course. Please be ready to leave in twenty minutes." The squat Hungarian beamed at Harry and turned to study the ops-room map, marked "Secret."

Twenty-two minutes later, Captain Harry Ford was in a Lynx helicopter with his NBC kit, his shaving gear, and a change of underpants and socks. After all, it was only going to be for twenty-four hours.

On the ground, Desmond MacSweeney watched the Lynx flutter away over the desert, the evening sun rendering its ripples and dunes in varying shades of pink and russet. He knew in his bones that he would not see Harry Ford again.

Riyadh was in the middle of a Scud attack when the helicopter reached the landing pad at Allied Command

Headquarters. Harry Ford had not been to Riyadh since the start of the war, and he peered out of the Perspex cockpit canopy as the rocket trails of three Patriot anti-missile missiles tore relentlessly upward into the night sky, disappearing momentarily into the low cloud cover. Then a couple of massive orange-yellow flashes seared the sky, and the Lynx rocked gently as the shock waves touched it.

Harry glanced at the man he knew as Fred Ester-gomy, who had watched the entire process, fascinated, without a trace of apprehension. Szabodo caught Harry's eye and winked, giving the thumbs-up sign.

The helicopter touched down amid a clatter of rotor blades into a cloud of swirling dust. Harry opened the door and moved forward, ducking his head although he knew that the arc of the rotors was not remotely close to touching him. Szabodo followed.

Harry tried not to let much surprise him, but he was impressed by the depth—it seemed like a hundred feet into the ground—as the express elevator descended from the nuclear-shelter basement. Finally it came to rest, and when he and Szabodo emerged, he was profes-sionally impressed by the high tech of the Allied War Bunker.

They were escorted by two Military Police sergeants and a tall, tanned colonel with General Staff tabs on his collar, who had met them on the landing pad and escorted them into the Command Nuclear Shelter. He seemed a professional, cheerful man who knew his way through the many security areas. Ronnie Szabodo had clipped on a plastic-covered pass with his photo on it, and to Harry's surprise, the tall colonel, who had intro-duced himself as Charles Malone, produced an identical pass for Harry, which had Harry Ford's own photograph, rank, and name neatly sealed within.

They walked along a corridor with rubberized floor

and gray walls, passing busy staff officers and enlisted ranks in U.S., British, and Saudi uniforms. A series of pale green doors on either side, identified only by numbers stenciled on them. At number 116, they stopped. Ronnie and the colonel had been exchanging desultory small talk, about the war and about some dancers at a U.S. Marine Corps party that had been held clandestinely so as not to offend the Saudis. Apparently the dancers had been quite something.

At the side of the door was a buzzer with a combination of numbers. Colonel Malone punched out a sequence, and inside the reinforced door an electronic lock clunked open. Malone opened the door and went in ahead of Harry and Szabodo. The two MP escorts stayed outside.

Inside was an air lock, and the party was briefly scrutinized before a second, inner door opened, and there was David Jardine, in shirtsleeves and the trousers of his fawn Prince of Wales-check suit.

"Come on in," said Jardine. "Have a good flight?"

"As flights go," the Hungarian replied. "We landed in the middle of a Scud attack."

"No! Really?" Jardine shook his head as if to say what's the world coming to. "Trouble is we're so isolated down here. There could be a nuke on the city and we wouldn't know it. Captain Ford. Welcome." He led them through to an inner office, with two desks, several phones of varying colors, and some Arab rugs on the floor. Also three comfortable armchairs and a wall map of the region.

Bloody armchairs, thought Ford. How very fitting for armchair bloody soldiers.

Jardine flopped into an armchair and seemed to read Ford's mind. "Grab a pew." He grinned and indicated a chair.

Harry laid his kit on the floor and sat down. Szabodo

opened a wall safe and produced a bottle marked Surgical Spirit. He glanced at Harry. "Vodka?"

"No, thanks."

Charlie Malone hovered at the door. "If you chaps need anything . . ."

Jardine lifted a hand. "Thanks, Charlie. Love the outfit."

Malone shrugged. "Bit butch, don't you think?" Then he left, closing the door behind him.

A clock ticked on one desk. An old-fashioned wind-up alarm clock, with a half sphere on the top. It reminded Ford of something out of a Tom and Jerry cartoon.

Szabodo poured two shots of vodka into cheap china cups. He placed one on the desk beside Jardine.

"Well, Captain," said Jardine, in fluent Spanish, "I hear you're having a good war."

Harry Ford gazed at Jardine. What the hell was going on? There was something about the man that commanded respect. Yet he was clearly not in the military mold. And Spanish . . . ? Harry had volunteered to go with the training teams to Colombia. That was before the Gulf crisis, and it had seemed like a good career move, but Johnny McAlpine had blocked it, saying Harry's Spanish was so good he might be needed in the future for something special. That had probably been prudent, but spooks? Harry knew Johnny McAlpine well enough to know he would want to keep his best assets out of the clutches of Century House.

Still, here he was in some space-age bunker, playing silly buggers with the funny people. Might as well show willing.

"Sí, señor." He used the Colombian accent because he was not so dumb. It did not seem likely they were interested in sending him to the Costa del Sol. "I am having a terrific opportunity to do what I do best."

Killing people, he thought wryly, and immediately sensed that he had communicated that to Jardine.

"I don't think you're being fair to yourself, Captain. I have made a most careful study of your file and we have spoken with many people who have come into contact with you. Some friends, some enemies. My office has a fairly comprehensive research capability, and while nothing compares with personal contact, I feel I know you quite well. And what you have the potential to do best is, I believe, as yet untapped." All this still in Spanish.

"Señor, I am a simple soldier. But it seems to me you did not fly me all the way to Riyadh—and unless you actually live belowground twenty-four hours in the day, your lack of tan suggests to me you have come out from England—just to ask me about the political situation behind the Iraqi lines. The man in the colonel's uniform might act the humorist, but he is clearly no fool. Now you speak to me in the tongue I was brought up with. Your accent, if I might say so, suggests the area around Vigo, in Spain. Perhaps, maybe, Ecuador, for many settlers there came from the north of Spain. So it is fair to assume you have responsibility for areas which use that language, rather than Arabic. Maybe then, señor, and with respect, we could cut out the time-wasting preamble. Why have you gone to some little trouble to bring me here?"

Jardine remained slouched in his chair. I'm getting old, he told himself, for the flight had left him exhausted. But let God in his celestial charabanc be praised. This boy might just fit the bill.

"Ronnie, leave us, if you would be so kind."

Szabodo swallowed the remains of his vodka and left, closing the door behind him. The alarm clock ticked sedately. Harry Ford wondered if there was a hidden microphone. The fact that the man whose plastic pass identified him as Frederick Estergomy should be addressed as Ronnie surprised him not one bit.

Time to flatter the candidate, thought Jardine. Time to spend a little top secret currency. They all love it.

"Just before I start, Harry"—he reverted to English—"you will be interested to know, and this is SIS only, that Modhafar al-Salim, the Intelligence major you hiked out of his bunker a few nights ago, is singing like a canary. He has volunteered to be infiltrated back into Iraq, to set up a cell of dissidents among the Ba'athist leaders." He inclined his head. "We're still assessing him but it might just work. Either way, we're in your debt." This intelligence was true, there was no point in lying, the Joe would sense it.

Harry met his gaze. "Do you mind telling me your name . . . ?"

"It's David. Harry, tell me about your work in Northern Ireland."

"I'm afraid I can't do that."

"Let me put it another way. I know already that you worked for two years undercover. Your work name was Richard Clark and your cover job was traveling salesman for Princewick, the children's-shoe manufacturer. Your team Two I/C was Captain Bill Fulton, whose work name was Bill Mackay, and your security-service area liaison was Mandy Symington, with whom you had a brief fling until she got engaged to a young Hussar officer attached to the Army Air Corps. Your prize informant was Liam Cassidy. Shall I go on?"

Jardine's eyes flicked over every detail of Ford's expression. Ford held up his hands in surrender. Both men grinned.

"What I meant was, tell me how you felt about it. Was it an assignment you enjoyed? How did you feel about living a lie? How many times did you fuck up? Times that only you could know about."

"Did I have an aptitude for it? Is that what you're saying?"

"Asking."

"Asking. Is that what you're asking? And if so, David, why? Why did you bring me off an important military operation to speak to me in Spanish and tell me little secrets and ask me if I enjoyed being a . . . a minor spy?" He fixed Jardine with a hostile gaze. Bloody SIS, who did they think they were? Arrogant bastards.

Jardine waited for a moment. The terrible beauty of his job was that, like in hunting, sometimes you just had to seize the moment. The complex games, the charade that Jardine and Szabodo had planned to seduce Harry Ford, Jardine's instinct yelled at him, were unnecessary. It was indeed like seduction, for it was easy to ignore that the quarry might desire precisely the same thing, even if until that moment they had not realized it.

Here goes nothing, thought Jardine. "You're absolutely right to ask these questions. I flew from England because your CO, for the very best of reasons, refused to lend you to us. Captain Ford, my name is David Jardine. I hold the rank of counselor in the Diplomatic Service and sphere controller, if that means anything to you, in the Secret Intelligence Service. I am responsible to the Prime Minister and the Cabinet Office for offensive intelligence in Denied Areas of Latin America. You are one of three men my colleagues and I believe could be vital, and I'm not exaggerating, to spearhead an operation to infiltrate the cocaine cartels of the region. I am breaking the rules between our services, Harry, by offering you a place in SIS. Join me, and it will mean resigning your commission. Oh, fine, my superiors can speak to the Army Council and smooth your departure so that you can resume your commission at the end of the contract. But it would mean saying good-bye, at least for a couple of years, to commanding your own SAS squadron. In return, all I can offer you is constant danger, loneliness, and a chance to serve your country in secret, without public honor or awards."

Silence.

"And this would be in Colombia?" Harry asked.

"In South America."

"And what about my wife?"

"She would be allowed to know you had joined the office, but as a black operator, that would have to remain her secret. Elizabeth has already been security cleared by your own people, so that doesn't present a problem."

Harry Ford thought deeply. He looked distinctly unimpressed. I've blown it, thought Jardine. Damn.

Then Ford looked up. Until that moment, he had not realized how much he had resented MacSweeney the Sloth's smug satisfaction in telling him he had just missed being decorated for gallantry. And he had been bloody gallant. Very bloody gallant, actually.

"Tell me about pay and conditions."

Oh bliss. Thank you, God, in your celestial vastness. You really are a sport.

Jardine sat up from his slouch. He lifted his untouched vodka and raised it toward the young soldier.

"You won't regret this," he lied.

———

London's Metropolitan Police have a department whose responsibility is countering subversion, espionage, and certain aspects of terrorism. It is called the Special Branch and was originally called the Special Irish Branch when it was formed toward the end of the last century, to combat the violent activities on the mainland of Great Britain of the Sinn Feiners and the Irish Republican Army, who were fighting a minor but deadly guerrilla campaign to achieve Irish independence. Over one hundred years on, the branch had broadened its scope and multiplied its resources, but the Irish aspect was still a major headache.

In 1919, independence had been won in twenty-six of the thirty-two counties that make up the Emerald Isle. But thanks to a deal between British prime minister Lloyd George and Eamon de Valera, the leader of the rebelling Irish, the northern six counties, predominantly populated by Protestants of Scottish descent, were not included in the independence agreement, and a vestigial element of the Irish Republican Army swore to liberate the North from British rule.

By the 1960s, their occasional bombs and the odd attack on border customs posts had come to be treated with resignation by the North and with a degree of affection tinged with exasperation by the more grown-up citizens of the Republic.

This status quo was rudely interrupted in 1969 by an awakening of the young and radical section of the Catholic minority in the Six Counties who united in protest of repressive treatment by the ruling government in their tiny substate, denied universal voting rights, equality of jobs or housing, and policed aggressively by the Royal Ulster Constabulary and its volunteer part-time police force, the B Specials.

Television cameras moved to cover their puny demonstrations. Comfortable viewers in less tribal, less primeval environments were made less comfortable by the violent reaction of the B Specials who moved in, cracking heads with their nightsticks and firing tear gas on singing, arm-linked kids, some students, some workers, many unemployed.

What a gift to the clapped-out, ballad-singing mafia that called itself the Irish Republican Army. A few rusty Lee Enfield .303 rifles were dug out from the peat, or the turf as they called it over there, a number of .45 Webley revolvers were taken out from Granny's thatched roof and carefully oiled. And the Boys, as they were affectionately known, fired a few rounds and took on the more powerfully armed and prepared B Specials and their illegal civilian counterparts, the Protestant Ulster Defense Association, the Ulster Freedom Fighters, and the Ulster Volunteer Force.

The London Parliament dispatched troops to the province, and its soldiers, who had no brief for either the B Specials nor the Protestant paramilitaries, were at first greeted as heroes, arrived to defend the downtrodden minority and restore normal life.

Now more determined radicals emerged. They exhorted the IRA to blow hot on this now glowing ember of rebellion. Fiercer gunfights followed. The example of terror tactics in other parts of the crumbled British empire was followed. In Cyprus, hadn't women out shopping been pistoled to death in front of their kids? In Kenya, hadn't the Mau Mau disemboweled British schoolchildren? And look at the results. Independence for all. And the leaders of those brave freedom fighters? Jesus, weren't they invited, after a few years in the jug, to form governments?

But the grandiose dreams of the IRA soon crumbled. The leaders of that time were educated, steeped, in the history of the original struggle against the British. They were not sure that the cycle of bombs and murders was going to be good for Ireland's future. The English were hinting, through secret negotiations, at a solution that would strip the Protestant ruling majority of its bullying power.

It was a dangerous moment for the handful of political extremists who lived on an adrenaline high of bomb blasts, gun oil, clandestine contracts, Che Guevara, the PLO, and the *Minimanual of the Urban Guerrilla*. Their burgeoning links with the Baader Meinhof and the

Basque ETA movement and the Russian Novosti news agency correspondent in Dublin would quickly dissolve if the movement weakened and opted for reason and negotiation.

After some lethal internal feuding the young Turks broke away from the old IRA and styled themselves the Provisional Irish Republican Army. The old movement called itself the Official IRA. In the schism, some cardboard lapel badges were taken by the Provos, but they omitted to take the pins required for attaching them so they treated their purloined badges with gum, and to this day the Provisionals are known in Ireland as the Stickies.

These were the thoughts meandering through the mind of the Special Branch sergeant on duty at London Heathrow Airport's Terminal One, as he observed the stream of passengers entering the arrivals hall from the Dublin flight. It was eight twenty-three in the morning. He recognized a group of three young political activists from Sinn Fein's Belfast Branch and he gave two of his detectives the nod to tag on and arrange a tail. He was so pleased with this minor alleviation of his boredom that he did not look twice at the middle-aged man in the well-cut blue topcoat who walked past, looking slightly harassed, as travelers do, carrying one shoulder bag and a leather valise. And even if he had recognized Mr. Justice Pearson, it would only have been to nod in approval of the "Extraditing Judge," as the *Daily Telegraph* referred to the possible future attorney general of the Daíl, the Dublin parliament.

Pearson had flown from Dublin using his own name. The chances of bumping into an acquaintance or member of the press while using a false identity were just too great to risk embarrassment, although he had an excellent reason for using an alias when traveling. For the Provos had issued a death threat against him because of his policy on extradition. Only that week, a superintendent from the Garda Protection Unit had called on him to discuss his personal security and had suggested using a pseudonym whenever practical. Pearson had said he would bear that in mind.

He took the underground to Victoria Station, a twenty-five-minute journey, and walked into Grosvenor Place, beside the high wall around Buckingham Palace. There he hailed a taxi and at nine forty-two got out in Judd Street, near King's Cross Station. He crossed Euston Road and entered the busy main railway station, where, by an astonishing coincidence, he spotted two members of one of the two teams of operators known as Active Service Units the Organization had on operations in England. He prayed they had not planted a bomb, because the resulting disruption would delay or even cancel his train to Edinburgh and that would upset his fairly tight schedule.

Pearson's involvement with the Movement was not known to the two terrorists, Gerard Price and Rosine MacEvoy. Price was thirty-four and Rosine, a dark-haired beauty of a girl, was twenty-six. With Price in a neat, dark gray suit and sober necktie, carrying an expensive briefcase, and Rosine in a tan skirt, navy-blue jacket, and plain, cream colored blouse, they looked like any couple of white-collar workers going about their business. Together with the other three members of their unit, they had to their credit four shootings; two car bombs, which had killed a politician and a general's wife; four railway station bombs, which had killed six members of the public including a twelve-year-old schoolgirl and a trainee priest; and a mortar-bomb attack on Downing Street that had nearly wiped out the prime minister and his war cabinet.

Pearson kept out of their line of vision and walked obliquely to the ticket office, where he purchased a first-class ticket to Edinburgh. The train was due to leave in thirty-four minutes, and the judge made one phone call, at precisely ten-twelve, to a public call box in Waverly Street, in Edinburgh, Scotland. His conversation lasted seven seconds. Then, as Price and Rosine strolled out of the station, the Irish judge walked toward the platform, half expecting the dull, ripping concussion of four or five pounds of Semtex plastic explosive at any moment.

He found an empty first-class compartment and spent the first part of the journey reading Helen Lane's translation from the Spanish of Mario Vargas Llosa's *The War at the End of the World,* an epic novel about South America that conveys most graphically the subcontinent's intriguing strangeness. Then he had lunch, not in the Pullman car but alone in his compartment. Some sandwiches that Mhairaid had made for him the night before, and an apple. He had told her these trips away were to do with secret consultations with an American-based multinational that was exploring areas for massive investment in Europe. They had offered him, he had told Mhairaid, the top legal job, with a salary four times his present one and a seat on the board. And although Padraic's offer of the attorney generalship would be a fitting pinnacle for his career, he would continue to talk with the Yanks until the more political cup had safely reached the lip.

"But then you'll take it, Eugene, you will, won't you?"

And Eugene Pearson had agreed that he would most probably accept the position. In the meantime, Mhairaid must continue to keep his trips abroad absolutely to herself and say he was away fishing with friends in England.

In truth, the judge was not at all sure whether or not he would accept the position. It was one thing being a senior figure in the legal establishment and working all the time for the Movement. But attorney general was too high a profile and the question he had to ask himself was, which would be of the greatest benefit to Ireland? For he really did believe that his secret influence on the Provisionals' Army Council was work for a patriot, which would one day, when he was dead and gone, be sure to put his name among the great Republican heroes of Ireland's lore and literature. How many attorneys general had ballads in their name?

The ballad of Eugene Pearson . . . He chuckled to himself, peering over his half-moon spectacles at the landscape flashing past. The engine driver was surely going too fast, driving like a maniac he was, as the carriages inclined away from the curve of the tracks and the clackity-clack, clackity-clackity clackity-clack of the wheels sounded in urgent rhythm.

When Pearson stepped off the train in Edinburgh's Waverly Station, he made his way to the taxi rank outside and paused, gazing around. Sure enough, a blue Jaguar car was parked across the street. It had one of those appalling toy cats that stuck by its paws to the window. They were modeled on a funny-pages character called Garfield and represented to the judge all that made Britain the Philistine nation it was since the onrush of the gutter press. A sense of humor was not high in the extraditing judge's list of attributes.

He crossed to the car and got into the backseat. The driver was a member of the Organization and had no idea of Pearson's identity, nor did Pearson know his. It was one aspect of a system Pearson had devised some years before, along with Martin McGuiness and Rory

O'Brady, to restructure the Provisionals and improve security.

The driver was about thirty. Hair neatly trimmed. Slightly overweight. He wore a heavy gold ring and his sports coat was of Donegal tweed. He eyed Pearson in the mirror as he started the motor.

"Will you be the man for the Milk Marketing Board?" he inquired in an east-coast Scots accent.

"Not me. I'm on my way to the Gaelic Literature Society."

The driver nodded, the exchange of identification phrases completed, and the car moved away, joining the afternoon traffic.

During the journey to the airport, which took thirty-one minutes, the driver opened his glove compartment and passed back to Pearson a large manila envelope, inside of which was a British passport with Pearson's photograph in the name of Kevin Edward Paterson, born in Glasgow in 1946. Also other documents, including driver's license and credit cards in the same name. The address was in Streatham, London. Pearson had already put his own documents into a flat leather wallet, which he had zipped into the false bottom of his leather shaving bag. The face on the false passport wore glasses with a light tortoiseshell frame. Pearson found an identical pair in the manila envelope, with plain glass except for bifocal reading ellipses on the lenses. Prepared to his own prescription. He put them on, blinking and looking around every which way to get used to them.

The flight to Pisa was by chartered airliner, taking its passengers to a football match in the city, part of the European cup. The team was Hibernian, an Edinburgh side. Kevin Paterson, occupation import agent, was one of the Hibernian supporters' club.

At seven in the evening the airliner touched down in Pisa in the middle of a thunderstorm. Eugene Pearson, with just hand baggage, was quickly cleared through Customs and Immigration. He checked that the car, a dark blue BMW 325 that had been purchased for cash in Rome one week before, had been left for him as arranged, in the airport car park. Included on his own key ring was a key for the BMW, slipped to him at his morning round of golf the previous Saturday.

Justice Pearson had been trained in countersurveillance and its evasion. He walked purposefully around the carpark, so as not to appear to be loitering. He stood by the entrance, glancing at his watch, all the time checking out the carpark and the various people around the area. Finally satisfied, he got into the car, started the motor, and drove off, pausing just before the autoroute to reconfirm his planned route to Florence and exchange the false identification papers for yet another passport and credit cards, this time representing him as a New York buyer for an antiquarian book dealer. Name of James Hanlon. There was indeed such a person. He was third-generation Irish/American and he had volunteered seven years before, at a Noraid benefit dinner, to do what he could to help the Cause. Stay away from Noraid, came the answer, seven weeks later, after the organization had checked him out, courtesy of a sympathizer with access to the NYPD computer at BOSI, or Bureau of Special Investigations, as the New York equivalent of Special Branch was called at that time.

From then on, the identity of Hanlon was available to the Organization for operational purposes. One phone call and the real James Hanlon would take himself off to a remote cabin in Connecticut for the duration of the impersonation.

By nine-fifteen, the BMW was winding up the steep escarpment leading from Florence to Fiesole, the small village that looked down on the beautiful medieval city. Halfway up the hill, Pearson turned in to the entrance of the old monastery, with friezes by Michelangelo, commandeered as Field Marshal Kesselring's headquarters during the German occupation in World War Two. It was now an elegant, exclusive, expensive luxury hotel with its own terraced gardens and a stunning view of old Florence spread out in the valley below the cloistered restaurant terrace.

The hotel reception staff were charming, imperceptibly aloof, and smooth as glass. Signor Hanlon was of course expected. He was led to his room through an ancient, crumbling courtyard rich with greenery in terracotta pots, with tiny swallows swooping in the eaves, up a stone staircase, and along a stone-flagged corridor, with hushed dark oak doors at regular intervals. He was reminded of his first day at Saint Dominic's, the boarding school in West Meath where he went to school to be educated by the Jesuits along with his elder brother Tom, now a housemaster at Ampleforth School in England and an implacable enemy of the IRA and all that it stood for. Eugene often grieved at the loss to the Organization of such a good brain. He had never dared to hint of his secret life to Tom, who was as terrible in rage as he was sublime in compassion.

The room, with bathroom off, which the under manager ushered Pearson into, was wood-floored, with Turkish rugs, four-poster bed, and shuttered window overlooking the hillside. It was like a monk's cell refurbished by *Vogue* magazine.

As he showered away the fatigue of an extremely long day, Eugene Pearson was experiencing a variety of emotions. The prospect of becoming attorney general was just beginning to become a reality. There was a very real chance that Fine Gael would achieve a working majority in the Dáil, Ireland's parliament. The discovery that he was up to his ears in the command and control of the Provisional IRA would result in his ruin. Of course the same was true of his present position, but somehow the possibility had been something he had disciplined himself to ignore. But that was before he had been so ruthlessly set up and exposed to blackmail by the evidence of the photograph of the Whore of Venice lying freshly murdered at his feet.

Pearson had no doubt that the entire clandestine visit to Paris and the meeting with Restrepo had been planned by Brendan Casey for that express purpose. Now not only was his voice, the principal dissenting one on the Army Council, silenced, but he had been cynically, even sadistically, forced by Casey to arrange the negotiation with the Colombian cartel and to take charge of arrangements for a cocaine-distribution network in Europe, Britain, and his beloved Ireland. With the clear instruction to keep it at arm's length from the movement, in the event of discovery. What a bloody pickle.

He was also apprehensive about the coming meeting with Restrepo. After all, the last meeting had been perfectly traumatic. Planning and running the Armed Struggle, whose currency was violent death and bereavement, was very different from having a middle-aged transvestite's brains blasted over your best suit. What in God's name did this next encounter hold? What new horror? For, bizarrely enough, that killing on the Paris bridge had been the good judge's first encounter with violent death.

He was also of a mind, after the meeting with Restrepo, if it went off without more bloodletting, to break the rules of his professionally organized secret life and visit the conservatory in Rome where Siobhan was studying music. He loved the child with such intensity it almost stopped his heart. Mhairaid always said don't bother the girl, she needs her own space, sure how often did you write home when you were a student? But four weeks was just a bit too long to be out of touch. He'd phoned three times from his judge's room to the place where she lodged, but the woman didn't speak much English and he wondered if she had understood his message asking Siobhan to phone home.

But what possible reason could he give her for turning up in Rome? Maybe Mhairaid was right. Give the girl her space, don't crowd her. Jesus, it was a problem, being a father. He decided to sleep on it. If an evening with the Colombian hoodlum's lawyer Restrepo could allow sleep.

Pearson turned off the shower and stepped onto the Florentine-marble tiled floor. It was a comfortable, soft stone with an almost cheeselike texture. He dried himself and wrapped a huge, fluffy towel around him, feeling drained and alone. The precise arrangements for meeting up with Restrepo had been vague, but the hotel was in an isolated situation and seemed to be quite confined, so they would doubtless just bump into each other. He was conscious of a growing erection, which somewhat took him by surprise. Probably some physiological concomitant of the long journey, the apprehension, and the shower. What was it Cyrano de Bergerac had said? If ten thousand men marched through the streets of Paris, brandishing instruments of death, they would be cheered and showered with roses. But if ten men marched through the streets of Paris brandishing instruments of life, they would be arrested and thrown in the Bastille!

Pearson smiled almost coyly and stepped boldly from the bathroom, his instrument of life leading the way, back into the impeccably tasteful wood-floored bedroom, to be confronted by Restrepo and an overweight Mexican-looking man in neatly pressed flannels and blue blazer, clean-shaven and wearing gold-rimmed glasses. Restrepo standing by the door, the other man sitting in the dark mahogany-and-leather chair.

Both men exchanged amused glances as Justice Pearson covered himself in an excess of embarrassment and alarm. Never in his entire life had he felt so completely vulnerable. Except on that bridge, the Whore dead at his feet, the noise of the Uzi buzzing in his ears.

"Arriba, hombre." Restrepo smiled. "Would you like me to ring for room service?"

"What? No, no. I was, um, I was just having a shower." His detumescence was instantaneous. His heart threatened to burst through his chest. Adrenaline made him gasp for breath, as if he had sprinted a hundred yards. His posture was distressingly defensive, he knew. Knees bent, shoulders hunched, hands trembling. His eyes flicked from Restrepo to the seated man, whom he knew in his bones—and in truth his skin crawled with the chill of it—to be none other than the murderous chieftain of the Medellín Cartel in person, Pablo Envigado. A man confidently reported to be trapped by police and DEA harrassment in his home province of Antioquia in the remote Colombian interior at the other end of the world.

"Forgive us for intruding, Señor Hanlon"—Envigado's voice was soft, with the sort of Spanish-American accent that Pearson had only heard before in old western movies, usually starring Charles Bronson—"but this room is clean, my people have had it swept." Pearson knew he meant free from electronic eavesdropping. "And I will be brief." The bastard, thought Pearson, he's not going to give me a chance to get dressed. And he just knew the man in the blazer, and the one in the camel-hair jacket, would be in the corridor outside. He didn't want to know about the kid on the motorcycle.

Envigado continued, "I have a great respect for your organization. And I wish you well in your struggle. The

English live in a surreal world, where they dream of colonizing us all, from Dublin to Bogotá . . ."

A simplistic view of international politics, thought Pearson, but he was in no position to debate the subject.

Then, out of the alarmed middle-aged man, arose his alter ego, the hawk-eyed, fearless, ice-tongued Justice Eugene Pearson, senior member of the bar, the nominal equal of Brendan Casey and Martin Murphy on the Army Council of the equally murderous, equally ruthless, equally bold Provisional IRA. Future attorney general of Ireland. The man of whom one day ballads would be sung in the schools and bars of Kerry and Kildare.

"Get the hell out of my room," he heard himself saying, his Celtic temper swamping his instinct for survival. "I'll see you both in the bar in fifteen minutes." He was still breathless, but this time with anger. "If you have a mind to conduct any form of business with me, bear in mind at all times, *señores,* I am protected by an organization that makes your gang of murdering bastards look like the Mormon Tabernacle Choir . . . !"

He was standing straight now, the towel pulled round him like a Roman senator's toga, his eyes fierce and intimidating, just like in court.

The man called Restrepo moved away from the door, walked across the bedroom, and, without the slightest warning, slapped Pearson hard on the face, pulled his towel off him so hard it spun the judge around, and swept Pearson's ankle away with a sweep of his impeccably shod right foot so that the man crashed on his scrawny hips to the floor.

"Fifteen minutes, Señor Hanlon."

He stepped over Pearson and walked to the open door. Pablo Envigado had already left.

Eugene Pearson hauled himself to a sitting position, doubling his knees up underneath. He reached for the

towel and covered his shoulders, trembling uncontrollably. He sniffed, close to tears of anger and shame. That
bastard Casey was responsible for this. And by God he
would pay . . .

The British army was run with surprising efficiency.
After a flabby period in the sixties and seventies, it had
become lean and battle-hardened, with victorious cam-
paigns in the Falklands and now in support of the United
States Army and USMC in Saudi, Iraq, and Kuwait under
its belt.

The twenty-year guerrilla campaign in Northern Ireland had honed its infantry and intelligence arms into
the most experienced counterterrorist force in the world,
and there had scarcely been a year when some of its
units had not seen action, somewhere in the world.

The management had grown up on the streets of
Belfast, in undercover operations against urban guerrillas in Ulster, in jungle fighting against the Indonesians
in Borneo, on counterterrorist operations in Cyprus,
Aden, Yemen, and Oman, and in the violent and ruthless
land battles for repossession of the Falkland Islands in
the South Atlantic. It had a high proportion of university
graduates. Several officers had been encouraged to
spend a few years away from the service, experiencing
life on the outside before returning with fresh ideas and
a more streamlined approach.

Flabby generals were no longer to be found. And
there was no better example of this new breed than
Robert Wolfe Anderson, Major General, Distinguished
Service Order, Military Cross and Bar. Wolfe Anderson
had taken part in most of the above. He had accomplished the rare feat of combining a successful, regular
military career as an Armored Division officer while

working his way up through Special Forces to command 22nd SAS Regiment, then Special Forces Group, until now he found himself directing Operations and Intelligence, British Forces in the Gulf, on Operation Desert Storm, directly under Commander British Forces.

Among Anderson's attributes was a straight-to-the-point, practical approach, and he listened carefully as David Jardine, with whom he had worked on joint operations in previous years, outlined candidly and succinctly his requirement to have Captain Harry Ford released from duty in the present theater of operations. Anderson's influence was needed to persuade the Army Board to accept the resignation of Ford's regular-army commission and for the door to be kept open for a three-year period so that the young officer would have the option of returning to the military after his contract with the Secret Intelligence Service expired.

Jardine put most of his cards on the table. He told Anderson that SIS needed Harry for a black infiltration operation. That the target was Pablo Envigado and that the prime minister was taking a direct interest. He did not mention there were two other candidates and that Harry Ford might not be the final choice.

The conversation took place strolling through the dark, palm-tree-lined avenues of suburban Riyadh. Jardine knew this was time stolen from the mere four-hour break that Anderson had in every twelve for essential sleep. But the soldier had given him the ten minutes Jardine had requested, with courtesy and his customary patience. He did not ask any unnecessary questions. It was clear to him how important the matter was to Century, for a sphere controller to fly out in person. In the middle of a war.

"When do you need him?" Anderson asked

"I'd like him to be back in the U.K. within two weeks."

They strolled on. Overhead, two Tornado fighter-bombers scored upward into the night sky, followed by two more, and two more after that.

"Well, there's no point in Harry going back on ops. It would be a pity for him to get slotted after you guys have gone to so much trouble. I understand you've already approached Johnny and he bombed you out?"

"Yep. Yes, I'm afraid so." And I don't blame him, thought Jardine.

Another two aircraft, closer this time, thundered over the city. F-111 Stealth bombers. Stealthy if you're deaf, that is.

"Well, the CO of the regiment is captain of his own ship, David. He's going to be a most unhappy soldier if you, if we, go over his head."

"Yes. Yes, I know, Robert."

"I don't know. Why does he want to leave? Harry Ford has all the makings of a general, you know."

"Couldn't he still . . . ?"

Anderson was silent for a few moments. He stood at the corner of the avenue, giving that question his serious consideration. Two U.S. Marine Corps ambulances raced past, lights flashing, sirens wailing. The noise died away. From the grounds of a luxurious villa floated the strains of the Doors. Jim Morrison singing "Come On Baby Light My Fire." An anachronism from another war. Jardine hoped this one would have a more satisfactory result.

Finally the tall major-general glanced at Jardine. "Sure. It's not impossible. If in fact he comes back." He appeared to have some kind of premonition. Or maybe it was the chill night air that made him shiver. "You people . . ."

Us people what? wondered Jardine. Us people will hang on to him? Or us people will lose him, leave him strung up by the balls by Pablo and his chums? He let the silence hang there. Only Jim Morrison intruded, a faint whisper, almost inaudible. *Come on baby light my fire . . .*

"I'll see that he's in London by Sunday week. The rest, the admin, is up to you. I've a horrible feeling I know what's in your mind . . ."

Gracias a Dios. Muchas, muchas gracias, God, you really are a most excellent sport.

"Thanks, Robert. Thanks a million."

"Well, now, I'm going to get some sleep, so bugger off."

David Jardine smiled. He offered his hand. Anderson gripped it, firmly but oh so briefly, as if he instinctively felt this was something he did not want to be part of.

———

The irony of it was that PeeWee Patrice was under police guard in the custodial wing on the eighth floor of Bellevue Hospital, with never less than three uniformed cops from the 14th Precinct to make sure his two homicidal, crack-pushing brothers did not spring him from custody. And in the morgue in the same hospital, the Jane Doe was still on ice.

Sergeant Eddie Lucco nodded to the cops sitting outside the door. One had quickly stopped working out his overtime when Lucco had emerged from the elevator. The other laid his cup of coffee on the rubber-tiled floor.

"How ya doin?" Lucco said, and without waiting for a reply opened the door and walked into the room. Another cop, in plain clothes, sat inside in the far corner, munching his midday meal. Pastrami on rye. A pretty black nurse was writing up PeeWee's medical chart.

PeeWee had been hurt worse than Lucco had first thought. The bullet had shattered the bone in his upper right arm, he had lost a lot of blood and had nearly died of trauma. Too bad. If the kid had reached his mini-Uzi, Eddie Lucco and Detective Vargos would've been down in the morgue sharing ice with Jane Doe and PeeWee's most recent victim, Narcotics detective Benjamin Ortega.

PeeWee looked real young lying there in that hospital cot, his arm in plaster and held in a kind of pulley. His lazy, dark eyes watched Lucco warily as the big cop pulled the gray plastic-and-metal chair out from the wall and sat at the side of the bed. The nurse recognized him and smiled shyly.

"Hi, Bernice, how ya doin'?" Bernice and her sister had been raped two years before, on a subway between Queens and Manhattan South, by a bunch of heroes called the Red Reboes. The sister had stabbed one of her attackers with his own blade. It had been Lucco's week on nights and the senior patrol cop responding to the incident had handed the violent death over to Homicide. Eddie had considered the girl had gone through enough, and after a stand-up row between the detective and the DA's office, she had not been charged with involuntary manslaughter and was left to get on with her life, which she had coped with bravely, even giving evidence against the survivors.

"I'm fine. How's life in Homicide?"

"Well, life ain't what I necessarily pay most attention to."

She grinned. "Contradiction in terms, right?"

"You got it."

He glanced down at PeeWee. Bernice got the message.

"I'll finish this later," she said, and returned the medical clipboard to the foot of the cot. "Patient's gonna be fine."

A brief smile on the stone face. "Yeah, we'll see."

The smile had gone. But his eyes twinkled as Bernice walked sedately out of the room as if she hadn't heard.

"Okay, Steve. Go eat your lunch out in the lobby."

"Sure thing, Sergeant."

And the plainclothes cop rose nimbly and loped out, clutching the remaining half of his pastrami sandwich.

The room was suddenly very quiet. PeeWee affected indifference, closing his eyes and pretending to rest. Lucco could see that the kid's chest was thumping with anxiety.

"Killing a cop was real stupid, PeeWee."

Silence.

"You ain't gonna be out on the street for at least fourteen. That's minimum. We'll see you get Judge Almeda, and he would make you into toast if he could."

PeeWee was acting out some James Cagney role he'd seen on TV. He was trying to breathe real slow. Only his fluttering chest betrayed him.

"So you know your rights. The DA has been talking to your lawyer and from here you're being moved to the prison hospital. Is there anything you want to say, anything to tell me that might help you, when the judge is figuring out what to hand down?"

"You ain't got no right hassling me in here, white boy, I knows ma rights." The angry whisper was a pale shadow of PeeWee's well-known loud and high-pitched tones. This boy sure as hell has been properly shot, thought Lucco, and wondered if Vargos, too, used illegal ammo. All they needed right now was an inquiry by some do-gooders.

"Be practical, PeeWee, I got Roberto the Cuban downtown. The man is giving me the most righteous dirt on you and your brothers."

PeeWee, to Lucco's surprise, smiled. This was an unexpected reaction.

"I say something funny?"

"Sure did, man. You're speakin like a black woman's child. Righteous?" He laughed, coughed, and lay back, exhausted but amused. "You make me laugh, that ain't good for me, man. Shoot me, that's just business, but have mercy. No more vaudeville, huh?"

PeeWee seemed genuinely amused. Lucco felt bad about calling him a piece of shit when he had made the arrest. Nobody was a piece of shit. Then he remembered Detective Benjamin Ortega lying there with half of his face missing, all over a crack bust that went wrong. How many kids had this twenty-year-old wrecked their lives? And he did not use it himself. Had to keep his brain sharp to push the dope.

"Anyway man, you gotta know about the stuff that's going down."

"What stuff's that, PeeWee?"

"Man, I'm tired, get the nurse in. I feel real bad, man."

"Tell me what stuff." This said gently, conversationally.

"With Mulrooney. The big Irish narc."

He's done a deal. The little bastard.

"Oh, that." This was called treading water, when you didn't know where the hell the conversation was going.

"Can he deliver?" Anxiety surfacing now. The kid's eyes wider.

"You'll have to do some time . . ." Is that right? Was that the right reply?

PeeWee looked thoughtful.

"Tell me about this witness protection program . . ."

Wow. Did PeeWee have that much of a song to sing? Lucco stared at the wounded killer. It was rumored that his older brother, Simba Patrice, was in direct contact with the Colombians, Velez and Cardona, who were the cartel's principal distributors in NYC. And yet, Lucco knew the DEA had bugged and tailed Simba every which way and, although the leader of the Blade Claws had pushed crack and heroin, along with marijuana, all over his turf, the eight-month operation had been called off because the one thing it had proved was the rumors about Simba being a direct link to the main target, the Colombians, were incorrect.

And now Piggy Mulrooney was doing a serious deal with this kid who had in cold blood gunned down one of his undercover detectives. Had the DEA not swamped PeeWee with surveillance? And if not, maybe it was the youngest brother who was quietly running the connection . . . Jesus.

The youth met his gaze. Eyes as old as time itself.

"PeeWee, you wanna stay alive, right? Just don't ever mention what you just said to me to any other person. Not your lawyer, specifically not your lawyer. Not any other cop. This is between you and Lieutenant Mulrooney, okay?"

PeeWee considered this excellent advice. The penny dropped. "You mean you didn't know . . ."

"Just like that. And I'll forget I heard it. Next time might not be so lucky."

He rose. That explained the SWAT-team camper he had seen on Twenty-eighth Street, parked across from the back entrance. And the muscular male nurses mopping down the already clean corridor outside.

PeeWee looked chastened. He continued to watch Lucco. No way was this Blade Claw going to thank a cop.

Lucco crossed to the door. Stopped, as if some small thing had crossed his mind. He turned back and bent over PeeWee. "You picked the one way to beat the rap that's smart, it's smart to help yourself, for we come into this world alone and we go out alone, right?"

PeeWee watched him carefully. What was the cop up to?

Eddie Lucco produced a photo from his pocket. It was a good-looking white girl, eyes closed. Looked like a stiff. PeeWee shrugged his good shoulder. Shook his head.

"Nothing to me, man."

"She OD'd on crack at Grand Central, coupla weeks ago. Five-five, one-twelve. Who would she get it from?"

"Man . . . you can get it from twenty, thirty doctors at the station, streets around . . ."

Doctors was what the Blades called pushers.

"Sure." Lucco shoved the photo back into his pocket. Turned to leave.

"Did she have a purse?"

Lucco stopped, staring at the door. The hairs rose on the back of his neck. "No."

He did not move.

"Only the Apache cuts purses around there. He can't get his junk no other way man. He watches some girl score, then slice slice, cuts and runs. Crazy thing is, he don't throw the stuff away. His place under the sidewalk is just filled with purses and stuff. He takes the cash, no plastic, man, he don't understand how to use it. Uses any dope, crack, he finds. Sells anything that looks pricey. Place to look. If your OD didn't have no purse, man."

Lucco listened to the silence. "Where is this place, PeeWee?" he asked, as if it didn't matter to him one way or the other.

———

The cloistered terrace restaurant at the Villa San Michele, perched on the side of a steep escarpment, had a stunning view of Florence by night. From within the cocktail bar came the strains of a piano playing melodies from a succession of Lloyd Webber musicals.

White-jacketed, black-tie waiters served the ten or twelve tables quietly and efficiently. The man in the camel-hair sports coat sat sipping an orange juice beside the al fresco bar on the terrace, with a clear view of the restaurant. His colleague had changed the blue blazer of the Paris rendezvous for a green worsted jacket and dark trousers. At first, Eugene Pearson almost missed him, for there were a couple of tanned men in their mid-thirties—one possibly European, the other olive skinned, with the high cheekbones and Zapata mustache of a South American—sitting at a table at the far end from the al fresco bar. They were casually keeping the area under observation. A bottle of Badoit mineral water sat on the table. No wine. They were picking at a mozzarella salad and fillet of fish respectively. And they each had solid, square-edged briefcases within easy reach. Pearson had no doubt these contained the ubiquitous Mini-Uzi submachine pistols.

As he paused beside the bar, ignoring the bodyguard in the camel-hair jacket, the IRA man counted one more winger loitering confidently and unobtrusively in the courtyard off the restaurant terrace. That one wore a long, cotton raincoat and kept his right hand in the pocket, casually prepared to use whatever serious weapon it was he kept slung from his shoulder. Then Pearson let his gaze fall on Restrepo and the other man. He had made a point, before he left Dublin, to have the movement's director of intelligence provide him with a full briefing on the cartel and in particular Pablo Envigado.

He had read papers furnished by sympathizers in New York, including NYPD classified documents. He had studied photographs and rare video recordings of Envigado and his advisers. Envigado attending a football game in his favorite Antioquian town, Santa Fe. Envigado at a bullfight near Medellín, being greeted by the crowd with applause and smiles, for had he not provided new housing, a hospital, and that very bullring for the local poor, who revered him as some kind of latter-day Robin Hood?

Eugene Pearson was therefore familiar with the shape and face of the Colombian godfather of cocaine. As he approached the table, there was no doubt remaining in his mind that this was indeed Pablo Envigado. Don Pablo, as his acolytes called him, with something approaching reverence.

Jesus, what a chance to take. The most wanted man in Colombia. The man the U.S. Customs, the DEA, and the CIA had lost eleven good agents between them trying to capture or kill. The man responsible for throwing Colombia into a state of permanent siege, who had ordered the "execution" of the previous president, Emilio Barco, for daring to agree to the extradition of the cartel's leaders to the USA on charges of cocaine distribution, conspiracy, murder, and extortion. The man the other, more civilized, cartel bosses had connived with the Bogotá DAS, the secret police, to have captured and killed in order to return to the earlier, more acceptable status quo, a time when the cocaine warlords would not sanction the murder of any cop above the rank of captain or any official above the status of minor circuit judge.

In a business where the regular method of buying a troublesome law-enforcement officer was to deliver, politely, the choice of a couple of million dollars anywhere in the world or the death of a favorite offspring, or wife, or brother, the sort of general mayhem indulged in by Pablo was neither necessary nor conducive to the proper conduct of Colombia's most lucrative industry, the refining and illegal export and distribution of cocaine.

Pearson had recovered from his assault and humiliation. He had realized only two alternatives were open to him, just as there had been on that hillside in Wicklow when Brendan Casey had ordered—there was no other word for it—him to proceed with the setting up of a deal between the organization and the Colombians to obtain the cartel's distribution concession for Europe, including his beloved Ireland, whose two great cities, Dublin and Cork, were already half-crippled by the rise of heroin and cannabis addiction. God knew he saw the results traipsing through his court. For addiction relied upon violent crime to finance the habit.

The alternatives were to submit to the total ruin of his professional life, dragging Mhairaid and his beloved Siobhan down with him in most desperate disgrace, the negation of his life's work for the Cause and probably his murder by turning himself in to the Dublin authorities. Or he could continue to control the cocaine scheme, Casey's brainchild (encouraged no doubt by the several fat cats the Armed Struggle had spawned, made wealthy by money laundering, extortion, pornography, and the tawdry prostitution of Belfast and Derry massage parlors) by accepting his appointed role and using his quite considerable intellect and cunning to somehow destroy it, and Brendan Casey, for whom he now felt an intensity of hatred, into the bargain.

Restrepo glanced up as Pearson approached. The judge had held a cold-water-soaked flannel to his face and the mark of Restrepo's hand had almost gone from his left cheek and jaw. He wore a good tweed jacket, from Brooks Brothers, with various ticket stubs and stuff from New York that helped to maintain his cover as James Hanlon, antiquarian book dealer.

Pearson was stiff from being thrown to the floor of his tasteful room. But he took comfort from the resolve he had found, in deciding to proceed deeper and more deeply into this dangerous venture, until he could devise some way, and by God he would, to wreck it most comprehensively, and in such a way that the finger could never point at himself, the patriot of whom, one day, songs would be sung in the smoke-filled bars of Erin.

Restrepo stood up and pulled a chair out for Pearson. He met the justice's gaze and seemed almost sympathetic, "Please join us, Mr. Hanlon. I sincerely hope there are no hard feelings about our earlier business consultation."

Pearson returned the stare. His eyes said, no problem, I am a man of the world. This is a tough game we're in. It was nothing personal.

"It was nothing personal," Restrepo murmured, as Pearson sat down, painfully.

"It's over. Let's look to the future." He looked into the hooded eyes of the other man, across the table. And in his heart, he swore to see him in hell.

"I am very angry with Luís." Jesus, it *was* Envigado, the ease, the . . . authority. Like Padraic, who was soon to be *taoiseach*. "He is living on his nerves and all the traveling had exhausted him."

"I see." I see? The bastard has slapped an Irish appeal court judge, and a patriot to boot, around the room and I sit here and say I see? Holy Mother of God give me the strength to see this thing through, the bastard, God forgive me.

"Luís. Apologize. Now."

Restrepo turned to Pearson. "I am sincerely sorry, *señor*. I behaved like an . . ." he paused politely as the waiter handed Pearson a menu and poured some white wine, a Chardonnay, ". . . like an animal." This last said quietly and with a degree of contrition.

"Forget it." Pearson smiled at him, which hurt his cheek. "But if I ever see you in a dark alley when this business is done, I'll pay three dagos to slit your bloody throat."

Envigado choked on his antipasto, greatly amused, and spluttered with laughter. "Spoken like a Colombian!" And confidentially, to Restrepo, in Spanish, "I like this man . . ."

Just the right touch, thought Pearson. You're a dead man, Restrepo, you don't mess with the Provos and walk away from it. He grinned.

"So tell me what you have in mind, gentlemen . . ."

6

UP SPOKE JAKE

The man was about forty-five. He was tall and skinny, with a long, angular face ingrained with the city's grime. He wore several shirts over a black T-shirt, their tails hanging loose outside his torn jeans. His hair was shoulder length and he had a bandanna strip tied around his forehead. He sure looked like an Apache, thought Lucco, one highly pissed-off Apache, as he was led by two patrol officers to a waiting paddy wagon, complaining loudly about his rights and swearing the filthy hovel below the manhole cover was nothing to do with him and he had just slept there that night because it had been raining and he had no place to go, because the New York mayor was secretly exterminating all Apaches within the city limits.

Joe and Albie Kovick were twins. They worked on the forensic detail, scene-of-crime squad, for Homicide, out of the 14th Precinct. Nothing escaped their initial searches. Eddie had read of English cops from Scotland Yard's famous Anti-Terrorist Squad suffering the embarrassment of turning over an IRA safe house in a London apartment, and four months later some house painters finding false papers, a few rounds of ammo, and a hit list of VIP targets. There was no way the Kovick twins would screw up like that. They were not great conversationalists, but when they left a scene of crime, you knew their combination of experience and intuition would have left the place stripped and filleted.

Eddie watched as they worked in the filthy lair beneath the sidewalk that the Apache called home. Joe would take a Polaroid photo, then start to remove the top stratum of stolen purses, wallets, valises, fast-food cartons, girlie magazines, discarded, crumpled white squares of paper like the one in the outstretched hand of the Jane Doe at Grand Central, filthy socks and grimy T-shirts, beer cans, and suchlike. Each item of interest would then be photographed separately, bagged in clear plastic envelopes, and tagged.

Joe would appear at the manhole cover from time to time to grab another handful of evidence bags and to pass the booty to a young detective in training called Walter Russell.

Eddie Lucco's instinct had been to climb down into the hole and root around, certain in his bones that somewhere in there was the evidence that would give him a make on that so scrawny, waiflike kid whose face looked like an angel's once the police photographer had cleaned it up and brushed her long, fair hair. He was too experienced to succumb to the urge, for nobody would come up with the goods faster and surer than the Kovick twins. But his sense of urgency was great. He knew Mulrooney and Jimmy Garcia from Missing Persons were right—the kid had got to him. Somehow, the pathetic cadaver had touched him and he knew that there was no way that this Jane Doe would be crated in an unmarked box and taken by the morose, jaded, occasionally wisecracking boatmen who made up the burial detail across the East River in the drab, gray dawn mist to be dumped in an unmarked grave in the potter's field, on that drab, damp island in the middle of the river.

It had become a point of honor.

He was so certain that this tip would pay off that he half expected to hear Albie or Joe shout, Hey chief, we got something. But all he heard were traffic sounds and the mournful hoot of a ship's foghorn on the Hudson.

He shivered and glanced at his watch. As far as the department was concerned, this was part of the Patrice/Ortega shooting. There just wasn't the time or money to use this sort of effort on a dead junkie.

"Hey, chief . . ." It was Albie Kovick.

"Yeah, what?"

"It sure stinks down here."

Three thousand and some miles across the Atlantic that Friday (it was a Friday when Eddie Lucco was turning over the Apache's nest), the Secret Intelligence Service's Sphere Controller, West 8, was adding more olive oil to the nicely transparent onions in the dented but large frying pan on the butane gas ring on the cooker in his comfortable, untidy rural kitchen.

"Spike's gone a bit lame, I wonder if he's pulled a fetlock. Don't use too much olive oil, it gets all gooey. Will you open the wine or will I? Jesus, what a week. How are things at the office?"

David Jardine smiled and put the cork back on the Olio di Oliva First Pressing Tuscan Olive Oil from Taylor & Lake of Oxford. "Dog's don't have fetlocks, you daft cow, he's probably strained a muscle. Don't open . . ." (by "open" he knew his enormous and adored wife

Dorothy meant "choose") "the Californian, my little dove, for this is going to be fairly rich, don't make faces, it'll be delicious. How about the, um . . ."

"I'll open the Barolo, that'll go with risotto, do we need that much garlic, David? We'll sweat like Etruscan navvies."

"It's good for the heart. Try the, um, Château de Bon Dieu, not the '78, there's a couple of bottles of '85, try one of those."

"Claret with risotto. Are you sure?"

"So what sort of week did you have?"

Jardine turned the gas down under the lamb stock, to which he had added the rind from the bacon he had chopped into pieces on the butcher's block beside the stove.

"Bloody bloody."

"Oh, that's nice.

"Bloody little Angus Agnew decided to interview the Belgian Comique Ensemble in French. Well, Belgian comic's a contradiction in bloody terms anyway and now we've got an interview in French where nobody laughs to be screened at ten-forty tonight with bloody subtitles. I could ritually disembowel the pretentious little shit."

Jardine burned his little finger on the edge of the stock saucepan he was laughing so much.

Dorothy wandered back into the kitchen from the back corridor, twisting a corkscrew into the neck of a bottle of claret with such relish it was obvious she was thinking about Angus Agnew.

"Have you any idea how many times you mention God in your conversations?"

"No, actually, I don't. Precious flower, that's the '78."

"Too bloody bad. You're lucky I got the right bottle, bulb's gone in the wine cupboard again." And with a *plop,* the cork was hauled out. "Where did we get the suntan, or don't we ask?"

"I was down in Riyadh."

"Oh, tra-la-la. Just like that? Isn't there a tiny war going on there, or something?"

"So they say. I had a bit of business with Charlie Malone. He's swaggering around dressed up as a colonel GS. It only took a couple of days."

"Dear Charlie. I can just see him. David, don't let the rice burn, it's time to add your stock. God, what've you put in it?"

"Bacon rind, it'll be delicious. And that was you mentioning God."

"With you it's different. Ever since you converted you seem to be in constant touch with each other."

"You make it sound like opting for double glazing."

"What about the Scud missiles, weren't you frightened . . . ?" Dorothy sat at the scrubbed-pine kitchen table, which she referred to as the refectory table. She leaned behind her and plucked two glasses off the Welsh dresser shelf without taking her eyes off her husband.

Jardine turned from the cooker and stepped across to her. He stooped and kissed her on the forehead, pushing her hair off her face. "I'm too thick to be frightened, you know that," he murmured, and let his hand linger on her cheek. Her hair still had the same particular aroma that had lingered after that first afternoon when they made love behind the cricket pavilion on his last ever day at Oxford. Dorothy had been twenty years old, stunning, honey-tanned, lithe, and athletic. Exactly his type. Now you could make two and a half of them out of solid, chunky, cigarette-smoking, successful Dorothy Jardine, the current-affairs chieftain of Television Centre. And now he loved her that much more.

But honey-tanned, lithe, and athletic was still a

pleasant alternative from time to time. He had mentioned that to God, via his Jesuit confessor, Father Wheatley, at Farm Street Church in London's Mayfair. And God, through Father Wheatley, had said he understood and forgave, but adultery was a sin and Jardine should try hard to remain true to his marriage vows. God had passed on this message to Jardine more than once, each time forgiving him for the confessed sin, provided he had sincere remorse.

Jardine had confessed further that he felt true remorse and repentance only at the fact that he could not, in all truth, avow that he felt any serious degree of remorse for his little treats, his little acts of naughtiness with the lithe and nubile if they were so kind—and it was rare enough—to take pity on his occasional craving for long limbs and the mutual, delighted panting of the ever so slightly depraved.

Father Wheatley had told him each Christian must weigh his own conscience in the balance. We are all found wanting before the example of Christ, he had said, and Jardine had agreed emotionally and intellectually. Do your best, my son, the priest had admonished, but do not make yourself ill with worry, we are all human. We are each of us frail. God loves us and rewards our sincere efforts to follow His example.

Amen, thought Jardine. And kissed Dorothy with infinite tenderness before returning to the risotto.

Dorothy gazed at him as he busied himself with the meal. She glanced at her tough, plump hands and back at her husband.

"You really are a soft big twerp . . ." She poured two glasses of wine, "So let's drink to your safe return. And the end of a bloody week."

"And the painful, lingering death of Angus Agnew, to be shown on prime time, without subtitles."

"Amen."

Home, for David Jardine, was a comfortable farm-house on the edge of a sprawling sporting estate on the Wiltshire Downs. He and Dorothy had bought it in 1973, along with the four acres of woodland and meadow on which it stood, with the proceeds of the sale of their three-bedroomed flat in London's Highgate and some shares his father had left following the old man's fatal accident as a result of a collision between his bicycle and a CND bus in Trafalgar Square, together with a fixed 5 percent mortgage arranged by a bank that had an informal and wholly deniable understanding with the Firm.

The farmhouse had a fair stretch of lawn and a number of apple and cherry trees, surrounded by birch woods to the east and north and descending gently to the orchard on the west. It had been built in 1638 for a local squire who had subsequently died in the cobbled courtyard, defending at swordpoint his son of nineteen who had lost a leg on Clay Hill during the second battle of Newbury and was being hunted by a troop of Cromwell's Scottish Horse. The house had been torched and the son slaughtered in the barn, where he had been hidden, but not before he had dispatched three Round-heads. Two with his horse pistols and one with a cavalry ax, hurled across the barn.

They were both buried in the estate's tiny church-yard, and Jardine and Dorothy placed flowers on their graves every spring, on the anniversary of the day in 1648 when Sir Richard and Guy Fotheringham had died gallantly. It was a quiet and unobtrusive little homage. Their daughter Sally and young Andrew always accompanied them when they were at home. The present parish vicar had made some patronizing remark about the "little ceremony" and had managed to convey a degree of disapproval, at which time David Jardine had politely inquired if the vicar and his live-in boyfriend had ever contemplated an informal little ceremony to sanctify their union. Relations with the vicar had, since then, remained in a condition of armed truce.

There were indeed sides to David's nature, thought Dorothy, as he busied himself with the risotto, that made him not a bad guy. The nice thing was, he did not seem to be aware of them.

For instance, when Sally had gone off the rails a bit in her last year at boarding school, it was David who had taken time out from some panic at the office, a panic resulting in the American invasion of Panama, to drive down to Dorset and bring the girl back up to the farm and sit with her and listen, and understand, and warn gently, and suffer the tantrums. Then he listened some more, forgave without being a bore about it, advised, and took her back down to school, where she just managed to scrape onto the academic path, passing her final A-level exams with sufficient to get into university, where she was now reading Biology and hoping to switch to medicine and seemed to have settled down.

Then, when Dorothy had hit the bottle, unknown to her colleagues in the BBC, and had behaved abominably to all of the family, it was David who had tackled her head on with the unforgivable but essential information that she was well on the route to becoming an alcoholic, that she would soon betray her weakness in some probably humiliating way, and that he really couldn't stand the idea of living with a bore of teetotaler who never touched a drop. "For you're a fucking survivor, Dot," he had said, "and you'll pull out of this fucking nosedive. But do it now . . . so that we can still get pissed from time to time, in the sunset of our years, without each little nip becoming a hand-trembling challenge to your, our, very fucking existence."

"You mean, you would still be around . . . ?" she had asked, through tears of rage at having been found out.

"Of course I would, you daft twat."

And he had been quite extraordinarily wonderful, helping with his patience, and listening. He was actually a born listener, which was probably why he was good at his job, and with his sense of humor—which he said was because he knew what his own failings were and if that didn't give you a sense of humor nothing would—he had forced Dorothy into drying out, then weaned her back to the land of the living, as he described it, where she could enjoy a glass or two of wine without that dreadful urge to glug down half the booze in England in order to blot out whatever it was that needed blotting out.

All in all, he's not a bad chap to have around, old David Arbuthnot Jardine, CMG, and just about okay as a chef. She smiled to herself and savored a mouthful of Château de Bon Dieu without a trace of guilt.

Happy days.

———

"Hello there." Malcolm Strong pushed his wire trolley from cakes and biscuits across to frozen foods, where Jardine was selecting a variety of Lean Cuisine packets to sustain him in his London flat.

"Um, don't tell me . . . Strong, Malcolm Strong."

"We met at Pellings, I dropped you off, ah, here. Actually. Outside here."

"Of course you did. I just couldn't remember your surname that's all."

The two men laughed. Slightly embarrassed.

"I was going to phone you at the Foreign Office but we've been up to our eyes with work recently. How many calories?" He was examining the Lean Cuisine packets. "Three hundred and twenty, my dear chap, you'll starve!"

"I eat two at a time," Jardine confided.

"Listen, the girlfriend's gone to her bloody aerobics classes tonight. Are you on your own?"

"Well, actually, I . . . yes. Yes, as a matter of fact I am."

"What do you say to a—do you like curry?"

"Love it."

"There's a little curry place in Smith Street, what do you say?"

"Well . . . as long as we can have a pint of beer first."

"You're on! What a coincidence, eh?"

"Remarkable." Jardine smiled and they pushed their lightly laden trolleys toward the cash desks, passing a squat Hungarian browsing over jams and condiments. "What's it called, this Indian restaurant?"

"I think it's the Light of India but I'm not sure. You know, it's the one in Smith Street just down from the Phoenix pub."

"I know the one. We could have a beer in the Phoenix then."

"Great idea."

And the two men paid for their purchases and left.

Ronnie Szabodo chose a jar of Frank Cooper's Oxford marmalade, mainly because he was such an irretrievable snob that he figured anything with the word Oxford in it must be a bit classy. He paid at the cash desk and strolled back to the office Sierra. Kate Howard was at the wheel. She leaned across and opened the door for him.

"You know, Kate, you're wasted in Personnel. Have you ever thought of transferring to the operational side?"

"Good Lord no," Kate replied. And by so lying, cleared the first hurdle, eagerness, with ease.

"Good girl."

When they had parked the car and arrived at the Phoenix, he held open the door to the welcoming fug of

150

the saloon bar aware, without seeming to look, of Jardine and Strong standing by the bar counter to the left of the door. "What'll you have?"

"Large Scotch," replied Kate, thereby clearing another hurdle, for abstinence was not considered trustworthy in a field officer.

Jardine and the lawyer sat down at the slightly cramped table in the Indian restaurant, which had turned out to be called the Mohti Mahal. They were relaxed and at ease in each other's company. They had been speaking Spanish since the second pint of beer. They now knew that they both liked sailing, medieval court music, and the Rolling Stones and that each had an irrational hostility toward TV soap operas. Jardine had listened to the few anodyne personal details Strong had parted with as if he was learning them for the first time. He was relieved to note once again, as he had at the bar in Pellings, that Strong was discreet without appearing to be secretive.

They reverted to English to order a couple of starters and agreed to share a lamb ghost and a chicken vindaloo, with boiled rice and a side order of tarka dal.

"And two beers," said Strong. The waiter bowed politely and withdrew.

"Do you smoke?" asked the lawyer, reverting to Spanish.

"Now and again. It's not really a habit."

"That's unusual, you must have incredible willpower."

"Not when it comes to the fair sex," Jardine said truthfully, and smiled.

"I smoke a pipe."

"You do?" Jardine showed more surprise than the intelligence might merit.

"Started this week. Jean bought me a Peterson briar for my birthday." (Last Tuesday, thought Jardine.) "And a jar of decent tobacco."

"Chap in my office smokes Dunhill. Quite like the smell, actually."

"David, you work in Protocol, right?"

"More or less." Here we go, thought Jardine.

Strong watched him carefully, evaluating his next question like a computer. After all, the guy was a successful barrister. Kate's research has estimated an IQ of 169.

"Only I have a cousin in the Foreign Office. She works quite closely with Protocol, arranging visits of foreign ministers, that sort of thing."

"And she's never met me . . ."

"She said at first you could not be in Protocol or she would've come across you. Then the next time we met, she seemed a bit evasive. Said you were very senior and one of the back-room boys. And she blushed. Victoria's a dreadful liar."

"Would never survive in my office." Jardine smiled candidly and held Strong's polite gaze. Good old Kate, she was really very good at choosing potential operators.

"Well, obviously it's none of my business . . ."

"My dear chap, I'm intrigued."

"No. Actually I now feel extremely stupid. I do apologize, my job's made me incurably nosy. I'll just shut up." He shrugged, slightly embarrassed.

Excellent, thought Jardine. The boy's a natural. "Malcolm, please go on. I always like to see how other people work."

"Well. I looked you up in the Foreign Office green book."

"Good old green book." The green book was a government publication that listed the names and career histories of every person employed by the Foreign and Commonwealth Office. They paused as the waiter put two glass mugs brimming with lager beer on the table, along with a plate of pappadums.

"And there you were. Quite a career. Berlin, Aden, Saigon, Moscow, Buenos Aires, Tehran, Equador. CMG to boot." CMG stood for Companion of the Order of Saint Michael and Saint George. The next one up the scale was a knighthood, the KCMG. "Now, Companions of Saint Michael and Saint George rate a mention in *Who's Who,* so I then took the liberty of looking you up there . . ."

My God, thought Jardine, he's interrogating me. Cheeky bugger. "And there I was."

"And there you were. School, army service, Oxford University. History and Modern Languages. Two years with the *South China Morning Post,* then HM Diplomatic Service. Hobbies medieval music, jazz, and sailing."

"I'm intrigued you went to so much trouble, Malcolm."

"No trouble at all. The books are all in my office." He broke off a piece of pappadum and spooned some spicy lime condiment onto it. "Only in England, eh?" He fixed Jardine with his amused gaze and smiled.

"Only in England what?"

"Only in England could a senior . . ." Strong glanced around, the restaurant was busy and no one was paying the slightest attention to them at their corner table. ". . . chap in your profession be listed in *Who's Who."*

He has balls, this boy, Jardine considered as the young lawyer followed through with a frank stare that must have disconcerted more than a few men under cross-examination at the Old Bailey. He sipped his beer and told Malcolm Strong the story about the Century service station, nestling under the great glass-and-concrete box that was Century House. Thereby tacitly acknowledging the charge against him. That he was a senior officer of SIS.

Strong seemed content with his small victory. The conversation switched to their respective ladies. Jean was in the wine trade and Dorothy, of course, was a television producer. Jardine noted with relief that Malcolm Strong was neither overly impressed nor particularly interested in the fact that his recent acquaintance was in intelligence. His point had been scored in nailing Jardine's coy cover with the Protocol Department.

Jardine switched the conversation back to Strong's career and it became clear how much the lawyer was enjoying it and how ambitious he was for the future.

"And you went straight from university into law."

"Well, I took six months off to go backpacking around South America." Jardine knew that. He had the itinerary.

"No military service?"

"In Argentina? No way. I'm a British citizen."

"I meant here."

"Well, there's no conscription."

"Some people do a three-year short-service commission."

"You did. Parachute Regiment. It's in *Who's Who.*"

"But you, it never attracted you. The idea."

"Not the military type, David. I don't like people shouting at me."

"Or being asked to kill people."

"I've thought about that. With this unpleasantness in the Gulf."

"And?"

"Wouldn't bother me. Quite frankly, if there was a war, a real, sixty-four-thousand-dollar war, like against

Hitler, or if Europe was invaded, I'd join up like a shot. I think most men would. Of my age."

"Army? Navy? Pilot?"

"I don't like flying. I suppose with my training, your sort of outfit would be the thing. But I would have to be one of the back-room boys. Analyzing information."

Jardine liked that. Strong did not use words like intelligence, or spooks. "Interrogating enemy agents, I don't know."

"Why that? Why not out in the field? You speak French and Italian. Spanish like a native."

"Well, I've no idea about undercover work. False identities, all that sort of thing. I don't even read John Le Carré, or watch that stuff on television."

This kid is too good to be true, thought Jardine. He leaned forward to lend weight to his next, casual words. "These are skills that can always be taught, Malcolm."

Strong glanced up sharply, his eyes reading Jardine's. It was the use of the man's name that had personalized it. There was a long silence, the muted buzz of conversation from the rest of the restaurant unheard.

"I'm going to say something which is probably quite crazy. David, is this some kind of approach?"

Jardine seemed to consider this, then he inclined his head in the affirmative. "It's not in the least crazy. You came to our attention some time ago. I must confess, your several skills and attributes have been considered at a high level. There is something you could help us with. I wonder if you would . . ." he raised his shoulders in a shrug ". . . entertain the notion. Or if we should, um, go forth and multiply."

Strong contemplated. He was a bright boy. So much so that Jardine wondered if Arnold Goodwin, who had arranged the chance encounter at Pellings, might have given the lawyer a hint. But Arnold was far too discreet for that.

And as Strong opened his mouth to speak, the Indian waiter suddenly loomed over them. "Is everything all right, sirs . . . ?" he inquired, with immaculate timing.

How did they know precisely when to interrupt at the vital moment, wondered Jardine. He glanced at the man. "It's absolutely perfect."

"Thank you, sahib."

"Quite delightful."

"Oh, you are too kind."

"Never tasted better. The tarka dal in particular is made in heaven. My compliments to your excellent chef."

Jardine's eyes had turned to flint. Even the betel-chewing waiter began to realize he might be in mortal danger.

"Most kind, sir. I will be telling the cook." He swayed his head and moved away.

Jardine turned back to Strong, who was grinning. "They choose their moments, those chaps. I'm so sorry, Malcolm."

"No problem." The lawyer became more serious. "So what happens next?"

Oh thank you, God. My heart is like a celebration mass, with organ voluntary.

"If you are free sometime tomorrow, I'd like you to meet a couple of colleagues of mine."

"Will you be there?"

"Of course."

"I'm free until two-thirty. Then I'm prosecuting Regina versus Grace."

"Eleven okay?"

"Eleven's fine."

"Good man." Jardine took a visiting card from his pocket with D.A. Jardine in copperplate. Nothing else.

He scribbled on it. "Come to this address. It's between Mount Street and Grosvenor Square."

"Not the big glass building, then? Where the gas station was?"

"We'd like to try and keep you very far away from there."

Slight pause. Jardine was not insensitive to the fact that this was the moment when the other man's destiny had changed its course.

"So this was no chance encounter?"

"Not in so many words."

"Excuse, sahibs, this is Ali, the cook." And the waiter indicated a tiny, extremely brown man in white apron and pantaloons, all smudged with curry of varying hues. "I am telling him of your kind words and he is being most excellently grateful. May I please offer you drinks on the house, if you please, gentlemens."

"A large whiskey would be very welcome," said Strong.

"Yes, please. Could you make that two?"

"Two whiskeys, straight away . . ." the waiter replied, and he hustled Ali back kitchenward.

"So," said the lawyer, relaxing in his seat, "Tell me about your family. Where is the boy at school . . . ?"

And as Jardine gazed at his catch, still not reeled in but well and truly hooked, he was reminded, somewhat disturbingly, of a line from Yeats: "The ceremony of innocence is drowned . . ." He could not remember what came before, which was probably just as well.

———

Dinner with Pablo Envigado and Restrepo had been strained. They had discussed the business of cocaine distribution in veiled terms. Anyone overhearing would have been forgiven for thinking they were arranging a fairly mundane commercial enterprise. The upshot of it was that the cartel was suggesting they would commence by smuggling cocaine to Europe by a variety of methods in monthly lots of around 3.68 metric tons, of which they expected to lose 30 percent to customs and police interception. This would leave 2.57 metric tons, or 2,576 kilos, of pure cocaine to be distributed clandestinely by the Provisionals to established narcotics wholesalers in each EEC country. The IRA would further police the onward distribution to pushers at city level, to ensure the security of the operation.

At no time would the Provos be required to be in touch with the users. Their contract with Bogotá and Medellín would be simply for the arranging, in close liaison with Restrepo, of secure reception of the drug in Europe by gangsters, who would then cut the drug before passing it on to the smaller fry, who would cut it again before passing it on to the pushers, who would cut it again (with chalk, or talcum, or anything that would pass) and put the result in small, square paper envelopes measuring about three inches by two.

In return for this service, two million dollars US would be paid into any of the sophisticated international banking systems used by the IRA to launder its funds from Noraid, embezzlement of EEC grants, social-security frauds, bank robberies, illegal drinking dens, prostitution, and pornography.

Envigado hardly spoke. The conversation was conducted in elliptical, guarded, and oblique terms by the man who called himself Restrepo. But Restrepo did inform the judge that Don Pablo, who was traveling under the name of Xavier Precioso, with a Spanish diplomatic passport to prove it, was seriously impressed with the IRA's improved and streamlined systems of fund acquisition and management, modeled on that evolved over seventy years of crime by the five families of the New York Mafia.

Pearson was too modest and security conscious to admit that he had devised the system. Also he was deeply grieved that Brendan Casey had soiled a perfect if illegal economic system with whores and filthy videotapes. And now drugs. The ultimate obscenity.

He smiled and thanked Don Pablo for the compliment. It was suggested that the next stage would be for the Provisionals to arrange a system of collection points and establish a courier network that would then be checked out and approved by Restrepo. Detailed information on the principal delivery points in Europe would be conveyed to Pearson once he had accepted, on behalf of the Provisional IRA, Envigado's proposal. Also a broad-brush briefing on the country-by-country requirements for making contact with the wholesalers.

The staggering scope of the operation had thrown Pearson. He was an experienced judge and he had made a point of informing himself of the most up-to-date documentation from the Garda Drugs Intelligence Unit and the Customs briefing on narcotics and stimulants in Europe. Cocaine was not a narcotic, it was a powerful stimulant.

Now here was Pablo Envigado in the flesh, sitting across the table discussing ten times more volume of the deadly white powder than the authorities had imagined in their worst nightmares.

"Let's take the night air, gentlemen. So that we can discuss details . . ." he heard himself saying, at the same time half reconciled to some fresh and appalling outrage on the part of the Medellín hoodlum's lawyer.

"I guess I will turn in, it's been a busy few days," said Envigado. "If you are able to look me in the eye, señor, and tell me we have a deal, then Luís has our authority to take it from there . . ."

Pearson sat perfectly still. He was sure that some-where out there in the dark, further down the escarp-ment, he had heard the sound, like air forced from a tire valve, of a silenced automatic weapon. And the faintest of cries. He was aware that the two Colombians were watching him intently. Waiting for a response. He was also aware that he was perspiring, he could feel the bead of sweat on his temple.

The white-coated waiters moved smoothly about their business. The muted buzz of discreet conversations came from some other tables. The tables immediately on either side of them were vacant. Pearson's ears were attuned to sounds that did not fit the environment, because of both his clandestine life and his profession. In Justice Pearson's court, momentous criminal hear-ings were sometimes punctuated by silences in which you could hear the proverbial pin drop. And Pearson probably could, his hearing was so sensitive.

But no one else seemed to have heard anything, and Pearson put it down to his fatigue, his discomfort at his predicament, and his clear knowledge that this roomful of unobtrusive and discreet, but heavily armed, body-guards was probably one of the most dangerous places in Europe at that moment.

The pianist in the cocktail bar off the restaurant terrace started to play "Don't Cry for Me, Argentina." Pablo Envigado met his eye and smiled. The sounds in the room returned to normal.

"Provisionally, and on behalf of my company, I accept your offer, Señor Precioso. The next stage should be a feasibility study."

"Oh, it is feasible," Restrepo said. "We would not be sitting here if we were not convinced of that." His cold gaze met Pearson's. Don't snow me, it telegraphed.

"I mean, which method of collection, transport, doc-umentation, and delivery is the most feasible. Also personnel. I have a suspicion you might imagine my company has more resources than is in fact the case."

Envigado patted his mouth with the snow-white napkin. "You two can take it from here. It's been a pleasure, buddy."

"Buddy"? Mary and Joseph, what a boor of a man.

"Anything we can take care of for you? While you're here?"

"In what respect?"

"In respect of getting laid. I mean . . ."—he leaned forward and gripped Pearson's wrist in an unwelcome gesture of familiarity—". . . we all know you got the equipment!" He grinned and his shoulders shook with mirth.

"I'll just have to wait till I get back to the wife," the judge said primly, instantly appalled at having conjured up a picture of Mhairaid as some kind of sex slut.

"Whatever you say. Luís, take the hombre for a little walk. Explain to him the details and fix for to see him again real soon. Okay? *Arriba*. I gotta go now, you fixed a couple chiquitas, right?"

It was Restrepo's turn to look discomfited. He was being made to look like Envigado's pimp. He said something in Spanish that clearly meant yes, sir, it's all arranged, a couple of Florence's most agreeable young chickens are even now in your bedchamber.

Envigado nodded, stuck a long cigar in his mouth, declined the match that Restrepo had instantly struck alight, got to his feet, and ambled comfortably from the restaurant, preceded and followed by his bodyguards, who deserved Oscars for accomplishing the drill without any of the civilians in the restaurant seeming to notice.

"Would you care for a coffee, señor? Or a cognac?" Restrepo seemed more relaxed than before, as if they were now equals, two senior employees of Pablo's.

If Pearson were to be one hundred percent honest

(and when, he reflected, was he last? When had the Cause last permitted him to be that?) there was no place in the world he would rather not be than here with this hoodlum.

He met Restrepo's gaze. The man was somehow less threatening since he had been revealed to be Envigado's creature. A dangerous creature, like a rottweiler in the wrong hands, but instructed, in Pearson's presence, to do business with him.

"Why don't we take a walk? Get down to basics. Why don't we do that?" he suggested.

Restrepo stubbed out his cigarette. He placed his napkin on the table and got to his feet. "As you wish. It's pleasantly mild for the time of year."

There was something so surreal about this banality that Pearson experienced a moment's mental dislocation so unbalancing that he was required to steal a deep breath to prevent hyperventilation.

As they left the terrace restaurant, the man in the green jacket, who had worn a blue blazer that dreadful night in Paris, was already in the small courtyard leading to the reception hall where a deconsecrated altar served as reception desk. He was deep in conversation with a short, swarthy, black-mustached man who looked like a local, in black suit, white cotton shirt with no necktie, dark cap clutched in his peasant's hands. As Restrepo and Pearson emerged, the two broke off their conversation.

Out in the courtyard with its parked Ferraris, Porsches, and other class machinery, the bodyguard in the camel-hair jacket was at the open trunk of a gray Lancia sedan, his eyes watchful.

Pearson felt a twinge of apprehension.

"Is there a problem?" he asked.

"I don't think so," Restrepo replied blandly, and led the way across the yard and up some wooden steps

Pearson had missed upon his arrival. "This path takes us over the ridge and into Fiesole, at the top of the hill." He started to climb. A third winger appeared at the top of the first flight. He wore a long, loose trench coat. There was no doubt about it, the Colombians had suddenly become very jumpy. He shrugged and climbed after Restrepo, his hip still stiff and painful.

Restrepo did not speak until they had reached a narrow path through the long, dry gorse on the saddle of the ridge leading to Fiesole. Pearson was thinking about Siobhan. There really was no way he could visit her at the conservatory in Rome. He would have to wait until he got back to Dublin, and if they still could not contact her by phone, then he would return to Italy under his own name and give the child a piece of his mind. She should think about her mother more. And himself. Sure, the girl was young and no doubt having a fine time, but five weeks was too rude. Pearson blamed himself. Next semester he would cut her allowance. Then she would have to keep in touch with her parents. The judge found himself suddenly angry with his daughter for her thoughtlessness.

"Vigo is our principal port of entry," Restrepo said. "Then Cádiz. We also ship to Casablanca. And Dakar, in Senegal. I understand your organization has a network in Vigo for collection and distribution of arms and explosives to the Basque ETA movement, the fighting communist cells that have succeeded the Baader Meinhof, and to the French Action Directe, which is regrouping. I don't know if you will choose to use the safe houses and transport system run by Devlin and the Lorca Group, but something similar would be advisable."

Pearson's heart almost stopped. Restrepo had just disclosed his awareness of one of the Provisionals' most precious secrets. Under the cell system created by Pearson, O'Brady, and Martin McGuiness, the clandestine

IRA operation code-named Lorca should have been known only to the group leader, Gerry Devlin, along with an Irish priest who traveled Europe liaising with other European terrorist cells and two men on the Army Council—himself, as policy coordinator, and the chief of staff, Brendan Casey.

It was now clear as daylight that Casey had already set up and committed the movement to a deal with the Medellín Cartel. Pearson was merely the office boy. And the fall guy.

But Eugene Pearson was nothing if not a survivor. Somewhere in all this, there was a charge to be leveled at the pipe-smoking Sinn Fein Member of Parliament for Armagh South. For it was in clear contravention of Article Three of the Rules of Membership of the Provisional IRA to disclose any information about members or operations to unauthorized persons or organizations. It was an offense that required a trial and the mandatory sentence was death. Oh yes, mused the judge, the Belfast hoodlum with intellectual pretensions was digging a fair-sized hole for himself this time. For, by discussing the Movement's secrets with outsiders, Casey had committed a capital offense.

It was maybe too early to level the charge, but if something were to happen to the Lorca Group that could be traced to Restrepo . . . then Brendan Casey might yet finish up with a headful of lead. And after the Whore of Venice and tonight's beating, stark naked, by Restrepo, that was a fate that the possible future attorney general wished most devoutly for his comrade on the Army Council.

David Jardine kept a small place in London.

Number 173 Tite Street was a maisonette, being the

attic and third floors of a spacious terraced house, with a small studio where Jessica, his sister, painted race-horses on commission, earning in the process a tidy income of around thirty thousand a year. The place had been left to her by Sir Harold Leese, the tea magnate, who had once been a lover of their mother and who chose to believe, wrongly and even eccentrically, according to the late Alicia Jardine, that Jessica was the fruit of his loins.

The Jardines, no relation to the famous Hong Kong taipan family, had been going through a difficult time financially since George Jardine, their racehorse-breed-ing father (a much loved and respected man who had announced the death of his favorite mare in the *Times*) had died in that tragic bicycle accident. Alicia had counseled her daughter that she should accept her doubtful inheritance and enjoy it, on condition that she shared it with David until such time as she might marry.

This was the comfortable, untidy place where Jar-dine stood at the front door bidding Ronnie Szabodo good night while inside, young Kate Howard warmed her stockinged feet at the realistic imitation-log gas fire, sitting curled on the rug Jardine had brought back from Kabul some eight years before.

Jardine lived there during the week and commuted to Wiltshire at weekends. Dorothy spent much of the week abroad, working on her current-affairs program, "Europe Now." Most weekends they spent together, often visiting Andrew at school in Dorset or spending lazy holidays and half terms with lashings of spaghetti and mending fences and stuff. Sometimes Sally would grace them with her presence from Cambridge University, bringing down a few amiable and intelligent friends who all dressed like refugees from some mid-European po-grom.

Szabodo stood on the step, bidding good night in

his courteous, Hungarian way, his vowels upper-class English, his consonants rooted in his Magyar past.

"Most constructive evening, David. Two hooked, one to go. When is the PM meeting with President Gaviria?"

"This week. I'm seeing Charlie in the morning, along with Giles. Then I have to work on the legend, and if you have time, perhaps you could help with that." Charlie was how the office referred to Sir Steven McCrae, who as chief of the Intelligence Service was designated "C" in official correspondence. And Charlie was the phonetic alphabet word for "C." Giles was Sir Giles Foley, permanent under secretary at the Cabinet Office. The complex, imaginative, and watertight false history, identity, and occupation provided to each black operative was referred to as a "legend." It was in fact a deeply planned and substantiated cover story.

Ronnie nodded and frowned. "Sure. Happy to. Don't forget the third candidate's presenting himself at Ryder Street at two."

"Okay."

Szabodo seemed to be lingering.

"What is it?"

The Hungarian glanced over Jardine's shoulder. "You know she wants to get into Operations?"

Jardine feigned astonishment. "Good Lord, really?" He held Szabodo's gaze. The man slowly grinned, shook his head.

"I can be really slow sometimes . . . Sleep well."

"You mind your own business. And Ronnie—"

"What?"

"You've pulled this show together single-handed. Thanks a lot."

"Don't snow me, old friend. Your secret's safe with me."

Szabodo grinned and turned away, stepping down to the pavement and walking off along Tite Street with the slight limp he had acquired (cultivated, unkind people might allege) after being shot in an operation that had come unstuck in a Saigon café in 1972.

Jardine poured a splash of Scotch into a heavy, plain crystal tumbler. He glanced at Kate, who sat curled comfortably on the rug by the fire. "Can I tempt you?"

She turned around, her hair falling over part of her face. The firelight lent a warm glow to her features. Not for the first time, Jardine noted her fine bone structure.

"I'd actually love a beer. Do you have any?"

"Sure. It's in the fridge."

She started to rise. "Shall I get it?"

"Help yourself." Jardine treated his section very much like an Oxford don, keeping open house in his untidy Tite Street sanctuary. His sister, Jessica, was traveling the world with a picture framer she had taken a fancy to and who was half her age. Actually, she was forty-two and the craftsman twenty-nine, but to Jardine that was as near half his sister's age as dammit.

Kate reappeared from the kitchen with a bottle of San Miguel in her hand, the beer foaming slightly at the top where she had uncapped it. She sipped from the bottle and crossed back to the hearth, turning to gaze innocently at Jardine, her head slightly to one side. Jardine was slightly thrown as his heartbeat quickened and his intention to have a quiet word about the next stage in recruiting the three Joes was abruptly threatened.

Kate didn't move.

He wondered if good-looking graduates in the behavioral sciences were aware of the effects of their own body language. Be still my foolish middle-aged heart, he told himself, the girl would faint with embarrassment if she knew what you were thinking. Let's behave with some propriety here, we don't ever mix business with pleasure. As in not ever.

Kate moved her head ever so slightly. And, it seemed in the firelight, her immaculate hips.

She smiled, maybe a little nervously. With just a hint of mischief.

"Well?" she said.

"Oh yes, please . . ." he replied, and crossed the room shyly to stop in front of the former Oxford cox and Assistant Director, Personnel, his dark gundog's eyes not leaving hers. He placed his tumbler on the mantelpiece, removed the beer bottle from her unresisting grip, placed one hand around her in the small of her back, pressing her lithe body to him, and with his other hand gently tilted her face up toward his.

The kiss was infinitely sweet and gentle. Her mouth tasted fresh and cool, the taste of youth. She relaxed into his body as his tongue explored it, caressing her teeth. She responded, tentatively at first, then with passion. He pushed her firm backside so that her belly pressed against his hardness. This was going to be fantastic. Reluctantly he ended the kiss and nuzzled her ear and neck tenderly, delicately bending his knees to guide them down onto the fireside rug, where they knelt, the fire warming their sides.

"David, I—"

"Ssh, not a word, *pas un mot*. Seize the moment, Kate, seize the bloody moment . . ." He let his hands slide down to her slender waist and pushed her jumper up, taking her brassiere in its upward course, exposing her perfect mounds, with flawless, pale pink nipples.

"Oh, God . . ." he sighed, and buried his face in her breasts, gently licking the cool flesh, noting it smelled lightly of Johnson's Baby Powder. How sweet, he thought, reaching for the hem of her skirt.

"David!" The voice just slightly tougher, as Kate with some delicacy eased the sphere controller, West 8, as South America was known in official parlance, off her chest and gently tugged her brassiere and sweater down over her superb little figure, using her doctorate in body language to signal that this was okay, nobody had any need to be embarrassed. Her tight skirt was by this time around her waist, and she steadied the rutting Jardine by the shoulders, then with considerable tact guided his left hand from her inner thigh.

This finally secured his full attention.

"David." Her voice was intimate and still full of promise . . .

"What is it?" His voice was hoarse with anticipation of pleasure.

"David, when I said, 'Well?,' well I can see what you thought . . . but you know what I meant, when I said that?"

Poor Jardine. He looked like a Labrador whose master has just thrown the scraps of a roast-beef dinner in the trash can.

"I was going to say, 'Well, what about Guerolo? Did you know about his adverse report?' "

"Oh my God . . ." he breathed, appalled, and carefully tugged her skirt back down past her stocking tops, neatly smoothing it back into decency, avoiding Kate's annoyingly understanding gaze. You stupid, sex-starved old bastard, he told himself, deeply ashamed.

"Oh, you poor child. Christ forgive me . . ."

Kate put her arms around him and hugged him, kissing him, like the good chum she was, on the cheek.

"No, you forgive me," she said. "I should've stopped you before it started. Only . . ."

He glanced at her, his stretched senses finely attuned.

"Damnit, David, I was curious."

She sat down, curling her legs under her, and smiled, full of mischief.

"Curious . . . ?"

"You have something of a reputation. Terribly nice, but terribly randy. Always considerate. Discretion itself. I was curious . . ."

Bloody women. "You've got me totally confused. Have I behaved badly or been teased dreadfully or what?"

He watched Kate carefully, the realization dawning that this could be part of her office strategy. And somewhere behind his annoyance lurked a hint of reluctant admiration.

"You're a lovely, cuddly, no-messing-about man. And you certainly got me going, I very nearly didn't stop you."

"So why did you . . . ?"

"Because it would upset our relationship in the office. I've seen it happen and so have you. I don't think you want an affair because I know that your wife is still the only girl in the world for you, even if that side of things has cooled. What you like is a quick, no-demands, highly carnal relationship, by mutual consent. I don't find that an unattractive proposition but I intend to go right to the top in the Firm and so my lovely, juicy urges will have to be assuaged out of Wonderland unless some unattached officer turns up. Sir, could you be an absolute darling and hand me my beer?"

She grinned and shook her hair from her face.

"I can't think why, but I could just about get to like you," Jardine said, and passed down the bottle of San Miguel. "Now what the hell do you mean, adverse report?"

"I just read it before we left the office. Further report on the special investigation you ordered from the nasty people, as Ronnie calls them." She meant the office's Security Investigation (UK) Section. "Subject Guerolo W., summer of '89 flew to Athens on two weeks leave, sent postcards back from Paxos to his mother and friends. In fact has been traced to the nudist colony at Mykonos."

"So he's a sun worshiper. So what?"

"It's an all-male nudist colony."

"Maybe he's shy."

"Plus, quote, over a period of three years, subject has on occasion visited two Anglican priests in Westminster who are known to spend their spare time entertaining pretty youths. I don't know, David. Maybe being a closet queen doesn't necessarily disqualify him from risking his neck among the dross of the Medellín Cartel. He's never put a foot wrong during eight years as a navy pilot. Very brave. Well thought of. Just something to take note of."

"What about his PV?" Positive Vetting was the procedure where the Ministry of Defense's Security Vetting Unit carried out an in-depth investigation of officers with constant access to top secret information. They traced police records, interviewed acquaintances and work colleagues, noting all snippets of gossip and innuendo, liaising with Special Branch and the Security Service, of which the Vetting Units themselves were a department.

Traders, banks, and "hostile references" were all interviewed, and unsubstantiated allegations would count if they were repeated by different sources. It was, on paper, a tough and unforgiving screen, but with the thousands of subjects in the navy, army and air force, including reserves, civilian employees, and five yearly reviews, while the SVUs chose to err on the side of caution, there was just too much workload on the investigators. If a subject passed his or her initial vetting by concealing some character or ideological horror, it was unlikely the system would find them out unless their subsequent behavior aroused interest. A most senior and well-loved patriot who had reached the very heights of the intelligence service had been forced to resign when he was found to have been a benign but enthusiastic homosexual throughout his many years of incomparable service to the nation.

Jardine was unimpressed with the Positive Vetting system, since playing safe, erring on the side of caution, was the name of the game, and that tended toward the hiring of the boringly gray and the weeding out of colorful and imaginative individuals. But rules were rules, and he had not risen to controller by ignoring them except when absolutely necessary.

"I couldn't contemplate him as a contract officer. Agent, fine. But we can't take a man with a good career, who's giving service to the nation, ask him to resign his commission, which is probably terribly important to him, and send him to Colombia where his little weakness might well see him cottaging down in the barrio among those urchins with angels' faces, whores' morals, and more pistols and machetes than Che Guevara's bodyguard. The boy's throat would be cut pretty damn quick." Jardine looked bleakly into the fake log fire. He was five thousand miles away in that seductive, dangerous place called Colombia. A country he loved more than any other in South America. He could see the round, big-eyed, Tartar faces of the beggar children in the shantytown barrios of Medellín and Bogotá. And the horror . . .

"If he was lucky, they would just cut his throat . . . ."

"It could just be rumors." Kate watched him carefully. He looked sad and, somehow, angry. "You know what tarts Security are for gossip."

Kate was surprised by a sudden realization that she

172

could fall for this big, intricate man, who hid his fine sensitivity under a careful mask of professional spook and slightly naughty boy. "I mean," she said, "say that's his inclination but he doesn't actually . . . you know. Do it."

Jardine looked at Kate in disbelief. She met his gaze. He smiled slowly, the real David Jardine almost revealed.

"Kate, do something for me." He touched her hand. She curled her fingers around his broad fist. "Take the meeting tomorrow in Ryder Street. Take it for me. Would you do that?"

"Of course . . ."

"If we cancel it the guy will know we've rumbled him. There's no need for that. He landed some bloody jet with the flaps jammed and its rudder shot off, instead of ejecting. Because his navigator's ejector seat had failed. Wrote off the aircraft but saved the man. That's how he got his Distinguished Flying Cross."

"I read that. The citation."

"So make sure his adverse report stays locked away someplace. There's no point in wrecking the man's life."

"Sure."

"I mean, sometimes I wish we could mind our own bloody business . . ." He looked so serious. Then he grinned and started to laugh at himself, "But if we weren't nosy bastards we wouldn't be here." He glanced at her, the gloom gone. Kate leaned over and kissed him very tenderly on the cheek, just beside his mouth.

"I think I'm going to go home," she said quietly. "I think that would be really sensible . . ."

"I know . . ." He touched her hair, nuzzling his face against hers. It's now or never, he told himself, and to his mild surprise did the decent thing. He kissed her briefly and got to his feet, reaching down to help her up.

In the small hall, he helped her to put on her coat

and scarf. Their hearts were both racing. Neither spoke. As he moved to open the door, they moved closer and held each other tightly. Kate looked up at him with her mischievous eyes.

"Good night then."

"Sleep well, Katherine."

They kissed, like brother and sister innocently courting incest. Then she opened the door and was gone.

Jardine stood gazing at the door. Women . . . Delicious, wonderful creatures. And that bloody pilot, what a shame. What a bloody waste of his department's budget. Oh well, Strong and Ford showed promise. The choice was now between them.

It was eight after eight in New York City. Eddie Lucco sat in his office, sifting through a mountain of bits of flotsam from the Apache's lair beneath the sidewalk. All neatly, antiseptically placed in transparent plastic evidence bags and labeled. The Kovick twins had done a thorough and intuitive job. Some of the purses had been emptied and their contents were irrevocably mixed up and parted from their homes. Others still had the contents inside. All the usual sad jumble of female users' purses and pockets, he had seen it a thousand times before. But generally one at a time. The evidence bags, just a fraction of the stuff the twins had removed, covered the floor behind him and the surface of two desks.

And suddenly there she was. Her hair blowing in a breeze, laughing, clinging to the arm of a good-looking guy. In a city that was not New York. It had a lot of real old buildings with slate-tiled rooftops and old church domes and stuff. Maybe South America. Maybe Europe. But the guy's face looked familiar. Eddie Lucco had seen that face someplace before. Hopefully on a mugshot.

For NYPD had a computer that could match this photo with any photo they had on file. With an interface to FBI and the DEA.

He lifted the phone handset and punched out a number.

"Mannie? I got a picture here, be a prince and help a guy out, would'ya?"

The photograph, in its transparent plastic envelope, was taken by Officer Stan Morgan, serving out his last month before retirement by making himself useful, with no particular role, just like in his very first months with the department thirty-two years before, from the 14th Precinct to NYPD's Intelligence Division offices on Hudson Street.

Morgan received a signature from Mannie Schulman's assistant, Jake Goetz, at the front desk.

Jake was thirty-two and had worked with Schulman for eight years. The two men were experts in photo identification, and each had a phenomenal memory for faces. It was a matter of pride that they would try to make an ID ahead of one of the most comprehensive computer Facial Recognition Systems in the West.

The younger man stood silently beside Schulman as the plastic cover was opened and the photograph removed with a pair of tweezers. They studied it for some moments. Somewhere out in the city, a police siren sounded, then faded away into the night.

"I know the guy. I've seen that kisser . . . But where in hell . . . it's gone. Something says to me counterfeit, I dunno. Girl means nothing," Schulman said. "Get a blowup and feed it to the machine. How the hell did Eddie Lucco hear we was working nights?"

"Mannie, I think I know who it is."

"So speak up, Jake, I ain't got all night."

"Could be a guy called Santos. Ricardo Santos. On

the DEA's airport watch file. Colombian. That's all I can remember. Could be wrong . . ."

Schulman smiled as he studied the photo, then glanced around at Jake. "Glad you upspoke. So start with the DEA."

But Mannie Schulman seemed less than pleased.

7

STANDING IN THE SHADOWS

As Malcolm Strong shaved and put on his comfortable Aquascutum double-breasted dark blue suit with a muted chalk stripe, wondering with mild interest what form his meeting with the secret world, in three hours' time, was to take, Judge Eugene Pearson paid his hotel bill at the Villa San Michele. He scribbled the signature "James Hanlon" with practiced ease on the Amex Gold voucher and retrieved the plastic credit card from the cool under manager, who might have been a smidgen less cool if he had been aware of the various personalities and happenings of the last twelve hours.

There was no sign of Restrepo and Envigado or any of their unobtrusive bodyguards. "The Mamelukes," Pearson had christened them, after the wicked and fearsome Caucasian slave guard of thirteenth-century Egypt, who seized the throne in 1254 and reigned for another three hundred years. At what stage would Pablo Envigado's Swiss watch of a security entourage turn around and bite him in the arse?

Pearson tipped the porter precisely twice the amount he had calculated was too much, reckoning that was what a New Yorker like Hanlon would have done. He was from Dublin after all, and had not heard how the glad-handed American of yesteryear had all but disappeared in the recession.

The judge drove his BMW 325 down the drive, curving left on the steep hairpin before joining the road that descended steeply from Fiesole to Florence. He glanced at the hotel gardener standing by a wheelbarrow on the bend of the drive, half expecting him to be one of Restrepo's men, but he was just a local, with the deeply lined, suntanned, and incurious face of a true Tuscan peasant.

As he motored carefully down the winding road toward the narrow plain and the river on the outskirts of Florence, Pearson switched on the radio. It was tuned to the "Voice of America" and the news was about Saddam Hussein and his threats to turn Kuwait into a sea of blood. The light traffic in front of him had slowed down on a right-hand bend. A motorcycle cop in tan uniform, white gloves, and shades waved them past the scene of some accident.

Drawing level, Pearson saw two *carabinieri* vans stopped on the grass at a slight angle where the hill rose steeply. There were two local police patrol cars and a gray Lancia sedan with a blue light on the roof revolving lazily. White plastic tapes sealed off the immediate area. Several men in green boiler suits, wearing rubber boots, were on their knees, sifting through the grass.

Then he saw them as the BMW cleared the second *carabinieri* van. Two crumpled white sheets, close to each other on the hillside, like enormous handkerchiefs dropped from the sky. Except from one protruded a pair of boots. From the other, one foot clad in a Reebok training shoe. A forearm lay, flung at an odd and final angle, beneath the Reebok owner's sheet. There was no blood on the white cloths, so the men must have been dead for some time before the police covered them. Also, there was no sign of a vehicle, unless the cops had taken it away. But you don't send a forensic team in for a traffic accident.

Pearson suddenly recalled the unsettling sounds he had wondered if he had imagined the previous evening, dining on the terrace with Envigado and Restrepo. A couple of muted noises, like a tire-valve popping. A faint yell. A scream?

He shivered. Clearly a double killing had occurred as he sat up there in that former monastery, nibbling at his *cinghiale in padella* and discussing the betrayal of everything he had believed the movement stood for, namely the honorable fight to free Ireland and establish a brave new socialist state, by getting involved in the filth and corruption of the cocaine business.

Then the road wound more steeply down and straightened out, the grisly scene receding behind them. Two more mother's sons, he thought, no wonder the Envigado security boys were spooked. No wonder that by the second cockcrow, at five-ten this morning, the villa was completely empty of its guests from Medellín, scuttled away as quiet as wolves in the night, with the soft footfalls of accomplices.

Dear God, wondered Pearson, first Paris, now this. Am I doomed to wander in strange lands, leaving death wherever I go?

Then, being a survivor, he took a deep breath, dismissed such fanciful indulgence, and turned the radio back on.

". . . between President Bush and General Colin Powell, at the White House yesterday.

". . . and now foreign news. A massive bomb explosion at London, England's King's Cross Station just ninety minutes ago has killed around forty and maimed many more. Among the known dead are three U.S. cheerleaders from Kansas University and a number of schoolchildren along with their teacher, a Catholic priest. More on that story as it comes in . . ."

Pearson turned the radio off. He had long ago deadened his emotions to such news. The Armed Struggle inflicted casualties on the innocent. But so did every war. However, with the flow of money from sympathizers drying up month by month, this was just the sort of botched operation the Organization could do without. There had been a time when the judge had in fact counseled the occasional carefully planned act of outrageous and cruel carnage. Calculated to seize the headlines and dominate the TV screens. One of the secret tenets of the planners of the Army Council was that no civilians are innocent. It was a phrase relayed from a seminar on the political use of terror held in Damascus in 1981, at which, in addition to representatives of the Provos, Yasser Arafat and George Habbash were present. Friend or foe, it was agreed, they could all be used to advance the terrorists' particular cause and keep it in the public consciousness.

No civilians are innocent. Eugene Pearson repeated the phrase to himself like a mantra as he motored fast toward Pisa airport. Not so fast as to attract some speed cop's attention, but fast enough, because they would need him back in Dublin to help the movement limit the damage caused by that unkind trick of fate in placing three American cheerleaders—doubtless all attractive and grinning with those wide American toothy grins—in the path of the bomb Gerard Price and Rosine MacEvoy had been planning when he spotted them on the railroad station concourse the previous day. Human placers were the movement's Smart bombs. The targets were never random.

The death of the Whore of Venice was a horror story that Pearson could not handle because he had never before encountered violent death, with blood and brains on his clothing and on his face. But forty strangers at King's Cross Station, in the heart of the enemy's safe capital city? Sure, weren't the Yanks doing exactly that to Baghdad? This was just business. And the grim-faced policy advisor to the Army Council of the Provisional IRA, his hip still painful from being dropped to the wood floor the night before, began to work out the wording of a press release. And a call to the boys in Noraid. They would have people in the media who would help to deflect American anger. The thought that there might also be disgust did not enter his reasoning.

———

At the same time that Eugene Pearson was checking in at Pisa airport in the name of James Hanlon for Alitalia Flight AZ 328 to Paris (the first leg of his return to Dublin), Pablo Envigado was fast asleep on board a TransCargo Corp Boeing 747, twenty-eight thousand feet over the Atlantic, eight hundred and four miles northeast of the Cape Verde Islands and on course for touchdown in northern Venezuela. TransCargo was a legitimate airline, but a number of its pilots had been approached by the cartel. Three had refused all offers and had seen their loved ones murdered before their own deaths. Others had accepted the offer of $100,000 for each contraband flight to Europe and West Africa, more in order to survive than to get rich quick. But of course they did get rich, and used to it. The crew flying Envigado and Restrepo back to South America were the wealthiest and most reliable of the cartel's TransCargo human assets.

And also at the same time, Malcolm Strong was being welcomed by Kate Howard on the first floor of the General Facilities Group offices in a quiet mews behind Mount Street, in Mayfair. He had presented himself to a long-haired, casually dressed young man of about twenty-six, working the switchboard downstairs in reception. After a few minutes, during which time he seriously wondered if he had come to the right address, this quietly attractive girl of about twenty-eight, with tailored tweed skirt and granny glasses, had greeted him courteously and led him upstairs to a wood-paneled corridor with a garish orange carpet, the discreet sounds of computer printers behind a couple of doors, and into an office with a desk and typewriter, filing cabinets and wall safe, and beyond to a spacious room with two desks, one on either side of the door, and at the far wall, facing the door, a sofa and two armchairs in a bad taste sort of sixties mock Bauhaus design. The windows were covered by net curtains and slatted blinds. Strong glanced at the ceiling, expecting to find strip lighting, and he was not disappointed.

David Jardine and a squat man who looked like a cross between a country squire and a building-site foreman rose and came out from behind their desks as the girl in the tweed skirt and granny glasses, with a way of moving that conveyed confidence, authority, and a disturbing desirability, ushered the lawyer in.

"Malcolm . . ." Jardine grinned cheerfully, extending his big paw. "Nice of you to come. I know you're a busy man."

They gripped hands. Jardine indicated the girl, who was of course Kate Howard. "This is Fiona Green, from our Personnel Section . . ."

"How do you do," Strong said. Kate smiled and shook his hand firmly.

"And this is Fred Estergomy, who works with me."

"My dear chap," said Szabodo, "I have really been looking forward to meeting you." The man's voice had a cultured confidence, with a hint of middle Europe.

"Pleased to meet you." Strong nodded, shook hands with Ronnie Szabodo, and stepped further into the room, glancing around, demonstrating by his body language that he was not there to be patronized or manipulated. Jardine and Szabodo glanced instinctively at Kate, who was watching Strong approvingly.

"Let's all sit down," said Jardine. "I'll sit here."

Strong took a seat at one corner of the couch, facing the door and opposite Jardine. Kate sat on the other corner of the couch and the Hungarian took the seat next to Strong. There was a ceramic vacuum pot of coffee and four cups. Also some cookies and milk and sugar.

"Did you find us without any trouble?" asked Kate as Jardine started to pour coffee for all.

"Took a taxi to Oxford Street and walked down."

There was a slight pause as the cups were spread across the coffee table toward each person. Strong was becoming convinced he was the victim of some sort of confidence trick. He did not know, or care, much about the secret service, but this, surely, was not the way it operated?

"Did you remember to bring your passport?" Szabodo asked. "I know it's bizarre, but the law actually insists we confirm your identity and nationality before divulging state secrets."

Strong took his passport from his inside pocket and handed it to the Hungarian. He watched as Szabodo flipped through it, then realized Kate was offering him sugar.

"One spoonful please." At least nobody was speaking in Spanish. "No milk."

"Thanks." Szabodo handed back the passport. "Can I be a real bore and ask you to sign this? It's the Official Secrets Act. You've signed it for your job with the Crown Prosecution Service, but if you would be so kind . . ."

"All it means, Malcolm," Jardine said, "is that in conversation with you this morning we are permitted by law to disclose certain classified, um . . . items. Of information."

Strong studied the printed, postcard-sized document while drawing his pen from his pocket. Satisfied, he scribbled his name.

"Do you mind us using first names? Is that okay with you?" Kate crossed her legs and held her cup and saucer in one hand, gazing at him through her glasses, which were slightly askew.

"No problem. I think I should perhaps ask you three for some ID, so that I know who I'm dealing with." He glanced at Jardine, who was staring at his coffee with something approaching disbelief.

"Has anyone tasted this stuff?" asked Jardine. "It's disgusting. Listen, after this let's go around to the pub and have a beer. Malcolm, Fiona and I work out of Century House . . ."

"Where the service station was," responded the lawyer automatically. Then thought, watch yourself, you're playing this man's game. And no one's producing ID, that's for sure.

"Just so. Fred is based elsewhere, but comes over to visit us quite often. My job is the acquisition of special intelligence, unobtainable by normal methods, from and concerning the South American continent." Jardine laid his coffee back on the table. "Special, or secret, intelligence is information which is actively protected by its possessor. The acquisition of it would cause grave damage to those trying to keep it secret. Part of my job is to keep an eye out for responsible, loyal citizens who might be interested in using their particular skills . . ."

"Plus others that we would teach them," added Ronnie.

"To travel in South America," Jardine continued, "using a cast-iron cover and with a generous allowance, while working clandestinely for SIS and protected by a contract of employment with us. It's quite a simple proposition, but a radical change of direction for an able professional man like yourself."

"A contract?" asked Strong.

Jardine and Szabodo glanced to Kate. She turned to the lawyer, removing her spectacles and peering at him in the earnest way of the shortsighted. "We offer co-opted officers in the field of clandestine operations a contract. It provides high insurance cover, both life and medical, a covertly accounted cash flow, and the accumulation of a separately banked salary. There's a generous tax-free lump sum on completion. The contract officer is bound by certain conditions, not the least being absolute secrecy."

Ronnie Szabodo explained the difference between controlled agents and contract officers, who were to all intents and purposes bona fide SIS personnel, for the duration of their employment.

Contracts were generally on a yearly basis, or when the assignment was completed, said Ronnie, and renewable by mutual agreement, prior to expiry.

The three intelligence officers watched Strong digest this preamble. He lifted his coffee cup, sipped, and grimaced. They smiled, like possible adoptive parents, waiting for the okay. Finally he looked up at them.

"David, you really are a shit."

Kate held her coffee in her mouth, narrowly avoiding

choking. If lack of enthusiasm really was a prime requirement, this guy deserved immediate acceptance.

"In what way?" inquired Jardine gently, his eyes the only part of his face not smiling.

"When you asked if I would do something for my country. Well, I assumed you meant here. In London. In situ. While holding on to my job. There is, and here I'm quoting: there is something you could help us with. Those were your words. I mean for Christ's sake, that's why I'm here. I didn't mind taking the morning off, but swan off on some spying jaunt to South America?"

And here Strong switched to Spanish, which, being his first language, was the one he reverted to when annoyed. "Thank you for nothing, señor. If I had wanted to live in South America I would be there right now. A year off my job? Give me a break, my friend, you're kidding. So thanks for the coffee. And adios . . ."

He rose. There was an infuriating, studied, understanding silence. As if he had done something completely predictable.

"How many cases of murder, assault, robbery with violence, and related crimes do you have awaiting trial, Malcolm, at the Crown Prosecution office, that are related directly to the importing, distribution, and use of cocaine?" Szabodo spoke quietly, gazing up at Strong. "Would you mind telling us, how many . . . ?"

Nobody else had gotten to their feet.

"Nine killings, either murder or manslaughter," replied the lawyer. "The others are in their hundreds."

"And how many killers under the age of twenty-three?"

"All of them. As you have obviously informed yourself." Strong was beginning to feel silly standing there in a huff, like some kid who had stamped his foot.

Jardine seemed to be studying his suede-booted feet.

Kate glanced up at Strong and smiled. As if humoring

a troublesome passenger on the subway. He became aware of a clock ticking on one of the desks.

"Malcolm, one of my tasks, from the Cabinet no less, is to assist the Colombian government to inform itself of the movements and plans, and corrupt inside contacts, of the cocaine producers' and distributors' version of the Mafia. Which you know, I'm sure, is called the cartel.

"I happen to believe that you are uniquely, well, almost uniquely, placed to perform a valuable service to this country and also to South America, by working undercover in order to gravely damage the flood of cocaine into Europe and the USA. We did not set up this meeting, which is of . . . great importance to us, in order to jerk off or have a laugh at your expense. I am permitted to tell you that considerable time and government money has gone into researching your background and special qualifications. Now please sit down and let's get on with this, shall we?"

The clock ticked away the seconds. Jardine still did not look up at Strong. The girl and the Hungarian watched him without expression. Strange things decide the fates of men, and as Strong studied those three people and listened to the clock, he was struck by the tremendous bond of competence, commitment, and . . . it seemed to be affection, between them. Nothing like that was to be found in the Crown Prosecution Service's arid corridors.

Thus this grown man, a serious legal professional, for a brief but fatal instant wished that he too could be a Musketeer. What piffle, he told himself. Grow up, Malcolm. Wise up.

And he sat back down and said, "I do apologize. Tell me more."

And Jardine's heart sang, for the lawyer had said that in Spanish.

One hundred and eighty kilometers west of the Rio Cauca, in the province of Antioquia, and ninety-three kilometers southwest of the ancient, picturesque, and dangerous (even by Colombia's standards) town of Santa Fe de Antioquia, is a remote area of uplands, pampas, and forest. There is an abandoned oil-drilling site, with a few derelict cabins. And a landing strip.

It was here that a twin-engined Beechcraft Bonanza touched down, its tires skiffing up two plumes of dust as they found the overgrown concrete runway, passing a rusty metal SHELL emblem at the base of a tattered wind sock.

Two Dodge six-wheel-drive all-terrain wagons were parked at the edge of the tree line. One was dull brown in color, the other a faded green. They had no chrome work or bright metal trim. The windows were of non-reflective, tinted, armored glass. The body shells were bullet and blast proof and the high suspension was stiffened to accommodate the armor plating by a company that made suspension parts for passenger aircraft. Each vehicle was fitted with radios that constantly monitored the national police and military wavebands.

There were also two short-wheelbase Jeep Renegade wagons, lighter and faster, equipped with shortwave radios for communication with the other vehicles.

Seven Suzuki 500cc mountain bikes were parked inside the forest, and their riders cradled MAC-10 submachine pistols as they watched and listened on their hearing-aid earpieces for instructions and information from the forty watchers scattered around the wooded slopes.

The Bonanza's twin-engined propellers feathered and their roar quieted to a well-tuned rasp. The aircraft taxied to a stop and turned on its length to face the runway for emergency takeoff, if that became necessary.

The Executive Bonanza's door opened and the bodyguard who had, in Paris and Florence, worn the camel-hair jacket jumped onto the ground. He now wore a tan leather jacket and carried an M-16 automatic rifle with folding stock and spare magazine taped, upside down, to the one slotted into the breach. He too had a hearing-aid earpiece and as he listened, his eyes swiftly and professionally scrutinized the environment from behind gold-rimmed Zeiss sunglasses. After precisely seven seconds he stepped forward and a second bodyguard, the one who had worn the blue jacket, jumped down. He carried a heavy, U.S.-manufactured M-60 general-purpose machine gun, its bandolier of 7.62 ammunition draped around his shoulders.

The job of those two, should the plane have flown into an ambush by the Colombian authorities, was to hit the deck and give covering fire to allow the aircraft to get back into the sky. Eleven such loyal soldiers in Pablo Envigado's small professionally trained army had died covering the boss's legendary hair's-breadth getaways.

But today, to the one with the M-16 and the Zeiss sunglasses, whose name was Murillo, nothing seemed amiss.

The forest was busy with the sound of birds and the grass buzzed with crickets. It was warm enough for that part of Antioquia, and there was not a breath of wind. Standing by the Dodge wagons were familiar faces. Envigado's security boss, Jesus Garcia Ortez, his nephew Jorge Envigado Rivera, and that guy from Miami who ran distribution there and in New Orleans. What the hell was his name? . . . Castaneda. Whatever, he was one of *el grupo,* the group, one of *nosotros,* one of us.

The men standing by the edge of the forest looked relaxed, with the exception of Santos. German Santos Castaneda, who, by his hunched shoulders and the way he shifted from foot to foot, appeared to be on edge. Probably the guy was in the shit with Don Pablo. The business of handling millions of dollars often proved to be too much of a temptation for the greedy. Murillo wondered if they would be leaving Castaneda buried among the trees near the airstrip, like the two DEA men who had believed they had infiltrated the cartel, one as a pilot, the other as a buyer. What a night that had been. Murillo and his buddy, Quintero, had assisted in the torture and interrogation of the two agents. What a bloody goddamn night.

Eleven seconds had now passed since Murillo had dropped down onto the runway. He raised his left hand and placed it briefly on his head to signal to the passengers and the pilot that in his, Murillo's, judgment, everything was okay. That was Murillo's responsibility. The hand signal had been taught to them by the British mercenary MacAteer, a very professional guy. Probably keeping his ass clean by making regular reports back to the British, but he posed no risk to the group's security, for, along with the other British, Israeli, and South African mercs who trained the cartel's foot soldiers, he was never involved or even aware of operations and was never allowed within a mile of Don Pablo or the main players.

Use them and lose them, was the attitude of the cartel, *el grupo,* to the employment of outside advisers.

The man who called himself Restrepo jumped down from the aircraft, followed by Pablo Envigado, who was shorter than the others but whose eyes were even sharper, even keener than those of Murillo and the other bodyguard, Bobby Sonson, who was part Muisca Indian, of the Zaque clan that had ruled the area around Tunja for over one thousand years before the arrival of the Spanish conquistadors.

The four men walked casually toward the tree line. An innocent might have expected one of the vehicles to have driven out to collect them, but MacAteer had taught them that satellite surveillance could identify anything on a landing strip, so the transport remained under the edge of the forest. Thus, whoever was seen arriving by plane, would simply disappear from view.

Jesus Garcia Ortez, the Medellín group's security boss, strode out from the trees to welcome his master. A ferocious-looking mongrel hound, big and rangy, a cross between a mountain shepherd dog and an Andalusian mastiff, padded at his heel. The dog was called el Diablo, and wherever Garcia was, Diablo was not far away.

As they met and Garcia fell into step with them, talking quietly, the Beechcraft's engines roared and the plane moved off down the overgrown concrete strip and suddenly its wheels were free of the ground. The aircraft climbed gently, gaining height, than banked and straightened, lost from sight, its drone soon receding.

Envigado listened carefully to Garcia, who was telling him about the latest successes of the DAS, the secret police. So many laboratories raided and burned to the ground. So many functionaries of the cartel arrested or shot in DAS raids. And as he listened, his eyes met the sad eyes of seventeen-year-old Jorge Envigado Rivera, the only son of his cousin and right-hand man, Carlos Envigado Rivera, who had died in a DAS raid on one of their safe houses in the old quarter of Medellín. Just three weeks before. The DAS had formed an ultra-secret special unit, and Rivera had been tasked with identifying its senior officers, with a view to reaching an accommodation with them. A fund of twenty million US dollars had been set aside, and the cartel's fiercest and most able assassins had been assigned to Rivera to enforce the alternative to cooperation.

Now Rivera was dead, his body so heavy with bullets from the 9mm Heckler & Koch MP-5 grease guns used by this new DAS unit that it was clear a point had been made. Don't fuck with us.

Envigado kind of liked the . . . tone of the new unit, which was proving to be his most dangerous enemy yet. He enjoyed the game of survival as much as his vast wealth. Football, bullfighting, smuggling—they were all good games for the *paísa* from Santa Fe de Antioquia who had murdered his way to control of the second most successful *grupo* in the Colombian cocaine cartel. The first most successful was run by the Ochoa clan, also from the Medellín region, but with pretensions to descent from the conquistadors. The Ochoas' Finca La Loma, a vast ranch on a hillside not far from Medellín, had been in the Ochoa family for generations.

Privately, among the Ochoas and the old family "gentlemen" cocaine cartel members from Cali in the southwest and the capital, Bogotá, Envigado was considered to be a thug and an upstart who had struck it lucky. Along with another gangster family, the Gachas, Envigado had carved, killed, tortured, terrorized, and shrewdly dealt his way to near supremacy in the business of cocaine in Colombia. Which is to say in the whole of South America, which is to say in the entire world.

But the old families of the cartel resented the gangsterism, the high-profile violence of Envigado and Gacha. And just one year before, Gacha's son had been released from prison in Bogotá, where he was being held on a murder charge, owing to "lack of witnesses," and followed (after three days of whoring and drinking in the Candelaria, the old quarter) by a team of American Special Forces, all Hispanics, all working undercover, to his father's ranch, where the two Gachas were gunned down as they frolicked with some nubile girls in and around the semi-Olympic-size swimming pool.

Envigado had little doubt that Don Fabio, the aging

boss of the Ochoa family, and the faceless bankers and industrialists in Cali and Bogotá, had assisted in the tracking down and killing of the Gachas. He therefore lived his life aware that death was a cold companion to his very shadow.

He chose his immediate circle with shrewd instinct. Any who caused him the merest hint of doubt were murdered, either by the loyal Murillo and Sonson or by Pablo himself. Now that the DAS was hounding him as their *numero uno* target, either for death or for extradition to the United States (the treaty agreeing to extradition of cartel members was the reason for Envigado's formal "death sentence" on former-President Emilio Barco, who had thus far survived), Pablo Envigado never slept in the same place two nights in a row. He did not use the phone, and his close circle were not allowed to mention him by his real name.

This ruthless personal security, coupled with a genuine affection for him from the poor and proud peasants and slum dwellers of Medellín and in Antioquia generally, who had a degree of admiration for the way he had declared war on the government, had thus far kept Envigado alive.

His boldness, therefore, in traveling to Europe for meetings with potential distributors, was quite extraordinary. He knew such boldness helped to keep the myth alive, and he was well aware that with careful planning, it was no more dangerous than taking a meal in Bogotá's excellent Hostería Salinas among the diplomats and government hierarchy. And Pablo liked to eat there at least once a month. My God, how he liked his life.

The European trip had been necessary. The IRA had sent emissaries to Medellín. It had been Casey's suggestion to use the Irish terror organization's clandestine networks to handle distribution of cocaine in Europe. But Casey was as prudent as Envigado, and he had constructed a scheme of Machiavellian beauty, whereby his most dangerous opponent on the Army Council of the Provisional IRA, Justice Eugene Pearson, would be coerced, not merely into agreeing to the deal, but into setting it up and running it, at arm's length from the Organization.

Envigado approved of the pipe-smoking Belfast man's devious and meticulous plan, and the *grupo* was quietly assisting its progress. It appealed to him to have taken the place of Libya's Colonel Ghaddafi as chief sponsor of the Provisional IRA. After all, the two organizations had the same methods, if not the same aims.

Envigado was not surprised to see German Santos with the others. For German's brother Ricardo was a key player in the intricate dance they were performing to Casey's tune, and German was the link with Ricardo, who should now be back in Colombia after several weeks in Europe.

". . . plus there's a problem with Ricardo," Garcia was saying.

Envigado continued to smile as if he had not heard. He did not say another word until they reached the tree line and German Santos Castaneda, from whom the others had detached themselves, was standing some way from him.

Garcia had sensed Envigado's latent anger and had not continued the conversation. He left the two men facing each other.

German Santos avoided Envigado's gaze.

"What's the problem, German Santos?" asked Envigado quietly. Somewhere in the forest, a monkey shrieked.

"Don Pablo. My brother is still in New York . . ." Santos forced himself to look Envigado in the eye.

"Why? Has he not had enough pussy by this time?"

"Don Pablo, Ricardo has lost the girl."

"Lost? What do you mean, lost?"

"Well, you know we have her parents' phone and mail intercepted. She has not tried to contact them. But Ricardo and her, they had a row. He thought she was killing herself with the powder. She wanted to try crack. He said don't be stupid. She went to bed in a sulk. He locked the door and went out for a beer. When he got back, she had phoned room service and had split. He's put the word out on the street. But the kid's just vanished."

Even the screeching monkeys were silent. The only sound from the forest was of a distant, busy woodpecker. And a hint of static from one of the bodyguard's walkie-talkies. These served to enhance the ominous quiet.

Envigado stared at German, who stared back frankly. A dead man already. His life Envigado's to do with as he wished.

"What word? On what street?"

"We're in touch with most of the mobs in New York. Also the police department. People are looking but we can't be too specific, for the kid has an important part to play. We don't want to identify her, for obvious reasons. I figure, personally, she's been hit by a car and is in a hospital. We're combing the hospitals but Ricardo does not have a photo of her."

"Ricardo . . . does not have . . . a . . . photo?" The others, standing away from those two, recognized a sentence of death when they heard it. In their heads, they thanked the Virgin it was German and not them.

"The Israeli who trained us taught us stuff like that. It would be bad for security for Ricardo to have a photo of that particular kid."

Envigado considered. Deep in thought.

"Do we have a photo?" he asked no one in particular.

"Of course, *jefe*." Jesus Garcia was thirty feet away,

but in the silence of the forest, everyone could hear the quiet conversation. "I have two photographs on file. Ricardo needed to know what she looked like. We had them snatched by . . . friends, in Rome."

Envigado nodded. He spoke to Jesus Garcia without looking around. "Get them copied and pass them to our friends in the NYPD. How fast can we do that?"

"We can wire them, *jefe*. Using the national police line for a routine communication."

"How secure is our man in the police wire office?"

"She's fine. She's a *paísa*. She has father, mother, two brothers in Lanoque. The brothers move paste for us."

Pablo Envigado frowned. "Today?"

"We can try. Certainly tomorrow."

"Tomorrow. Okay. Luís . . ."

Restrepo moved to join him.

"Luís, fly to New York. It's that important."

"Of course."

"Meet up with Ricardo. Tell him his brother dies, real slow, if the girl is not found and delivered here in Antioquia by the weekend." Envigado gazed without malice, indeed with some sympathy, at German, who ran the Miami end of their operation. And New Orleans. The man was a millionaire in his own right. "German, it's not personal. You're free to go just as soon as your cocksucking brother gets his little junkie down here in one piece."

He nodded, his mind already on other matters. He patted German Santos Castaneda gently on the shoulder and moved toward the waiting Dodge wagon. Its engine started and Murillo held the door open.

To his embarrassment, German Santos could not stop his hands from trembling violently. Sonson indicated he should get into the second truck.

———

The next day, while Restrepo was on Avianca Flight AV 82 from Barranquilla, on Colombia's Caribbean coast, to Miami, where he would change to American Airlines Flight AM 106 to New York, Eddie Lucco was sitting in the New York office of the Drug Enforcement Administration, getting the lowdown on Ricardo Santos, who was the guy in the photo with Jane Doe from Grand Central Station. And the staff of David Jardine's South American section were, among many other things, arranging the various administrative processes that would remove Captain Henry Michael Alcazar Ford from the officers' list of the British Army and Malcolm William Strong from the Crown Prosecution Service, enlist them as contract officers with the Secret Intelligence Service, and house and train them.

———

Two hundred and nine miles west of Century House, Justice Eugene Pearson was sitting in the coffin storeroom of a certain Dublin undertaker, along with the other five men who made up the Army Council of the Provisional Irish Republican Army.

The subject was damage limitation with regard to outrage in the United States of America over the deaths of American cheerleaders in the King's Cross bomb explosion.

The press and the CNN television news network had published horrific scenes of the carnage, with one particularly distressing picture of a hysterical, once-pretty teenager from Wisconsin with one leg severed above the knee and an eyeball out of its socket on her blood-spattered face.

"There's no call for publishing photos like that," said Ciaran Murphy, the Sinn Fein leader. "That's bad taste pure and simple. I think it's time we threatened a few editors. All they're interested in is selling bloody newspapers."

Eugene Pearson closed his eyes at this. Jesus Mary and Joseph, the day the hoodlums and Long Kesh semieducated political illiterates from Derry and Belfast threw out Rory O'Brady, Daithi O'Connell, and the rest of PIRA's founding fathers was a sad day indeed. They had usurped the leadership in a swift and devastating coup during the political movement's Ard Fheiss, its annual conference, in Dublin in 1984, berating the old guard from the platform and so humiliating them, Chinese Mao style, that they had been forced to walk out from the conference and, in a face-saving press release later that day, announce the formation of a breakaway outfit, Republican Sinn Fein. But although RSF had acquired a few supporters and some arms and explosives from the extremist Irish National Liberation Army, it had never amounted to anything.

Eugene Pearson had seen it all coming and had quietly allied himself to the victors in the power struggle that, remarkably, had been achieved without bloodletting.

It was, in fact, Pearson who had written much of the script for Sinn Fein Vice President Martin McGuiness, whose denunciation from the platform had forced the split, wiping out the power base that had run the Provisionals from Dublin in the Irish Republic and transferring it to the commanders of the Provos in British Northern Ireland. To the men who were doing the killing, who had got their hands wet.

The Provisionals were now hell-bent on the "one big push" strategy, which required a great deal of money, in order to use to maximum advantage the tons of weapons and Semtex explosive contributed by Libya's Colonel Ghaddafi in 1987. Hence Casey's plan to use Colombian drug money.

Pearson gave his advice briefly and succinctly, and the others, even Casey, listened intently. For the judge had a good brain and he knew instinctively how even the worst embarrassments, like the catastrophic bomb at a Remembrance Day parade to honor British and Irish war dead in Enniskillen, or the machine-gunning of a baby girl by the psychopath Martin Sheehy in Germany, could be minimized, and on occasion turned to advantage.

It had been Pearson's idea to bring Sheehy back from active service and kill him as he spoke on the phone to the man he most trusted, the pipe-smoking Brendan Casey. It had been a tacit signal, to those who observed such things, that the baby had been Sheehy's mistake and not the Organization's. And the disciplined Provisionals had executed him for it.

After the main business was over, Casey and Pearson went into the cold store, a white-tiled room where the cadavers were kept prior to embalming. It was professionally soundproofed. They ignored the blue-veined, naked corpse of an eighty-year-old bookseller from the university bookshop and Pearson reported on his meeting with Pablo Envigado.

Casey listened intently as Eugene Pearson outlined the details of the cartel's proposal. Pearson did not mention the humiliating incident in his hotel room, when Restrepo had slapped him about and left him naked and bruised on the floor. Neither did he reveal that Restrepo had indicated he was in possession of some of the IRA's most vital secrets.

Instead, Pearson told the chief of staff that he had accepted the cartel's offer of two million dollars cash, each month, in return for the Provisionals' handling the wholesale end of cocaine distribution in Ireland and Europe but excluding the United Kingdom mainland, where counterterrorist measures were too sophisticated to risk security by entering into contact with the criminal underworld, except perhaps among the immigrant population. And his research had shown that their principal drug use was limited to marijuana and heroin, except for quantities of crack being peddled by the Jamaican crime syndicates known as "Yardies," who had their own sources of supply and who were too violent and volatile to risk dealing with.

Casey gazed thoughtfully at Pearson.

"You've come round a long way, Eugene. It wasn't so long ago you said over my dead body. To this enterprise."

The judge stared coldly back. "That was before I was most comprehensively blackmailed. Photographs now exist of me standing on a bridge in Paris, with a man being murdered in my arms."

"Ah yes. I was forgetting," Casey said blandly.

Pearson merely shrugged. Not rising to the bait.

Brendan Casey's instinct abruptly told him the man was holding something back. Something Pearson believed might give him an edge. It was there in the chill atmosphere, a tangible danger, apparent with disturbing clarity to the Provisionals' chief of staff, who was as complete a survivor as Pablo Envigado.

And yet Pearson's capitulation seemed complete. "I agreed to set up a network," he said. "They bring the stuff into Spain and the African coast. I'll use contacts with the Germans and our friends in Amsterdam. I'll report to the council in ten days with a plan for approval."

"I would like to be in on the planning stage, Eugene."

"We'll have to clear that with Ciaran," replied Pearson. And the primly confident way the judge said it revealed abruptly to Casey's almost feline intuition precisely the advantage that Pearson was nursing. It was probably Lorca. The fucking Lorca Group, in Vigo.

Even when he'd let slip that piece of information to Restrepo—a bit of hard info to boost the movement's profile—a few weeks back in Medellín, Casey had known it was a slip that might come back and bite him.

The structure of the IRA's hierarchy was such that no one man had complete authority over the others, not even Casey, the chief of staff, and command appointments were rotated to avoid any personality cult.

There was however, one job with arguably more real, lethal, power than Casey's, and that was security boss. Responsibility for the Provos' security was the most vital role of all. For it concerned their very survival.

Ciaran Murphy, in tandem with his public, political face as deputy president of Provisional Sinn Fein, working out of the Falls Road in Belfast, was the Provos' director of security and security investigations. Any man or woman being tortured in some shebeen back room, and there were generally a few, or in one of the organization's remote barns in South Armagh, was there on the authority of Murphy, the former butcher's apprentice from Turf Lodge who had learned the Cuban Marxist doctrine of urban terror and guerrilla warfare from more formally educated internees in the H-Blocks of Long Kesh prison back in 1974.

Internment had been the British government's biggest mistake of the current struggle, when hundreds of men and women were picked up in dawn raids throughout the Six Counties and thrown into captivity without trial or appeal.

The lists used by Britain's Security Service, MI-5, had been absurdly out of date, and the net had been spread ridiculously wide. No finer recruiting scheme could have been devised for the Republican resistance movement, and no finer university of the politics and techniques of guerrilla, literally "little war," than the segregated and self-administered camps within the internment camps of the Kesh and MacGilligan.

Ciaran, bright, cunning, ruthless, and photogenic, had emerged to command elements of the Provisional IRA, including the Belfast Brigade, and had taken turns with Gerry Adams, Brendan Casey, and Martin McGuiness as chief of staff, operations director, and director of security, which was his current role. And the word was that Murphy was the most ruthless of them all. The horrific reports coming out of Kuwait and Iraq about the nightmarish sadism of Saddam Hussein's torturers had prompted an instruction from the Provos' Army Council to Murphy to "watch it," for there was a farmhouse on the border in South Armagh, not far from the Newry–Dundalk road, where a cellar had been dug and carefully concealed, originally to hold some of the tons of Ghaddafi's arms, then converted to an "interrogation facility" that rivaled anything the Iraqi secret police could dream up.

By allowing Restrepo to know about the IRA's Lorca network, operating out of Vigo, Brendan Casey had committed a cardinal breach of security. The fact that he considered that as chief of staff, he had the authority, did not alter the potential gravity of the sin. His almost psychic sixth sense told him that this was Pearson's edge. Restrepo must have let slip to the judge that he knew about Gerry Devlin and the Vigo operation. And of course Restrepo would. He was a pro. Divide and rule would have been his motive for the "slip."

Casey stared at the cold white tiles of the room, the blue-veined legs of the dead bookseller, awaiting embalming, just within his peripheral vision. He felt comfortable that he could justify to Murphy his decision to impart secret information to Restrepo and Pablo Envigado. After all, they had entrusted him with secrets of their own, and Ciaran Murphy was the only person in the organization who knew and had agreed that Casey was to travel clandestinely to Colombia.

Casey realized he had started to perspire, in the minus eight Centigrade temperature. He forced himself to relax. Then he smiled calmly. For didn't he have the judge by the balls? And in ways Pearson could have no inkling of. Yet.

Brendan Casey turned to face Pearson, "Something happened in Florence, Eugene. Something's upset you. What was it?"

Pearson watched Casey's face, which betrayed no emotion. The cold air was forming particles of frost on the Belfast man's beard.

"As a matter of fact, Restrepo roughed me up. In front of Envigado. They apologized after but it was a calculated thing."

The two men gazed at each other. Many a man doing time had seen that look in Pearson's cold eyes.

"What a bunch of hoods. And where were the two wingers I arranged for you?"

"Wingers?"

"I asked our Italian friends to watch your ass. Just in case the Colombians tried to pull another Paris."

Suddenly Pearson had a clear recollection of the two bodies sprawled under the white sheets on that Tuscan hillside.

"How many?" He asked slowly.

"Just a couple. Local lads from the Brigate Rosse." That was one of Italy's terrorist outfits. They had a good relationship with the Provos.

"Really." Pearson rubbed his hands, which were blue with the cold. "I think Restrepo's boys took them out. There were a couple of bodies on the hillside below the hotel. And a bit of, um, tension. The night before."

Casey gazed at him. He nodded, reluctantly impressed.

"They just don't care, these fellas." Casey unlocked the door and pushed it open. As he stepped into the undertaker's coffin store, his round steel-rimmed glasses instantly misted up. He removed them and polished the lenses on his tie, deep in thought. "Eugene, you say to Ciaran whatever you have to, okay? I still want in on the planning phase."

He nodded and strode to the door. His personal minder, Colm Meade, opened it from the other side and the two of them were gone.

Pearson stared at the door as it swung shut. His heart was pounding with anger. Just you wait, my brave boyo. Just wait till the Lorca Group comes tumbling around your ears. Then his blood chilled. Never in his life before had he actively contemplated harming the Movement. This was madness.

Suddenly he longed for Mhairaid. And Siobhan. Where the hell was that lovely child? He resolved to fly out to Rome and bring her home. After all, she was only eighteen, and his heart ached to hear her gentle laughter. At the end of the day, she was what it was all for. A new Ireland, the fighting done. And time for the family.

He would fly to Rome on Friday. Using his own name. Loving fathers needed no lies or shadows.

8

INCIDENT AT BELLEVUE

Two-thirty in the morning. A few lights at Century House were still burning.

Some bright security mastermind had exercised his paranoia, which was after all what he was paid for, and had come up with an example of what was known among security masterminds as the "what if" syndrome. This particular "what if" was, what if the Soviets, or the Israelis, or the Chinese, or whoever (everyone knew the unspoken candidate was the dear old USA) what if somebody had obtained a schematic layout of the great glass box, with a diagram, similar to those on chocolate candy boxes showing which is coffee, which is marzipan, truffle, and so forth, illustrating which departments and sections and sphere controllers and so on toil on which floors and behind which windows?

Then all the interested party had to do was observe which windows were lit up at night in order to divine what global regions were causing unusual activity and what type of SIS action was being taken, i.e. analytical or offensive and suchlike.

So the mastermind wrote a paper suggesting that in order to confuse the nighttime observers, someone should run around the building switching on various permutations of lights, so that when there was trouble in Zimbabwe, say, those parts of the glass box handling information and agents in Finland, Borneo, Peking, and the Middle East should also be illuminated, with some groups staying on till the wee hours and others being switched on briefly, for a couple of hours after work.

The really important offices were all underground, so the exercise was more of a waste of the taxpayer's electricity than anything else.

David Jardine glanced at his watch. Two-thirty-two. He shut his eyes tight and opened them again. They felt as if he'd been working all day in a wheat field. Or down at the fort playing with CS gas. It was in fact a combination of fatigue and cigarette smoke.

When he straightened his back, most of the vertebrae below his neck, in the thoracic region, crunched and ground against each other, almost going into spasm.

The business of finding and recruiting two possible operators for Op Corrida had taken up more time than Jardine could afford. South America was not the secret intelligence backwater it had been before the Argentines invaded the Falkland Islands, Las Malvinas as they called them. Then Prime Minister Margaret Thatcher had called for two independent study groups to deliver comprehensive updates on the entire South American subcontinent. One group from inside government service, the other from the private sector: bankers, captains of industry, and journalists. A distillation of their combined conclusions was that, although the region had always been considered, by Europe, to be a United States sphere of influence, the truth was that in many Latin

American countries, the gringos were not particularly liked and, while some nations and political groups were happy to take American dollars, few were prepared to enter wholeheartedly into commercial or political union with the USA.

It was the advice of the report to Margaret Thatcher that where there appeared to be a vacuum left by the unpopularity of the USA there were opportunities for Europe, spearheaded by Great Britain, to move in and benefit in terms of trade and influence. Britain was, to the British government's surprise, quite popular in many parts of South America because, probably by an accident of history, she had supported various revolutions in the previous century that had resulted in victory for the forefathers of many present-day governments. A British brigade had fought alongside Simón Bolívar, and that made Britain okay in the eyes of many South Americans.

The decision had been taken: move in where the Americans have dropped the ball. Keep the American government informed, and don't let's fall out. But as was pointed out to President Reagan, better a South America under Western European influence than under the communists. Thus a secret understanding had been reached, and, most of the time, the USA was well aware of and agreeable to the various moves being made to increase British interests in Latin America.

Thus West 8 was a busy and well-funded sphere of interest for the Firm. It had been a good promotion for Jardine and he had handled it with surprising delicacy and skill. All government departments were clamoring for his section's product, and not least had been the Home Office's Customs and Police Departments, fighting a growing battle to stem the flood of cocaine and marijuana from South America via Europe and West Africa.

So along with the glamor of flights to the war zone of Saudi Arabia and the convoluted minuet to recruit Malcolm Strong, David Jardine was coping with the controlling of sixty-one top secret clandestine intelligence-gathering operations in almost every country in the subcontinent. To be accurate, those sixty-one belonged to fourteen principal operational code names, and each had a case manager, with subordinates, all working through Bill Jenkins, with occasional help from Ronnie Szabodo. But the tall, scar-faced sphere controller still had to keep himself *au fait* with every operation and contribute his experience, point out warning signs, kick some ass, and from time to time save the hide of some agent who was too close to the ground to see the awful shadow of discovery looming over him.

Two-thirty-three. Time for a beer. And some shut-eye. There was a room beside his office, with a campaign bed and a tiny washroom, complete with cramped shower.

Jardine stared down at a folder marked "CONFIS-CATE," which was not an instruction but the name of an operation. Where did Mrs. Brownlow dig them up? he wondered. The words had become hazy. His head was beginning to hurt. He stretched his arms above his head and yawned, loud and immoderately.

"Hello, you old bastard." It was Steven McCrae. The chief. "Sorry to butt in on a good stretch. But the PM's seeing Gaviria tomorrow and he's asked me for an update on Colombia. Not to mention, of course, but just to feel confident he's one hundred percent in the picture."

Silence.

David Jardine turned slowly and stared at McCrae. Sometimes, if an operation was taking place in another time zone, a prolonged operation, the people concerned lived in the building and switched their routine to that time zone. The boss must've done that, therefore it must be bloody important. Or important to him, which meant it was probably to do with China, which was not only a serious sphere but was where Steven, Sir Steven, had run an operation of legendary success and danger (legend created and nourished regularly by Steven McCrae) in the late seventies.

And butting in on a good stretch? Jesus Christ, the man must be taking English lessons from Ronnie Szabodo.

Jardine smiled brightly and tugged a bottle of Scotch from his lower drawer. "Colombia. Now be a sweetheart, Steven, and point it out on the map for me, would you?"

McCrae shook his head. "I remember when you were only senile . . ."

He flopped down on a well-worn green leather chair with wooden arms. The chair that Jardine had been looking forward to stretching out in with a cold beer.

Jardine poured two shots of whiskey into two tooth glasses from the same drawer. Shoved one across his desk toward the chief.

"Help yourself."

"What's this, whiskey?"

My God, the man should be a spy. "No, it's hemlock, actually."

"Hemlock?"

"That's a joke, Chief. It's called Lagavullin and it comes from Isla. It's a single malt. There's gin if you prefer."

"Getting just a tiny bit uptight? Tough work running a sphere, isn't it? David, how's the Corrida thing progressing?"

Jardine sniffed at his whiskey. "I've recruited a couple of Joes. They start training on Tuesday."

"You don't waste much time."

"I got the impression, in the Prime Minister's office, there was not much time to lose."

Jardine glanced at McCrae, his Scotch still not touched. The scar on his face was more obvious when he was tired.

"It's been a confusion of errors."

Comedy of errors, you illiterate twerp. There were those who said, in places where they could not be overheard, that the top job should have gone to another. A younger man than was usual, but an able intelligence officer and strong politician who would fight the service's corner. Steven McCrae tended to be all things to all men. But those who advised on such appointments had chosen him. Jardine shrugged. He was, at forty-eight, probably as close to the sun as he was going to get. Maybe director of operations, as a final appointment, in a few years, as a pat on the head. Maybe not.

For some reason he found himself thinking of Sir Richard Fotheringham, dying sword in hand on the cobbled yard of their seventeenth-century farmhouse, giving his life's blood for his wounded son, half sitting, half lying, on the loft of the old barn, horse pistols in hand, sweating and nervous as hell, Jardine didn't doubt.

He met McCrae's gaze. "I plan to choose one to infiltrate the cartel. The other to establish himself, long term, in Bogotá. Two separate operations. Training and evaluation will take ten weeks. During that time, I'll establish a small cell in Medellín. To service the man inside the cartel. I should be receiving raw product in about four months."

"We're receiving raw product already."

"Not top grade, A-one from Don Pablo's table."

"Can you accomplish that . . . ?"

"I can certainly do my best." Jardine sipped his Scotch.

McCrae gazed at Jardine. "You had every right to be very angry."

"For what?" What? Angry? What had he missed?

"I had given the impression we were much further along the road to this. With this infiltration."

"So you took the liberty of bullshitting them." This was a quote from *The Blues Brothers*, which Andrew, Sally, and Jardine had watched on home video no fewer than eleven times. They knew every line of dialogue and sometimes, when the family was all together down in the farmhouse, they would mouth the script along with the actors John Belushi and Dan Aykroyd. Dorothy thought they were quite demented.

"I did not, actually, bullshit anyone." Obviously C was not *au fait* with the movie. "It was just, you know how bloody discreet we all are. The secret world."

"Secret. Right."

The ringing noise of cold steel in his imagination sent shivers fluttering over his spine. Imagine. Fighting those bastard Lowland Scots horse troopers of Cromwell's, they with their brutal, curved hangers of German steel. Sir Richard with an elegant basket-hilted sword of Toledo blue.

"So when the PM said, a few weeks earlier, I don't want to know the details but doubtless you chaps are well inside the cocaine problem, in its country of origin, I just smiled enigmatically. You know the way we do."

Jardine had not been to one of the exclusive English boarding schools, like Steven McCrea. He had gone to a solid local grammar school and had sweated for his place at Oxford. But his children had both been through the system. Sally at Tudor Hall and Andrew, who was still at Sherborne. He could just imagine the boss, aged fifteen, in the fifth form, sitting on his study bed, knees bent, legs pulled up, scruffy shoes unpolished, earnestly holding a similar conversation with Smith minor or whoever, over some comedy of confusion in the queue for central feeding.

"Yes, I often get myself misunderstood like that." Two-fifty-one, please, dear Lord, I must sleep soon.

"And he now believes we're that much further involved."

"Yes, Steven, I gathered that."

"Probably told HM for all I know."

HM, Jardine deciphered, was Her Majesty. The Queen. He doubted, somehow, that she would be religiously following the comings and goings of her Secret Intelligence Service on a day-to-day basis, fed by titbits from the prime minister.

"Oh, I really don't think so. Steven, I can't *invent* product. Giles Abercrombie's doing a great job, running the station out there. He has a bloody great network of informers. I'll dress all that up and you can flash that at Downing Street."

McCrae contemplated this. Gazing into his whiskey glass. "Point is, old son, four months is too long. We can't afford the luxury."

"I wouldn't like to think you were putting your hands on my operation, Chief."

"I wouldn't dream of it. But if you like, I'll send a directive down from my room." He always referred to his office as his room. Just to remind people he had been to Cambridge.

"Got the point, sport." Jardine drained his glass and rose to his feet. He uncorked the bottle and offered a refill to McCrae.

"No thanks. Must press on. And David . . ."

"Yes?"

"We require serious product coming out of Medellín within seven weeks. You can call on any resource we have. If you've chosen your operators with your usual skill, I have no doubt you'll succeed. Good afternoon."

And Sir Steven left. It was a couple of minutes before three in the morning. Unless one was working Peking time.

Jardine stared at the door as it swung shut. He rubbed his face with the heel of his hand, sighed, and dialed a number.

He waited patiently as it rang. Finally Bill Jenkins, his operations manager, answered. Bill lived in Paddington and Jardine had a mental picture of the man's neat bedroom and his wife, Pam, asleep beside him.

"Sorry to disturb your slumber." Jardine's voice was unmistakable, not so much because of its timbre as for its easy authority.

"No problem," lied Jenkins, doubtless cursing his boss.

"Were we going to send Adrian back to that place?"

Adrian was the code name for an agent who had spent months each year for the last four years training the cartel's bodyguard. Unfortunately, they had been extremely security conscious, and he failed to get more than a sniff of what was going on. His name was MacAteer.

"Not in the immediate future."

"Where is he?"

"Up north, asleep, I imagine. Like any sane person."

"Bring him down first thing in the morning. I need him to brief my Joes."

"Is that wise . . . ?"

"No. But time's running out. I want a man on the ground in five weeks."

"Shit."

"You said it. Sweet dreams."

Three days later, Harry Ford was collected from Heathrow Airport and flown by helicopter to a remote country house in Wales. A slightly stunned Malcolm

Strong was already there. The best instructors SIS could provide had four weeks to turn them into secret agents.

———

Lia Asunción was a pretty, well-rounded girl of twenty-six. She worked in the Communications Department of the Policia Nacional, in Bogotá. She had the flirtatious good looks that were typical of so many Colombian girls, perhaps more European in character than many in Colombia's polyglot society. This marked her as a *paísa*, as native Antioquians were known. The Spaniards who had first settled there in the seventeenth century had, unusually, kept themselves to themselves, and many *paísas* were similar to Europeans, or perhaps Israelis, for many of the original settlers had been descended from Sephardic Jews who had arrived in Spain in the first and second centuries from northern India, via Phoenecia.

Lia's two brothers owned a couple of trucks and ran a transport business. They also worked for the cartel, running coca paste from laboratory to laboratory in the wilds of Antioquia. Lia had gone to university in Bogotá and after graduating in English and History had taken a job with the Convention Center, working as a telephonist and secretary, before befriending a lieutenant in the Policia National, who had helped her get a position as a civilian clerk in the Communications Department. One of Lia's functions was to operate the telex and fax system between the department and English-speaking police agencies around the world. She was a bright and cheerful girl, efficient and reliable. And she was the cartel's agent, inside the Policia Nacional's headquarters, in Bogotá.

When Lia was asked to pass the photos of the missing girl, hidden among a series of routine inquiries, to someone in the New York City Police Department, she knew just who to telex, and the query was in the right hands, in New York, before Restrepo got off the American Airlines flight from Miami to JFK.

And while Restrepo, Murillo, and Bobby Sonson were checking into the luxury Pierre Hotel, on Fifth Avenue, using Spanish passports that identified them as garment-trade executives, a reply was flashing down the wire to Lia Asunción in Police Headquarters, Bogotá. The reply stated that the photograph matched that of a Jane Doe found dead at Grand Central Station two weeks before. It further informed that NYPD Homicide was in possession of a photo that showed the girl, in some southern European city, in the company of a known cocaine dealer called Ricardo Santos Castaneda.

By the time Restrepo had tipped the porter, locked his bedroom door, and phoned the street pay phone where Ricardo Santos was waiting, Jesus Garcia Ortez, Pablo Envigado's security boss, had been informed by an intermediary of the swift result of Lia's research.

Restrepo arranged a discreet meeting with Santos. He told his bodyguards the arrangements and took a long, warm shower. He dried himself and flopped down on the kingsize bed, gazing out over the treetops of Central Park. Twenty minutes complete rest, he promised himself. Then get dressed and take the meeting with Santos. It was imperative that they find the girl, although in New York, the task was next to impossible. Restrepo guessed that she had taken a plane back to Rome after her row with the darkly good-looking Ricardo Santos. Maybe even back to her parents, in which case the—

The phone rang.

Restrepo answered. A coded message from a garment factory in Barcelona (where it had been sent from Medellín) told him the girl was dead. It was imperative, and this was from the *jefe*, the chief, that Santos be taken off the street and questioned. Restrepo was to "tidy up" and use his own judgment. There were to be no loose ends. Then Restrepo was to return to brief Don Pablo on the whole ball of wax.

Forty-two minutes later, it was five in the afternoon and Sixth Avenue was packed with office workers marching from the many skyscrapers in that part of Manhattan and relentlessly finding subways and taxis and automobiles in parking lots to spirit them home.

Ricardo Santos stood near the Radio City entrance. It was starting to rain. A dark blue Cadillac stopped at the sidewalk. At the wheel was a Colombian who worked New York as a taxi driver and chauffeur to the *grupo*, the cartel. He had a wife and five children in Cartagena and his discretion was guaranteed. He also knew the town and had all his papers in order.

The rear door opened and Bobby Sonson got out. He glanced around the environment, then to Santos, who stepped forward, smiling, and got into the back of the Cadillac, where Murillo was waiting. Sonson shut the door and climbed into the front passenger seat. The car moved away, joining the traffic.

"Where's Luís?" asked Santos, relaxing among his own kind.

"We're just going to see him," replied Murillo. And that was all he said as the Cadillac drove to a construction site in Brooklyn, with a view of the East River.

Ricardo Santos was fished out of the river three weeks later. It was impossible to identify the body, on account of its head was missing and the hands too. He had, stupidly, told everything he had to tell during an appalling eight hours of questioning by Restrepo, aided by Murillo and Sonson. The Colombian driver had been found shot in the driver's seat of his cab at dawn the next morning—that is to say, three weeks before Santos was taken from the harbor—in a part of Queens where four similar murders had taken place.

This was Restrepo being "tidy."

The night of questions had established that none of Santos's underworld contacts, hunting for the girl, had been aware of her real identity. That was good. Also, the girl had had no suspicion about why this handsome (once handsome) young South American millionaire was really taking her from Rome to Colombia. That too was good. But Ricardo had enlisted the help of Simba Patrice and his street gang, the Blade Claws, to try to find her. That was dumb.

And Simba's brother, young PeeWee Patrice, was in Bellevue Hospital under police guard and facing a murder rap for shooting an undercover cop. That was bad. And the girl had in fact gone missing not a few days ago but over two weeks back. Ricardo had tried to find her on his own first, before alerting the cartel.

That was fatal.

All in all, the visit to New York by the man who called himself Restrepo was not dissimilar to a latter-day visit to Rome by the Visigoths.

———

While Eugene Pearson was disembarking at Leonardo da Vinci airport near Rome and passing through immigration using his own name (a novel experience) on his search for his daughter, it was Eddie Lucco's Saturday morning and he and Nancy were taking their delicious time about doing what it was they most liked to do on a Saturday morning. Or a Tuesday. Or a Friday, or whenever.

Just as this thing they liked doing best was gathering a head of steam, and they were both sweating although it was cold and foggy outside, the phone started to ring.

Being a sensible man, Eddie placed his wife's and his own contentment first and ignored the phone for a while. But its continued ringing finally intruded too much and spoiled the moment. Lucco gazed at Nancy. She watched him, amused. He kissed her gently on the side of the mouth, then reached for the receiver.

"Eddie, I thought you were out." It was Pig Mulrooney, the Narcotics lieutenant who had PeeWee Patrice in a Witness Protection Program.

"No kidding." Lucco frowned at Nancy, who clearly intended to keep the proceedings alive.

"I just got word the Claws are taking heat from some spics, looking for that kid you got on ice at Bellevue."

Lucco stared at Nancy's glistening black hair. He stroked her shoulder. "Friends of Rikki, huh?" By Rikki he meant Ricardo Santos.

"There's also a fuckin angle which worries me. I can't explain but I got a bad feeling."

Lucco's blood turned to stone. Sometimes, like a few good cops, he got those premonitions. He did not know what was going down, but it was going to be bad. "Where are you?"

"On my way to the hospital. I got somebody there maybe I should move."

"Yeah, I hear you. I'm on my way." Lucco put the phone back on the hook. Nancy glanced at him. There was something about the way she sometimes looked at him that still drove him crazy. So he touched her tenderly, at first . . .

And that brief delay probably saved his life.

The first thing Eddie Lucco saw, when he turned onto East Twenty-eighth Street, was the living body of a nurse, arms and legs flailing, dropping like a stone from the eighth floor to the street. He stood on the brakes, a van ran into the back of his car, and the woman hit the street without bouncing. Lucco shouldered open his door and started running toward the hospital side entrance, hearing, because he was half anticipating it, the crackle of gunfire high above, and the sound of breaking glass. Maybe he imagined it, but later, he thought he had heard faint sounds of screaming. Still running, he glanced at the crumpled body of the nurse. She was very obviously dead.

The side entrance loomed closer and a man appeared from inside the lobby with blood on his leather zip-up and white shirt, holding an Ingram submachine pistol, which he immediately pointed and fired straight at Eddie Lucco, whose years of training and experience had conditioned him to hit the deck and roll for cover, from where he could radio for assistance. But instead he dropped to a crouch, drawing his .38 and shooting back, his reaction automatic and coldly angry. Nobody shot at Eddie Lucco, people had to know that, for word soon got out on the street and all the guys had thought this through. There was no way out for anyone dumb enough to shoot at a New York cop.

Ignoring the adrenaline rush, he squeezed off four loud, booming shots in rapid, relentless succession, as slugs from the Ingram hit the street and cracked past his head. The man was hit and jerked backward, dropping the Ingram, which clattered onto the step.

Lucco scuttled for cover. Reaching the front of a parked Buick, he reloaded and as he bobbed up glimpsed the wounded assailant pulling himself back into the shadow of the lobby.

Lucco aimed fast and shot the guy twice in the upper legs, then, using cars and the wall for cover, he moved forward to reach the lobby. To seize the enemy territory. Lucco had been a marine. He knew from combat.

The wounded man was bleeding profusely. People were screaming. The sounds of gunfire continued, sporadically, from the upper floors. Eddie Lucco stooped and rolled the assailant, a swarthy Hispanic type, onto his front, expertly cuffing his hands behind his back. Then he holstered his revolver, picked up the Ingram, removed the magazine, checked it had about eighteen rounds unused, and pushed through the double swing doors and into the hospital lobby, Ingram in one hand, detective's badge in the other.

The first thing that registered was alarm bells ringing shrilly. Two civilians, a white-coated doctor and a nurse, lay dead or gravely wounded on the rubber-tiled floor. There was blood on the walls and bunches of terrified nurses and patients in various rooms off the lobby and corridors. A uniformed patrolman, gravely wounded, was being tended by a group of nurses and a young intern.

In the moment it took Lucco to register this, he knew precisely what had happened and where the gunfire was coming from. He glanced at the elevator and thought no way was he going to get trapped in that cage so he moved to the stairs and started upward, moving as fast as was prudent, through layers of shrilly ringing alarm bells, like a diver coming up from the deep.

By the time he reached the eighth floor, the bells had been joined by the whoops and wails of growing numbers of police patrol cars and ESU (NYPD's SWAT team) response vans drifting up from the streets below. He paused on the landing below the corridor. Because of the alarm bells he was deprived of one vital sense, his hearing. He got his breath back, holding the Ingram ready, and edged upward and inched around the corner, his heart thumping powerfully. In the corridor, a scene from Goya. Maybe eight bodies. There were the three "hospital cleaners" who were undercover officers from the witness protection program. The two Homicide cops who had been stationed outside the door to PeeWee's room. And two Colombian button men, one of whose faces was no longer recognizable. The other was known to Lucco. Big-league hoodlums, the one with the face owned a bar in Miami and had a private pilot's license.

One of the witness-protection cops was still breathing, and Benwell, from the 14th Precinct was moving slightly, his back a mess of blood. In fact there was blood everywhere. Suddenly the alarm bells stopped.

Somebody, cowering somewhere, a woman, was sobbing.

Now Lucco's ears started to work. Everything was strangely still. He moved, this ex-marine cop, aware each second could be his last, eyes and ears everywhere at once. Only one thing required of him right now. To stay alive.

He reached the open door to the guarded hospital room, stepping over Benwell and the overturned chair, along with a police notebook with overtime calculations unfinished. PeeWee was comprehensively assassinated. He had been shot with both machine gun and shotgun, from the doorway and from close range. His drip feed had been knocked over by Pig Mulrooney, who sat propped in the corner next to the bed, Colt .45 automatic clutched in his dead hand. Blasted in the chest by a shotgun, his big, Irish cop's face unmarked. Its expression was not one of surprise, it was more . . . regret.

Lucco's instinct was still one of self-preservation. His already sharpened senses were now approaching overload. Was there someplace he had overlooked? Some muzzle even now pointed in his direction? He sidled along the wall and, one eye on the doorway, hunkered down and glanced under the bed. To come face to face with a petrified Bernice, the nurse whose sister had killed her rapist, her face streaked with tears of fear and horror. Her eyes big and white in her plump and beautiful black face.

Lucco mouthed, silently, "You okay . . . ?"

She nodded, terrified.

Lucco mouthed, "Stay right there . . ."

She nodded.

He raised a finger. "Don't move from there . . ."

Then, the tension somehow relieved by the brief contact with another, living, human being, he moved back to the door. From other parts of the building, shouted words of command. The squawk and static of police walkie-talkies. Still more wailing sirens drifting up from the street below. This was disaster. At least seven officers down, a serious narcotics witness wasted. And Mulrooney, in his last phone call ever, had linked all this to Ricardo Santos and the Jane Doe.

Who was lying right here in this building. In the morgue here. At Bellevue.

A chill breath touched Lucco.

"Fuck . . ." he breathed. And moved out fast and headed for the stairs, going down three at a time to the first floor, where the morgue was. On the sixth, fourth, and third floors he was almost shot by cautiously ascending ESU teams and was required to yell "police officer police officer police officer . . ." as he headed for the cadaver closet, also imparting information such as "six officers down on the eighth." And "dunno . . ." to very natural inquiries as to the whereabouts of the armed and dangerous perpetrators of what CNN reporters were already referring to as the "massacre at Bellevue."

The morgue was silent.

The green doors swung shut behind him. He stared at the two half-finished cups of coffee and the checkerboard on the gray-topped metal table. He stepped quietly toward the set of doors that led to the rooms where the dead were kept in refrigerated containers that slid neatly into the walls.

A door opened and a squat Hispanic woman, aged

about fifty, with the high cheekbones of the Andes tribes, emerged. She wore green coveralls and rubber boots. Latex gloves. And was carrying a bulky, black, rubberized garbage bag that seemed heavy. She gave Lucco an incurious look as he stood there holding the Ingram and shuffled past.

Lucco's hair rose on the back of his neck.

"Hold it right there," he said, watching the doors. The woman stopped, resigned. He motioned to the black, bulky, rubberized bag.

"Empty it." He gestured, his stomach heaving, the awful presentiment of its contents too much to accept.

"Qué?"

"Empty the goddam bag. Right now. On the floor."

The woman shrugged and laid the rubberized bag on the tiled floor, tipping it up and shaking its contents out. The sight and smell were dreadful but so was the relief that hit Sergeant Eddie Lucco, for among the assorted visceral discards from a couple of autopsies, each in its own sealed bag, was no sign of what he had been dreading. The head and hands of that unknown waif. The unclaimed Jane Doe. Who was somehow tied in with the bloody mess on the eighth floor.

Lucco moved on to the chamber where her body was being kept. One of the green-coated attendants was there.

"Hi, Sergeant, what kinda gun is that?"

Lucco stared at the man. Sort of let the Ingram hang loosely at his side. "You been playing checkers back there?"

"Sure. It ain't against no law, is it?"

"Didn't you hear the excitement?"

"Few sirens. Man, this is a hospital."

Wow . . .

"And everything's okay."

"Sure."

The man stared at Lucco, quite relaxed and obviously wondering what the hell he was getting at.

"There's been a shooting, in the hospital." Lucco indicated the Ingram. "I'm just checking this, um, this area."

"Well, everything's fine."

"You got a JD serial zero eight zero one."

"Yup." The attendant shrugged. "She still there, man. She ain't goin' noplace."

Lucco was beginning to feel stupid. There were cops out there who needed his input. "Just check out her tray for me, wouldya."

"No sweat. You wanna look for yourself?"

"No." Spoken too fast. Too quick. What's going on here, Eddie? This is just another cadaver for chrissake. NYPD cops don't flinch from a glance at just another corpse. He shrugged. "Sure."

"No? Sure . . . ?"

"Come on, come on, I ain't got all day."

"Sure thing, Sergeant." The attendant strolled over to a row of drawers set in the wall. "Oh eight oh one . . . here we go."

And he rolled out the tray with Jane Doe lying there, her skin blue-white. Eyes closed. Her hair if anything slightly longer, crisper, and lackluster from the freezing temperature. Lucco for some reason felt embarrassed to see her lying there naked but they would think he was crazy if he suggested putting on a shroud. Suddenly the dreadful events of the last few minutes hit him. He felt dizzy and to his horror realized he was going to vomit.

Stop that right now, he commanded himself. This Homicide officer did not vomit when faced with a cadaver even if he had just waded through blood and seen the massacre up there on the eighth and had risked this so precious breath called life. And traded lead with some asshole trying to kill him. What a goddamn day and it was only ten-forty-two. Plus it was his day off.

Lucco started to smile and swallowed the stuff in his gorge. What a goddamn day. You flint-hearted hard-nosed bastard wop cop.

"Okay?" The attendant was watching him kind of strangely.

"Yeah. Listen, there's been a major incident here. Eighth floor. Number of dead."

"How many?" This was a professional question.

"Eight. Nine. Something like that."

"Thanks for the word, man. I'll get the morgue ready."

And the attendant slid Jane Doe back to her icy rest.

———

Eugene Pearson paused on the stone staircase, on his climb to his daughter's room. He stopped and gazed through the arched window in the thick outer wall at the Aventine Hill and the treetops and domes and red slate roofs and the haphazard scatterings of statues and ruins that made Rome so timeless and magnificent. My God, Siobhan was so lucky to be studying here.

The house was owned by the conservatory administration and its floors were noisy with a cheerful anarchy of wind and string instruments practicing as Pearson continued his climb. He smiled as he remembered only a year ago struggling with Siobhan's trunk as they man-handled it up those stairs. It had been her mother's trunk at Trinity College Dublin and the exclusive Saint Margaret's Convent before that.

A couple of girls clattered down the stairs, laughing and conversing in English, with East Coast American accents. The judge felt slightly apprehensive about being an interloper in his daughter's world. After all, maybe

Mhairaid was right and the child merely wanted to feel trusted, that she could cope. Needed her own space, was the modern way Mhairaid had put it.

He reached the fourth floor and stepped along the polished wood corridor. Even the brass lintels had been polished gleaming bright. Some doors were open, and he glanced into the cramped, attractive sitting rooms, each with two or three bedrooms. A flautist was attempting an intricate passage from Monteverdi's "Venetian Mass." Hesitant, stopping, then starting again. He smiled. What a brilliant place in which to be privileged to study.

Room 412 had three names on the door: Andretti, Thompson, and, most reassuring to see it there, Pearson.

Eugene Pearson tapped gently on the door. Let her be in, he was praying, let my lovely girl be on the other side of this door.

The door was opened by a dumpy black-haired girl of about twenty. There was a smell of cooked pizza from inside. He could see that the window looked out over terra-cotta tiled roofs and across a valley to part of the Aventine Hill and blue sky beyond.

"Prego?" The girl inquired, sulky at being disturbed on her Saturday afternoon.

"Pardon me. Is Siobhan Pearson in . . . ?" He smiled. "You see, I'm her father."

The girl stared at him with a hint of insolence. Without a word, she sauntered back inside, leaving the door open. He wondered if he was to follow. Then a lean, short-haired girl of about the same age came into the short passage between door and sitting room. She was pale-faced, for Rome, and wore a single earring in the shape of a Nuclear Disarmament symbol. She wore black lipstick, a black T-shirt, and no bra.

"Mister Pearson?" She came from the USA, some-place in the Midwest, he imagined. Maybe farther south.

He smiled again. "Is Siobhan around? I just hap-pened to be in Rome." And shrugged, trying to look casual.

"She's not back yet."

Praise the Lord, at least she's here. "When do you expect her?"

"Well . . ." The girl, Thompson, he guessed, looked embarrassed. "I'm not sure exactly." She glanced back into the room. "You'd better come in."

And Justice Eugene Pearson followed Sally Thomp-son into the sitting room. As he did so, a door to one of the three bedrooms closed. The sullen plump girl ob-jecting to his intrusion. He glanced around. Among various homely touches was a framed photo of Pearson, Mhairaid, and Siobhan on the last day of term at Saint Margaret's. All smiles. Another family milestone. He glanced at the American girl. She watched him uncer-tainly.

"Would you like a cup of coffee?"

"Where is she?"

"Still in Venezuela, I suppose . . ."

Venezuela . . . ??? The judge stared at her. "Vene-zuela?" he inquired politely, expecting it was the name of a restaurant, or a nickname for some part of Rome.

"With Richard."

"I'm sorry . . . ?" So the child had a boyfriend. That was natural.

"Richard. Mr. Pearson, you did get her letter . . . ?"

"When?"

"Oh . . . about four weeks ago. She tried real hard to phone you. And her mom. There just never was a reply. Then she phoned the courthouse but you had gone fishing."

"I tried to phone here a few times but some Italian woman never seemed to understand what I was asking . . ."

"Well, Siobhan wrote to you. I know because she gave it to me to post. Then Richard said he would post it. And she wrote again, the night before they left, and she tried phoning again that night but we were all having a party and it all got kind of impossible, I guess. Siobhan's, well she's very impulsive, right? She said she would phone you from the airport."

"Before they left for where?" The judge's stare had replaced the mask of dithering father.

"For Venezuela . . ." She stared at him. "Oh, my God, don't tell me you don't know."

"Let's assume I don't."

"Won't you sit down?"

Slight pause.

"Not just yet."

"Do you mind if I smoke?"

"No."

Sally Thompson tugged a Gitane from its blue pack and lit it with a match from a book of matches with the name of some nightclub. She exhaled nervously. To put her at her ease, and with an awful mixture of growing anger and foreboding, Eugene Pearson sat down. Venezuela . . . ?

The girl relaxed somewhat. "He's okay. Real nice guy. Family owns this big ranch. In Venezuela. His uncle, well he said it was his cousin really but he's that much older so he calls him uncle, he conducts and composes piano and he's professor of music at the university there. Richard showed us magazine articles and a book the man wrote. And three LPs. Enrique Lopez Fuerte, people in the conservatory had heard of him." She paused, watching Pearson warily.

He willed himself to hear it all.

"Richard?" He asked, casually.

"Well, he liked being called Richard but being Venezuelan his real name's Ricardo. They were inseparable all last term. That's why she came back a few days early, after the Christmas vacation. And she took the term off, to go to Venezuela and study piano under Fuerte. The dean said it wouldn't count in her credits. But you know Siobhan, when she decides to do something."

"Where precisely, in Venezuela . . . ?" asked Judge Pearson, in a still, quiet, dangerous voice.

"Hell, I don't know. She wrote down the details in the letter she sent you. She was real worried about you and her mom. Her not being able to get through on the phone and all. But she read in the paper about you being, um, congratulated on some verdict you gave, and she was thrilled for you. Those last few days before she went passed in kind of a whirl."

"Do you mind if I take a look in her room?"

"Go right ahead."

"Then I'll need to speak to the dean."

"He's never around at the weekend . . ."

"And this Richard. Ricardo. What's his full name?"

"Oh something real Spanish. You know, several names, *de* this and *y* that."

"But you don't remember."

"I'm really sorry. Maybe she'll have phoned. While you're out here. Is her mom at home?"

And at that juncture, the cold prescience of eternity laid its icy hand on Justice Eugene Pearson. As clear as a clear winter's day in the mountains of Mourne, the voice of his beloved daughter was suddenly suspended in that room overlooking the rust red roofs and the Aventine Hill.

It said, simply, "Daddy . . ."

And Eugene Pearson, with Celtic insight, knew from that chilling moment that his daughter, his life's joy, needed him desperately.

———

The Bellevue massacre had hit the headlines and TV news screens around the world, replacing the King's Cross bomb outrage in many editors' priorities, which put it after the Gulf War but ahead of sports and weather. Eddie Lucco's boss, Homicide Captain Danny Molloy, was descended upon by the Feds and by the chief of New York City's Narcotics Task Force, Marvin Kelly. The upshot of this was that the FBI and NYPD Homicide would jointly investigate the massacre, while liaising with Narcotics and keeping each other fully informed. Lucco was assigned to the case, working under Molloy and a DEA man, Special Agent In Charge Don Mather.

Sergeant Lucco was known to be close to the facts before and surrounding the crime, and his solid and growing reputation in Homicide led to him being given responsibilities usually assigned to a lieutenant. He chose Detective Sam Vargos to be his partner in the investigation.

———

That had also been the week in which Captain Harry Ford and Malcolm Strong had begun their indoctrination and training as contract operators with the Secret Intelligence Service.

They had been taken to a country house in Wales on the edge of the Brecon National Park, a wild and remote region of the country with a sweeping panorama of hills, wooded valleys, and steep mountainsides, laced with streams, fields of boulders, and treacherous bogs. The weather there was constantly variable and the finest early-spring day could become a torrential storm by midafternoon. It was an ideal place to test the mettle of men who had chosen (or had been chosen) to step just that bit further beyond the norm of human endurance, both physically and mentally.

The house was in eighty acres of secluded grounds, surrounded by fern-floored woods of fir and pine. It was discreetly protected by concentric tiers of electronic fencing and peeling signs that declared in English and Welsh Gaelic: Welsh Water Authority Sewerage Analysis Plant. Keep Out. Men dressed as rural workers patrolled the area with dogs and guns. The inner perimeter, protecting twelve acres, was thirteen-foot-high chain-link fencing, with razor wire coiled from base to angled top. For all its comfortable, rural beauty, once you had arrived, it was not a welcoming environment from the outside.

Week One had been crammed with interviews, tests, medical examinations, language assessments, physical training, introductory lectures, weapons training, and individual-initiative and character-reliability trials. There was no moment, awake or asleep, when the instructors and assessors were not observing, goading, encouraging, coaching, or stretching the two recruits.

Throughout this time, Strong and Ford did not see David Jardine nor Ronnie Szabodo nor Kate. Jardine was in Quito, Ecuador, being taken by Giles Abercrombie on a tour of SIS agents and meeting officers of other government agencies, including Her Majesty's Customs & Excise, who were at the head of Britain's battle to keep cocaine and marijuana out of the United Kingdom, and with the British military attaché. He also met with the senior Colombian DAS officer commanding the new, secret DAS unit that had filled Pablo's cousin so full of lead, and he renewed a long acquaintance with the squat, hooded-eyed General Xavier Ramón Gomez, a trusted and recently retired DAS officer who had been deputy director of DAS Counterintelligence and remained an invaluable asset to the British and Americans in the fight against the cartel. Jardine also liaised with the local chiefs of the USA's Central Intelligence Agency, Drug Enforcement Administration, and Federal Bureau of Investigation.

Given his incomparable powers of concentration and his innate talent for asking the right questions, five days of unending research among those people brought David Jardine comprehensively up to date on all available intelligence concerning the players in the Bogotá, Cali, and Medellín Cartel.

He left Quito with Ramón, using the passport and papers of a British executive with a firm of construction insurance assessors, on Avianca Flight AV 82 to Bogotá. There, he rented a car and simply drove around the known environments of the cartel players, both the serious and the insignificant, using his up-to-the-minute intelligence briefings and his instinct simply to soak up the atmosphere, get the vibes—an outdated expression his kids would have giggled at—and to identify which faces were cool and confident, which were running scared. His Spanish was without a trace of accent and his cheap, off-the-peg clothes and unobtrusive manner left him more or less unnoticed and unremembered. He still enjoyed this aspect of the job more than any other. He knew who they were, what many of them had been saying and doing very, very recently, but the hoodlums and dealers did not even know he existed. It was like being a ghost and it was the result of twenty years as a field operator with the service. The notion that Strong and Ford were expected by the chief to be able to accomplish the same in five weeks left the big sphere controller cold with anger.

Ramón had provided three bodyguards, trustworthy men working for his own private-sector security company, who shadowed Jardine so discreetly even Murillo and Bobby Sonson would never have noticed them. And Ramón and his wife Beatrix had, on the Friday evening, taken Jardine for supper at a traditional *hosteria* in downtown Bogotá's Candelaria, the old quarter where embassies warned their staff and visitors it was too dangerous to venture after six in the evening. There had been dancing and a cabaret of folklore mostly featuring high-spirited and alluring Colombian girls flashing their wonderful legs and stamping their feet in a way that could only be described as suggestive. The aquardiente flowed and the sphere controller, West 8, fell in love, yet again, with Colombia and almost all of her delightful, noble, and fun-loving people.

At nine-forty, Ramón and Beatrix drove Jardine to Bogotá Airport. They shook hands warmly and he passed through the various stringent controls, comfortable and satisfied. But alert, for it was during moments like these when an operator was at his most vulnerable. Mind already on the flight home and planning a visit to his favorite pub or a romp with his girlfriend, or whatever. And it was precisely at moments like these when more than a few operators had nose-dived, surprised and annoyed with themselves, into the grave, like pilots doing aerobatics at night. Blindfolded.

First couple of days on operations, last few days before coming out. These were the most dangerous times. As Jardine relaxed into his comfortable First Class seat, and the Avianca 747 climbed and banked to avoid the precipice of mountains beyond the Bogotá runway, and the lights of that sprawling, intriguing city dropped away, he made a mental note to impart that wisdom to the two Joes who had just sweated out a most uncomfortable first week in Wales, so very far away from this, their ultimate destination.

Then he fell fast asleep.

9

BREAKFAST WITH PABLO

For Malcolm Strong, the week had been humiliating. He had been shouted at and insulted by a variety of men and women, some of them lacking the basic intellectual requirements he would have imagined necessary for espionage. He had been set written tests so simple that he assumed there was some astonishing brain behind them.

He had sat through terminally boring instruction on the theory and practice of intelligence and its relevance to government and had had one or two quite interesting eye-openers on the truth about the who and the how of the Secret Intelligence Service. He had been given case histories to read and to lecture on, pointing out why each had been successful or dreadful failures, then case histories that stopped short and he was required to explain why each would have succeeded or failed. Also there was the appalling experience of being wakened every day at five in the morning and the awful runs that had started with one mile, and another after physical training at five in the evening, rising by varying distances each day until now, on his second Saturday, he had gasped and retched through four miles at five-thirty in the morning after a cold shower (naturally) and the same distance in the evening.

Every muscle in his body ached and his arms actually felt too sore to lift the knife and fork to eat his supper of steak, fried egg, beans, and fries. He gazed across the table in the small dining room at the man he knew only as Parcel. His own stupid nickname was Baggage. He hated Parcel with a deep and increasingly dangerous hatred. The man ran ten miles each day, with a sort of rucksack on his back. He was deeply tanned, lean and muscular, with amused gray eyes and the sort of fair, drooping mustache Strong associated with gay bodybuilders in Surfers' Paradise.

Ten miles. The training workouts had been humiliating. Strong's Five BX plan, which he had done religiously for years, had, so the paperback workout book assured him, brought him steadily to the fitness equivalent of a twenty-four-year-old aircrew pilot. So when the track-suited instructor with muscles on his cheekbones had asked him to assess his fitness on a scale ranging from totally unfit to athlete, he had ticked "average plus." What a bloody mistake.

Meanwhile, as he had almost wept his way through sit-ups and push-ups and something invented in hell called burpees, always in groups of sixty, Parcel the athletic robot was glistening in sweat and pumping iron and skipping in the thousands, with would you believe fucking great weights *on his ankles*. How Baggage, the former Malcolm Strong, barrister at law, hated the man and, indeed, the absent David Jardine and the entire God-rotted band of psychopaths and sadists who lured ordinary decent people into this hell. No wonder they made you sign an oath of secrecy. Decent people would be outraged. Oh, yes, and they dragged you out of bed just as you had escaped into sleep and threw you into a cellar or rolled you in the mud and yelled questions at you. Woe betide you if you ever claimed your name was anything other than Baggage. Unless of course you wanted to be slung off the course and onto the next train back to normality. To Wonderland. And there was no way Baggage would have given those bastards the satisfaction.

Which meant that once again, the Jardine/Szabodo recruiting team had chosen correctly.

———

During the week that had passed since the violent incident at Bellevue Hospital, Eddie Lucco was deep into investigating the massacre, which pointed at Colombians silencing PeeWee Patrice because he knew too much, which meant he must've been a serious link, at the age of twenty, between the cartel's New York people and the street. David Jardine was doing his thing in Ecuador and Colombia. And Eugene Pearson was back in Dublin, deep in communication with the Venezuelan embassy in London, then, through Dublin's Ministry of Foreign Affairs, with the Ministry of Education in Caracas, inquiring about the whereabouts of the music professor and composer Enrique Lopez Fuerte in order to trace the man called Richard, or Ricardo, who had eloped with his daughter.

The news had not been encouraging. Señor Lopez was somewhere in the mountains. Composing. Yes, he did often keep open house for young musicians. It would not be unusual for a nephew, or cousin, to turn up unannounced, with a nineteen-year-old girl of pale, waiflike beauty, from a conservatory in Europe. And of course, if he could be found, Justice Pearson would be informed immediately. And the girl would be politely required to telephone her anxious parents.

Mhairaid was angry with her daughter for her thoughtlessness, and desperately worried. The dinner party she had arranged for Padraic O'Shea, the probable next *taoiseach* of Ireland, Desmond Browne, the blood-stock dealer, and their wives, went ahead, for nothing could get in the way of Eugene's future as attorney general. But it lacked the magic of that earlier dinner, and Siobhan's being missing cast a gloom over the occasion.

———

When Jardine arrived back in Heathrow Airport, it was raining. Dorothy was in Lyons working on her European current-affairs program. He took a taxi back to Tite Street and after a hot bath settled down with a pot of coffee and started to make plans for the covert infiltration of either Strong or Ford into Colombia. He had ceased to be angry with the chief's directive—that hard intelligence was to be coming out from deep inside the cartel in seven, actually six weeks now. For the demand was so impossible that steps would have to be taken. And nobody was more adept at the political chicanery of life near the top of SIS than the Jesuit convert David Arbuthnot Jardine.

He glanced at his watch. Six-oh-eight. He reached for the phone and dialed a Dorset number. He listened to the ringing tone for a few seconds, then a very polite, youthful voice, full of energy, replied, "Drake's House."

"Good evening to you. I wonder if I could have a word with Andrew Jardine."

"I'll just go and find him . . ."

Jardine waited patiently, doodling the letters PM and DRINKS, WHERE? on his pad.

". . . Dad?"

His heart melted at the breathless, enthusiastic voice of his son.

"How are you?"

"Where were you?"

"South America."

"Well, thanks a lot!" (For not taking me).

"It was really wonderful. Fabulous native dancing girls and great beer."

"I hate you. Dad, are you coming to the parents-masters?"

"When is it?"

"Tomorrow evening. You forgot."

"No, I didn't."

"You little liar . . ."

"I did not forget."

"Did you bring anything back?"

"A carving of a pig."

"Oh, terrific."

"It's very old. Muisca Indian. Quite sweet really."

"I'll forgive you. So are you coming?"

"Of course."

"It starts at six but I think the head man wants to rabbit on about university and stuff, in the Memorial Hall."

"I'll be there. Mum's in France."

"Yeah. Lyons. She phoned."

"Any horrors I need to know before I walk blithely into the PTA?"

"No, well, um . . ."

"What?"

"Piers asked me to look after some beer for him and Patrick busted me."

"Have you done your time?"

"Next weekend. I'm gated."

"Give you time to do some work."

"Yes I suppose so."

"So I'll see you tomorrow. You want to have dinner?"

"I've, um, I've got a sort of detention."

"Smoking?"

"I don't smoke, Dad. Late work."

"Kids. Can't live with them . . ."

"Pass the beer nuts." They laughed. This was a line from an episode of "Cheers," which they sometimes watched when they were not glued to reruns of *The Blues Brothers*.

"Okay. Be good."

"Ditto."

Silence.

"You hang up first."

"No, you do."

"I'm going now."

"Good-bye."

"God bless. Love you." And Jardine put the phone down, smiling. He would drive on to Wales, after the parents-masters meeting and wine with the housemaster. Maybe an office driver would be better. Maybe if Kate was going down tomorrow she could . . . That's enough of that, David. Behave yourself.

He phoned the duty officer at the glass box and made arrangements for a driver to collect him from Tite Street and take him the hundred and twenty-five miles down to Dorset and then to the Honey Farm, as the Welsh country house was called, on account of its cover as a sewerage laboratory.

Then Jardine phoned a good friend who was a government whip and who lived in Lord North Street, in Westminster. After the usual pleasantries, he got to the point. "Alec," he asked casually, "are you planning any drinks thingies in the near future, where Himself will be present?"

"Actually, this Wednesday, just a few of us, would you like to be included?"

"All politicals?"

"No. Master of Magdalen. Controller of BBC Something. About ten souls, is that all right?"

"You really are a sport."

"So what will you come as? How do we introduce you?"

"Diplomat. Back-room boy."

"See you Wednesday."

"Thanks."

Jardine worked steadily for another couple of hours, then retreated to his bed. He thought with fondness of his son, whose whole life was ahead of him, of his daughter at university, and of Dorothy, down in Lyons with the current-affairs film unit. But his last images, as he fell asleep, were of the bars and dangerous streets of Bogotá, of the smiling girls and the players in the cocaine game among whom he had moved, ghostlike, just the day before. And, perplexingly, of Kate Howard, kneeling there in front of him, the flickering flames from the fire reflecting on her superb body, her skirt up around her waist, tugging her jersey down over those perfect spheres with the pale pink nipples.

He woke at seven-thirty, showered, shaved, and put on a comfortable pair of cord trousers, cotton shirt, and pullover. He pulled on his favorite pair of old leather boots, made to measure ten years before in Peru. He zipped them up, making a mental note they needed a spot of polish, shrugged into a worn anorak, and left the flat, triple-locking the door. He strolled along Tite Street, savoring the damp, cold English air, all the time checking, out of habit, for tails, couples in parked cars, the windows overlooking his front door, cyclists stopped and studying street guides, things like that. Things that

Harry Ford and Malcolm Strong would have time to learn, he intended to make damn sure of that.

The pure sound of choirboys singing a Venetian mass in another part of the church filled Farm Street Catholic Church, the headquarters of the Jesuits in England. The comforting smell of incense hung in the air. Here Jardine felt he was finally home. His conversion had surprised all but Dorothy. And the chief of that time, an owlish man, with podgy jowls and keener eyes than any bird of prey and a ready sense of humor. A brilliant medieval scholar, if not the ablest spy master in the trade, he himself was an Anglican and played the organ in Westminster's Saint Mathew's Church whenever the business permitted. He had always made time to talk late into the night with David, sometimes in the office, sometimes in a restaurant called Lockett's in Marsham Street, where he kept a modest flat. He understood Jardine's need to have a religious base, to make some ethical sense of the work they were at that time engaged in. And since David Jardine was a man of some style, and a romantic to boot, his need to embrace and to be embraced by the Church of Rome came as no surprise, and Maurice had given his blessing. The chief's subsequent disgrace, when he was found to have been profoundly sexually deviant throughout his forty-odd years with the firm, met with less condemnation from Jardine than from most of his colleagues, who had felt damaged and betrayed. For in addition to David Jardine's several faults was a rare generosity of spirit and the compassion that can only stem from one who understands too well that we are each of us frail in the morality stakes.

"Father, it has been five weeks since my last confession."

The sphere controller, West 8, sat squeezed into the confessional box, the choir's "alleluia" and "pie Jesu" warming the stone vaulted roof, high above.

"Have you sinned in that time, my son?"

"Yes. Forgive me, Father."

"How?"

"Sin of lust, Father. Sin of untruthfulness. Sins of pride."

The voice of the priest on the other side of the grill was familiar and comforting, for it was the man who almost always heard his confession and who usually gave him communion.

"Tell us, my son . . ."

And Jardine recounted his affair, the end of his affair, with Nicola who was now pregnant, but not by him, and his lustful feelings toward Kate, plus a little peccadillo with a lithe and willowy creature in Quito, Ecuador, who ran the PR for a well-known airline and had, for reasons best known to herself, decided she rather liked him. These facts, as in all his confessions, were suitably sanitized, told to the priest in a carefully disguised form, in order to give no hint of the nature of Jardine's employment and to safeguard the nation's secrets. God, he knew, would understand, so long as he truly repented. Which he didn't really. And that of course was the subject of yet another confession.

God, via Father Wheatley, did not seem to think too harshly of David Jardine's confessed sins, and a moderate number of "Hail Marys" and "Glory Bes" were handed out in return for His forgiveness.

Jardine left the confessional and knelt for some time in prayer. Father Wheatley sat quietly behind the confessional grill, contemplating the nature of the tall, complex man whose voice he had come to know well. The priest was about forty-five and he was well used to confessions being made in some form of code in order to protect third parties or to avoid embarrassment.

There had been, however, from the start of the scar-faced man's irregular visits, an easy professionalism with which he translated his confessions into a code, and Father Wheatley had found it intellectually challenging to try to figure out precisely what it was that David Jardine did for a living. He had resolved not to make inquiries but to use his brains. Then one day an altar boy had told the priest that his mother was a chauffeur for the Diplomatic Service, and one time at Mass she had nudged her son and whispered that the tall man was a spy. Father Wheatley smiled as he collected his things. He still had no idea what the man had really confessed. But that was not for *him* to interpret.

Jardine left the church and walked down South Audley Street, through some narrow street to Park Lane, and across to Knightsbridge and the Pizza on the Park, where he ordered a considerable breakfast and flirted with a slim and attractive Australian girl, whose name tag announced she was Jessica, while glancing through the Sunday papers.

He determined not even to think about Kate, for an affair with her, the girl was right, would be complete madness. And he remembered the slight scent of baby powder on her wonderful little orbs.

He turned to the music page of the *Sunday Times* and read a review of a performance of Purcell's *Faerie Queen*, which he would dearly love to have seen, when he noticed, across the spacious room, at a table by the window looking out onto Knightsbridge, a slender, tall, rangy girl with long, fair hair. She was talking animatedly to a man of about sixty who looked distinguished, even in polo shirt and some kind of baseball team wind cheater. Why the hell was his face familiar? Dick Longstreet. Of course. Last but one United States ambassador to the Court of Saint James. A millionaire banker from Boston who had been an outstanding success with the British of most political persuasions. Self-made, courteous, sharp as a knife, and close friend of the present and former Presidents. U.S. Marine Corps pilot in Korea. Dick Longstreet had become a confirmed Anglophile and he was on the board of a major British shipping company, which brought him back to London fairly often.

And the girl, who radiated quiet good humor and cool self-confidence . . . where had he seen her before? Then the ex-ambassador grinned hugely and shook his head, laughing at something she had said, and David Jardine realized this was the girl he had noticed in Hereford, when he was in Johnny McAlpine's house, getting out of a car with Johnny's wife and a couple of SAS bodyguards. She had made them laugh too. And in the kitchen, he had heard their voices, but when he and Johnny had gone through to have a cup of tea with Sheila, the girl who made people laugh had gone. And here she was. What the hell was she doing with Longstreet?

Then it clicked. File 8/2007 - P/r 411, Ford, Captain Henry Michael Alcazar, Scots Guards and X Squadron, Special Air Service Regiment. Wife, Elizabeth, née Leadbitter, b. Fort Worth, Texas, twenty-seven years ago. Ed. Houston, Vassar, Lady Margaret Hall Oxford. Father deceased. Mother m. 2nd. Richard Longstreet, President, Longstreet Banking Corp. Former US Ambassador London.

The girl who made people laugh was Harry Ford's Texas-born wife, Elizabeth. And here she was, in the Pizza on the Park, with her stepfather. Jardine was tempted to go over and introduce himself, but what could he say? Hi. I'm a spy, and you don't know it yet, but your brave and fearless husband is going to risk his neck because he's coming to work for me.

That would have been silly, for neither man was permitted to communicate with the outside world, and Harry's wife did not even know he was back in the country, although Johnny McAlpine's wife Sheila had quietly taken her aside and explained that Harry was no longer on dangerous operations and she might be seeing him shortly. So Jardine ignored them, enjoyed his brunch, read the papers, paid Jessica, the good-looking Australian waitress, and left. As he was leaving, she, the girl who was Elizabeth Ford, glanced across at him and her expression was one of . . . interest?

He pretended he hadn't noticed and began the long walk back to Chelsea.

The office car, a dark blue Jaguar on this occasion, took Jardine straight from the parents-masters meeting at Andrew's school in Dorset past Illminster on the A303, on to join the M5, then north and west to Wales and, by twenty minutes after midnight, delivered him to the night janitor at Dylif House, which was the official name for the Honey Farm.

He went straight to bed and was wakened at seven by Benedict, the retired Royal Navy Chief Petty Officer who ran Dylif House with the efficiency of a master mariner and the courtesy of a 1930s butler. Benedict put a mug of strong coffee on the bedside table and opened the curtains. For once, the sun was shining.

"Good morning sir. Touch of frost but clear blue sky. Spot of rain forecast for late afternoon."

"Morning, Mr. Benedict. How is Mrs. Benedict?" Jean Benedict was the cook and resident dietitian. She could present a meal fit for royalty or the solid high protein, high calorie, and carbohydrate sustenance required to fuel Parcel and Baggage through their initial ordeal.

"She's fine, sir. That hip replacement's given her a new lease on life."

"Amazing, really, what they can do."

246

"And she says to thank you and Mrs. J. for them flowers. And Mrs. Jardine for going into hospital to visit her."

"I'm glad she's well. How are our new boys?"

"Well, one, if you ask me . . ." Here Benedict was being the soul of discretion. He knew perfectly well that Jardine had a comprehensive knowledge of his two Joes' backgrounds. "One of 'em has been a bloody athlete, or a commando or something. So the physical's been a piece of cake. *And* the psychological warfare." (He meant hauling them out of bed at all hours and dragging them down to the cellar or out into the mud and interrogating them.) "He's done it all before, so this week's just been a bit of a dawdle, on the physical side. The other poor fellow, Baggage they've called him, damn near killed him it has. But he's getting angry, and I don't know, but he seems better at the brainbox side of things."

"Baggage? Oh, dear."

"Early days of course." He produced a duster as if by magic and picking up Jardine's boots, one by one, deftly produced the ghost of a shine, then glanced at Jardine keenly. "Rush job, is it?"

Jardine, sitting up in bed sipping his coffee, met Benedict's gaze. "Absolutely not. I don't send my Joes off at half cock."

"Well, maybe the directing staff have got the wrong idea . . ." Benedict's seafarer's eyes, set deep in weatherbeaten skin of crinkled leather, held Jardine's.

Chief Petty Officer Benedict has just passed on his opinion. Loud and clear, thought Jardine. And worth heeding. If Strong and Ford were being driven too hard, it was because Ronnie Szabodo was eloquently registering a protest at the directive from the top floor. There was no way that a responsible outfit could take a man off the street and train him in five weeks. Not unless there was a war on.

"Great cup of java, Chief. My regards to Jean."

Benedict nodded, placed the boots neatly beside the bedroom chair, and left the room without another word.

At eight-fifteen, Jardine was in the director's office, which was the old conservatory above the ground-floor library, overlooking the wooden huts where the whole gamut of skills required in the business of espionage were taught.

The Intelligence Service had a number of these facilities, mostly old country houses around the country from Cornwall to Ross and Sutherland in the northern mountains of Scotland. Some were used as safe houses to hold and debrief defectors. Others were training establishments or retreats for operators who needed to recover from physical or emotional injuries. And a few were used for the indoctrination and training of just one or a very limited number of men and women recruited to work for that other side of SIS, the side that never went near Century House or ninety-five percent of the people who worked from there. These were the black operators, whose identity was known only to their re-cruiters and the most secret cell within Personnel (Re-cruitment/Administration). Their pay and other financial arrangements would appear on no accounts section's list. And any examination by a hostile, or friendly but curious, service of their deep-cover identities would check out comprehensively, with no item of detail being spared.

If, for example, the black operator's cover was as a computer salesman with, say, Peking as his territory, then a genuine computer company would have him on its books and would pay and administer him and pay him commission on any computers he sold. And the staff would accept him as a regular employee and thus unwittingly add to his legend, as it was known in the trade.

Thus it was vital to the security of the service and for the protection of the identities of Strong and Ford, who were known to the directing staff only as Baggage and Parcel, that they should be trained and evaluated away from prying eyes and with their anonymity protected.

They were, therefore, the only two recruits undergoing indoctrination and training at the Honey Farm. Short of not recruiting anyone at all, it was about as secure as the system could make it.

The director of this particular course was Ronnie Szabodo. He poured two cups of tea, added milk and sugar to his and milk to Jardine's. He turned away from the table by the window and grinned, his gap tooth visible. He was wearing rust-red cords and a dark blue fisherman's sweater over a tattersall check shirt, the very model of an English gentleman.

"I decided to chuck them in at the deep end, David. The soldier's taken to it like a gundog at a three-day trial. The lawyer's hating every minute of it, but right now, I'm still sure he's our man. Or would be if we had the time to train him properly . . ."

Jardine kept his own counsel. He picked up his cup and gazed out over the grounds. "It's very dangerous over there right now. Gaviria has used the fact of being a new president to try to ease the state of siege. Pablo had declared war on the elected government of Colombia, Ronnie. The previous president, Barco, was his number one target, closely followed by General Maza, the DAS director. The DAS feel they're closing in on Pablo, who they claim is trapped in Antioquia, although I have my doubts. With Barco gone and Gaviria in the palace, the DAS has been authorized to sound out the quote less violent elements of the cartel unquote. They're talking about deals, Ronnie. And they've lost nine undercover operators since January, native Colombians every one . . ."

"Using natives is tricky, David. Too many chances of their legend being compromised."

Jardine gazed out of the window, where a score of dead flies lay on the once-white ledge. "Parcel and Baggage . . . Maybe that's how we think of them. Poor bastards."

"Why is it, every time we do this, you act like a virgin? . . . With the greatest possible respect."

"Because, Ronnie, every time we do this, some piece of political, departmental . . . act of stupidity gets in the bloody way." He felt sure he recognized several of the dead flies on the window ledge as leftovers from last year's abortive Paragon operation, when four operators had been held in Training and Evaluation for much *longer* than had been desirable because the director of operations had become nervous about four West Indian officers being sent on a mission without one white face to act as nanny. The situation had given rise to an exchange of memos ranging from outrage about racial attitudes to farce in a now famous paragraph from the Top Floor on the subject of black operatives. (In the event, Jardine had downgraded the men to agent status, increased their expenses, invented a white case officer, and achieved results that were still earning admiration from clients in Whitehall.) It was not an episode he felt proud of.

"Remember Paragon?" he asked Szabodo. "This time the problem's the opposite. How am I to outwit the Top Floor and squeeze some more weeks?"

"Knowing you, you've already started . . ." And the Hungarian grinned and held his boss's eye until finally, Jardine smiled.

Szabodo relaxed. "Thank God for that."

"So ease up on them, will you?" Jardine asked. "Now that I've got the message."

"Just a bit. I don't think even you will negotiate the twenty weeks we need."

"No," Jardine replied. "Neither do I."

"What'll you do if neither makes the grade?"

"I'll go to Bogotá myself and recruit a local agent." Jardine's reply was automatic.

"I've worked with worse." Szabodo relented. "Find me ten weeks and I'll give you two operators we can all be proud of."

Jardine drank the last of his tea, "I'll do what I can . . ."

Pale sunlight filtered through the windows of Hut K. Wisps of steam curled lazily from an electric kettle that stood on the floor, near the roller blackboard. Two men in gray tracksuits sat at a long table, listening to the cooing of wood pigeons and the distant, anxious warble of a bullfinch.

Harry Ford and Malcolm Strong were being talked to by a tiny, birdlike woman called Agnes, who wore thick, blue-tinted glasses with large lenses. Ford guessed she was Austrian. She was about sixty and her subject, which she related to them quietly in a conversational tone, was the psychology of living your cover day and night. Harry was bored by her relentless chewing over what she called the eleven cardinal points of clandestine work using a legend and false identity, and his attention was beginning to wander. It had been ten days since he had arrived back in England, and half of his thoughts were with his Special Operations troop out in the Gulf, operating deep inside Iraq, while the other half were longing for Elizabeth, with her long, superb legs and her passionate and imaginative addiction to sex. She was the most cool, elegant, controlled and . . . carnal woman he had ever met. Which was almost exactly two years before.

She had just won a good Classics degree at Oxford and he had been instantly attracted to her Vassar-cool, educated American voice and her self-deprecating sense of humor. They had met at a horse race, a steeplechase, when Harry had ridden the horse that came in last and her gentle amusement at his frustration had made him feel better.

He had known she was more or less living with a successful photographer, about twelve years older than her twenty-four years, and it had been with some diffidence that Harry had asked her if she would have dinner. The dinner date was followed by a visit to Hereford, where she had spent a chaste night with a couple of his friends in married quarters. Then there were two more dates and another Saturday at the races, as spectators this time. It had begun to rain and Elizabeth had taken his hand and started to run, at first he thought for shelter, but they had run and run, as the downpour got heavier, until the racecourse was a couple of hundred yards away and they had clambered over a wooden fence and found themselves in a field of wheat waist-high and drenched in the rain. And she had pulled him to the damp earth and had kissed him with a hungry and disturbingly knowledgable lust, tugging at his trousers and taking him at first gently, then with worldly urgency, as the squall rippled the wheat, their clothing saturated in the torrential downpour.

They had spent the weekend in her bed, at her flat in Highgate, North London, astonishing each other with their staying power and tenderness and invention, to the music of Tina Turner and an English Gothic band called the Cure. And she had fallen totally in love with him. And he with her.

Elizabeth had phoned the photographer, who was working in Los Angeles, and in a sometimes tearful conversation of forty-one minutes had told him their affair was over and that she had found the man she wanted to spend the rest of her life with.

The wedding of Harry Ford and Elizabeth Leadbitter was held three months later, in the Guards Chapel, beside St. James's Park in Westminster. SAS officers are recruited from the cream of the British Army, with only about eight out of one hundred volunteers passing the carefully devised selection course, which was physically exhausting and intellectually demanding. Captain Harry's original regiment, his parent regiment in army parlance, was the Scots Guards. Thus the attractive couple were married in the Guards chapel, and after a honeymoon in the Caribbean, they had moved into married quarters in Hereford, where Liz had settled in and made friends with the other young wives with surprising ease. She was popular and lacking in pretension. They spent their times together making love, going to the races, sailing her little boat, which had been a twenty-first-birthday present from her stepfather, and eating and drinking with others in the close and supportive family group that was the real strength of the regiment.

Halcyon days.

". . . in the not impossible event that you bump into someone who knows you, let us say, at a bullfight in Antioquia, maybe Medellín? Pablo still shows up at bullfights. And if you've done your job you should be right there with him. In his entourage." Agnes was asking him a question.

Harry glanced at Malcolm Strong, who raised his eyebrows, meaning he had no idea what to reply.

"I would ignore them. Um, particularly avoiding eye-to-eye contact."

"Okay, they wave their program at you and try to attract your attention. Yelling out your real name."

"You mean Parcel . . . ?" asked Harry innocently and Malcolm grinned.

Silence. Agnes was watching him. Harry was getting bored with SIS. He had worked undercover in Northern Ireland, drinking in shebeens and betting shops with some of the most dangerous men and women of the Provisional IRA. The Army Intelligence course for that work had been comprehensive. Quite frankly, the Special Forces captain couldn't see why he had to go through this rigmarole. He spoke Spanish. South America was the target, probably Colombia, where he had already volunteered to serve with his regiment. It would be simpler just to point him at the target and say, go on Harry, worm your way inside this or that cocaine outfit. Here's your cover ID, here's your emergency contacts. And here's your satellite radio frequencies, times, and codes.

For God's sake, that's what Harry had been trained to do. He was beginning to think the much-vaunted Intelligence Service had no comprehension that other outfits in the system ran agents and conducted secret operations.

And they were not all that smart. For Agnes had just let slip what he, and no doubt Baggage too, had suspected all along: Pablo Envigado was the principal target of this endeavor.

———

As Parcel and Baggage sat with Agnes at the Honey Farm, Pablo Envigado had just finished eating breakfast on the veranda of a *finca,* or ranch, eighty miles south of Santa Fe de Antioquia. It belonged to a loyal and trustworthy friend who had, prudently, gone to Chile on business. One or two gauchos exercised horses on the pampas stretching beyond the veranda. Servants loyal to the *grupo* attended them, and the usual armed body-guards were in evidence. His guests, sharing breakfast with him, were the man who called himself Restrepo and German Santos, the millionaire boss of the Miami end of the cartel's distribution syndicate and brother of Ricardo Santos Castaneda, who had been murdered (after his night of torment at the hands of Murillo and Bobby Sonson) by Restrepo, on the orders of Pablo. His headless, handless body was not to be found for another few weeks, and at that time it rested in the silt at the bottom of the East River, shoved around aimlessly by the tide.

"So, German, *amigo mío,* Luís has brought good news back from New York."

German Santos had shed a few pounds and looked stressed and haggard, although he had been treated courteously and as an honored guest. He visibly relaxed and accepted a cup of freshly made coffee from Envigado. "They found the girl?"

Envigado nodded, smiling benevolently. *"Sí.* The girl has been located."

"Thank God . . ." German Santos crossed himself. "Are they on their way here?"

"Why, yes, *amigo.* In fact, that could be them now." And he smiled and gazed over Santos's shoulder into the distant prairie. The syndicate boss, relieved, turned in his seat to stare across the pampas, beyond the gauchos and their ponies. It was the last thing his eyes recorded.

Pablo Envigado laid his 9mm Sig Sauer P226 automatic pistol on the white-and-blue checkered tablecloth, its boom-boom still reverberating around the veranda.

German Santos's corpse slowly toppled sideways off the chair, which fell with the weight of it. His head had exploded, leaving a dark crimson mess, like a sea anemone, at the top of the corpse's neck.

Restrepo met Envigado's gaze, which was vaguely challenging and slightly flushed with the lust of killing. "He would have been unreliable. Once he found out."

Envigado nodded sadly, his lust spent. "At least," he said, "poor German has been spared the grief of his brother's death."

And even Restrepo was touched by a breath of horror as a genuine tear ran down Pablo Envigado's cheek.

"Oh, yes. They were fine boys . . ." Don Pablo sighed. And crossed himself before returning to his breakfast as two trembling servants removed the carcass.

———

Don Mather was special agent in charge of the New York Office of the Drug Enforcement Administration, the DEA, which led the fight against the illegal importing and distribution of cocaine into the USA. He listened with growing respect as Sergeant Eddie Lucco explained the results of his investigation into the Bellevue massacre.

They were in the DA's office, and along with District Attorney Tony Faccioponti, present were an FBI special agent, an investigator from U.S. Customs—because where Colombians were involved in spectacular murder, drug smuggling was inevitably a factor—a lieutenant from NYPD Narcotics Division, and Lucco's boss, Homicide Captain Danny Molloy.

"Okay." Lucco gazed at the men sitting around the office. "Here's the story, from my viewpoint. PeeWee Patrice is running a territory dishing out crack, smack, and Mary Jane. His older brothers are working for *him*.

256

Ten days ago, a Narcotics bust goes wrong and a detective goes down. I pull PeeWee for that and in the arrest he is shot while going for his piece. By my partner." Lucco suddenly had a vivid recollection of the black kid's face as he was knocked down by the big wadcutter, flat-nosed slugs from Vargos's 9mm Glock automatic. Surprise and . . . frustration, at being beaten to the draw. That kid sure had a lot of spunk. He continued, "PeeWee is under police custody in Bellevue and while there Narcotics makes a deal with him to turn state's witness. They must consider his evidence to be pretty damn important because the kid is a cop killer. Therefore he musta been able to finger the Colombian angle, this I'm deducing so don't close the shutters on me, Frankie, come on." Frank Schneider was the Narcotics man present and they never discussed their undercover work with outsiders. "And Pig Mulrooney puts him on the WPP. Now me, I'm also, among lotsa other shit, investigating some Jane Doe who OD'd down at Grand Central a few weeks back. When I get a whisper from PeeWee where to find the JD's purse. I follow this angle and presto, one photograph of the kid, the dead kid, laughing and smiling someplace in Italy, probably Rome, with her arm around one Ricardo Santos Castaneda, who ain't no bit-part player."

"Brother of German Santos, the Miami end of the cartel . . . ?" asked DA Faccioponti, examining his stainless-steel Rolex Oyster Perpetual Datejust. Faccioponti rode a Harley Low Rider to work and generally accoutered himself more like a Top Gun Aggressor pilot than an NYC lawyer. He saw himself as some kind of expert on organized crime, which, reflected Lucco, was probably why he had got the job.

"The very same guy. So I put out some telexes, asking around, who is this dead chick and what was she doing in Rome with Ricardo. And like when? Last year on vacation? When? Then I get a whisper Ricardo is in NYC. Then I get a phone call from the Pig, maybe, I dunno, maybe an hour before he is killed. Eddie, he says to me, it appears there are some *paísas* in the city, probably led by Rico, Ricardo Santos, the guy in the photo with my Jane Doe. They are leaning heavy on the Patrice brothers in order to locate her. Only. Except. They are looking for a chick they think is still alive. Pig tells me at the end of this phone call he is on his way to Bellevue, to protect his asset, on account of these grease-gun cowboys leaning on the Patrice family, and I figure I'll join him there."

"Why?" asked the deadpan FBI agent, looking at Lucco as if he was to blame for the whole goddamn massacre.

"I got a bad feeling about this, okay? When Mulrooney says quote I got a bad fuckin' feeling about this, which is his exact fuckin' words on the phone, so at that moment did I." His unblinking eyes stared into the Fed's. "If you were a cop, you would understand."

Cool down, Lucco, thought Mather. Even Feds don't care to be insulted.

"So you decided to go along to Bellevue, to back him up?"

"Sure. But it was all over."

"Apart," observed the FBI agent, "from the one you shot. Several times."

"Read my report." To some embarrassment, it was rapidly becoming clear that Eddie Lucco did not like Feds.

"Sergeant Lucco proceeded to the scene of the primary crime, disregarding the risk to himself," said Danny Molloy, to Lucco's surprise, for they had never much liked each other. But Molloy was going to let no shit be directed at his department.

"Go on, Sergeant Lucco." Faccioponti relaxed, leaning back on his wooden chair, adjusting the slide on his red-and-yellow suspenders. "You're making a connection between this Jane Doe and the incident at Bellevue. This is good. I'm interested."

Wonderful, thought Lucco. Faccioponti's "interested." This is my lucky day, the DA has finally remembered my name. Wait till Nancy hears. The DA had recently invited Nancy to have a drink with him in the 21 Club, just off Fifth Avenue. He had no idea the big Homicide cop was her husband.

"I believe either Ricardo Santos Castaneda, or serious cartel men associated with him, ordered PeeWee to be blown away, pronto, to silence him. And they musta known and accepted that would involve killing a number of officers and anybody else who got in the way."

"And the Jane Doe?"

"That's the angle I'm working on. We have a photo of her alive, and a photo of her dead. Maybe she was Ricardo's girl. Don, could you see if she's been noticed in Miami? Maybe that's where she comes from."

"Or Colombia. Has anyone considered maybe she's a *paísa*?" The FBI agent wasn't so dumb. "Some of them could pass for Caucasians . . ."

"Sure thing," said Don Mather. "I'll wire the girl's photo to the Policía Nacional in Bogotá."

Lucco let the conversation lap around him like cold wavelets on a beach. He was surprised to realize he felt resentment. That these . . . strangers should be discussing *his* Jane Doe. "Maybe I should coordinate that," he heard himself saying.

"Why?" The FBI agent again. "Contact with the Colombian police is a federal function."

Molloy grunted and shifted on his chair. "NYPD is investigating a multiple homicide, including the murders of seven of its officers. We have first call on all aspects at this stage, including the JD, whose burial has been held up on a warrant obtained by Sergeant Lucco, who is the Homicide officer investigating her death, which, as an autopsied suspicious OD, falls within our jurisdiction."

God bless America, mused Lucco. Molloy is fighting in my corner.

Don Mather looked up from tying his shoelace. "We can channel it through you. While conducting our own inquiries where appropriate."

"Sure." From the FBI.

"Okay, gentlemen, reality time," Faccioponti said urbanely, "I have the mayor's office on the line nine times a half hour. Seven cops have been murdered. The populace is outraged. Right now the drug connection takes second place. If there's a lead from the dead kid to the killers, let's go for it."

That was the end of the meeting. The officers left independently of each other. On their way along the corridor to the elevator, Eddie Lucco glanced at Molloy.

"Thanks, Danny," he said.

Molloy grunted. They reached the elevators. He glanced up at Lucco. "Son, if you're gonna stay lieutenant, you're gonna have to be a whole lot more agreeable to the Feds. They're not rivals, they're . . . associates. When we deal at this level."

"Lieutenant?"

"Yeah," replied Molloy gruffly. "I figure if we make you up to acting lieutenant it's gonna give the Division more voice in this thing. And if you get a good result, well, you heard the DA, this is city business. I figure you would get to keep the badge . . ."

That night, Acting Homicide Lieutenant Eddie Lucco took Nancy to a terrific Italian restaurant in Soho called Barolo. They drank a bottle of good wine and dressed up for the occasion. Eddie wore his necktie loose and the top button of his shirt unfastened. However much they promoted him, he was still the hard-assed cop from Queens.

Dorothy Jardine and the controller of BBC 1 television stood deep in conversation in a corner of the oak-paneled library. The drinks party at government whip Alec Maberly's Georgian town house was taking place on the first floor, where a stair landing opened onto the library on one side and the drawing room on the other. A pale, oyster-colored carpet, laid wall to wall, lent a spacious air when the solid, stripped-pine doors were left wide open, and guests drifted from one room to the other, picking up a prawn here, a canapé there, and sipping excellent white Burgundy, a Pernand-Verge-lesses '82, or a fine claret, Château Guillot '83. For those who had had a tough day, or who preferred harder liquor, there was a crystal pitcher of Maberly's lethal Bloody Mary.

"The secret, old boy," he was confiding to David Jardine, who had incautiously started on his third Dartford crystal tumbler of the stuff, "is just the right quantity of celery salt." He beamed. "And, of course, tons of bloody vodka."

Jardine grinned and sipped some more. As he lowered the glass, he noticed the prime minister being talked to by an ancient and stooped but broad-shouldered Tory peer, Lord Greffake, whose backing was vital even for the Leader. The prime minister was listening courteously but watching Jardine thoughtfully. As their eyes met, he nodded in the big spy master's direction. A warm and friendly nod, Jardine perceived.

Then he noticed a young man of about thirty-four, lean and fit, confident and wearing an almost well-cut suit in light gray, of a pattern that tried but did not quite succeed in passing itself off as Prince of Wales check. Also, the youth—or so Jardine considered him—was wearing an old Etonian tie, a sure sign of insecurity and bad manners. Eton ties were not worn in Town. Even Jardine, a grammar-school man, knew that.

"You know Michael, I understand?" said Alec, possibly too casually.

"We've met." Michael Watson-Hall was a bright, top-stream civil servant at the Treasury. And as Jardine and Alec Maberly observed him, the svelte and attractive Nicola Watson-Hall entered the room from the landing, her figure immaculate in a clinging, black silk jersey dress. Jardine could see that she was wearing stockings. She had had her hair cut in a 1920s gamine style, short at the back, with a seductive fringe. She flicked her hair off her brow and smiled winningly at Alec, her host, her gaze lingering for an impersonal second on Jardine, who nodded gravely. Then she turned to her husband.

"Damned attractive, Nicola. Don't you think?" asked Alec Maberly casually.

"Very nice girl. I like a bit more meat, myself."

"Pregnant, I hear." Alec helped himself to more of his lethal Bloody Mary from the crystal pitcher, glancing keenly at Jardine, or so David Jardine imagined.

"Good age to start a family," he replied, shaking off the fairly recent image of Nicola bent over the one armchair of that tiny flat in St. James's, glistening with sweat, gripping the arms of the chair and gasping, "Oh yes, yes, you bastard!" eyes fixed on the mirror as he swelled inside her on a crest of never-to-be-repeated mutual pleasure. The senior intelligence executive gazed around the room and absorbed the muted buzz of ruling-class conversation with studied nonchalance.

He noticed the prime minister speak gently to Lord Greffake, then detach himself, meeting Jardine's glance.

"Your turn, old man," murmured Alec Maberly, whose job it was to miss nothing.

Jardine moved to the corner by an oak bookcase and a fading winged armchair that created a private space. The rooms had several such havens, and not by mischance.

"I see you're braving one of Alec's Bloody Marys." The prime minister smiled.

"Can't resist them," admitted Jardine candidly.

After a pause to ensure they were not being overheard, the prime minister inquired, "How is the project going . . . ?"

Jardine was overjoyed. He had not been required to raise the subject himself. "It could have a serious chance of success, sir," he replied, and was gratified to note the PM's immediate disquiet, "if I was only allowed sufficient time to prepare my, um . . . players."

There was a whole evening's conversation in the way he had said that, and the prime minister was first among his equals precisely because he understood so much that was unspoken. He contemplated for a long moment, then gazed shrewdly into Jardine's eyes. Finally, he asked softly, "How long do you need?"

"Fourteen weeks, Prime Minister. In truth, twenty. But fourteen will suffice. To go in fully prepared."

The muted chatter of conversation went on behind them. Jardine knew instinctively that Dorothy had noticed him deep in conversation with Himself, and she would be intrigued and quite proud.

"Monumental breach of discipline, I imagine. You coming to me with this."

"I imagine so, sir."

"And it wouldn't do to, um, repeat the occurrence."

"Point taken." Jardine glanced at the nation's leader, who had something close to a twinkle in his eye.

"I take it we have not had this conversation . . . ?"

"What conversation, sir?"

"I'll see what I can do."

"Thank you, Prime Minister." They met each other's gaze and smiled. Jardine, grimly satisfied, turned to place his vodka glass on a shelf of the oak bookcase. "I was delighted to read that your daughter had won a Latin prize . . ." he said, making small talk. But the prime minister was already moving off, back into the room, smiling his charming, you are the most important person in the room smile at the master of Magdalen College, who bowed his head gravely and cut dead Dorothy, who had been deep in conversation with him.

Dorothy glanced at David. He raised his shoulders imperceptibly, and she shook her head, amused.

10

DEATH BY PASTA

The pain of Siobhan's eloping with some Venezuelan called Richard or Ricardo was hurting Judge Eugene Pearson's relationship with his wife Mhairaid. It was also affecting his performance in court.

Such traumas affect different people in different ways. Pearson, never a gregarious man, became more remote than ever. In the bar of the Shelbourne Hotel, where Restrepo had quite correctly guessed, or known, that he took a whiskey some evenings before going home, the judge had become conspicuous by his absence, as some wag on the editorial staff of the *Irish Times* had put it.

Mhairaid was, herself, desperately worried for the girl, for sure wasn't Siobhan just out of school and a convent school at that? But she knew—although Eugene was too deeply brooding and perhaps, thoughtful, to mention it—that her husband blamed her for adopting the apparently easygoing attitude of giving the girl her space. Letting her do her own thing.

Mhairaid was at least certain no drugs would be indulged in, for it had been a subject she had broached a few times with Siobhan and it was obvious the child had thought that one through, and in Dublin, whose heroin and dope junkies littered, literally, the streets and AIDS hospices, there was plenty of opportunity for consideration. No, they had always enjoyed a fairly ideal mother-daughter relationship. Open and affectionate, and without the rather cloying sentimentality and possessiveness that, sadly, colored the judge's adoration for Siobhan. In her darkest thoughts, Mhairaid had a couple of times wondered if . . . but no. Such thoughts are to be banished from the remotest corners of the wife of a future attorney general. And if there had been a problem, surely Siobhan would have said.

Justice Eugene Pearson would have been mortified if he had been privy to Mhairaid's innermost, half-formed, suspicions. Not even suspicions, more musings. But he had more on his plate than the problem of Siobhan and the prospect of becoming attorney general of the Republic of Ireland. The Army Council was waiting for his plan to set up a separate, clandestine organization to receive and distribute several tons of cocaine powder at its purest state to certain European organized-crime syndicates, in return for two million dollars each month.

Now Pearson was no wimp. He had served the Cause since 1970, risking his reputation, his liberty, his family, and his life in precisely that order, for Eugene Pearson had thought it through in his customary methodical and logical manner. And the comrades with whom he shared control of the Organization were serious men who earnestly, and murderously, intended to be recognized as the real power brokers in the Irish Problem: the Provisional Irish Republican Army and its political face, Provisional Sinn Fein.

Thus, he was able to divorce personal and family

problems from his primary commitment, and, ironically, Siobhan's disappearance (for that was what it had to be considered as) had one positive aspect. Eugene Pearson's colleagues and the attorney general's office knew about it, and had agreed without demur when he had requested a couple of weeks' leave, pleading family business.

Contrary to media-guided popular opinion, both in England and the USA, British and Irish security organs worked closely together in monitoring and endeavoring to thwart the movements and operations of the Provisionals. It was therefore a hallmark of the Organization's professionalism and experience that it continued to survive and operate with a degree of efficacy. This clandestine proficiency was, of course, precisely what attracted the Colombian cartel to doing business with them. Meetings of the full Army Council were conducted in conditions of great secrecy, and as rarely as practical considerations would allow.

There is a *loch*, as lakes are known in the Gaelic, in the county of Kerry between Killorglin and Glenbeigh. The first is a tiny hamlet straight out of folklore, where once a year, in the fall, traveling folk and horse traders and all manner of men and boys, women and girls, hellbent on enjoying themselves, descend on the place for the ancient, some say pagan, festival of Puck Fair. A live billy goat is put on the top of a rickety wooden tower, maybe forty feet high, and Killorglin and its several bars come alive to the sounds of penny whistles and ancient skin drums, known as *bodhráns,* and laughter and horse dealing and *ceilidh.*

The second, Glenbeigh, is about the same size or smaller. It caters for a different class of Irishman and plays host to the many professional people who motor from Dublin and Cork to enjoy the best fishing and golf in all Ireland (say some; the claim itself fuels many a night's heated argument, which is the Irish tradition, and lubricated in the traditional Irish way).

During the Civil War in Ireland, when the IRA took on the elected government of Eamon de Valera, in the immediate years after Independence, families in the Killorglin-Glenbeigh area were split asunder, and many brothers and fathers and sons fought bitter skirmishes against each other, depending on whose side they had chosen. By the last decade of the century, the wounds had long healed, even after so much bloodletting, and the greatest affection, kind of rough and unspoken maybe, was to be found among the descendants of the combatants. And indeed, until a few years before, among the aged former enemies themselves.

The *loch* is called Caragh Lake.

Eugene Pearson and his colleagues on the Army Council sat in the sun on a steep, wooded shore on the edge of Caragh Lake, watching a small, clinker-built, varnished wooden dinghy some hundred yards offshore, with two men in it, idly fishing. Their M-16 carbines within easy reach on the floor of the boat. No fewer than fourteen other wingers, or bodyguards, mostly local men, watched over the surrounding area. They were not, with two exceptions, what were described by the authorities as terrorists. For the Organization was only fielding twenty-six active operators throughout the Six Counties, England, and Europe, and those could not be squandered in a mere security operation. Also, the Army Council—none of them men the Garda Special Branch or even the Brits could prove a thing against—were not inclined to risk being found in the company or the vicinity of a dozen or so wanted men, for Eugene Pearson was not the only member of the ruling elite who led a completely double life and was not even known to be inclined toward Republican politics.

Thus, the men (and three young women) protecting

the Army Council were not active "soldiers" but trusted supporters. Only five of them were armed, although they were all trained in the use of weapons. The others relied on their personal radios and a system of watchers, of sympathizers, who would know if the Garda Special Branch even entered the county boundary.

It was against the Provos' standing orders to open fire, or even exchange fire, with Irish citizens, which included cops, unless under very exceptional circumstances. So the precautions surrounding one of the Army Council's rare meetings, which inevitably took place in the comparative safety of the Republic, were more to avoid identification and therefore breaches of security than anything that threatened life or liberty. The men (and woman) of the Army Council were most careful never to touch a gun or a bomb, or even to be seen in the company of known activists. Except for those who had a parallel role with the political Sinn Fein, a public face, at Provo funerals. And except for Judge Eugene Pearson, who had been photographed with the murdered Whore of Venice in his arms, blood and brains on his face and a false passport in his pocket. Oh, yes, Brendan Casey had him by the balls all right.

Warm, golden light drove down in shafts through the branches of the pines and elm trees, motes of woodland dust suspended in its rays. The grass was dry and smelled of the turf of long ago, when Mhairaid was eighteen, and the long Friday nights and Saturday mornings' games of rugby, played through trepanning hangovers, were the most exciting and violent things in the experience or expectation of the earnest legal student who was once Eugene Pearson.

"So, Eugene. I understand you have come round to . . . espousing a . . . marriage of convenience. Between ourselves and certain men from the land of the tango."

Pearson gazed at the leader of the Army Council,

elected by his peers to direct the Armed Struggle. Declan Burke was a committed Marxist, self-educated, and very well at that. He would have been a hard-line Stalinist in a different country, at a different time, of that Pearson had no doubt. It was this man who had liaised in the mid-eighties with Yuri Polganin, the KGB FCD (First Chief Directorate) operator who had worked out of Dublin with the cover of Novosti news agency correspondent. It had been Polganin, as the dark clouds of Perestroika whispered over the steppes and into the Warsaw satellite countries, who had introduced the Organization to Ghaddafi's cousin in Vienna. And therefore put in train the arrangements for the Libyan leader's gift of four shiploads of Semtex plastic explosive, assault rifles, handguns, nightsights, and handheld rocket-launchers that were now stored in underground bunkers in the Republic, in England, and in Europe. Lacking the funds to exploit their potential for carnage to the desirable full.

"I find myself obliged to agree," Pearson replied, ignoring Brendan Casey, who was sitting with his back to a pine tree, puffing gently on his Peterson pipe with its curled stem of briar. The aromatic smoke mingled with the smell of grass and warm wood. Crows cawed in the upper branches, and somewhere, a blackbird was advertising for a mate.

Burke had come up the hard way. He had been interned in the early '70s and from inside the prison camp at Long Kesh had been responsible for the discipline and security of his group, few of whom were at that time Provo activists. He had taken part in the hunger strikes and was down to ninety-six pounds when the British caved in to sufficient of the strikers' demands for the protest to be called off.

A wiry, muscular man before his twenty-seven-day fast, he had soon regained his physique, and on being released back into the community had joined the Derry

Brigade and had made his name in the movement with several bomb attacks against seemingly random civilian targets in crowded places such as the Le Mon restaurant and the Droppin Well bar. The campaign was masterminded by the then Army Council, including Seamus Twomey and Rory O'Brady, and had been advocated by a young lawyer called Eugene Pearson, who believed the sheer scale of the carnage would so horrify and outrage the British public that the London government would be forced to sit down and negotiate a withdrawal of British troops, and British rule, from the North.

Such operations, at Pearson's suggestion—adopted by Twomey, Casey, and O'Brady—were broadened to include a parallel bombing campaign on the British mainland, and for a few bloody months, Londoners endured the dull, empty thuds of explosions, with their attendant shattering of glass and metal, and human flesh.

The strategy proved counterproductive, and even the armchair terrorists of Noraid in the USA were forced to counsel a more selective approach to the killing.

Pearson's next move had been to visit New York, where he sounded out Irish Republican sympathizers and returned with a fresh strategy, in which British soldiers and their families, along with cops in Northern Ireland's Royal Ulster Constabulary, were targeted. The success of this move encouraged the Movement, and money from the USA flowed in greater abundance. This, together with the help in arms, explosives, and training organized by the Soviet Union's KGB, via Czechoslovakia and the Palestine Liberation Army, gave the Provos a new lease on life and emboldened them to their highest moment, when a massive explosion ripped apart the Grand Hotel in Brighton, in the south of England, almost killing Prime Minister Margaret Thatcher and wiping out several prominent Conservatives and their wives.

Now, seven years later, here were Pearson and Burke, the judge and the former bomber and unrepentant Marxist-Socialist, among the small clique running the whole bloodstained business. A testimony to relentless patriotism and single-minded hard work.

"And you have a cunning plan . . ." Burke said to Pearson.

"The task is fairly simple." Pearson deliberately shifted his gaze to draw in the others, including Casey. "Sancho Panza (this was their code name for Pablo Envigado) wants a simple reception and primary distribution facility, with total security from infiltration or detection by other means. He also wants the next stratum of distribution to be advised and monitored for security."

Silence.

"And that's it?" asked Casey, disingenuously, since the entire enterprise had been his brainchild in the first place.

"It's a two-tiered operation. Since, for some reason, somebody saw fit to compromise our Lorca Group by mentioning it to Sancho's lawyer, I have decided to use Lorca as our managing unit. It will mean detaching that circuit from other operations and keeping it at arm's length from the Organization, which is a pity."

"Can you think of a cell more suited? If so, I would be glad to have your thoughts." This from Ciaran Murphy, the Provos' director of security, who, while not a member of the Army Council, had been co-opted for this particular meeting because of the extreme sensitivity of the subject under discussion.

Pearson kept his eyes off Casey. Clearly the chief of staff had gone to Murphy and disclosed his security gaffe in mentioning Lorca to the Colombians. And clearly he had contrived to make it appear to have been a masterful piece of the negotiating mosaic. And it suddenly struck Pearson that, without his blind hostility toward Brendan Casey, it was quite apparent that the Vigo-based Lorca Group was ideally suited for the task.

"No, Vigo is my choice," said the judge, as if it had been his idea all along. "And if there was a better one, I would not have chosen Lorca."

Burke smiled and squinted out across the loch at the two wingers in the boat. One of them had caught a small fish and they were both laughing as they landed it.

"I have other arrangements to make," Pearson said primly. "Setting up an alternative and parallel reception point. With the agreement of the council, I leave tonight, should the basic, ethical question be resolved in favor of proceeding."

Even the blackbird fell silent.

The faint laughter and low voices of the men in the wooden dinghy out on the glass-calm water of Caragh Lake, sounded somehow ominous.

"And what . . . ethical, question is that, Eugene?" asked Declan Burke softly, still watching the fishermen-bodyguards.

As Pearson glanced around the others, one at a time, for all the world as if he was sitting in his Dublin courtroom (he was even wearing the half-moon spectacles), he was suddenly visited with a clear recollection of the afternoon just ten days before, in his daughter's room at the conservatory in Rome. He had a sharp mental picture of where the two armchairs were, and the rugs, and the table with the graduation photo on it. And the vivid clarity of Siobhan's voice, saying, simply, "Daddy . . ."

And his blood went cold.

"Cocaine is evil," he found himself saying. And his gaze hardened as he examined each of his comrades—disparate backgrounds, disparate morals, but good intellects. And bound together by a common cause.

"The ethical question is unavoidable and we have to address it. Do we, for money, assist in the massive importation of drugs into Europe? And do we insist that none of it finds its way to Ireland? For that would be impossible to enforce, once the stuff is in the hands of organized crime, which these days knows no frontier. Therefore, on the one hand, we have a public policy of punishing street pushers in Dublin, Cork, and elsewhere in the Republic, and on the other, we would be taking two million dollars each month for putting the bloody stuff there in the first place."

"It's heroin pushers we're hitting," said Ciaran Murphy. "Horse and cannabis. Cocaine's a yuppie habit."

"Not these days. It's processed into crack and PCP. Dangerous and sometimes lethal. Do we want to be responsible for spreading that stuff into countries that are not hostile to the Cause? And onto the streets and campuses of our native land? You have to address the ethical question. And you have to address it now, at this meeting." Pearson removed his glasses with a sweep of his left hand, very much the skilled and practiced advocate.

Out on the lake, the men in the wooden dinghy had settled down. The blackbird had started to sing again. Ripples appeared here and there on the glasslike surface of the water and the gentle *plop* of rising fish could be heard.

Declan Burke had folded his gray suit jacket and lay stretched on his back, using the folded jacket as a pillow. He wore a sleeveless sweater, knitted no doubt by Roseen, his wife, who was a prodigious knitter and had kitted out half the Kesh in socks and scarves that winter of '72.

"Here's how I see it," he said to the branches overhead. "Tell me what you think. The Colombians have targeted Europe, that we know. For it's in your report,

Eugene. And with their resources they will succeed. . . . Whatever we do."

"So why not take the funds and use the money for the final push?" This from Casey.

"I'm not suggesting it's not tempting," Pearson said. "What I'm asking is, do we, the Army Council, accept moral responsibility for our actions? If, indeed, at the end of this meeting, that is our decision."

Casey shot him a fierce look. It was clear that Pearson had made the others stop and think.

"How about whacking anybody pushing it in Ireland? And simply arranging safe arrival into Europe . . . ?" This from Murphy, who used every invitation to sit with the Army Council as an opportunity to have a voice in the shaping of events.

"Eugene's right, Ciaran." Casey tamped down the tobacco in his pipe. "There's no way we can keep cocaine out of the country, now that it's flooding into Europe. So the question is, can we accept that responsibility? On behalf of the Organization? I mean, we already run protection, smuggling, massage parlors, and escort agencies. Not to mention bank jobs. It's long been accepted we raise funds from activities that are not exactly . . . legal, begging the judge's pardon." He smiled and drew contentedly on his pipe.

"Then there's the damage question," Pearson said. "For if a breath of this ever gets out, we're going to lose support from the grass roots. Sinn Fein would have you out on your ear, you two."

Pearson directed this remark at Casey and Murphy, who were, quite separately from their clandestine leadership of the Provisional IRA, chairman and vice-chairman respectively of its legal, political counterpart, Provisional Sinn Fein, which regularly at elections won just over one percent of the democratic vote in the South and about four percent in the British-occupied Six Counties.

"There's things going on every day you would think would shake and horrify the grass roots, Eugene." As Casey spoke, Pearson remembered him standing on that hillside in Wicklow, spouting his "fuck the grass roots" diatribe with cold contempt. No chance of such an outburst in formal session of the council.

"You'd expect them to have walked in droves, after the Tower of London bomb." Casey was referring to a bomb placed among a roomful of schoolchildren in the museum at the Tower. It had happened way back in the seventies, but the Cause lived on a selective history going back six hundred years and kept vital in song, legend, and political rationale. Twenty years ago was like yesterday. "Or the machine-gunning of targets in front of their kids. Or the brothels. The grass roots are horror junkies, they're hooked on violence, they're more like Jim Rourke than we are." Jimmy Rourke had been a Provo soldier who had taken to masturbating in the getaway car after a killing, so consumed was he with sexual arousal and blood lust. He was buried in Milltown cemetery, summarily executed for having brought the movement into disrepute.

"I think dealing in drugs is different," Pearson said quietly. He noticed the imperceptible exchange of glances between Casey and Burke. Jesus God, they were already doing it.

Burke looked Eugene Pearson straight in the eye. "If we decide to proceed, Eugene, what . . . action will you take? Does it, for instance . . . embarrass your day job?"

Pearson felt the anger rise in his throat. He held his temper. Oh boy, it was going to be sweet to destroy those two, Casey and Burke. The Cause was being betrayed and with it, the fine people of Sinn Fein. He had seen it before. Power corrupted. And the power of death and more death . . . that was a drug ten thousand times more powerful than cocaine.

He held Burke's gaze coolly. The Whore of Venice, the slapping around in the Villa San Michele, the manipulation by Casey . . . oh yes, they were going to pay. But not just yet.

"I shall play my part to the best of my ability. I am policy advisor to this council. I will not ever shrink from spelling out unpalatable facts, or from predicting possible areas of damage to our . . . our future in Ireland's history."

"Well said," said Mary Connelly, the only woman on the Army Council. Mary was unknown to the public. A lecturer in Applied Mathematics at Trinity College in Dublin, Mary had one operation with an Active Service Unit on the British mainland to her credit, around the time of the Harrods bombing. Thirty-six years of age, she had been born in Belfast, off the Falls Road, and had joined the Organization on her return from the London School of Economics. A natural operator, she would doubtless have finished up dead, in jail, or on the platform of Sinn Fein had not Brendan Casey read a paper she had written on the insecurity of the Provos and how a cell system could make its leaky operations watertight. The paper echoed the words of advice given by Abu Nidal to Casey and Burke at a secret meeting in Cyprus some weeks before, and Mary was taken out of active service and assigned to the Organization's planning staff. She applied for a job at Trinity, moved to Dublin, and religiously kept out of politics and away from known Republican activists.

She smiled from under a rogue strand of raven-black hair. "Gentlemen, we can't keep the fight going for another twenty years. Some bright fucker's going to realize our irrelevance. So let's do the deal. Take as many million dollars as it takes. Screw Envigado and blow the Brits out of Ireland."

The men chuckled. Bravo, said Casey. Out on the lake, the hollow sound of oars on rowlocks as the two wingers shifted position, taking it slow and easy.

"Any dissenters?" asked Burke, gazing around and allowing his gaze to end on Justice Eugene Pearson.

Silence.

"Excellent. Your plane leaves tonight, you were saying, Eugene . . ."

And that is how the last shreds of innocence began to fall from Judge Eugene Pearson's tattered conscience.

———

There is a diner in Greenwich Village in New York City called Morta da Pasta. It's cheap and busy, on Waverley between Mercer Street and Fifth Avenue, not far from Washington Square, right in the heart of New York University campus. Death by Pasta. And it has a bar, cocktails half price during happy hour.

Acting Homicide Lieutenant Eddie Lucco sat at the bar, leaning against the counter, half facing the room and occasionally gazing out through the windows at the street. He had fought to retain control of the case and with the backing of Danny Molloy and the DEA's New York SAIC (Special Agent In Charge) Don Mather, had succeeded. And he was at a dead end.

Sure, everybody knew the multiple homicide at Bellevue had been perpetrated by Colombians, "the" Colombians as the DA and the Feds had taken to calling them.

But what specific Colombians?

Lucco had been living out of the 110th Precinct for a few days, buying favors from detectives and uniformed officers who had stoolies and undercover operations and access to wiretaps by the Narcotics Task Force, a joint NYPD/DEA/U.S. Customs team that had the Colombian immigrant population in Jackson Heights infiltrated, wire-tapped, surveilled, photographed, flattered, and bribed to saturation point.

If there was word on the street, the combined intelligence of the 110th Precinct and the Narcotics Task Force would hear it. Even if there was word in bars, men's rooms, on the phone or in certain bedrooms, they would still hear it.

But nobody was talking. The word on the streets was *nada*. Zero. Zilch.

This meant either they did not know, or the killers were too heavy even to mention in taproom or barbershop gossip. Lucco did not favor one theory more than the other. He was too experienced a detective.

DEA Miami had never seen the Jane Doe. Ricardo Santos Castaneda had not been seen in Miami for over five months. His brother, German, was known to have flown to Barranquilla about three weeks ago. He had not been seen back in his usual haunts, which was unusual, since he liked to keep a tight grip on his business interests, the wholesale distribution of cocaine and enforcing discipline in the cartel's Miami operation.

The dead Colombians—there were four, including the guy Lucco had shot in self-defense, who had bled to death before the paramedics could save him—had all been identified. Two were from Miami, two from Bogotá, having entered the U.S. two days before from Mexico, using the genuine Mexican passports of two food importers who had open-ended U.S. visas. Of the two from Miami, one had owned a bar in Bayside and worked as a pilot for a Miami air-charter company. He had done time for assault with a deadly weapon and smuggling marijuana, and had beaten charges of kidnapping and conspiracy to murder. The guy was rich and kept two girls, one in an apartment in Coral Gables, the other on a big cruiser berthed at Key Biscayne, the laid-back, causeway-linked island playground for Miami's major players. The other deceased from Miami was a charter-boat mechanic who had at one time served with the Colombian Policia Nacional before quitting the force and buying himself a U.S. work permit. He had been suspected of working for the top end of organized crime as a contract killer. That suspicion had proved to be correct.

The two Colombian nationals were private-sector "security consultants" who ran a lucrative business providing bodyguards in Bogotá, where there was always a place for a well-trained professional in that line of business.

And there the investigation stopped.

The one big surprise item was that none of the dead Colombians had been a known associate of Ricardo Santos, or even of his brother German. Obviously this had to point to a theory. But what? Lucco was confident he could keep his investigation looking good. But pretty damn soon the DA was going to lean on the chief of police, who would lean on Danny Molloy, who would advise Eddie Lucco to get into bed with the Feds or turn in the brand-new lieutenant's badge.

Well, the Feds didn't know squat. Lucco knew this from the damn-fool questions they had been asking around town. And the badge? While pleased to have the extra money and the clout that goes with promotion, every time he looked at his shiny new badge, with "Lieutenant" on the top and no detective's serial number on the lower half, and thought of his worn-smooth, faded, and beat-up-looking old detective's badge of seventeen years' service, he couldn't help thinking, "Now that was a *real* badge."

" 'Nother beer, Eddie?"

The kid behind the bar was a student, working his way through college. What nobody else in the bar knew was that the student had already done two years on the beat and was planning to come back to NYPD with a bachelor's degree and a place in Homicide if he could hack it.

"Sure, Tony, why not?" Lucco let his eyes wander around the diner's two rooms. The place was doing good business. The Italian food was delicious and the service typical New York-brusque but with a big heart. He glanced at his watch. Ten after seven. Soon the campus dormitory houses around tree-lined Washington Square would be alive with students hanging out, rapping, or even studying. This was where Nancy had studied before getting a post-grad scholarship to Harvard. Eddie had met her while he was working undercover as a precinct detective, before Homicide. They used to hang out around the neighborhood. And quietly and without fuss fell in love. Although they had not figured it until she went to Massachusetts, to Harvard. He had stood it three whole weekends, then drove through a rainy night, like in some French movie he had seen, and as the car had cruised around, searching for her apartment, there she was, walking in the early-morning rain, looking miserable.

They had gotten married three weeks later. Lucco smiled at the memory.

Tony slid a bottle of Corona beer, Colombian beer, the best, across the counter. Behind the wood-and-glass panel, facing the bar, making a passage from the entrance door to the manager's desk, a tall, loping, confident/furtive Rastafarian appeared, coming into the diner. Lucco's demeanor did not alter, but inside his heart beat faster and he was one hundred percent alive. For the man coming in, with his ebony handsome, maybe originally Somalian features, was none other than Simba

281

Patrice. Leader of the Blade Claw street gang, dope peddler, pimp, and killer of at least eleven of his fellow men.

He loped directly to the bar and sat next to Eddie Lucco.

"What'll it be?" asked Tony.

"I hear you made lieutenant," Simba said.

"You don't say," replied Lucco, casually flicking open the middle button of his tweed jacket.

"An' you is handlin a certain . . . investigation." His voice was real deep and carried an attractive Caribbean lilt. Investi-gay-shun, is what he said. And every instinct Eddie Lucco possessed told him that out of nowhere, the break he was patiently waiting for had arrived.

"I'm listening," he said, watching the street beyond the windows. And the door. People who gunned down seven police officers were not going to worry about a pasta joint. The detective's eyes narrowed as he glimpsed Snowblind, one of the Blade Claws, loping past the window, then crossing the street and leaning against a fire hydrant, turning casually to gaze at the door to the diner.

"I got eight soldiers out there man, but relax, man, they're just takin care of me . . ."

Lucco glanced at Simba. Eight armed Blade Claws loitering around Washington Square at this time of evening, with the regular pushers (this was not Blade Claw turf) and undercover cops doing their thing, was a recipe for mayhem. He had already checked out Simba's mini-Uzi under his purple baseball windbreaker. Working on his hunch, Lucco turned his back to the room and rested his elbows on the bar counter. Tony, who was a good boy and was going to make a good cop, casually crossed to the tape system, which was playing Eric Clapton's "Lay Down Sally," and turned up the volume, not so much as to annoy the customers, but sufficient to make conversation at the bar unintelligible.

Simba leaned back, facing the room. Nobody had noticed anything unusual or threatening. Waiters and waitresses barged in and out of the kitchen door beside one end of the bar, carrying pasta, soup, ice cream, stuff like that. Or empty plates, on the return journey. Simba's head was not far from Lucco's. "You been asking about some pale chicken. OD'd at Grand Central."

"Sure."

"I spoke with her when she was alive."

Eddie Lucco's expression did not change. But his skin began to tingle. On his fingers, and on the backs of his hands. He felt a vein on the side of his muscular neck beating strongly.

"Uh-huh . . ."

"She was with Ricardo, you know who I mean, man?"

"Spell it out."

"Santos, okay?"

"She was with Ricardo Santos?" Lucco glanced to Tony, who was adding up his checks. Without returning the glance, Tony nodded. He knew he was a vital witness to this otherwise deniable conversation. Lucco hoped he was writing it down.

"When?"

"About a month ago. Then Rico puts the word out, the chick has walked out on him. He's going crazy. He wants the town turned upside down. So we keep our eyes open. Now this is interesting. He is not just the love-crazy fool, or pussy crazy, wanting his woman back."

Eddie Lucco sipped his beer and waited, ever patient.

"No, man. This dude is running so scared he can't shit."

"Now why would that be?" Lucco murmured, as if it was not really important.

"I don't know, man, but word is it sure got his ass wasted."

"Ricardo is dead?"

"This I hear. Also a Colombian taxi driver found with his head shot? Yellow cab? Queens? Morning of the hit when my brother PeeWee is taken out . . ."

Big mistake, reflected Lucco, killing PeeWee without reckoning on his brothers' taking revenge.

"PeeWee was a tough kid. I'm sorry he went like that."

"Man, that is the way we are all going to go, you kidding? This is our life, we chose it. So be it, baby, it gonna be our death too."

Terrific, time is short and we got a philosopher, that's great.

"Tell me about the Jane Doe."

"Say what?"

"The girl. Rico's girl."

"Okay, she was just a kid. Maybe eighteen. She an' Rico took a few lines of good stuff, soon as they got off the plane."

"Took it?"

"Bought it. From, uh, off the street." From Simba, in other words.

"You said you spoke. Whaddid she say? Was she Hispanic?"

"She spoke like a British kid, okay? All right, maybe softer? Not la-di-dah, just, maybe Boston, I dunno. This was her first time in NYC, she told me that. Kid had a neat voice, looked good. But trouble, she was into crystal like it was gonna be banned tomorrow."

"Well, it's banned right now."

"Figure of speech, man."

"What else did she say?"

"Uh, she wanted to do some crack." This said quietly. Simba was no fool and he did not intend to incriminate himself.

"So what did she say? What exactly . . . ?"

"She got no chance to say nothin', for Rico told her no fuckin way. He put her back in the car."

"That's it?"

"She was mad at him. They was having an argument. Now, the guys who iced my brother . . ." Simba's eyes were themselves like ice as he gazed at the street where his "soldiers" waited. ". . . they were from out of town. Nine dudes. Colombians. Working direct for the top man, you know who I mean. They had heard PeeWee had done a deal. It was PeeWee who looked after that side of the business."

"I need a name."

"That's all, man. I figure I owe them for PeeWee. If I reach them first, they're meat."

"Pal, you've told me nothing . . ."

Simba, who clearly felt the drama of the moment—him moving, with armed escort, into rival turf to speak with the cop investigating his brother's murder—leaned his back against the bar, deep in thought. Lieutenant Lucco realized that here was not some colorful street-gang warlord. Simba Patrice was a tall, dissipated, murderous, self-preening punk.

"You come all this way to tell me the Colombians blew away your kid brother, who was the only Blade who could finger the Colombians you deal with? Mister, you're fulla shit. Now get outa here before I bust your ass."

"The girl."

"So you met the kid and now she's dead. Who sold her the crack?"

"I dunno, baby. Rico locked her in the hotel room. She called room service and got out."

"Rico tell you that?" No man had ever called Eddie Lucco baby. He figured it must be some Blade Claw form of address, or hip talk from the street. He tried hard, but he could never keep up. Bay-bee, was how the guy said it.

"Rico told me."

"So who sold her the stuff?"

"Man, she scored, that's all. This is the city, man."

"So what's the point of this, Simba? Why are we talking?"

"The point is, the guys who wasted your cops and my brother . . ."

The Eric Clapton number had ended. They sat quietly, listening to the hubbub of customers in the diner. Lucco sipped his Corona beer. Tony put on another tape. Some Ben Webster tenor sax, cool and blue. Lucco wondered if there really were any breaks for Homicide cops, for Homicide lieutenants. He had had more luck as a sergeant. And he missed that seriously worn detective's badge. When flashed, it had announced, this is an experienced no-bullshit New York cop. Do not fuck with this man. Now, the new, shiny, lieutenant's badge, Jesus *what* had Simba just said?

Simba had just said, "The point is, babe, their instructions were, find the girl. The girl is *prima importante*. Then take out the stoolie. That's my brother they was talkin' about. But in that order . . ."

Eddie Lucco turned and stared at Simba Patrice. He studied him hard. The man did not flinch.

"And Ricardo Santos . . . ?" he asked, his eyes fixed on Simba's.

"Somewhere during the three days these spics were in town, man. What I hear is the guy is taken to Brooklyn down by the river and some dudes heard some screams that went on all night long, I mean, babe, there's a bunch of bums live down there. It's some fuckin place been building for years, man."

"And the taxi driver?"

"What I hear is, this spic moonlighted for the *grupo*, the cartel. People was surprised when he was found killed like that, for he was well in with his people. Know what I mean?"

"Let me get this straight . . ."

"Make it fast. I gotta be out of here." Simba flinched as Lucco's eyes glinted.

"The spics come into the city specially to find that kid who Rico arrived with from JFK . . . ?"

"Sure. Correct, I gotta—"

"Relax. And they grill Rico, who you hear is now deceased."

Simba nodded, becoming more apprehensive. His skin glistened with sweat and he smelled of fear. He was constantly checking his route out of the diner and the street outside.

"Then the hospital is hit, PeeWee and fifteen other people die, including four of the *grupo* team. Anything else?"

Simba eased himself off the bar. Stood up. Glanced around. The message was he was going now. "They were staying at the Hampton House. The girl told me."

"Was that the second time you saw her? When she came back and you sold her the crack?" Lucco remained sitting, his right hand inside his coat, holding the butt of his .38 Smith & Wesson, thumb on the hammer, watching Simba intently.

Simba remained motionless for a long moment. Then he smiled, slowly, the smile becoming a grin on his handsome features.

"Man, I didn't sell her nothin' . . ." And he sauntered out as if he did not have a care in the world.

As Eddie Lucco watched him leave, and the Blade

Claws out on the street glanced around professionally and moved off with their leader, Tony glanced up from his busy scribbling on the check pad. "So who was the girl? And what makes her so important?"

"You tell me, Tony, and you got a place in Homicide tomorrow . . ." And Lucco reached across, took the check pad with Tony's notes, and walked through the door to the kitchen, leaving the diner the back way, out of customary prudence.

The Hampton House is a big and luxurious hotel on Central Park South. It has 214 rooms and a number of suites. To describe it as impersonal is maybe unfair, but if you wanted to stay in NYC and not be noticed, the Hampton is as good as anyplace. The duty assistant manager was from California and was naturally relaxed and courteous. His name was John Bordek. When Homicide Lieutenant Eddie Lucco appeared at his front reception desk, accompanied by Detective Sam Vargos, John's first instinct was he wished they would tighten their ties, which both men wore loose at the neck, top shirt button undone.

He listened politely as Lucco explained the nature of his inquiry. Then he punched in the relevent details on the computer.

"Let me see . . . Castaneda . . . or Santos . . ."

Clickety-click, went the keyboard. Clickety-clickety-clickety.

Lucco and Vargos waited politely, gazing around the lobby at the Japanese businessmen, English and Americans from out of town. South Americans. Germans.

John Bordek looked up, smiling helpfully. "I'm terribly sorry," he said, "no one of that name has stayed here, not since before Christmas."

"When is the last time somebody with either of those names did stay here?" asked Vargos.

"I really couldn't say. Not without a printout," replied Bordek.

"Tell you what, John," Lucco said, "I would like to speak to the doormen who were on duty four weeks ago, also the room-service persons and the chambermaids, can you fix that for us?"

"No problem. Except some of them will be off shift, or taking the day off."

"That's okay. I'll come back when they're here."

"You're going to ask them if they can ID a photograph, right?" Bordek grinned. This was just like the movies.

"While I'm talking to the doormen, maybe you could fix for Detective Vargos to interview the room-service staff."

"Sure thing, Lieutenant."

Lieutenant. Eddie Lucco grinned to himself. He kind of liked the sound of that.

The doorman studied the photo of Ricardo and the Jane D.

"Hey, that has to be Rome right? *La bella Roma,* am I right?"

"How about the couple? Did they stay here?"

"Don't ring no bells. Let's ask Louis, him and me do different shifts. Come on."

The doorman led Lucco to the porters' and doormen's room beside the front doors. Louis was smooth, olive-skinned, and cheerful. He studied the photo, holding it this way and that. Outside, an excited group of Japanese businessmen were gathering in the lobby and moving out through the doors to fan out, it seemed, and conquer New York.

"Sure. That's Mr. Enriquez." And Lucco saw that the doorman was sure.

"Okay, let's go sit in the lobby. Where it's private." The big detective turned and led the way. Louis stood up, picked up his jacket, and followed. The duty door-man, disappointed, went back to work.

Back in the lobby, Eddie Lucco found a couple of seats beside a high marble wall, screened from the rest of the lobby by a group of English advertising executives who had just arrived, mingling momentarily with the departing Japanese.

Louis sat in the other chair. Lucco handed him the photo for the second time. "Take a good look," he said. "Make sure."

"It's Enriquez. And that was the girl, the kid who took a walk."

What was it Simba had said? *The chick has walked out on him. He's going crazy . . .*

"Whadda you mean? Took a walk . . ."

"He comes down to the door. Asks me if I've seen her, um . . . he does not say a name. He says, have you seen the young lady I am with? Well, I remember because if she was with him, we'd both've seen her, right? It was a dumb thing to say."

"What else?" A name, we're getting close to a name . . .

"Well, she never turned up. After that." No, thought Lucco, she was lying on a slab at Bellevue.

"And Enriquez . . . ?"

"He stayed on a couple more days. Then he checks out. But he hands me a C-note and says if she comes back, asking for him, to phone some number. But she never did."

Gently, Eddie, said Lucco to himself . . . "You got the number?"

"Sure." Louis took out a battered pocketbook and took out a scrap of paper from the hotel's courtesy-phone pad. It had a number on it that Eddie Lucco recognized as being in Jackson Heights. In the 110th

Precinct, where the serious Colombian players were gathered. He took the piece of paper.

"Thanks, Louis. Anything else?" This was a question no good cop could ever leave an interview without asking, even if the subject had just confessed to multiple murder and quadruple rape, theft, and assault.

"The kid was a real good-looker. But Jesus, man, she was so young."

"Underage?"

"No way, the hotel wouldn't have let them check in. I guess she was about eighteen, nineteen. That photo don't do her justice, Lieutenant. She coulda been a movie star." The cold light of logic suddenly struck Louis. The logic of why he was sitting here talking to a cop from Homicide. He looked Eddie Lucco in the eye. "Aw fuck, the kid's dead, right?"

Lucco nodded.

Louis looked suddenly tired. "This fuckin town, man . . ."

Vargos had about the same result from the room service and housekeeping staff. Some remembered the couple, who had booked into a suite with kingsize bed. Mr. Enriquez had wanted a room with a view of Central Park but had had to settle for one looking back, down Sixth Avenue. The couple had ordered champagne and later had gone out for dinner. Nobody knew where. The next day, they had stayed in bed till about nine, then had gone out shopping. One of the chambermaids remembered shopping bags from Gucci and Bloomingdale's. And Banana Republic.

The girl had sent down for Coke and chicken sandwiches. About ten in the evening. The room-service boy had let himself into the sitting room and had heard knocking from the bedroom door. He opened it and the girl had laughed and said her stupid boyfriend had absentmindedly locked her in while she was taking a nap. She had tipped the boy ten dollars and, he remembered thinking it was strange, had put on a jacket and left the suite with him, not touching the chicken sandwiches, and taking the elevator to the first floor.

And that was it. Jane Doe went out into New York City and sometime between then and ten before seven the next morning, she had scored, had her purse stolen by the Apache, and died, inhaling her own vomit, ODing on crack that had been cut with too many impurities, which made her a Homicide case.

Lucco wondered if he would ever find out what she had done between ten at night and six in the morning. He remembered Simba Patrice's broad grin. "Man, I didn't sell her nothin'. . . ."

What the hell had he meant by that?

"Plus I got a name," Vargos said. They were in the tan Dodge, unmarked car, on the way over the potholes and through the rush-hour traffic, moving east on Fifty-seventh, crossing Madison. Vargos was driving.

Lucco watched the truck in front, the mounted cop sitting on his horse at the curb, talking to a tall black youth who seemed relaxed, hands on hips. The police radio was crackling and squawking. Car horns were hooting in desultory gestures of impotent impatience. It was like, Where were you when you heard Kennedy was shot? Lucco knew he would always remember this moment.

"No kidding," he replied casually. "What is it?"

And Vargos told him. He nodded. Yeah, that was the kinda fey, other worldly name he should have figured the waiflike corpse would have.

"How about her family name, her second name?"

"Gimme a break, Eddie. It's a start."

11

GOD AS A
SPORT

I don't actually know what the hell you're playing at,
David."

Steven McCrae lacked the ability to get coldly angry
in the way previous chiefs had. David Jardine thought
he was behaving childishly. Which probably made him
more dangerous. They were in the men's room at their
club, in St. James's. David Jardine was washing his
hands. Sir Steven was finishing his business at the
urinal.

"Not quite with you, old boy."

"Really? Okay, how about this . . ." McCrae hitched
up his zipper and ran some hot water. Steam misted the
lower half of the mirror over his washbasin. "I do not
take kindly to the foreign secretary and the cabinet
permanent under secretary, individually and separately
. . . and if that's a coincidence I'm Regius Professor of
Poetry at Peking University *fuck!*" This last expletive on
account of the water being at scalding temperature when
he plunged his hands into the basin. Jardine suppressed

a smile. ". . . taking me aside," continued McCrae, "and inquiring . . . precisely, precisely was the word they each used, primed obviously, by the head man. Precisely how long it takes to train a secret agent, that was precisely the absurd, inelegant expression they used, to infiltrate a hostile target and live his cover. With any reasonable chance of success . . ."

"My dear chap. That's the sort of question they ask all the time. Are you all right? Try plunging them into very cold water."

"On being asked that damn-fool question twice in the same day, I was obliged to tell them, at least four months, sometimes more than a year. . . . Even then I could sense your devious bloody hand at work. God, do you think the skin will peel off? It bloody hurts. Then at five-fifty, just before I left the office, I am informed by the PM, on the secure line, that he feels terrible about rushing us into something, vis-à-vis your, um, business. And would we please think in terms of twelve weeks' preparation, starting from whenever we commenced training."

"Well, that was handsome of him."

"David, that was a stupid thing you did. I don't think you've done yourself much good."

"Look, this is not the place, but I really don't know what you're talking about . . ."

"Cut the crap, there's a good chap." McCrae glanced around. The cubicles were all empty. He lowered his voice and leaned close to Jardine, keeping his scalded hands in the basin of cold water. His hair smelled of one of those lotions Top People's barbers use and his breath of Fisherman's Friends, a powerful mint-and-eucalyptus breath freshener. He was about two inches shorter than Jardine, which still left him taller than average. Jardine watched him balefully in the mirror. He continued to lather his hands, out of politeness, since he could hardly walk away.

"Okay," continued McCrae, "you will extend the training period to ten weeks from day one, which was two and a half weeks ago. And I require to have a man in on the ground, establishing himself and his cover, twelve weeks after that. With product emanating, say . . . three weeks after that. Is that quite clear?"

"Emanating . . . ?"

"Coming out," said the former Cambridge don, appalled at being reduced to what he referred to as media English. In other words, communicating. "The prime aim in all this . . ."

Jardine was more than interested to learn what the prime aim was now to be. Prime aims had a habit of shifting like the desert sands. And as the officer responsible for their personal safety, as far as was possible Jardine was determined to be aware, as the sands shifted, what precisely it was that Baggage or Parcel was expected to do. Once he had wormed his way into Pablo Envigado's confidence. And here the prime aim, in its latest form, was about to be revealed, in the washroom of one of London's oldest gentlemen's clubs. The Americans would have been appalled. And to tell the truth, so was David Jardine, but it was not the moment to lecture the chief on security.

And at that moment, Warwick Small, the best-selling novelist, walked in, tanned and chain-smoking, deep in conversation with a former member of the Firm, Donald Flower, who had become slightly seedy and was making a living in PR.

"Evening, Steven," said Small as he stepped up to the pissoir. "How is the delightful Annabel?" Sir Steven McCrae had recently remarried, having been widowed for two years. His new bride was the daughter of a director of the Bank of England. Annabel was twenty-three years his junior.

"She's fine, thank you, Warwick." McCrae dried his bright red hands gingerly on a towel. Jardine was already at the door. Sir Steven nodded to Flower. "Donald . . ."

And he left, following Jardine.

"Who was that chap with the chief?" asked the novelist.

"Dashed if I can remember his name," lied Flower, who was more discreet than he pretended.

———

At eight-ten the next morning, in Dublin, in Judge Eugene Pearson's fine town house, Mhairaid Pearson went through her morning routine of grinding fresh coffee beans, putting toast in the toaster, slicing a grapefruit and cutting out the heart, then taking a fruit knife around the edges, then cutting the flesh into eighths. Devlin, the twelve-year-old cocker spaniel, had already been out and done his business, taking longer now each morning.

On the news was word of the latest developments in talks between Dublin and London on the future of Northern Ireland. Also, masked gunmen of the Protestant Ulster Volunteer Force had sledgehammered their way into a council house in Newry and shot to death a thirty-eight-year-old father of five in front of his wife and two of their children. And in the Persian Gulf, Stormin' Norman seemed ready to invade Kuwait and roll right on to Baghdad with the aim of annihilating Saddam Hussein and his cabal.

Eugene Pearson came downstairs, fully dressed, in a brown suit and discreet necktie, striped shirt from Hilditch and Key in London where, each June, he bought his shirts in batches of six, and comfortable leather sneakers, which he had mail-ordered from an advertisement in *The New Yorker,* of which he was an avid reader, although he did not understand many of the jokes.

Mhairaid heard the sound of his battered leather suitcase being laid down in the hall.

"I hope you get the job in the end, all this traveling around the world you're doing . . ."

Pearson sat down at the kitchen table and poured himself a glass of orange juice. "It's not around the world, Mhairaid, it's just Europe."

"Anyway, Padraic's ahead six percent in the opinion polls, not that they're always right. But it looks like Fine Gael have a good chance." She poured some muesli into a bowl and placed it on the table in front of him. "And he's set his heart on you being attorney general. My God, we've both worked for it all these years, Eugene."

"Is this milk fresh?" Pearson asked with his customary grace.

"Will you be away long?"

"About five days. Sit down and eat something, you don't need to dance attendance on me like this . . ." He knew it was because she felt guilty about Siobhan's disappearance.

"I think Devlin's got prostate trouble, he takes forever to squeeze out a pee these days." This veterinary turn the conversation had taken was abruptly terminated by the flutter and slap of the morning mail being dropped through the letter box in the front hall.

Mhairaid turned and moved out of the kitchen, leaving the door to the hall swinging. Eugene Pearson sat staring at the door, milk jug held over the muesli.

The sound, the rustle, of envelopes being picked up and sorted through. It seemed to take, like every morning when he was home, forever. Then Mhairaid came back into the kitchen, studying the pile of four or five envelopes.

"There's one from the bar association. A letter in Joe Leeson's writing. Phone bill . . ." She beamed, elated. "And a letter from Siobhan, with a Venezuelan stamp."

The silence in the room was complete. Pearson's heart pushed inside his chest. He laid down the milk jug with shaking hand and stared at Mhairaid who, tears on her cheeks, sat down, offering the envelope to him. His heart softened. Gently, he put his hand on hers. Squeezed it.

"Why don't you read it out loud . . . ?"

She sniffed, nodded, and carefully opened the envelope with a clean breakfast knife.

"God bless her, it's a long letter she's writing."

"When did she write it?"

"The nineteenth. Five weeks ago. But it was posted only eight days ago . . . Look." Mhairaid handed Pearson the envelope. The Venezuelan stamp was franked Caracas.

Pearson's heart was pounding with relief. "Read it to me."

"Dear Mum and Dad, life in Rome is great. I have tried to phone you but the line is always busy, or there is no reply. So while I'll tell you all about it when we finally get to speak, here goes . . . help, exclamation mark. I'm so nervous. Anyway, I've met this lovely fellow. He's from Venezuela, that's in South America as if you didn't know. And although he wants to get engaged I've said not till I graduate and not till my mum and dad give you the once-over. He has invited me to Venezuela for a few weeks, to study under the famous South American composer, Enrique Lopez Fuerte. Anyway, I really want to go, and since I'm away from home anyway, it's not as if it's a big drama, so by the time you get this, I'll be either airborne or in Venezuela, from where I'll phone the minute I get there. How is Devlin? Give him a big tummy tickle from me. Please don't worry about me . . ."

And so the letter went on, with a postscript explaining that she had not had a chance to post the letter before they left Rome, and here it was, posted from Venezuela, the flight had been fine and she was a wee bit tired so she would phone when they got to Fuerte's place in the mountains.

Eugene Pearson and Mhairaid read the letter a few times, together and separately. It was as if an enormous curse had been lifted off the judge's house. They embraced and to Mhairaid's surprise, he got quite amorous.

A short while later, she drove him to Dublin airport and he caught Aer Lingus Flight AE 112 to Paris. There he became an American citizen called Daniel Rooney, a Boston-based corporate-law consultant, with all the requisite papers and passport.

As Rooney, Eugene Pearson rented a Peugeot 205 GTi and drove south to Lyons. The journey took him six hours and forty minutes. At 9:37 P.M., in the rue de la Victoire, he parked the car, went into a small bar with a faded yellow awning, ordered a cognac and an omelet, and handed the car over to a French sympathizer, a lawyer for Action Directe—the French urban terror group, almost destroyed by the authorities a few years before but now quietly regrouping—who would return it to Paris, using the Rooney documents.

The Dublin judge now metamorphosed from Rooney to become a London real-estate dealer called Michael Kenneth Donaldson, using a passport supplied by a Pakistani immigration adviser based in the north of England who traded in stolen British passports at £8,000 a time.

From Lyons, Pearson took an overnight train to Biarritz, on the southwest coast close to the Spanish border, and was met at the station by a fifty-five-year-old woman called Marie Laportière, the Communist sister of one of the founders of the Basque ETA movement, fighting for independence from Spain. Marie was one of the ETA-B members who worked in support of the Provos' Lorca Group, which was based in Vigo, a coastal port four hundred miles away, on the far side of the Pyrenees. She ran a small real-estate business on both sides of the border.

Marie Laportière gave Judge Eugene Pearson a breakfast of warm croissants, hot chocolate, and cheese. And a bottle of Kronenbourg beer. He consumed it without making conversation. Then she drove him in her Renault 20 to the border and into Spain. The customs and border guards waved them through without formality.

Eighty-four minutes later, Pearson was left by Marie Laportière in Murguia, a village in the Spanish foothills of the Pyrenees, and he waited there for two hours until a battered Dodge pickup, once dark blue, now faded and scarred, pulled up beside the tiny bar where he had been reading Vargas Llosa's *The War at the End of the World* and drinking coffee, beer, and Perrier water. A scruffily dressed but still good-looking girl of about twenty-nine jumped down from the cab and went into the bar, bidding Pearson good day in Irish Gaelic as she passed.

Eugene Pearson took the precaution of going to the john before he left the bar and climbed into the cab of the pickup, clutching his valise. He glanced at the girl, as she climbed back in.

"Waiting for a bus, were you?" she asked, once again speaking in Gaelic as she started the motor and crashed the gears, moving the truck back onto the road and making a U-turn, heading southwest.

"You're late," replied Pearson. In the same language.

"I asked you a question," said the girl, taking her right hand off the wheel and letting it move to her lap.

Eugene Pearson sighed. "I was hoping to meet a friend. He's a doctor . . ." He said this in English, reciting the second recognition phrase, which was like a password for this one specific encounter.

"You've maybe got the wrong village."

"He likes to drive up here for a game of cards."

The formalities completed, the girl nodded, relaxing. She moved her hand away from her waist, where, under the worn leather jacket, was the butt of a 9mm British service automatic that she had removed from the body of a British undercover soldier, in a builder's yard off the Falls Road in Belfast while the man was still jerking in his death agonies.

"We've had a hell of a lot on. Gerry and Father Michael are helping the local lads get ready for a blitz."

Pearson knew that. The Basque ETA movement was planning a summer of terror in Barcelona, Bilbao, and Madrid. They lacked technical expertise, and the Provos' Army Council had authorized Lorca to supply it. That was now going to have to stop, since Lorca was to be separated from the Provisional IRA for its next task, receiving and wholesaling cocaine, arriving in vast quantities from Colombia via Cuba and Panama.

"You were late, Rosaleen," repeated the judge. "That just won't do. I was extremely vulnerable there. We're lucky no cops came along. Or Guardia Civil.

"For fuck's sake, I said I was sorry."

The Dodge slowed down and the gears crashed once again as Rosy stood on the clutch and brakes, then gunned the big motor and turned the truck left, joining a road that was signposted Bilbao 82k–Santander 127k. The scrub on either side of the descending, winding road was dry and parched. They passed a huge black billboard cut out in the shape of a black bull, advertising some beer or coffee or something.

Rosy Hughes was aware that it had been a long

silence since their brief exchange. She determined not to let it bother her and concentrated on the road. Then, sod it, she thought, and switched on the tape deck. It was a singer called Sinead O'Connor, singing "Nothing compares to you. . . ."

"Let's get a couple of things straight, you and me." His voice was disconcertingly mild, "I am the most senior man you have ever met in the Organization, except of course for your former boyfriend." He was referring to Brendan Casey, who had agreed to Rosaleen being sent to Europe with the Lorca team in order to avoid a scandal, for Casey was married and lived in a council housing scheme in Derry with his wife and three kids.

"You are not to be late for a job again. And you are not to use profanity. Not because I'm a prude, but because it draws attention to a pretty woman like yourself, and in this game that's the last thing we need."

Rosy Hughes glanced at him. She shrugged. "You're the boss."

"Yes, I am," said Pearson. "I have no doubt you will get used to it." And he let his chin drop onto his chest and fell sound asleep.

Rosy Hughes was quietly furious. Was she not a tight and proven member of an Active Service Unit? And had she not killed for the Cause? Seven men, three women, and a couple of bastard Prod kids who happened to be passing at the time? She resolved to make this relic from the days when Dublin called the shots pay for his arrogance.

And that was Rosy's first mistake.

———

While Parcel and Baggage, aka Harry Ford and Malcolm Strong, completed their initial training and basic

indoctrination into the theory and practice of espionage
under the direction of Ronnie Szabodo, David Jardine
was hard at work, spending a great deal of time away
from the great glass box with a clandestine outfit working out of a small travel company's offices just off
Victoria Street, Westminster, in an ancient mansion
block of nondescript companies and trading agencies.
Numbers 199–203 Buckingham Gate. This department
of the firm was part of the Directorate of Operations and
was designated D-Ops (CLD). CLD stood for Clandestine
Logistics in Depth.

Its function was to provide the best background to a
legend, or cover story, that the experience, imagination,
and technology of SIS could devise. One of the aspects
that fascinated David Jardine was that, whereas in the
old days it took months, sometimes years, for a spy to
live his cover before being played into an operation, CLD
was now able, by a variety of techniques, to create a
history for the operator so verifiable, so accurate, that it
would be virtually impossible to disprove its authenticity
under the strongest and most professional, that is, KGB,
Mossad, or CIA scrutiny. And one of the greatest accomplices to this form of counterfeiting was the trusty and
ever more state-of-the-art computer. In its many forms.
For once one computer asserted that Joe Brown had
rented this automobile, or traveled on this airline, or
served this jail term . . . every other computer with
access (legal or illegal) just had to believe the lie
because computers are essentially dumb, and—and this
was what Jardine found so beautiful—pass it on out-
ward, in ever-spreading ripples, until the lies became
true. A few good actors—Intelligence Service agents
inhabiting the real world of the computers' data, with a
row in a bar here, a shared joke there, a lost-property
query, a telephone complaint, a fistfight, an arrest in a
public place—pretty soon transformed those lies into

real memories to life's unsuspecting spear carriers and bit-part players.

Thus, a trail of credit-card purchases, airline flights, hotel bills, automobile rentals, small purchases, and business transactions was being laid around South America, the Caribbean and Europe. This phase was code-named Operation Obfuscate, and it was building up the Op Corrida black operator's legend even before it had been decided if Baggage or Parcel was to be selected. A cover identity had been chosen for each of them, and so thorough was Jardine's trail-laying that two legends were being authenticated, so that either could go. And if one fell by the wayside, then the other could follow.

And suddenly, the way they do, another week had passed.

Thursday. 4 P.M. Hallelujah, thought Jardine. Tomorrow's Poets day. He planned to take a helicopter down to the Honey Farm, read Malcolm Strong and Harry Ford their assessments, kick some ass, annoy them to the point that anyone less than committed would tell him to stuff the whole enterprise and if, as he devoutly hoped, neither did, surprise them with a three-day pass and their own cars. With orders to be back at the Farm, ready for work, at 8 A.M. Tuesday.

Then he would helicopter back to London, have a mid-course conference with Ronnie Szabodo and the officer from Personnel (Recruitment/Planning), as he was disciplining himself to think of Kate Howard and her orbs and thighs.

David Jardine had never been able to fool himself. He knew when he had sinned, or was about to sin, or was contemplating it. Ever since he had converted to Catholicism he had slept less restlessly and had been less . . . uneasy within himself. He believed in his God, accepting Him as some kind of infinitely omnipresent, omniprescient . . . Forgiver? . . . Planner? . . . Almighty Force for Good, in constant battle with Evil?

Yes. And no.

David Jardine had the gall, or the ignorance, or the innocence, to think of his God as a sort of Chum, with total knowledge of, and understanding of, this one soul among billions, David Arbuthnot Jardine. When he prayed (which he more often than not did in a disgracefully informal way, such as saying, Dear Lord, you really are a sport!) he unquestioningly believed that he was in safe hands and that, provided he did not tear the arse out of it, God the good sport would help him to find solace and forgiveness. But he was no innocent, this David Jardine. He knew firsthand that life was appallingly shitty for many people all of the time, and for most people, some of it.

He also knew firsthand that there were, at the most unexpected moments, wonderful things to be moved close to tears by. A sudden breathtaking landscape, some exquisite piece of music, an act of stunning, thoughtless courage, the sound of his children's laughter in another room, or Dorothy's knowing, forgiving glance.

The poorest, most desolate soul, he mused, can always find a glimpse of something comforting, a shaft of sunlight, a memory . . . or a ray of hope.

But being no saint and a less than perfect Christian, there was always the business of sin, without which, Jardine wondered heretically, would there be any need for God? If so, God bless sin, he thought, and crossed himself for the blasphemy, for he enjoyed his visits of worship and contrition to Farm Street Church.

And right now the sin he was contemplating involved Kate and he knew it was lust and he knew he liked the girl and respected her and he was too old for her and that he was getting sex-starved after Nicola, wife of the ghastly Michael, had so abruptly ended a satisfying liaison. He knew that it was bad for office discipline and if she fell for him he wouldn't feel anything half so decent and certainly not anything remotely permanent and it might mess up her personal career plan and happiness and for all those reasons, now that he had thought it through, he would let the matter drop.

He wasn't a satyr after all. Thank God the girl would never find out what a silly old fool he had been close to making of himself.

The phone rang. It was an interoffice secure line.

Jardine lifted the receiver, realizing he had been staring at a top secret file on the progress of Op Obfuscate while daydreaming about God and Sin and Sex. And coming down on the side of decency, for once.

"Hello . . ." he said, with quiet authority. A light on the phone base indicated the call was coming from Century House.

"David?"

He smiled. "Yes . . ."

"David, this is Kate. Are you busy?"

"I've got another hour on Obfuscate. Then I'm taking a helicopter down to the Farm."

"You watch out with helicopters. I've heard of this thing called a Jesus nut."

"It beats the traffic. We're all meeting tomorrow though. Is that still on?"

"Apparently the whole machine depends on this one small nut, holding the rotor blades onto the spindle. I just wondered if you would make it back in time."

"Oh, I'll be there."

Silence.

"Great. See you then."

Jardine smiled. "There's room for one more. Do you want to come?"

"I, um, someone's just come in. See you tomorrow."

And the line went dead.

Jardine took the receiver away from his ear, glanced at it, and laid it gently back on the phone rest. Noble notions of decency receding, the way they do, for that had sounded just a touch . . . promising.

And he hummed as he flipped through the file, initialed it, called for the clerk to take it and lock it away, washed his hands, grabbed his jacket and overnight bag, and was still humming as he climbed into the office Sierra to take him to Battersea Heliport.

6:28 A.M. Myg Trefwny Wood, Dylif, Wales. Pine needles soft underfoot, on a firm base of earth and grass. Rain from two days and nights of steady downpour weighed the overhanging branches and dropped in heavy, cold lumps. A man, barely visible, lay motionless in the undergrowth beneath a row of pine and fir trees. He wore a soaked, torn, once-blue jacket and dark gray trousers, solid with mud. His trainers were soaked and mud-caked. He had a torn piece of thick plastic, with a hole cut for his head, worn over his clothes and tied at the waist with a length of thick hemp. In his left hand, a prismatic compass, in his right, a muddy scrap of paper, on which was sketched a map of the area. His chin was rough with stubble. He peered through the dismal morning light toward an abandoned hut. From within, a clink of metal. Low mutter of voices.

Is it safe . . . ? He strained to decide, his red-rimmed eyes sunk in his cheeks, his body stinking like a wet hog.

And just five weeks before, this sinewy, dangerous creature of Myg Trefwny Wood had appeared at the Old Bailey, London's central criminal court, in the case of Regina v. Bloom, bewigged and gowned, and plumper, arguing most eloquently the case for the prosecution of a white-collar thief who had purloined seven million sterling from unsuspecting investors, in many cases their lives' savings, and for whom there was no redress from the insurance companies because of some minuscule small print which meant that there was no liability to honor.

Malcolm Strong aka Baggage had prosecuted the case with vigor because he did not appreciate the idea of smug Mr. Bloom, who was apparently now bankrupt, walking free to enjoy his wife's untraceably acquired millions, and the lawyer had been grimly satisfied to see Bloom go down the steps for seven years.

Now here he was, sixteen pounds lighter, fit as a fiddler's rat, and nothing in the world was more important than to make contact with the occupants of that hut, give the correct recognition phrase, and be directed to the last rendezvous where, according to Tojo's briefing, there would be a vehicle waiting to take him back to the Farm, and egg, sausage, fried bread and ham, many mugs of scalding coffee, and a hot, wonderful bath. He was disturbed to realize he might maim anyone who got in his way.

The first three weeks had been taken up with fitness training and basic indoctrination into the theory and practice of espionage, with particular reference to operations in Denied Areas, clandestine communications—including Dead and Live Drops—legend protection, survival in a PHE (Permanently Hostile Environment), observation and memory training, weapons and demolitions handling, close-quarter combat, aggressive/defensive driving, map reading and astral navigation, under the direction of a variety of SIS instructors who had come to earn the grudging respect of the two candidates, as Parcel and Baggage were from time to time referred to.

Tojo was the nickname he and Parcel had given to the squat course director, who had two bullet scars on his left forearm and who spoke bad Spanish but fluent French, and according to the fit, muscular bastard Parcel, excellent Russian. Baggage supposed it was natural that bloody Parcel would, in addition to skipping with fucking weights on his ankles, know Russian.

Still, Baggage had beaten Parcel in stripping and assembling seven pistols and submachine guns, their component parts mixed inextricably, while hooded and blindfolded, much to Parcel's chagrin . . . actually, that wasn't fair. Parcel had winked at him and said, "Not bad . . . for an amateur." I'll give him bloody amateur, had thought Baggage.

Something had stirred, something had moved, imperceptibly, among the roots of a dead pine tree, closer to the derelict hut, from which smoke was beginning to curl in the moist air of the drying day.

Baggage had no intention of being taken prisoner. Not again.

The first couple of night exercises, when the inevitable had happened and the instructors captured them, the interrogations had been fierce and tiring and bewildering and . . . uncomfortable. But the resistance to interrogation course, of which those exercises were part, was thorough, and Baggage was intelligent enough to know they could only go so far.

Then, into week five, everything had gotten much more serious. All of the instruction was now conducted in Spanish, with new directing staff who spoke fluent Argentinian and Colombian dialects. He had been captured once, in a small town nearby, when they had been carrying out a brush pass exercise. That is, when you take a pass from someone without acknowledging their existence. Maybe they leave a newspaper on a café table. Maybe a roll of film passed in a bus queue, a kid selling flags for some good cause. Anyway, just as Baggage had taken the pass from a young woman pushing a pram—she had dropped a fluffy toy and he had stooped to pick it up—he was blackjacked, hoisted off his feet by three men in workmen's clothes, and thrown into the back of a van that had seemed to be loading from a nearby store.

A sack had been shoved over his head, he had been handcuffed and hog-tied. The questioning and beating had started right away. In Spanish. Always in Spanish. What is your name, they had gone on and on, and his reply of Baggage had been greeted with guffaws of laughter.

At one stage he had been thrown down some stairs into a cellar. There had been rats. That interrogation had lasted three days, without sleep, and it was rough. In fact, brutal. Twice his hood had been removed and a "doctor" had asked him if he wanted to pull out, to resign from the course, to be released from his contract.

The moment this charade is over, he had vowed to himself. But not yet. I'll defeat those bastards first.

Then, a mistake (a deliberate mistake?) by one of his jailers had resulted in Baggage whacking the guard across the face with a wooden toilet seat and half strangling him with the down-chain from a cistern. And making his escape.

He had found himself in a yard at the back of Dylif House, on the far side from the wooden huts, and it was about three in the morning. He had broken into the main house and had been found the next morning, fast asleep in the bed of one of the instructors who was out searching for him.

Although nobody said anything remotely complimentary, it seemed they were quite pleased with Baggage from that point.

Yes, something was definitely moving in the roots of that dead pine tree.

Baggage lay perfectly still. He had reached his hiding place while it was still dark, the sound of his movements masked by the heavy rain. This was no longer a game. Fuck them all. He would survive this . . . nonsense. He would make contact with the stupid "agents" in their absurd derelict hut, after making sure it was safe, because if he got caught he would face more interrogation, like the last time.

The movement among the roots was more apparent. It was a man, carefully and professionally observing the environment around him. It was Parcel, his face camouflaged with dried mud. Gingerly he rose from the roots and moved, alert and cautious, toward the hut. There was only one door, hanging broken on its frame. The windows were boarded up.

Baggage, still as a fish at the bottom of a pool, watched, his breathing silent.

Parcel stood at the door. Baggage heard a voice, quiet and low, reassuring, from inside the hut. Parcel replied. Then another, questioning voice. Parcel, cautious, replied again. Then he heard quite clearly, a voice in Spanish say, "Well done, *amigo*. Here are the coordinates for your final rendezvous . . ."

And as Parcel moved into the doorway, like ghosts, out of nowhere, seven instructors from the Farm were suddenly standing behind and around him, rising from the very ground. There was a brief scuffle, not really a fight, and Parcel was hooded and wrapped in a poncho, handcuffed and hog-tied, struggling furiously and swearing in Spanish all the while. A vehicle motor started up, and a covered pick-up truck pushed its way out from the brush and low fir branches. Parcel was bundled in. All the players in this charade climbed on board and the truck moved off, soon lost in the forest.

Baggage did not move for another hour and twelve minutes. Even when he needed to relieve himself he did not move. He lay patiently, cursing SIS and everyone remotely associated with it. And their children. And their children's children.

At eight-nineteen, a solitary figure climbed down from the branches of a fir tree. It was a girl in jeans and anorak. She was soaked and shivering. Cautiously she approached the hut, checking out its surroundings. Then she took a piece of chalk and scrawled on the wall beside the door before turning away, passing the motionless Baggage, and disappearing back into the woods.

Eight minutes later, Baggage cautiously rose from his hiding place and approached the hut, his senses as acute and stretched as a hunting cougar's. The only sound was the drip . . . drip . . . drip of the drying forest.

Written on the door were eight numerals. They told Baggage where to find the vehicle that would take him back to the Farm.

He walked for two hours, hiding when he felt, or heard, any human presence. The "vehicle" was a bicycle, with both tires flat. Coldly furious, Baggage mounted the bike and started to pedal. After four or five minutes on the sandy hillside track, which thank God descended gently into a green Welsh valley, the sound of a Land Rover could be heard approaching.

Baggage quickly dismounted, rolled the bicycle into the undergrowth, and dived into a clump of ferns behind a log.

The Land Rover appeared around the bend that Baggage had just passed. To his dismay, it slowed to a stop. He pressed his face into the earth, as if, if he could not see them, they would not spot him.

He heard a door open. Then low voices, speaking in English. Then a gentle laugh. The sound of feet on the track, coming through the grass toward him. And suddenly there was someone right beside him. With a great growl of rage, Baggage rose like a tiger from the ferns and dived at the enemy.

David Jardine swayed gently to one side and flipped the storming Baggage onto his back. Ronnie Szabodo stood nearby, grinning broadly.

"Good morning, Mr. Strong," Jardine said, which was the first time in five weeks Baggage had heard his own name. "Let's all go for breakfast."

Breakfast had been everything Malcolm Strong had dreamed about for four days. Three fried eggs, fried bread, beef sausages, mushrooms, crisp bacon, canned tomatoes, black pudding—which was a kind of meal and blood and spice sausage—two tumblers of full cream milk, hot Colombian coffee, freshly ground, toast, butter, and Frank Cooper's thick-cut Oxford Marmalade. And the hot bath, followed by a long shower, where he had washed his hair twice, and the luxurious shave, his tanned and leaner cheeks dabbed with Geo F. Trumper's astringent West Indian extract of limes. Clean linen, fresh socks, his jeans, cotton shirt from Blazer, and navy lamb's wool sweater from the Brooks Brothers shop in the City. His well-worn, comfortable docksiders from Timberland. Malcolm Strong felt refreshed but deeply fatigued. Exhausted but content, his anger with the system that had put him through so much lessening as he relaxed into the by-now familiar surroundings of the brick and wood hut where his room was. Everything spotlessly clean, the wooden floors polished, his bed linen crisp and turned down invitingly. He glanced at his watch . . . six minutes before David Jardine and Tojo wanted to see him in the director's office in the main building, which was the two-hundred-year-old Dylif House.

Strong (Baggage) lay down on the bed and checked

his watch. It would take two minutes to walk from the spider, as the hut complex was called, to the main building. That allowed him a good three minutes of complete and absolute rest. Baggage was learning.

Harry Ford was first to enter the main building. He gazed around the spacious entrance hall, not sure where to go. A small, lean woman in green overall entered, carrying a metal bucket and a mop, cigarette jammed in her mouth. Ford asked her how to get to the director's office, speaking in Spanish without giving it a second thought. The cleaner looked at him as if he was from outer space.

"Sorry, love. Can't understand a word you're saying . . ."

Ford tried again in English. She told him it was up the stairs, along the corridor, through the fire doors, down three stairs, unlocked door on left, up some stairs and that was where the director's office was.

As Harry Ford (Parcel) made his way to the office, he was not a happy man. He had started this SIS course with a feeling of déjà vu, for Special Air Service selection and training techniques were designed to supply soldiers who could operate clandestinely deep inside enemy territory in small teams or on their own, able to pass for local inhabitants. The running, the workouts, the weapons training were like a quiet ramble for a Kentucky mountain hound. The lectures and observation and memory tests had been similar to those he had taken at the Army Intelligence School at Ashford, in Kent, prior to working undercover in Northern Ireland.

He was aware that some form of selection procedure involved a choice between himself and the not-all-that-fit, slightly overweight candidate he only knew as Baggage.

At first, Baggage had really not been in the running, except for the facts that he was obviously highly intelligent and spoke fluent Spanish, with an Argentinian accent. But the guy had guts. He had persevered, although the physical exertion was clearly hurting. He had, Ford had overheard, done very well in the interrogation phase. And the plump, once plump, bastard had gone and beaten Captain Harry Ford, SAS, at assembling weapons, blindfold in a darkened room, when the various component parts had been mixed up. Then, and this was what really hurt, Harry Ford had been captured at that bloody hut in Myg Trefwny Forest after a four-day exercise that had been fairly grueling, even by Special Forces standards, out-tradecrafted, fieldcrafted, whatever you like to call it, by the Intelligence Service hoods on the ground. And taken, not for the threatened interrogation but for breakfast and a clean-up, when who comes in, laughing and joking with the senior hood, Jardine, and Tojo, the Hungarian training director, but a very lean and filthy, but triumphant Baggage. Who had apparently lain patiently, watched Ford making a balls of it, chosen his moment, and succeeded where the SAS hero had failed.

And suddenly Harry Ford saw the funny side. He was still chuckling as he found the director's office, knocked casually, and entered.

The room was sunny and had probably been a conservatory when Dylif House was a family home. David Jardine sat behind a desk with two blue folders laid in front of him, one with "Parcel," the other with "Baggage" on white labels on their covers.

"Take a seat, Harry," said Jardine, who opened the "Parcel" folder and sat reading it, without looking up.

After a few moments, there was a knock at the door. Jardine did not bother to reply and eventually the door opened and "Baggage" came in, glancing around politely.

"Sit down, please," said David Jardine, not looking up from his reading.

After four long minutes, during which Jardine studied both folders, he glanced up and gazed thoughtfully at both men.

"You have both scraped through to the next phase," he announced. "Now it's real. Now we're going to help you try to stay alive, not for humanitarian reasons, but because a dead operator is no bloody use to me."

He stared at each of them. "Does either of you have any problem with that?"

They stared back at him with something approaching hostility.

Silence.

"Fine," said Jardine. He slid two envelopes across the desk. "These are the keys to your cars, which I've had delivered here. Go home and see your loved ones. Report back on Tuesday. Nine A.M."

Strong and Ford stared at him. They took their car keys from the envelopes. Was this a trick?

"What do we tell our families? How much can we tell them?" asked Malcolm Strong.

"You decide. You've done the course. We trust you." Jardine stood up. "Have a nice weekend."

And that was that.

Eddie Lucco sat in the backseat of the unmarked police car, the tan Dodge, sipping chocolate malted through a thick straw, which was essential in order to suck the real, ice-cold, thick, sludgy pieces without taking the plastic top off the tub. He felt around a carton of taco chips mixed with melted cheese on the seat beside him without taking his eyes off the entrance, across the street, to the Chirimia Bar, which was between a five-and-dime store and the *vallenato* record shop. *Vallenato*, he had been told by Luís, the Colombian immigrant the 110th Precinct had suddenly produced to work as a street guide for Lucco and Vargos, was a type of Caribbean music popular all over Colombia.

Chirimia was the name given by Colombians from the Andes and the Caribbean coast to a wandering street band, according to Luís, who was mostly Tayrona Indian, with some Spanish and some Scottish blood, he claimed, as a result of a liaison between his great, great, great, great grandmother, a Tayrona weaver, and a pirate, name of J. Murdo MacLeod, who sailed with Teach out of Cartagena. Eddie Lucco soon learned that this irregular, lent to him by detectives in the local precinct, loved Colombia with as much intensity as he hated the *paísas* of Antioquia who, he alleged, were too goddamn smart for their own good. His three brothers and his father had been taken out from a bar in Barranquilla, up the coast from Cartagena, along with seven others, and machine-gunned by guerrillas of the Ejército Popular Nacional, which was not a group anyone had ever heard of before. Local rumor had it the EPN was a group of renegades from the Fuerzas Armadas Revolucionarias de Colombia who did not like the FARC's inclination to follow the now-respectable M-19 guerrilla group into the democratic political arena.

This lecture on the intricacies of Colombian revolutionary politics succeeded in confusing Acting Lieutenant Eddie Lucco more than somewhat. However, he grunted instant understanding when Luís related that the killers were reputed to have carried out the massacre as contract enforcers for the cartel, which had been defeated in recent attempts to press-gang local Tayrona Indians for work in the vast jungle cocaine laboratories, small fortresses built by the cartel to process cocaine paste from almost every nation in South America. The freedom fighters were just hoods. That figured. No problem in understanding that.

He also could see that Luís had a serious reason to wish the cocaine pushers and local mafia barons ill, and his initial reservations, discussed over several beers with Vargos, at working with a Colombian, even one with U.S. citizenship, were fading fast. In fact, his several weeks in Jackson Heights, the district that had become known as Little Bogotá, where the 110th Precinct was located, had impressed upon him that Colombians were hard-working, hard-playing folk with considerable charm, national pride, and one hell of an ability to smile in the face of adversity.

Eddie Lucco found that he instinctively liked Colombians. And since the most dangerous men he had ever come across—men who had shot, knifed, and tortured New York's Italian Families, the Irish Mafia, and the bloodthirsty Yardies into making room for them, and dealing with them, taking their supply—were also Colombians, Eddie Lucco was aware that the killers he was seeking would probably be equally charming and fun-loving and attractive . . . and lethal.

The Chirimia Bar was the subscriber to the telephone number Ricardo Santos, the late Ricardo according to Simba Patrice, had given to Louis the doorman (who knew him as Enriquez) at the Hampton House, along with a hundred-dollar bill. This was the best lead Lucco had, and he had organized a watch on the place during working hours. He had also obtained a wiretap on the bar's three phones. Transcripts, translated from the Spanish and sometimes unintelligible English, revealed nothing special.

As Lucco watched, Sam Vargos came out from the bar. Sam was second-generation American, but his Cuban parents still spoke Spanish and his wife was Puerto

Rican, so like many New Yorkers he was bilingual. He wore jeans, plaid shirt, brown sweater, and a beat-up old leather jacket. It was a cold New York day, and he rubbed his hands and his breath hung around him like a scarf of mist as he approached the car.

The plastic seat squeaked as Luís slid across from the driver's side and Vargos got behind the wheel and hauled his door shut. There was a faint noise of static coming from the car radio, which was netted into three frequencies—Homicide Control, the local network, and the 110th Precinct. Any outside communications would be patched through Homicide Control, at Police Plaza, Manhattan South.

"So?" inquired Lucco.

"So like before, It's a regular bar, with what you expect. Guys drinking beer, chewing the fat. No juke box, *gracias a Dios*. Two bartenders and the manager . . . just like yesterday and the day before and like that."

"What fat, like what fat do they chew?"

"Men, women, bicycle racing, football. Wages. The Giants. Price of beer. C'mon. You know. Eddie, just because you got four cars sitting around here, and fifteen on foot, don't blame me if the result is a big zero. Is that tacos? They sure smell good."

Eddie Lucco sighed and passed the half-empty carton of tacos and melted cheese over to his partner. He gazed, deep in thought, at the back of Luís's neck. The guy was remarkable. He never got in the way, he always had a good, helpful answer if asked, and he was happy to work the outrageous hours this investigation needed. And serious detectives from the 110th had vouched for him, some had even entrusted their lives to his discretion. And yet . . . this Luís was a Colombian. Lucco instinctively felt more than the usual distrust a cop feels for a civilian, and a sense of fairness made him realize how much the cartel and related criminals had damaged

Colombia's standing and reputation in the eyes of even unprejudiced people like himself. After all, Eddie Lucco was Italian American and he had nothing but contempt for the Mafia. So every Colombian was not a dope hoodlum, or in the cartel's corrupt grip. That figured, and Eddie Lucco knew if he was to get anywhere in this investigation he was going to have to trust more than a few of the inhabitants of Little Bogotá.

Then, just at that point in his musings, he was struck by an idea that Captain Molloy would later tell him was what any sensible detective woulda done the minute the place was wrapped in surveillance.

"Sam," he said, "get three officers into that bar right now. Tell them the pay phone will ring a couple of times, then stop, then ring again. I wanna know the reaction of whoever takes the call. If he speaks to somebody, I wanna know who. If he writes a note and passes it, *capisci?* And if he, or somebody he's communicated with, leaves the bar, I want them tailed all the way. Whatever it takes."

"You bet," Vargos said and picked up the radio handset that looked just like a mobile phone. He started to organize the job. Meanwhile, Eddie Lucco used the other handset to call in a favor, which resulted in a complaining detective heading for a pay phone on Hudson Street, near the river.

Seven minutes later, three undercover detectives with Lucco's detail were inside the Chirimia Bar.

In the Dodge sedan, Lucco spoke with Homicide Control and was patched onto the regular phone-company line. He punched out the number of the bar pay phone.

The big detective listened as the ringing tone sounded a few times. Then a voice answered, "Bar Chirimia, *quién es?*"

"Señor Enriquez, *por favor* . . ." requested Lucco, in a very passable Spanish accent.

"Quién?"

"Enriquez," Lucco repeated, and went on to say he had been given this number to call, by Señor Enriquez, who had asked for some information.

There was a long silence. Then a new voice came on the phone. "There is no Señor Enriquez here," it announced.

"Señor Enriquez said for me to call this number," the detective insisted. "He even wrote it down."

There was another silence. Then the voice said, "If he comes here, where can he find you?"

Eddie Lucco's pulse quickened. He gave a number that checked out as the pay phone down on Hudson Street, saying he would be there for the next couple of hours.

"I don't know him, but if somebody calls that asks if there's been a phone call, I'll give him that number, okay, *paisano?*"

"Muchas gracias," replied Lucco, and ended the call.

Inside the bar, the bartender who took the call, Alejandro Domingo, went back behind the counter, continued to work for another half hour, then took off his apron and told the junior bartender to cover for him. He washed his face and hands in the john, observed by two undercover detectives. Then he put on a quilted parka and a wool hat and left the bar.

Alejandro Domingo's journey across the street and along four blocks to the El Paradiso Travel Agency was observed by twelve detectives, male and female, on foot and in five unmarked vehicles. A hasty and illegal wiretap on the travel agency's phones was just in time to catch a call to the Hudson Street pay phone. The number rang and rang. Lucco cursed the cop who had promised to be there to take the call. Maybe he got held up in traffic or some emergency. So much for favors. Lucco could see the whole lucky break turn to dust. Eventually, some guy, some civilian—it sounded like a vagrant, high on cheap wine—picked up the receiver. The ensuing conversation was complete confusion and when the caller hung up, it was fair to guess he would blame Alejandro for writing down the wrong number. No harm was done, because all the wiretappers needed was the caller's voice on tape.

This tape of the confused conversation was rushed across town to the NYPD Intelligence Division, where voiceprints of known criminals, including narco players, could prove identity as accurately as fingerprints.

The voice of the man in the El Paradiso Agency was that of one Juan Baquero Camacho, wanted in Miami on suspicion of cocaine trafficking.

Eddie Lucco leaned back on the seat of the unmarked sedan, smiling with relief. He offered his upturned palm to Vargos, who slapped it in congratulation.

"So now we got a lead . . ." Lucco said, and gazed deep into Luís's eyes as the man grinned back at him.

MARRAY SAITH

12

THE RED MAN THE
JUGGLER SENT

David Jardine stood at a window of his corner office
on the eighth floor, gazing across the rooftops of Lambeth. After so many years, he no longer noticed the
clock tower of Big Ben on the far side of the river, or the
flag fluttering from the Great Tower of the House of
Lords, just over a mile away. He was watching a Concorde airliner scoring its way across the evening sky,
heading west toward Heathrow Airport. On board was
(he knew, because he had a printout of the passenger
manifest in his hand) a man traveling under the name of
Luís Osorio Restrepo using a Peruvian passport. His
profession was lawyer for an international banking consultancy, Banco di Commercio Principal, with offices in
La Paz, Caracas, Rio, Geneva, and Barcelona.

Jardine had been aware for some time that Restrepo
was one of Pablo Envigado's most trusted advisers.
Reports from the Paris office of the DST, the French
internal security service, advised him that Restrepo had
recently attended a meeting of bankers in Paris to dis-

cuss financing a Japanese car-assembly plant in Argentina. He had stayed at the Hotel Crillon, along with two "aides," who were probably bodyguards. The next evening he flew on to Geneva. Ninety minutes before his flight departure there had been a gangland-style killing of a known cocaine distributor, a Venetian restaurant owner called Montepalcino, on the bridge leading to the quai Anatole France. The coincidence was drawn to the attention of interested parties, including Jardine's office. The fact that the report had reached him six weeks after the event did not surprise him. That was quite typical of intelligence bureaucracy in action.

David Jardine knew that Pablo Envigado had been Montepalcino's supplier, and that the Venetian transvestite had handled part of Envigado's European concession. Jardine had no doubt that Envigado's lawyer had been tasked with finding a wholesale organization to replace that of the murdered man, who had apparently been known in the underworld as the Whore of Venice.

While he pondered the reason for Restrepo's visit to London, Ronnie Szabodo, Kate Howard, and Bill Jenkins sat in his office, quietly reading Jardine's operational plan for Op Corrida, including a comprehensive update on what was known in the trade as a three-dimensional trail being laid across the Americas and Europe, creating legends for Parcel and Baggage.

As the thunderous, always dramatic, noise of the Concorde receded, Jardine could not hazard a guess at what Restrepo was going to do in London. Undercover agents of Her Majesty's Customs Special Investigation Unit were on hand to tail him wherever he went, but Restrepo would assume that and behave accordingly. It was a minor mystery, but one thing was certain, wherever Restrepo went, it was on *el grupo*'s business.

He shrugged and turned back from the window to

the others in the room. Heather, his Scottish P.A., was quietly pouring fresh coffee for everyone.

Kate sat, legs crossed, a wisp of hair over her nose, glasses slightly askew. Jardine noticed that her crisp, pink cotton shirt had one button loose just above the waistband of her Jaeger tweed skirt. He knew it was Jaeger, because when he had gallantly said he liked it, Kate had told him where she bought it. She must have realized he was gazing at her for she glanced up, met his eyes, and went back to the file.

Jardine looked away and met the gaze of Ronnie Szabodo, who gave an infinitesimal, world-weary, amused shake of his head and returned to study his Op Corrida file.

"Everyone ready . . . ? There's a rather good film at the Chelsea Curzon. I was rather hoping to catch the eight-ten performance."

"What is it?" asked Bill.

"*Cyrano de Bergerac*. With Gerald Depardieu. I hear it's very good."

"Okay." Szabodo peered for a last moment at his file, then closed it. "I'm ready," he said, and looked at his watch. Jardine found himself wondering if Ronnie had a little tartlet, as the Hungarian had once bizarrely termed a well-known politician's mistress. Someone to ease the boredom of that untidy bachelor flat that Szabodo called home.

"It's Gerard. Not Gerald," announced Kate, removing her glasses and cleaning the lenses on the loose part of her crisp, pink cotton shirt.

"I'm sorry?" Jardine glanced at Szabodo, hoping for some reaction to his carefully thought-out plan.

"Gerard Depardieu . . ." murmured Bill Jenkins, penciling some comment on the margin of his top secret copy of Op Corrida.

Coffee had been a bad idea. And the briefing room

would have been a better place. The briefing room with beer and sandwiches.

"I think this plan is quite good." Szabodo dug his pipe into a plastic wallet of Holland House tobacco. "It could perhaps even work." He grinned his gap-toothed smile.

If he leaves the office with his denture in, it's definitely a Friday-night tartlet, thought Jardine, who found himself watching Kate as she crossed her legs and put her spectacles back on, middle finger of her right hand pushing the bridge delicately.

"It's important." He switched his gaze, first to Ronnie Szabodo, then to Bill Jenkins. "It's important Pablo notices our man, our operator. Thinks he's making the approach. Not the other way round . . . Here's a notion of mine, you won't find it written down and when I've told you—thanks . . ." he accepted a fresh cup of coffee from Heather and settled, half leaning, half sitting, against the leading edge of his desk, ". . . you'll understand why . . . Heather, be a darling and guard the outer office."

He waited, politely, until Heather left the room, closing the door to her office, which shielded Jardine from casual visitors. Then he explained his plan. The others watched and listened with growing interest and occasional disbelief as his idea, prosaic on paper (for Jardine's masters were prosaic people) took wings. And a degree of outrageous . . . genius. The boss had something of a reputation for idleness, trusting to his rare intuition and original flare to keep him at the top table. And here he was in action, producing original thinking, and flare, in spades.

It began to seem, in that charmed room on the northwest corner of the great glass box, that there was nothing David Jardine did not understand about Pablo Envigado, the cartel, Colombian politics, the Colombian people, human nature, and the nuts and bolts of espionage as an art form.

But among the impressive and original thinking was a bombshell, and when he had finished, the room was silent.

Jardine sipped his coffee, which had become lukewarm.

"Well, that's certainly very cheeky," said Bill Jenkins.

"Questions . . ." Jardine invited.

Kate and Jenkins glanced to Ronnie Szabodo, who had the most experience of the unorthodox in offensive intelligence work. He studied his pipe bowl, the tobacco reduced now to fine ash. After a moment, he stared hard at the boss.

"David, clearly you have thought this one through but why, and this is what I think is worrying us all, why do you think you can trust, um . . . Dolphin?" He was referring to the bombshell, which involved someone, code name Dolphin, who was to be a cornerstone of David Jardine's plan.

Jardine met his gaze and for a long moment didn't speak. Finally, he said, "I know I can." And the quiet way he said it brooked no further discussion.

And since there were no further questions, that was the end of the meeting. The atmosphere was thoughtful and subdued as the others collected their notebooks and tobacco pouches and spectacle cases and things. Subdued because Jardine's plan had taken them completely by surprise. It required, it depended on, the help, trustworthiness, and discretion of an international criminal, doing twenty years to life in a Miami penitentiary. Szabodo was reluctant to have a row, there and then, but you would not need to be a graduate in body language to see that he meant to take the matter up at the earliest opportunity, in private. He was also clearly annoyed that Jardine had not discussed it with him beforehand.

They made small talk while Heather came into the room and collected the numbered top secret Corrida files to be taken back to the Secure Room.

As Bill Jenkins moved to the door, he paused and looked across to Jardine. "If you think it's wise . . ." (Sir Steven would have said "prudent") ". . . it's just, we're putting our Joe out on a limb. Sticking his neck on the block."

"Bill, this is not the Little Sisters of Mercy."

"Yes I do know that." Bill had good reason to be concerned, because his job would be to provide the necessary operational backup. It was Bill who was running Operation Obfuscate. He pressed on. "Let's say that it works. The Dolphin cover . . . How, precisely, David, does our man bring himself to Pablo's attention? Always accepting we can make Pablo think *he* has noticed *him.*"

"Oh, I'll think of something," said Jardine, meaning he already had but was not ready to discuss it.

Ronnie Szabodo glanced at his watch for the third time in thirty minutes, glowered at David Jardine the way only an Eastern European can do, wished everyone (else) a good weekend, and left, followed by Bill Jenkins.

As Jardine stepped over to the window and gazed out at London's darkening sky, pitter-patters of rain suddenly whispered on the windows, muted by the blast-proof coating with which they had been treated. Kate put her spectacles case into her purse, then picked up her knitted cardigan from the back of her chair. With their colleagues gone, they were both very aware of each other's presence.

"Cyrano . . ." she said, glancing at him as she pushed the rogue strand of hair from her face.

"That's the guy," Jardine said, and as he turned to say something flippant, he was ambushed by her gaze. In the name of God, David, he said to himself, let's not have a repeat performance. And he mastered a matter-of-fact expression, as if she was just a pleasant colleague. But that fooled neither of them.

The rain whispered relentlessly against the blast-proof windows. On the bookshelf beside him, the antique clock gently ticked the time away.

"I've been meaning to see that. So damn busy . . ." She smiled, shrugged. "It'll be off before I get around to it."

She turned and moved to the door. David Jardine lifted his jacket and patted the inside pocket, checking his wallet was there. As Kate got to the doorway she turned to say good night.

It's now or never, thought Jardine. "Look, Kate, I'm going alone."

Kate looked at him. She matched his this-is-no-big-deal expression. "Do you mind if I come . . . ?"

"Just as long as you don't eat popcorn and rustle candy papers." He grinned. "See you downstairs in . . . half an hour?"

Slight pause. The phone started to ring. Kate nodded. "Okay."

She moved to the door. Jardine lifted the receiver. "Hello."

The voice on the other end was from the Metropolitan Police Special Branch, Joint National Unit, a young and ambitious detective chief superintendent, Andy Laing.

"Mr. Jardine?"

"Andy, how the devil are you?"

"That bloke." Ambitious young Special Branch executives did not waste time on small talk. He was the coordinator of intelligence between the police, customs, the Security Service, the Inland Revenue Investigation Unit, and MI-6, as David Jardine's outfit, the Intelligence Service, was sometimes called. The "bloke" referred to was Restrepo.

"I'm listening."

"He stepped straight off one plane and onto another."

"Going where?"

"Geneva. He phoned the manager of his front company's Geneva office and they're having a late supper at the Hotel Richemond."

"What's arranged?"

"We sent two officers on the plane, doing man and wife. The Swiss customs will notice chummy and it's over to them. Well, actually, we were wondering if it could be over to you people. If you could tail him, in Geneva."

Jardine knew these words meant good-bye to Cyrano and the tantalizing possibility of nuzzling those perfect orbs, with their scent of Johnson's baby powder. And those thighs . . .

Damn the Firm, the Outfit, the bloody Service. He should have left the office early. Even probationers knew why half the intelligence world ran for cover at three-thirty on a Friday afternoon.

"Of course. I don't know how we're placed there right now. But our NDO" (Night Duty Officer) "knows everything there is to know, who's who and where and . . . I'll see what we can manage. Bit short notice. Fax me the details, would you? For my own number. And get your married couple to keep surveillance on the target until we can relieve them. They might very well be needed, I suspect we'll need every spare body."

"Roger on that. Bloody Fridays, sod's law, isn't it?"

And the cop, for whom David Jardine was beginning to feel an immoderate antipathy, hung up. On an impulse, Jardine lifted the receiver of his internal phone and punched out Kate's office number. The phone rang for some moments, then Kate answered, slightly breathless.

"Hello?"

"You're going to hate me . . ."

"It was that bloody phone call wasn't it?"

"It was the bloody phone call. I have to organize a watching job in, um, in Europe. Chum of our major player actually. Could take all night."

"You want any help?"

"What?"

Kate was not involved in operations, except where their plans involved the selection of black operators, like Baggage and Parcel. Ronnie Szabodo had warned, or gossiped, to Jardine that she was hell-bent in getting into the operations side of the business, the sharp end of the Firm's work. Lady Luck moves in mysterious ways, and a Friday night, when everyone has pissed off for the weekend except for a few brave souls and cipher clerks on overtime, with a sudden . . . emergency, he supposed . . . was just about the one circumstance when an assistant director personnel (Recruitment/Planning) might find herself in the right place at the right time.

"I said, do you want any help? I was only going to the pictures . . ."

Jardine smiled. "If you like. But I warn you, this could take hours."

"Shall I bring something from the canteen?"

"We're pretty self-sufficient up here. Oven, freezer, and two hot plates. Lean Cuisine, toasted sandwiches, and frozen pizza. It's better than the Ritz."

"I'll be right there." And she was gone. Jardine gazed at the receiver and shook his head. Was it lack of the ever so slightly depraved Nicola Watson-Hall's superb and no longer available body? Or genuine affection for Kate?

And what on earth could they get up to in the office? Jardine had heard rumors, but not at controller level. That would be too undignified. And what if Steven McCrae barged in, living in another time zone, to find one of his senior executives . . . it did not bear thinking about, and Jardine found himself chuckling at the thought. "Sorry to butt in on a good bonk" . . . you had to laugh. Then he glanced up to see Heather standing in the doorway, ready to leave.

"Anything else, David?"

David Jardine had completely forgotten Heather existed. He stared at her, guiltily. Heather knew all about Restrepo, and one aspect of her job was to keep records of the South American desk's regular liaison with Scotland Yard's Special Branch. And Customs. And Heather too dreamed of, one day, being tapped on the shoulder and led into the world of Real Secrets, which remained almost impossible, since she had no university degree.

Jardine smiled and ran his hand through his unruly mop of hair. "Actually, something rather interesting has just cropped up. And you speak French, don't you? How would you feel about working late? We'll need to liaise with the Swiss service." And, as an afterthought, "Kate's coming up to lend a hand . . ."

Heather grinned and sighed with happiness. The fact that her boyfriend was even then on his way from the Foreign Office to meet her at Brooks's Club in St. James's for a cocktail and dinner did nothing to mar her contentment.

Jardine shook his head ruefully. He was in grave danger of becoming Nice and that would not do. "Okay, go and ask the duty officer, *very* politely, if he could pop up for a quick chat. Plus I need a street plan of Geneva. And the architect's plans of the Hotel Richemond, which is in Geneva. Also please get a cipher clerk up here to net into the Berne embassy and Geneva outstation pronto."

And that was how, by the time the man who called himself Restrepo got off the Swissair DC-9 and passed through Customs and Immigration, a team of SIS and Swiss intelligence service watchers were in place, in and around the luxurious five-star Hotel Richemond, with its stunning view of Lake Geneva and its floodlit, hundred-foot-high fountain.

Jardine was grateful to Andy Laing at Scotland Yard for his information, but he had made the decision, even while they were speaking on the phone, that there was no need to involve police, customs, or any law-enforcement agency in the Swiss surveillance operation. For the very last thing that Op Corrida needed was for Restrepo to get himself arrested. Because Restrepo was to be a major player in the game David Jardine had planned for the Firm's infiltration of the Colombian cocaine cartel. Restrepo, and the man in a Miami jail, code-named "Dolphin."

The northern Spanish town of Vigo is perched on a near precipice, with winding streets leading down to the port below. Some of the best bullfights can be seen in Vigo. There is a bar and diner for local workers, truck drivers, and crewmen from the liners and cargo ships that are the life's blood of the community. It does not figure in any guidebooks or good-food guides, but it has clean, red-plastic-topped tables, wooden kitchen chairs, and a glass-fronted counter, where fresh-caught fish and shellfish are displayed on a bed of crushed ice. No matter the hour of day, Alfonzo the owner always seems to be cooking something on his big, burnt-black aluminum griddle. The wine is in unlabeled bottles, the white a pale yellow color and the red the purple/violet shade of strong paraffin, with a bouquet to match. The beer is cold and Alfonzo stocks a mixture of Spanish and French. No German, because Alfonzo's father and mother were killed fighting for the other side in Spain's civil war in 1938, blown apart or buried under rubble by the bombs dropped by Adolph Hitler's Condor Legion, which was using Spain's ferocious conflict to gain valuable blitzkrieg experience.

Eugene Pearson munched a forkful of shrimp paella at a long table in the back corner, under a faded bullfight poster featuring a matador called Ordonez. Beside him was a crop-haired man of about fifty, wearing a cheap black suit, black shirt, and priest's dog collar, with a small gold crucifix on his lapel. His name was Father Eamon Gregson, and he was a member of the Catholic Church, absent from his teaching position at a seminary in County Cork and under formal warning of dismissal and possible expulsion from his order because of his peregrinations around Europe on Sinn Fein business and the hints and allegations that were beginning to reach the ears of his bishop that he was a senior member of the Provisional IRA.

Sitting facing Pearson was a lean, tanned man who wore a dark blue sweatshirt under a black leather jacket, faded jeans, and dusty, brown leather boots with thick rubber soles. His jaw was unshaven, with three or four days' growth. This was one of the most wanted men in Europe. Gerry Devlin. One of the team who had planted the bomb in the Grand Hotel, Brighton, that had killed several leading members of the British government and just missed Margaret Thatcher.

Like Brendan Casey, he had started his Provo career as a street killer, preferring, like Casey, to get so close he could touch his unsuspecting victim before using the big .45 Colt automatic pistol, a present from the fan club in New York City, to do the business. Two shots to the face would take the back of the head off. Sometimes he had liked to see the look of sudden fear, as the target's last emotion was oh fuck why me oh please God no don't. Devlin had to admit it, he enjoyed that millisecond when he was recognized as the instrument of Republican death.

After all, what was the use of being a fuckin' terrorist if you couldn't terrorize the opposition? Then he had found he quite enjoyed doing it with people watching. At first his own unit, then strangers who just happened to be in that street, or that bar, or that gas station. Then, inevitably, the wives and kids of the subjects, as he liked to refer to his victims. It was like . . . there was nothing to describe the utter power, the orgasmic triumph, of blowing apart some RUC cop, or some carpenter who had ignored warnings to stop working on army contracts, or some Protestant bastard Unionist. While the bastard Prod piglets squealed in fear and the bastard Prod bitch mother-wives peed themsleves in horror and disbelief.

It had gotten to the stage when he felt, more and more, the urge to tear off his black ski mask and point a quivering finger to his face and yell, "Yes! Look!! It's me, Gerard Mary Devlin! The Angel of Republican fuckin' Death!!"

But that would have been a breach of discipline and the Organization would either have sent him off to New York City to recover his sanity and work in some bar, or worse . . . Nobody in the movement would forget the salutary fate of Jimmy Rourke, who got a Provo trial and two slugs in the back of the head for jerking off in the getaway car after doing the business.

So after twenty-nine "contact jobs," as opposed to bombs, where it was less personal, Devlin had gone to

Brendan Casey and Ciaran Murphy and said enough was enough. Could they give him something else? To his surprise, they had said they were putting together a new team to liaise with the Basque ETA-B group in northern Spain. Word had got back that the existing Barcelona unit was drinking and whoring, indiscreet and boastful. One soldier had accidentally killed two Basque students he had been instructing in bomb-making. His laconic signal had been that they had "failed the practical."

Devlin had done Spanish at school, under the Christian Brothers. He had been hidden in Spain on eight occasions when the heat focused on him, the most serious being when word came from a tout who worked in the RUC as an electrician that the SAS had brought a team over from B Squadron—four covert-action specialists, all staff sergeants and close-quarter battle instructors—with Gerry Devlin's death as their single aim.

Not unnaturally, PIRA intelligence took a keen interest in the SAS, which had an aptitude and a taste for ambushing and killing that inspired reluctant respect. Maybe even fear. The Hereford Special Forces Regiment had tangled with the boys on several occasions, and the hard truth of the matter was they had always provided yet more Provo funerals, with few losses to the visiting team, as the SAS was called in the Belfast Brigade of the IRA.

During his eight sojourns in Spain, Gerry Devlin had discovered a natural competence for the Spanish language that had never surfaced at school in Belfast. So Brendan Casey sent him to reorganize the Basque liaison team (this was three years before) with instructions to sort it out, restore discipline, tighten security, and present a plan for further action in support of the Republican Cause.

When Devlin had arrived in Barcelona, the situation was worse than anyone in the Organization had imagined. There were few left-wing activists or radical students who did not know each member of the Provo Active Service Unit by name. And not their cover names, their real ones.

There had been six members of the Active Service Unit, or ASU, and five Spaniards who knew far too much about the Organization. By the time Devlin had finished, all but one of them were dead. Four in a car that crashed through a wall on a precipitous mountain road in the Pyrenees and exploded as it tumbled to the bottom of a ravine a thousand feet below. Two in a gas leak in the Barcelona apartment they rented. One by drowning, and three executed on a remote mountainside on the road to Banyuls, on the French side of the border, after being made to dig their own grave. Executed by Devlin himself, who thus restored good order and discipline. The survivor was a brother of Ciaran Murphy, who was sent back to the Republic with Devlin's coded report.

Murphy's young brother—so shaken he was later transferred to the political wing, Sinn Fein, as a ballot counter—returned to Ireland and at his debriefing affirmed that Gerry Devlin had reestablished the Provos' reputation and standing among the most serious and able of the Basque ETA group, who had taken to referring to Devlin as "the red man the juggler sent." Which was a quotation from Yeats's poem "The Tower."

Now Brendan Casey, who had been educated in Belfast's Long Kesh prison and majored in Kalashnikov, Semtex, Co-op Mix, the *Minimanual of the Urban Guerrilla*, Marx, and Mao, had never known a line of Yeats (except, of course, for "A terrible beauty is born . . . ," which is how the Movement saw itself) and he therefore imagined from that moment on that the freedom fighters of the Basque Separatist Movement had nicknamed him "the Juggler." He was pleased with the sobriquet and took to signing and referring to himself as that. And who was going to point out the chief of staff's lack of erudition?

Gerry Devlin had then outlined his plan for a one hundred percent secure and professional Active Service Unit, which would keep liaison with ETA to a minimum, and he recommended that the unit should move to Vigo, on Spain's northwest coast, where it could arrange a pipeline for weapons and explosives arriving by sea from Ghaddafi and the Eastern bloc, which, at that time, was not yet a dead duck.

The Army Council agreed. Their chief fixer for arms acquisition, liaison man, and negotiator with the KGB and the PLO, as well as with Ghaddafi, was the traveling priest, Father Eamon Gregson. And since the KGB link was drying up in direct ratio to the march of perestroika, he was dispatched to Spain to assist Devlin in establishing the new group, which Devlin christened Lorca.

The need to send someone reliable from Belfast to assist the fledgling Lorca Group prompted Brendan Casey to kill two birds with the one stone, and he ordered his mistress, the seasoned street killer and bomber Rosaleen Hughes, to Vigo, thereby silencing murmured criticism from the more prudish members of the Provisional movement, who did not approve of their leader committing adultery.

All this passed through Eugene Pearson's mind as he picked through the remnants of his supper, sipped his wine, and watched the other two. He had just informed them of the reason for his journey.

The Army Council, he told them, had decided that Lorca was to cut itself off completely from the Organization. Thanks to Devlin's ruthless skill and natural caution, the unit was secure and unsuspected. Devlin and the priest were to set about preparing and establishing a reception facility, with distribution and couriers, to receive and pass on several tons of pure cocaine every few weeks to European wholesalers. Their secondary task was to examine, test, and report on the security of the principal criminal networks they would be dealing with. They were not to deal with any that were not 100 percent watertight.

Pearson had explained the rationale—that the movement needed several million dollars for the final push to take the Armed Struggle to the streets of Britain and make no place in Europe safe for Brit soldiers, or even tourists. The strategy of the big push was that an outraged and terrorized British public would force the government to come to the table. Sod Dublin *taioseach*, Charlie Haughey, and the endless conferences between elected representatives. The Provisional IRA would dictate its own terms to the enemy.

To Pearson's mild surprise, it was Devlin, not the priest, who voiced moral objections, very much in line with his own. Using his relentless legal logic, the judge patiently spelled out the reasoning of the Army Council, emphasizing there was no other way to raise the badly needed finance.

Father Gregson quietly added his support to Eugene Pearson's argument.

Devlin sat, deep in thought. It was obvious from the way Rosy Hughes glanced at him, from time to time, from her table covering the door and the dark street beyond, that they were now more than comrades. That did not bother Pearson. In fact, since they were both normal young people, it was better that they should keep their sex lives within the cell.

Finally Devlin raised his head and gazed long and hard into Pearson's very soul. Pearson stared back, used to the theater of Provo hard men.

"Okay," Devlin said. "We're here to serve the Cause. Give me four days to sever any connection with other comrades. Then Lorca will be alone and unknown."

Eugene Pearson did not even want to speculate on how Devlin was going to ensure that those few Basque ETA guerrillas who had some marginal contact with the Lorca Group would cease to present a (previously necessary) security loophole.

"There's a fellow coming to meet you," said the judge, "from Bogotá. As a matter of fact, he only needs to meet one of you."

"That'll be you, Eamon," Devlin said to the priest, who inclined his head. By Christ, thought Pearson, there's no question who's running things out here. And he knew that his deepest, most secret intention, to somehow scupper this cocaine link, would have to start taking shape very soon. Apart from his strong legal and ethical objections, the Struggle would be gravely damaged when, as inevitably it would, word got out that Irish freedom was being bought with the misery of thousands, addicted to drugs courtesy of the IRA. Too many good men and women had sacrificed life and liberty for the Cause to be thus soiled.

"While you're sorting out your own . . . arrangements," he said, refusing the offer of a cigarette from Gregson, "Eamon and me will buy ourselves a boat and rent an office and warehouse space down on the docks. I've brought some documents with me that make you local manager and supervisor respectively of an up-and-running European haulage and salvage company."

Devlin gazed at the judge like a rottweiler that had not decided if it was going to obey orders or have its owner for supper. "What's it called?"

"RSTE. Routiers et Sauvetage Trans Europe. Head office in Marseilles. It has eight Mercedes container trucks and three tugboats. We set it up three years ago, run by a family with no police record and no overt sympathy with the movement or the cause."

"But Irish." Devlin stared at him.

"As Irish as you, Gerry."

"And what've they been up t'll?"

"Road haulage and salvage. Building their cover. The idea was to use them for arms smuggling. But we already have more bloody Semtex and Kalashnikovs than we know what to do with."

"So this is their first piece of business?" asked the priest.

"They are not to know about this business. All they are doing is providing bona fide cover for the operation."

Gerry Devlin lifted his glass of Coca Cola and peered into it. Then he grinned. "They always said you were a thorough fella, Eugene. I'm impressed. And this . . . business, does it have a name?"

Eugene? Who in the name of God did this Belfast thug think he was talking to?

Pearson smiled back. "Legitimate. Its code name is 'Legitimate.' "

And as Alfonzo, the owner/cook/barman, yelled something in Spanish to a bent old woman who was cleaning the tables, while he stirred a pan of frying prawns, cigarette jammed between his lips, Devlin and Father Gregson nodded their approval.

"Legitimate . . ." murmured the priest, speaking in Gaelic. "I like that."

———

6:48 A.M. Geneva. A joint SIS and Swiss intelligence service surveillance operation had the Hotel Richemond under observation from inside and every street around. Waiters, boot boys, chambermaids, guests, each group had been smoothly infiltrated by the teams of watchers.

Taxi drivers, street cleaners, couples in parked cars, covered the exterior. Motorbike riders and a variety of nondescript vehicles waited to tail the target anywhere he might go.

The evening before, he had booked into Suite 356 and phoned a discreet and pricey madam who had sent him a stunning ash-blond call girl, whose face and figure were known to readers of glossy women's fashion magazines, worldwide. Her fee was $3,000 for the two hours she spent with him. Judging from their conversation, which was, admittedly, limited since Restrepo obviously believed time was money, they had met a few times before. She knew what he liked, and the expressionless Swiss and noncommittal SIS teams monitoring the listening and viewing devices planted in sitting room, bathroom, and bedroom of Suite 356 observed drily that if any sexual tryst was worth $1,500 an hour, the twenty-three-year-old fashion model certainly gave the Colombian his money's worth.

At ten after ten, he strolled into the cocktail bar beside the incomparable Terrace restaurant, looking cool and refreshed and smelling of, reportedly, just a hint of carnation essence, which is what he had used in his bathtub.

His partner was already there, the bona fide manager of the Swiss office of Banco de Commercio Principal, and after a club soda, he had ushered the man into the restaurant where they had dined, Restrepo on Tartar de Saumon and Filet de Loup, sauce Nantaise, his companion on Ouefs en Gelée, followed by Turbot, sauce Champagne. The wine was a 1983 Corton Charlemagne, a smoky but intriguingly tart white burgundy. They also drank some mineral water. After the meal, they had coffee. The Swiss manager of the Banco de Commercio took a cognac, but Restrepo did not.

The bill for the British taxpayer for the two SIS watchers who ate at the next table came to 312 Swiss Francs, which was about $214. It was money that could have been better spent, because Restrepo confined himself to small talk and discussing the Japanese car-assembly project.

Also, and this puzzled David Jardine, his watchers reported there was no sign of the usual discreet, unobtrusive bodyguards, normally the hallmark of a *narcotraficante*, a baron of the cartel mafia.

At five minutes to twelve, the Colombian lawyer said good night to his colleague and went up to his suite, where he watched TV for about seven minutes before going to bed.

At 6:48 A.M., he had wakened, gone to the john, showered, and phoned Swissair to confirm his flight out of Geneva at 12:30 that day. He had then rung the concierge and asked for a car to collect him at ten o'clock, which suggested he had plans before going to the airport.

Dennis Telford, a steady, cardigan-wearing Englishman from the Zurich outstation, remarked drily, "If he's planning another bout of sex, one might have to resort to some kind of tranquilizer. Last night was really far too torrid for an innocent like me." A mild joke, and apparently taken seriously by his Swiss service liaison man, because shortly after eight-thirty, a Swiss probationer arrived with a small pharmacist's envelope, inside of which were two 5mg tablets of Valium. Not only were they the only drugs in evidence that day, but they arrived too late, for the man who called himself Restrepo had vanished, under the noses of thirty-four trained experts in the art of surveillance.

David Jardine sat at his desk, his shirtsleeves pushed back to the elbows, his scar livid with fatigue, and stubble on his unshaven jaw. London was an hour behind Geneva, and it was five past seven when the secure phone rang, linked directly to the SIS operations chief in Geneva. He nodded as the voice informed him of Restrepo's disappearance. He listened and made appropriate noises as the voice alternately explained and apologized. Finally, he thanked the caller most courteously, agreed that all airports and airstrips out of Switzerland, together with land borders, should be watched, but suggested that was a job best left to the Swiss authorities themselves.

"Thanks, Jimmy. Go and grab some rest. Cheers." Jardine replaced the receiver and pushed at his tired face with the heels of his hands. Then he stretched and linked his hands behind his head, not entirely displeased with this turn of events.

He had sent Heather home around three o'clock in the morning. Kate and he had been taking it in turns to grab some sleep and man the phone. He had briefed Kate that the operation was a straightforward exercise in observing the man called Restrepo and monitoring his visit to Geneva. There was no need, he felt, to burden her with more than that. But Kate Howard was nothing if not perceptive and astute. So when David Jardine had taken his first spell of rest, warning her not to waken him unless the Swiss authorities looked like even *contemplating* an arrest of the Colombian lawyer, she realized that, not for the first time, the real aim of SIS, personified by David Arbuthnot Jardine, was to discreetly, and covertly, protect their target from the heavy hand of the law.

At 5 A.M. Jardine had taken over and Kate Howard had slept for a couple of hours in Jardine's inner sanctum of his office.

Now, lying on the quilted sleeping bag on the campaign bed, covered by a huge tartan traveling rug—which Jardine had proudly told her had belonged to his late father's favorite racehorse—Kate lay awake, gazing at the small dressing table, her skirt neatly folded on it, her blouse over the back of a small wooden chair. The sleeping bag and the cushion that served as a pillow smelled of David Jardine. His astringent bay rum cologne, with a faint aroma of cinnamon; his hair, which she remembered from that evening when he had made a pass at her. It reminded her of the scent of youthful hair, some masculine hair conditioner, mingled with . . . body sweat, but fresh. Somehow attractive. She half expected to see a cricket bag, or rugby shirt, lying thrown in a corner, like in her younger brothers' rooms at school. *That* was what Jardine reminded her of . . . a big, overgrown schoolboy.

She had found, when she had been on the Oxford University rowing team, to her confusion and surprise, that some friends of her eighteen-year-old brother could be more attractive, in physical terms, than many of the muscular, handsome giants she was training with every day of the week.

As her final term came to an end, Kate Howard had been contemplating a year-long assignment with an anthropological expedition to Papua, New Guinea. Then her tutor had invited her to dinner at Magdalen College and introduced her to a quiet, articulate Scotsman in his early fifties who listened intently to her various comments on rowing tactics, body language, current affairs, and her plans for the future. He had kind, intelligent eyes, which did not quite hide a ruthless streak, and the suspicion of a lurking temper if crossed by the unwary.

He had told her he worked for the Ministry of Agriculture and Fisheries.

Anyway, about a week later she had received a letter from this man, inviting her, before committing herself to Papua, New Guinea, to make a trip up to London and take an interview with a colleague who might have something of interest to offer her, careerwise.

Kate had gone to London, more out of curiosity than anything else, and had found herself taking coffee in an office in Queen Anne's Gate, just behind Broadway, in Westminster. The Scotsman had introduced her to a woman of about forty with a gentle sense of humor and a habit of holding her head to one side when listening and gazing directly into Kate's eyes without blinking, or so it seemed. After an hour of questions, courteously relieved by casual conversation, they had told Kate that, in their opinion, she could find interesting and rewarding employment within their own government organization. Which was neither the Ministry of Agriculture, nor Defense, although more closely linked to the latter. It was the Intelligence Service, sometimes called MI-6, and Kate, in her innocence, had politely inquired if that was anything to do with MI-5, and what did it actually do?

"MI-Five, my dear," said the Scot, "is the government's Security Service. Its job is to protect the nation from foreign espionage, subversion, sabotage, terrorism, and to keep our most important secrets safe from hostile curiosity. They work closely with the police, in particular, Special Branch."

"Our job," said the tall, gentle woman, in her unaffected, educated voice, "is to do to other countries around the world precisely what MI-Five exists to protect us from. To satisfy our government's curiosity about *their* secrets, which they tend to guard quite jealously."

"MI-Five are the policemen. We are the pirates," explained the Scot with a twinkle in his patient, understanding eyes. "Plus, we get to travel. And we have more dress sense." And from that moment, Kate Howard was hooked. Piracy had always appealed to her.

The Firm liked her and she had risen well, and quite

rapidly, to be one of several personnel executives, at the age of twenty-nine. Responsible for the Personnel Section's part in the recruiting and selection of contract operators, even in the most secret and deniable areas of the clandestine side of her employers' work. She hugely enjoyed being thus trusted and she knew that trust was well placed.

And now, here she was, in the very heart of that area of the service that was her whole ambition . . . Operations.

Or was it merely the threshold . . . ?

Either way, she felt a thrill of fulfillment at being involved, at being part of Corrida. She knew in her bones that if she played this carefully, Kate Howard might one day find herself abroad, *on the ground*. She asked God, in her innocence, to fulfill that wish.

It would perhaps have been better for her if God had chosen that moment to give Kate Howard a sign, like in the Old Testament. A warning.

But in His wisdom, He did not.

Kate had heard David Jardine's end of the conversation with the Swiss station, and it seemed that Restrepo had given everyone the slip and the operation was being aborted. If her instinct was right, she suspected Jardine would be pleased the Colombian lawyer was still on the chessboard, free to play on, and be played against.

A couple of times during the night she had felt something approaching tenderness for the big, complex man who was quietly and steadily preparing, in Corrida, one of the classic coups of espionage, if it succeeded. Despite his transparent interest in her, Jardine had behaved like a perfect gentleman and he had clearly been at pains that Kate should not feel uneasy.

There was a gentle tap on the door.

"Are you awake?"

"Yes . . ."

Slight pause.

"Kate, our chum has vanished. I think we can safely shut the shop and retire to our respective beds."

Kate smiled and rose, splashed water on her face, brushed her teeth, and dressed. Feeling fresher, she opened the door. Jardine glanced up from his wall safe, which he was locking.

"Would you like to come back for some breakfast . . . ?" she found herself asking, and her pulse quickened.

David Jardine grinned slowly and straightened up, arching his aching back. "Why the hell not . . . ?"

Juan Baquero was not the kind of guy to show his emotions, least of all to strangers. He fixed his expressionless brown eyes on Eddie Lucco and ignored the DEA Wanted File the detective was holding up for him to read. His photo, taken at Bergins beer bar on Bayside, in Miami, must have been snapped by some undercover cop. So be it.

Expressionless he may have been, but inside, his stomach was in knots. The *grupo* had a set routine for its contact men working abroad. Normally, they would choose a man and wife, maybe with kids. They would move into a comfortable house or apartment with easy access to an escape route in case of a bust. They would live modestly and without drawing attention to themselves. They would drive unremarkable cars that would have been paid for with cash. They would work in some business that was legitimate, with good reason for sudden travel and high turnover of funds. They would pay social security and taxes and would avoid getting booked for speeding or running up parking tickets.

The *grupo* had a network of such people. Some

would be active, others just getting on with their unremarkable lives, ready to go to work whenever, as happened frequently in the endless war with the DEA, an active cell got blown or even attracted just a little heat.

Now here was this Homicide lieutenant with the Italian name asking about a Señor Enriquez and showing Baquero a secret DEA file with Baquero's photo on it.

Juan Baquero's bowels nearly embarrassed him as the realization it was All Over zapped him and engulfed him in its enormity. For he had a real wife back in Bogotá, and three really great kids, aged five, seven, and eleven. Protected by servants and bodyguards, who were also their jailers, although Esperanza, his wife, would not be aware of that.

The *grupo*'s routine was simple. Now that he was blown, Baquero would, as soon as possible—within minutes even, within seconds, if that were feasible—walk out of the El Paradiso Travel Agency, make no phone calls, contact no one, take a taxi to a helicopter charter company in Manhattan, rent a helicopter from the two gringos who ran the outfit and who knew him from the travel agency, and fly himself to a prearranged location in Long Island, from where he would be flown in an executive jet to Nassau, and from there by fast boat to Cuba, then onto a regular flight to Bogotá, using one of six passports he had access to from the *grupo*'s people in Panama City.

And when he arrived home, in Colombia? He knew his fate would be in the hands of Jesus Garcia, Pablo Envigado's ruthless security boss.

It was all Baquero could do to keep from messing himself, as fear churned his vitals.

Eddie Lucco was still watching him. The bastard was smiling.

"Well now, Juan," he said, in English, "this does not have to be the end of the world . . ."

They were standing in the travel agency's front office. The two men and the girl clerk who worked there had left for the night. Juan Baquero Camacho had noticed the tan Dodge parked across the street, with three men inside. At first he had wondered if it was heat from the Cali families, who, it was rumored, were unhappy with the way Don Pablo's violent war against Colombia's judges and elected government was getting in the way of business. Rumors abounded that the Cali people were intent on destroying Pablo Envigado and that they were quietly checking out his operations abroad prior to taking them over. Which would involve some serious bloodletting unless Medellín issued orders to acquiesce, and Juan Baquero could not imagine that scenario.

In fact, when Eddie Lucco had flashed his Homicide lieutenant's shiny new badge, Baquero's first instinct had been one of relief. Until the sober truth dawned with the revelation that he was wanted by the DEA.

He ignored Lucco and let his gaze wander around the office, with its rack of brochures for cheap vacations around the USA, to Mexico, South America, and to Europe. There was even a bargain flight and six nights in Leningrad, but none of the Colombians in the neighborhood had availed themselves of the offer. Although two Jews from Bogotá had taken the brochures.

He fought to control the trembling in his limbs.

The big detective folded the DEA file carefully and put it back in his inside jacket pocket. His partner, Sam Vargos, stood slightly to one side of Baquero on the edge of the *narcotraficante*'s field of vision. He had not taken his eyes off the Colombian.

Outside, a fire engine's siren was approaching. A laughing, ordinary family of Colombians strolled past the window and paused to gaze at the color posters of sunny climes far away. One round-faced, healthy youngster flattened his nose grotesquely against the glass and peered in, studying, without interest, the two cops and Baquero in his predicament.

"I said," said Lucco, "this does not have to be the—"

"I heard you," Baquero replied. But two cops had come into his shop and they were not here to purchase a bargain vacation to Rio. People would have noticed.

Beyond the window, the kid wailed as his mother tugged him away from the window, leaving an imprint of mist where his face had been pressed. Oh yes, it would not take long for word to get back to the *grupo* that Juan Baquero Camacho had been leaned on by the law.

Baquero turned to face Lucco, summoning up the will to give a cool but insolent response.

"Save your breath," said the acting Homicide lieutenant. "There was a shooting here two nights ago in the alley behind the Chirimia Bar. You play ball, Juan, and I'll send officers to every store and bar in the neighborhood, I'll even go to a few myself. With Detective Vargos. So nobody will get too suspicious about you getting a visit from the cops."

"What do you want? Is it money . . . ?"

Eddie Lucco and Vargos exchanged glances, their turn to remain expressionless.

"I'm outraged," Lucco said. "This is police business. Tell me who this is."

He produced the photo of the Jane Doe and Ricardo Santos in what had been identified as the Piazza Santa Cicilia, in Trastevere, Rome's artists' quarter.

"I never seen them. Don't know." Baquero shrugged. The photograph was the coup de grace, the nail in his coffin. He remembered like yesterday young Ricardo Santos coming to him, meeting him in the bowels of a multistory carpark. Scared out of his mind, for he had lost the girl, this girl in the photo the detective was holding, and he had begged Juan Baquero not to tell the *grupo*, to cut him some slack, just for a few days. And when Restrepo had come to town, like Attila the Hun, for some reason he had never found out that Baquero had stalled, breaking the cartel's strict security rules, to help Ricardo. And with Ricardo dead, so the rumors went, Juan Baquero had felt secure. Only now the cops were here, asking the worst kinds of questions, and already word would be out on the street, he was sure of that.

He was dead. He could already hear Esperanza's howls of grief. Don Pablo might take over his children's education. He had heard the boss sometimes did that.

Lucco leaned closer, speaking quietly, "Okay. Let me make it real easy for you . . . The male is one Ricardo Santos Castaneda. Deceased. I know that . . . Who is the girl?"

Baquero considered. Was there really a chance the cops would give him breathing space? After all, if they visited every business in the street . . .

"What about the file . . . ?" he asked, so low they had to strain to understand him.

"Well, that's a DEA file, Juan. We're Homicide. Catching you is their business, not mine . . ."

Even to a hardened dope dealer and Medellín agent like Juan Baquero, the stone-faced cop could seem reasonable and reliable. It was an essential weapon in Eddie Lucco's armory.

Baquero considered. Would the cop keep his word? And what about the one who just stared and never spoke?

Hallelujah, thought Lucco, he *knows* . . .

"Just you and me, *señor*. Please. *Por favor.*"

"Sam, wait in the car."

Vargos shrugged, dropped his cigarette butt on the floor, ground it with his heel, and sauntered out. The door squeaked as it opened, and again as it swung slowly shut behind him. Acrid smoke from the not-quite-extinguished cigarette stub reached their nostrils. Somewhere outside, a dog began to bark.

Slowly, Juan Baquero lifted the photo from Lucco's fingers and studied it. He nodded.

"This is a girl who came to the city with . . ." He could not bring himself to utter Santos's name, so ingrained was his habit of secrecy and discretion.

"When?"

"Couple a weeks ago. She walked out on him. He was going crazy to find her. But he never did."

No. He never did.

"Who was she, Juan? Tell me who and where she came from and I'll drop the heat, you got my word."

Silence. Baquero was clearly struggling to choose from a variety of chilling options. Then he handed the photograph back, mumbling, "The kid was being taken to Bogotá. The uh, certain people wanted to make her their honored guest."

Suddenly, Eddie Lucco began to see a chink of light. "Honored Guests" was how the cartel referred to its kidnap victims. So Jane Doe, found dead of an OD of impure crack on the floor of a women's rest room at Grand Central Station and now frozen on a slab at Bellevue morgue, belonged to somebody important, important enough to get her kidnapped. And not even in Colombia, but from Rome, in Europe. Jesus. No wonder Ricardo had gone crazy looking for her. And by walking out on him, the waiflike child had condemned Santos to a death that the detective did not want to imagine.

"Who was she . . . ?"

"*Señor* . . . That is all I can tell you." He looked desperate. "The kid is an English speaker. Ricardo said the, certain people, needed to put pressure. On her father . . . That's it." He was trembling at the enormity of his actions. Informing on the cartel had only one future. "That is the fuck *it.*"

"Who is her father, Juan?"

"*Señor,* I do not know. I swear it. *Madre de Dios.* I don't know names . . . I, that's it." Perspiration rolled off his forehead and down his cheeks.

Eddie Lucco watched Baquero closely. There was no more to be squeezed out of the guy.

"Juan, you wanna get into the car and come in from all this . . . ? We got a witness protection program."

Sure, ask PeeWee Patrice and seven dead cops.

Silence. Baquero was weeping, silently. Tears coursed down his cheeks. He sniffed and shook his head.

"You gonna turn me in now, *señor?* To the DEA?" This guy surely had had some good experiences from the police.

"No," replied Lucco, keeping his gaze on the man's face and ready for a gun to be produced. This was just the sorta time a detective could find himself with chalk lines around him on the floor.

Baquero sniffed again, his face wet with tears and stuff. Lucco sighed and passed over the fresh hanky Nancy had put in his pocket that morning. He winced as the small Colombian blew his nose. Then Baquero glanced at him, eyes bright with fear. "And you gonna go around the neighborhood? Like this was for the murder you said?"

Eddie Lucco glanced at his watch. He had promised to take Nancy to see some Woody Allen movie. She really liked Woody Allen, and he pretended he did, for her sake.

"Sure," he said, trying to figure how he could persuade some guys from the 110th Precinct to do that.

Then, "Anything else you wanna tell me?"

"I told you too much. *Ai, señor.* I am a dead man . . ."

"Yeah, well, you change your mind, call me." And Lucco handed the pusher a purple-and-green business card with FiFi Moreno printed on one side and the number of Eddie Lucco's stoolie's phone on the back.

He walked out and straight across the street to a flower shop, signaling to Vargos, who was back in the Dodge, to follow him.

Eddie Lucco kept his word and the street was subjected to intensive door-to-door questioning by a team of detectives and uniformed cops, apparently investigating a casual killing two nights before. He thought about putting a real pro tail onto Baquero but that would endanger his new informant. So when Juan Baquero Camacho left the El Paradiso Travel Agency at eight after seven, he was left alone. His mutilated body and that of his "wife" and Caribbean Indian housekeeper were found at eleven-oh-four the next morning. His hands and feet were bound. His eyes were taped, and his tongue had been cut out and stuffed into the gaping red slit where his throat had been.

"Don't blame yourself," said Captain Molloy, biting into his lunchtime pastrami on rye and waving at Lucco to make a space in the mountain of files and sit down. Outside, in the 14th Precinct's Homicide Department, phones were ringing and detectives punched out reports on the office's three ancient Remington typewriters.

"The guy was dead," Eddie Lucco observed laconically, "from the minute we walked into his place of business."

"And you figure he was on the level . . . ?"

"Sure. Our Jane Doe was being kidnapped on the express orders of somebody real high in the cartel, maybe Pablo himself."

Molloy studied Lucco's typewritten report, smearing the pages with grease from the pastrami. He nodded. "Not bad, for a brand-new acting looie. Now exactly who is this kid's father? That somebody in Colombia would want to put the grip on him . . . ?

"I'm working on that."

"No kidding. Listen, maybe it's time you spoke to some outside help." Molloy meant the FBI.

"Not yet."

"And how does this figure, about the incident at Bellevue?"

"It's a connection. If Santos is dead, and I believe Simba Patrice . . . I think the same people who did that number are responsible for the killings there."

Molloy nodded, chewing ruminatively. After a minute he burped, tapped his chest, reached for a glass of water, and glanced across at Eddie Lucco.

"Okay, Lieutenant. What the fuck are you waiting for? A fuckin commendation?"

And Lucco took his weary self out into the streets of the city and pressed on with his investigation, aware for the first time, with an uncomfortable feeling of apprehension, that his career, maybe his very life, had been inextricably touched by that pathetic teenage corpse to whom he had tried so hard to administer the kiss of life.

Look at the people who had been involved in some way . . . PeeWee, Pig Mulrooney, Ricardo Santos, Juan Baquero. All murdered. Eddie Lucco stopped at a bar with a pay phone and called Nancy at her office. Her secretary told Lucco she was in court. The big detective thanked her and put the phone down. Relieved to have time to figure out how to say it. To tell her she should go stay with her mother for a few days.

For with his inherited Neapolitan streetwise prescience, Lucco knew that his name and interest had finally come to the attention of the Colombian cocaine cartel. And that could be fatal.

13

SINS OF THE FATHER

The dockside at Vigo was hot. The first serious hint of spring sported a faded blue sky, and the muting of everyday sounds that is somehow the companion of real hot weather pushed the stutter of generators, the clanking of monstrous quayside machines, and the occasional blast from some unseen tugboat's siren into a comfortable, lazy murmur. Only the cries of sea gulls seemed as sharp as ever, and the smell of warm, thick, tarlike oil, mingling with the tang of the sea and the harsh aroma of salted, fresh-caught fish, made one feel alive.

Eugene Pearson sat on a rusting iron mooring bollard, his left foot resting comfortably on a coil of hemp rope as thick as a man's leg. He lit a small cheroot, one of a pack of five he had bought at Alfonzo's diner, up there on the cliff that seemed to hang, suspended, over the harbor.

Three fishermen in a small, wooden skiff slowly skulled the craft, low in the middle and high at bow and stern, into view from behind the massive front of a Russian coaster, the *Strantsvuyuzhchik*, which, the priest had informed him, meant "Wanderer." For Eamon Gregson had learned Russian in order to communicate better with the KGB in his negotiations for arms and training facilities for the Organization. "Wanderer" . . . a sobriquet the good judge felt might well be applied to himself, for his life had become a series of peregrinations for the Cause.

Maybe when they were singing, in future generations, when Ireland was one nation once again, of his part in the struggle, they would call Eugene Pearson "the Wanderer." It would have a good, rousing ring to it when accompanied by fiddle and recorder and *bodhrán,* and the voices of a good number of patriots, fueled with just a touch of the hard stuff.

"Will you ever give me a hand with this timber, or are you intending just to sit there contemplating your navel . . . ?" called the priest as he struggled out from the warehouse they had just rented with a couple of long planks, nailed together, on which he had painted the legend "R.S.T.E." and "Director P. Dalton," which was Gerry Devlin's working name in these parts.

Pearson sighed, watching the skiff glide past with its three fishermen, reminding him of that afternoon on the shore of Caragh Lake when he had raised the Ethical Question and had found himself outflanked by the rest of the Army Council.

"Sure thing. I'm your man." He stood up stiffly, squinted in the strong, hot, sunlight, took a last drag of the cheroot, which was only half finished, and flicked it into the harbor. Good God, if only half the fellows he had sent to the cells could see him now . . . He smiled to himself and turned to Gregson, noting with approval the neat lettering, painted yellow and white on a deep blue background, and suddenly found himself thinking of his lovely child Siobhan, and could almost picture her, sitting at the feet of that South American composer on some mountainside *estancia* in the Andes with her precious boyfriend. And his smile faded. The bastard. What right had some dago to steal his child . . .

"Take that end," grunted the priest. "And walk it gently toward the ladders."

A man wearing a camel-hair jacket stepped out from the shadows beside a tall, mobile crane. It was Bobby Sonson, although Pearson only knew him as one of Restrepo's wingers.

Instinctively, Eugene Pearson glanced to his right, and there, sure enough, was a steel-gray BMW 750i sedan, with the other one, the one who had worn a blue blazer in the Georges Cinq a million years ago, who was known to his *compadres* as Murillo, standing by the open front passenger door.

Luís Restrepo (the man half the Swiss Intelligence Service was still combing the streets of Geneva for) climbed out from the back and raised a hand, reminding Pearson of that TV detective, the one with the glass eye and the filthy raincoat whose gimmick was to seem to leave, then turn back and say, "Just one thing, sir," before he went for the jugular.

"How very excellent to see you again . . ." Restrepo called to Pearson, and the judge flinched inside, wondering what fresh horrors the Colombian gangster's lawyer had brought to continue the torment of a suffering patriot.

"Likewise," Pearson replied, little dreaming the nightmare Restrepo was to inflict upon him this time.

Pearson introduced Restrepo to Eamon Gregson, using the Priest's alias of Patrick Dalton. As they strolled around the interior of the warehouse, the judge explained that regular comings and goings of R.S.T.E.'s trucks and cargoes would establish the outfit's bona fides with Spanish customs and local police. The shipments of cocaine should arrive irregularly, by a variety of methods. Pearson had done his homework thoroughly, making full use of his access to Irish Customs and Interpol data on smuggling methods, with particular reference to those the authorities complained of finding most difficult to counter. Shipments of concrete from West Africa, with the pure cocaine packaged in identical sacks, buried deep inside the concrete powder. Furniture shipped from the Azores, Panama, and Latin America by returning European diplomats and professionals who had been working abroad. Religious ornaments whose plaster-of-paris content was fifty percent cocaine, easily separated by a simple technique. His ingenuity was impressive, certainly to Gregson, although Restrepo, while listening politely, had clearly been around the world a couple of times as far as the illegal movement of cocaine was concerned.

Pearson told the Colombian lawyer that the warehouse would soon be filling up with crates and regular merchandise. They would be using eight long-distance articulated trucks to deliver consignments around Europe. As they reached the office area at one side of the warehouse shed, partitioned off by old, dark wood panels and glass windows, he was aware of the two bodyguards standing in the open entrance. Silhouetted against the hot grays and whites of the dock, with just a glimpse of faded blue sky.

The office door swung open and it was cooler inside. Cool and bare. He suppressed a wave of nausea as a black rat glanced at them from one dark corner and scuttled away into the shadows.

"Patrick will be your point of contact here."

"Are you with the Lorca Group, Patrick?" asked Restrepo politely.

"I don't think you need to concern yourself with such

360

matters," replied the priest in fluent Spanish. "As far as you are concerned, I am Patrick Dalton, and my . . . operation is answerable to this gentleman here." He indicated Eugene Pearson.

"All the details regarding code names, recognition phrases, visual signals, and hand-over arrangements for moving the product on to the European wholesalers are on these," Pearson said, handing Restrepo a manila envelope, inside which were two 3.5 inch computer discs. "The code for getting into the program will be given to you when I am satisfied with your end of the . . . arrangements. With the arrangements for payment, and with your security."

"I'm impressed." Restrepo put the envelope into his inside jacket pocket. "But this is nothing more than I expected. Presumably Señor Dalton will arrange insurance for my principals' product for the period between the merchandise arriving here safely and reaching the wholesalers . . . ?"

"Insurance?" asked the judge, slightly thrown.

"Insurance, señor. We are talking about many millions of dollars' worth of product. What happens if it walks? While in this gentleman's safe custody?"

"My life is the insurance, sir," said Gregson. "We are not criminals, you know."

Restrepo gazed at him with amused patience. "You know, one of the leaders of Fuerzas Armadas Revolucionarias de Colombia used the same expression to me. At the time when they were protecting our laboratories in the Cordillera Oriental." He glanced at the open office door. Bobby Sonson was just visible, standing in the warehouse, cleaning his sunglasses with a dark silk hanky. "While I appreciate, and would probably, certainly, take you up on your offer . . ." his dark, flintlike eyes dissected Gregson like a surgeon's scalpel, "my group was thinking of something more . . . tangible. And since your organization has little in the way of funds . . ."

"Well, presumably, we would forfeit part of our financial benefit." Eugene Pearson was not prepared to let this hoodlum threaten an able and experienced comrade like Father Eamon Gregson.

"Your financial reward would not cover the scope of what is at risk here," Restrepo remarked calmly. "Don Pablo has come up with a rather more interesting . . . arrangement." He strolled past them, leaving the office section to its dust and the black rat. Pearson glanced at Eamon Gregson and followed.

The heat on the quayside was quite strong when they emerged from the warehouse. Two Spanish workers had stopped and were staring at the freshly painted sign, and the BMW, and the group coming out into the harsh sunlight.

Restrepo ignored them and, putting on his sunglasses, walked casually to the edge of the dock in the shadow of the tall mobile crane. He stood opposite the prow of the Russian cargo ship, gazing out across the harbor at a white-and-gold Greek cruise liner that was majestically entering the harbor escorted by two fussing tugboats, like terriers trying to corral a thoroughbred.

As Eugene Pearson and Gregson followed, and the two bodyguards discreetly positioned themselves—one between Restrepo and the two Spanish workmen, the other between the BMW and the same two men—one of the Spaniards approached Pearson, who glanced at him coldly, without pausing his stride.

"*Hola, señor . . . Se acuerda de mí? Hay trabajo para nosotros?*" He was asking if there was going to be some work. It was not unreasonable, with the new sign and the obvious preparations to open some kind of business there.

"Would you ever see to that, Patrick?" said the judge,

and Gregson paused to greet the two men politely and explain about the new haulage company and the number of stevedores and porters it might need from time to time. The experienced operator, like Gregson, knew instinctively that any attempt at secrecy would raise hackles and arouse curiosity and gossip as fast as horseshit attracted flies, so he could not have been more open and courteous in his response.

Eugene Pearson reached Restrepo and stood beside the Colombian, who stood, hands in pockets, deep in thought, gazing out at the liner, pink-faced passengers in rows along the rails. Even at this distance, they seemed slightly apprehensive, for few of them were adventurous travelers, and one or two had probably won the cruise in a Sunday newspaper competition. Pearson was discomfited to realize that he was actually concerned about Restrepo's reaction to his plans and proposals for the smuggling and illegal distribution of several tons of cocaine into Europe. For while he secretly abhorred the whole idea and was privately sworn to destroy the Provisional IRA's ambition to grow rich on drug money, he was still sufficiently proud of his undeniable planning skills to be confident that his proposed clandestine cocaine . . . pipeline, was not unimpressive.

He waited, patiently, for Restrepo to make his comments. It occurred to him that this was the first time he had ever met with Pablo Envigado's henchman without some ghastly misfortune or physical violence befalling him.

Not a bad plan, though, he mused. The fellow won't have much to cavil about with a professional plan like that. After all, this is the top echelon of the Provisional Irish Republican Army you're dealing with, Mr. bloody Restrepo.

"I understand your daughter is studying piano under

a very good friend of Don Pablo's," said the man who called himself Restrepo.

And the bottom fell out of Judge Eugene Pearson's life.

——————

The ceiling had a molded frieze running around the junctions with the walls, disappearing where the fitted wardrobes had been added. There was a plaster rose in what had been the center, before the wardrobes had been built. The light fitting was solid, lacquered brass, with three opaque, pale white coral glass or Perspex shades in the shape of fin de siècle–style lotus leaves.

There was a vestigial tidemark where water had once leaked from the apartment above. It had almost gone, and resembled a watermark on expensive writing paper.

The wallpaper was duck-egg blue and faded sand-colored, in a mottled, cloudlike design. His gaze moved from the ceiling to the dressing table, the couple of quite good Regency chairs, which had not been re-covered, and the framed prints of strong, hot, Mediterranean or Mexican narrow village streets with glaring-white stucco houses, red or green doors, and terra-cotta slate rooftops.

Jardine's shirt lay half on one of the Regency chairs, half on the floor. With the exception of one sock, which needed darning, the rest of his clothes were still in the other room. Kate Howard's once-crisp cotton blouse lay across the end of the bed, and he let his mind drift idly over recollections of the last few hours, which had combined tenderness with lust and enthusiasm with invention. Altogether a highly enjoyable respite from the trials of work and a marriage that, while never boring, lacked a certain *je ne sais quoi* on the erotic side.

Lacked a certain anything, truth be told. So David Jardine did not feel the remotest twinge of guilt (something he would feel obliged to mention to his confessor, next trip to Farm Street) as the relaxed, firm, smooth-skinned, and slightly damp body of Kate Howard slept, as comfortable as a child, wrapped around him, legs and arms entwined.

He stroked her hair gently as his mind wandered over his plan to infiltrate either Malcolm Strong or Harry Ford into Colombia, using a convicted criminal to provide a solid keel to the legend, the cover story. The stroking caused Kate to wake, drowsily. Her eyes flickered, and when she raised her head and gazed up at Jardine, he held her more tightly and without more ado they made love.

When the controller West 8 awoke from a profound and comfortable slumber, it was one forty-five in the afternoon and he lay there listening to sounds from the kitchen as Kate made breakfast, or lunch, or whatever.

He hoped she had not realized just how starved of such delights he had recently become, but all in all, the pleasure at lying there in her warm bed, while the aroma of frying eggs and bacon became just discernible, was definitely one of life's great moments. Those little oases of forbidden pleasure really did make life worth living.

But the professional in him was slightly thrown by having broken a personal rule, for this was the first time he had gone to bed with a woman from the Office. Still, provided they both were discreet about it, and God knew that was what they had been trained to be, what harm could it do?

At a time when the commitment against the Colombian cartel was claiming more and more of his time, David Jardine began to persuade himself that such a liaison was just about right for the moment. And who could object?

And could this new relationship damage his chances of rising to the very top? Because oh yes, David Jardine was a damn sight more ambitious than he ever let on, even to himself, half the time. He would make a good Chief of SIS. He had all the qualifications and experience. And indeed, reputation. And Sir David did not sound half so fine as Lady Dorothy. The good Lord knew he owed her that, and being David Jardine, he intended to deliver.

So who could possibly object?

Only the present chief. Sir Steven McCrae. And he had, for all that he was a tight-arsed, prim little fellow, never indicated the slightest frown at Jardine's occasional . . . peccadilloes. So that was all right.

He hauled himself out of bed and padded to the kitchen with its sizzling bacon and eggs and Kate in what appeared to be a very long woolen sweater, busy slicing fresh bread for the toaster.

Jardine stepped through the door. He kissed her gently on the nape of the neck and wrapped his arms around her from behind.

She grinned, trying to concentrate on the cooking. "David, off you go before you get hot fat on any of your more delicate parts. There's tons of hot water . . ."

Jardine glanced at the spitting frying pan with mild alarm. Then he went off to the bathroom, where he ran a luxurious hot shower.

And in the shower, he hummed a song from Purcell's *The Faerie Queen*, which was a sure sign he was in high good humor.

As the water cascaded over him, David Jardine congratulated himself on having landed on his feet. Just as long as Kate didn't take the relationship too seriously. He would hate her to get hurt but he reckoned, shrewdly as it turned out, that she was much too ambitious to let anything get in the way of her own career plans.

An excellent prospect then. He smiled at the recollection of their mutual pleasure and decided there was no harm in this auspicious beginning to Kate Howard becoming the once enthusiastic, but now joyously pregnant, Nicola Watson-Hall's successor.

Humming the bit where Oberon, the Faerie King, slightly drunk, woos his coy paramour, Jardine turned off the shower, stepped out of the tub, and dried himself on an enormous blue bath towel. He peered at his face in the mirror and winked to himself, thinking you lucky bastard Jardine, and felt not the slightest guilt at such chauvinism.

There was thick stubble on his jaw and he wondered if the dear girl kept one of those dinky little razors ladies used to shave their legs and under their arms.

Idly content, he flicked open the mirrored vanity cabinet above the washbasin and there he saw, on the top shelf, and hidden to persons of average height but not to a man of six feet and three inches, not only a man-sized Gillette razor, with spare blades, and a can of Anteus Pour Hommes shaving foam, but nestling in the back left corner, a pair of men's cuff links. A pair, to be specific, of one man's jade and gold cuff links, with the Chinese symbols for *leung,* or dragon, most delicately carved on each surface.

The very cuff links, unmistakably, irrefutably, specially made by King Antiques, of Swire house in Hong Kong, for the then Head of Station, China Station, new chief of Her Majesty's Secret Intelligence Service, Sir Steven McCrae.

Jardine stared silently at the evidence. His admiration for Kate Howard's unswerving determination to get precisely where she wanted in the Firm, coupled with her patience and immense discretion, did little to comfort the damage to his limitless self-esteem.

And like a child whose ice cream has dropped to

the ground, he sighed, the impish tunes of Purcell's baroque opera forgotten.

Damn.

Well, good luck to the girl. He would shave with Steven McCrae's razor, dress and take breakfast or brunch or whatever the hell it was, and leave with a kiss and without rancor, leaving the delectable Kate Howard to discover in the fullness of time that this would be the last time.

What a shame. And not a breath about the bloody cuff links . . .

———

In New York City, Acting Lieutenant (Homicide) Eddie Lucco and his wife Nancy sat in a movie theater in Queens, watching the latest Woody Allen movie. It was three days since Nancy had been persuaded to go stay at her mother's for a few days. She had made it a condition that they saw each other every evening, or as often as his work would permit. Lucco smiled indulgently as Nancy chuckled at innuendos and laughed outright at some obscure intellectual pun.

It was a good place to sit quietly and figure out something that had been nagging at him for the three weeks since the murder of the Colombian travel agent, Baquero. And for the sixteen days since a bloated, headless, and handless corpse had been fished out of the harbor under the gaze of a bunch of tourists peering down from the crown of the Statue of Liberty. The body revealed evidence of a severe beating and worse. Burn marks and traces of sulfuric acid indicated a horrific and slow death. This tied in with the information from Simba Patrice, that Ricardo Santos Castaneda had been tortured and murdered.

The autopsy had shown the cadaver had been in the

water about twenty-one days, which corresponded to the night before the killings at Bellevue Hospital.

So all in all, Eddie Lucco figured the body was that of Ricardo, brother of German Santos, boss of the Miami end of Pablo Envigado's cocaine smuggling and distribution operation, who himself was missing from his usual haunts, and lover (and would-be kidnapper) of the Jane Doe who still lay, ice-cold, in a refrigerated drawer at the Bellevue morgue. Whose father was important— which presumably meant rich—enough for Escobar to arrange for his daughter to be lured from Rome to South America, to be held for ransom. But why? Eddie Lucco had been comprehensively briefed by the DEA's New York office and he knew that Pablo Envigado only resorted to kidnapping in order to put pressure on opponents, like newspaper owners, straight politicians, and judges. Kidnapping a kid from Europe just did not make sense. Unless her father was prominent in the anti-cocaine war. It sure as hell was a mystery.

Two things had to be done. One was to identify the dead kid, which had become Lucco's number one obsession, in order to identify the father, so that he could be given the worst news any father could ever receive. Lucco had already decided he would do that in person, even if it meant flying to Europe.

The second was more worrying. Why had Ricardo been tortured and killed by his own people? Because he had lost the girl. Why was she *that* important? And more worrying . . . Baquero's information seemed to indicate that the Colombian who arrived in New York as the cartel's enforcer had been armed with copies of the photograph Eddie Lucco had found after pulling the Apache from under the sidewalk and painstakingly sifting his hoard of stolen purses et cetera.

If the cartel had access to NYPD confidential information, it meant there was nobody Lucco could trust until that source had been identified and neutralized.

It also meant he could not reveal how close he was getting to identifying the J.D., for that would endanger her father. He could not quite figure out the logic for this last feeling, but his detective's intuition was usually okay on such matters.

He gazed at Woody Allen and Mia Farrow and smiled obligingly as Nancy rocked with laughter.

Manny Schulman.

Or his sidekick, Jake somebody. In the NYPD Intelligence Division's photo computer office. It had to be one of them.

Or both.

Eddie Lucco relaxed and reached for the popcorn. That was why he loved Woody Allen movies. They gave him time to think.

The next morning, he hung his jacket over the back of his chair and went up to the 14th Precinct's ninth floor to chew the fat with the Kovick twins, Joe and Albie, the forensic guys who had so expertly cleaned out, photographed, and catalogued the contents of the Apache's lair, under the sidewalk in the garment district.

For the umpteenth time, he quizzed them about the passports they had found. Many of them unreadable, they had been there so long. But there were none that could remotely have belonged to, and therefore, identified, his Jane Doe.

"Man, you know if it was there we woulda found it . . ." complained Joe.

"Yeah." Lucco scratched his head and accepted a plastic cup of lukewarm coffee from Albie. "I figure the boyfriend Ricardo musta took it off her. When they had the fight and he locked her in the hotel room."

"Word is Ricardo was the stiff they fished outa the river, wid no hands and head," observed Albie.

"So all his stuff could be back in Colombia by now," mused Joe Kovick, who went on, "including the J.D.'s passport."

Eddie Lucco gazed out the grimy window and across the street at a couple of stenographers in the office opposite. One was filing her nails and the other was talking animatedly, gesticulating with her hands and arms. He wondered if the Jane Doe had been a secretary, or a typist like that. "Yeah . . ."

"Which means we're no closer to a make."

"You said it."

"Except," remarked Albie, watching Lucco suspiciously. "I heard you guys scored a name for her . . ."

"Just a first name," replied Lucco, cautiously.

"Like what?" Albie Kovick was the most trustworthy cop on the force. This was what paranoia did to a guy. You could not start suspecting guys like the twins.

"Shivon. Shivonne. I looked through whole lists of names, can't find another one like it." Eddie Lucco gazed thoughtfully at the Kovicks. "It isn't Polish, is it . . . ?"

"Nah. Shivonne . . . Wasn't that the name of Pig Mulrooney's wife? His widow. She was at the funeral."

Lucco stared at Joe Kovick. Of course. "Mrs. Mulrooney. Was she Irish too . . . ?"

"Who knows, but that sure is what it sounded like. Sheevonne. Yeah. Could the Jane be a mick?" This was said by a Polish American detective who intended no offense whatsoever. Eddie was a wop. They were Polacks. Vargos was a spic and Irish colleagues were micks or Paddies. This usage was limited to close colleagues and was intended to indicate ethnic group empathy. It could, however, be dangerous, because if the recipient was having a tough day, you could end up with a black eye.

"So what the fuck was she doin' in Rome?"

"Well, that's for you to find out. You're the fuckin detective . . ."

One thing about NYPD is you are never far from the Emerald Isle. It took Eddie Lucco exactly eight minutes to discover that the name was usually spelled Siobhan. By ten after ten, which was ten after four in Europe, he was speaking on the phone to the Interpol officer in Paris who handled liaison with the Rome police. He also faxed a message to a cousin of Captain Danny Molloy who was an inspector with the Dublin CID, which was their detective bureau. It inquired if any female aged between fifteen and twenty, first name Siobhan, had been reported missing in the last fourteen weeks. Or missing while on vacation in Italy or Europe generally.

Sometimes a case would stagnate for months, then things suddenly started to happen. To Lieutenant Eddie Lucco's mild surprise, this was not one of those times.

Then late at night his phone rang at home, just as he was getting ready to switch off the TV, heave his frame from his favorite chair, and turn in.

"Yeah . . . ?"

"Mr. Lucco?"

"This is him."

"Mr. Lucco, you gotta stop pushing against us." The voice was gentle and reasonable, with a hint of Hispanic accent.

"Who the fuck is this?"

"Oh come on, Lieutenant." A gentle laugh. "You know who the fuck this is . . . So ease off on the kid from Grand Central and do yourself a favor."

"Get the fuck off the line, you scumbag."

"That wife of yours. Nancy. Nice-looking broad. Staying with her mama, that was wise, Lieutenant. Her mama has a real nice place on Long Island. I like the porch and the swing chair. Hey man, let's hope they both live to get to use it in the summer. You might even live to see another Woody Allen movie."

Click.

The caller had hung up.

Bang! Bang! Bang! Somebody was hammering on the apartment front door. Eddie Lucco's heart nearly jumped out of his chest. He scooped up his gun and holster, and by the time he reached the door—the side of the door, for he knew guys who had been blasted through the wood—the leather holster had dropped away and the Smith & Wesson was cocked and held ready, two-handed.

Silence.

His heart was still battering at the wall of his chest. Memories of Bellevue flooded back.

Somewhere, out there in Queens, a fire engine's siren blared and the throaty roar of its powerful motor vibrated in the deserted night streets. And closer, the wheezing of the apartment block's creaky elevator. He strained his ears against those sounds to figure out what was going on right outside his door.

Then the buzzer sounded from the downstairs main entrance. He started, for it was right beside his ear. If he answered, it would give his position away for any wise-guy waiting outside the apartment door.

The noise of the fire engine receded.

The buzzer sounded again, then, from way down in the street, the roar of an automobile engine, a squeal of tires, and another squeal of rubber, and the roar moved away fast.

Silence.

Eddie Lucco checked that all the bolts and locks on his steel-backed front door were fixed. Then he made his way around the apartment, switching off all the lights.

Then he phoned Vargos and asked him to get hold

of some backup and come right over. Also to send two patrol cars of uniformed cops to check on Nancy at her mother's. And to stay around the clock. Then he phoned his wife out on Long Island. She sounded sleepy.

"Hi, kid. Listen, you know being a cop's wife is endless joy, right?"

"Jesus, Eddie, what shit are we in now?" asked the Harvard-educated attorney.

"Nancy, are you keeping that piece within reach . . . ?"

"Yeah, sort of. It's in a drawer."

"Get it right now. Keep it in your hand. Two squad cars are coming to baby-sit. Don't let them in if they don't say the right words."

"Squad cars . . . ?"

And they talked quietly for a few more minutes. Then:

"Eddie, I hear them." A pause as she moved from her bed to the window.

"Stay away from the window."

"I see them. Two prowl cars. One's stopping. The other one is turning around. It's stopped on the other side of the street. Two officers in uniform. One's a sergeant. Hold on . . ."

Lucco heard the window being opened.

"Officer. What's the problem?"

Pause. Lucco strained to hear, without success. Then to his relief, Nancy came back on the line. "It's okay, he said the right thing. Said to tell you his name is Kaplan. Steve Kaplan. From the One Oh One. You still owe him a beer from Da Nang."

Eddie Lucco relaxed. God bless America. That was the fastest response he could've wished for. Cops still looked after their own, for they knew any time of any day they might need the same fast service.

"Honey, I love you. You try and sleep." They both laughed grimly.

"You take care. I'm fine. Don't worry about me, okay?"

What a goddamn woman. He could just picture her out there in '49 with the covered wagons.

"I'll phone back about seven."

"Sure. Eddie . . ."

"Yeah?"

"Are you okay?"

"Yeah, yeah, I'm fine. Nancy, you're . . ."

"Get off the line, you big dope."

"Catch you later." He replaced the handset.

Silence. He half expected the phone to ring. And it did. Calm now, he lifted the receiver.

He half expected no one to speak.

And they didn't.

Just a soft . . . chuckle. And the caller rang off. He laid the receiver back on its rest and sat there on the floor, his back against the wall, his face and clothing drenched in sweat. He held the Smith & Wesson gently in his hands, resting on his knees. And wished there was somebody he could shoot.

Twenty-seven minutes later he listened to the discreet noise of three cars stopping down below, the comforting squawk of radio static, and the sound of car doors closing.

Vargos had a key. They each had the other's keys, for times like this. Lucco relaxed and waited for his partner to make it up to the fourteenth floor. With backup.

The entry-phone buzzer sounded three short, one long, three short. The code he and Vargos recognized each other by. Lucco moved into the darkened hallway. His eyes had become adjusted to the lack of light. He had his .38 in his right hand, a slim flashlight in the other, held at arm's length from his body so that if somebody fired at the light source he would not be seriously hurt. Unless the firer was an extremely bad shot. Or was familiar with the technique.

Footsteps sounded, coming up the many flights of stairs, also the static squawk of personal radios. After several minutes, the footsteps arrived on the landing outside his front door. He could hear the rasping of air being gulped into tortured lungs. Then Sam Vargos's gruff voice, never more welcome.

"Eddie, you okay in there . . . ?"

"Sure."

"We're checking all the way to the top floor but it's clean I think. Hey, Ed, are you expecting a delivery?"

"No. Why?"

"There's a goddamn box at your door."

"Don't touch it."

"Whadda you think my name is . . . ?"

"Why, Officer Turkey, of course." This harked back to a cartoon movie they had sat through five times while tailing a Mafia hoodlum who spent every afternoon watching an endless program of Bugs Bunny and the rest of the Looney Toons funnies in a theater just off Times Square.

"Ed, stay back, go to another room okay? I'm gonna radio for a sniffer dog to take a look at this."

"A sniff."

"Say what?"

"You mean take a sniff at it."

"Yeah, very droll." Then Vargos was obviously speaking to others on the landing and on the stairs. "Guys, let's clear this area right now. Jack, Shaun, nobody on the stairs or in the elevator, let's go."

So the dog came. The sniffer dog. And it was not a bomb in that box. It was a human head. It was the head of Simba Patrice. As Eddie Lucco remarked to Sam Vargos as he took two beers from the fridge and studied the thing, now resting on his kitchen table, "He looked real scared that day in Morta di Pasta, Sam, but not half so fuckin scared as that look on his face right now."

You hard-assed bastard, he thought to himself, and prayed forensic would get here real soon and take this nightmare out of his kitchen. Jesus, thank Christ Nancy was at her mother's. She got real fussy about her kitchen.

He sniffed and his nose wrinkled. He held the cold beer can against his cheek and said softly to Vargos, "Sam, you know what?"

"What?" asked Sam Vargos, who looked distinctly green.

"I think this head is past its sell-by date."

He met Vargos's eye and the two men started to laugh, the perspiration wet on their faces.

———

The rolling, densely wooded mountains west of Santa Fe de Antioquia reach around eight thousand feet at their highest. Rivers and mountain streams flow down the myriad steep-sided valleys toward larger rivers and into the Rio Cauca, beside which stands Santa Fe, an old Spanish colonial town that was founded in 1581 by Jorge Robledo. It is a small town, with a population of around eight thousand souls. It would be a tourists' paradise, like so many places in Colombia, if it were not for the cocaine wars and the Cuban-influenced guerrilla movement, the Ejército de Liberación Nacional, the Maoist revolutionary fighters of the Ejército Popular de Liberación, and a general confluence of bandits and men (and women) who have become used to living the outlaw existence.

Its architecture is stunning, with slate rooftops, white stucco, and four churches of simple, elegant, traditional Spanish design. There is a police presence, and a small detachment of soldiers, mostly conscripts from the Antioquian region, but in the interests of their personal safety those representatives of law and order keep a prudently low profile.

High in the La Cruz hills to the west is an *estancia* and plantation of 30,000 acres where carnations and coca plants are cultivated by a small army of content, well-cared-for peasants. The *estancia* is known locally as La Cama de Mariscal or La Cama Matrimonial after a conquistador and *mariscal*, or marshal, of Spain who, it was rumored, built the original *estancia* as a secret hideaway for himself and his fifteen-year-old bride, Isabella, the daughter of a Spanish colonial governor who had forbidden the union. The conquistador and his child wife lived the rest of their lives high up there in the wooded hills, under the discreet protection of Jorge Robledo, founder of the town of Santa Fe.

There is no historical record of this romantic story, and the location of the *estancia* appears on no known map or chart of the region. Even local peasants and ranchers deny knowledge of the place to outsiders, and any serious questioning as to its location has proved to be dangerous to the health of the inquirer.

There is a long veranda under a sloping tiled roof, and almost English lawns, neatly tended, in a series of terraces, from which a spectacular view can be had of the valley descending, tumbling, down several thousand feet to, in the distance, the pink and rust tiled rooftops and church towers of Santa Fe.

It was on the second of those terraced lawns that two men sat on antique wood chairs of simple design at a table covered with a snow-white linen cloth, a pitcher of lemonade between them. One of the men, wearing a white cotton shirt, open at the neck, where a plain, gold crucifix could be seen, was Pablo Envigado. The other was dressed in the black coat and low-crowned, round black hat of a Jesuit priest. He was very old, perhaps in his eighties, and wisdom mixed with a lifetime's fatigue was etched in every one of the many lines on the aged priest's face.

They spoke in a relaxed but not informal manner, Envigado treating the cleric with proper respect. When a servant approached, or one of Pablo Envigado's close aides, their conversation would cease. And no one knew, at that time, the momentous subject of their discussions. For this was not the old priest's first secret visit to the man known throughout this region, his home territory, as Don Pablo. The two had been brought together by the man who called himself Restrepo some weeks before.

His spies had informed Pablo Envigado that when the priest left whichever hideout he had been brought to for those discussions, the old man would go directly to Medellín for talks with the intelligent and attractive woman the new President had appointed his counselor for Medellín affairs.

Don Pablo had nodded, unperturbed, and thanked his informers for the information. And the priest's visits had continued.

And higher on the terraced lawns, in the shade of the veranda, two men of equally differing ages sat painstakingly at work with pens and ink pads and woodcut blocks and magnifying glasses. They had the lined and Oriental features particular to the Vietnamese of the Hue region, and they were grandfather and grandson. Both wore thick glasses, and the older man had a white, straggling goatee that gave him the look of a Buddhist sage.

They were members of the Nghi family, whose mastery of the art of forgery dates back to the eighth century in the Vietnamese calendar. The CIA had recruited five Nghi family forgers and housed them in a secret place in Saigon, where they spent the entire period of the war creating immaculately accurate falsifications of North Vietnamese, Chinese, and Russian passes, documents, and of course, currency, for the quickest way to subvert a nation's economy is to flood the economy with worthless banknotes.

At the end of the war, certain members of the Nghi clan quietly disappeared from their CIA employment and were subsequently decorated by the North Vietnamese government for their work as secret agents. Others took their chances with the Americans and fled to the USA, where their particular talents ensured they were never unemployed (or short of cash).

With his annual gross profits from cocaine of over $2,000,000,000, Pablo Envigado was able to run his operation like a ministate, with political, economic, security, and intelligence advisers of the highest caliber. Thus it was natural that he would come to hear of the existence of the Nghis, and inevitable that he would acquire them for his own purposes, which were essentially identical to the work they had done for the CIA.

On that day, however, while Pablo Envigado and the aged priest sat deep in discussion down on the terraced lawn, Huynh Tan Nghi and his grandson, Le Xuan Nghi, were laboring over a sheet of writing paper pressed between two sheets of glass, with faded blue ink writing, in English, in clear, neat penmanship, which started "Dearest Mum and Dad . . ." and ended "All the love in the world, . . ." and a spirited flourish of a signature, "Siobhan."

Each man had a writing pad on which he was recreating the dead girl's handwriting. The younger man had mastered her signature to perfection.

Their biggest problem right then was that they had nobody they could trust to advise them precisely what an eighteen-year-old piano student from Dublin would write to her parents from a composer's hacienda in the wilds of the Andes mountains.

14

DICING WITH THE MAN

David Jardine's work brought him into regular contact with the Central Intelligence Agency's London Station, the United States Drug Enforcement Administration, working out of the American embassy in Grosvenor Square, and the U.S. Customs Special Investigations Office.

The influx of cocaine from South America and the USA into Europe and England was quietly reaching unmanageable proportions. Four years earlier, the DEA had warned the British government that lowering street prices of the drug in America would make Colombia's traffickers turn their attention across the Atlantic. Subsequently, at a high-level press briefing at New Scotland Yard, the deputy commissioner, Sir John Dellow, had told assembled editors and media chiefs that the cartel had targeted Europe.

He warned that Great Britain and the Continent should brace themselves for a battle against the violence of the Medellín Cartel, and the internecine warfare that had accompanied the *grupo*'s acquisition of the United States market.

Because such a process—establishing a cocaine distribution network, or series of networks—took time and had many teething problems, public interest soon waned, for the streets were not immediately filled with crack addicts; the promised urban gang battles, high-speed car chases, and general Uzi-generated mayhem failed to hit the front pages and TV screens of a spoiled and sensation-hungry media.

Then certain metropolitan slum areas in France, Germany, Holland, and Britain became focal points for shootings and gang slayings, often by youths in their teens, which, the press were slow to realize, were the harbingers of the very future foretold by Sir John and subsequently rubbished as panicky overreaction on the part of Britain's police.

The murder of the Whore of Venice in Paris was recognized by the French police, and by international law enforcement agencies, as a move by the cartel to tidy up its European distribution plans. The press had shown some interest, but the war in the Gulf was dominating headlines and TV screens and it took, as Judge Eugene Pearson well knew, something like the bomb in the crowded concourse of King's Cross Station and the massacre of a few pretty midwestern cheerleaders to grab the front pages. So the Whore's killing was a three-day wonder.

All this Jardine pondered as he gazed around the long conference table in the CIA briefing room, below the underground carpark below the American embassy in London's Grosvenor Square.

Sitting around the table were the CIA station chief, Jim Polder, his deputy, Ed O'Keefe, DEA boss SAIC (Special Agent In Charge) Elgin Stuart, U.S. Treasury Special Agent Joe Lamb, and a good-looking woman from the U.S. Customs Narcotics Division, Amy Lubitz. Representing the British were Jardine, the head of SIS London Station, Allan Gilbert, and the Firm's Director of European Operations, Frank Cottrel.

Jim Polder's secretary, Denise Stuart, was married to DEA boss Elgin Stuart, which kept the Stuart family well placed to cope with the essentials of embassy intrigue and survival.

"So what was Restrepo doing in Geneva without his usual protection team?" Elgin Stuart pushed an index finger against the woolly stubble that covered his mahogany-brown features. His eyes flicked around the room. Jardine liked Elgin's eyes. The man always looked ready for a good joke, but in fact, when he was amused you were lucky if you got more than a broad grin, and the eyes . . . they never stopped working. The man was a serious professional.

"Possibly," said David Jardine, "something he did not particularly want Pablo to know about."

"Like what . . . ?" Stuart's conversations were conducted in a lazy, laid-back way that promised, at any moment, to develop into interrogations.

"My dear chap. He screws a cover girl. Dines with a, reasonably, legitimate bank manager, then disappears from sight." Jardine raised his broad Savile Row-clad shoulders. "If it's Switzerland . . . could it be money? I hardly think so, for the man virtually prints his own."

Now what on earth have I said? wondered Jardine. For he had not missed the infinitesimal frisson that had passed between O'Keefe, Deputy Station Chief for the agency, and Joe Lamb, from the U.S. Treasury.

"David, if you show us yours, we'll show you ours," said Polder, the CIA boss, whose craggy features and deep, intelligent eyes reminded Jardine of the real spies who used to inhabit the intelligence world, instead of the polygraph-sanitized, moderate-social-drinking joggers and careful drivers with stable home lives who conducted the business now, making safe analyses from satellite photos and electronic eavesdropping.

"Sure." Jardine often lapsed into American speech patterns when dealing with Americans, for whom he had a warm regard. He also had a warm regard for Russians and Colombians and he spoke their languages just as fluently.

"I have information," he went on, "that Restrepo is holding discussions, in secret, with the Colombian prime minister's office. And with the Cali and Bogotá barons of the cartel. To find some formula that will persuade Pablo Envigado to give himself up. Clearly Gaviria's inherited commitment to extradite *narcotraficantes* to the USA will be a major topic of those . . . negotiations."

"And why would the Cali and Bogotá people be interested in Envigado getting locked up?" asked Amy Lubitz, from Customs.

"Because everyone's sick of the violence. In the seven years since Pablo took on the authorities, since his campaign of narco-terrorism started, the whole status quo has been rocked. Cocaine is Colombia's principal export, just as whiskey is Scotland's. Envigado's addiction to the Scarface way of doing things is considered uncultured by the self-styled descendants of the conquistadors." David Jardine gazed around the table. "An accommodation is in the cards."

"How will Restrepo sell that to Pablo Envigado?" This from Elgin Stuart.

"Maybe he won't. But my information is that's what he's trying. And I have no doubt your own sources tell you the same."

"Thanks for sharing that with us, David," said Polder, smiling deep into Jardine's eyes, for he knew that the

SIS executive had not told him a thing the agency was not already aware of.

Then Polder frowned, deep in thought. His own colleagues looked alarmed. Was he actually going to divulge a real secret? To the British? The little cousins, as they were known in Langley, the CIA's Virginia base. The equivalent of a couple of hundred Century Houses. In real-estate terms.

"David, I hear Restrepo has been seen with one Brendan Casey, the IRA chief of staff. This was in Santa Fe, in Antioquia. Some time ago, I'm afraid. It came out of an intelligence trade we've just done with Tel Aviv."

The others busied themselves with files and notes. Jardine held Polder's gaze. This was the CIA formally putting it on record. Putting the books straight. David Jardine knew they had known all along, he could tell, with that almost witchlike intuition of his. It came as no surprise. But Polder's tactics were clear. For he obviously believed it was only a matter of time before SIS found that piece of information out for themselves.

Which probably meant that Polder had gotten wind that David Jardine was very close to infiltrating a black operator deep inside the heart of Pablo Envigado's cocaine cartel.

Now who had leaked that?

He had an instant recollection of those bloody cuff links on the top shelf of Kate Howard's vanity cabinet.

Bloody Steven McCrae. Arse-licking to the Yanks.

Jardine continued to look at Polder. He made his face devoid of expression. Then smiled politely.

"Thank you, Jim. I'll feed that into the system . . ."

And Elgin Stuart nearly smiled.

David Jardine strolled out of the embassy garage, unobtrusively located at the back of the building, and walked into Burnes Mews between Upper Brook Street and Upper Grosvenor Street in the heart of London's exclusive Mayfair district. He was well aware that Brendan Casey had visited Colombia early the previous October. In fact there was not much he and his colleagues did not know about the Provisional IRA. Its members, active and supportive, were all known, even those on the chief of staff's secret list of trained members not yet assigned to Active Service Units.

Their personalities, family backgrounds, and voice-prints were constantly updated. Their whereabouts were generally well known, as were their past histories, including bombings and shootings, as well as participation in interrogations and the torture and execution of informants and other miscreants in the eyes of the Organization.

In fact, just about the only times those relatively few serious, active IRA soldiers went missing from the British war machine's overwhelming surveillance, eavesdropping, and network of informers were the vital times, the lethal times. When an Active Service Unit had been sent to work, either in England or on the European continent, its members disappeared from their usual haunts. In the twenty-year campaign of urban and rural terrorism, the Provos had devised some ingenious and, in other contexts, quite entertaining schemes to give the impression their soldiers were still drawing their unemployment benefits or seeing their probation officers or whatever.

And the detectives of the Royal Ulster Constabulary's Special Branch, the undercover soldiers of the 22nd Special Air Service Regiment and the 14th Security and Intelligence Group, along with agents of the Security Service deployed throughout the postal and communications facilities, the social services, hospitals, pubs, clubs, and brothels, had become just as adept at second-guessing the other side's scams, illusions, and deceptions.

However, bombs continued to go off, visiting cheerleaders and schoolchildren and soldiers' wives and infants were still being visited with death and mutilation. The attacks varied constantly and ranged from the obscenely cowardly, such as tying a man to the seat of his car and forcing him to drive into a military checkpoint in the certain knowledge he would be blown to pieces while his children were held at gunpoint just a mile or so away, to the bold and imaginative, like the mortar attack on Downing Street while a cabinet meeting was in progress. The missiles delivered from homemade mortars hidden in a van that was parked in the middle of Whitehall, where security was tight, and fired straight through the paper-thin roof, to miss their target by only a few feet.

The driver had calmly climbed out, leaving his van at an angle on a busy intersection, climbed onto the back of a motorbike, and disappeared into the morning traffic, the bike wobbling slightly in the rain.

That, mused Jardine, was an attack worthy of any Special Forces unit, and at the SAS memorial service he had been attending at the moment the attack took place, only three hundred yards from its target, quite a few of the men of the Special Air Service, gathered to remember their founder and father of the regiment, Sir David Stirling, confessed wry admiration for the impertinence and style of the perpetrators. On this occasion.

He made his way down Park Street to Mount Street and strolled across Berkeley Square and up the slight incline of Hay Hill to Dover Street, turning right into Grafton Street. He reckoned he would be five minutes early for his lunch appointment with Harry Ford and his wife, Elizabeth, whom he had not yet met.

Eleven weeks had passed since Harry had been

processed out of the British Army and into civilian life. On paper, he was working as a trainee consultant for the Defense Equipment Division of the multinational banking conglomerate IRRC. The personnel and accounts department of the U.K. office of IRRC had all Harry Ford's employment documents, and the security division had processed his security clearance and issued him with a corporation ID card with the third-highest security clearance, which was exactly correct for his appointment.

Somebody called Harry Ford, or so the computers believed, was quietly and unremarkably working his way through training.

In fact, both Harry and Malcolm Strong had just completed six weeks of their Tradecraft and Hostile Environment phase, which followed the five weeks of Evaluation, Indoctrination, and Selection at the Honey Farm.

The training had taken them to Spain, Scotland, and back to the Farm. In addition to practical exercises, where they had been required to infiltrate unsuspecting (but not "hostile") environments, the relentless physical training and instruction in weapons, hand-to-hand fighting, clandestine communication, self medical treatment, and theory and practice of intelligence gathering, analysis, and prediction had continued without letup.

Both men had changed. Harry Ford was less arrogant and ready to rely on his physical competence. Malcolm Strong was more physically self-assured and less quick to assume his was the only intellect in town.

Both had done well, and even Ronnie Szabodo had reluctantly agreed that either man could soon be trusted to do the business without the entire enterprise resulting in catastrophe, by which he meant the death of the operator and political and professional embarrassment for SIS.

The evening before, Jardine had taken Strong and his live-in girlfriend, Jean, who was four years older than the trainee agent, amusing and entertaining, to dinner at an Italian restaurant in Richmond, a London suburb about six miles from Chelsea, where he had never eaten before and would probably not visit again, although that was a pity, for the food had been exceptionally good.

Jardine believed it was time to get to know his Joes a bit better. He knew some agent runners did this much earlier in the relationship, some indeed became great chums with their protégés, but this, he knew from grim experience, could unbalance one's judgment, particularly when that streak of frigid ruthlessness that was the real stock in trade of the office was called for.

So, eleven weeks into their new lives, Parcel and Baggage had proved there was a place for them in the Firm's business. They had been absorbed, all unwittingly, into the ethos of the British Intelligence Service, which was so different from Harry Ford's Special Forces or Malcolm Strong's world of Crown prosecutors, Special Branch, and criminal law. Only now did David Jardine take the step of becoming more than just a cold, charming bastard of a boss—which is how he knew they thought of him—and step into their own lives, their homes and family existences, to extend the hand of friendship and gently let their two women know just about enough to become indoctrinated themselves, members of that very, very small team that was a black agent's limited world. The agent, his trainers, his controller, and, if necessary, his woman. That was the limit of his horizon. No camaraderie. No drinks with colleagues. No office to go to. No group reunions.

Jardine sighed with genuine compassion as he mounted the couple of steps into the lobby of Brown's Hotel. Those poor bastards, he had wooed and charmed them into the netherworld of black operations. He had supervised their punishing training and reeducation. He had made them into potentially able, intelligent, professional spies who would take a life, if need be, in a suburban sitting room or in the washroom of a movie theater, which was altogether different from ex-Captain Harry Ford's gallant and fearless performance as a soldier, behind the lines in Iraq, just fourteen weeks before.

Never mind, he told himself, that's the job and you do it with your eyes wide open, my lad. And he wondered, idly, precisely why Steven McCrae had told the Yanks about Corrida. Or if he had. Sometimes the whole ball of wax just got too complicated. He envied the spies of fiction who seemed to function with psychic computers for brains, and four-dimensional memories.

And there, standing in the lobby, was Ford, grinning warmly, looking comfortably immaculate in a dark blue double-breasted suit from Jardine's own tailor. Jardine knew that, because he had read the file.

"You're five minutes early," Jardine said, gripping the younger man's dry and firm hand, returning with a smile the steady, honest gaze of his fledgling operator.

"Good training." Ford laughed and gestured to the tall, slender young woman beside and slightly behind him. "David, this is Elizabeth. My better half."

At that moment, some waiter in the hotel lounge beside the lobby dropped a tray of glasses and silver and immediately on its heels the hotel fire alarm went off shrilly, then ceased just as abruptly. The whole interruption lasted just under two seconds.

"My word," said Jardine coolly, "talk about alarums and excursions . . ."

But it was a moment he was never to forget. As long as he lived. He should, perhaps, have permitted himself to be more superstitious.

"So you're the man who came down to Hereford that day . . ." said Elizabeth, taking his hand, and she laughed, her eyes full of mischief, in such a way that Jardine found himself laughing too. And she chuckled, holding his gaze, and he grinned like a fool. And she hadn't really said anything terribly funny.

This was the girl he had seen through the window of Johnny McAlpine's drawing room in Hereford, flicking her hair that way he was to come to know so well, and the three young SAS bodyguards had laughed at something she had said. And he had heard her in Sheila McAlpine's kitchen. And Sheila had been animated and amused.

Then, where the hell was it? Yes, in the Pizza in the Park, one Sunday a few weeks back. Elizabeth Ford was the girl with Dick Longstreet, the former U.S. Ambassador to London, her stepfather. And he had been laughing at some comments of hers as she had leaned across the table and flicked her hair and angled her head that way that David Jardine was to come to know so very, very well.

"I must plead guilty," he said. And he never said a truer word.

Harry Ford sipped his gazpacho and gazed around the restaurant at Brown's Hotel. He had never been there before but he liked the space and old-world plush, the paneled walls in the lobby and the well-mannered deference of the staff. For Harry liked the quality things in life. Appreciated them. And he was pleased that the SIS contract was paying him almost twice what his pay had been as a captain in the Special Air Service. Most of which he would be able to bank, he had worked out, because he would be off on this daring mission old Thunderbox, the nickname Baggage had coined for Jardine, had recruited them for.

He watched Jardine with interest as the man relaxed and listened patiently to Elizabeth, whose Texan charm had been honed by an exclusive school in Virginia and at Vassar and whose mind had been schooled at Lady Margaret Hall, Oxford.

Despite her breeding, her good looks, and her barely restrained energy, Elizabeth Ford had rare common sense, inherited, Harry had decided, from her Scottish ancestors, who had arrived in America in 1657. Her mother had been born a MacPherson, descended from some of the first MacPhersons in America, who had pioneered their way to the Mexican border and had created a minor dynasty before losing most of it in the Wall Street crash of 1929. Elizabeth's mother had married a young medical student, James Leadbitter, who had gone on to become a wealthy surgeon before his death from cardiac arrest in 1980.

Leadbitter had been in the army reserve, and he had volunteered for service in Vietnam, as a surgeon, rank of major. Thus Elizabeth was born on the base at Fort Worth, on June 14, twenty-five years and eleven months before this lunch with a senior officer of the British Intelligence Service.

The senior officer seemed amused at something Elizabeth had just said. She flicked her long hair and glanced at Harry in a way that still made him feel a tug of adoration. With just a touch of lust.

"David's been telling me who you're working for. Harry, I'm deeply jealous. I spent three years at Oxford just waiting for someone to ask me to do something like that."

Her voice was deep, Jardine noted. With a hint of something . . . animal. The girl had a way of addressing one with an elegant sincerity that barely disguised a wicked sense of humor. And the eyes communicated wisdom, together with a degree of vulnerability that was not unattractive.

"She means she's not impressed," said Harry Ford.

"She is actually . . . terribly impressed," his wife

said. "I mean, has *anyone* ever said something sensible when you tell them this sort of thing?" Elizabeth turned to watch David Jardine with an earnest expression.

Jardine liked her straightaway. Pleased that his Joe should have such a wife, for a Joe's most deeply personal life, his woman, was fairly vital. It was fairly vital for the Joe to have a stable and rock-solid relationship to think about when he was so very far away, alone, and, there was no way to duck this, in grave and constant danger.

"It's really no big deal." He smiled. "Most of it is shoving paper around. Meeting people on boring committees. Harry's luckier than most. He's going to travel quite a bit."

Her eyes did not miss a trick. She glanced at Harry with just a trace of concern, of . . . foreboding. Jardine realized he was going to have to stay wide awake with this Elizabeth Ford. She turned back to him. "And exactly how dangerous is this boring new job?" The eyes said I'll kill you if he gets suckered into something stupid.

Jardine held her gaze.

"Darling, really . . . I'm a big boy," protested Harry.

Without looking at her husband, Elizabeth said, "No, you're not. I know about spies, my stepfather was an ambassador." She searched David Jardine's face, scanning it like a Gypsy. He felt she was getting too accurate a reading.

"Elizabeth . . . we're very glad to have Harry in the service. He was doing much more dangerous things before. In the army. I don't know how much you know about that . . ."

He glanced around for a waiter, using his apparent distraction to observe how they handled his remark.

SAS soldiers were all positively vetted by the Security Service and they were, to a man, as close-mouthed as nuclear submariners. Their families rarely knew where they had been or what they had been doing. That was the legend. In fact, the more sensible of them sometimes let their wives know just enough to feel part of the regiment family. And some of the more long-serving soldiers' wives knew a great deal.

Harry Ford, trained to conceal his feelings, both by his army undercover experience and by the Honey Farm, did not bat an eye. Elizabeth did not glance at her husband. She merely watched Jardine until he had attracted a waiter, who was now hurrying over.

"Obviously more than you read in the papers," she said, "but not much. They're reading more in *Newsweek* about what the regiment did in Iraq than any of us down in Hereford have heard."

Not bad, thought Jardine. If only she spoke Spanish they could have gone in as husband and wife. He recognized a woman of spirit and, he suspected, of courage, when he saw one.

"Well, Elizabeth, he was appallingly brave. If I hadn't stolen him for a life in the shadows he would have been highly decorated."

"But he is going to be." She glanced at Harry proudly.

"I'm sorry?"

The waiter reached Jardine's side. "Sir . . . ?"

"I wonder if we could have a bottle of the Pichon Longueville '83. I hadn't realized you had it on the list."

"Of course, sir, will that be instead of the Bon Dieu?"

"Yes. Thank you."

The waiter moved away. Elizabeth Ford continued, "Sheila McAlpine took me aside and told me. Maybe I shouldn't say . . . Harry, is it all right?"

The young man nodded and remarked to Jardine, "Elizabeth told me this morning, didn't you know?"

"I don't keep up with the military, we hardly ever meet." Jardine felt a hot anger rising. What the hell was

Johnny McAlpine, the commander of 22 SAS, thinking about? The whole idea was for Captain Harry Ford to disappear from notice.

"MC. Military Cross. It's being announced next month, along with all the other Gulf awards." Harry looked as pleased as a schoolboy. "And I thought they'd passed me by."

"Congratulations, Harry, I'm delighted for you. Having read your operational history, I would say it's long overdue." And David Jardine grinned warmly, gripping Harry Ford's fist. He made a mental note to have the man's name removed from any published list. "You see?" He smiled at Elizabeth, who seemed aware that he was concerned. "He won't be doing anything remotely like that for us . . ."

And she smiled and nodded, as if to say "Oh yeah . . . ?"

The lunch continued and it was a success. Jardine swiftly got over his small rage. He realized that if he had a fault (if? he knew he had hundreds) it was that he was obsessive about having total control of his operators. It was for their own good, and for the watertight requirement of the office. So Johnny McAlpine had rewarded a brave officer. The man deserved no less. And Johnny had gently cocked a snook at SIS, which the Special Forces boss did not consider to be a superior organization. Finally Jardine smiled and relaxed. His aim was to bring Elizabeth just sufficiently into the fold, to feel SIS had accepted her as well as her man. It was common sense, it meant Harry did not have to lie to her about his employment, and it meant she could be gently indoctrinated into the very real necessity to keep her husband's SIS connection absolutely secret.

By the end of the meal, as they sipped coffee and the remains of the second bottle of claret, Elizabeth leaned back in her seat and lit a cigarette. Jardine wished he could ask for one, but he was trying, yet again, to give up.

"There are a couple of people in the office I would like you to meet, just socially. So that you get the measure of the sort of people we are, Elizabeth. Also so that you can have a point of contact. We take very great care of our own. And when Harry is away, training or whatever, I want you to feel the family is always here to help. Whether it's some problem with funds or just a shoulder to cry on. Okay . . . ?"

She examined his eyes. Decided he meant what he had said, and smiled. "Thanks. I felt kind of . . . deeply suspicious, I guess. You people do not have a wonderful reputation in certain quarters."

"Really . . ." Jardine held her gaze. "I have no doubt we deserve that."

And after a moment, she shook her hair off her face and laughed.

Harry gazed at her like a man on his honeymoon, Jardine thought.

He never did understand what had started, even then, or what was to happen in the weeks to come.

———

Mhairaid Pearson was in seventh heaven. Margaret O'Shea, wife of Padraic, and Deborah Browne, wife of Desmond, the millionaire bloodstock dealer with a stud on the Dingle Peninsula, were in the sitting room (Mhairaid knew it was infra dig to call it a lounge) taking afternoon tea from the china Eugene's grandmother had left them. It was Delft porcelain and a collector's dream. But conversation was not about the tea service. They were talking about the news, just announced that morning on the radio, that Padraic O'Shea had been elected leader of Fine Gael, the main opposition party in the

Daíl, the Irish parliament, and with current polls showing Charlie Haughey's ruling Fianna Fail party dropping
in the voting forecast, it was a fair chance that Padraic
would be next Prime Minister, the *taioseach*. Excitement
was high.

"Margaret, I can just see you. You'll be far too grand
ever to speak to the likes of us . . ." Deborah leaned
toward Mhairaid and jogged her saucer and cup at her
like a tipster at Cork races. "Make the most of it. This
time next year she'll be with the prime minister of
Pakistan's wife or out shopping in Washington with
Barbara Bush."

And then the phone rang.

"Excuse me," said Mhairaid, and crossed to the old
rosewood escritoire, inherited from her great-uncle
Colm, the one who had the big Georgian house in
Connemara, godforsaken place. The wood had a fine
patina on it. Mhairaid cherished the notion she could
get about four thousand for it at auction. But she would
never have parted with it.

She lifted the reciever. "Hello . . . ?"

"Mhairaid, good day to you . . ." It was the future
taoiseach himself.

"My word, Padraic, you're getting so famous I
thought you would have a flunky to do your phoning for
you. Is it Margaret you'll be wanting, she's right here."

Muffled chuckle. "As a matter of fact, it's Eugene. I
phoned the court but they said he's taken a holiday.
Where is he? Fishing, I suppose . . . Tell him I want a
big, brown trout would you?"

"He's taken a few days off, but he's due back anytime
now. I'll get him to phone you, will I?"

"Tell him I'm counting on him joining my team,
Mhairaid. He's been just the judge for these troubled
times. No fear, no favor. And he'll be just the attorney
general for us, if we get in next time."

Mhairaid's heart beat faster with pride. "I'll get him to phone just as soon as he comes in."

And she hung up, turning to the others. Smoothing her skirt fussily. She smiled, brightly, "That was your Padraic, Margaret. It was Eugene he wanted . . ."

And Margaret smiled back knowingly. They didn't mean to exclude Deborah from their exclusive places on the inside track, but everybody loved to have a secret, after all.

Meanwhile, at exactly that moment, Judge Eugene Pearson was standing in a storeroom above a famous Dublin bookshop near the university. Books and boxes of books were piled high against the walls and in rows throughout the room, making alleys. Quiet, dusty alleys of text books and biographies and histories and translations and reference books covering every conceivable discipline.

Pearson stood in one of those rows, hidden from the three old Georgian windows that were too grimy and dusty for anyone to see through, in any case.

His battered leather traveling bag was on the floor beside him. He sweated slightly in his raincoat, the collar haphazardly turned up, rainwater dripping from the hem, making mercurylike globules on the book-dusty floor.

His necktie was slightly askew. And a vein on the side of his temple was prominent, registering every beat of his pulse, which a medical man would have guessed as being about ninety to the minute.

Facing Pearson was the lean, bearded, pipe-smoking Brendan Casey. Two quietly dressed Provo wingers relaxed on the landing outside the storeroom door, blocking the only approach from a steep flight of polished wood stairs leading up from the cashier's Dickensian office on the ground floor.

Casey filled his pipe and gazed at Pearson through his gold-rimmed aviator glasses.

"And he gave you a *letter?*" he said, sympathetic and incredulous.

"He said Siobhan is staying, studying, at a very good friend of Pablo's. Pablo Envigado."

"Yes. Envigado knows many people . . ."

"In the name of the Blessed Virgin, Brendan, the bastards have kidnapped my daughter!"

"Did they say that, Eugene?" Casey fumbled in his tweed coat pocket and fished out a tobacco pouch.

"Not in so many words, but that gobshite Restrepo, he hands me—me, the child's father—a letter she wrote and asked somebody to post to me."

"Sure, maybe they were just being helpful. Saying listen, Eugene, your daughter's in a strange land on the other side of the world. And since we're doing stuff together, we'll make sure she's all right . . ."

"And suppose something goes sour? Suppose we cut loose from the cartel? What then?"

Casey held a burning match over the bowl of his Peterson pipe and sucked in a calculated fashion. Soon the tobacco had taken alight, and thick puffs of aromatic smoke wove layers of haze around the book alley. He seemed deep in thought. Then finally his eyes lighted on Pearson, as if he had just remembered the judge was still there, and distraught.

"Well now, Eugene," he said. "It'll never come to that, so Siobhan will be fine. And probably a damn better musician for the experience."

Eugene Pearson stared at Casey, who met his gaze innocently but transmitted a cold message. The bastard. This was all part of his scheming. He had second-guessed Pearson, realized the judge would scupper the cocaine plan, probably most ingeniously and unattributably, if he could. And it was Casey who had arranged with Restrepo for Siobhan, his darling baby, to be lured to South America—Venezuela or Colombia, it hardly seemed to matter—and held hostage until such time as the Organization had its cocaine program up and running, and set up by the man the London *Daily Telegraph* had hailed as the enemy of the IRA, the voice of reason and maturity in Dublin justice.

Pearson's eyes narrowed as he stared back at Brendan Casey, whose demeanor was just short of . . . mocking. There were men in Irish prisons who would remember that same expression of Pearson's until the day they died.

"I do expect the full cooperation of the Organization in securing her safe return to Dublin. Believe me, Brendan, neither you nor your sick killers will survive any other course . . ." His voice was so low, so filled with bile, so potent with . . . confident threat, that Casey, who was used to life on the edge, felt the putrid breath of that pale, skeletal goddess called Fear.

It was the moment when each knew one would not survive this business.

"Fine, Eugene. We understand each other. I'm glad the Vigo arrangements are going so well."

He paused for a moment, studying the judge's face. Then he smiled coldly. "And you must be too . . ." And Brendan Casey, chief of staff of the Provisional IRA, turned and strolled out of the storeroom, taking his wingers with him. Leaving Judge Eugene Pearson, perspiring, heart racing, dripping rainwater on the dusty floor and wreathed in a haze of pungent tobacco smoke.

"Whadda you wanna do? You wanna come off the case?" Captain Danny Molloy tried to relight the remaining three inches of a six-inch Swan cigar, glancing across at Acting Lieutenant (Homicide) Eddie Lucco.

Lucco had cut himself shaving. He had not slept the previous night, driving out with five colleagues for escort—and those were guys on his squad doing that in their own time, just like they would expect from him—to Nancy's mother's place on Long Island, where he had explained to his wife that he was on a case where the lowlife concerned had threatened to harm her. And they had the ability to do so.

Nancy had listened carefully, without interrupting. Eddie Lucco had gotten the idea she was listening more like the increasingly successful attorney she was becoming than Mrs. Eddie Lucco, wife of a New York cop.

He had explained about the Bellevue massacre, about PeeWee, and Baquero the Colombian travel agent, and about Simba Patrice; and about the phone call that showed the Colombians even knew the two of them had been to a Woody Allen movie; and how a mutilated, headless, and handless cadaver fished out of the harbor below a gawping group of tourists on the crown of the Statue of Liberty was most probably that of Ricardo Santos, who was a tight member of the cartel but had pissed off Pablo Envigado in some particular. Nancy had pushed a spoon around her mug of coffee—it was ten after four in the morning—and had examined her wedding ring thoughtfully, turning it around on her finger as if she had just discovered it. Then she looked him straight in the eye.

"What the fuck is this leading up to, Eddie?"

"Hey, come on gimme a break—"

"Are you trying to tell me we have to lay low for a while? If that's what you're leading up to, fine."

"No kidding . . . Nancy, that's great."

"But if what you're leading up to is that I, Nancy Lucco, née Starshinsky, am to be taken off to some log cabin in Vermont, or worse, an apartment in Seattle, forget it, buster."

"Nancy, don't be stupid."

"Don't call me that." Nancy hated being called stupid. She said it was worse than any cussword.

"Okay, okay . . . But honey—"

"Honey is worse."

"Nancy—"

"Better."

"Nancy, gimme a break. I gotta job to do."

"Me too."

"I just don't wanna get you hurt."

"Ni moi non plus."

"Say what?"

"I don't want you hurt."

"I can handle it."

"Me too."

They were both angry, staring aggressively at each other across the table. They were in her mother's kitchen. The house was infested with cops. The two patrol cars out front. Lucco's five colleagues, including Sam Vargos, in the front room, watching a game show in Spanish on the TV with the sound turned real low in order not to waken Nancy's mother, Mrs. Starshinsky, who, incredibly, was still fast asleep.

"Aw, Christ, Lucco . . ." Nancy suddenly had tears in her eyes. Lucco's family name was reserved for serious stuff. "What the fuck is goin' on here? Just yesterday we were at the movies."

"Day before."

"Yeah, yeah, be a cop if it makes you feel good."

She pushed a tear off her cheek. Eddie Lucco's heart melted and he leaned across the table and kissed her, hard but gentle, on the mouth, then held his cheek close to hers. He could feel the cold, wet salt of her tears and his throat constricted. What a fuckin mess.

Nancy whispered, nuzzling her face to his, "But if you're not coming, I won't go. You work, so do I. We don't let some cheap hoods send us running for the hills, Lucco. Not you. Not me. Now do we go to bed here or at our own place, for I gotta get to court at ten in the morning . . ."

"We can stay at Sam's sister's, she has a place in the Bronx. And you'll put up with two cops around you, one will be a woman, around the clock."

"You knew I wouldn't go away. How come . . . ?"

"Because that would be sensible . . ."

. . . As Eddie Lucco watched Danny Molloy puff on his cigar, on the frayed end of a piece of cigar, he smiled at Nancy's spirit and worried about her. She would be in court right now.

"No, Danny. I want to stay with the case. I figure maybe I'm getting someplace . . ."

Molloy sucked on the cigar and wrinkled his nose, taking the butt out of his mouth and staring at it with a degree of hostility. He nodded.

"Like where exactly?" His pale blue eyes swiveled to fix on Lucco.

"Okay the *grupo* has caused multiple homicides, including the murder of seven cops, and tortured and killed one of their top honchos. Why?"

Molloy looked at him askance, as if to say I don't fuck with rhetorical questions.

Eddie Lucco shrugged. "Because they don't want the Jane Doe to be identified. Why?" He flinched as Molloy's eyes narrowed. "Because they don't want her next of kin to know she's dead . . ."

Silence. The big Homicide cop could be stubborn at the damnedest times. He took off his watch and held it to his ear, listening intently. And asked the captain, "Are there thirty days in this month or thirty-one? I can never remember . . ."

Molloy gazed at the damp and frayed end of his relit cigar. He threw it across the room into a metal trash can, drab-green in color.

A clock on the wall clicked its minute hand one more minute onward. Outside, the wail of a squad car, rapidly dying away.

"Okay, wiseguy. Why?" asked Molloy.

Lucco smiled inwardly. "Because she was being kidnapped, taken to Colombia by Ricardo. Her father is somebody in Europe."

"What part of Europe?" asked Molloy, and Eddie Lucco, about whom the Colombian lowlife suddenly knew everything, including about his mother-in-law's porch seat and when he went to the fuckin movies, decided this was not a good time to reveal just how close he was getting to an ID.

"I'm working on it."

"I heard word you got the Jane's first name."

"Sure. It's Siobhan."

"Which I heard you found out is Irish. You could've asked me. I march in the parade, goddamnit."

"Maybe. You know Europe, they could be living in Italy, or anyplace."

"So you ain't got a definite lead . . . ?"

"I'm working on it."

"Okay, you got seventy-two hours, then we get into bed with the Feds. City Hall is going apeshit about results, Eddie. Get me some collars, charge some dumb spics, I gotta produce something for the press. This is not a good year to have seven dead officers and nobody in the slammer."

Lucco stared at his chief. The wall clock clicked on another minute. "Well, maybe I should shoot a couple or three, resisting arrest. How about three with serious histories? Three from Bogotá or Cartagena, I know a couple of short-order cooks work a chophouse over in

Queens. Sam and me could stage a gunfight. Display the cadavers to the 'Six O'Clock Show.' Case solved."

Molloy was bent half out of sight, rummaging through a cardboard carton under his desk. Eventually he surfaced, pink faced, with a whole fresh five-pack of Swan cigars. He blinked as he watched Lucco, not taking his eyes off the acting lieutenant as he unwrapped a cigar.

"You had a tough night, kid. But that's no excuse for insulting the badge. Things is tough enough."

He fumbled for his gas lighter. Flicked at it. The flint was gone. He watched as Eddie Lucco laid a book of matches from the Chirimia Bar on the desk and pushed them toward him.

"It was a dumb thing to say," said Lucco.

"Accepted. Now get outa here and drink some strong coffee and do your goddamn job. And Eddie . . ."

Lucco stood up, feeling childish and stupid. "Uh-huh?"

"Some fuck in this New York Police Department is second-guessing you and feeding stuff to the fuckin enemy. I want you to know I made a confidential request to Internal Affairs. They'll find out who it is. In the meantime, watch your ass and don't forget to sleep a couple of hours from day to day . . ."

Lucco met the captain's unblinking gaze. The man had seen it all before.

"Sure thing." And he turned and walked out.

In the precinct garage he climbed into his tan Dodge, then changed his mind and borrowed a car that belonged to the Vice detail, a dark green Mustang with a big V8 under the hood. As he drove out into the streets of New York, his own order of priorities was different from City Hall's. Number one, I find the worm in the apple. He'd been kind of busy, but events last night had pushed identifying the *grupo*'s link into NYPD right to the top of Eddie Lucco's personal list.

He swung the Mustang left into the traffic and headed for the offices of NYPD Intelligence Division. Manny Schulman. Or his assistant, Jake. Photographic computer librarians.

You wouldn't need to be a detective to work that one out.

Huynh Tan Nghi, white-haired and wispy-bearded, bore a remarkable resemblance to Ho Chi Minh, a fact that Saigon's CIA operatives used to joke about when he worked for them on the top secret counterfeit program, code-named "Arapaho," during the Vietnam war. He had two of Ho's characteristics, the ability to survive in a hostile environment and the knack of keeping discreetly in the background.

He sat at his work table near the veranda of the *estancia* at Cama de Mariscal, high in the La Cruz Hills, with a spectacular view down the valley to the meandering Rio Cauca and the pink and rust rooftops and white church towers of Santa Fe, in the province of Antioquia. He and his grandson, Le Xuan, had perfected the handwriting of the girl, and they had prepared three postcards saying simple things like "weather fine," "South American food is terrific," and "hospitality here is great." The signature "Siobhan" was now natural and indistinguishable from the sample letters Señor Restrepo had brought back from his last trip but one. Huynh was aware that visit had been to New York, but he was careful, being a survivor, not to admit to the knowledge.

So he worked patiently at the address for the postcards: Mr. & Mrs. Eugene Pearson, 54 Phoenix Road, Dublin, Eire, and in brackets [Republic of Ireland]. At no time did he permit himself to wonder why he was doing this particular work of forgery.

As he worked, white-jacketed servants prepared a table on the next terrace. White linen tablecloth and three comfortable chairs. A pitcher of yogurt drink, peach flavored, which was Don Pablo's favorite, a pitcher of iced tea, and a picnic cooler stocked with Corona beer, which was for Señor Jesus Garcia, the *grupo*'s security boss. The pitcher of iced tea caused Huynh's otherwise inscrutable face to cloud with mild apprehension. Señor Restrepo was the one who drank iced tea, and Huynh had a feeling in his bones that the item of forgery he was engaged upon might be his last unless he contrived to work his old trick of remaining unnoticed.

Restrepo was a type he knew well; Saigon had had its share of brilliant psychopaths, both with the Viet and with the Americans. And the French. And the Russian illegals, whose papers he had been able to provide, unknown to his CIA employers.

And Huynh knew that there was a strong chance that Restrepo might have a sudden notion to have him terminated so that the secret of his work on those postcards would die with him. Why else had his grandson Le Xuan been excluded from access to the family Pearson's address in Dublin, Eire?

So as Pablo Envigado, Jesus Garcia, and the man who called himself Restrepo emerged on the wood-and-white stucco veranda, conversing easily among themselves, old Huynh Tan Nghi quietly and unobtrusively folded his work materials and vanished, ghostlike, from the grassy terrace, its lawns cut as immacuately as, according to Don Pablo, they were in English aristocrats' country *fincas*.

Pablo Envigado poured some peach yogurt drink into a glass. His crisp white shirt was open to below the breastbone and a fine gold chain was visible, from which hung his flat emerald St. Christopher, a present from his hometown of Sabaneta, from where he took his family name—grateful for the schools, hospital, football stadium, houses, and concomitant prosperity he had given to it from his vast cocaine wealth. He watched Restrepo carefully as the lawyer relaxed in his chair. The *padrino,* as Envigado was known among his own, trusted Restrepo more than his own family. No one had proved himself time and again more than Luís. But this Irish connection worried Envigado. He had met Brendan Casey and had not been impressed. The man was a political zealot who imagined that a twenty-one-year campaign of mainly stupid bombings and killing that had gotten precisely nowhere would suddenly, as if by magic, achieve some kind of result.

Envigado did not like political zealots. Colombia had been torn apart by them until they had kidnapped the daughter of a member of the *grupo.* He grinned to himself as he remembered how very quickly their zeal had evaporated as the cartel's soldiers demonstrated such unimaginable ruthlessness that the girl had been returned pretty damn quick. And the Marxist and Maoist freedom fighters had come to an accommodation with *el grupo.* Namely, they provided areas of Colombia where no cops or soldiers dared to go, and men to guard the coca-processing laboratories.

Casey was a *cabrón*, an asshole. But useful, for the IRA had certainly run rings around the British and their European neighbors, quite a few of whose governments had been taken in by the propaganda of the Cause and who turned a blind eye to the comings and goings of the Irish psycho-romantics. Lenin had coined a phrase for *cabrónes* like that: "Useful Idiots." The KGB and the Cheka before it had scored some great coups by the manipulation of Useful Idiots.

And a deal with Casey's organization was possessed of certain obvious benefits. Provided the security of the cartel's cocaine distribution was not jeopardized. But Luís Restrepo could be trusted to see to that.

No, Pablo Envigado was . . . worried? Maybe mildly concerned was more accurate, about another matter. This business with the dead girl in New York. That was untidy. And seven dead New York cops. Why make enemies where there was no advantage? Still, it would not be long before that end of the arrangement was settled.

"So, *amigo mío*. Tell me about this New York detective, and why you are advocating his murder . . ." The *padrino* smiled and sipped his yogurt, gazing down the valley as the evening sun glinted on the solid golden bells on the church towers of Santa Fe. Bells that no man would dare to steal, for they were gifts from Don Pablo Envigado himself.

And Restrepo quietly briefed Envigado and Jesus Garcia on Eddie Lucco's relentless and patient police work, which was, correctly, based on the hunch that if the dead girl could be identified, the investigation into the murders of seven cops and the others who got in the way at Bellevue would be that much easier.

"He is one stubborn guy, *jefe*. It's just a matter of time before he gets to one of my best sources inside NYPD. And we own it for would you believe five thousand dollars a month?"

"If we took out every cop who was investigating us, we would have no time for business." Pablo Envigado glanced at an exceptionally pretty girl servant, just into her teens, a lithe and coffee-colored creature from Cartagena, who was brushing leaves from the stone steps leading down from the higher terrace. "Why would it be a problem? If he identifies the dead girl."

"Okay," said Restrepo. "We agreed to Casey's suggestion to bring the judge's kid here, to keep the pressure on that we started with the Whore of Venice killing. Pearson is the greatest known danger to our business with the IRA."

Garcia nodded his agreement. "The man is a judge, an idealist. The idea of dealing with us, *jefe*, it must be eating him."

"He would fuck us if he could . . ." Restrepo watched Envigado carefully.

The cartel boss frowned. "I thought you had this under control." Suddenly the sounds of the mountainside died. The birds, the wind in the trees, the swish and scrape of the girl sweeping.

"I watched him in Vigo, he's doing the job thoroughly. With notorious professionalism." Restrepo used the word "notorious" in the South American sense, meaning most excellent. "Don Pablo, so long as he believes we are holding his daughter . . ." Restrepo shrugged, ". . . we have him by the balls."

Jesus Garcia, who had been listening carefully, wiped the beer from his mustache and spoke. "If he learns the girl is dead I don't think the photos of him with the dead Whore will restrain him. He hates you, Luís, he hates cocaine, and from what I hear from other sources . . ." Jesus Garcia, being the *grupo*'s security boss, always liked to have other, undisclosed sources. ". . . he believes this deal will wreck his organization and its so-called Armed Struggle. I agree with Luís Restrepo. The judge would fuck us if he could. The man is no idiot, we have to assume he has already taken steps, some . . . insurance. So, killing *him* would not solve the problem."

Restrepo leaned forward, "*Jefe*, the New York *tombo* must be stopped. I've seen these scenarios develop very fast." He raised his hands in frustration. "He really is one stubborn cop."

Envigado frowned, deeply thoughtful. He gazed down on the rooftops of Santa Fe. A gentle breeze was starting to cool the mountainside. Pablo Envigado reached for his red pullover lying on the grass beside his chair. After a while, he looked away from the view down the valley, and when he spoke, he seemed to have dismissed the subject of Eddie Lucco from his mind. "I have met five times with the priest, the one from Medellín . . ."

Restrepo nodded. The priest referred to was the very old man who had been sitting at that very table on the terrace when the Nghi grandfather and grandson had been perfecting Siobhan's signature. He had been acting as a go-between, in conditions of almost medieval secrecy, in a dialogue—one which would be denied by all parties concerned—between Pablo Envigado and a beautiful woman who was President Gaviria's personal Counselor for Medellín Affairs, a euphemism for counselor for sorting out the goddamn mess that was the cocaine capital of the world. Her name was Esperanza-Francesca Arranga de Toro.

The subject of the secret negotiations—known only on the *grupo*'s side to the three men present—was a hypothesis that went: what if Pablo Envigado were to give himself up? What if he was tired of constantly being on the run? What if he realized he had bitten off more than he could chew when he declared war on the government and judiciary of Colombia and sentenced the previous president to death?

What if the Colombian parliament, the oldest democratic body in South America, canceled the treaty that automatically extradited *narcotraficantes* to the USA and long prison sentences, served usually in Marion, where top-security prisoners were kept in an underground complex where they never, ever saw the sky?

What if a deal could be struck, using Colombia's

legal code, that allowed confessed crimes to be treated more leniently?

And, bottom line, how much stir would *el padrino* really have to do in return for giving himself up and ordering a halt to the violence that was tearing the country apart?

Don Pablo relied on Restrepo for advice on such sensitive matters. He trusted him more than any brother. And as he brought his *consejero* up to date on the secret talks with the eighty-four-year-old priest, Restrepo listened quietly, occasionally asking a sensible question.

"Okay, I suggest these are the most important things, *jefe,*" he said gravely when Envigado had finished. "One, to make sure you do not have to spend too long inside; two, to protect you from your enemies, namely all the cops and judges and politicos you have purchased over the last ten years; three, to ensure your comfort, and, above all, to make the action look like that of a hero of Colombia, which is how the *paísas* of Antioquia and many others throughout the country see you. And of course, to be able to control the business from inside jail . . ."

"And how do I do that, *amigo mío?*" Pablo Envigado asked softly.

"By making it clear you are calling the shots. For instance, the location of the . . . hospitality the government would provide. I suggest you stand firm on your prison being specially built, and in a symbolic location."

"Where?" Envigado grinned, sipping his yogurt. "Do you really imagine there's a chance in hell of giving myself up to those *huevones?* I mean, good friend, I am merely seeing this old guy to hear what he has to say. It informs me about the way the enemy is thinking."

Madre de Dios, thought Restrepo, as he caught the mood swing, there is no way on God's earth I am going to seem to be pushing the boss into surrendering.

"Hell, yes, Pablo. But try pushing them into a corner. Before we send them the old *brujo* back piece by piece." *Brujo* was the Spanish word for a tribal medicine man. Restrepo meant the priest. "Let's see just how far Gaviria will crawl . . ."

Pablo Envigado stared at Restrepo for a long moment. Then his eyes brightened and he roared with laughter. Jesus Garcia smiled thinly, looking at Restrepo with a thoughtful expression.

"Luís, my good friend and most notorious counselor! That's exactly what we'll do . . ."

Restrepo nodded and quickly changed the subject. "Now, *padrino*, this New York *tombo*. He can be dead by midnight, just give the word."

Envigado stopped laughing. He placed his tumbler carefully on the snow-white linen tablecloth and drummed his fingers thoughtfully on the surface. Then he shook his head. "We disagree on this . . ." And he glanced sharply into Restrepo's eyes. "Luís, what is the point in directly outraging the New York Police Department? We have a good business going in New York City."

Restrepo lifted both his hands in the air in the merest, politest hint of exasperation. "We have already killed seven New York cops. I don't think we are their favorite people."

"Call yourself a fucking lawyer, Luís Restrepo Osorio? The target was a stool pigeon, those cops died in a regular piece of the war between us. They're pros. That was not . . . personal. But blow away a lieutenant of detectives . . . ? That would be a direct and outrageous insult and a challenge. Why do that? Keep it businesslike in New York. We don't want a war with the cops, and we don't want to frighten off our outlets. Come on, *amigo*, tell me another way we can get to Lucco."

Pablo Envigado relaxed and wiped an insect off his nose with an index finger. Jesus Garcia offered him a

handkerchief and Envigado dabbed at his nose delicately, then his eyes returned to Restrepo. "What would
we do if the cop was in Bogotá?"

"Buy him, or kill his family if he couldn't be bought."

"So try that first." His eyes held those of Restrepo.

The cartel lawyer frowned, then slowly smiled. "Why
not . . . ?" He drank his glass of iced tea all at once, his
gaze wandering to the pretty child-servant from Cartagena who was brushing the steps leading down to the
next terrace. "I'll see to that myself."

Envigado watched Restrepo gazing at the young girl.
"You can be in Barranquilla in three hours. You want a
few minutes with little Isabella? She has no pubic hair,
not one little wisp. But Jesus, how she loves it."

Restrepo stood up, placed his glass on the table.
"When I return. There's work to do."

"You know, Luís," said Pablo Envigado, "sometimes
I think you prefer working to fucking. *Amigo*, that worries
me."

"Don Pablo, I work for you and I fuck on my own
time."

All three men laughed, and Restrepo turned and
strolled across the immaculate grass toward the villa
that had been built in the seventeenth-century for a
mariscal of Spain and another girl-child called Isabella.

Envigado watched him go and said to Jesus Garcia,
without taking his eyes off Restrepo, "Why does he want
me to go to prison, Jesus Garcia?"

"*Jefe*, you pay for his advice, it is good he gives it
without fear."

"If this priest business is more than just a game to
keep the heat off while they think we're negotiating . . . I
will skin Luís Restrepo Osorio."

Jesus Garcia inclined his head gravely. "I know you
will, *padrino* . . ."

M U R R A Y   S M I T H

15

IMMEDIATE HEAT

David Jardine had taken final council of his Recruitment, Training, and Selection Team. He had driven down to the Honey Farm and had interviewed the six instructors and four course lecturers just prior to their departure for leave or other assignments. For in a few days, Dylif House would be silent and deserted, apart from Mr. Benedict and his wife, now fully recovered from her hip-replacement operation.

He had read the files along with the course director, Ronnie Szabodo, and had spoken at length with each of the team who had made able and professional agent material out of the two men they knew only as Parcel and Baggage.

He had flown back to London in one of the unmarked olive-drab Lynx helicopters seconded from the Special Duties Wing of the Royal Air Force. Some conscientious professional had taped the legend "Water Authority" in white on each side of the tail assembly and Jardine had made them take the stuff off. No words were sometimes better than nonsense. But not always.

At a meeting in the briefing room, with beer and sandwiches, he had consulted the original team of Bill Jenkins, Kate Howard, Tony Lewis, and, once again, Ronnie Szabodo, who was without equal as a trainer and selector of black operators. The general consensus had been that there was not a great deal to choose between the two candidates. Malcolm Strong had the greater intellect but Harry Ford had real and valuable experience of undercover operations with the SAS and with 14 Intelligence and Security Group in Northern Ireland.

Strong had scored a grade of 17, which was high, during his course at the Farm. Ford had scored 15, which was well above average. The SIS psychologists who had mixed with the two, using the cover of low-grade instructors, had assessed Malcolm Strong as a self-reliant, mild introvert, with no psychological hang-ups, strong self-esteem, and high intelligence. They scored Harry Ford as self-reliant, uncommunicative, strong-willed, with strong latent aggression, possibly lacking in self-confidence and with high intelligence. Strong was considered by all who knew him as very steady and slightly boring. Ford was reckoned to be tough and determined and very charming.

Both men had scored way above average in the various skills and tradecraft exercises. Their South American Spanish had been tested, and either could pass as an Argentinian, even in downtown Buenos Aires.

"There is no doubt," Ronnie Szabodo had observed, "that either Joe can do the business."

"In which case, David," Kate Howard had remarked, rubbing her spectacles on her cream poplin shirtsleeve, "the decision is really up to you . . ." And she had looked him in the eye and smiled, relaxed and friendly.

She must have understood about the cuff links, mused Jardine, and he had smiled back.

The sphere controller, West 8, had nodded, thoughtful, and said he would decide during his visit to Miami, which was to take place in four days' time.

"David, are you absolutely set on this Dolphin thing . . . ?" Szabodo had asked. Jardine had noticed the false tooth was neatly in place. It must be a tartlet, he'd thought. And he had replied quietly, yes, he was absolutely set on the Dolphin thing. And Heather had walked in, as if on cue, and had confirmed his arrangements for traveling to Miami and meeting a local representative of the CIA, who would take him to the North Dade Detention Center in Dade County, Florida, where Dolphin was serving twenty-five years.

That had been two days ago. Now he was sitting in Farm Street Church, praying for forgiveness.

How the hell could it have happened? He felt so utterly ashamed of himself. For at least twenty-four hours afterward he had seriously contemplated resigning.

Every ground rule he had set himself in his private life—right then he considered his rather lonely personal odyssey to be little short of pathetic—chasing those little "treats," as he had thought of them . . . all discarded in one afternoon of unrepeatable, unacceptable, sweating, rutting, licking, cries-of-lust, glistening, bursting, delicious . . . lunacy.

It had in truth been lust fulfillment to die for but this time he had gone too far. David Jardine was essentially a private man who was always able to remain in control of any situation. That was one of his greatest strengths.

But now he had caught a breath of the remorse and shame the sort of person he despised must feel, the sort of person to whom sexual adventure was not limited to the occasional bit of friendly naughtiness, where no one got hurt, but who had become a victim of his id, his animal needs dictating his actions with contempt for his civilized instincts. Jardine was never unaware of the satyr within him, but he had believed, apparently wrongly, that the beast had become tame, if not domesticated. His behavior, just the day before, had been quite . . . appalling.

Worse. It had been a total and unforgivable betrayal.

For Jardine had committed a sin so cardinal that he found himself in a situation he could neither cope with nor endure. His heart raced at the enormity of his misdemeanor and he struggled to formulate words for his imminent confession. For, being in a job like his, no priest, no confessor, could be privy to the real world of the nation's deepest secrets.

Reasons of security alone dictated that his every confession, where it related to the Firm, must be encoded in such a way that God would understand and the priest, the medium, did not learn anything remotely compromising.

And as he knelt there, comforting wafts of incense drifting among the drafty pews, the sound of matins being chanted by seminarists and warmed by yellow rays of sunlight drifting down from the high stained-glass windows, David Jardine already knew that of course he would cope, of course he would endure. But for the first time since his conversion he felt genuine shame and deep remorse for the unforgivable situation into which his overeager, ever-ready, shameless priapus had thrust him.

"Father, it has been three weeks since my last confession."

"And have you sinned, in that time?"

"Forgive me, Father . . ."

The comforting voice of Father Wheatley murmured from the other side of the confessional grill. "How?"

"Sin of pride, Father. Sin of anger. Sin of lust."

"Tell me, my son . . ."

And Jardine, more subdued than Father Dermot Wheatley could remember, recounted his various minor transgressions, then took a deep breath and explained what had happened with Elizabeth Ford, the wife of a man who worked for him. A man whose work was lonely and dangerous, and who needed to have a rock-steady home to keep him going when things got worse than rough. And even as he intoned his version of his sin, paraphrased so that the priest could have no inkling about the nature of David Jardine's work or the business of Op Corrida (a confession that might have been made, he had carefully thought through, by the director of a large city firm or an insurance organization), even during his metaphorical prostration before the Lord he could not rid himself of recollections of her hand on him, of her long linen skirt dropping to the floor, of her immaculate skin and her glistening, long hair, of her moistness and her urgency and her . . . incredible skill and so deliberate, jaw-slack, lust-wet surrender to pleasure. And her breathtaking instinct for mutual, imaginative coupling—with him, a virtual stranger.

He realized with guilty confusion that this was absolutely and very definitely not the sort of musing for the confession box. Should he confess *that* to Father Wheatley? No fucking way, he thought then, oh Dear Lord, once and former chum, please forgive me! He wondered for an insane second if he was in the grip of some outrageous evil influence and realized promptly that the only outrageous influence was the hedonistic thing at present hanging its head limply between his legs. The cobra, Nicola had called it: once it rises, nothing will stop it from having its victim.

". . . does she feel about what happened? Have you spoken to her since?" his confessor was asking.

"Father, this took place only yesterday. I am going abroad on business in a few hours. I don't expect to see her till I get back."

"When will that be, my son?" Not a trace of condemnation in the man's voice.

"Um, just after the weekend."

"Do you think, do you intend, to carry on the liaison?"

"Good God, no. Sorry, Father. Forgive me. No, not, um, no. You see, there's too much at stake. Her husband relies on me. And on her. It really is a most sinful thing I have done . . ."

"Good Heavens . . ."

And the ghost of a chuckle from behind the grill.

"Father . . . ?"

"I really do believe you feel true remorse."

David Jardine stared at the grill. He was perspiring with anxiety. He smiled grimly. "I really do . . . I feel dreadful."

"Well, then. We might make a good Christian out of you yet, David."

———

Miami International Airport was hell to get through once one had disembarked from the seven-hour flight from London's Heathrow Airport. Jardine always traveled First Class because when the office had decided its senior executives should economize and travel Business Class, he had assumed, for foreign journeys, the work name and cover of a man who would never travel any other way. His papers and passport revealed he was Alistair Norwell, director of Hall & Gregg, a small family bank in the City of London. The charade was not intended to be a particularly deep cover, which was just as well, for when the other passengers joined a long, snaking, meandering queue to pass through Immigration and Customs, Jardine was met by a large, plump man of about forty, wearing a dark, loose-cut, lightweight suit, cream button-down shirt, and sober necktie. He was John Consadine, chief of the Miami and south Florida CIA office.

It took four minutes for the SIS officer to be whisked smoothly out of the MIA terminal and into a waiting airconditioned, dark blue Buick.

Jardine was surprised there was no driver and said so.

"This is my car," Consadine said. "In fact it's Joni's. She says hi and we're all going to Key Biscayne for dinner tomorrow night, although I have to warn you, this is not the season for your favorite stone crab claws . . ."

"How is Joni?" asked Jardine, watching the mainly Hispanic inhabitants of that quarter of Miami as the Buick smoothly cruised out from the airport.

"She's fine. Maybe put on a few pounds since you last saw her in Caracas. But it suits her."

Ninety-seven minutes later, David Jardine was shown into a spartan room in North Dade Correction Center. The walls were pale green and the floor was gray rubber tiles. Light came from four white rectangles in the ceiling. There was a table and two chairs. As the door behind Jardine closed and he heard an electronic lock clunk shut, a narrower door on the facing wall slid open, and the man he had traveled three thousand eight hundred miles to see stepped through, ducking his head slightly, and blinked in the light. Then he recognized Jardine and his lean face crinkled into a smile.

The two men shook hands and sat down.

"David. You're the last bloody person I ever expected to see again," said Spencer Percy, a most charming,

Oxford-educated rogue, who was serving a twenty-five year stretch for international marijuana smuggling on an impressively grand scale.

"You look older," Jardine said.

"Come back in twenty-four years and two months," said Percy with a wry movement of his face that might have been a smile.

The two men sat silent, comfortable in each other's presence. Behind them, beyond an armored glass window, two guards put a large Harrods carrier bag on a counter and started to check a number of items, which they produced from the bag with the air of magicians, not quite sure if the trick would work.

"I brought you some stuff. Bath Olivers, Lea and Perrins, Trumper's Lime. About six months' worth of *Spectators* although it's not quite the same as it used to be . . ."

"By MI-Six standards, that's quite a comprehensive bribe. What the hell do you want?"

"Do you remember a conversation we had back in 1981, late August, I think?"

"I was in Brixton prison. Of course I remember."

"You made me a promise."

"Oh shit. And you've remembered . . ."

"Do you . . . ?"

Percy gazed at Jardine, who settled into his uncomfortable chair, crossing his long legs. "I might."

In September 1981, Spencer Percy had pleaded a most unlikely defense to a charge of importing fifteen tons of marijuana from Colombia via the West Indies and the north of Scotland. Enough dope, it was calculated by some newspaper reporter, to provide every adult in Britain with a spliff, or joint. One of the main lines of his defense was that he had been working since his days as an undergraduate at Balliol College, Oxford, as a paid agent of the Firm, SIS, MI-6, the Intelligence

Service, whatever. And that any activity related to drug smuggling was entirely due to his patriotism and conscientious application to his top secret assignment on behalf of HM government. The details of which he could not discuss, even at the risk of losing his liberty. His lips were sealed.

Such a defense was inspired nonsense. It was true that Percy had been asked by a junior intelligence officer with the Firm to report on an Irishman who dabbled not only in marijuana but was known to be in the IRA. Percy was paid several times for his information and was even given a larger sum in order to open a boutique in the south of France in partnership with the Irishman.

The office had soon dropped Spencer Percy, however, when they learned that his dedication to providing enough dope for everyone in the world to get stoned—regularly—was going to land him in deep trouble, and probably soon.

Spencer Percy's intellect was way higher than most, even than most highly intelligent people, and he knew he could embroider and hint and elaborate and by his very reticence convey a strong impression that he had never left the secret world with a reasonable chance of success. For he knew that SIS, the government's most secret and deniable organization, which had no legal existence under any statute and therefore did not, officially, exist, would never in a hundred years permit any mere criminal case to bring it out of the security closet in order to confirm or deny the accused's outrageous defense.

However, the Firm was occasionally imaginative enough to take advantage of a situation, and David Jardine, at that time deputy director, UK Operations, had visited Percy in Brixton prison, London, and had struck a bargain with the disciple of dope. He had laid it on the line, gently pointing out to the trafficker that several of the lawyers and investigators on Percy's case were well connected, as was the way of things in London's professional society, with its Mafia-like network of gentlemen's clubs and military and old-school-tie associations.

It merely required a blank look or a frown in the bar at White's or Boodle's, its exclusive neighbor in St. James's Street, to keep the office's bland hands off Percy's defense or, by the merest shake of the head, to damn it.

And David Jardine and Spencer Percy had had a long and very private conversation, during which Jardine had made his own assessment of the man. Jardine was eventually convinced that Percy loathed and despised heroin and cocaine dealers just as much as he believed with almost messianic conviction that a little bit of hash was good for you. The two men also liked each other, and the real intelligence operator had foreseen a possible benefit for the Firm.

Thus, quite improperly, they had reached a sort of a deal. If SIS decided to sit on its hands and let Spencer Percy take his chances in court, neither confirming nor denying the man's untrue claim to have been working for the secret world, he would repay the debt at some time in the future.

Percy had, to universal astonishment, been acquitted by the jury and he had walked out of the Old Bailey, as surprised as anyone, a free man.

But from that moment, it was clear that Spencer Percy was destined to spend serious time behind bars, and the story of how a young DEA agent decided to devote years to that end, pursuing the amusing, gently arrogant trafficker across continents, using every modern surveillance technique available, had become a classic of contemporary law enforcement.

And now, ten years after Percy had sauntered from

the dock at the Old Bailey, here he was in North Dade Detention Center and the Secret Intelligence Service, in the person of David Jardine, was here to collect.

"But my dear David. How on earth do you know you can trust me . . . ?"

Jardine grinned. "That's exactly what my colleagues asked."

And they both laughed, to the surprise of the watching guards beyond the armored glass window.

"But by God, Spencer. It would not do to mess with me." This remark was made by David Jardine very casually. Without a trace of a threat. Except in his eyes, where the message was frigidly, ruthlessly clear.

"You mean things could get worse, for *me* . . . ?" Percy searched Jardine's face for a trace of humanity. But there was none to see. He shrugged. "Okay. What can I do . . . ?"

Then Jardine quietly explained what he needed. He made it clear he was intending to hurt cocaine trafficking in general, and the cartel in particular. Percy listened carefully and watched Jardine intently, looking all the time for a trap, for some sign that this was a ploy by the authorities to stick him for a few more years in the jug. But because Jardine was being straight, not disclosing any details but quite obviously having decided to trust him, Spencer Percy accepted that the request was genuine.

"And you believe they'll make contact with me, to check out your Joe . . . ?"

"I'm sure of it."

"You know I'm being moved to Butner prison? That's in North Carolina."

"Yes." Percy could study for a degree at Butner, under a scheme they had with Duke University. He wanted to do law.

"And they can still reach me there?"

425

"What do you think . . . ?"

Percy chuckled. He nodded. "I'll do it. You know why?"

David Jardine held the convict's friendly, amused gaze. "Why, Spencer?"

"Because any man who turns up in North Dade, Miami, with a couple of bottles of Lea and Perrins sauce and a handful of Bath Olivers is quite clearly in serious need of assistance."

And they both laughed.

"Don't throw away the wrappers." Jardine smiled and stood up to leave.

Percy rose, unwinding himself, and shook hands with the sphere controller, who towered above him. His grip was firm. "Good luck, David. Something's worrying you, I can see that. Don't take life too seriously, it's all a game."

"Do you believe that?" asked Jardine.

"I have to," replied the man with another twenty-four years and two months of jail in front of him. He smiled, slightly shyly, and turned back toward the prisoners' door.

Jardine watched him go. His hunches were based on a mixture of experience and intuition. He had learned to trust them. His Joe, whichever one he chose, would have a twenty-four-carat backup for his legend. For international dope dealer Spencer Percy would now confirm their mythical business relationship, stretching back six years. Details of which were printed on the wrapping paper of Bath Oliver biscuits Jardine had given to him.

As to which of the two candidates he would choose, Jardine put his mind to that while he walked along the bleak coffee-and-gray corridor on his way to a side entrance, and freedom. Even after a brief visit he felt he would be glad to get out of the claustrophobic atmosphere of the correction center.

Malcolm Strong's situation was clearcut. The guy presented no problems and could be fed into Op Corrida the next day. The same day even. But when he concentrated on Harry Ford, guilty thoughts of his Sunday afternoon with Elizabeth intruded. Okay David, grow up, he thought. Let's not be ungallant enough to blame the girl, but it does take two to tango. Maybe we could just pretend it never happened.

And as the prison warder unlocked the side gate and Jardine glimpsed the Buick, with John Consadine sitting at the wheel (for this was no official occurrence and there would be no record of the British spy's brief visit) he had a brief recollection of that moment last Sunday. He had promised Harry he would take her for a coffee to explain things, put her mind at rest, on the Sunday morning that Ford and Strong had been flown, without prior warning, to separate safe houses in Bogotá and Barranquilla respectively. At the Hard Rock Cafe, off Piccadilly at Hyde Park Corner, he told her, in that patently sincere way of his, how Harry had been sent to Hong Kong on a training exercise, nothing at all dangerous, and would possibly be gone for some weeks. She could expect some mail from him, infrequently, via the office and could write to Harry any time, via the office of course. As he was giving her this spiel, of which Harry was aware, in order to allow her to be free from anxiety, Elizabeth had suddenly glanced into his eyes, her face mostly hidden by the most enormous hamburger, with lettuce and mustard and cucumber relish oozing out from the bun and through and over her fingers, smearing her face, and he had met—and understood with appalled clarity—what that glance, that unmistakable glance, meant from one enthusiast to another.

The glance, long and amused and unambiguous, had said "Fuck me."

It had not been a glance like Kate Howard's, when he had made such a turkey of himself that night on the hearth at Tite Street. In fact the difference between the two glances was so . . . light-years apart that he had wondered how he could have made such an embarrassing mistake. No. Elizabeth, with the long, athletic legs and the burnished model's hair and that deep, animal voice, was saying with her eyes, now, you bastard. I want you. Are you as keen as I know you are, you lecherous, amoral bastard?

And of course, David Arbuthnot Jardine, CMG, was precisely as keen as she had figured he was and he had reached across, gently taken the hamburger and bun from her wet fingers, placed two ten-pound notes on the table, and led her by the hand from the Hard Rock Cafe, where the sound system, jukebox-fed and close to the threshold of pain, was belting out the Mick Jagger number "You Can Make It If You Try" . . .

The pain and anguish he was going through since that afternoon of remorseless, agile, devouring, guilty pleasure was killing him. He had broken his cardinal codes of honor in every particular.

Christ, it had been incredible . . .

And if they just pretended it had never happened . . . ? Hell, you're only here once. Maybe they had both deserved one little treat.

He smiled and strolled over to the Buick.

"Success . . . ?" inquired Consadine, who believed Jardine had been speaking to Spencer Percy about a possible deal if Percy would reveal details of ongoing marijuana-smuggling routes into England.

"You know that little shit," Jardine said. "Sure he'll talk, but first can he please get moved to some prison in North Carolina. He wants to study. For a law degree, would you believe?"

"Butner," contributed Consadine. "That's Butner prison, they have an arrangement with Duke University."

"Really . . ." David Jardine nodded sagely as the high, mesh security gates swung open and the Buick headed for Interstate Highway US 1. "That must be the place."

———

A few hundred miles north, Sam Vargos wove the unmarked Mustang through the evening rush, heading toward an apartment block on Broadway not far from Lincoln Center. Eddie Lucco sat beside him, using the radio frequency netted to Homicide headquarters in Police Plaza, Manhattan South. A client had been found dead in a bondage and S/M prostitute's premises. Lucco had been listening without listening, the way cops do, without paying much attention, when he had heard the dead guy had his throat cut and his tongue pulled through the slit. Just like the poor jerk Baquero, who had fronted for the cartel as a travel agent in the Colombian quarter in the 110th Precinct.

"Maybe you oughta put the light on," suggested Vargos as he whooped the concealed siren and did outrageous things, fighting through the solid traffic.

"Nah . . . Right now, Sam, we don't need to be too outstanding." He meant too obviously a police car.

Vargos glanced at his partner. It was not too often the boss got careful.

Manny Schulman's eyes were wide open. His cheap nylon shirt was crimson wet. His tongue hung grotesquely from the nine-inch gash which, the pathologist reported later, had sliced his Adam's apple in two. The human tongue is quite a long affair when it is completely excised, and it lay down on the dead man's chest.

A camera flash lit up the grisly, stinking room and reflected momentarily off the lifeless eyes.

"His big mistake," opined Acting Lieutenant Eddie Lucco, "was getting into bondage."

He walked around the cadaver, which was suspended in a complicated and bizarre arrangement of chains and leather straps from a pulley in the ceiling. Manny's hands were handcuffed behind his back, his ankles in leg irons with chains fixed to an adjustable block on the floor. Apart from the bloodstained shirt and a pair of brown nylon socks he was naked.

"Musta been his ultimate thrill," Vargos remarked, indicating the murdered man's hard-on, which looked ready to burst out of its skin.

"They do that in cases of violent death. Sometimes," said the pale-faced, slightly spotty forensic photographer, a kid whom Lucco had not seen working on his own before. Must've been promoted, thought the detective. Christ, we're all getting old.

"Yeah, sure," he said.

Two fingerprint men were dusting the place for fingerprints. Dr. Henry Grace, the Bellevue pathologist who moonlighted for Homicide, stepped out backwards from a closet in the wall, holding a glass slide in one hand and a pair of surgical tweezers in the other. He glanced briefly at Lucco and smiled a wan greeting. Eddie Lucco had heard he was now on a bottle and a half of bourbon a day. He understood entirely.

"How ya doin', Doc?"

"Never better." Grace put the tweezers on a wood-and-metal table that looked like a medieval torture rack, which is more or less what it was. With great care, he slid the glass slide into a plastic exhibit bag.

"Who you got in there . . . ?" Lucco indicated the closet.

"Anita Frankenheim. Dominatrice-in-residence. Deceased."

"Frankenstein?" asked Vargos, in mock error.

"You said it."

"How?" asked Lucco, strolling around the room, looking for something normal, something everyday, that might have been left by the killers.

"Slug in the head. Entered left ear. Most of her brains are on the wall just beside the door here."

Lucco realized he was listening to a very groovy blues number, mostly instrumental, by John Lee Hooker. He seemed to recall it was called "Baby Lee." He looked around for the source and saw the sound system, an Aiwa. The compact disc was programmed to repeat that one number.

"How the fuck can a guy pay to get tied up and abused to good sounds like that . . . ?" he wondered, never failing to be amazed by human perversion.

"I put it on when I came in," said Dr. Grace, removing the small brown paper-wrapped bottle of Jack Daniels from his lips. "I like to work to music."

Lucco scratched his head and met Vargos's gaze. Vargos was grinning.

"Right," replied Lucco. "I knew that . . ."

"You know what they call a killing like this, Ed?" If he drinks any more we'll have to carry him out, thought Lucco. "They call it a Colombian necktie."

Lucco and Vargos exchanged glances.

"No kidding," said Lucco.

"So I figure this was done by some cocaine outfit."

Eddie Lucco gazed around the chamber where New Yorkers paid about four hundred dollars for an hour's torture. What was the matter with these guys? Maybe they did not have mothers-in-law.

The door opened noisily and a squat, balding man who bore an uncanny resemblance to the movie actor

Danny de Vito breezed in, followed closely by two detectives from the local precinct. His name was Sergeant Milt Gaynor. Homicide.

"What the fuck is this? You go for a pastrami on rye and when you get back the 14th Precinct is crawling all over the fucking evidence. This connected with your big case, Eddie? You want it, you can have it, I got a family of three, kid of five months, murdered for a few ounces of crack. You can have this Eddie, it's all yours pal."

Lucco smiled. "Just sightseeing, Milt. We're outa here."

And Lieutenant Eddie Lucco walked past Gaynor and left the murder scene, followed by his partner.

Outside, he said, "Sam, make sure we get copies of Milt's investigation, would you do that?"

"No problem."

And they got into the unmarked green Mustang just as the Colombian, sitting in a panel truck parked across the street, received a phone message that meant do not proceed with Lucco's murder. The button man, who did in fact work as a short-order cook in Queens, removed the magazine from his silenced MAC-10 Ingram machine pistol, swiftly unscrewed the silencer, wrapped the piece in an oily rag, put it back in its canvas case, and lit a cigarette, Mustang brand, from Bogotá. He watched with hooded, lazy eyes as the two cops drove away. They would never know how close they had come. He shrugged and started the motor. He had a party of fourteen to cater for that night.

In Bogotá, the north of the city is considered safer than downtown, or the university quarter, or the picturesque old quarter, the Candelaria. And the neighborhoods east of the Avenida Caracas, which bisects the city, are considered marginally safer than those on the west. All things of course are relative. North Bogotá is a pleasant area with high, modern buildings of generally tasteful design and considerable construction work. Apart from the ceaseless peregrinations of dark-windowed sedans, backed up front and rear by all-terrain jeep wagons filled with armed bodyguards and usually flanked by a half dozen alert and dangerous-looking men on powerful trail motorbikes, submachine guns slung over their shoulders, there is less menace in the streets here and a comparative absence of the grim-faced and jumpy Policia Nacional and military jeep patrols with manned, heavy machine guns encountered the nearer one gets to the center of town.

There is a sprawling commercial and leisure complex just north of the Chico district in North Bogotá, between Carrera 7 and Carrera 20, called Unicentro, with apartment blocks and nondescript condominiums around it, and beyond the northwest corner, a hotel, designed and built with great care to reflect the architectural history of the city (much, perhaps most, of Colombia's new architecture has been carried out with deference to good taste and the country's Spanish heritage). It is built of terra-cotta-colored brick in the form of an old Spanish citadel, with inner courtyards, flying buttresses, and Castilian projections on the upper floors. There is a courtyard fountain and a comfortable café that doubles as a breakfast room. It also has a bar, decked for some unfathomable reason in plaid, with prints on the pine walls of Scottish clansmen. This bar is called the Glasgow.

The hotel is La Fontana. The bar, the Glasgow, is approached by a carpeted corridor, and apart from the bartender's door, back of the counter, there is just the one entrance from the corridor. There are thick padded leather seats and polished oak tables.

All in all, thought Harry Ford as he nursed a cold
Kronenbourg beer and casually memorized the layout of
the bar, not a good place to be if one was of a nervous
disposition, a place like this with only one way in and
out and a corridor to get trapped in. But at that time,
Bogotá was not the ideal place for someone of a nervous
disposition. There were three men standing at the bar
counter, well dressed and speaking Peruvian-accented
Spanish in quiet, patrician tones. Harry had overheard
that two were staying at the hotel and one was a diplomat, commercial attaché, at the Peruvian embassy. In a
corner to the right, at the table next to the wood panel
that made the exit/entrance even more of a death trap,
forming a short extension from the corridor beyond, sat
an aristocratic-looking Argentinian with his slender,
poised, well-groomed wife and elder daughter. The couple had three daughters, aged about eight, twelve, and
sixteen. Harry Ford had seen them in the café at breakfast—an elegant, impeccably mannered family. Well,
perhaps the two younger daughters were a bit boister-
ous, but their good nature helped take the edge off the
slightly strained atmosphere of the cafeteria with its
sumptuous array of breakfast choices, from muesli and
scones through passion fruit, melon, and pineapple to
salami, cold ham, cooked ham, eggs—scrambled, fried,
or poached—sausages, steak, and gammon. There was
a variety of fruit juices and yogurt drinks in tall, cool
pitchers. Including peach yogurt, which seemed to be a
favorite.

The place was well staffed and attentive, with two
white-coated assistant chefs serving the hot food. The
clientele was clearly wealthy, sophisticated, and cosmopolitan. There were Japanese, Koreans, Germans,
and South Americans from all over the subcontinent. No
English that he could identify, and not a single American, for gringos had a poor impression of Colombia

from the media and felt they could be kidnapped or gunned down anywhere at any time.

Harry Ford smiled inwardly and sipped his beer, for he realized that was more or less exactly how he, the SAS hero, now a fully trained and indoctrinated MI-6 spy, was feeling. Just a mite strained and apprehensive. He was sensitive to atmosphere, and that had kept him alive in places like Republican clubs in Londonderry, cattle markets near Dundalk in the Irish Republic, Basra in Iraq, and the Panshir Valley in Afghanistan. He understood full well the strained atmosphere in the Fontana's elegant café and had been grateful for the normalcy of the two little Argentinian girls, whose guessing games and giggling and occasional squeals of laughter made the place seem a little less like the anteroom to hell.

The girl with the well-groomed Argentinians in the Glasgow bar, the oldest daughter, sat straight-backed with the poise and elegance of a dressage rider, which, with her background, she probably was. Three times, in the three days Harry had been at the Fontana, she had waited for a moment when her parents' attention had been diverted and glanced, head slightly tilted forward, directly into Harry Ford's eyes. Held the gaze for a second or two, then ignored him completely, but with an enigmatic smile on her olive-skinned, slender, classical features.

The child was about five-seven, with an agile slimness, tiny waist, and the beginnings of little breasts. When she wore her hair loose, it fell over her shoulders and halfway to her waist. She was one of the most beautiful adolescent girls Harry had ever seen. And she knew it.

The secret agent was young enough (yet in some ways a thousand years old, having killed around twenty men in combat) to understand she was just practicing when she held his gaze like that, just flexing her flirting muscles, to see if she could interest a grown-up man.

And understanding this, he always returned the gaze courteously, with the merest flicker of interest, and a smile like he used to give his little sister's friends that meant, "Don't worry, I know you're just kidding."

He relaxed and returned to pretending to read the *Espador* newspaper, which carried details of the latest killings in Medellín, where a bunch of people had been machine-gunned as they left a football stadium, and of the slaying of five of Bogotá's sewer children—children who lived in the city's sewer conduit pipes, some of them born to fourteen-year-old girls themselves sewer children and living their entire, often brief, lives down there in the sewers, emerging to beg, to steal, and to prostitute themselves. Another five had been shot. The paper hinted, with remarkable editorial courage, that the killers were cops, encouraged by a perverted and rogue Policia captain who was notorious for that kind of thing. Sometimes the victims were gang-raped first.

Harry Ford of course was not anywhere near Colombia. Harry Ford was working on his first assignment after training for the Defense Equipment Division of the international banking conglomerate IRRC, somewhere in Southeast Asia. The personnel records and any number of computers from American Express to Hertz Rent-a-Car said so. His airline trips were well documented and his passport, Harry Ford's own passport, had been through all the airports and presented to all the hotel desks where the trail, the secondary legend, was being laid. The legend that would confide to any inquisitive researcher precisely what Captain Harry Ford, MC, had been doing since he left the Special Air Service.

And Harry's pay was paid into his bank, the Bank of Scotland in London's Haymarket, by the Accounts Division (UK)/Personnel of the IRRC, which really believed he existed and was working in Southeast Asia. Some-place in Southeast Asia. He even sent reports back and made the occasional sale. This mythical Harry Ford.

No, the man sitting in a corner of the Glasgow bar in the Hotel La Fontana was Señor Carlos Nelson Arrigiada, a Chilean national who was known to use the alias Miguel José Guerra and was wanted for questioning in Florida, Nassau, Caracas, Madrid, New Delhi, and Bang-kok in respect of certain narcotics agencies inquiries into marijuana trafficking. This information was avail-able only to persons with classified access to interna-tional law-enforcement agencies' protected computers. Persons like Luís Restrepo, legal counselor to the Medel-lín Cartel, *el grupo*.

Harry Ford's task, for the moment, was to blend into the Bogotá scene. Bogotá was alive with informers, police agents, cartel agents, guerrilla agents, DEA as-sets, CIA agents, British Intelligence assets, and a score of others, all watching and reporting back to their re-spective (and often several) clandestine employers.

Ronnie Szabodo and an SIS officer known to Harry only as Jack, who was in reality Bill Jenkins, had played him into the work of establishing his cover by a training exercise in Spain. He had passed that, and the exercise had continued, changing gear from exercise to an oper-ation in the field. He had been indoctrinated into the cover, the legend, of Carlos Nelson Arrigiada, and even after the months of training and learning every facet of the espionage operative's craft, the former special forces officer had been amazed at the nth-degree thoroughness of the Firm, who had created Carlos specially for him with all his habits and idiosyncrasies, so that by the time he was primed, it was ready, like one of his Savile Row suits, to shrug into and find as comfortable as an old jacket.

Harry Ford knew every day and night of his legend,

going back to his schooldays. Carlos Nelson had few relatives, but those who remained were a doctor in Chile, a rancher in Argentina, and a neurologist in Zurich, along with an assortment of aged aunts and young cousins scattered around the remoter parts of South America. He also had relations he had never met, in Devon, England, descended from the family of one Sebastian Nelson who had settled in Chile in the early nineteenth century and who had created a degree of wealth for the Arrigiada family, who farmed vast swathes of Chile.

Much of this was easy to assimilate for it was based on Harry Ford's own South American antecedents, translated from Argentina to Chile because the Firm had excellent relations with the Chilean intelligence service, which had already quietly fed into their various national computers enough data to support the history of the hitherto mythical Carlos Nelson, as he became known to Chilean narcotics police and customs, who then maintained a genuine watch at ports and airports for the marijuana smuggler, whose photo in their files was one of Harry, snatched surreptitiously when he was coming in from an exhausting exercise back at the Farm in the early days of training. He had a three-day stubble and looked suitably disreputable.

His task right now was merely to settle into Bogotá. The Bogotá DAS were unaware of his presence but when, as they very quickly would, they made discreet inquiries around friendly international security and law-enforcement agencies, they would learn that Carlos Nelson was a small-time (by Colombian standards) but modestly well-heeled marijuana trafficker who had at one time been connected with Spencer Percy, the biggest Mary Jane dealer of them all, now doing twenty-five years in an American correction center.

He smiled an infinitesimal smile as the remarkably

beautiful Argentinian teenager lowered her head and glanced briefly in his direction.

As to what his new employers, the Firm, the Office had in store for him, he could only hazard a guess. He had no idea that Baggage was settling quietly into Barranquilla with a similarly watertight legend, keyed-up and waiting to work.

And he had no idea that David Jardine had not, at that precise moment, chosen which of them was to risk his life by bringing himself to Pablo Envigado's notice and infiltrating the cartel.

———

So Manny Schulman had been passing stuff to the Colombians. Eddie Lucco shook his head as he leafed through the thick printout ledgers itemizing every communication from NYPD's Intelligence Division to the rest of the USA and foreign police departments. He had just about used up all his favors in this goddamn investigation. It seemed a hundred years since he had raced down into the womens' rest room at Grand Central Station, wiped the vomit off the kid's face, and tried, even though the coldness of the limbs shouted the truth, to bring her back to life, breathing his warm breath into her cold, pathetic lungs.

Siobhan . . . an Irish kid, en route from Rome with her handsome boyfriend, Ricardo Santos Castaneda, now deceased. A waiflike child of disturbing, fair-haired beauty, wasted by a dumb case of poisoning from bad crack.

He had no doubt that she had walked out of the Hampton House, made her way to Simba Patrice, hanging out near that amusement arcade where Lucco had shot PeeWee, Simba's brother, and pleaded with him for a few lines of crack. And Simba, being Simba, had exacted his pleasure as payment.

What was it he had said in the Morta da Pasta? Standing there at the bar, when Tony the bartender had been making surreptitious notes of the conversation . . . "Man, I did not *sell* her nothing . . ."

No. She had sold something. Siobhan, Jane Doe Number Zero Eight Zero One on a slab at Bellevue, the cause of serious mayhem in New York City, had sold herself, in return for the crack she imagined would give her a new experience.

Well, it sure had.

And Eddie Lucco read, his experienced detective's head nodding, unsurprised, the record on computer printout IDIV/377629/NY BOG-CMBA/16430391, which contained a series of routine inquiries from the Communications Department of the Colombian Policia Nacional in Bogotá. Among them were three for the Photographic Computer ID Office, that is, Manny and Jake, and one of those consisted of a photo of the girl, with a routine inquiry asking if she had been admitted to hospital or had been arrested or what. And the code, when Lucco checked back painstakingly, along with Sam Vargos, over a period of three days, matched a steady number of other inquiries that seemed innocent until you had the key, which was that every single one would have been of interest to the cartel.

Manny had faxed back the Missing Persons' photo of the dead Jane Doe, her face wiped clean and her hair brushed neatly by some thoughtful photographer. Eddie Lucco wondered if that had been the same kid who was in the brothel, photographing Manny's suspended, throat-cut cadaver, with the blood-wet shirt and the obscenity of chains and handcuffs.

Well, that was the fax that had sealed the fate of Ricardo, of PeeWee, Pig Mulrooney, and a dozen other murder victims in NYC, giving Homicide Lieutenant (Acting) Eddie Lucco his biggest case, his most headaches, and some serious personal danger.

Siobhan, Siobhan . . . who the hell are you? And he was disturbed to find himself rejecting, not for the first time, the desire to go back to the morgue at Bellevue and stand gazing down at the blue-gray, refrigerated body of a kid who had just wanted a taste of the wild life.

Lucco left the Intelligence Division offices and said good night to Sam, who was going to drive the Mustang back to the 14th Precinct and take his own car home.

Eddie Lucco strolled among the fast-walking, purposeful evening rush hour crowds, the rumble and incessant hooting of traffic making him feel glad he was not driving. The newsstands were full of the latest grease-gun slayings in the city. He had little doubt they were the work of the sole surviving Patrice brother, Abdullah, who would have set about revenging his siblings' murders the only way Abdullah knew how. The big cop shrugged his shoulders, thinking the chances of Abdullah Patrice getting any of the *grupo* who had really been involved were just about as good as Abdullah's own chance of surviving till the end of the month. In other words, zilch.

It was not till he was at West Forty-third, going north on Sixth Avenue, that he became aware of the seven or eight men accompanying him. They wore a variety of clothes, a couple of blue-collar types, three businessmen, a hobo, and so on. As he stood on the curb, watching the Don't Walk sign across the busy street, a dark blue Cadillac stopped at the sidewalk and he felt two gun muzzles jammed hard into his ribs. The back door of the Cadillac was opened by one of the three businessmen standing beside him. Although Lucco did not know it, this was Bobby Sonson.

"Relax, Eddie," said Sonson. "I'm taking you to meet a guy who has some information. Keep your gun. We ain't gonna hurt you."

The accent was Colombian.

Eddie Lucco felt his heart stop, then kick itself on, but not as steady as it had been a mere second before. He glanced around at the opposition. The ex-marine in him told him this was no time for heroics.

He shrugged and climbed into the car.

Murillo was already inside. Two more Colombian hoods swiftly squeezed in and the Cadillac shot off, riding a red light.

Murillo nodded to him without hostility, one professional to another, and reaching across, lifted Lucco's jacket and relieved him of the Smith & Wesson short-barreled revolver. He flicked open the chamber, dropped the six copper-nosed bullets into the palm of his right hand, flipped the chamber closed, one-handed, and returned the gun to its owner. Eddie Lucco took it and slid it back, impotent, into its chamois leather and steel spring shoulder holster.

Twenty minutes later, the Homicide detective was led into a warm and comfortable room in a luxurious town house off Madison near the Armory. There were oil paintings on the walls, expensive leather furniture, and Oriental carpets to deaden the footfalls of the place's loaded inhabitants.

A well-groomed man of medium height entered. His shoulders were broad but the rest of him was lean and fit looking. His hair was longer than was fashionable in New York at that time and his dark gray suit was of impeccable, Italian cut. Crocodile sneakers, of course. And a plain gold wristwatch that could have been pawned to provide a life-support system for a pricey hospital.

"Lieutenant Lucco. My name is Luís Restrepo Osorio." He did not offer his hand and he made no attempt at stupid pleasantries. "I am here to make you an offer, on behalf of my principals."

Eddie Lucco did not need to ask who they were.

"So make the fuckin offer, I got a busy day."

———

Nancy Lucco was having a good day in court. She was defending a young commodities broker who was accused of insider dealing. It was becoming clear, on day one of his trial, that he was taking the rap for his senior partners in the respected Wall Street firm of Lewis, Jasper and Hodges. Her cross-examination of old man Hodges, one of New York's top socialites and president of the exclusive Manhattan Sailing Club, had elicited occasional traces of fluster from that millionaire pillar of the community.

Those moments had not gone unnoticed, and the judge, Judge Almeda, whose photograph still hung on the wall of a bar he used to play jazz piano in while working his way through college, had actually held her eye and given the ghost of a wink. A tacit signal he did not actually mind Nancy following a line that was receiving continuous protests and objections from the prosecuting attorney.

She wished Eddie Lucco could have been in court to hear her, watch her working at her best, and in the court of Judge Almeda, his hero. If she had known it was going to be Almeda, she would have phoned the 14th Precinct and told him. But he had been so tied up with the Bellevue Massacre investigation that they had hardly seen each other the last few days. She still had two detectives assigned by NYPD to provide protection, they were sitting in court at that moment, and all in all it had been kind of tough. Eddie had not phoned her at Sam's sister's place till late the night before and she had been worried about him. He had sounded fine, maybe tired, and . . . thoughtful. Yes, she sure would be glad when this investigation of his was over.

Then, to her pleased surprise, she glimpsed her husband's tall, spare frame edging into the courtroom, past the cop by the door, and sitting near the back. He saw her grin and he nodded, glancing at Judge Almeda as if to say whadda you know . . . ?

Or strike me pink. Strike me pink was a phrase they had heard, watching some black-and-white TV movie with British actors. Dudley Moore or somebody had said, with a London accent, "Well, strike me pink!" and Lucco had cracked up. He thought it was the funniest thing he had ever heard. But Lucco did have an infantile sense of humor. And ever since, he sometimes came out with the expression, and Nancy would generally respond with "Jesus, Lucco."

There is a good Chinese restaurant near the court and Nancy insisted on taking Eddie there for a quick lunch. She was on a high, with the case going so well.

"Whadda you think, Eddie? It looks like the judge is going to throw this one out . . ." She ignored the two detectives who had squeezed into a table nearby with a view of the door.

"Ni ho mah, Miss Lucco . . ." The tiny, very old Chinese waiter, whose face had that baby-face sheen of the over seventies smiled. He dished out two long menus with the deadpan skill of a cardsharp.

"Ni ho mah, Freddie. Give us two chicken chow mein and a side order of water chestnuts and two Cokes, how about it?"

"You got it." And Freddie the diminutive Chinese waiter moved away.

"Chow mein," said Lucco. "And Coke. Don't I get to order?"

"Eddie, don't be childish. *And* it's Judge Almeda. Good omen, right?"

Acting Homicide Lieutenant Eddie Lucco glanced at the two detectives from the Protection Detail. They were too busy studying their menus to be interested, anyway the place was noisy.

There is a well-known phenomenon: when two people are very close they become telepathic, like most animals. True or not, when Lucco gently touched Nancy's wrist she glanced at him sharply. "What's wrong?"

Her eyes searched his face. The last few weeks had not been easy, but to keep sane, Nancy Lucco had dismissed the Colombian menace from her mind. As far as she could, living in a strange apartment, under armed escort. So when she asked what was wrong, she meant how much worse is it now?

Lucco held her hand, caressing it from habit and affection. It was something he did when he needed comfort, which was something even flint-faced NYPD detectives needed from time to time.

"You know in this business," he said quietly, "a cop sometimes gets made an offer . . . ?"

Nancy glanced around, then examined his face. The man seemed to be in silent pain. "A bribe?"

"Gimme a break honey, don't tell the world."

"Well the . . . offer does not exist that could turn you, Lucco."

"Sure, but they presented a very strong case. I said I would think about it."

"You . . . ?"

"Come on Nancy, you know me or what?"

"You stalled them."

"Sure."

"Because you want to . . . what? Set them up? Go back with a wire?"

"You're kidding. They would make salami outa me, with a wire."

"Eddie you have to report this, you know you gotta report it."

"I can't report it, those guys have eyes and ears you wouldn't believe it."

Nancy had never seen him this worried before.

"How much are they talking about?" she asked.

He told her. And even the two protection cops looked across as she said, "Jesus Christ . . ."

And Lucco raised a hand to them in greeting and smiled. The two cops nodded and went back to their menus as their waiter arrived with two Chinese beers.

"How about Internal Affairs?" Nancy was beginning to feel her day turning sour. A better than average day, too. But this was not the first bribe Lucco had been offered. And although mind-numbing, the amount was not a consideration. Not for Lucco. It had to be something else.

She touched his hand.

"Okay, what else . . . ?"

Lucco scratched the back of his neck. Freddie the Chinese waiter appeared with two glasses of Coca-Cola, packed with ice and condensation frosting the outsides.

"Chow mein just coming," said Freddie, and glided on among the other tables.

Nancy had not taken her eyes off Lucco. He watched her till Freddie had moved away. He quit scratching his neck, and after gazing casually around the restaurant, as if he had not a care in the world, checking out the other lunchers, he faced her, leaning forward slightly and said, "I got twenty-four hours to reply. During that time we're both safe. If I say no, or just don't get in touch, they take you out."

Nancy instinctively touched her throat, tugging nervously at her gold chain with the small silver Star of

David on it. A present from Lucco when she had told him good Catholics were not allowed to marry Jewish girls.

"Go to Internal Affairs."

He shook his head.

"How about the Feds?"

His eyes narrowed.

"Okay, forget I spoke." They sat in silence. Nancy sipped her cold drink. "This is serious heat."

"It's life and death, nothing in between. This is immediate heat."

"Lucco, you can't even contemplate taking it."

"I have to tell you honey, I look at you and I looked at you in there today, conning Almeda . . ."

"I was not conning him, you dick, that was serious advocacy."

"I was proud of you. They have to make you a partner, you win this you have to do that."

He gazed at her sometimes with so much love she felt guilty. Not because she loved him any less but because she knew the one thing she wanted to give him more than any other, their child, was proving impossible. And from what he had just said, time was not on their side. And Lucco would make the perfect father for a Polish Jewish, Italian Catholic New York kid.

She took his big hand and raised it gently to her cheek, she pressed it to her face and kissed his thumb, near the palm. When she looked across to him, her eyes brimmed with tears. He nodded, moved. He knew, like the animals do, precisely what she had been thinking.

"Fuck them, Eddie. You handle this, whatever you do will be straight and fine. Just . . . fuck them." And two tears ran down her left cheek. Then she blinked and like the pro she was stopped any more from following.

Eddie Lucco touched his wife's face, squeezed her hand gently, and took it away, his eyes not leaving hers.

He swallowed and smiled, the anger in his eyes not a good portent for his enemies.

"Sure. I guess I needed to hear you say it. I'll fuck them good. Now you get back in there and destroy the DA's case, I want to be married to a partner, boy, then we really could afford to move to the East Side . . ." He glanced across to her protection officers, thinking they must have wondered what the hell was going down between the Luccos, but the two detectives nearby were taking delivery of their food.

Lucco was outraged. "How come they got served first?"

"Maybe they have influence," Nancy said.

"Just make sure they pay their check. I can't stand cops on the make."

Nancy gazed at him, so scared the flesh on the backs of her hands felt cold. But at the same time, and to her surprise, elated. Lucco often talked about his first partner, a grizzled veteran of forty-one who had died trying to rescue a suicide, a bridge jumper (she had survived, owing to some bushes breaking her fall), who had told him about the difference between a little heat, serious heat, and immediate heat. Immediate heat was totally dangerous, life threatening, and . . . his word, addictive. Nobody who had not lived on the very edge could ever appreciate the addictive nature of that much adrenaline.

Well, now Nancy knew what he meant. Suddenly the serious heat, the danger from the cartel, had taken on a dreadful immediacy.

"Tell me how much again . . . ?" she asked him quietly.

And he leaned closer and murmured, "Four million."

"Jesus Christ," she said, quieter this time. "I suppose we're safe till your deadline expires, when's that?"

"Midnight."

Freddie arrived with their food.

"What kept you, pal?" asked Lucco, the way New Yorkers do, and while the small Chinese waiter placed the dishes on the table and muttered something about the kitchen staff, he held his wife's gaze for a long moment.

"Life on the edge, huh?" he said.

"They should put their orders on separate spikes," announced Freddie. "That way no more mix-ups."

"You said it," said Lucco, loosening his necktie another couple of inches. And Nancy shook her head and smiled.

16

CEREMONY OF INNOCENCE

Two letters and three postcards from Siobhan had assuaged Eugene and Mhairaid Pearson's terrible anxiety for their daughter's safety, but while Mhairaid was still in the dark about her child's whereabouts, Judge Eugene Pearson was now aware that she was in the hands of the cartel.

Restrepo had told him Siobhan was being well cared for, was indeed studying piano at the feet of the Venezuelan maestro, and that the girl had no idea she was not free to leave. And of course she was completely free to leave the moment Pearson flew out to Bogotá, which should be quite soon, when he was satisfied with the cartel's arrangements for delivery of the cocaine to Vigo and with the security and discretion of the wholesalers the Lorca Group would be distributing to, so that he could impart to Restrepo the key to the two 3.5-inch computer discs he had given to the Colombian lawyer. Then he would return to Ireland with his beloved daughter and sit back and watch the Organization's funds swell at the rate of two million dollars each month.

This situation trapped the judge in a dilemma of classic proportions. Of course the cartel deal would provide more than enough funds to take the terror initiative and blast the pubs and dance halls, the airport terminals, crowded bus stations, and shopping malls throughout the British mainland and carve a swathe of death and mutilation across Europe wherever there were Brit soldiers and their families. Indeed, there would even be sufficient funds to purchase more sophisticated ground-to-air missiles in order to realize one of Judge Eugene Pearson's most often argued notions at secret meetings of the Army Council, which was to blast a jumbo jet out of the sky as it approached Heathrow Airport, just outside London.

By the Blessed Virgin, two or three of these would soon bring the Brit Government to a negotiating mood, make no mistake, ruminated Pearson as he strolled from the Law Courts, through Phoenix Park, to a certain primary school, St. Madeleine the Miraculous.

But his fierce antagonism to illegal drugs and his silent oath to destroy the IRA connection before it got under way stood second only to his need to bring Siobhan safely back from South America. Therefore even the devoutly wished scheme to visit another Lockerbie airliner disaster on the neat suburbs of West London would have to wait until the money could be obtained from more respectable methods, like bank jobs or the vast rackets in the Six Counties and in Kilburn, London, that were skimming tens of thousands a year from the British Social Security, or from threats to contaminate food products from vast supermarket conglomerates (an idea of Pearson's). But cocaine? Eugene Pearson felt contempt for Casey's notion that the grass roots Provo supporters could be kept in the dark, or that they would not care about the Organization pushing drugs on its own doorstep.

But time was running out. The road haulage and salvage company was operating routinely, the European crime syndicates—which were to distribute the cocaine onwards to smaller traffickers and eventually to the streets and playgrounds that, apparently, were such a lucrative part of the market—had been contacted and were ready to do business and it merely remained for a representative to fly to Bogotá and hand over the keys to the computer codes that would provide the cartel with details of times and places for delivery of around two hundred tons of cocaine over a six-month period.

Waiting for him at St. Madeleine's were Declan Burke, Brendan Casey, and Mary Connelly, gathered for one of the rare and, of necessity, furtive meetings of the Army Council of the Provisional IRA. Its purpose was to give formal approval to Pearson's report on Lorca, which was now set up and ready to go. Pearson also wanted to raise the matter of a counterproductive killing that had shocked Irish listeners to radio news reports that very morning.

Until the bastards had kidnapped Siobhan as a hostage against his good behavior, it had been Pearson's intention to recommend Brendan Casey, the Provos' chief of staff, for the final visit to Bogotá. In Casey's absence he had planned to tip off the American Drug Enforcement Agency and Spanish Customs with details of the Vigo operation. But now it had become imperative he make that journey himself. Nothing was more important than bringing his precious baby home to Dublin. There were plenty of good places she could study music in Ireland. There must be. He would find one. That was for sure.

And as he passed a group of junkies huddled around

a pusher, just inside the gates of Phoenix Park, thin and ashen faced and shivering with cold or anticipation or both, he could not contain a grimace. Somehow, he had to work out how to get Siobhan back safe and sound and still find some way of wrecking the council's suicidal plan to fund itself from drug money. For the story was bound to come out one day, and that would destroy the movement's integrity in the eyes of honest patriots who had fought for more than twenty bloodstained years to free the Six Counties from the English yoke.

He reached the plain green wood side door of the primary school. The squeals and happy yells of two hundred youngsters playing reminded him this was lunchtime. He wished he had remembered to bring a sandwich.

"Mr. Hannah?" The aging Sister smiled, her old face pink and serene, deep inside her wimple. "Come away in, sure are your friends not expecting you?"

Eugene Pearson climbed down some stairs to a subterranean maze of tiled corridors and pipes and boilers and small storerooms. The nun indicated a door at the far end of one corridor and, ducking her head, turned and went back the way they had come.

Inside the storeroom, a jumble of desks and piled cartons of infants' coloring books and poster paints and all the paraphernalia for educating four- to seven-year-olds played hosts to the Army Council, meeting in furtive and secret session, of the Provisional IRA.

"Welcome, comrade," said Declan Burke in the Irish tongue. "Congratulations on a good and thorough piece of work."

"The young girl and her granny who got killed this morning . . ." began Pearson without preamble, laying his briefcase down and pulling a wooden straight-backed chair toward him ". . . was that IPLA?" IPLA stood for Irish People's Liberation Army and it was a murderous (even by Provo standards) bunch of psychos who enjoyed all the business and life-style of killing and had seized on the Cause as an excuse for it.

"It was us, Eugene." Brendan Casey sat on an infant's desk and seat set, holding a flame over his pipe. A draft of air snuffed it out. "I've ordered an inquiry."

The incident referred to had taken place at seven-thirty in the morning of the same day. A sixteen-year-old Protestant girl had been taken out of a car driven by her maternal grandmother in the village of Ballynahinch, in the North, stopped at gunpoint, made to lie on the ground and had been shot through each knee, each elbow, and finally, writhing, sobbing, and vomiting in agony, twice in the face. The grandmother had climbed out of the car in an attempt to stop the horror and had been shot three times in the stomach with the U.S.-issue M-16 one of the four hooded attackers had been wielding. The girl's wounds were caused, an autopsy later established, by .45 slugs from a Colt combat automatic. It had taken the grandmother three hours and eight long minutes to give up the breath of life. Her intestines had been spilled for yards in every direction on the asphalt where she lay.

The killers were reported, by shocked Catholic workmen who witnessed the murders, to have whooped and cheered as they drove away in a stolen car that was later found burned out on the outskirts of the IRA's safe haven of Dundalk, in the Irish Republic.

"An inquiry is an internal matter. In the meantime, who's handling the press?" Pearson regretted the loss of Danny Morrison, who had been an able handler of the press until his imprisonment for conspiring to execute a tout.

"Liam."

"Well, I hope he's up to it. What's the line?"

"The Prot kid was a hardened killer with the UFF. Four scalps, we've provided details."

Eugene Pearson looked mildly surprised. "Was she now . . . ?"

The others smiled patiently at his innocence, exchanging glances as if to say, "Isn't he sweet, the silly old fool."

"No, she was nobody, Eugene. But we have to turn it to our advantage. The granny got in the cross fire. Death regretted et cetera." He picked up a colorful infants' textbook called *ABC of Wonderful Things* and idly flicked through it.

"Great operation you're running, Eugene," said Declan Burke, the president of the Army Council. "Now who's going to take the codes to Restrepo in Bogotá . . . ?"

"I thought Mary," said Casey, inclining his head toward Mary Connelly, the university lecturer at Trinity. Another fait accompli, thought Pearson.

"I'll go," he announced, brooking no argument. "I've seen it through this far, I might as well see it to the end . . ."

"The end, Eugene?" asked Casey, still gazing at the *ABC of Wonderful Things*.

"Of phase one."

Silence. The shouts of schoolchildren above the cellars were barely audible.

Burke and Mary Connelly glanced to Casey. This boy is calling the shots now, thought Eugene Pearson. If I don't put a spanner in his wheel he's going to be the next bloody president. He raised his shoulders and relaxed against a table on which were heaped boxes of crayons and cartons of basic alphabet books.

"Plus I will be able to bring Siobhan home . . ." His eyes fixed on Brendan Casey. There was no mercy in his heart.

Casey actually looked away first.

The silence was by then truly awkward.

Declan Burke cleared his throat. "Then of course you must go. How is the bench taking your absences? Your trips abroad?"

"We get a fair amount of leave, Declan. Don't you worry about that."

Perhaps it was to ease the tension, to clear the air. To bring Pearson right back into the heart of things. But to his own surprise, the president of the Army Council found himself saying, "Mary's had quite a coup. Did you know we have access to a fellow in the MI-6? Working out of Century House no less. He thinks he's a right clever fellow, but Mary, bless her heart, has got the measure of him. Isn't that right, Mary . . . ?"

Mary almost blushed and said yes that was so. And Judge Eugene Pearson was admitted to the tight and close-mouthed circle of the Provos Intelligence Planning Staff (Burke, Casey, and Mary Connelly) and the encoded confessions of one David Arbuthnot Jardine, CMG, which the Englishman had told in his own form of code, but had been tape-recorded in the confessional by Father Wheatley, who was originally official IRA but had come over to the Stickies when volunteer Bobby Sands had been the first but not the last Provo prisoner to die in Long Kesh during the hunger strikes.

After an altar boy had mentioned to Wheatley that his mother, a government chauffeur, thought the tall man was a "spook"—as the boy, doubtless a loyal subject of the Crown, had put it—the priest had passed the information to Sinn Fein's London intelligence officer. Jardine had been discreetly shadowed by members of the Intelligence Cell Structure in London and his connection with Century House had been established.

Thereafter, every one of David Jardine's confessions heard by Wheatley were taped and posted to Dublin, where the quite brilliant Mary Connelly had them decoded by one of her colleagues, who was not only a sympathizer but a translator of rare texts and one of the team who set the *Irish Times* crossword puzzles. Thus, David Jardine's supposedly anodyne confessions to his chum, the Almighty, were being studied by the Provisional IRA on a fairly regular basis.

Often the exercise was either meaningless or of no interest, for South America was not a sphere of activity or fund-raising for the organization. But since the Provos began playing footsy with the Medellín Cartel, anything involving the British and Colombia had become of great interest. And Mary's erudite colleague had pulled at the entrails of Jardine's confession about screwing some trusting subordinate's wife and had just a suspicion that SIS were planning to put a man inside Pablo Envigado's Medellín Cartel.

"So you be careful, Eugene," admonished Burke.

"And tell Pablo, not Restrepo, for I don't trust the fucker, that the Brits are trying to get into his knickers. And anyone who turns up out of the blue should be hung over some hot coals till he spits out the details of his apprenticeship." Casey laid the *ABC of Wonderful Things* back on the desk with some reluctance. "Particularly if Pablo thinks he noticed the fella first. For that's the way the Brits operate, right, Mary?"

"And he'll speak South American Spanish like a native," said Mary, "and his background will check out unless they really pick at it. But pass it on, Eugene. It'll do the Organization a bit of good."

Eugene Pearson contemplated this. It was quite impressive, if true. Sometimes Mary had some weird and wonderful ideas. He nodded. "Most impressive, Mary." Then he glanced at Brendan Casey. "Why did they shoot the girl in the first place?"

"You know Martin, Eugene. He'd been waiting since

four in the morning on a tip there was an RUC typist used that route on her way to work. He just got pissed off and blew the kid away, he's highly strung, young Martin. You know what it's like, at the sharp end." His cold gaze bored into Pearson's head. "No you don't, do you? Well, good luck in Bogotá . . ."

And Casey tucked his pipe back in his pocket and left the room, picking up his three wingers in the corridor and climbing up some stairs to emerge into the playground and stroll off, patting a couple of flaxen-haired little girls, twins maybe, on their flaxen little heads.

Mary Connelly left to return to the headmistress's office, where she was researching a talk on primary education.

Only Burke and Pearson were left.

"How's Mhairaid?" asked Burke.

"Right as rain," replied Eugene Pearson, and he left the room, nodding to the president, and struggled with feelings he had never experienced before. If he had been a seminarist, they would have been called "doubts."

Beneath the port window of the Boeing 747, as the aircraft banked steeply to the left, David Jardine watched the rooftops of Chelsea drift past, and the serpentine meandering of the River Thames, where a couple of tugboats, towing chains of barges, and a scruffy white motorboat plied their ways.

The speaker system was asking everyone to fasten their seat belts and put the backs of their seats to the upright position. Jardine complied, leaving his backrest one notch from upright, which was more comfortable and which, he felt, was his small contribution to civil disobedience against officialdom.

"Your jacket, Mr. Norwell." The hostess smiled and handed him his lightweight linen jacket, which he had purchased in Brooks Brothers, on Madison Avenue, four years before. The Americans made looser fittings than the tight, tailored English cut, and being a big, well-muscled chap, oh all right putting on a few pounds, Jardine felt more comfortable in slightly more generous jackets.

He thanked the girl and laid the jacket on the seat beside him. The window seat. He always sat on the aisle, just in case there was ever a requirement to move fast. Then, as the rumble of landing gear trembled the floor slightly and groaned audibly, he touched his half-full glass of California chardonnay and sighed with sheer pleasure.

For David Arbuthnot Jardine was essentially a hedonist. He knew that pleasure, bliss even, came in short supply, rationed by the gods, and was often followed or indeed abruptly interrupted by life's shitty stick. But to be a hedonist is to be an optimist and he was sane enough to recognize the good moments and savor them, and to thank his chum, God, for them. Although he had given God a wide berth recently, for he felt the Elizabeth Ford episode had not earned him many brownie points.

However, this was always a moment he savored to his very bones and sinews, suspended like a returning god of some pagan era over England, his England which he loved far far more than Eugene Pearson (of whom Jardine was still unaware) loved his Ireland. It was the earth, what Russians call their *zemlya*, and the history and the people, including the West Indians and Asians and other immigrants and stretching back to the Sir Richard Fotheringhams with their mad, heroic sacrifices, and not some vague, rancorous idea wrapped in that dread word patriotism. It was the earth, his England, that David Jardine loved with a deeply personal . . . affection.

Not that he would admit such a thing to anyone. Except maybe his children, for he believed it was his place to help them to shape themselves. Without pushing. Jardine preferred not to push, which sometimes confused those whom he suddenly pushed with unexpected and chilling ruthlessness.

As the Boeing began its landing approach, the hum and groan of ailerons and flaps being trimmed reminded him of sailing on the Dart Estuary, and the neat suburbs of Slough beneath the port and starboard windows loomed ever closer. He thought about his conversation with Spencer Percy at the North Dade Correction Center, and about his supper of blackened dolphin (which he was always assured was not actually *dolphin,* like Flipper, intelligence which he chose to accept) sitting outside at Sundays on the Beach, a marvelous, sprawling old wooden shack restaurant and bar on the Key Biscayne waterfront, straight out of Hemingway, with marlin-fishing boats and a yacht harbor and the prettiest, charmingest, sexiest young waitresses and big gray pelicans sitting brooding, like old men of the sea, on weathered wood piles jutting out from the calm harbor water, and herons, tame and at the same time aloof. There had been live ska music played by sleepy and smiling West Indians from the nearby Bahamas, with that lazy, sensual backbeat of heavy bass that always reminded Jardine of his mother's old Bendix washing machine, circa 1957.

John Consadine, his CIA host and chief of the south Florida office, and his wife, Joni, had been warm company and his conversation with John had been mutually rewarding, with each man bringing the other up to date on many intelligence matters of mutual interest concerning the West Indies, Cuba, and Central and South America.

As the monstrous tires of the Boeing 747 hovered for milliseconds over that last, enticing inch of unspent flight, the tall SIS man watched the shadow of the port wing on the runway. And being David Jardine, the briefest recollection of Elizabeth's face—slack and flushed, on the point of ultimate pleasure, her tongue caressing her lip, her eyes fixed on his, sharing their hedonistic, decadent, secret addiction to sins of the flesh—intruded and occasioned the merest smile on his countenance. For being David Jardine, he was already beginning to forgive himself the unforgivable.

He went through passport control as Norwell, unnoticed by any of the teams of watchers that frequent airports—the Customs Special Investigation Branch, Police Special Branch, Immigration Service, and, occasionally, people from Box 500, as the Security Service, was known and from his own service.

He walked swiftly across the Terminal 4 concourse, through the automatic doors, and out to the bus and taxi ranks and the private-car collection point. He looked around for Stevenson, his office driver, and to his delight and surprise, there was his own car—a slightly beat-up Mercedes 300 TE estate car, dark blue in color—with Dorothy leaning against the side, hands in the pockets of her slacks, a vast wool sweater that she had bought while on location in Norway three winters ago stretched over her vast frame. A Gitane cigarette hung from her mouth and she gazed at Jardine with that half-amused, half-reproachful look that had driven him wild when he was a student at Oxford and that still aroused feelings of the deepest affection he had ever known. He supposed it was called love. And he was well aware just what sort of a bloody hypocrite that made him.

He laid his valise down by the back of the car and

hugged Dorothy so tightly she asked him, gruffly, "What's up? Somebody shoot at you again . . . ?"

"Not this time. Maybe next."

A mild breeze tugged at the trees and long grass around the little churchyard. David, Dorothy, Andrew, and Sally Jardine stood by a long double gravestone laid with freshly picked flowers. They wore formal clothes, Andrew in his Sherborne school charcoal-gray suit, with white shirt, shoes polished (for once—that had been the subject of a mild debate the night before) and a necktie that he had won for playing cricket for his house, in his house colors, of which he made little but was actually quite proud. Sally wore a long silk skirt and purple jersey wool top. Dorothy wore a dark blue cotton blouse, floral-patterned silk skirt, and her best navy leather shoes. Jardine wore his other Huntsman suit, the dark grey herringbone double-breasted, with a deep maroon tie patterned with tiny white parachutes between blue wings, the tie of the parachute regiment in which he had served after Oxford and before being plucked from Wonderland and honed into an able and indeed ambitious spy by a young and slender, always laughing, always totally mad Ronnie Szabodo.

"Dear Lord," said Jardine, without a trace of embarrassment or affectation, "please accept these our prayers for the comfort and grace of the departed souls of Sir Richard Fotheringham and his beloved son Guy, who died near this spot, on this day, in your year, oh Lord, 1648, defending to the death their home and their king . . . and all that they believed was right and just, without hesitating and with no thought of compromise. Or surrender."

The wind rose momentarily, tugging at the wire

fencing and carrying the sound of sheep from the lea, moaning through the elm trees at one corner of the churchyard. "And grant us, dear God, the strength and the faith to live our lives with the same courage, knowing that sometimes there are more precious things than life itself and that each of us, once again, dedicates our life to your grace and to our country, and to our family." He paused for a moment, then nodded to Andrew, who bless his heart was able, this year, to conceal his profound embarrassment at this ceremony dreamed up, with no liturgical basis, by his sometimes quite eccentric dad.

"Amen," said Andrew gravely, avoiding his sister's eye, for Sally was in danger of damaging herself as she attempted to suppress a relentless attack of the giggles. Only the trembling shoulders and one knee pressed against the other gave any hint of her predicament.

"Amen . . ." said Dorothy, deliberately ignoring her daughter.

Sally made some kind of muffled noise.

David Jardine stood in silence for some fifty-eight seconds. Behind the sound of the wind, he could imagine the ring of cold steel, the short, muffled reports of young Guy, his left leg amputated below the knee, the bandaged stump still bloody, using his double-barreled horse pistols to dispatch several of his father's killers before dying of flailing saber cuts at the hands of the Roundhead Scottish horsemen.

Then he stood erect, hands clasped, thumbs touching the outside seams of his trousers.

"See you next year, chaps," he said, then added, "God willing . . ." And Dorothy glanced at him.

It was twenty-nine minutes past six.

In New York City, five hours behind England, it was twenty-nine minutes after one. Eddie Lucco, in need of a shave and one hour and twenty-nine minutes into his wife Nancy's death sentence, in accordance with Restrepo's terms, sat in a rented Ford sedan, parked on the rooftop parking lot of a multistory carpark near the United Nations building. It was a hot night, and a spectacular display of atmospheric electrics gone haywire flickered and crackled in the black sky some twenty miles east of Queens, accompanied by the muffled, rumble-tumbled rumble of earth-shaking thunder. It reminded him of Vietnam, when he used to sit in a foxhole listening to B-52s carpet-bombing the Ho Chi Minh Trail across the border in Cambodia.

He checked his wristwatch. He was worried. This had been a mistake, he should have been with Nancy. Sure she had five armed cops (he had sent Sam Vargos and two Homicide buddies to reinforce the two officers assigned by Headquarters) and two neighborhood prowl cars protecting her, but that kind of help had not kept PeeWee Patrice alive.

Ninety minutes now, ninety minutes past Restrepo's deadline. And those guys did not fuck around. Lucco took a deep breath, a couple of really deep breaths, to steady his nerves. After his lunch with Nancy, when he had laid it on the line and she had told him whatever he decided to do was all right with her, so long as it screwed Restrepo and the *grupo*, he had arranged a covert meeting with a man he had come to trust more than any other outside the police department and who knew the cartel better than any cop. Eddie Lucco had called Don Mather, the Special Agent in Charge of the DEA's New York office.

The big homicide cop had learned from sources on both sides of the law that Mather was a rock-solid guy who could be trusted implicitly. Plus he liked the man on a one-to-one basis from their work together on the Bellevue Hospital slayings.

They had met in the same rooftop car lot at five twenty-one that evening. Lucco had told Mather every particular of Luis Restrepo Osorio's attempted bribe, of the offer no man would find easy to refuse—four million bucks in cash, anywhere in the world, or the bloody murder of his wife. Nothing personal. This was just business.

Frankly, Restrepo had said, we would take no pleasure in hurting your lovely wife. So please accept the money.

On the one hand, this was just a pricey variation on the kind of "offer" New York cops, detectives mainly, got all the time. But on the other, forgetting the stupendous amount, the *grupo* would most certainly and efficiently, and doubtless with maximum cruelty, carry out their threat. And real soon.

Mather had listened, after Eddie Lucco had checked him for a wire, because the big cop did not trust anyone anymore. And they had talked out on the roof, away from their cars and any directional microphones.

The DEA chief had not seemed surprised by Lucco's story. He had asked Lucco if he would stay right there. He understood the cop's problem immediately. It was not uncommon in Florida and Las Vegas. And of course in Colombia itself. Lucco had emphasized the midnight deadline and Mather had assured him he would take advice from the DEA's deputy chief in Washington and "some other people" and come back with, he hoped, an effective response to what was, essentially, a hostage situation without the other side even bothering to kidnap the victim.

Eddie Lucco had agreed to stay put. Not to try to phone Nancy or anyone else. So for the past six hours, the normally manically busy detective had done just that. He gazed at the electrical storm, deciding to give it another half hour, then he was outta there.

The noise of tires ascending, bringing an automobile up each ramp from floor to floor, had become familiar over the long hours. Each time, Lucco had held his gun easily in his lap and watched the ramp to the roof in his rearview mirror. Each time had been a false alarm, but this time the screeches of rubber got louder and he could see the glow of approaching headlights. He opened the door and slid out into the night on the roof. He was standing in the shadow of an air-conditioner vent when a white Porsche 928 growled into view from the ramp. It parked beside his rented Ford.

One man got out. It was Don Mather. He strolled to the edge of the rooftop lot and stopped to light a cigarette, gazing out over New York City and the electrical storm. He did not seem worried by Lucco's absence from the parked Ford.

After a careful examination of the environment, Eddie Lucco emerged from his cover and crossed gently to Mather, resting his back on the parapet and checking out the ramp and other points of egress.

"Eddie, I've spoken to my director in Washington, and to somebody I trust at the Treasury. Also the Special Investigations director at Justice." Mather glanced at his wristwatch, "I'm sorry it's taken so long, but I needed to ensure the integrity of the operation. And get approval at the highest level."

"What fuckin operation, Don? What are you talking about?"

Silence. Down below, a ferryboat, windows lit, moved upriver. A helicopter rose from the East River heliport, dipped and fluttered above Brooklyn, heading toward JFK Airport.

"Okay." Mather leaned back and looked Lucco straight in the eye. "I am required to tell you, Lieutenant, you don't have to do this . . . But I figured you knew that, for you could've gone directly to NYPD Internal Affairs. Which is by the book, which is what you should've done . . ."

Lucco knew what was coming. He had always known.

"It's not a safe proposition. It's not attractive to any decent cop and believe me, we know you are one straight guy."

Eddie Lucco watched Mather's face. His wife was technically dead. "You want me to take the dough." The big cop raised his shoulders and glanced, pointedly, at his watch.

"Buddy, you don't have to do it. But if you agree, you would be working as a federal agent, under my direction. The money would belong to the U.S. Treasury. You will have committed no crime."

"No wires . . ."

"Eddie, we're talking something sophisticated and important to the whole fight against these people. Once they make you, with a four-million-buck handout, they will not be satisfied with you taking the heat off the Jane Doe investigation."

"They'll be back."

"You would be on Pablo's payroll. Everything they ask you to do for them, it's going to tell us all about them. It will be like having a direct line to their operation here in NYC."

"And Nancy might just stay alive. Always figuring they have not made the hit already."

"Of course." There was nothing else to say.

After four long minutes of private deliberation, Eddie Lucco nodded. "So I better phone this asshole."

London was a city of contrasts. The polished, high-tech complexes of commerce, banking, fashionable shopping areas like New Bond Street and Knightsbridge were only yards away from scenes of Dickensian squalor and neglect, with the dispossessed living rough out of cardboard boxes, their worldly goods clutched in pathetic plastic supermarket bags. The rat population of the metropolis was growing at a rate that was so alarming the statistics were suppressed and classified under the Official Secrets Act.

Nowhere was the contrast so in evidence as on a narrow street, perhaps more Hogarthian than Dickensian, which nestled under the edge of, towering above it, Waterloo Station, the glass-and-concrete monument to British rail travel at its most hygienic and spaciously modern. The street was known, and had been for over two hundred years, as Mepham Street.

One side of Mepham Street is a high wall of soot-stained and crumbling old red brick, the rampart and buttress that separates the citadel of high-tech glass and efficiency, Waterloo, from that rodent-scurrying, vagrant-infested urban ravine.

The other side is similar, with a series of vaulted, tunnel-like apertures, some of them converted into storage spaces, workshops, a hand carwash and a public house, as the English call their bars. The pub is called the Hole in the Wall, for that is what it is, and from time to time its patrons find conversation drowned by the thunder and rumble of railroad trains passing on the many tracks overhead. The Hole in the Wall, however, serves some passing excellent beer and an eclectic Irish stout called Murphy's. Less bitter than Guinness, but black and full of body.

David Jardine and Ronnie Szabodo tended to repair to the Hole in the Wall from time to time, for they could be sure that no one of any authority, or pretensions to social acceptability, would venture near the place.

At two fifty-three on the day after Jardine's return from Florida, the two intelligence officers from the South American Sphere of Interest emerged from the Hole in the Wall with a couple of pints of Murphy's inside them and strolled past several of the railway arches before stopping and holding a quiet review of their most secret plans for the imminent implementation of Operation Corrida. It was a conversation held, perhaps appropriately, the way things were to turn out, against a background of flickering shadows inside the perpetual gloom of an open vaulted arch, and tall orange and yellow flames from a bonfire built by a Dante-esque group of furtive, long-haired hoboes, with string tied around the waists of their ragged overcoats, woollen caps, and bent hats pulled from some rag and bone heap. They moved and argued among themselves, fighting, as if underwater, for possession of a milk bottle filled with God knew what kind of stupefying liquor.

Jardine watched this tableau as he listened to Szabodo outlining the cases for and against Malcolm Strong and Harry Ford, who had both scored top grades for their infiltration into Colombia, settling into their bespoke identities and legends. The lawyer, Strong, in Barranquilla, the soldier, Ford, in Bogotá.

"Actually, David, as a matter of fact, either man can do the business. They were well chosen in the first place. Both first-class operator material."

"But the lawyer gets your vote . . ."

"The soldier . . ." Szabodo stuck his hands deep inside his topcoat pockets, hunched his shoulders, and gazed at his feet as he scuffed one shoe against the ground. He sucked in air, deep in thought, and the gap in his teeth was evident. He kept the denture in his pocket, Jardine knew that. The thing went in and out of the Magyar's mouth with practiced speed and precision, whenever the need arose. "The soldier. He's very good. No problems with him at all. I suppose, being a spy, David, not a military man, I tend to shy away from using them."

"I was a soldier . . . once," Jardine remarked. "For a few years."

"You had a good Oxford degree, David." Oxford to Szabodo was like Valhalla to a Viking or Miss Porter's to Emily Post.

"Harry Ford's a Special Forces soldier, Ronnie. He's not your marching up and down and shiny boots sort. Takes combat in his stride. Enjoys it when the bullets are flying. I must say it always terrified me. And he is now a fully trained operator. I'm not fussed about his mildly adverse psychological profile. What the hell do they know?"

"Bullets were never my cup of tea," replied Szabodo, and David Jardine smiled, for he knew his companion had dropped Molotov cocktails down the long gun barrels of Russian T-54 tanks during the unequal battle for Budapest, in September 1956. The squat Hungarian had two bullet holes in his left forearm and a bayonet wound from a Tartar paratrooper who had pinned Ronnie's left thigh to a wooden floor before receiving eight bullets from a young man, attached to a British newspaper, who had been supplying Budapest's freedom fighters with medical packs, morphine, plasma, weapons, and ammunition. That young man was now sixty-two, mused Jardine, retired from SIS and running a yacht charter business in the south of Spain, along with a stunningly good-looking woman he had met when she worked as a waitress in one of St. James's Street's more exclusive gentlemen's clubs.

David Jardine turned his gaze away from the surreal shadows dancing on the archway wall and studied

Ronnie Szabodo for a moment. His seemingly irrelevant memories had just reminded him, if reminding was needed, why he should heed Szabodo's carefully considered advice.

"If you have doubts about Harry . . ." he said.

Szabodo looked pained. He screwed up his eyes as the flames rose higher, beginning to roar. "I think he lacks the . . . *gravitas* of Strong."

After a long pause, Jardine scratched his forehead. "Here's how I'm thinking. The lines along which . . . On the one hand we have steady-Eddie, cautious but full of initiative Malcolm Strong. On the other, Harry Ford is more able, with his background, to save himself, and therefore our good name, if a wheel comes off. He's experienced, as opposed to well-trained, in survival over hostile terrain and in evading capture. Plus, psychologically, he's been through dangerous work like this before. So he has actually proved himself." Jardine shrugged. "Just to be devil's advocate . . ."

"David, I've said my piece. The decision is of course yours."

Two of the hoboes were locked in silent struggle for possession of the milk bottle, each with two hands wrapped around it. One wore woollen, fingerless gloves. The other, a battered felt hat, with an uncommonly high crown. The scene reminded Jardine of a 1960s movie by Ingmar Bergman, or maybe Luís Buñuel, the Spanish surrealist.

"All right, Ronnie," Jardine heard himself saying. "It's going to be the soldier." And he was visited by a vivid and disconcerting memory of Elizabeth Ford's glistening thighs, her head lolling in ecstasy.

Damnit, Jardine, he assured himself, this is a profoundly thought-through, professional judgment. Personal considerations do not enter into it. The madness with the girl is over. It's a closed book.

"Get Strong out of Barranquilla and into Holding."
Holding was a safe house in Caracas, Venezuela, which
had a long and ill-protected border with Colombia.
There the passed-over of the two candidates would wait,
maintaining his cover, until the chosen operator had
been successfully played into Op Corrida.

"Fine." Szabodo turned to glance at a black taxi,
which was waiting beneath the high, crumbling wall
below Waterloo Station. He nodded and the taxi engine
started, the car moved forward and stopped near the two
men.

"You're taking a helicopter from the Ministry of Defense roof to RAF Northolt, a bigger, faster chopper to
Brize Norton, and RAF jet transport to the NATO airfield
outside Madrid. Fly Madrid Bogotá, you will be there in
time for breakfast. Everything is ready for you to play our
Joe into the game. Now, David . . ."

David Jardine sighed. Sometimes the Magyar fussed
like a Jewish mother. "Yes, Ronnie?"

"Are you prepared? Is there anything you need from
us here?"

"No, thanks. It's time. Let's go . . ."

And the two men climbed into the black taxi and it
drove off. The driver knew where to go, for he was
employed by the same people who paid Jardine and
Szabodo.

As the taxi drove out toward the Cut, the disputed
milk bottle slipped from the grasp of the struggling
vagrants and smashed on the grimy cobblestones. The
bonfire flames whooshed higher as spirit splashed from
the shards and ignited.

17

PICADOR

Mary Connelly eased herself gently from the leaden leg and arm of Maude Burke, now fast asleep and snoring gently, which was how their lovemaking usually ended. She patted her lover on the rump and made a mental note to waken her and drive her to the Abbey Theatre in time for the end of the last act, so that Maude could mingle with the emerging crowd and be collected by her husband, Declan, company secretary for a chain of butchers' shops and president of the Army Council of the Provisional IRA.

Mary padded her chunky frame across the bed-sitting room to the kitchen, lit a gas ring, and filled a beat-up old kettle from the faucet at the sink. She lit a Marlboro cigarette and walked quietly down the short, narrow corridor to the bathroom, where she dropped the plug in the big, old off-white bathtub and turned on lashings of hot and cold water, splashing some orange-and-walnut oil into the water from which most satisfying clouds of steam were already ascending.

She relieved herself and flushed the wc. Then, relaxed and satisfied with the evening so far, she peered at her reflection in the fast-misting-up mirror above the washbasin, pushing her unruly dark hair this way and that.

"Ah, Jeysus, Mary," she thought to herself. "You were once the prettiest girl and look at you now." Too many nights working for the Organization, writing planning papers, working out briefing documents for Active Service Units. Writing up security instructions. *And* holding her job at Trinity, marking essays, preparing lectures.

Her poor face could do with some more fresh air. The chunky corpus with more exercise. She was smoking too much. Eating too much junk food, but she never could be bothered to cook properly for herself. And the booze. Well, least said about that.

She had just decided to put on the new Sinead O'Connor tape and pour herself a glasseen of good Jamieson's whiskey, preparatory to rousing Maude and sharing the hot tub, when the knock at her front door caused her to jump with alarm. Jesus Mary and Joseph now who could that be?

There it was again. Knock-knock-knock. Knock knock.

A student handing in a late essay? Surely not. They were all out getting pissed or burying their heads in Synge and J.P. Donleavy, which was their work for this month.

Dermot Burke? No chance. No Provo would ever risk being seen like that, out of context, a butcher's clerk on a university campus. Not a chance.

Knock knock knock.

"All right, all right, in the name of Saint Philomena of the one leg I'm coming, damnit."

She glanced in at Maude, who was snoring gently through the minor commotion, smiled, and pulled the door to the one room shut. Almost shut, for there was a pile of books on Parnell blocking its arc.

Mary Connelly pulled on an old raincoat—her Easter Rising Mac her colleagues on the faculty jokingly called it, never guessing how close they were to the truth—and crossed to the door.

"Who is it?" she called.

"Finbar MacMurragh," answered a vaguely familiar voice, and when she cautiously opened the door, Mary Connelly was confronted by the dripping wet figure of Judge Eugene Pearson, his raincoat soaked and rainwater running from his brown felt hat. He was holding a briefcase.

Of course, Finbar MacMurragh was the wee man's code name. She tried to suppress a laugh.

"Well, Finbar, I'd ask you in but I'm just going to pop into the bath. Unless of course you would care to join me?"

Pearson almost jumped back down the stairwell. Mary smiled. She had judged the good judge bang to rights.

"Mary, it's just a couple of quick questions, can I come in . . . ?" He was peering past her at the gap of light in the bedsit doorway. "It is important."

Mary bit her lip. The last thing she needed Judge Eugene Pearson to see was the wife of the president of the Army Council lying sprawling, naked but for her cultured pearls, snoring the sleep of the sensually sated.

She lowered her voice to a conspiratorial, almost inaudible breath. "Come in, but go directly into the bathroom, I'll tell you why when you're in there . . ."

The bathroom was damp with steam, and Eugene Pearson blinked and removed his wet felt hat. Mary slipped in and closed the door. Perspiration was running down their faces almost before they started to speak.

"Eugene, make it fast, I have a fellow in there and

the last person I want him to see is you . . . what the hell are you doing here?" Mary Connelly was no fool. She knew attack was always the best form of defense.

"A fellow? Oh. I see." He pursed his lips and frowned. His white shirt collar was going limp in the orange-and-walnut-scented steam. He lowered his voice and said something, but the roar of the running tapwater into the steaming tub rendered him inaudible.

"I can't hear you," said Mary.

He put his face close to her ear. "I need to have details of this British official. The one who goes to confession."

"Why?"

"Sancho Panza is no fool." Sancho Panza was the current code name for Pablo Envigado. "I need the facts, if he's to believe us. And that will do us a lot of good . . ."

Mary sighed. This was a subject that required careful consideration. Disclosing sources was never a good idea. Even to the Movement's policy advisor.

"I don't know, Eugene . . ."

"Remember I have been admitted to the circle. I need to know."

Christ, any moment now Maude is going to wander in here, doubtless brandishing the enormous pink dildo, oh God this is no way to conduct an Armed Struggle.

It took Mary Connelly precisely one second to figure out which was the greatest risk. On balance, it was not her fault she was wrong.

"His name is David Jardine. He runs South American intelligence operations for SIS. He lives at 143 Tite Street, in Chelsea, and at Fotheringham Manor near Marlborough, in Wiltshire. He goes to confession at Farm Street Church, irregularly. And he seems to be attempting to put a man inside Sancho Panza's outfit. A younger man, with a very pretty and very horny wife. Eugene, why not stay and have a bath with me? With us both . . . my boyfriend is very kinky . . ."

She laughed as the hurried footsteps of Eugene Pearson grew fainter, and the downstairs door banged shut.

The door to the bedsit opened and Maude Burke stood there, in nothing but her cultured pearls.

Mary gazed, still chuckling, into her eyes, and pushed the front door shut, very gently.

———

Pablo Envigado was running, feet pounding, breathing hard, his shoulders bumping against the earth and rock of the tunnel. The smell of damp, stale earth was in his nostrils and the adrenaline was flowing. The mistake had been to get comfortable at La Cama de Mariscal. The clean air, the stunning vista, looking down the valley to the rooftops and church towers of Santa Fe. He had been able to think there, to reestablish control of *el grupo*, which had been slipping from his hands during the last two years, constantly on the run.

The real mistake had been, of course, to declare war on the Colombian government and administration, to sentence the previous president, Barco, to death. He had not appreciated that sovereign governments could take a vendetta back to you. And they had more soldiers.

El padrino generally moved every few days and even then he had narrowly escaped capture eight times. And on a number of occasions he had been taken. Then discreet negotiations, somewhat along the lines of those being conducted by Restrepo in New York, had taken place. Suitcases with millions of American dollars had taken the place of the prisoner and Don Pablo Envigado had survived to run his slice of the cartel.

As his feet thudded on the rock and earth floor of

the escape tunnel, Envigado's ears rang with the blast of explosions, the hammering din of gunfire, and the clattering roar of swarming Huey helicopters, as two groups of crack Colombian antiterrorist commandos and the Policia Nacional's paramilitary Narcotics Unit attacked from all sides.

This had been the first time they had brought the helicopters right up to the point of attack. It was normal for the special troops to get out a mile or two from the target so that they could achieve surprise by approaching silently, on foot.

Jesus Garcia, Envigado's security boss, had anticipated such an attack.

But today's raid, at dawn, had taken the *grupo*'s complex and heavily armed guard system by complete surprise. The two lazy, menacing swarms of helicopters had seemed to be heading further up the valley, and since military operations against the FARC guerrilla group had been intensifying over the past few weeks, the sight was not unusual. Then they had suddenly banked right and left, swooping fast toward the hacienda and the terraces, and teams of special troops had dropped to the ground, firing with deadly precision.

Envigado's personal bodyguard numbered forty-one men and they were fierce, ruthless, and highly trained by British and Israeli mercenaries. In the ensuing firefight, series of running firefights, Jesus Garcia and the twelve core bodyguards, all men of the caliber of Murillo and Bobby Sonson, had coolly and swiftly gotten *el padrino* and his key people, including the two Vietnamese forgers, with all their essential equipment, down into the cellars, into a long mine shaft with a crude, rope-operated elevator, and sixty feet vertically into the mountain, where a fresh tunnel had been prepared weeks before, and along which the escapers were running, cool and silent, conserving their energy.

Jesus Garcia and Bobby Sonson's brother Franco trotted in front of him, Garcia's big mongrel dog, Diablo, padding on ahead. The dog had been known to rip out the throat of someone attacking his master.

Franco carried the heavy M-60 light machine gun and Garcia had a Spas-Franchi 12-shot combat shotgun, every second round loaded with ten ball bearings, every second round loaded with one hundred flechettes, thick steel needlelike darts that tumbled forward, like a swarm of hornets, at two hundred miles per hour and would shred a man into something unrecognizable.

Also, thought Envigado, who was interested to find himself enjoying this brush with capture, possibly death, there were unmistakably British voices, British-accented Spanish being shouted, as the first wave had dropped the last twelve feet from the choppers and started firing stun and CR gas grenades, moving in an economic, well-rehearsed way, as if they had already practiced the attack on a mock-up. Which is what the renegade SAS man MacAteer had taught the *grupo*'s own soldiers.

Pablo Envigado smiled as he loped along the musty tunnel. The British SAS were known to be in Antioquia, mostly tracking and training, and carrying out reconnaissance missions, along with the army's crack Force 9 Commando.

They had tailed Gacha's son, released from jail when murder charges against him were dropped (for no good reason, with hindsight), and after three days of whoring and drinking the dumb kid had driven with his bodyguards directly to his father's hideaway. Three days later, they had been gunned down in the swimming pool, in an attack not unlike the present one, except no helicopters had gotten so close.

Jesus Garcia's inquiries had revealed that the Special Air Service had carried out the tracking and covert observation in that operation. Using secure satellite communications that went directly to their base at Hereford in England, then were relayed back to the Force 9 Operations Team, on the ground in Colombia.

Not bad, thought Don Pablo.

"Hey, Jesus . . ." he grunted as they ran.

"Sí, jefe . . ." Garcia did not look back.

"Los hombres ingléses son muy buenos. Maybe we should get some for the *grupo.* I would feel much safer I think . . ."

And they laughed as their feet hammered on the rock and dank earth floor.

A big wide-winged heron flapped lazily just above the glass-flat surface of the Bahia de Las Animas, the bay within the larger Bay of Cartagena, directly across from the Club de Pesca, a harborside restaurant that was part of the Fuerte de San Sebastian del Pastillo, one of the series of forts and fortlets, dating from 1533, when the town was founded by Don Pedro de Heredia, a conquistador from Madrid.

Harry Ford sipped his Dos Equis beer and tapped the Mustang cigarette against its pack. He had never smoked much, maybe a few at parties when he was at Sandhurst, the royal military academy, or after a steeplechase when he had ridden well. He had liked the idea, the image, of smoking. And he had occasionally bought some classy and rare brand from the smart tobacco shops around Mayfair and Piccadilly. Sobrani or Benson's Turkish filters. Camel was a neat packet. And Salem mentholated. Mostly, he admitted to himself, it was for the image rather than the tobacco.

But those last few days, he had found himself smoking for . . . comfort. He had always believed that the most dangerous places by reputation were, on balance, safer than certain rough neighborhoods in any big city. In a region of dangerous repute it was not too hard to stay out of trouble by keeping one's profile low and not taking stupid risks.

But Colombia was different. Harry had sensed it the moment he stepped off Avianca Flight AV 82 from Rio de Janeiro, bearing the passport and four-dimensional legend of Señor Carlos Nelson Arrigiada. Travelers seemed reluctant to move from the heavily guarded and patrolled arrivals terminal until they had identified their welcoming relatives or friends or business colleagues waiting in the dark, outside the armored glass windows, under the watchful eyes of more soldiers and *policia* and DAS agents, all armed with submachine guns or self-loading rifles, except for some of the DAS men who carried pistols in belt or shoulder holsters.

It had seemed, once you stepped out from the last, umbilical link with the rest of the world, that there was no going back and everyone's life expectancy would drop from years to hours.

Harry had experienced very similar feelings on his first posting to Northern Ireland as an army lieutenant, seconded for a tour with 14th Intelligence and Security Group for undercover work.

Then, he had stepped gingerly off the London–Belfast shuttle, carrying a battered canvas valise and a rucksack slung over his shoulder. Wearing faded jeans and a sports jacket with a Dublin outfitter's labels. And fully expecting to be gunned down by the Provos before he reached the two staff sergeants who would be waiting for him in the carpark.

But he had survived that day and the next, and Harry had soon gotten used to Belfast and Derry, Fermanagh and South Armagh. Ireland was in fact a very peaceful place, and most of its inhabitants, outside the ghettos, had never seen a single incident except on television.

The beauty of the countryside and the quiet good humor of its people, of all religious and political persuasions, had soon won yet another admirer, and he and Elizabeth had actually holidayed on a cruiser on the breathtaking Fermanagh lakes, mooring at a different village each night, and enjoying great crack (as in conversation) with folk in the local bars.

Three weeks into Colombia and he knew that although this was a totally different scene the population had much in common with the Irish, and he easily recognized the way they had of indicating, without saying it, that they were sick and tired of the violence and had nothing but contempt for those who visited it upon them.

However, where the Six Counties had the Provos, the INLA, the Protestant UDA, UFF, and UVF, addicted to their life-style of murder and psycho-romanticism, the long-suffering, hospitable, and essentially gentle Colombians had the various elements of the cartel (increasingly dividing into competitive factions), the procommunist FARC guerrillas, the Cuban-inspired ELN, the Maoist EPL, and a host of rural bandits and urban criminal gangs with access to cocaine and marijuana money. Add to that mixture unofficial right-wing death squads, understandably nervous and trigger-happy teenage conscripts on many street corners, a legion of heavily armed private bodyguards, and teams of undercover cops and secret agents, plus many private citizens who carried pistols for protection, and the scale of the problem, thought Harry Ford, one could begin to appreciate.

And yet . . . he gazed out across the harbor, still watching the gentle, graceful heron, feeling perspiration run down his spine in the drenching humidity, listening to a salsa band, its bass line thumping steadily and very lazily. Hospitably. It wasn't really too bad, this Colombia.

Bogotá had been, had felt, very dangerous, like Beirut without scars. But this Cartagena, it was so . . . tranquil. Sure there were armed soldiers on many street corners, sure he had been rousted out from his Renault 9 on a couple of VCPs (Vehicle Checkpoints), but what a town. The old town was built on and around the various fortifications. The hotel he had checked into was comfortable. The Caribbean locals were courteous and good-humored. The girls, well . . . Colombian girls were without a doubt the most alluring and attractive in the whole of South America. They flirted and they seemed to share the great joke that sex was fun. Anathema to the strait-laced Europeans and Yankees.

He lit his cigarette and relaxed, glancing at his watch. The message he had received, suitably coded, in Bogotá was, leave with what you might need for a few days, fly to Cartagena. Book into the Capilla del Mar hotel. On your second day, if you are absolutely sure you have not attracted a tail or any kind of interest, go at lunchtime to the Club de Pesca and order a Dos Equis beer. Take a pack of Mustang cigarettes and ask for two menus. You will be joined by a Señor Armando Torres Tejada. He is the brother of the wife of a Peruvian friend, Andreas Quesada. Her name is Lydia. You last saw her at the Quesadas' Christmas party in Lima.

And as he smoked the Mustang, a tall figure loped through the open-air restaurant, weaving among the tables. He wore a striped cotton shirt outside his linen trousers and a scarf around his neck, knotted in a slightly piratical fashion.

As Harry Ford might have guessed, Señor Armando Torres was none other than his SIS controller, David Jardine.

Jardine's Spanish was as flawless as Harry's, and the two men played out their roles—for any interested eavesdroppers—comfortably. They ordered *calamares en ce-*

bolla and *corozones de lechuga al chef* to start with, followed by *mariscos Sebastian del pastelillo* for two, all of which was an assortment of freshly caught seafood, for which the Club de Pesca was justly renowned.

While they made small talk about Armando's sister Lydia and Peruvian society gossip, Jardine doodled and scribbled idly on the back of the buff-colored menu, which ran to several pages and included a potted history of the fortifications and local tourist information. The message conveyed to Harry Ford in David Jardine's economic scribbling was a comprehensive briefing on precisely how he was to proceed, as Operation Corrida's main player, to come to the notice of Pablo Envigado. The briefing, while essentially simple, like all good briefings, took both lunch courses and longer to impart.

As the tall, elderly waiter withdrew, after serving coffee and two more beers—bringing to three each the number consumed with the meal—Harry Ford, deep in thought, tugged a cigarette from its pack, then, remembering his manners, offered one to his boss. Jardine accepted and produced a Zippo lighter with the logo of a Peruvian football team.

Harry exhaled, and Jardine glanced at him briefly. He appreciated the younger man would be shocked at the thing he had just been ordered to do. But what was it he had said to Ronnie Szabodo? This was not the Little Sisters of Mercy.

"What's on your mind?" he asked, in Spanish.

"I want to be absolutely sure I have this right . . ." replied the ex-Special Forces man.

"Well, so do I, *amigo mío.*" Jardine glanced around, raised a hand to their waiter, and mimed he would like an ashtray.

Harry Ford tapped part of the scribbled doodling on the menu. "That's pretty final. If I understand correctly . . ."

"I hear, the way one does, on the grapevine, that our mutual friend has been making inquiries on the same subject. It's the sort of small . . . gesture he needs right now. It would be nice if you could beat him to the draw."

"You think he would understand? That my motives had been the same as his? If I did this thing? And why on earth would he be sufficiently interested? To try to seek me out?"

"My dear Carlos . . . I have not the slightest doubt." Jardine smiled and thanked the waiter as he laid two clean ashtrays on the table. The waiter departed. Jardine met Harry Ford's gaze. The boy was anxious, which was not only understandable but a good sign. A Joe without adrenaline was a liability to himself and his employers. "We are not amateurs in such matters. Men like our friend are, happily, predictable. Believe me, if you move first, Señor Keats" (Keats was the operational code name for Pablo Envigado) "will want to make your acquaintance. The man is quite a character you know. With something of a sense of humor."

Harry frowned, touched for the very first time by intimations of that . . . fear that becomes the constant companion of the lone operator. There were things about this operation he was not being told. "You know him . . . ? You know him, don't you."

"Not terribly well. But we have met a couple of times. Once at a soccer game. Once at his wife's sister's . . ."

There was a period of mutual silence. They listened to the lazy beat of the salsa band, the laughter of three couples at a long table by the edge of the harbor restaurant.

Finally the younger man shook his head. "You know, you never cease to amaze me . . ."

Jardine smiled quietly, realizing he had come to respect Harry Ford. The soldier had a degree of style, with higher than average intelligence and a dry sense of humor. He felt convinced he had made the right choice, and for the right reasons. He was not prepared to consider what might have been the wrong reasons.

"Anything you need," he said, "I want you to use this man."

And he handed Harry a business card, with the name Xavier Ramón G. and in Spanish, Public Relations and Business Consultant, with a phone number in Bogotá.

"He's our local support and a trusted friend." Jardine was using the term "friend" in its professional context, meaning a fully paid-up and cleared agent of the British Intelligence Service. "He will provide whatever you need. There is, however, no requirement for him to know what you're up to."

"Sure. No problem . . ."

Jardine was suddenly ambushed by a feeling of real compassion for the fledgling operator. For after all the months of training and a few weeks settling into his legend, the fun was over. Here was a sphere controller sitting with a black operator at a table in Cartagena, at the end of the world, sweat running down their backs, turning the operator loose into a subculture of cocaine barons, secret liaisons, and the constant possibility of torture and violent death.

"Any questions, *amigo?*"

"Um." Harry glanced at him, suddenly quite shy. "How is Elizabeth?"

He watched Jardine, who seemed to be concentrating on a two-masted schooner gliding by, on its engines, two rigid inflatables on davits at the stern, and a tiny gyrocopter fixed with webbing straps to the deck.

After a few seconds, David Jardine met Ford's inquiring gaze. "She's very well. Asked me to tell you she loves you, and all that stuff . . ." And he nodded sagely, like a good buddy, no trace showing of his revulsion with himself for the glistening, lust-slick orgy of delicious coitus he had so very recently celebrated with this trusting recruit's wife of one year.

What a bastard he was. In truth he should probably resign. There was no getting away from it. But not right now. Not with a Swiss watch of an operation up and running.

Harry Ford grinned. "She's a great girl. My friend, look after her for me. Will you promise to do that? I'm sure everything will be absolutely fine. But I'd, um, feel better."

There is no place in successful agent running for emotion. No one knew that better than David Jardine, CMG.

Excessive care for a Joe can bring the whole reason for a mission into question. And guilt, Jardine told himself as the sweat in the small of his back turned cold, can be given no quarter. Human intelligence operations require profound ruthlessness. Which is why he had run to his Jesuit conversion like a bug to a safe, dark crack in the floor.

He fixed Ford with his gravely responsible look. "Yes, Carlos. I promise."

Jardine glanced back at the schooner leaving the Bay of Cartagena, a huge heron lumbering gracefully from the surface of the mercury-calm water. The fact that the boat was operated by the U.S. Drug Enforcement Agency, monitoring shipments of cocaine from the Caribbean coast, was not something young Harry needed to know.

"Is this your lunch or mine, Armando?"

"I think lunch is the least I can do," Jardine said coolly, and indicated he would like the check to a group of waiters standing near the doorway to the kitchens.

"Anything else I should know . . . ?"

"Not that I can think of."

"Well, then." Harry Ford rose and picked up the

menu David Jardine had been scribbling on. "I'll be on my way."

Jardine remained sitting, much as he had a sudden impulse to stand up and grip his brand-new operator's shoulders, grasp his hand and wish him all the luck he was going to need. Instead, he nodded, raising a languid hand.

"Go with God . . ." he said in Spanish.

"*Estamos hablando* . . ." replied Ford, which meant something like "catch you later."

Twenty hours later, David Jardine was arriving for the fourteenth time that year at London Heathrow Terminal Four, on Flight BA 216 from Miami. He had slept well on the plane, traveling First Class as usual, and he took the underground train to Victoria and walked the two miles down Victoria Street, across Westminster Bridge, up Westminster Bridge Road to St. George's Circus. By eight-twenty in the morning, he was in the tiny room off his inner office, showered and changing into fresh linen and his favorite Prince of Wales double-breasted suit.

There was a knocking at his office door and he emerged from his inner sanctum to find Mrs. Brownlow standing there with a mug of tea and a plate of hot buttered toast. Plus a folder of updates on all current operations.

"Cecily, what would I do without you?"

"Make your own bloody toast," replied the Section P/A with irrefutable logic. "David, there's rather an odd letter arrived at your house in the country."

What can she mean, odd? A bomb?

"It's not a bomb. It's a letter. Posted in Dublin. Maggie wondered if you would like her to open it."

Maggie was the daily help down at the farm. She had

worked as a housekeeper at one of the office's safe houses in Wiltshire before her husband had died, and she had proved ideal for the Jardines. Dorothy got on well with her and she was security cleared and knew her way around all the shortcuts in communicating with the Firm.

"Maybe she should just post it to me at Tite Street. Bloody Maggie, she really is nosy."

"Actually, David . . . She really is just going by the book. The handwriting made her wonder. That's all. She's never bothered us before. Except with the, um, Cuban thing."

The "Cuban thing" was a KGB major who had written to David Jardine at his country home, warning of an informer in a circuit Jardine had spent years painfully building up in Guyana. Maggie had had a sixth sense about the letter, which was addressed to "Commander" Jardine, with "most personal" written on the back. And it just didn't seem normal, so she had phoned the office and a score of agents' lives had been saved.

So perhaps Maggie's feeling about some letter from Dublin should be taken seriously.

"You're absolutely right, Cecily. Ask her to drive to a pay phone. Ring my secure number here."

The precaution of phoning in from a randomly selected pay phone was elementary security tradecraft.

"I took the liberty. She's phoning at three minutes past ten."

Jardine stared at Mrs. Brownlow. She stared back, daring him to protest. He grinned. "Quite right. We mustn't forget the Cuban precedent."

"You look absolutely shattered, even with a shower and that suit fresh from the cleaners."

"I'm fine. Okay . . . more pressing business. Let's have Ronnie and Bill in here at ten-fifteen. Plus all the Corrida data."

"Right away." She turned to leave, then glanced back. "Don't let that tea get cold."

"Thank you, Mrs. Brownlow."

Jardine knew she liked that mock reprimand, suggesting she had overstepped the bounds of familiarity. Cecily Brownlow shrugged and left, closing the door behind her.

The controller sighed, rubbed the heels of his hands over his face, then lifted the folder of case and operational updates and tried to concentrate, but the concise, neatly typed sentences were not making much sense. David Jardine loosed his necktie, stretched his arms, and leaned back to relax in his leather seat, a present from Dorothy. When the phone on his desk rang, it jerked him out of a deep slumber. It was exactly four minutes past ten o'clock. He lifted the receiver.

"Yes?"

"They said to find a phone box."

It was Maggie.

"Have you opened the letter?"

"They said I should wait for you to tell me to . . ."

"Fine. Do it now, please open it now."

He listened to the rustling and her breathing, the sound of sheep *meah*-ing someplace near the pay phone. He pictured a solid, red, English phone box, as British as policemen's helmets, until he remembered the ghastly yellow and black and glass booths that had sprouted like Luddite insults all across some of England's loveliest countryside.

She was probably speaking from one of those.

"It's opened," she announced, and Jardine suppressed a smile. For some reason the audible pantomine preceding that announcement reminded him of a fifties radio comedy show whose name he had forgotten.

"Jolly good."

Silence. He could hear her breathing. And the sheep.

"Any chance of reading it to me . . . ?" He inquired sweetly.

"Here's all it says . . . The Tower. W.B. Yeats. Fifty-seven to sixty-four. Penguin Poetry Library. 1991."

Jardine swiftly scribbled that down.

"And you're quite sure that's it . . . ?"

"That's all."

"Written or typed?"

"Typed."

"No signature or message?"

"That's all."

"Turn the paper over. Any little full stops or dots on the 'i's or punctuation marks? You remember the drill."

"I'm looking. I brought a magnifying glass . . ."

"You really are a pro."

"And I can do without patronage, thank you very much."

Jardine knew she meant "without being patronized," but it seemed churlish even to harbor the thought.

"Anything . . . ?"

Pause. More breathing. More sheep. Finally:

"No. That's your lot."

"Thanks. You're a star. And I really do mean it. Listen, I'll send somebody down for it, and the envelope. It'll be someone you know."

"Right then. I've got a kitchen floor to scrub. You shouldn't let those dogs in there when they're wet. Leave matted hairs everywhere, they does."

"Thanks again. Good-bye." David Jardine replaced the receiver. He stared at the words and frowned. Clearly they were the key to some form of unsophisticated code. Presumably the real message, the one to be decoded, was going to arrive at Century House, or at Charles Street where the Foreign Office was located, or at his club or indeed at the Tite Street apartment. He frowned.

How odd.

"Heather . . ." Jardine called. Heather appeared in the doorway. "Be a darling and send someone for a copy of poems by W.B. Yeats. The Penguin Poetry Library edition, would you? And send young Jeremy down to my place in Wiltshire to collect a package. Tell him I need it here soonest. Maggie, my daily, will give it to him."

"No problem." She smiled and turned away.

Jardine opened the update file and found he could concentrate, refreshed after his catnap. The telephone rang again. He lifted the receiver.

"Yes."

Heather's voice. "It's Mrs. Ford."

"Who?"

"Captain Ford's wife."

"Oh. Put her through."

His pulse quickened as he waited for Elizabeth to come on the line.

"David . . . ?"

"Hi."

"How are you?"

"I'm well. Harry sends his love."

"You've seen him?"

"Spoke to him. Briefly."

"How is he?"

"Busy but happy."

"He's such a baby. Listen, just say no if you don't want to, but would you like to have lunch?"

Absolutely not. Not again. No no no. We're going to pretend it never happened. You and your glistening flat belly and your tongue. "Why the devil not?"

"I'm at my mother's place in Kinnerton Street, that's near Belgrave Square."

"I know Kinnerton Street."

"Why don't we have some cold salmon, would you like that? Do you like salmon?"

"With your mum?"

"She's in New York, with my stepdaddy."

This is madness.

"Listen, Elizabeth, how about a plate of spaghetti? There's a wonderful Italian restaurant near you, it's called Mimmo d'Ischia, you won't find better in London. I'll be there from . . . one-fifteen. There are a couple of things we have to get straight. All right?"

Good man. I knew you could do it. David Jardine felt better about himself. The girl was just wonderful. He completely understood her liking for outrageously inappropriate sexual encounters, but not with him. No way.

> New York City
> is ever so pretty . . .
> In the night . . . time . . .
> New York City
> was never this pretty . . .
> In the day . . . time . . .

Homicide Lieutenant (Acting) Eddie Lucco bobbed his head in time to the music from a pair of mega-ghetto-blasters on the sidewalk near Times Square. Two male hookers, transvestites—one in a pink tutu, the other in a microsheath black wool tube dress and garter belt and stockings, with bright red lipstick, like the lead in the Rocky Horror Show—were hip-hop dancing to the tune. There was something so laconically outrageous about their performance, and about the world-weary way a cop on horseback was ambling his roan mare past, ignoring them, probably not noticing them, so common was the sight in these parts, that Lucco grinned as he tapped the steering wheel in time to the beat.

"At least we could take it out and look at it . . ." said his partner, Sam Vargos, sitting beside him in the un-marked Dodge sedan.

"No fuckin way. We might just be tempted, Sam."

He spun the wheel gently and avoided a legless man on a makeshift wood trolley, propelling himself laboriously along the gutter, with cardboard placards front and back alleging VietNam Vet Aids Blind and Tone Deaf, which brought a wry smile to the two detectives' faces.

"Way to go . . ." Lucco glanced in his mirror, relaxed. It was a warm night and spring had come. Nancy had been offered a partnership after Judge Almeda had thrown out the case against the young yuppie who had been set up. Plus old man Hodges had been suspended pending investigation into insider dealing. And Nancy's firm had been asked if she would consider representing him.

"Maybe we could just . . . give in to temptation, Eddie. Four mil to you, one to me. I ain't greedy."

"Well, don't think I haven't thought about it, good buddy."

"Every fuckin minute, right?"

"Couple of times a day. But see, I wanna live in this town. And the Justice Department got no sense of humor."

"We could spend a few bucks. I mean for chrissake."

Eddie Lucco turned into Broadway and stopped at the curb. The car radio squawked a continuous monotone of crimes occurring throughout the city. He tugged his wallet from his pocket and counted out three fins.

"Here."

"Oh, this is my cut, right? Generous . . ."

"Sam, I never thought money would come between us."

"Five million could come between me and my firstborn. I ain't fuckin kiddin. With or without?"

"With cheese. No ketchup."

"I thought you wops liked tomatoes."

"Sure. That's what I said."

Vargos shook his head and climbed out from the car, the plastic seat squeaking as he moved. He shut the door, leaving the lieutenant with his thoughts. Two weeks had passed since Lucco had phoned the number Restrepo had given him and said he wanted to negotiate.

At ten before nine the next morning, he had rendezvoused with the Colombian lawyer beside an Oldsmobile with one wheel off and jacked up and a breakdown truck behind it, on the Brooklyn side of the Brooklyn Bridge. Four Hispanic-looking men with trail bikes relaxed and exchanged smokes just behind the scene. It was abundantly clear—with the press of traffic zooming by, with commuters unwilling to stop in that neighborhood—that any attempt to stage a stakeout or an ambush would have been impossible.

Eddie Lucco had been taken to the far side of the breakdown truck and checked for a wire. Once again his revolver had been emptied and handed back to him with expressionless courtesy by Murillo, Restrepo's Tartar-cheekboned, cold-eyed bodyguard.

After this Restrepo had joined him, leaning against the truck, just as relaxed as could be, gazing at elaborate graffiti on the filthy stone wall.

"Negotiate is not a word we often take seriously. My principals."

"Señor Restrepo, I'm a cop. I know when I'm being shortchanged," Eddie Lucco said in accordance with the briefing he had received from Don Mather, the DEA's New York chief.

The rumble and shudder of constant traffic made quiet speech difficult to hear. At one point there had been a dangerous moment when a motorcycle cop had pulled up to see what the trouble was. The trail bikers' hands had automatically moved to the sinister bundles on the backs of their bikes. But before the big detective could defuse the situation, the man in breakdown company coveralls had crossed to the motorcycle cop, grinning, and produced an FBI ID wallet, forged by the younger Nghi, spoken a couple of sentences, and the cop had laughed at something the guy had said, kicked his bike into gear, and roared off, joining the constantly moving rush-hour queue.

Restrepo was watching Lucco, sizing him up. "Tell me about it."

"Pal, I'm right in there at the center of things. Buy me, you get more than just the soft pedal on the Bellevue killings."

"More how . . . ?"

And Homicide Lieutenant Lucco had told Restrepo he could replace Manny Schulman in spades. To have a Homicide lieutenant was going to make life that much easier for the cartel in NYC. Particularly one working with the Narcotics Task Force.

"How much?"

"Four million dollars to wrap up the Bellevue stuff and lose the Jane Doe investigation. Another two for ongoing business."

Restrepo had scratched the back of his hand. Lucco noticed the lawyer had a touch of eczema or something. No fuckin wonder. He had heard that was brought on by stress.

"Five million, Lieutenant. For the lot."

"Deal."

"You know what happens if you fuck with us."

"Everybody knows that, Luís." Eddie Lucco had smiled inwardly. Restrepo did not like this New York lowlife calling him by his first name.

"Nancy." Restrepo began to pick at one expensively manicured nail. "You don't mind if I call her that? Nancy would be picked up somewhere, sometime, taken to someplace, maybe down by the river where we chopped up Ricardo. Gang-raped. Mutilated. Then I would send some to you. And the rest we would probably make into stew."

"Sir, what kind of a dickhead do you think I am?"

The Colombian gangster's lawyer had smiled. Sir. He liked sir. Lucco knew he would. He had done the course. All hoodlums liked being called sir.

So the deal had been agreed. Eddie Lucco was now a made cop of the cartel's. He had insisted that he would only deal direct with Medellín, and would only be given top-level assignments so as not to debase his value to the *grupo*. Restrepo was no fool and he saw the wisdom of that. The fact that it left Lucco with most of his time to be just an ordinary homicide detective made sense, for it would keep suspicion off this new, valuable asset.

And Nancy could move around freely.

Eddie Lucco had reported all this back to Don Mather. He had also insisted on bringing his partner Sam Vargos into the secret, otherwise it would have been impossible to make the operation work.

Mather had agreed. Unknown to Eddie Lucco, he had kept Vargos's involvement to himself. Mather knew what to worry head office with and what could just be left to let ride.

The money had been paid into BCCI in Nassau, the Bahamas, and only Lucco had access to it. The one thing Restrepo had warned him was to not withdraw any funds from BCCI's New York branch. Miami would be okay. And any flaunting of sudden wealth that would alert NYPD's Internal Affairs or the IRS would result in the account being abruptly closed and certain steps taken. There was no need to specify the steps.

Lucco had taken Sam Vargos for a walk in Central Park and told him the whole setup. Vargos had nodded gravely and asked, without a trace of a smile, when it would be cool for them to travel to Nassau with their wives and Vargos's kids, withdraw the lot, and head for Shangri-La.

Then he had smiled.

Eddie Lucco watched his partner amble across the sidewalk with two hamburgers and two extra-large Cokes. As Sam got into the car, Lucco reflected on the fact that he had passed on the entire results of his homicide investigation to Don Mather, who had promised to take very quiet steps to try to ID the teenage Jane Doe lying cold in the morgue at Bellevue Hospital. For that was still Homicide Lieutenant Lucco's number one priority . . .

"Like this . . . ?"

"Mmm, Jesus . . ."

"Like this . . . ?"

"Oh, God . . ."

"Do you like that? Do you like it?"

"Oh, you bastard, you horny bastard . . ."

David Arbuthnot Jardine eased himself gently, tantalizingly against her rump, her back pressed to his thumping chest as he delicately smoothed Dewberry 5-Oils Lotion from the Body Shop in King's Road across her breasts, the nipples straining erect under his experienced fingers.

"This is definitely the last time . . ."

"Oh, God. Awww . . . Oh, yes. Yes!"

Later, as Elizabeth rolled on one silk stocking, sitting on the one armchair in the tiny service flat in St. James's, she flicked her long, fair hair, which had fallen over her face, and fixed Jardine with that direct gaze of hers. He was standing by the vanity unit, tying his paisley-pattern necktie as he looked in the mirror, meeting her reflected gaze.

"Why?" she asked, in the intimate, friendly way she had of talking to him in private.

"Elizabeth, put on some knickers, I can't think responsibly when you look so . . ." he lifted his shoulders, ". . . delicious. Like some Degas wanton."

"Why should it be the last time?"

"Oh hell, you know why."

"Listen, David, I've explained to you about Harry. God knows I love him but I just can't help the way I am. And with the world he works in, not just with you people but before, with the SAS, it's . . . okay, this is me being selfish, but I can't let him down. So by and large, this part of me, which is a very real part—"

"It's a wonderful part," said Jardine softly.

"It just has to be sublimated. I go for a long swim. Work out at aerobics. Ride Benjamin."

"Lucky Benjamin." Her lover grinned. Benjamin was Harry and Elizabeth's sixteen-hands steeplechaser. Jet black with one hell of an ancestry.

"Look, he's going to spend a huge part of his life away from me and I really don't feel any guilt about this. It's not as if I make a habit of it, for God's sake."

She stood up and pulled on her underwear, lowering her head and looking at him in a way he found vulnerable and provocative. The decadent-child look, he had whispered to her, more than once, the scent of her hair in his nostrils, the cobra rising.

"I know you don't," he said gently, tightening the knot in his tie, sliding it under his shirt collar. "I really do."

"You mean the snoopers would have found out."

"Sure." He lifted her Jean Muir dress, slub brown wool, and handed it to her.

"Thanks," she said sulkily.

"Darling Elizabeth, it has to stop for two very good reasons. One is that your husband has placed his life and his career in my hands. He trusts me implicitly and—with this one, absolutely major exception—he's quite right to." Jardine sighed and pushed a hand through his thick hair. He obligingly fastened the two top buttons at the back of her dress.

Down below, the whirring tick of a black London taxi's diesel engine. For years Jardine had thought the sound came from their charge meters. What a dorp, he thought, using his children's terminology. He wondered who it was dropping off. Maybe some tourists, for they often used this expensive and ideally located block of rental apartments. As did a High Court judge and a national newspaper editor, for the same reason that the controller West 8 did, to steal a little secret pleasure in the middle of life's hurly-burly.

"And the second reason . . . ?" she inquired, putting her elegant head to one side and watching him carefully.

David Jardine met her gaze. There was a long silence.

"You know the other reason," he said.

And as they watched each other warily, Elizabeth raised one finger and wagged it at him slowly, in admonishment.

"That is too naughty, David. We agreed at the start, this is a divine arrangement between like-minded friends. Don't play with emotion. Or the whole house of cards will come crashing down." And she stepped across to him and gazed solemnly up into his eyes.

"We mustn't kiss," whispered Jardine, as their mouths drew closer, "and this must really stop . . ."

And when they kissed, it was as if for the first time, the thunderbolt kiss of love, and it left them breathless and . . . afraid. And it lasted, that kiss, for many hours. Hours that were to change their lives.

It had been two weeks since their lunch at Mimmo's when David Jardine had told Elizabeth Ford, evenly and honestly, why their one afternoon of delicious lust would have to be consigned to pleasant and secret memory.

Maybe a romantic Italian restaurant had been a fatal place to attempt such a sensible gesture.

By coincidence, in Bogotá, during the time that the endless kiss was taking place, Harry Ford was about to carry out the first and carefully planned phase of his part, his leading role, in Operation Corrida.

As he loaded the magazine of his Sig Sauer P-226 automatic pistol, his hands were steady, and the smell of gun oil was like an aphrodisiac.

Just west of the Javeriana University district in Bogotá is a road that climbs up into the National Park and is used as a shortcut to circumvent the heavy traffic around Carrera 7 and the Avenida Caracas. On the approach to the steep hillsides of the National Park, which is not a place to venture alone or in innocence, are a number of barrios, or shantytown slum dwellings. Sometimes the Policia, occasionally with the help of raw conscripts from the Army, move in and force the slum dwellers to move out.

From some parts of the foothills and from the barrio road, the tall white tower of the church on the peak of Cerro de Monseratte can be seen, high above. Monseratte has become a source of inspiration for pilgrims who flock to the statue of the *Señor caido,* the Fallen Christ, sculpted in the seventeenth century by Pedro Lugo de Albarracin, to which many miracles have been attributed.

Captain Rodrigo Tabio Barbosa sat in the passenger seat of a police jeep, lighting his fourth black cheroot of the morning. He watched through his dark sunglasses as grubby urchins wandered around the barrio's rough wood and corrugated iron shacks, with Indian blankets draped to afford a modicum of privacy. One particular plump male child, of maybe six or seven, had caught his attention a few weeks back and he stared, thoughtfully, as the boy walked this way and that, following some of the older kids, who were talking and arguing among themselves.

Jaime, his driver, a Policia corporal, could be relied upon to keep his mouth shut, for Tabio had made damn sure Jaime had taken part in the last "running of the chickens," or *corrida de los pollos* as Rodrigo Tabio called it in his language. Jaime, like the other seven cops in Captain Tabio's detail, had, one by one, been terrified into taking part in the gang rapes and killings of urchins from the sewers, the sewer children whom the *Espador* newspaper and the Bogotá TV station were now campaigning to rescue and rehabilitate.

Rodrigo Tabio's was no sinister, extreme right-wing secret campaign to rid the streets of penniless beggars and cutpurses. It was part of no organized move by the rumored Fascist elements who knew how to take the law into their own hands. Every South American state was plagued with those. No, Rodrigo Tabio Barbosa was that form of human mutation that crops up in all societies, from the most primitive to the most highly civilized.

He was a clinical psychotic who harbored an obscene compulsion to spoil, torture, and sadistically put to death that which most of mankind would find defenseless, vulnerable, and physically attractive.

He had realized his nightmarish compulsions when his work as a cop on antitheft patrol took him into the sewers and barrios and shantytown slums. It had started as an accident. He had been creeping gingerly through a trenchwork, where work had long since stopped on some municipal reparation, in pursuit of two teenagers armed with knives, when a sudden sound had made him whirl around. There had been a shape, a movement, and he had fired four slugs, in self defense. The figure that slumped forward, spewing blood, was that of a ten-year-old sewer child. He had heard a flurry of small footsteps disappear down one of the five sewer tunnels beyond the trenchworks.

The sound of terrified breathing had taken his attention to the left and there, in the gloom, the whites of little eyes. Up to that awful moment, Tabio had been guilty of an honest mistake, a mistake for which, in the violent city of Bogotá, few would have blamed him. But then the madness had gripped him. Madness with a dreadful calm. Madness with the foul, cemetery breath of putrid lust.

And after that, Captain Rodrigo Tabio Barbosa had ensnared his acolytes one by one, some sickened by the horror, others resigned to descent into total evil, for they believed they would be dead meat to choose any other path.

Why did even one of them not go to his superiors?

Because evil can hypnotize. Those seven cops, those seven eternally damned cops, had become Tabio's creatures as surely as any of the undead in Haiti's voodoo communes.

Zombies of Rodrigo Tabio.

After watching the plump barrio urchin child through his dark sunglasses, Tabio tapped the dashboard with his short cane, his policeman's cane, and the corporal started the engine and the jeep moved on, passing the children playing and arguing, oblivious to the sinister shadow that had lain upon them.

Now it was the case that certain detectives in the Bogotá Policia criminal department had their suspicions about Tabio, but the guy was just too clever to get caught in his dreadful enterprises. Those men had families and children of their own, but the workload of Bogotá cops was deadening and the random murders of unknown, unclaimed sewer kids, while crimes for investigation, were way down the list in the capital city of a nation that was enduring 25,000 homicides every year, many of those in Bogotá.

One particular group of detectives had resolved to get Captain Tabio. The Policia Nacional had a remarkably high proportion of honest cops, considering the blend of bribe and deadly threat that was *el grupo*'s and the guerrillas' way of keeping out of jail. Such men were murdered at a rate that made figures for Allied casualties in the Gulf War look sissy. Their common danger and common decency bonded them tightly. By coincidence, several of them had been trained by Colonel Xavier, Ramón G., the former DAS director of Security and Counterespionage and trusted agent of David Jardine's, when he had been assigned in the late seventies to the Police Anti-Terrorist Training School.

This group had leaked rumors about Captain Tabio to the editors of Bogotá's press and TV current affairs programs. That had resulted in the stories that Harry Ford had read in *El Espador* while sitting in the Glasgow Bar at the Hotel La Fontana, flirting gently with a beautiful sixteen-year-old Argentinian girl.

When the leaked stories had seemed to have no effect on the Policia top floor, the group of concerned detectives took a step that might seem radical outside Colombia. They went in for a little *palanca*, which is to say a connection with somebody of influence when the legal route has not worked. The *palanca* they employed was Don Pablo Envigado, the Robin Hood of Antioquia.

At this time, Don Pablo had been saddened to learn during his conversations with the eighty-four-year-old priest—who was acting as intermediary between Escobar and the president's Counselor for Medellín Affairs—

that his growing reputation for extreme violence was losing him the sneaking affection many of the ordinary people had felt for him and his colorful career.

In his declared war against the authorities to force them to renounce the extradition of arrested *narcotraficantes* to the USA, Don Pablo had imagined he would have the support of every red-blooded Colombian. But he had deployed car bombs in several major cities, and such indiscriminate and random atrocities were losing him the goodwill of his traditional and maybe romantic nationwide following.

So the detailed dossier on the evil Captain Tabio could not have been presented to him, with a supplication by the Antioquian grandmother of one of the group of concerned detectives, at a better time. This was just the sort of act of natural justice on behalf of the oppressed people that Pablo Envigado and the Medellín Cartel needed to arrest the waning of popular support. And a plea from a bunch of *aguacatos*, of *tombos*, of cops? What a cinch!

And Bobby Sonson and Murillo, fresh from New York, where Restrepo had just bought a lieutenant of Homicide, had been dispatched to Bogotá with orders to terminate most publicly the odious Captain Tabio and his bunch of murdering pederasts. And to make damn sure Colombia knew it was Don Pablo who had ordered it.

Such a move takes a few days, maybe a couple of weeks, to set up properly. Killing Rodrigo Tabio would have been too simple for words, but the kind of theater that Pablo Envigado had specified . . . that took planning and patience.

Thus, when Captain Rodrigo Tabio Barbosa sat his enormous bulk down at a table on the patio of the small restaurant in the foothills of the Parco Nacional, just above La Merced district, and the ensemble of four musicians began to play some *vallenato* music, quiet and lazy, just the thing to eat lunch to, it was Bobby Sonson and Murillo who entered quietly and sat at a table in the corner. There were maybe five tables outside, and the middle-aged *patrón* with his son and daughter came out to fuss over the *policía* captain and the two high-cheekboned, cold-eyed strangers.

The other tables were soon occupied, two by businessmen up from the north of the city and one by four kids from the local TV station.

Tabio ordered a starter of *jamón Serrano,* followed by *churrasco Argentino.* He blew his nose into a dirty blue kerchief and reminded the *padrino*'s son to bring him two beers. Not one but two. The TV-station kids definitely remembered hearing that.

The owner's daughter had just laid down the first course, the *jamón Serrano,* when a man of medium height, some said, others declared he had been taller than average, wearing a plaid wool jacket like the Indians of Santa Marta sell when they come to the city, walked in, passing the four musicians and ignoring the *patrón* who very courteously had pointed out all the al fresco tables were taken but there was plenty of room inside.

The tall, or medium-sized, man, aged about thirty, had walked, straight-backed, to the table of Captain Rodrigo Tabio Barbosa and asked in a loud, clear voice (which bore the accent of Argentina said the businessman, Cali, swore the TV-station kids), "Are you Captain Rodrigo Tabio Barbosa?"

Tabio had wiped the beer from his mustache and his plump cheeks with the same dirty kerchief he had just blown his nose with.

"That's me," he said, his eyes searching the stranger's face from behind the dark sunglasses.

"Are you the Captain Tabio who has been buggering

the infants of Bogotá and wiping the manly reputation of our police force in the sewers? Killer of fatherless children? I need to be sure I have the right cocksucker, so speak up, *hijueputa*."

With a roar of anger, the fat cop swept his table aside and rose, the pistol he had surreptitiously drawn thrust at the stranger and firing. *Bang! Bang!* But those two shots were drowned in a machine-gunlike succession of deafening reports from the Santa Marta jacket pocket of the stranger, which erupted in flame and afterward had wisps of smoke curling from the blackened, torn cloth. Tabio stumbled backward, his fleshy frame shuddering as five of the fourteen rounds fired struck resisting bone structures in his blubber-wrapped skeleton.

The man was dead before he staggered over his upset chair, but the stranger continued to fire until there was nothing left of the psychotic cop's face.

In the stunned silence, the stranger lifted his pistol from the jacket pocket, dropped the spent magazine into the palm of his red-gloved hand, and in a millisecond had slotted a full magazine into the butt. The pistol was a Sig-Sauer P-226. By this time everybody had noticed his red wool gloves. In fact that was the one detail of description they all agreed upon.

He walked past Bobby Sonson and Murillo, who had risen, Mini-Uzi and Colt .45 automatic gripped, ready for action.

"Nos vemos," he said to them courteously as he passed right by their table, ignoring their pieces, and fixed each in turn with a brief, calm, but somehow frightening stare.

Trying to describe that stare later, they could only say, limply, it had been the stare of a fellow professional. It had said, "Guys, I'm no danger to you. But don't fuck with me." And it was not every day Bobby Sonson felt his blood chill.

The kids from the TV station had a field day. They got photos of the assassinated police captain and were on the six o'clock news, recounting word for word the sentence of death the killer had pronounced. And his casual farewell to the two unknown armed men who had discreetly vacated the scene almost immediately afterward, looking slightly stunned.

"Nos vemos . . ." he had said. Meaning "catch you later."

And the red gloves. Everyone knew about the killer with red gloves.

The group of concerned detectives were pleased.

David Jardine watched a videocassette of the TV report, sent directly from the SIS man at the British Embassy in Bogotá. He watched it in his office in the company of Ronnie Szabodo, who opened two bottles of Dos Equis from the cooler and passed one to his boss without taking his eyes off the screen.

"Nice one, David," said the Hungarian, and Jardine inclined his head graciously.

Pablo Envigado was furious. Not one mention of his name. This was not what he had ordered. Then the phone rang and it was Jesus Garcia, his security chief. When Envigado heard the whole story—that some *cabrón* had hijacked his natural justice, cartel-executes-child-killer-plan—his rage was terrible to behold.

Then, just as the psychiatrists at Century House had predicted, Don Pablo suddenly started to chuckle. His rage spent, he flopped into a chair on the patio of the house in Medellín, close to the Jardin Botanico Joaquin Antonio Uribe, whence he had been spirited by Jesus Garcia after the raid on the Cama de Mariscal in the mountains above Santa Fe.

His laughter was genuine, and it brought his body-guards and Luís Restrepo running out from the villa.

"Que pasa, padrino?" asked one of the bodyguards.

Still laughing, Pablo Envigado turned to Restrepo. *"Que tumbada, hombre!"* he said. What a rip-off!

"Some *huevon* has hijacked our goddamn plan. Some asshole has just shot the psycho cop . . . ! *Que pueria!"* Which meant he thought the whole thing was really wild.

"What do you want me to do, Don Pablo?" asked Restrepo. "Did Sonson and Murillo fuck up?"

The richly amused Pablo Envigado shook his head, gasping for breath, smiling broadly. "Hell no, they're good boys. I'll tell you what I want you to do, Luís, *amigo mío* . . . Find this guy. I like this son of a bitch's style, man."

He snapped his fingers a few times. Like he was ordering a side salad. "Find him and bring him to me. I will have dinner with him. And maybe later . . . breakfast?"

And he rolled his eyes and the others laughed. For they remembered what had happened to German Santos Castaneda, the doomed brother of Ricardo, who had lost the Irish girl Siobhan Pearson in New York City. Breakfast with Pablo could be fatal.

18

MATADOR

Light but endless rain fell, slanting in a mild breeze, all over Lambeth, the sort of rain the English call drizzle. It pattered onto shallow puddles and ran trickling down the drain just outside the Goose and Firkin pub on Borough High Street, not far from Saint George's Circus and the squat glass box where analysts and operations controllers and cipher wizards and section chiefs, scientists and armorers and security teams and planners toiled in the clandestine service of their country.

David Jardine's large feet, clad in the pair of soft leather boots he had had handmade for him in Peru several years before, splashed on the wet pavement as he strolled in the rain, deep in conversation with Ronnie Szabodo, who was carrying a golf umbrella with "Guards Polo Club" printed on its fabric. Jardine wore a battered old oilproof zip-up shooting jacket, with thorn tears and a couple of stuck-on patches of lighter material. He squinted at the welcome sight of the bar as they approached it. He had already decided to have one of the ham salad rolls with tear-jerking helpings of strong Coleman's English Mustard.

"The Vigo stuff checks out," Szabodo remarked. He was referring to the unsolicited and therefore highly suspect information that had arrived from Dublin, giving very precise information about the hitherto unknown Lorca Group of the Provisional IRA and its link with Colombian cocaine coming into Europe.

"Collateral . . . ?" asked Jardine, aware that if other sources confirmed the Dublin stuff, then whatever game the sender was playing, such high-grade intelligence would do his section no harm at all. Or his own reputation, although he had disciplined himself to let that take second place, for subjectivity in the grading and analysis of intelligence was like the sun's heat to the wings of Icarus.

"Spanish station," replied Szabodo. "They took a very discreet look at the Routiers et Sauvetage company. The names of the directors and of the principals check out. They sneaked a couple of photographs of the girl and the older man. CT Desk confirms they are probably Rosy Hughes and Father Eamon Gregson." CT was Counter-Terror.

"Probably . . . ?"

"You know Dennis," replied Szabodo. Dennis Weston was intelligence coordinator of the office's encyclopedic Counter-Terror Desk. "Probably is good, coming from him. Any joy from Forensic . . . ?"

When David Jardine had returned to his Tite Street apartment on the evening of his lunch at Mimmo's—which had, with a degree of inevitability, become an afternoon with Elizabeth at her mother's Kinnerton Street flat—he had not been surprised to find a thick envelope with a Dublin postmark on the mat beside an electricity bill, a parking ticket, and a special offer from American Express.

The four sheets of flimsy paper inside the Dublin envelope had been covered in a jumble of letters that made no sense at all. This was the encoded message to which the few lines of poetry by W.B. Yeats from the Penguin Poetry Library would provide the key, as advised in the letter sent to the farmhouse in Wiltshire.

That particular system of cryptology was as old as espionage itself. It had been used in the Crusades, in ancient Greece, and in the land of the pharaohs. Essentially, if the communicator holds (ideally, in his memory) a few lines of text, poetry being easier to memorize, and the only other person in the world who is aware that those lines form the basis of a code is the person to whom the communication is addressed, all manner of secret coded messages can be sent, based on starting at one randomly selected letter anywhere in the text, moving backward or forward or up or down, as indicated in the initial part of the message.

Exhausted by that time, jet-lagged and physically drained, David Jardine had not felt inclined to stretch his brain, and he had called the night duty officer at Century House, who had sent a skinny youth with a ponytail and an earring on a big BMW motorbike to collect the envelope. The first letter and the book were already with the cryptographers on the third floor.

When the sphere controller had arrived in his office at nine the next morning, Mrs. Brownlow had presented him with a mug of hot black coffee, buttered toast, and a plastic folder with the contents of the Tite Street letter decoded. It had been based on the key contained in a few lines of Yeats's poem "The Tower."

And I myself created Hanrahan
And drove him drunk or sober through the dawn
From nowhere in the neighbouring cottages.
Caught by an old man's juggleries

He stumbled, tumbled, to and fro
And had but broken bones for hire
And horrible splendour of desire,
I thought it all out twenty years ago:

There was such an awful element of synchronicity in those lines that David Jardine resolved to discover the identity of his secret correspondent. So in addition to following up the Lorca Group/Colombian-cocaine angle, he had asked his security manager, Tony Lewis, to have the SIS Technical Directorate submit the envelopes and their contents to a detailed forensic examination. Also handwriting experts and psychologists had been asked for their thoughts on the contents to attempt to identify the sender.

"Forensic," Jardine now replied to Szabodo, "tells me the paper is milled in Hampshire and sold all over the country, including the Irish Republic."

"Well, that is actually *another* country, David."

"You know what I mean."

"Wars have been fought over less."

"A war is being fought, Ronnie. The ink likewise, from a Ball Pentel Fine Point R50, made in Japan, violet in color. Envelope number one, that is the one sent to my farmhouse, your good old Basildon Bond. Envelope number two is a buff, long envelope from a batch purchased by the Irish Civil Service, Legal Department."

"All adding up to something quite genuine."

"All adding up to a self-indentured source on the Brothers' planning staff." The Brothers was how David Jardine referred to the Provos.

"An educated person."

"They're all pretty well educated, they have a better education system than we do. But yes. The choice of poem was quite inspired. It tells me a great deal about the person who chose it."

"Unless," remarked Ronnie Szabodo with a deal of good sense, "it was chosen at random."

"There is a whole seminar waiting to be held on the subject of how the brain chooses at random. Random can sometimes be very telling. Kate has a few theories on the random quotient in human choices."

They reached the entrance to the pub. Szabodo let his umbrella down with some difficulty. The steady rain fell on his shoulders as he held open the door for Jardine. Then he stopped and remarked, "If our self-indentured Dublin friend is accurate, Lorca is gold dust."

"That's right," Jardine replied. "It's reasonably interesting . . . One might imagine." Which meant he had no intention of discussing it further.

The Hungarian shrugged. They stepped inside. The place was full and noisy, with students and local office workers and staff from the eye hospital. A slim middle-aged man in a black suit, like an Italian undertaker, was sitting by himself at the battered upright piano. Jardine noticed the man was wearing a black eyepatch. A piratical undertaker, he mused, as he gently eased his tall frame through the crush to the bar.

"Yes, squire?" asked the barman, who had once been a detective sergeant with the Metropolitan Police Special Branch until he had opted for a saner life. If he recognized David Jardine from earlier times he had never shown a flicker of it.

"Two pints of Borough Ale," said Jardine, "and two ham salad rolls. And if you don't call me squire, I won't call you sergeant, how's that?"

Rudi, the corpulent barman, stared hard at Jardine, then forced a tight smile and moved away to pour the beer.

"I hate being called squire." Jardine rubbed the bridge of his nose. The break had been almost perfectly reset, but not quite. Twenty years before, such things had been more rough and ready. Rainwater dripped from his hair. "You're not going to do much about that, are you?" said the Hungarian, shrewdly. "About the Dublin stuff . . ."

"D'you know, Ronnie, I really don't see why anyone should hold them back. I have a . . . I can't help feeling they come from some guy at the very top. Close to the top."

"A dissenter?" The reason they could discuss such sensitive matters was because the noise in the pub that lunchtime was deafening. Even the honky-tonk piano could hardly be heard above the din. And when they spoke they kept their mouths close to each other's ears.

"Exactly so. And this unknown Joe, not unknown for long I sincerely trust, believes they're knee-deep in a policy disaster of their own making. For once it's known they're pushing crack in the back alleys and dance halls and playgrounds of a dozen countries, including their own, and how can they stop it, once they have passed the stuff on? They won't recover from that. So why the hell should we bring their plans to anyone's attention? Let's keep an eye on it, that's our job. But I don't actually see it as any part of my remit, to save those murdering bastards from themselves . . ."

And he reached across to the barman, who had poured two pints of beer, and took the first tumbler. "Cheers, sport." He smiled at the long-suffering Rudi.

It did not take Restrepo long to identify the executioner of Captain Rodrigo Tabio.

Murillo and Bobby Sonson had not been so completely thrown by the deafening stream of bullets and the horrific death of the psychotic Bogotá cop as the others present. Trained and hardened killers themselves, they were far more accurate witnesses to the murder than the waiters, the *vallenato* band, the businessman, or the kids from the TV station. While Harry Ford's red gloves had distracted the others present from giving any kind of realistic description, the touch merely indicated to the two *grupo* soldiers that here was a professional at work.

And when he had passed, giving them that cold, chilling stare that seemed to reach a thousand miles deep into the very soul, they had perhaps been momentarily frozen into inaction, but every detail of the man's face was recorded as accurately as a close-up photograph.

When the two Colombians had sat with Jesus Garcia's computer photofit operator, it had not taken more than a half hour to produce what to all intents and purposes was a photographic likeness of Ford.

Hundreds of copies of this were then taken all around Bogotá and discreetly shown to bartenders, car-hire staff, bank clerks, prostitutes, some tame cops, taxi drivers, restaurant waiters, and of course rental agencies and hotel staff.

A cleaner at the Hotel La Fontana, an honest woman from Mompos in Bolívar Province who believed she was talking to a local detective (perhaps she was), had no hesitation in identifying the likeness as that of Señor Carlos Nelson Arrigiada, in Suite 303.

Bobby Sonson and Murillo let themselves into the room without difficulty, and a thorough search of Señor Nelson's belongings and of the room produced—taped in waterproof and concealed behind the icebox in the suite's kitchen—a metal box containing gun-cleaning oil, a pistol-cleaning kit made by a Chilean company, a silencer for an automatic pistol, and forty-three rounds of ammunition. The man's clothes had been purchased all over the world, from Buenos Aires to Hong Kong, Bombay, and Miami. There were tourist maps of Singapore, Marseilles, Tangiers, and Bogotá.

A polite word with one of the desk clerks produced details of Nelson's Chilean passport, and within seven hours, Jesus Garcia was in possession of Carlos Nelson's Interpol, U.S. Immigration Service, Colombian DAS, and the Royal Hong Kong Police computer files, in addition to the Chilean Narcotics Bureau file, all of which established that Nelson was a marijuana trafficker, wanted internationally for narcotics smuggling and a one-time known associate of Spencer Percy, the king of marijuana, now languishing in Butner Prison, North Carolina, where rumor had it he was going to study law under some arrangement the jail had with a local university.

Jesus Garcia and Restrepo had received this intelligence along with reports on the movements of Carlos Nelson, who was being most comprehensively tailed by an army of the *grupo*'s best watchers, who ranged from elegant couples to teenage student types and eleven-year-old street urchins.

Six days of watching established that the man was very quietly and professionally dealing with serious marijuana growers who had come into town from their plantations to do business with him.

It was discovered from his credit-card details that Carlos Nelson banked with BCCI in the United Arab Emirates and that he had access to several million dollars, discreetly spread around South America and the Caribbean.

Finally, word came back from a trusted Mafia don whose son was doing eight to ten in Butner. Yes, Spencer Percy remembered Nelson. He was a cool dude but a little bit crazy. A *tabacotraficante* certainly, one of the best, but a bit quixotic. He would slug it out with the worst gorilla if some girl was getting hassled. And word was he sometimes moonlighted as a hit man, which was why Percy, essentially a nonviolent Peter Pan from the flowers and mantra era, had let their business relationship drop.

Don Pablo Envigado was pleased when he heard this.

"I told you I liked this guy," he said to Restrepo as they waited to receive the ancient priest who was continuing his efforts to negotiate *el padrino*'s surrender to the Colombian authorities. "Arrange lunch with him. That would amuse me . . ."

In Dublin, Judge Eugene Pearson sat in his room and tried to concentrate on the day's case, which was an appeal against extradition by a former low-grade diplomat who had sold Irish passports to illegal immigrants and Middle Eastern terrorists while posted to the Irish embassy in London. The argument by the defense was not the usual one, that the man would not receive a fair trial in England; it was that even though the offenses had occurred in London and the north of England, the defendant had enjoyed diplomatic privilege and had been immune from prosecution.

It was a difficult judgment because it would be quoted in any future legal arguments as a precedent. There was no political pressure on him, one way or the other, and Pearson's inclination was to deny extradition, but he felt the man had let Ireland down badly and he decided to call the prosecutor in and come to an arrangement that if extradition was denied, the minor diplomat could be arrested immediately and charged with theft of Irish government property and with criminal conspiracy. The problem there was that conspiracy was one realm where he had always refused to extradite to the United Kingdom and the British press would delight in showing up the glaring inconsistency.

As he wrestled with the problem, Justice Pearson's concentration became increasingly permeated by the punitive stress of the more pressing dimensions to his life.

He had betrayed a major operation of the Organization, an offense with only one punishment. Yet while the prospect of being found out caused him attacks of near panic, he felt no sympathy for those individual members of the Lorca Group who were bound to suffer. For the British were reputed, with good reason, to be ruthlessly efficient at killing off known Provo soldiers whenever they could be found on active service. And gender was no barrier.

The judge had no doubt that his move was ethically and ideologically correct, for Brendan Casey's cocaine project was beyond moral justification and worse, much worse, would be ultimately damaging to the Cause.

But the bloody English Secret Service man, Jardine, had not taken any action that Pearson could see. He had included in his coded letter a message to be inserted in the London *Daily Telegraph* personal column: "RJ loves Florence by night. Remember the 9th." This would acknowledge receipt of the betraying information.

There had been no such message in the *Telegraph*.

Pearson resolved to communicate once more, giving even more comprehensive details this time. Cover names, dates, communication secrets. His heart was heavy and it was no wonder he found it hard to concentrate on some little gobshite who had sold a few passports.

Then there was Siobhan. Jesus how he loved that child. And there she was, a virtual hostage of the Colombian drug barons. What sort of father was it who could get so embroiled in a political ideal that he puts his own child at risk? Cold logic told him the answer was that the risk came with the territory, but when it happened, the pain was never less.

Still, at least she was writing now, and Restrepo had promised that Siobhan could return with Pearson when he flew out to Bogotá with the final operational details and the key to the computer discs that gave chapter and verse on the minutiae of Operation Legitimate, as the smuggling and distribution of Colombian cocaine into Europe had been code-named.

And at the back of his mind, Eugene Pearson became aware of the enormity of his predicament. Once on the slippery road of betrayal there was no going back. A few hints to the British Intelligence Service were not going to convince. He was going to have to pass on copies of the two 3.5-inch discs, along with the access codes, in order to shaft most comprehensively Operation Legitimate's chances of success.

In for a penny, Eugene, he told himself, in for the full thirty pieces of bloody silver. There was a tap at the door and Dennis Mallory, his clerk those last six years, stuck his head around.

"Just to remind you, Judge, it's ten past twelve," he said.

"Why thank you, Desmond," replied Pearson, and his clerk nodded and withdrew.

Padraic O'Shea, the next *taoiseach* if the electoral polls proved correct, had telephoned him at breakfast time when he and Mhairaid were in the middle of the mother and father of rows over Siobhan and why Eugene was taking it so calmly, her being out there with all those dagos and him not insisting on her coming home right away. Why any halfway decent father would have flown out to Venezuela, where Mhairaid believed the girl was, up in the mountains with some piano player, and dragged her home on the next plane. And so on, like that, in that vein . . .

Padraic had asked Pearson if he could spare a couple of minutes, maybe a sandwich and a glass of something at lunchtime, at O'Shea's office in the Daíl, the Dublin parliament buildings.

Eugene Pearson had said of course, and he presumed it was to do with the attorney general's post, which he had decided to accept. When he came off the phone, Mhairaid was somewhat mollified, for if there was one thing she cared about almost as much as her daughter Siobhan, it was the prospect of becoming wife of the next Attorney General.

At four minutes to one, Pearson was striding through the main entrance to the Daíl, acknowledging the nods and how-the-devil-are-you's and good-day-to-you-Eugenes, aware and enjoying the fact that, given the tight and gossip-ridden society that was Dublin's, there was not a man or woman in the building who did not know Judge Eugene Pearson was tipped to be the next attorney general. Life was not so bad, really. And once he had that power, he might just set about using it to defuse his enemies in the Organization.

He strode along the corridor to the polished wood door with a white-and-black plaque that had the name of Padraic O'Shea on it. He knocked and entered.

The room was spacious and had two windows overlooking the city, with a few treetops to lend grace to the view.

Padraic O'Shea was standing at one of the windows, his jacket hung on a peg by the door, and he was wearing the gray cardigan that Mhairaid had given him three Christmases ago. He seemed deep in thought, gazing out over the trees and rooftops.

Two plates of sandwiches and two cans of beer with two plastic tumblers were on a low table, around which was a leather couch and two leather armchairs, all very old and none of them matching.

"One o'clock on the dot," said Pearson, by way of announcing himself.

When Padraic turned around, he seemed older, more tired, the cares of the body politic on his features. He smiled a tired smile, like a big, ample-bellied, sad bloodhound.

"Well now, Eugene," he said, moving to one of the old armchairs, "will you be having a glass . . ."

"Just the one, Captain," Pearson replied, smiling and crossing to the couch. Captain and doctor were the honorary titles they had bestowed on each other at Trinity College, a thousand years before.

Padraic O'Shea opened the cans and poured out two beers in silence. Creating the moment, decided Pearson. Creating the appropriate atmosphere of *gravitas* to discuss the next government and Pearson's place therein.

"Thanks, Padraic," said Pearson, and took one of the plastic tumblers of Heineken lager. He admitted to himself he was quite nervous. It had been a long, hard haul from litigation counsel to this, the top of the pile.

O'Shea grasped his own beer and raised it, still somber. "Your very good health . . ."

"*Slainthe maithe,*" replied the judge. Good health to you.

They sipped and set their tumblers back on the table.

Here it comes, thought Pearson, savoring the moment so he could recount it to Mhairaid, and later, to Siobhan, the acme of his career.

"Eugene . . . I have to run the list of my future cabinet and senior government officers past the security people, G2 and the Garda Siochona Special Branch. You being a legal type will appreciate that."

"Of course. It's routine." What was he getting at?

Padraic O'Shea looked Pearson straight in the eye.

Padraic was one of the straightest men Eugene Pearson had ever known. "Well, everything's fine, except when I submitted your name there was a bit of a hiccup."

Pearson's heart stopped beating.

"What do you mean?"

"The Secret Service, and of course we don't acknowledge the existence of such a thing, and very small it is too, just a few bright men and women. But very professional. And very accurate. They don't seem to be entirely thrilled with you." O'Shea watched Pearson closely, his eyes still friendly, but more distant than the judge had ever seen them. For the man was a survivor.

Pearson held the party leader's gaze. He raised his shoulders and turned his palms upward in a gesture he had meant to mean I've got nothing to hide but he wished he hadn't, for he felt it had made him look shifty, like an Arab camel trader.

"Padraic, I have no idea what you're on about."

O'Shea sighed, clearly embarrassed. "Well, it means there is some sort of security question mark about you being appointed to the government, Eugene. I'm sure it's nothing and it's probably some damn computer error. I mean, can you shed any light on it? Is there anything maybe I should know?" He chuckled. "Wild orgies in the Appeal Court chambers after dark? Secret pot smoker? Debts? Gambling? Listen, if that's all, make a clean breast of it. Sometimes that's enough to make them happy."

Eugene Pearson, never the bravest of men, something Brendan Casey had figured and had used to trap him into the continuing and ever growing nightmare, very nearly fainted. He felt the blood drain from his head and he quickly replaced the plastic tumbler of beer as his hand began to tremble. His heart was pounding and he found it hard to breathe.

"Eugene, are you all right, old friend . . . ?" God, how he hated Padraic O'Shea for his purblind *decency*.

"I'm fine. Just makes me very angry, that's all. Bloody Castle." He meant Dublin Castle, where the small but efficient Intelligence Service had its offices. "How dare they?"

"I would feel precisely the same. By God, I'm glad I witnessed your reaction firsthand, there's obviously some ginormous cock-up. Leave it with me, I'll have to have a word with Sean" (Sean Gant was the chief of Irish Intelligence) "but we'll get to the bottom of this. And you've not to worry, we'll have you on the team because I want you there. Best man in Ireland for the job, so to hell with the spooks. Have a sandwich, it's lamb and tomato . . ."

When Eugene Pearson left that appalling lunchtime engagement, he could not think straight. He had always known that at some time, and whenever it came it would be the wrong time, his double life, his long and secret involvement with the Provisional IRA, might turn around and bite him in the arse. But that did not make the intimations of disaster any more palatable.

Fortunately, he still had a few aces up his sleeve. He had sufficient material to blackmail the several extremely high-placed politicos and government luminaries, bankers, lawyers, and pillars of Dublin society who were also secretly and closely linked to the Organization. So there was no possibility of a trial or even a public scandal. But the attorney general's post was clearly no longer on offer. Padraic O'Shea was the last man in the world he would have wanted to let down and he only prayed that no word of this security problem would leak out.

And even as he walked briskly down the street, away from the Daíl Building, he was working on a scheme to defuse the situation. One far-fetched, maybe, but not impossible move would be to identify himself to David Jardine, the London MI-6 man, spill the beans completely about the whole Provo movement, identifying the two operational ASUs (Active Service Units) on the British mainland, the two sleeper units, the two units regrouping in Europe, and all the stuff on supporters, safe houses, and arms caches. In return, he would ask Jardine discreetly to let Dublin Castle surmise he had always been an asset of the British and . . . oh God, what nonsense! He recognized that he was a man on the verge of total panic. And glancing at his watch, he realized he had fifteen minutes to get back to his courtroom and pass a precedent judgment on that little shit who had sold stolen Irish passports to all and sundry.

It occurred to him he could sling the man into prison pending a judgment and that was what, one hour later, the good Justice Eugene Pearson did.

————

There was something about Elgin Stuart that David Jardine instinctively liked. In fact there were quite a few things. The man was shrewd and canny, to the nth degree, but unlike many government functionaries who inhabited the secret environment, Stuart wore his authority lightly and with profound common sense.

It came as no surprise to Jardine that when Stuart had decided to do business with SIS rather than the Security Service, Special Branch, or the Customs Special Investigation Unit, the Mississippian should choose the man who could do DEA most good, while at the same time furthering the beginnings of a good personal relationship. One that had started in that underground conference room at the American Embassy when the CIA station chief had gravely informed SIS, in the person of

Jardine, that the Provisional IRA was playing footsy with the Colombian cartel.

Elgin Stuart had looked down and smiled at the barefaced effrontery of the move, designed to observe protocol, for Jardine clearly knew that the CIA had been sitting on that information for many months.

And it was also no surprise that when Stuart decided to do business with Jardine he should invite himself across the River Thames to Century House, for Elgin Stuart had been a soldier in Vietnam and he knew the old military adage that time spent on reconnaissance was seldom wasted.

"The glass box, eh?" Stuart grinned, his brown eyes amused, the whites of his eyes more a sort of café au lait color, complementing the rich darkness of his skin. He lifted the cup of coffee he had preferred to a bottle of Dos Equis beer and gazed around David Jardine's office, which the controller had instinctively decided to use rather than the visitor's room, which could have been any room in any government office and would have conveyed a somewhat frosty impression of cool disinterest, which was what it had been designed for.

No one was more astute or sensitive to atmosphere than Elgin Stuart, and he appreciated the gesture as he took in the sailing photographs, the antique carriage clock, photos of Dorothy and Andrew and Sally, a wall map of South America, some presentation plaques from other agencies, and a framed pennant which was the insignia of a KGB Spetznatz unit that had roamed Kabul and the Khyber Pass for weeks until Russian military intelligence learned that no such unit appeared on the KGB's books.

The unit, 129th Spetznatz, State Security, had been made up of a mixed SIS and Special Air Service team, all fluent speakers of Russian and Afghan tribal dialects.

It had been a considerable piece of cheek, extremely

hazardous, and the leader of the outfit was KGB Major Arcadi Andreyevitch Modin, alias David Arbuthnot Jardine.

Beneath the pennant hung a framed group photo of the "Spetznatz" unit in Russian warm-climate fatigues. Jardine saw Stuart looking at the photograph and told him the story, with a few extremely funny anecdotes thrown in.

Laughing, the DEA man said, "But you did do some damage, David . . . ?"

Still smiling, Jardine replied gently, "Just a bit."

Elgin Stuart nodded. One tough dude, he was thinking to himself. He decided he had come to the right place.

"Okay," he said, "last time we met was in the tank, up in Grosvenor Square."

"Correct."

"Jim Polder fed you some intelligence that must've really shook you . . ." Stuart gazed innocently at the wall map of South America.

"I'm always grateful for information, Elgin."

"Along the lines that the IRA are getting into bed with Don Pablo."

"I don't immediately recall Jim getting that specific."

"Well, that's who it is."

"Interesting. But not surprising, eh?"

"But that's not why I came down here."

Elgin Stuart was a master of the unfinished communication. Jardine was warming to him. Maybe Elgin and his wife in the CIA office would like to come down to Wiltshire. Dorothy would like him. "Really. It was for the coffee, right?"

"We have a problem in New York City . . ."

"We being . . . ?"

"DEA." And Elgin Stuart told Jardine the whole story about the Jane Doe at Grand Central several months before, about Homicide Lieutenant Eddie Lucco's professional obsession, about the massacre at Bellevue, the murder of the travel agent, Simba Patrice's head, and the fact that Manny Schulman (deceased) had been a made man of the cartel. He did not mention or hint that Eddie Lucco had become a secret DEA agent and had taken five million dollars from Restrepo in a classic cartel move.

But David Jardine's intuition led him to the logical conclusion. He knew Stuart had figured this, and he appreciated being trusted so quickly.

"And the Homicide officer, he's still in . . . grave danger, I imagine?"

Elgin Stuart gazed into Jardine's eyes. He smiled slowly. "Whatever way he jumped, there's no safe way of dealing with *el grupo,* right?"

"You say the cartel. Who in particular?" asked Jardine, and with some reluctance, the DEA man passed on the name of Restrepo. This was a key item of information, for it linked, for the first time, the Jane Doe case to Pablo Envigado and therefore to Operation Corrida.

Suddenly Jardine was more than politely interested.

Stuart explained that the Joint Task Force and DEA Washington needed to learn the identity of the dead girl, or more accurately, the dead girl's father, so that they could make some sense of why it was vital to the Colombians that he remained ignorant of her death.

"Because the poor fellow believes the cartel is holding his daughter hostage, sticks out a mile, Elgin. Sure you won't have a beer?"

"I would love a beer. Okay, now the *grupo* does not take hostages except to put on pressure, they got enough money, so ransom is out."

"Identify the girl, you identify the father. Or indeed, the other way around . . ."

"You got it." Stuart caught a bottle of Dos Equis as it

soared gently over David Jardine's desk from the cooler at his feet. Jardine pushed a bottle opener toward him.

"I brought you all the details . . ." Stuart took a thick buff envelope from the inside pocket of his gray three-piece worsted suit. He looked like a bank executive, and Jardine reckoned that was definitely *not* what Elgin had worn down there in Mississippi, or in Puerto Rico, where the DEA man had done some outrageously brave things in the fight against dope dealing. Jardine knew this because he had Elgin Stuart's file in his desk drawer. He always took such precautions, but in this instance it had made impressive reading.

In the buff envelope were several sheets of paper covering more or less what Stuart had just told Jardine, plus the girl's name, Siobhan, the autopsy report, and scene-of-crime reports on the various subsequent murders. And the two photographs, one of the dead face from Missing Persons, the other of the laughing kid with Ricardo Santos in Rome.

Jardine nodded. He knew what Elgin Stuart was doing. He also understood why the New York Homicide cop had been touched by the case. The child was so waiflike, so . . . vulnerable. Jesus, what a disaster for her parents, whoever they were.

He looked up, expressionless. "We'll find out who this is. And who the father is. Would you and, um, Denise, like to come down to Wiltshire some weekend? It's not far by American standards. We could have lunch."

Stuart gazed back with his baleful brown eyes. "You'll find out? Just like that? Not, *try* to? Hell, David, that's confident."

"I'll find out." Jardine met the penetrating stare. "We will move reasonably fast on this one."

Stuart frowned. He still found British understatement utterly confusing. "That's good?"

"It's pretty good. And you will be the first to know. Okay?"

The DEA man stared at Jardine for a long moment. "So what's happening on the cartel front, David?"

"Nothing you chaps don't know about," David Jardine lied coolly. "I mean, that's your territory, Colombia."

The two men smiled. They understood each other perfectly.

One other person knew that it was Harry Ford who had killed the obscene Captain Tabio, of the Bogotá Police. That man was Colonel Xavier Ramón Gomez, recently retired from the Secret Police, the DAS, where he was deputy director of Security and Counterespionage.

Ramón now ran a small but efficient private security company, with lucrative contracts with the various American, European, and Japanese corporations who had invested millions in Colombia's natural wealth—mineral deposits, oil, coffee, fruit, and the like. Colombia is rich in many resources other than cocaine, and the hooded-eyed former intelligence officer was determined to help protect all opportunities for honest endeavor from the scourge of guerrillas of whatever political flavor, dope barons, and gangsters.

Being a realist, he sometimes reached accommodations in those remote regions where the rule of law could not be enforced, regions where the FARC, the ELN, or the cartel held sway. But his fierce pride in his personal integrity, and those he employed, made it obvious that he regarded all those outfits that had given Colombia the reputation of being one of the most dangerous and lawless countries in the world with the deepest contempt.

How, then, did he reconcile such transparent honesty and patriotic pride with the fact that he had been a trusted agent of the British SIS for so many years?

Only another Colombian could answer that. And maybe David Jardine. For as long as Ramón could further his battle against terrorists, bandits, and drug dealers, he would get into bed with the devil himself.

Therefore, rule number one in dealing with Ramón (Jardine knew it would be hubris to imagine one could *run* the man) was never ask him to do anything that might damage his own country or its people. Since Her Majesty's Government had no desire other than to assist the elected Bogotá government to stabilize the nation, that had never presented a problem.

Also, if Ramón became aware of SIS operations or policy, he always reserved the right to pass on the relevant details to his president. It might seem a strange arrangement, but it made sense to those who understood the predicament of brave and honorable men caught in those times.

Ramón had been warned by his friend David Jardine to expect Señor Carlos Nelson to be in touch.

When Harry Ford had made contact and explained tersely what he required—the weapons, the vehicles, the maps, the documents—Ramón had provided them without question. He had no idea what Ford's real name was but he knew it sure as hell was not Carlos Nelson, although the man was clearly a South American.

The items were supplied and Xavier Ramón had added them to SIS's account, which was always substantial and always meticulously honest.

But one of the items had been a Sig-Sauer P-226 automatic pistol and three hundred rounds of ammunition, along with cleaning kit and a screw-on silencer.

And in the inventory of Nelson's possessions in Suite 303 at La Fontana, the result of a discreet search by Ramon's trusted subordinate, Jaime, two days before the shooting, was included a pair of bright red, wool gloves.

Why did Ramón have Harry Ford's rooms turned over? Because he was one of the greatest survivors in Colombia. David Jardine would have expected no less, and he had warned Harry about those little foibles of the man who was his principal point of contact in Operation Corrida.

Now Xavier Ramón was on his way to meet Carlos Nelson for a routine encounter, to service the agent's requirements, if any.

The rendezvous was the bar in the Hosteria de la Candelaria, in downtown Bogotá, in the old quarter. The bar boasted a laid-back band who dressed in bullfighters' outfits and played salsa versions of seventies rock 'n' roll, like "Stone Free" and "Honky Tonk Woman" . . .

He had resisted running a DAS computer check on Nelson, just in case the security programs worked, for a change, and recorded the search. He was also meticulous about honoring his arrangement with SIS, as far as he possibly could, while remaining a loyal officer of the Secret Police. The DAS.

But did he not retire? Was Colonel Xavier Ramón not a retired officer?

Perhaps.

As Ramón approached the *hostería,* he spotted Jaime and two of his men disguised as beggars. The blue-and-white bandanna sticking out from Jaime's pocket was a warning signal. It meant it was not safe for Ramón to proceed with his meeting. And so he strolled a little way past, then stopped to gaze in a camera-shop window, stuffing his hands in his pockets and watching the reflection of the entrance to the hotel bar.

The blue Cherokee jeep, the three hard men on Suzuki 800cc trail bikes, dressed like something out of the movie *Road Warrior,* which was one of Ramón's favorites. He had the tape at home. They had *grupo* written all over them.

Then he spotted Restrepo and Jesus Garcia, walking past the jeep and going into the bar.

A sudden chill overtook Ramón and he quickly and none too casually glanced around the environment, looking for undercover cops or DAS anti-cartel teams. Carlos Nelson had chosen the wrong bar to be in if the place was going to be raided by the authorities.

But the area seemed quiet. Anyway, the man who called himself Restrepo could go where he liked. There was no warrant out for his arrest.

Only rumors.

Inside the bar of the Hostería de la Candelaria, Harry Ford lit another cigarette. His fifth of the day. He couldn't believe he was becoming a smoker. He had spotted two wingers, two serious men, among the several body-guards discreetly looking after their charges.

The two serious men did not seem to be looking after anyone in the room, but their eyes worked a nonstop assignment, checking everyone there, every new arrival, every departure. The only person in the bar, Harry had begun to realize, that they showed no interest in, after a keen once-over when he had arrived, was himself.

Those professionally observed facts told the SIS man two things. One, that the wingers were ensuring the environment was safe for their charge, who had not yet arrived. And two, that it was himself their charge was coming to see, to speak with, or to attempt to blow away.

The two men could perhaps be detectives from some elite squad. They were clearly expertly trained, and the techniques they were using were classic Hereford techniques, even down to the ways they silently communicated with each other.

That meant they were either DAS or Colombian Army Special Forces operators, for elements of 22nd SAS Regiment—until recently comrades in arms of Harry's—had been training those units for the last eighteen months. Or they were cartel soldiers, trained by the renegade SAS noncom MacAteer.

Harry Ford watched the smoke linger above the tip of his Mustang-brand cigarette and nodded to the lithe coffee-colored girl behind the bar. She smiled back, full of allure and fun, and opened a bottle of Corona beer. God, those Colombian girls were something else. One of the wingers Harry was watching in the mirror behind the bar rose and strolled out, touching his ear, which meant he probably had a radio hearing aid, in contact with others on his protection team.

They could only be cops with such sophisticated devices. Or *el grupo*, which, Harry Ford's briefings had instilled in him, could afford anything they wanted in the way of ordnance or equipment.

He took a deep, controlled breath, stubbed out his cigarette, and smiled briefly back to the bar girl as she slid a glass of ice-cold Corona across the counter to him.

And suddenly the feeling of apprehension had gone. Harry Ford was calm, his pulse, if anything, lowering. For he was a trained man and the game in which he was a pro player had just commenced. The two men he had walked past on his way out of the restaurant in the National Park, where he had blown away the sadist cop, had just entered, exchanging brief eye contact with the remaining winger still sitting beside the door, his back to the wall.

One had held a mini-Uzi, the other a Colt .45 automatic.

"Nos vemos . . ." Harry had said to them, convinced it was going to turn into a fast and unequal shooting match, but they had remained perfectly calm and he had walked out, climbed onto the big Yamaha, and roared away, off the road and up into the remote slopes of the National Park.

"Nos vemos." Catch you later. And here they were.

Bobby Sonson moved casually to one end of the bar and leaned his left elbow on the counter, watching the right-hand side of the room. Murillo placed himself on the other end of the bar, covering the left-hand side.

And still they hadn't even glanced at Harry.

Who the hell was coming? While conversation in the bar went on, most people in the room oblivious to any drama, and the band played "Jumping Jack Flash" (he's a gas, gas, gas), Harry sipped his beer and very casually turned from the counter and faced the door, gently flicking open the middle button of his old tweed sports coat. If this was a hit, he knew he could drop the three targets in the room and whoever came through the main door.

The music from the band had suddenly changed to quiet but dramatic Spanish flamenco, with much strumming of guitars. He felt like a matador waiting for the arrival of the bull . . .

Then two men entered. The second of the serious wingers, the one who had left the bar touching his radio hearing aid, followed close behind, making eye contact with his colleagues. The new arrivals wore sober, expensive clothes, with plain shirts and quiet neckties. Handmade shoes. There was the slender, broad-shouldered one with longish, well-groomed hair, and a shorter, pox-faced one with lantern jaw, swarthy features, muscular build, and artisan's hands. Both had a relaxed demeanor and total disregard for the rough and dangerous clientele in the bar that stated, with no room for misinterpretation, we are bad people, the worst in town.

The long-haired one looked at Harry and held his gaze, an amused smile flickering, his eyes lazy but not hostile. Like an alligator who is not yet hungry.

There was no pretense of a chance encounter. The two men approached Harry, and his eyes did not leave them, at the same time keeping himself aware of the other wingers. Targets, as they had become to Harry Ford the professional soldier.

The two men stopped a couple of feet from him. Amazingly, nobody else in the bar seemed to be aware of anything unusual.

"Señor Nelson. I am Luís Restrepo Osorio. I don't know if that means anything to you."

Did it ever.

Harry Ford knew everything David Jardine knew about *el grupo* and that included Luís Restrepo, his strange visit to Geneva, his place in Pablo Envigado's cartel, and his presence in Paris when the Whore of Venice had been found dead on a bridge, his head shot away.

"Buenos días, señor. Encantado de conocerle . . ." Ford smiled coolly. Enchanted to meet you. "How about a beer?"

"As a matter of fact, I have come here"—the glance with which Restrepo dismissed the bar and its clientele insinuated he would never have been there from choice—"to invite you to lunch."

"I already have a lunch date."

"Of course, with Colonel Ramón."

Shaken like a jet fighter taking a hit from an air-to-air missile, Harry Ford's training took him through the first of what Ronnie Szabodo had warned him would be the series of "nasty surprises" that were part of the everyday life of a deep penetration agent, operating among clever and dangerous enemies.

"Exactly," he replied calmly.

"The good colonel is across the street. His people noticed my men here and have warned him off. They're quite professional," Restrepo remarked in an offhand way.

"You mean he probably won't be coming to lunch," said Harry, and smiled as if in approval of Restrepo's superior muscle.

"So shall we go?" Restrepo watched him, no trace of tension on his face. And why should there be, thought Harry Ford, he has all the aces.

"Señor Restrepo. What possible interest could you people have in me?"

"Come on, *amigo*. Lunch, for God's sake. It's not going to kill you."

Harry stared deep into the Colombian gangster's lawyer's eyes. "Boy Scout's honor?" he asked, and Restrepo and Jesus Garcia burst out laughing.

"I told you . . ." chuckled Pablo Envigado, stuffing a forkful of rice and fish into his mouth, then waving the fork at Restrepo, who sat next to Harry Ford at the round table in Salinas, one of the better restaurants in the classy, diplomatic district of North Bogotá. ". . . this is one helluva guy . . . Boy scout's honor . . ." He wiped a tear of laughter from his eye. "Señor Nelson, you mind if I call you Carlos?"

"Not in the least, *padrino*," replied Harry.

"You see? And well brought up too," Envigado said to Restrepo, then turned back to Harry. "I hear you play polo."

"I play eight," said Harry, truthfully. An eight handicap was good.

"And you shoot people you don't like."

What would David Jardine, the ace operator, have done, faced with a direct statement accusing him of cold-blooded murder? Harry Ford contemplated acting dumb, saying I don't know what you're talking about. Certainly he would not be there unless Envigado knew everything. But having touched first base, Harry did not want to seem too eager a catch.

"I don't know what you're talking about," he said.

"You looked my two best men in the eye." Envigado indicated Murillo and Sonson, sitting at a table by the door. Then he took a folded piece of paper from his pocket and handed it to Ford. It was the computerized photofit circulated around Bogotá.

Harry studied the picture. It was truly a better likeness than his passport photo. He shook his head in admiration at the *grupo*'s efficiency and passed the paper back to Pablo Envigado. "The guy was a *cabrón*. He should have died slower."

Restrepo and Jesus Garcia glanced at Envigado. The hubbub of restaurant conversation seemed loud, suddenly. Then Pablo Envigado nodded approvingly:

"Está chevere. That's nice. Spoken just like me when I was your age. What are you doing seeing a *tombo* like Xavier Ramón?" *Tombo* was Colombian slang for cop.

"I need some clout here, it's strange territory. The man is so straight, if I can persuade him of my honesty and integrity, he can smooth things, open doors."

"You planning a little exporting maybe?" Envigado grinned, chewing another mouthful.

"We'll see." Harry found he was enjoying this game.

"I understand you know Spencer Percy."

Was there nothing this man did not know? "I didn't

think you knew him." Spencer Percy hated cocaine, everybody knew that.

"I like his style," replied Envigado. "Just like I like yours . . ."

And I quite like yours, pal, thought Harry. The most wanted man in Colombia, with teams, battalions, of soldiers and paramilitary police scouring the country for you, and here you are in Bogotá a couple of miles from the Presidential Palace and the DAS Headquarters you recently blew up in an attempt to kill General Maza, the director. Eating in a smart restaurant among diplomats, bankers, and politicians. The simple but efficient disguise of gold-rimmed glasses, a clean-shaven face, four false dentures capping his own teeth, a different haircut, and a bespoke tailored English suit, plus the sheer, calm confidence of the man all conspired to leave him unnoticed by the exclusive clientele. That plus the presence of around thirty of his soldiers, discreetly in place at other tables and outside among the cluster of waiting cars, each with one or two bodyguards for the important men eating at Salinas.

"So what can I do for you, Señor?" Harry affected (without too much trouble) to look anxious and perturbed. "After all, my little enterprise is no threat to you . . ."

"I hear your little enterprise has got you on wanted lists all over the world."

Harry Ford shrugged. "I enjoy the life."

Pablo Envigado dabbed at his mouth with a pale green linen napkin. "You hear that, Luís?" He jabbed his fork at Restrepo, who smiled patiently. "He likes—the—*life* . . . Now that I can understand. Listen, Carlos . . ."—his attention switched back to Harry—". . . things are getting pretty hot for you out there. It was a shrewd move trying to con Ramón into smoothing your path here in Bogotá. But take it from me. That is one deeply suspicious hombre. And so straight he shits standing up. You're a clever young fellow, *amigo*, but Ramón will fuck you sideways and you'll be extradited to the USA before you can break wind."

He waited as a waiter poured more wine. Harry Ford noted it was a Batard Montrachet '83. Only the best for Don Pablo, he thought. I could get to like this.

A helicopter fluttered fussily over the rooftops of Lambeth, probably from the police traffic department, for it was approaching the rush hour. Its rasp could be heard inside the corner office of controller West 8 in Century House.

Ronnie Szabodo was as close to excited as David Jardine had seen him. He was reading a deciphered signal that Harry Ford had sent from Santa Fe in Antioquia.

Two weeks had passed since that lunch with Pablo Envigado in the heart of Bogotá. Harry's signals had come in regularly, as one might expect from an experienced SAS troop commander, and each transmission had brought more details of his successful infiltration right to the heart of the Medellín Cartel.

At the lunch in Salinas, Envigado had warmed to Carlos Nelson. Jesus Garcia's sophisticated security investigation into the stranger had uncovered exactly what the Corrida team in Century House wanted him to do.

So neither Restrepo nor Garcia had any real reason to object when Pablo Envigado, in typical quixotic fashion, had invited Carlos Nelson to join him, to work for him, become one of the *grupo*'s organizers, reorganizing his enforcement structure and maybe, if things worked out, investigating the increasingly obvious attempts of the Cali branch of the cartel (the more "civilized" de-

scendants of the *conquistadores* to the south) to destroy
the excessively violent domination of the cocaine trade
by the Medellín *grupo*.

Harry had protested, saying he had lined up a couple
of excellent marijuana deals, cocaine was not his territory and he preferred to be his own boss. He was aware
from the start, and communicated this in his signals,
that Restrepo, although he held his tongue, did not like
the idea of him investigating the Cali *grupo*.

Join me, Don Pablo had declared, and I shall show
you riches and excitement you have never dreamed of.
Then he had grinned and added that when he wanted
something, he did generally succeed in getting it. He
revealed to Harry that he was aware of every detail of
the marijuana deals and asked how much the young
polo player expected to make after covering his expenses.

Over half a million dollars, Harry had replied.

Then Pablo Envigado had instructed Luís Restrepo to
arrange for Harry Ford to receive $80,000 per week for a
fifteen-week contract, and the secret agent had felt he
could reasonably appear to give in gracefully.

"Bit mean for a player," Jardine had remarked to
Szabodo. "Trifle mean for a chap at the top table . . ."

And the Hungarian had shrugged. For Envigado had
been known to pay more than that for his top aides.
Restrepo, for instance, was on a retainer of two million
a month.

"Maybe he's on a kind of . . . probation?" suggested
Szabodo.

Now, two weeks later, Harry Ford, agent Parcel, had
impressed the Corrida team with the quality of his
intelligence on subjects concerning the cartel. Locations
of cocaine laboratories, identities of cartel executives in
Colombia and overseas, both in Europe and in the USA.

Much of this early information was known already, but that corroborated the accuracy of the operator's product.

Ford/Nelson was not party to *el grupo*'s innermost secrets but he was doing better than the Corrida team had dared to expect. And the signal Ronnie Szabodo held in his hands gave details of a forthcoming visit by Envigado to a coca laboratory not far from the Forbidden City above Santa Marta in the foothills of the Sierra Nevada mountain range. That was fresh and high-grade secret intelligence from a Denied Area, which was exactly what Jardine's business was all about.

"This is very excellent, David." Szabodo fumbled in his jacket pocket for his tobacco. "If those dates and locations are accurate, we could send some SAS boys from Cartagena to lead an arrest and destroy by the Army and Force Nine."

"It's worth considering." Jardine opened the back of his carriage clock and fitted the key into the winder mechanism.

He touched a button on his intercom.

"Sir?" Heather's voice.

"Heather, get hold of Director Special Forces, would you? Secure line. If he's not available, try Colonel McAlpine down in Hereford." And he switched off the intercom.

Szabodo blew through the stem of his pipe, trying to dislodge a piece of tobacco. "Something's worrying you, David. What is it?"

Jardine finished winding the clock. He shut the back gently and placed it on his desk, setting the hands to the correct time.

"Lovely tick. Safe and steady. Like a good operator . . ."

"You still think eighty thousand is not enough?"

"Bit mean, that's all."

And Heather rang to say the Director SAS was on the

secure line and the Firm's man in the Dublin embassy was on the other.

David Jardine briefly outlined to Director Special Forces, an SAS Brigadier and an old sparring partner, that he had a possible strike, arrest, search, and destroy operation imminent in Colombia within range of the Special Forces teams operating in support of Colombian authorities out of Cartagena army barracks. They agreed to meet at HQ DSF, in London later that day.

Then the sphere controller lifted the other handset.

"Toby. How are you?" Toby Maitland was the senior SIS man in Dublin. His cover was as Press Attaché but nobody in the Dublin intelligence and security organs was taken in by that, and they generally went out of their way to be helpful.

"David, the girl called Jane . . ." He meant Jane Doe.

"What about her?"

"Well, there is talk about a legal chap here. Very high up the tree."

David Jardine wished his junior colleagues would learn it was not always necessary to speak some form of gobbledygook they imagined was guarded speech.

"He's a counsel?"

"Higher."

"Fine, he's a judge. Get on with it, Toby."

"Well, he has a daughter of that name." There was a crackle of static on the line. "David?"

"Still here."

"And the word is she's disappeared. Venezuela, apparently. Look, would you like, is it worth me sending a fax?"

God preserve us, thought Jardine.

"Well, that would be really splendid, Toby."

Toby sounded pleased. "Really? Will I do that now, David? Or can it wait? We have something of a flap on here. This is the embassy wine-tasting evening and I rather rashly volunteered to set the thing up, ha-ha."

For a millisecond, Jardine wondered if Maitland was talking in code before he realized the man was serious.

"Now that would be most helpful, Toby. You see, people are getting killed over this."

"Oh Lord. It'll be with you in seconds."

"Thanks a lot. And Toby . . ."

Toby sounded chastened, as well he might. "Yes, David?"

"Good luck with the wine tasting."

It took David Jardine seven minutes after receipt of Toby's fax naming Judge Eugene Pearson as the father of Siobhan Pearson, previously reported missing through Irish diplomatic channels, to contact the electronic-radio-monitoring division of British Intelligence, known as GCHQ, in Cheltenham in the West of England.

He requested printouts of all conversations between the Irish Foreign Ministry and all South American countries that mentioned the names Pearson, Siobhan, Judge, music, or—a brainwave this, as he studied the photo of Siobhan with Ricardo Santos—the name Ricardo or Richard. Also details of all telephone conversations to and from the judge's Dublin home and his chambers at the Criminal Law Courts over the past six months.

By ten o'clock the next morning, David Jardine was able to telephone Elgin Stuart and tell him SIS could confirm the probable name of the Jane Doe was Siobhan Pearson, daughter of one Judge Eugene Pearson, widely tipped to become the next attorney general if O'Shea's Fine Gael party won the next election.

They agreed that this knowledge should be classified top secret and that neither agency would inform the Pearsons of their tragic loss. For it was of vital importance to both agencies, for different reasons, to learn just what it was about Pearson that made the cartel so keen to put pressure on him.

And that same day, Eugene Pearson mailed copies of the two 3.5-inch discs he had given to Restrepo to Jardine's Tite Street apartment. He posted the access codes, which the cartel did not yet possess, to Mr. David Jardine at the Protocol Department of the Foreign and Commonwealth Office in Charles Street, off Whitehall.

EL DIABLO

19

EL DIABLO

Crows rose above the treetops, and their hoarse, misanthropic screeching seemed somehow fitting to Eugene Pearson's mood. He watched Brendan Casey, who seemed deep in thought. It had been his duty to inform the chief of staff that everything was now in place and the Lorca Group was ready to receive its first consignment of cocaine from the cartel.

He had also asked for the military wing, the Provos, to hold on to the initial consignment of two tons of cocaine, worth hundreds of millions of dollars, until he and his daughter, Siobhan, returned safely from Bogotá, where it had been arranged, in secret communication with Restrepo, that she would be reunited with her anxious father.

"I don't know, Eugene." Casey kicked at the bed of pine needles at his feet. They were in a wood forty miles north of Dublin, not far from Dundalk. Wingers lurked nearby, like ancient dun-colored tree men from the swamp of Eire's beginnings, guardians and perpetuators

546

of a lore of blood and myth and freedom enslaved. A myth that sustained Judge Eugene Pearson in his total commitment to the Armed Struggle and his complete intention to destroy the cocaine link before it could damage his beloved Ireland and the purity of the real fight.

In his not inconsiderable brain, Pearson had achieved perfect serenity on the subject of his anonymous messages to British intelligence. Of course the British were the enemy until such time as they cleared out of the Six Counties, but right now he perceived that Brendan Casey and his close little clique of misfits were the greater danger to the movement and to Ireland in the short term.

In his first communication to the spy David Jardine, he had slanted the information to make it appear the Lorca Group were renegade Provos, at odds with the professional and patriotic leadership of the Armed Struggle.

In his second, the one accompanying copies of the two 3.5-inch computer discs he had given to Restrepo, Eugene Pearson had emphasized the point. Lorca was disowned by the Army Council. It was a lie, but it would save the movement after the cauterizing internal struggle to come.

For the second thing Pearson had resolved was that, on his return to Dublin with his precious child, Siobhan with the face and hair of a wayward angel, he would kill Brendan Casey. And by so doing would finally, and ironically, arrive at the sharp end of the Armed Struggle.

He planned to do it at just such a meeting as this one. He would use a knife, one quick slashing thrust across the throat after diverting the bastard's attention. Pointing away and saying, what's that?

He had tried a case like that five years before. The graphic way the killer had admitted her crime and the method, the girl had worked in a slaughterhouse, she made it seem so simple.

Pearson had been impressed.

And he had practiced until he could perform the movement in his sleep. At first it had been for self-defense, or when the final push of the Struggle arrived. For it was and remained the Provisional IRA's most secret intention, once the British ran scuttling out from the Six Counties, to create a popular uprising like those in Bulgaria and, many years earlier, in Cuba. And to seize power from the elected Daíl. To create a one-nation state. Thirty-two counties united under Provo rule.

That was Eugene Pearson's dream. But the trick with the slaughterhouse knife would be put into practice sooner.

As he watched Brendan Casey and waited for a response, he smiled slightly. Jesus, the man's neck was just beautifully presented right now. When the time came, it was going to be so easy. He would have a typed proclamation ready to show to the wingers. An official sentence of death, signed by Declan Burke and Mary Connelly. That was the thing about Irish patriot fighters. They were literate to a man. And they would accept anything written down, provided it was eloquent and had a few semicolons.

Republican revolutionaries had a fondness for semicolons; any study of their proclamations, with their reasons for bombings and maimings, would reveal the truth of it.

"I don't know," repeated Casey. "A contract is a contract, you know that."

"Jesus Christ man, they've got my daughter."

Casey's baleful eyes fixed on Eugene Pearson. He nodded a few times, as if in time to some silent tune. Finally he grinned, his gold filling glinting in the beams of setting sun.

"Sure. Why not . . . ?"

Relief flooded Pearson's heart. For a moment he almost rescinded his private sentence of death, so grateful was he.

"When will you go, then?" asked Brendan Casey softly.

"Within the next couple of days."

"Will I send a coupla fellas with you? We don't want anything to happen t'll ye."

"No, no." The judge met the man's expression of concern with a self-deprecating smile. "I'm invited to a law conference in Florida. So there's a reason for me to go that far as myself. Then I'm onto a plane to Bogotá. One night there. Meet Restrepo, hand over the access codes, collect Siobhan, maybe have dinner with her in the old quarter, they say it's quite lively, kids like that, don't they? Then back to Miami on the next plane, sod the law conference, and fly home directly. Her mother will be over the moon."

Casey gazed up at the cawing crows; the sky was darkling. He nodded, and let his gaze fall on Pearson. "Well, good luck, Eugene. We'll see you anon . . ." And he turned and strolled away, comfortable on the floor of pine needles.

Somewhere, an owl screeched.

The air-conditioning in District Attorney Faccioponti's office had gone haywire. It alternated between sullen uselessness, adding humidity when outside it was a fresh, spring day, and surges of arctic air that left the Bellevue Investigation Group, which is what the ad hoc collection of interested law officers had become, frozen to the marrow.

An arctic phase had just ceased, abruptly, and Eddie

Lucco rubbed his hands and folded his arms, nursing the loose-weave tweed jacket to his chest. Don Mather tucked his hands under his armpits. The FBI agent and the Customs special investigator looked like they had the flu.

"You guys are all wimps," said Faccioponti, relaxed in striped Brooks Brothers shirt and red suspenders. Lucco had heard the DA worked out during lunch breaks and stopped off at a tanning salon on his way home. The guy was a dickhead. And he had asked Nancy out, for the third time. There was no way he could avoid knowing that she was Mrs. Lieutenant Eddie Lucco and that offended the detective more than somewhat.

"Okay," said Faccioponti, "to sum up, the perpetrators of the Bellevue killings were members of a Colombian hit squad, with orders to silence PeeWee Patrice before he could testify to a grand jury on the subject of illegal cocaine dealing in the state of New York. They were led by a senior member of the cartel, who came to NYC for the job. At the same time, a leading cartel player, Ricardo Santos Castaneda, was probably murdered. Santos had lost a girl, identity unknown, who had arrived with him from Rome. We have no record of their flight because they were traveling under false passports. Said passports must've been remarkable forgeries, or Immigration would have picked them up. The girl went to Simba Patrice, brother of PeeWee, for some crack action, slept with Simba, and was subsequently found dead of an overdose of impure crack. Jane Doe, as she now is, is being kept on ice, as a result of a warrant obtained by Homicide Lieutenant Lucco, working out of the 14th Precinct, because that is the precinct where the death occurred.

"Lieutenant Lucco has ascertained that the cartel was in the process of kidnapping the girl in order to put leverage on her father, who is somehow important in

Pablo Envigado's scheme of things. He is European, probably Irish, and Jane Doe has, as a result of some excellent detective work, become Siobhan Doe. Probably.

"Simba was murdered by the cartel, doubtless because he was known to have spoken with Mr. Lucco, but also because he might have been told by the dead kid more than he could be permitted to know. And also because he posed a danger to the cartel, because he had no sense of humor about them killing his kid brother." And as an afterthought: "Have we anything new on the third Patrice brother? What's 'is name?"

"Abdullah," said the Customs agent.

"He's disappeared." Lucco relaxed as the air conditioner breathed warm, moist air into the office. "Word is, he's taken off for the Caribbean till the heat's off. 110th Precinct want him for the killing of five Colombians in Queens. Including a short-order cook who turns out to have been a button man for the *grupo.*"

"Sensible guy," remarked the FBI agent.

"So, fellows . . ." Faccioponti spread his arms, palms up. ". . . who the fuck do we present to the New York voters? If all the killers have gone . . . ?"

"I'm trying to get some names. Even a couple." Lucco stretched his long legs and realized his shoes were the least shiny in the room. "Then we could announce them and start extradition proceedings in Bogotá."

The immediate laughter this suggestion got did nothing to assuage his increasing disenchantment with the meeting. Mather shot him a sympathetic glance.

"Fact is," said the DEA man, "Eddie has performed miracles." There was a murmur of agreement. "But sometimes that's not enough. Tony, there is nobody in the United States we can finger for the Bellevue killings.

Once Eddie drags a few names out of his stoolies—can you do that, Eddie . . . ?"

Lucco nodded.

"Then we publish wanted pictures and lift them next time they show their faces, anywhere in the country."

"That's it?" asked the DA. "What the hell do we tell the mayor's office?"

"Well that's your problem sir," Eddie Lucco said, lifting his eyes from his worn footwear. "We just do the easy work."

And this time the smiles were in sympathy. The FBI man hid his amusement by opening his briefcase.

Faccioponti tapped a pencil on his desk, making a sound like a woodpecker. "Any other bright remarks, Lieutenant?"

Lucco leaned back in his seat, touched his fingertips together, and rubbed the bridge of his nose, his eyes not leaving Faccioponti's face.

"Sure, Mr. Faccioponti . . ." And in Neapolitan Italian dialect he said gently, "Keep your fuckin hands off my wife. Understand?"

Faccioponti's face went scarlet. The tapping pencil fell silent.

The three non-Italian speakers in the room, FBI, Customs, and DEA, looked on without understanding.

"So share the joke," said Cortez, the Customs man, who had the best idea of what had just been said.

"It's an old joke, from Naples, Italy." Lucco smiled coldly at the DA. "It would probably lose something in the translation. You think, Tony . . . ?"

There was a long moment as the DA quietly regained his cool. The redness in his face began to recede. He nodded slowly. "Hard to translate." He stared hard at Lucco, then shrugged, avoided his eyes and addressed the others, "So what are the chances of identifying this Jane or Siobhan or whatever her goddamn name is?"

The others all turned to watch Eddie Lucco. He seemed to consider the question, then shrugged. "Right now? Zilch. But we won't let it drop. The case is ongoing."

After the meeting, as they walked to the elevators, Don Mather and Lucco let the others go in the first car.

"That was good," said Mather. "Eddie, you have to start using some of that dough. They'll get suspicious if you don't touch it."

"Sure. How much?"

"Buy a car. Take some cash. Take Nancy on a vacation someplace nice. Give some to your buddy."

"How much?"

"Oh . . . thirty grand."

"Shit!"

"Like they said. Don't use the New York bank. Go to Nassau, or Miami."

"We need a new icebox. And a rack to hold our CDs."

Mather grinned. "Thirty grand should cover it."

"When?"

"Soon as you like. And Eddie. Just remember. That money belongs to the U.S. Treasury. And whatever you purchase, I need receipts. Everything you and Vargos buy will belong to the government. *Capisci . . . ?*"

"You speak Italian?"

"My sister's married to one. Now, Eddie, listen to this. What I am about to tell you, and it's because I trust you and you deserve to know, is the highest security classification and not for repetition to a living soul . . ."

Eddie Lucco nodded. "Sure."

Don Mather glanced around. Then he took out his pocketbook, opened it at a blank page, April 17, Lucco would never forget, and wrote, in block letters "Siobhan Mary Pearson."

As Homicide Lieutenant Lucco read the three words

for the fourth time, his chest constricted. A tear made him blink before it coursed down his granite face. Embarrassed, he turned his face away and sniffed, wiping his face with his sleeve. When he looked back, Mather, affecting not to have noticed, was scribbling another name . . . "Judge Eugene Pearson. Dublin Criminal Court of Appeal. Ireland."

Eddie Lucco read and absorbed. It was as much exhaustion, after those months of relentless work, as emotion. But at last the child was close to finding a peaceful resting place.

"And no one, least of all him . . . is to know this. This is a high-stakes game, Eddie. Okay?"

Lucco nodded, meeting Mather's gaze. "Thanks Don. I appreciate it."

"So start thinking about a trip to Nassau, or Miami. And enjoy. Nobody said this job couldn't be fun."

The hard-faced New York cop sighed. Then remarked, "I think I'll get a white Ferrari."

And he laughed as he turned away and Don Mather called after him, "Just you fuckin try . . . !"

Harry Ford watched Pablo Envigado and the ancient priest, sitting at a wood table in the shade of a tall, twisted-limbed tropical tree that he felt he should have known the name of. He could just imagine the deep and sonorous Cockney voice of Lofty Wiseman, the SAS noncom who ran Survival Training at the time Harry was new to the game.

"What do you mean, you don't know the name of Ithyocantus Onomatopoea? You *duck!*" That's the sort of thing Lofty would have said. The man was encyclopedic about trees and roots and berries, on every continent and in every climate. The big Londoner had also been

with him on his first combat mission, someplace in
Southeast Asia. Someplace where the great British public had no idea their Special Forces were fighting.

There were three colorful parrots in the tree, minding
their own business. The Envigado entourage had moved
to a banana plantation on the slopes of the hills above
the Rio Mulatos to the west of the town of Brunito, near
northern Antioquia's Caribbean coast and the Gulf of
Uraba.

As Harry observed Pablo Envigado and the old priest,
he scribbled on the writing pad on his knee, roughing
out a set of training and operational guidelines for the
Medellín Cartel's enforcement teams. Enforcement in
the *grupo*'s context meant ensuring that nobody resisted, double-crossed, or endangered the day-to-day
operations of the cartel. At the lowest level, it meant
taking peasants and urban slum dwellers out of their
hovels and shooting them in front of their families,
leaving the corpses in the street or wherever as a grim
reminder of the long reach of Don Pablo. At the highest,
it meant burning down a millionaire's factory or blowing
up some Supreme Court judge's villa, or the Bogotá
Headquarters of DAS, with considerable loss of life, to
make precisely the same point. Nobody crossed *el padrino*, the Godfather.

While such a program was horrifying, there was no
facet of the cartel's operations of which Harry Ford was
not fully aware, so the details, although sickening, came
as no surprise. And while he (and his controller, David
Jardine) would ideally have wanted a place in Envigado's collection and distribution networks, with details of
all laboratories thrown in, it was not unexpected that a
new arrival would be given a task no undercover law-
enforcement officer would find himself able to go
through with. Arranging and directing cartel death
squads was a sensible test for any new *ejecutivo* of the

Medellín *grupo*, and in fact Ronnie Szabodo had warned
Harry to expect just such a first assignment during the
final briefing sessions in Spain, prior to his infiltration
of the Colombian underworld.

Harry Ford had no problems about that. He knew
that the presence of one secret infiltrator was not,
overnight, going to save lives. His task was to get so
close to Envigado that, when the time was right, the
man could be trapped and delivered to justice. But not
before—and this had been repeated again and again—
he had been able to furnish SIS with a comprehensive
picture of the entire workings and personalities, future
plans, and European links of the whole of the Colombian cocaine cartel. Not only Pablo Envigado's Medellín
Group, but the Cali and Bogotá elements, the post-
Noriega links with Panama, the Bolivian and Brazilian
players, and the more recent and hard-to-penetrate Ecu-
adorean cocaine laboratories and distributors.

It was a tall order, and one that suited an ambitious
high achiever like Ford down to the ground. He knew
that if he lived, and he intended to, and succeeded
where the DEA and the CIA had so far failed, his reputation in his new career would be made. For this was still
the same Harry Ford who had dropped deep behind
enemy lines in Iraq, completing a whole basketful of
dangerous and strategically valuable missions with the
sole aim of furthering his career in Special Forces.

It was still at the back of Harry's mind that, after a
successful year or so with the Secret Intelligence Service, he could return to the SAS, command a squadron,
then, if everything worked out, be strongly in the running
for promotion to lieutenant colonel and the job he had
dreamed of since he had been an officer cadet at
Sandhurst, nine years before. Commanding Officer,
22nd SAS Regiment. Even as he analyzed the gruesome
list of names for the cartel's murder teams, Ford felt a

warm glow of satisfaction that his career plan was well on target.

Pablo Envigado got to his feet and courteously assisted the frail priest to stand up.

Murillo, leaning against one of the twisted-limbed tropical trees, spoke briefly into a walkie-talkie handset. From the other side of the plantation's hacienda, Harry could hear the unmistakable whine and swish-swish of the Augusta-Bell 212 helicopter starting up.

The helicopter belonged to the *grupo*, but its papers were in the name of a documentary movie company based in Medellín, and the pilot was a German/Bolivian cameraman and adventurer who had several movies on South American wildlife and conservation of his environment to his credit. He worked out of a small office in the Antioquian capital, along with his pretty twenty-nine-year-old Colombian wife, Mia, who owned a bar in the fashionable El Poblado district.

As Pablo Envigado talked politely to the old man, the noise of the helicopter rose to a thunderous crescendo, and by the time the ground was trembling and the great, roaring arc of the rotor blades appeared over the hacienda's pink slate roofs, he had been reduced to shouting into the ear of the priest, who quite clearly could hear nothing intelligible.

The machine lifted noisily above the roofs and moved sideways, hovering delicately, swirling the grass flat and causing Harry Ford to hold his notepad tightly in the downdraft, then descending until its skids had touched the lawn.

Envigado and Murillo gently led the old priest to the helicopter and helped him to clamber into the cabin. When Murillo had fastened the man's safety harness, the priest raised his right hand, his ancient and shiny-cheeked face beaming, and made the sign of the cross, apparently blessing Don Pablo Envigado. He was still doing this as the landing skids left the ground and lifted up and up, passing directly over Harry, who had to spread his feet to avoid being blown over.

Then suddenly the clattering din became a fluttering rasp, then a swish-swishing buzz, then it was gone.

Pablo Envigado pushed his hair back and strolled toward the veranda where Luís Restrepo was waiting.

As he climbed the couple of steps, he glanced across at Harry Ford—Carlos Nelson as he knew him—then back to Restrepo.

"You know what he says, the old man . . . ?"

"No, Pablo. What does he say?"

"He says I could design my own prison, anywhere I want, have my own bodyguards and access to secure telephones."

"Yes, but it's still prison, *padrino.*"

"Also, I could be out in two years, debt to society paid."

"And what would you do then, Don Pablo?"

Envigado stroked his mustache, which was growing back quickly. His eyes lit up with a degree of enthusiasm and not a little humor. "Luís," he replied with a grin, "I'm going to get myself elected."

"Elected to what, Pablo . . . ?"

"To Congress. Permit me to remind you, Colombia boasts the oldest democracy in South America. And I intend to take my place there. The people will elect me, have no doubt."

"And if they don't, *padrino?*"

Pablo Envigado's eyes glinted, the smile fading. "We'll make sure they do, Luís." And he glanced at Harry Ford once more. "You and Jesus Garcia and Carlos there. I have no doubt between you we can raise a few votes . . ."

And when he chuckled, Restrepo felt suddenly cold.

———

"This is nice," said Elizabeth.

She was standing at an ironing board in the living room of the Tite Street flat wearing one of Jardine's old white shirts, the collar of which had frayed too much for office use but was just right for cricket matches, played on the village green near Fotheringham Manor. She was ironing a pale blue shirt of Jardine's, one of a pile of four or five, still warm from the dryer.

David Jardine glanced up at her from the floor where he was sitting, his back against an old winged library chair, a heavy Dartford crystal glass of malt whiskey beside him, a copy of the collected poems of W.B. Yeats on his lap.

"Yes. But it's not right," he replied, and she gave him a long look as if to say don't be such a frump. And for a brief second, Jardine had a subliminal, intuitive flash of Steven McCrae bucking like a ram on top of Kate Howard, his Swire House jade-and-gold cuff links glinting and twinkling. It was Thursday night. And Sir Steven always dismissed his driver on Thursdays. And his bicycle remained chained to a pipe in the underground carpark. In fact, one of the tires was pretty flat. Previously, Thursday nights he had cycled home, to Dulwich. But these days his wife believed he was doing secret things that could not be discussed. It was one of the bonuses of the job, not having to account for one's movements. Surely to God, wondered David Jardine, my own little dalliances are not half so tacky. So distastefully . . . absurd.

"What would he say?" asked Elizabeth Ford who could, on occasion, mildly surprise her lover with a perception that drew upon natural wit and a depth of learning. Hardly surprising, for the girl had a good degree from Lady Margaret Hall. Jardine chose to ignore the coincidence that Dorothy had also graduated from LMH, a generation before. The thought that Elizabeth had things in common with his wife, similarities (actually she was not unlike Dot at the same age, for Dot had once been a rare beauty) disconcerted Jardine. For it made him feel . . . unfaithful. And he had never once felt that before.

"Who?" Although he knew full well the girl meant Yeats.

" 'And pluck, till time and times are done," Elizabeth recited, "Golden apples of the sun . . . Silver—' "

She hesitated, and he was suddenly touched to see that she was moved close to tears.

" '. . . Silver apples of the moon.' Oh Lord, look at me." And she dabbed at her wet face with the blue shirt she had been ironing. "Damn Mr. Yeats, he always does that."

Even a few days before, David Jardine, romantic and hedonist, Catholic convert and searcher after life's little treats, would have risen, taken the shirt, tenderly dabbed the tears away and very gently made love to her. But now that he knew, now that he knew as clearly as he had ever known anything, that he was in love with this Elizabeth Ford, with her eyes and her mouth and her voice and that way of looking at him that for the first time ever totally destroyed his accustomed, cold-hearted control of such situations. Now that he knew *that*, things had gone too far.

For this was another man's wife. And the man had trusted his life to her seducer. He did not need Father Wheatley's relentless forgiveness to tell him it was not, actually, on.

Jardine winged a swift prayer of repentence to his erstwhile Chum, who was beginning to transmogrify from that cozy, comfortable image into a very serious, omniprescient Deity of the Major League. And there was not, at that moment, the hint of a smile on His imagined countenance.

"He's a lovely poet," remarked Jardine with studied casualness and, avoiding her eye, lifted his glass of Scotch. "I too shed the odd tear. From time to time . . ."

The drop had been a bastard. Free-fall parachuting on a blustery, moonless night was not Staff Sergeant Joe Moody's idea of a good time. True, the night-vision glasses, while cumbersome, at least revealed the terrain in varying shades of luminous green. But with steeply sloping mountain ridges and clusters of tall trees, easily confused with clusters of stunted bushes, it had been a dodgy business and he had found it difficult to keep his stick of four men together as they ran out of sky.

The theory was that you relied on altimeter and preset barometric canopy release, but a number of SAS soldiers had become part of the landscape owing to high-altitude landing spots hitting them at 120 miles per hour when the "fail-safe" equipment had made a marginal error. Thus, Sergeant Moody chose to rely on the Mark One Eyeball.

They had landed safely and two hours before dawn had reconnoitered and marked a safer drop zone for Bravo Company of the Colombian Army's Elite Force to parachute in, using static line chutes in rapid, multiple exits from the tailgate of a Hercules C-130, flying at 110 knots. The aircraft was six hundred feet above the narrow valley, eight thousand two hundred feet above sea level for a mere twenty-three seconds, in which time it had spewed out eighty-seven officers and men with their containers of weapons, ammo, medical packs, and rations.

The column then moved quietly and efficiently out of the valley and four miles along a steep wooded slope where, just at first light, they paused and took cover, listening, watching, and resting. Some chewed on chorizos, or munched chocolate candy bars.

The four SAS soldiers slipped away and a few minutes later had made contact with four of their colleagues led by Alistair Reid, a twenty-eight-year old Parachute Regiment captain on his second tour of duty with the SAS.

Joe respected Reid, a short and lean officer who had long since won the approval of the powerful cabal of battle-hardened senior noncoms who liked to believe they ran 22 SAS Regiment. He had served in Colombia on four previous assignments, had traded bullets with crack killers of Hezbollah in Beirut, killing two and capturing one, and had worked undercover in Northern Ireland, impressing with his quiet, level-headed way of getting on with the job.

Reid had spent the previous eight days with his three soldiers, keeping a cocaine-processing laboratory under surveillance. The men had made a complete record of the number of workers, the security procedures (which were assessed as "piss-poor"), the location of rest and work cabins and huts, kitchens, and latrines. The number of armed men was also recorded, and the location of a radio hut, which was being eavesdropped upon by a United States military satellite, orbiting many miles above the planet.

Their briefing at the Cartegena barracks had told them good intelligence, graded A-1, intimated Pablo Envigado might be visiting the laboratories at 11:30 A.M. on this particular day. They did not need to know that the information came from SIS, or that it had been obtained by Harry Ford, now deep inside Envigado's inner circle. So the SAS men remained skeptical, for there had been many false alarms and the commandos had little faith in intelligence "posers" who did not have to put their asses on the line.

However, the SAS team's hands-on observation of the site had revealed probable signs of preparation for a VIP visit. Signs that any soldier was familiar with.

Captain Alistair Reid and his seven men discussed the situation and agreed the most likely landing zone for Envigado's helicopter or light aircraft was a flat area one mile from the laboratory complex, where fuel drums and flares had been found hidden under the tree line. Reid sent two of his team back to maintain observation on the laboratory site, then led Joe Moody and the Colombian major commanding the Elite Force company, along with his master sergeant, to the landing strip, which was a half mile from their position.

By the time the twin-engined Embraer Xingu I light aircraft, with six passengers, was commencing its approach run, there was no sign, no flattened grass, broken branches, disturbed ground, to intimate the presence of ninety-five deeply professional, seriously experienced, heavily armed Special Forces soldiers waiting, faces blackened and shapes invisible and silent, among the trees and scrub below.

Not even Harry Ford, sitting beside Jesus Garcia, behind Pablo Envigado and the pilot, could see any trace of the ambushers. And while he had not been warned, he had transmitted so much intelligence about Envigado's future movements that he half expected some kind of action on the ground.

Heavy metallic, well-oiled sounds just audible above the noise of the engines came from Murillo and Bobby Sonson in the back two seats as they prepared their weapons.

The sixth passenger was Pablo Envigado's personal chemist, a lean, bespectacled man of about forty, who ran the quality-control side of the *grupo*'s business. He was simply referred to as *el químico*, and Harry had failed to elicit even a first name for the man. For this trip to the Sierra Nevada's wildest and most inhospitable region, *el químico* had attired himself in a baggy pin-stripe suit with candlegrease stains on the lapels and the trouser legs, a white shirt with pale green stripes, the collar size too big for his scrawny neck, a yellow silk necktie, and a scuffed pair of Reebok trainers. His watch was a forty-dollar blue plastic Swatch, with naval signal flags marking the hours.

El químico carried a bulky attaché case in which he kept his testing equipment.

Harry had caught a whiff of BO from the man, which explained why the fastidious *padrino* had sat him at the back of the plane.

Pablo Envigado tightened his safety straps as the pilot lined up the deceptively gently approaching landing strip—dropping his left wing, adding a touch of throttle to the left turbo-prop, easing it, pulling the nose up a fraction, quick-checking the landing gear, already lowered—and the tops of the trees rose level with the cabin windows, then blocked out the cloudy sky.

Harry Ford watched the tree line keenly as it flashed past. Then he caught sight of a group of men, eight or nine, some wearing the loose clothes and *ruanas* of the Magdalena peasants. With gaucho hats, baseball caps, and one battered fedora. All heavily armed and watching the arrival of the Medellín cocaine boss with expression-less faces.

The landing was technically proficient but bumpy.

"We fit new landing wheel assemblies and shock absorbers after every rough landing . . ." grinned Jesus Garcia, as if reading Harry's mind.

Behind them, as the pilot reversed his propellers and slowed down, the tail rising and bucking slightly, Bobby Sonson and Murillo slid the doors open, unclipped their safety harnesses, and cocked their weapons, Sonson with the M-60, Murillo with a Belgian FN 7.62 FAL

Parachutists' self-loading rifle with folding stock and Israeli Hit-Eye 3000 sniperscope.

Harry carried an American automatic AAI close-assault shotgun, loaded with thirteen rounds, every second round loaded with twenty ball bearings, every second round with eight one-gram flighted steel flechettes, which were like masonry nails and would rip a man apart.

Those three weapons had been carefully chosen to provide heavy medium-range continuous lead (the M-60), accurate elimination of individuals (the 7.62 sniper rifle), and close-quarter widespread antipersonnel blasts (the combat shotgun).

In addition each man carried other weapons. Harry Ford had his Sig-Sauer P-226 pistol and an Ingram MAC-10 submachine gun, with thirty-round magazine of .45 bullets. Also a machete and two hand grenades, one phosphorous, one high explosive.

Jesus Garcia, Envigado's security chief, carried a MAC-10 and a 9mm Biretta pistol, his principal task in the event of unpleasantness being to stick close to the *padrino* and spirit him to safety while the heavily armed Murillo and Sonson and the new man, Carlos Nelson, would hold off any attackers.

The twin engines roared briefly, then fanned and whispered to a quiet rasp as the pilot brought the aircraft to a stop, turned to face back down the strip, and feathered his propellers.

Sonson dropped to the grass and moved out beyond the wingspan. He knelt down, carefully checking the tree line. Behind him, Murillo dropped from the other doorway and ran to the rear of the plane, kneeling and watching the clearing.

Inside the Xingu, Harry Ford crouched in the left door, shotgun ready. *El químico* peered out of the cabin's Perspex windows. Jesus Garcia moved back and paused in the right door.

Harry could see the reception party at the edge of the forest. Then Sonson raised a hand and touched his head. Harry smiled. MacAteer must've taught them that. He jumped from the plane, and the instant he hit the dry grass he could smell the land, the earth, the trees, even through the aroma of high-octane aircraft exhaust. As he scanned the tree line and the landing strip, he experienced once more that precursor of an adrenaline high; his senses sharpened and his perception rose to an animal alertness. Behind him, he felt, sensed, the thump of Garcia's feet hitting the ground. Then Sonson rose cautiously and, glancing back, waited for Envigado and the chemist, who walked past Harry Ford, followed closely by Jesus Garcia.

Harry got up and instinctively moved to cover the left rear as out of the corner of his eye, he became aware of Murillo covering the right.

They had gotten exactly, almost exactly, halfway from the aircraft to the trees, every pace a step away from a fast scramble into the plane and a fighting takeoff, when Harry knew, with the cold and total certainty that only much combat experience can bring, that they were not alone in that flat wooded valley. He knew because—and Elizabeth had laughed when he had tried to explain he meant it literally, without hyperbole—the hairs on the back of his neck had actually lifted. This had happened to him before, and the MO at Hereford had smiled when Harry Ford had asked him about it and had merely replied that not every man who felt that sensation, which was a primeval vestige, lived to report it. For it was the ancient senses telling the corpus and the brain that danger was imminent and potentially terminal.

Harry glanced at the others. Only Murillo looked

back, and his eyes told the SIS man he too had the foreboding.

They walked on, getting closer to the trees and the murderous-looking reception party, who were all watching Pablo Envigado, slightly awed as the legendary *padrino* approached.

Harry's senses were by then so acute it seemed the cold mountain air was going directly from nostrils to lungs to fingertips and eyes and ears. There was going to be action, and he knew it was going to be soon. He caught Murillo glancing at him and he nodded, a silent pact between them to get Don Pablo to safety the moment it started.

He could almost sense the grass growing and at the same instant realized there were no bird sounds coming from the forest of stunted trees.

Alistair Reid, face blackened and camouflaged to be part of the forest undergrowth, felt two groups of three pulses against his wrist. The SAS Research & Development Cell, back in Hereford, had come up with some original inventions over the years. This one, the Combat Pulse Communicator, CPC-4, was a rubber wristwatch band with a radio receiver and transmitter in place of the watch. It could operate on up to fifteen frequencies and essentially it functioned like a tap on the shoulder.

The team had a series of agreed signals, which could get quite sophisticated. The beauty of the system was that it was silent and not detectable by radio scanning or monitoring devices.

Two groups of three meant that the point man had seen hostiles, up to thirty strong, approaching the ambush area—in military language the killing ground, although it was the intention of the Colombian Elite Force to capture Pablo Envigado alive. It was his bodyguards who were to be killed.

Alistair Reid breathed deeply and slowly, his finger

lying along the trigger guard of his cocked and loaded Armalite M-16. The forest was so silent, and the other soldiers so well concealed, he had a momentary qualm that the Colombians had gone, leaving just himself and his SAS team.

He had advised the Colombian major to place thirty men on one side of the track leading southwest from the airstrip to the laboratory, a group of twenty a half mile northeast, under the tree line, to take out the aircraft as soon as the shooting started, twenty soldiers to cut off the laboratory site from sending reinforcements, and twenty-five deeper in the woods to catch anyone who had escaped the ambush and fled away from the killing ground. Suddenly, like a radio being switched on, the ambushers could hear quite clearly the voices of the reception party and the new arrivals as they approached.

His wrist felt three groups of two pulses. This confirmed that Pablo Envigado had been identified. Reid's mouth was suddenly dry. Jesus, he was going to be the man who had taken Pablo! Not yet you haven't, he wisely cautioned himself. Don't anticipate the outcome of a firefight, just get on with it. The immortal advice of the late Squadron Sergeant Major Paddy Nugent.

Then five heavily armed but casual, careless men appeared in his rifle sights. They would be allowed to pass through the killing ground in order to lead the men behind them into the ambush. One of his SAS team and four Colombian Elite Force would take them out when the trap was sprung.

Then two rapid groups of five pulses, a pause, and one group of five.

Reid frowned. That was the signal for "friendlies among hostiles." It was normally only used in hostage situations. Intrigued, he let the five enemy point men pass to his rear, out of the main ambush area. Then others entered, six *paisas* who had passed earlier going up to the airstrip. Then some senior guys from the laboratory site, then, hallelujah, Pablo Envigado and some real hoods, seriously armed and paying keen attention to the track and their surroundings. They seemed jittery and very professional, one was walking virtually backward, his twelve-shot AAI Combat Shotgun held lightly but ready for instant action. That target was somehow familiar. Then he swung around and moved to catch up.

It was Harry Ford.

Captain Alistair Reid's brain, adrenaline-fueled and working like a computer, reminded him Ford had been spirited away from the SAS regiment by the funny people, SIS. Now here he was in a wood eight thousand feet up the Sierra Nevada, in northern Colombia, one of the cartel's top bodyguards.

Reid had a maximum of six seconds to decide if he should call off the ambush. Was something going on here that was more important?

He decided, correctly, to proceed and pulsed the code that meant avoid hostage. It was the best he could do. He took a deep breath and exhaled slowly, nestling the butt of his M-16 tight against his shoulder. I'll take out the bastard with the M-60 first, he thought, and lined Sonson up in his sights, tightening his finger on the trigger when some asshole opened fire too soon . . .

The first thing Harry Ford became aware of was the relentless trickling of water on the flat stones of the mountain stream. Then the rustle of a light breeze whispering among the branches of the surrounding trees. Then the pain in his left arm and the shadow of Murillo kneeling over him. The bastards, they're torturing me, was his first instinct. Then he lifted his head from the damp, grassy bank, where he was half sitting, half lying, to watch, slightly disinterested, as the *grupo* bodyguard tightened a tourniquet on his arm, just below the shoulder. His shirt, sweatshirt, and leather jacket sleeve had been cut away, and white muscle glistened where the pink and red flesh lay opened like a tropical fruit, split open.

His right hand rested on the AAI combat shotgun stock. It was hot, and the smell of cordite was in the air.

As he recovered consciousness, he became aware of the crackle and rip of a continuing firefight about a mile away above the bank of the stream, beyond the steep slope rising, tree-covered, above them.

He tried to catch Murillo's eye but the man was busy with the tourniquet.

Harry turned his head, feeling weak, to his right and there was Pablo Envigado, face earth- and blood-streaked, shirt and leather zip-up torn. But he was grinning and watching Harry intently.

"You're one hell of a guy, Carlos . . ." He offered Harry a water flask and Harry took it in his right hand and drank a few mouthfuls, feeling his senses return and a little strength too.

"How is it?" Envigado asked Murillo.

"Flesh wound. The bleeding is arrested, *padrino*." Then Murillo turned and gazed into Harry Ford's face. A trace of a smile cracked his leather Tartar-cheekboned countenance. *"Hola, hombre.* You are one very tough motherfucker." He shook his head, flopped back to rest against the banking, and tugged a pack of Mustangs from a pocket of his army surplus combat jacket. He took two out, lit them and passed one, without glancing at him, to Harry, who accepted it and stuck it between his lips. There were only three of them. No sign of Jesus Garcia or the chemist in his baggy, grease-stained pin-stripe suit, and while Harry seemed to be the only one wounded, Envigado and Murillo were clearly shaken and exhausted.

Then Harry Ford remembered it all. The sudden din of at least a platoon of infantry firing all its weapons onto the track. Men spinning, men lifted off their feet, men with limbs and parts of their heads shot off in the bedlam of lead, and his instinctively blasting a path directly into the ambushers, as he had been taught and as he had successfully practiced twice before.

He remembered Murillo right beside him and Jesus Garcia firing his MAC-10 left-handed from the hip, Envigado gripped by his other hand. Harry lobbing his two grenades into the ambushers. Phosphorous and high explosive, one-two, the pins pulled by his teeth, right hand blasting away with the combat shotgun and Jesus Garcia's chest and abdomen exploding and Harry twisting half right and firing instinctively at the same moment as his eyes met those of the target's just four yards away—the blackened face was Alistair Reid's and it had been too fucking late, the trigger was pulled, it was already pulled, the look of disbelief on Reid's face, instantaneously turned like the rest of him into raw red meat by wide-spread flechettes from the 12-gauge that tore the SAS captain obscenely apart.

Harry Ford's chest heaved as the moment flooded back. Envigado and Murillo were too exhausted to notice. Exhausted, why?

Yes. The tunnels. Just as the reception party, trading bullets but outnumbered and outfought, fell all around him, Harry had thrust Pablo Envigado over a number of bodies—Colombian soldiers and Captain Alistair Reid, still twitching—and plowed on into the thick undergrowth, followed by Murillo and several others, including Bobby Sonson, who was using his big M-60 machine gun to deadly effect, hosing the surrounding area—Special Forces and *paísas,* it made no difference—and suddenly Murillo appeared in front of them and with a frantic desperation located and hauled open a concealed trapdoor beneath the exposed roots of a lightning-blasted tree.

The ambushers were everywhere, closing in. Harry's and Sonson's AAI Shotgun and the M-60 held them off until Sonson pushed Harry down the trapdoor hole and jumped in after him, finding a ledge from where he kept on firing.

The last thing Harry had heard as he stumbled with Murillo and Envigado along the warren of tunnels, was the steady thunderous rasp of the M-60. Then there had been a booming explosion. He noticed blood trickling from Murillo's right ear. Concussion.

And his arm, it must've taken a bullet, slicing across the flesh, in the exchange of lead.

And Alistair Reid. Altered in a millisecond from vital, fighting machine to bloody, life-spent rag doll.

Alistair had been at the wedding of Harry Ford and Elizabeth. Harry remembered him singing some bawdy Scottish folk song, face flushed, pint pot of beer in hand. Alistair had really enjoyed the wedding, which had been at the Guards' Chapel and at the officers' mess in Chelsea Barracks. The two men had never really been close and had never been on operations together, but Reid was a good soldier and a likeable man.

What a fuck-up. What a fucking way to die . . .

Harry Ford sighed, his chest constricting. He shook his head, close to tears. Then Envigado leaned across and touched his right arm.

"Everything has changed, Carlos. Everything is different now . . ."

Harry slowly turned and stared at Envigado. Right, you fucker, he decided, you're dead. Just say your fucking piece and then I shoot you. Murillo first, to be prudent, then you. At least your stinking hoodlum's head will go toward the Alistair Reid account.

He smiled, still weak. *"Sí, padrinó . . . ?"*

"You saved my life, Carlos Nelson. The man you killed, he had switched his M-16 from poor Jesus to me. I will never be closer without coming face to face with the Virgin Mary."

"Any time, no problem . . ." replied Harry, his right hand closing around the pistol grip and trigger of the AAI shotgun. He struggled to remember how many shells were left in the magazine. The fourth he had used in the firefight.

"Don Pablo does not forget such things. Carlos, you are my brother. And you are two million dollars richer. Two million U.S. dollars, *amigo mio*. Anywhere you want it. In used notes, tens and fifties if you like. Or a bank draft, or in a suitcase. You name it."

Harry Ford stared at Pablo Envigado. Murillo was looking at them as if to say, "I risk my life ten times a week and you don't give me goddamn trunkfuls of money."

"Don Pablo, you already pay me. I was just doing what any of us would have done. In the *grupo.*"

Pablo's eyes narrowed. "If you're not gonna take my money you offend me. Are you trying to insult me, Carlos Nelson . . . ?"

At that moment there was a rustle of grass, a thump of feet, and Bobby Sonson jumped down onto the bank of the stream from the wooded slope above, clutching his M-60, about twenty shells left in what had been a bandolier of five hundred, filthy, torn, scratched, and bloody, looking as happy as a hound dog at a boar hunt.

His chest heaving as he fought for breath, Sonson grinned. "There were English, *padrino*, shouting. I heard English voices. That was the damn SAS again . . ."

In the distance, the faint tak-atak-atak and dull explosions of a fierce gun battle that was still raging.

"Los hombres ingléses . . ." Envigado leaned over and grinned, looking deep into Harry Ford's eyes. *"Son bastante letalos.* Maybe we should recruit some for the *grupo . . ."*

"You don't need them, *padrino,* with a tiger like Carlos on our side," said Murillo, who was a survivor from way back. He grinned at Harry.

"So what do you say, Carlos? *El Tigre?* You gonna take my two million dollars or am I gonna have to kill you?" Envigado's teeth glinted as he grinned, fiercely exultant, having escaped yet again.

Harry gazed at Pablo Envigado, aware of Sonson standing over them. He lifted his right hand from his shotgun and offered it to *el padrino,* who gripped it firmly.

"I don't deserve it. But of course I'll take it, *padrino.* I could use it." And at that moment, when he looked back on it, Harry Ford was still working, still behaving like a loyal officer of the British Secret Intelligence Service. It was maybe the last such moment.

"Bienvenido al grupo, Carlos, now you are a blood member of the Medellín Cartel . . . And an honorary *paísa!"* Envigado embraced Harry Ford, kissing him on both cheeks, then remarked, in that sly way of his, "There will be maybe some more millions if you stick with us . . ."

"And six feet of earth above you if you don't," said Bobby Sonson, grinning and picking at his teeth with a match. And as Pablo Envigado and Murillo helped Harry to his feet, they all laughed grimly and moved off across the stream toward their emergency rendezvous, four miles away.

There, an Allouette III helicopter of the Colombian Parco Nacional, piloted by an Antioquian from Sabaneta,

Don Pablo's birthplace, took them to Barranquilla airport on the Caribbean coast, from whence they flew, in an amphibious Grumman Goose belonging to one of the major international oil corporations, to a remote stretch of the Rio Mulatos, thirty-seven miles upriver from the coastal town of Mulatos, which was in the province of Antioquia. The Goose was the oil company's air ambulance, and by the time it landed on the river Mulatos, the doctor/copilot, whose sister was married to an accountant with the *grupo,* had sterilized Harry Ford's wound, sutured it, dressed it, and put it in a sling.

On the trek to rendezvous with the helicopter, Sonson had remarked on the fact that *el químico* had actually been cut in two by the ferocity of the ambushers' gunfire. Ford noticed that Envigado would probably have been more saddened by the death of a good horse.

Restrepo was waiting on the banks of the Mulato with transport to take Don Pablo and the others back to the safety of the banana plantation. He listened to Envigado's account of how Carlos Nelson had saved his life with something less than wild delight.

That night, when Harry Ford would have preferred nothing more than a stiff rum, maybe in a mug of hot milk, and a long, deep sleep, he found himself guest of honor at a traditional Caribbean *guateque,* a feast, on the terraces of the plantation *finca,* with much music and lithe, sensuous, almost naked dancers performing the *cumbia* and earthy, arousing folk dances from the Caribbean coast, heavily influenced by Africa and the local Indians.

Wonderful music and much aguardiente and rum punch.

Harry imbibed the liquor in order to forget the pain of his shoulder wound and just to stay awake. A beautiful, wanton creature of about sixteen years, wearing just a short, flounced, white cotton skirt, twirled away from the *cumbia* dancers and lowered herself onto his lap, wrapping her arms around him and kissing him urgently and passionately on the mouth.

Harry responded, knowing that Pablo and Restrepo were watching. Then, as the revelers clapped their hands and the folklore band led the way, the girl took his right hand and guided him across the grass and up the couple of steps onto the veranda, swaying her hips in time to the music. He bowed and nodded to Don Pablo and the others, in the fashion of such affairs, and when they reached the door to his bedroom, he kissed the dancer long and fiercely to great applause and yells of encouragement. Then he unlocked the door and they went inside.

The others went back to their party. Only the occasional squawk of radio static from walkie-talkie sets of the many armed and able cartel soldiers guarding *el padrino* indicated this was different from most other parties in fun-loving Colombia that night.

Pablo Envigado and Restrepo sat on a higher terrace watching the dancers, the spit roasts, and the partying members of the *grupo*.

"What do you think, Luís?" asked Envigado, helping himself to a line of the purest cocaine in the world from a white-gold spoon that hung from a white-gold chain around his neck.

"All our inquiries indicate he is a serious man. The fact that he has never done time, Pablo, means he must be pretty smart. He is reputed to be a violent man, but only with proper reason."

"Can I trust him?" Envigado looked sharply at Restrepo, holding his gaze.

"He did save your life. He did not want to come into our group. You insisted." Restrepo shrugged. "What do you have in mind?"

"With poor Jesus gone . . ." A tear rolled down the

cartel boss's cheek. Restrepo looked on, impassive. "I have a mind to make Nelson our *jefe de seguridad*. He is a good man, he is a realist, and he is ambitious."

"Yes, I had noticed that."

"And with Jesus Garcia's job, Luís Restrepo . . ." Pablo Envigado's teeth glinted as he smiled. ". . . he won't be looking at yours. Tell me about this latest offer. From the woman in Medellín . . ."

Pablo Envigado's threshold of concentration was low, maybe as a result of increased indulgence in his own commodity. He had switched to the subject of negotiations with the Colombian government.

"They say you can specify where you would consent to live during the period of your . . ."

"Jail. Say the word."

"While you were in . . . prison. If that was what you decided to do."

"There is only one place I would go. Provided it was staffed by the military and not the cops. We've bought too many *tombos*, killed too many of their women and their litters. I know who has been on the take since 1982. They would rub me out like that. That's why they're trying to kill me, Luís . . . That's why." When Envigado stared into Restrepo's eyes, he was close to tears. "They don't want justice, *amigo mío*, it's my silence they are so desperate to secure."

"Only one place, *padrino*. Where?" asked Restrepo softly and as if there was no serious probability. He examined his perfectly manicured hands.

The strains of a *chirimia* band drifted up from the *guateque*. They were playing an old tune, "Las Golondrinas," about two swallows who met on a flight from Spain and who died above the battle for Cartagena between British pirates and the brave defenders. Their souls, says the song, are forever in Colombia, part of the land, part of the sky.

"Sabaneta," replied Pablo Envigado. "If we can negotiate what you have suggested, it could only be on the mountainside, above my beloved Sabaneta . . ."

Restrepo stared at the flickering fires on the terraces below, his head nodding to the music. He raised a hand, as always, refusing a line of crystal from Don Pablo. What he had, in fact, suggested gently, a little bit at a time, to Pablo Envigado was that if a deal could be done with the new Colombian president, Gaviria, whereby it could be guaranteed that the cartel chief would not be extradited, would not be charged with serious crimes like murder or conspiracy, and if he could choose the place and manner of his incarceration, with full personal protection and access to his family, then maybe it might be a sign of great wisdom to surrender, to call off the state of war with the authorities, wind down the disproportionate use of violence from the Medellín *grupo,* and come out in two or three years, the slate clean, millions waiting and who knew . . . ? Why not a place in Congress? Envigado had bought his way into Congress before, and there was no reason why he shouldn't do so again.

To Restrepo's mild surprise, the godfather seemed to be seriously entertaining the idea.

Or was he just testing? To see if Restrepo wanted him out of the way?

"Me, I wouldn't trust them, Don Pablo. At least living like this . . . you are free. And we have you in our midst. That means a lot to us, *padrino.*"

He turned to face Envigado, his countenance a model of concern and trustworthiness.

Pablo Envigado nodded. Patted his hand on top of Restrepo's. "If only they were all like you, Luís . . ." he said, moved. "If only. And this man who saved my life. We could use a few like him. And Murillo, and Bobby Sonson. Tigers . . . you should have seen them. My God, it was only this morning. Hell, what a battle. We fought like tigers, you should have been there."

"I thank the Blessed Virgin for your safe return."

"So, Luís. Do we make this Carlos Nelson Arrigiada a millionaire?" He grinned, tucking his white-gold spoon back into his shirt. "Or do we slit his throat while he sleeps the sleep of exhaustion from combat, flight, pain, and lust . . . ?"

Restrepo realized he had the man Nelson's life in his hands. And while there was something he did not trust about Nelson, with Jesus Garcia gone there was no one outside Pablo Envigado's endless gang of greedy and second-rate relations who Envigado trusted to do the job. It might have been considered a drawback that Carlos Nelson did not know the other elements of the cartel, the Cali and the Bogotá *grupos*. But this, on reflection, did not worry Restrepo.

"Let's make the man a millionaire and give him Jesus Garcia's job, *jefe*," he replied.

Pablo Envigado stared at him and slowly smiled. He nodded.

And at six the next morning, Harry Ford woke with his shoulder and stitched upper-arm wound a solid rock of agony. The sixteen-year-old dancer lay sound asleep beside him looking like a contented child, her little cotton skirt hanging on one of the corners of the wooden bed. And on the floor, on the rug at his side of the bed, a large valise, opened and crammed with used U.S. dollar bills in tens, fifties, and hundreds, just crammed with them.

As Harry stared, he heard a low chuckle and looked up to see Restrepo standing there, immaculate in crisp, white linen shirt, jeans, and polished riding boots.

"Buenos días, señor," said Restrepo.

"Buenos días, cóm' está?" replied Harry, painfully wriggling to sit up in bed.

"Very well, thanks. Well, Carlos. There is your two million dollars."

How the hell, wondered Harry Ford, do I keep this for the Firm? How do I account for it? What if we get busted and the money disappears?

"I would rather have it put in a bank somewhere," he said, as if a suitcase full of two million dollars was a commonplace sight.

"Take my advice, *hombre*," said Restrepo, "the first two million should always be kept in cash. But if you like, I can have it put in a numbered account in the Bahamas."

"I think I can probably manage that myself." Harry Ford smiled and Restrepo smiled back.

He nodded. "Sure." And after pouring Harry some peach yogurt he asked him to take on the job of the dead Jesus Garcia . . . security chief for the Medellín Cartel.

After some demurring, saying he was only a simple marijuana dealer, Carlos Nelson agreed to accept the job for a few weeks till Pablo Envigado could find somebody more qualified.

And for the rest of the day, as Harry Ford lay in that room, visited by the doctor to change his dressing and by countless well-wishers, he could think of nothing else but that suitcase stuffed with two million dollars lying beneath him under the bed.

If Bobby Sonson had not appeared when he did on that bank by the stream on the Sierra Nevada, his M-60 and his high adrenaline causing Harry to abort his intent, seconds away, to kill Murillo and Pablo Envigado, things might have turned out less tragically.

Harry had dozed for an hour or so in the afternoon when suddenly he was alert and wide awake. Someone was trying to get into his room. There was a scraping sound at the door. As he reached his right hand under the pillow for his Sig-Sauer pistol, the door swung open abruptly and the late Jesus Garcia's big mongrel hound, Diablo, pushed its way in and padded across to the bed. His eyes were slits of yellow and it was quite easy to believe the peasant's rumors that he was half wolf.

Diablo paused, his tail moving slowly, thoughtfully, and watched Harry intently with a very serious expression on his face.

Harry gazed back into the yellow slits, which widened, revealing deep brown eyes.

"Hello, old fellow, what are you doing in my room . . . ?" he asked gently.

And laying its huge bearded head on the bed, the dog let out a "hrrumph" sort of sound.

Harry Ford stroked the coarse fur under its ear.

"Well, Diablo," he murmured, "I suppose *someone's* going to have to feed you . . ."

For Jesus Garcia was dead.

El Diablo looked Harry straight in the eye, which was mildly disconcerting, as if he was taking stock of him. Then he wagged his tail and turning, ambled to the door and lay down, heavily, across the threshold. Ready to protect to the death his new master.

20

A FLUTTERING
OF WINGS

You haven't fallen out with Padraic, have you?" Mhairaid Pearson sat at the bedroom mirror, putting rollers in her hair.

"What makes you say that?" asked the judge, standing in his shirttails, folding his trousers neatly before draping them over the back of a chair.

"Only I bumped into Margaret this afternoon, down in O'Connel Street. She seemed a bit cagey."

"Well, Padraic and I haven't fallen out." Pearson took off his shirt and placed it neatly in the laundry basket. "But I may as well tell you, Mhairaid, I have told him I don't want the A.G.'s job." He meant the attorney general's position.

Mhairaid froze, her hands at her hair, and stared at his reflection in the mirror. Then she twisted around. "Why ever not . . . ?"

Pearson stepped into his pajama trousers. "This job I've been discussing, with the multinational. It's one eighty thousand sterling. And it's a five year contract with a bonus at the end. I didn't want to lead Padraic up the garden path, that would lack . . . probity."

He climbed into bed and picked his copy of Mario Vargos Llosa's *The Wars at the End of the World*. His wife stared at him, dumbfounded.

"Don't you think that's something we could have discussed?" she said, leaving her hair sticking out at an angle and trying to keep the anger from her voice. The last few weeks had been one row after another. Until now, mostly about Siobhan.

"It happened when I went around to the Daíl to see him. To tell you the truth, I have shouldered so much responsibility over the years, and what with this worry about Siobhan, something so awesome as A.G. would probably be the death of me." He put the book down on the quilt and gazed at her over his half-moon spectacles. Sure enough, she mused, he does look awful pale and drawn. There were dark shadows under his eyes.

"Mhairaid," he said in the Gaelic language, "I'm so tired . . ."

She gazed at him. This was not the man she had married. She knew, with her woman's intuition, from the way Margaret O'Shea had seemed embarrassed somehow, inhibited, that he was not telling the whole truth.

"Do you remember how we used to share everything . . . ?" she asked, feeling as tired as he was claiming to be. Was it really worth the effort?

"I'm going to use this trip to Florida to visit her in South America. Try to bring her back . . ."

Mhairaid's heart missed a beat. For some reason, although she had only half admitted it to herself, she had begun to feel she would never see their beloved daughter again.

"How will you know where to find her?"

Pearson smiled weakly; he looked close to exhaustion. "I've still got a few contacts. Some Interpol people," he lied. "They're going to try for an address. By all accounts this composer fellow's a good man. I didn't want to raise your hopes, Mhairaid, but the business is more advanced than just perhaps . . ."

Mhairaid Pearson just sat there. On the dressing table behind her was the pile of three letters and five postcards from Siobhan. And never one phone call. She had said on one postcard the maestro would not allow a telephone in the mountainside villa where she was staying.

"You bring her back, Eugene," she said, pale as death, and buried her face in her hands.

Eugene Pearson got out of bed and went to comfort her but, sobbing bitterly, she pushed him away.

———

When a prima ballerina or an opera diva takes the stage, the spotlight upon her, it is the culmination of years of training, months of preparation, and impossible without the behind-the-scenes backup of dozens of people, from the director to the most junior messenger.

It is very much the same in espionage, when the highly trained deep-penetration agent is directed and supported by a sometimes considerable number of men and women, from his controller to local agents who service dead-letter boxes and more risky brush passes (where two strangers are momentarily in the same place at the same time, like a washroom or on public transport).

His messages are collected or received by clandestine radio transmissions, deciphered, decoded, and analyzed by experienced teams of intelligence professionals. His welfare in the field is monitored as far as possible, and other factors, sometimes unknown to the operator, also obtain.

In the case of Operation Corrida, one of the other factors was that David Jardine, a prudent man and agent runner without peer, was receiving low-grade but reliable intelligence on the cartel and on its newest executive, Carlos Nelson Arrigiada, from Maria Esperanza, the sister of the wife of Bobby Sonson's brother Franco. Maria lived in Bogotá but frequently visited the town of Sabaneta, in Antioquia, where her sister lived in a comfortable villa of white stucco, with pink slate roofs and sprawling gardens tended by several peasants, for her husband was a serious bodyguard of Don Pablo's inner circle, and that was a profitable situation.

Maria worked for Colonel Xavier Ramón. He had a stable of minor agents throughout Colombia, and their constant stream of reliable gossip and reported indiscretions provided him with the raw material for his reports to his various clients, the FBI, SIS, the Mossad, for which they were always grateful and paid good money. The collated intelligence thus acquired also gave him sometimes vital information for his endless fight against his country's worst enemies—the *narcotraficantes*, the urban and rural guerrillas, and the small mafias of organized kidnappers and brigands.

Since Carlos Nelson, agent Parcel, remained in ignorance of Maria Esperanza's existence and since, like many prima donnas, he could not conceive of anyone remotely approaching his skills, he could not have known that his London controller was, that Tuesday morning, with a warm spring sun cheering the corridor outside the West 8 Communications Room, deeply disquieted because of a secret signal received from Ramón, who transmitted under the code name *Pillastre*, which was the Spanish word for scoundrel.

Ramón's signal informed Jardine of what he already knew, that Harry Ford had succeeded, amazingly, in taking the place of Jesus Garcia as security chief for the

Medellín group of the cartel. It also informed him that Pablo Envigado had given Carlos Nelson two million U.S. dollars for saving his life. This was not intelligence Parcel had communicated to Century House in his several full and comprehensive messages, transmitted by sophisticated, clandestine satellite radio.

"What do you reckon, Ronnie?" Jardine leaned his back against a wall map of Colombia and watched Ronnie Szabodo study the decoded message from Ramón.

After a long pause, Szabodo handed the printout back to his boss. He scratched his shoulder and met Jardine's gaze. The tall sphere controller was sporting a considerable purple-blue bruise on his left upper cheek and around his left eye. It was not a bruise David had had when he left to meet Lieutenant Colonel Johnny McAlpine, who had helicoptered up to London from Hereford for an urgent meeting with the SIS man at the Special Forces Directorate in a Ministry of Defense building in Chelsea.

Upon Jardine's return to the glass box, Mrs. Brownlow had sent out for a chunk of raw steak and there had been a couple of long telephone conversations with the brigadier commanding SAS, who had been in Afghanistan with Jardine in the bogus KGB Spetznatz unit. The brigadier had offered to fire Johnny but David Jardine had absolutely insisted that the matter be dropped. He had said that he, in the same position, would have done precisely the same thing.

In fact, when he had walked into the Special Forces director's office and straight into a solid right from the boss of 22nd SAS Regiment, who stood almost a full head shorter, for one awful moment he thought his affair with Elizabeth Ford had got him his just deserts.

But when he had learned the reason for McAlpine's rage, David Jardine wished most earnestly his first assumption had been the correct one. For signals from the SAS commander of Operation Isolate, the SAS presence in Colombia, had reported in accurate detail the escape of Pablo Envigado from the ambush on the Sierra Nevada and the killing of Captain Alistair Reid by Harry Ford, who had been identified and actually photographed on the trail from the airstrip into the killing ground.

"What do I reckon . . . ?" replied the Hungarian. "I reckon if *I* had walked into an ambush, with every bugger and his sister firing at me, I would shoot back and try to get the hell out of there."

"You think I was wrong not to warn him . . . ?"

"I think you were right. But since you did not, then David, I have to ask you, did you not, even subconsciously, intend our man to do precisely what he did . . . ? I mean, saving Pablo's life is a fine way to get right to the top table."

"Well, that wasn't on my mind, what do you take me for?"

Silence.

"I just don't think you can complain about a black eye, do you?"

Jardine stared at Szabodo, not flattered by what the Hungarian was hinting. "Okay, I admit it was a two-way gamble. If they had captured Envigado, that was a good result. HMG presents public enemy number one to the Colombian government on a plate. President Gaviria owes our prime minister one. That's what we do, and so does the SAS. We further British foreign policy by covert means."

"And if Pablo had survived," said Szabodo, "and if they had both escaped, which was always a possibility, so much the better. Hell and damnit, David, Harry Ford actually saving the man's bloody life, that's a dream ticket."

Jardine sighed. He hitched up his trousers and tightened the belt a notch. He had been losing weight recently. The problem of whether or not to warn young Harry that he might be walking into an ambush up on the Sierra Nevada had exercised him greatly. He had prayed in Farm Street and had confessed, with true repentance, about his relationship with Elizabeth, explaining he had never intended something that had started as a jolly romp to turn into a passionate and potentially destructive love affair. And he had told God, in his coded way of confessing, that he was worried about the effect that was having upon his professional responsibility to her husband. Who was in a most dangerous situation.

Emotionally, and to ease his conscience, he had wanted to warn the boy. But professionally it would have been a mistake. Not for the arcane and mildly paranoid reasons suggested by Ronnie Szabodo, but because the golden rule, Jardine's golden rule of agent-running, was never allow the Joe to be in possession of any sensitive information he, or she, did not absolutely require to function.

Jardine had had no warning that Pablo Envigado intended to take Harry with him to the laboratory. It was probably a spur-of-the-moment thing. Therefore, in all truth, there was no substance in Ronnie's suggestion that David Jardine, master spy, sitting at the center of his espionage cobweb had cunningly arranged the present situation. Or the possibility of an SAS death.

"Every time the SAS sets up an ambush or any other operation, Ronnie, each man knows he's putting his life on the line. Even so, as God's my judge, I'm horrified . . . devastated, by Captain Reid's death. I met him a couple of times on Op Isolate and I would like to have attended his funeral, but under the circumstances that might have been less than diplomatic."

"Nonsense, you should go. They're too professional to take it personally . . ."

Jardine laughed and touched his bruised cheekbone ruefully. "Oh, really?"

"That was in the heat of the moment, and no one will know, except the handful involved, they're too professional. No one will know our Joe was there."

"He killed a brother officer, Ronnie. A man he had served with." Jardine strode across the room to Heather, who had wandered in clutching a sheaf of signals to be sent to various stations and agents in South America, and gently turned her and propelled her out, closing the door and bolting it. The girl went quietly, without protest, used to her boss's eccentricities.

"A guest at his wedding, for God's sake."

David Jardine sat down on the chair normally used by Eric the cipher clerk. He toyed absentmindedly with Eric's almost too-neat row of felt-tip pens, pencils, and erasers. When he glanced up at Szabodo, there was no trace of self-doubt on his face. "I would have considered the whole fuckup to be just that. A tragic accident, the kind that will always happen when big boys play with guns."

"If Harry had only told you about the two million dollars . . ." Szabodo finally understood.

David Jardine drummed his left hand on the desk, on Eric the cipher clerk's desk. Then he picked up a pencil, one of Eric's immaculately sharpened HBs, and snapped it between his fingers, rising abruptly and cold with anger.

"What did we miss? What's in his selection assessments to hint that the first time somebody shoves a suitcase full of cash at him he would turn bad? Did the bloody fool not imagine we would find out . . . ?"

"You said eighty thousand was a trifle mean . . ." For additional intelligence, reliable crumbs of gossip from the table of *el grupo,* via Maria Esperanza, alleged that Carlos Nelson had been on a hundred thou a week from the very beginning.

"Ronnie, we have to face it. The man is not reliable." He rubbed a big hand over his face, over the undamaged right half of his face. "And worse. If he killed Reid in order to get even further in with Pablo Envigado, in order to become rich, then he is also a murderer. Jesus Christ, tell me I'm wrong . . ."

And you're screwing his wife, thought Szabodo, who missed nothing. God help you, my friend.

"I don't think you're wrong," he said grimly. "If he killed the soldier in self-defense, which is Harry's version, and incidentally the story I urge you to stick to, that would be a casualty of war. Even if he killed Reid to strengthen his cover, that would be . . . ruthless. But not unacceptable. This is not, as you like to remind us, the Little Sisters of Mercy. Leave it with me, David, I'll devise some kind of . . . litmus test." Ronnie Szabodo felt sorry for his former protégé who was now his boss. But he knew that David Jardine came into his own in adversity, in what Szabodo termed one hundred percent, twenty-four carat fan shit-hitting crises.

And even as he watched, the sphere controller seemed to slough away his anger and anxiety.

Jardine stuck his hands in his trouser pockets. He nodded, once more calm, cold, and precise, "Thank you, Ronnie. The testing of Ford is a matter of urgency. I mean hours rather than days, and I think we should bring Tony and Bill in on this. There could be other explanations."

"Of course."

"We must take steps to protect the service, but I really do want to give young Harry the benefit of every doubt . . ."

The two men exchanged a brief glance. Before we

kill him was the unfinished part of the controller's comment.

Judge Almeda must've been about twenty-seven when the photograph was taken. Homicide Lieutenant Eddie Lucco sat at the bar nursing a Wild Turkey and water and contemplating the framed black-and-white photo. He liked Almeda, who gave no quarter, and he thought it was kinda strange that it was a criminal trial before his hero that got Nancy the offer of a partnership in her law firm.

"You okay, Eddie?" The bartender, another ex-marine, asked as he passed, using a slack moment to clean up and tidy the counter.

"A-okay."

"Sure." The bartender did not press it. But he had noticed the big cop was less than content these days.

"Great piano player, that guy. You know he's a judge? Played here, the Algonquin, coupla speakeasies. Just to pay his way through law school."

"No kidding . . ." answered Lucco, and his eyes narrowed as the door opened and in walked Minnie the Moocher, who clocked the lieutenant, performed an almost burlesque right about-face, and exited, all without expression or pause.

After a long silence the bartender remarked, "You know they say us guys are like psychiatrists. Guys chew over their beefs wid us, an' like that."

"You don't say," Lucco replied, and finished his bourbon in one long swallow, got off the barstool, lifted a battered navy blue canvas traveling bag from the floor, and walked out.

The bartender shrugged. "Funny guy . . ." he remarked to the mirror.

Outside on the sidewalk, Eddie Lucco crossed the street, walked a couple of blocks, checking for tails, nodded to a yellow taxi, which pulled up at the curb, climbed in, and told the driver to take him to La Guardia Airport.

At La Guardia he phoned Nancy who was working late at the office.

"How you doing . . . ?"

"I saw a great place in the Village. Two bedrooms, a big living room, bathroom, a second john with a shower, ancient kitchen, and a huge hall you could put a dining table."

"Nancy, the Village . . . come on, that ain't the East Side."

"It's nice, Eddie. It's really us."

In the departures hall, a disembodied voice announced the departure of an American Airlines flight to Denver, Colorado.

"Eddie . . . ?"

"I dunno . . . We can afford better."

"The village is neat. It's fun, it's cosmopolitan, it's . . . kind of raffish. What's the matter, when you sold your soul did you sell your good taste?"

"Cheap shot."

"Shit, Lucco, I'm sorry."

"And never, ever apologize."

"Sure. When's your plane?"

"Soon."

"So do I forget that one and keep looking? Maybe something ritzy by the park? What the hell, I can afford a mortgage now."

"Do you have to put some kind of deposit down?"

"For a Central Park penthouse? Hey, first you have to get past the residents' committee . . ."

"For the place in the Village."

"Two thousand bucks."

"So do it."

"We should go together."

"If you saw it, I'll like it, gotta go, love ya."

"Back tomorrow?"

"Sure thing. Big kiss." And Lucco put the receiver down and ambled through the hall, still checking for surveillance even as he passed the airline staff and went through the gate for the Miami flight.

———

And at Charles de Gaulle airport in Paris, Judge Eugene Pearson was disembarking from Aer Lingus Flight AE 212 from Dublin. There was a certain lightness in his step for the first time in weeks because within the next twenty-four hours he believed he would be reunited with his daughter, who, he reflected, must be a much-improved pianist, concert standard maybe, after all that master-class tuition at the feet of Enrique Lopez Fuerte.

He made his way to the transit area and studied the TV monitors for information about the onward flight to Miami. He was traveling Air France Flight AF 43 and he saw that it was leaving on time, at 1400 hours. That gave him time for a cup of coffee and a snack. He was carrying one valise, as cabin baggage, and Mhairaid had packed some clothes and underwear for Siobhan, and the latest Swatch Watch as a small present, the way mothers do.

He was relieved he had no time to visit Paris, once his favorite city. For the memory of the horrific murder of the Whore of Venice had never left him, and there were times when he woke bolt upright in the middle of the night, trying to brush the blood and brains off his face.

There was considerable police activity in the airport, and Pearson's trained eye noticed a number of undercover detectives disguised as leather-jacketed rebels of both sexes, ordinary travelers, and very fit-looking baggage handlers, the latter probably from the Groupe d'Intervention Gendarmerie Nationale's Antiterrorist Unit. For there had been five bombings in Paris over the past two weeks, the work, so Mary Connelly had told him, of an extreme right-wing oufit trying to discredit the Lebanese Hezbollah, who were rumored to be desperately searching for a politically profitable way to get rid of their several western hostages on the instructions of Iranian intelligence, whose leaders' number one priority was to emerge from the disastrous ostracized limbo earlier Ayatollahs had cast them into and rejoin the real world.

Certain extremist French organizations had, according to Mary, planted car bombs and thrown grenades into a Hebrew school, claiming to be a Lebanese fundamentalist terror group.

Eugene Pearson shook his head at the complexity of it all. Even as a senior IRA man, he got lost in the plethora of initials and labyrinthine logic of European revolutionary politics. His one concern was not being caught in some outrage as he waited to board his flight for Miami. He could even see a certain wry irony in such an event.

As he sat at a table in the transit lounge and perused the menu, he earnestly wished that all those groups could sit down and plan their work, of whatever political persuasion, in such a way they did not get in each other's way.

"*Un café, s'il vous plaît,*" he said politely to the Algerian waiter, "*et une petite baguette, jambon, tomates avec de la moutarde mais pas trop forte, la moutarde.*" And he was proud of that, for he had been listening to teach-yourself-French cassettes for months, years, to tell the truth, and he liked the sound, perhaps even the fluency, of what he had just said.

"Monsieur est très gentil . . ." murmured the waiter, and departed.

Très gentil . . . mused Eugene Pearson. Bejaysus, you don't know the half of it. And he grinned as he sat there on his own, for nothing could get in the way of his pleasure at the prospect of seeing Siobhan again.

———

Harry Ford was busy and at the same time alert. This was his first serious protection assignment since succeeding Jesus Garcia to become Pablo Envigado's security chief. The job was to keep the Medellín godfather number one, alive, and number two, at liberty, while he made one of his occasional forays into the heart of his enemies' territory.

Envigado's enemies were not, of course, other gangsters; they were the law-enforcement agencies and the Colombian army.

Harry sat in the front seat of the second Renegade jeep beside the driver. Behind them were Pablo Envigado and four bodyguards. Franco Sonson was just behind Harry Ford, in constant radio contact with the convoy of five armored and blast-proof jeeps and patrol wagons, windows blacked out, crammed with armed men, and with twelve powerful, dusty trail bikes front, rear, and alongside the convoy, constantly changing position, their riders wearing goggles and bulletproof vests, with MAC-10 grease guns or Uzi submachine guns.

They were on the outskirts of Medellín traveling at a steady forty miles an hour, monopolizing the fast lanes, not stopping for red lights or for traffic with the right of way at intersections.

VIP protection is part and parcel of SAS operations,

and Harry was thoroughly skilled in the work. But he had to remember to live his cover as Carlos Nelson, the hard and ruthless marijuana dealer, and be seen to be doing the job competently and using his brains without seeming to be too professional, which would have aroused suspicion.

The object of this foray was for *el padrino* to have lunch with his friends and relations from Envigado and Santa Fe. It was the kind of outrageous, magnificently dangerous gesture that had made him a legend throughout Colombia and something of a hero to his brother Antioquians.

The restaurant, as the convoy approached, was a most fashionable, low white building, built around a courtyard on a slight ridge overlooking the city.

Franco lifted his radio handset from his ear and leaning closer to Harry Ford, confirmed that the advance party had men in the restaurant and in the carpark. Others patrolling the streets reported no suspicious police or military activity.

The convoy swept into the courtyard around which the restaurant and bar was built. Armed soldiers of the *grupo* were everywhere. The second jeep pulled up at the entrance and Harry was out before it had come to a stop and ran up the steps and into the dining room, which he knew from studying an architect's plan of the place was on the right, beyond the cashier's desk.

Armed men were on the door and as he went through the doorway, Harry was greeted by a strange sight. It was a Sunday and about forty customers, dressed in their best, families, tables of well-heeled young people, mothers and fathers and in-laws and so on, were all sitting perfectly still with their hands, palms up, on the snow-white linen tablecloths where they could be seen.

Standing all around the walls, one side of which was mostly window looking out onto the courtyard, were seventeen of the *grupo*'s men, facing inward, covering the diners with their Uzis and shotguns, and Mac-10s.

As Harry entered, the seated diners turned to stare at him. He stopped and quickly checked out each table. A few macho-looking honchos, but no one had that relaxed, objective, deceptively gentle look that was the hallmark of somebody who might pull his piece and go apeshit.

He glanced at a table by the door. It was piled high with an assortment of pistols and revolvers, switchblades and a couple of mini-Uzis. Normal accoutrements for a gentleman or his bodyguards out to lunch in Medellín.

Harry adopted a relaxed stance and spread his arms in apology.

"We are real sorry to interrupt your Sunday lunch, ladies and gentlemen," he said in his slightly Argentine-accented Spanish. "But you made the mistake of choosing the best place in town . . . the classiest, with the most beautiful ladies, and the men . . . ? Well, hell, they must be millionaires to eat here."

One or two of them laughed, some nervously. One or two of the men did not think he was being very funny. But still, no potential heroes.

"Okay, we do not intend to inconvenience you if you do not inconvenience us. Today we are taking lunch with some friends. That's all. Nobody will be harmed, nobody will be robbed. Gentlemen, your personal weapons will be left right there for you when we depart. Oh, just one thing, please keep your hands on the table at all times. If you have food, please continue to eat and enjoy. If anyone's hands move below the table level, or if anyone stands up, they will of course be shot." He glanced at the kitchen and the maître d' entered with four black-coated, black-tie-wearing waiters, flanked by two hoods with MAC-10s.

Harry Ford nodded to the men behind him and there was a slight gasp from the customers as Pablo Envigado strolled in with his wife and two of his cousins, a well-known bullfighter from Cali, and three extremely beautiful women wearing Karl Lagerfeldt and Yves San Laurent-type clothes. Franco Sonson and eight of the cartel's top bodyguards surrounded them.

The maître d' advanced and bowed, welcoming *el padrino* with, for once, genuine obsequiousness and wormlike groveling.

Pablo Envigado waited until his guests were seated at the round table by the door, then raised his arms to the trapped Sunday lunchers. *"Buen provecho . . ."* he wished them, and sat down.

Harry did not join his employer. His job was to ensure their complete safety. Envigado and his friends ate and drank, chatted and laughed just like any other group out for lunch on a Sunday.

Harry meanwhile listened to continuing updates on the security situation in the surrounding area. All was quiet. Almost as if the other side had deliberately stayed away.

Finally the meal was over, and Pablo Envigado and his wife led their friends out to the waiting jeeps, engines running and motorcycle outriders revving up.

Harry Ford moved to follow, then turned back and faced the diners. "Thank you for your understanding. And for your patience. Please enjoy the remainder of your Sunday lunch in peace. And order whatever you want from the kitchens and from the bar. Champagne, scotch . . . aguardiente. You are all the honored guests of Don Pablo Envigado, and he will pick up the bill." Harry turned to the appalled maître d' and grinned. Franco, watching him, thought this Carlos Nelson could look as wolflike as the dog, Diablo.

"That's right, maestro . . ." Harry said to the maître d', "You'll just send the check to Don Pablo Envigado."

"An honor," spluttered the maître d', who was also part owner, as he contemplated the loss of a month's profit.

Ford nodded approvingly, then drew a thick envelope from his inside jacket pocket and handed it courteously to the man. The envelope was not sealed and it was crammed with $100 bills. "Just kidding. We always pay our way. After all, we can afford it . . ."

And the laughter of the relieved guests was still in his ears as Harry climbed into the Renegade jeep and the convoy swept out of the courtyard and across Medellín, carving its way through the traffic, which pretty quickly got out of its way.

I could get to enjoy this, mused Captain Harry Ford, MC.

The transition from able, courageous, ambitious SAS officer to deep-penetration intelligence operator had not seemed such a complete change of course to Harry, as it had to, for instance, Malcolm Strong. When Elizabeth had asked him about his reaction to David Jardine's initial overture and his evaluation and operational training at the Honey Farm, Harry had thought for a moment, then replied the whole chain of events had a certain . . . inevitability. It was as if he had always been aware of the course his life would take.

As for this latest development—suddenly finding himself with two million dollars, earning about another seven thousand every week and a quite separate monthly retainer of a hundred grand—somehow Harry Ford had always known he would be desperately rich one day.

He had arranged with Restrepo to have his first $2,000,000 banked with BCCI in Abu Dhabi, earning 18 percent interest on a term deposit, rolling over (apparently the banking term) every Thursday, which meant that in, say, six months, the money would have in-creased to over 2.3 million.

Did he realize he had broken the rules? Well, how many instructors and SIS trainers had dinned into him, time and time again, "There are no rules in this game, except fulfill your task, obey your instructions, and Don't Get Caught"? What the Hungarian referred to as the Eleventh Commandment.

So Harry Ford knew it was dishonest for him to salt away a few million before arranging for Pablo Envigado and Restrepo to die in an ambush, which Harry would set up, ostensibly to take the Cartel's two top men alive. But espionage was a game of lies and deception, of being economical with the truth. And where was the harm? He was not stealing the bloody money. And during the six months he had set himself to acquire around three or four million (for there was so much cash floating around the *grupo* it would be difficult for a man in his position to avoid it) he would be fulfilling his secondary task: to obtain sensitive intelligence about the Cali and Bogotá groups and the cartel's plans and operation methods of smuggling cocaine into Europe.

Harry was not entirely sure he could keep Envigado alive that long, and being no fool, he was aware that with the *padrino* dead or in jail, his own life expectancy with the *grupo* would be brief. It was Pablo who had been amused to take him to the heart of the family. The others simply tolerated him, with an underlying degree of resentment.

Well, no problem. He would keep the thing going as long as possible. And aim for the ideal result—Pablo and Restrepo dead, and therefore silent, a few million tucked away, a secret hero's return to England, where he would terminate his contract with the Firm, a decent interval of a few months, riding and training a few good horses, playing a bit of polo. Then he and Elizabeth would move to Argentina, buy a ranch, and live in the style Harry Ford had always known would somehow come his way.

It was a pity about poor Alistair Reid. And Harry was deeply upset by the accidental killing, for even in the heat of a firefight, he felt his training and his unusually quick reactions should have worked to save the man's life. It haunted him that maybe Reid had aimed off to avoid killing Harry, and he had not been quick enough to do the same for his brother officer.

Be that as it may (a favorite expression of Elizabeth's, whom he was beginning to miss), he was now in tight with Pablo, who believed Harry had deliberately saved his life.

Funny things, those lightning-fast "limited actions" as the British Army quaintly called brutal, deafening, bowel-churning gunfights that erupted between enemies on the ground, face to face and hand to hand. Every survivor's recollection was always slightly different, always subjective, for the primary instinct had taken over. And the primary instinct was always to stay alive. Every time.

Now because of that instinct, his reputation with these hoodlums was rock solid. Harry relaxed in his seat and, glancing in his mirror, caught the eye of Pablo Envigado, who winked.

"*Que puteria, Carlos. Está chevere, sí?*" Meaning "isn't life fine."

Carlos Nelson grinned. Oh yes, life was indeed just fine.

"Walked into a door . . . ? Dad, what exactly do you do with the secret service?"

David Jardine paused the chopsticks on their way to

his mouth. They were eating in a small Chinese restaurant in Wardour Street, in London's Soho. Andrew was up in town for an interview with a personnel officer of BBC Television for a four-day Job Experience course where, if he was successful, he would learn what it was like to work in TV drama. Dorothy had managed to get him the interview but from there on it was up to Andrew.

"Oh, jolly boring actually. Various government committees. Travel abroad, visiting some of our diplomats. Writing endless reports. Do quite a few of your chums at school have dads in, um, my sort of work?"

Andrew grinned, ladling chicken chow mein into his mouth. "I don't know . . ." he mumbled. "I tell them you're in Protocol."

"Good boy." Jardine felt guilty that he had, as an automatic reflex, just interrogated his son. "Nervous about the interview?"

"Uh-uh." Andrew shook his head. Then finally, for a moment, his mouth was more or less empty. "Way I look at it, if I get it I get it. If I don't, it's their loss."

Jardine laughed quietly. The confidence of youth.

"Who are you playing this weekend?"

"Bryanston."

"You'll smash 'em."

"Dunno. They're very good this year. Excellent fast bowler, somebody McCrae."

"Roddy?"

"Yeah."

Jardine smiled. Roddy was Steven McCrae's youngest boy. Which Andrew probably knew. He caught his son looking at him and grinning.

He touched his cheek; the bruise was almost healed. "Dear oh dear. We'll make a Jesuit out of you yet . . ."

After lunch, they emerged into Wardour Street and David Jardine steered Andrew away from the amusement arcades of Old Compton Street and put him in a taxi for his interview at the BBC television center at White City, giving the boy a tenner for the journey and an extra ten for his pocket. Dorothy was up in Morayshire, in Scotland, interviewing a former cabinet minister who claimed to be in regular touch with Saint Joan of Arc, who appeared to him on the long, deserted beach at Culbin Sands.

And as the black taxi receded, with Andrew already thinking about other things, the sphere controller suddenly knew that he was in the wrong place at the wrong time.

He had managed to keep out of his mind, during lunch, the fact that he had an assignation with Elizabeth at three, for Andrew's presence would have made him feel too bad.

He had managed to keep out of his mind the fact that, while he relaxed with his son, an expensive and deadly serious game was being planned by his Operations and Security managers, headed by Ronnie Szabodo, in order to trap Harry Ford into betraying himself, into proving that he had turned into an unreliable and potentially dangerous negative asset.

There was a deeply secret and always denied procedure in SIS for dealing with clandestine operators who were seriously compromising the service. It was a procedure that did not allow for the survival of the transgressor.

And just as Harry Ford had always known he would reach the point in his life where he then was, so did Jardine—standing there in Wardour Street, with heavy drops of rain landing on his head and on his shoulders—realize that the boy would not, in all probability, actually be in Colombia if the man running him had not wanted to have Elizabeth all to himself. Just for a few weeks' fun. Just for a few weeks' carnal knowledge, old boy. For with hindsight, Agent Baggage, Malcolm Strong, was quite clearly the candidate Jardine should have chosen. God knew everyone had tried to tell him.

"But at the end of the day, David," Szabodo had said, "It's your decision . . ."

David Jardine shivered. He felt wretched. But as the realization grew stronger that the time had come for him, for him personally, to sort out the whole bugger's muddle, he found a deadly calm. A cold resolve.

He raised a hand and a taxi pulled up.

"Where to, guv'nor?" asked the driver.

"Tite Street, first call, then wait if you would be so kind, and take me on to Heathrow Airport."

"Now that's the kind of fare I like, guv."

And Jardine climbed in, pulling the door shut, and the taxi moved away.

Summer sunlight fell across Jardine's vacant desk and the carriage clock ticked patiently each passing second. Beyond the corner windows a rainbow hung over Parliament Square.

The atmosphere of peace and lazy, late-summer-afternoon tranquillity struck Ronnie Szabodo as he stood silent on the threshold, gazing at the empty chair and the photo of 129 Spetznatz on the wall behind. He was clutching a file with the preliminary results of the intelligence analysts' reports on Harry Ford's most recent clandestine signals.

They did not make encouraging reading. The service had been canny and experienced even in the time of Queen Elizabeth the First, over four hundred years ago, and it was still beyond equal in recognizing the signs when an agent was hiding things or consistently misleading his masters.

This is an empty room, thought the Hungarian, gazing around. It was like a house whose owner had died or moved away.

"He didn't come back from lunch," announced Heather, reentering the outer office from somewhere. "Will he be coming back . . . ?"

Szabodo closed his eyes. "I hope so," he replied.

ADVICE TO TRAVELERS

21

ADVICE TO TRAVELERS

If the Miami branch of the Bank of Commerce and Credit International had opened at its regular time that Friday morning, if it had not been closed until two in the afternoon for a special audit, then Homicide Lieutenant Eddie Lucco would have carried out his intention to withdraw thirty thousand dollars in cash, buy a 1975 three-liter Ford Mustang coupe at Jerry's Special Autos in Coral Gables, completely restored, for nine thousand, fill it with gas, and drive north on U.S. 1, aiming to be back in NYC in time for brunch with Nancy next day.

It was a dream coupe, right out of the movie *Bullitt* with Steve McQueen, who was, secretly, how the cop saw himself. Even Nancy did not know that.

The previous night he had stepped off the American Airlines flight from New York, rented an unremarkable Dodge sedan, and booked into a nondescript hotel in Coconut Grove, where the top floor was a noisy nightclub and Spanish was the main language.

It was hot and humid and Lucco had put on a

lightweight pair of linen trousers and moccasins, with his shirt worn outside, his detective's badge taped to his right ankle and his snub-nosed .38 Smith & Wesson in a holster taped to the other. He had driven to Bayshore, where there was a whole complex of bars and eateries, live music and street theater, and in Bergin's Bar there, right on the waterfront, the manager, a good-looking divorcée from New York, recognized a kindred spirit and guided him through a couple or three of the several hundred kinds of beer they had.

When she heard Lucco was looking to buy an automobile with some class, but not too pricey, the manager said he could do worse than take a look at Jerry's Special Autos and she introduced him to Jerry, who was sitting along the bar.

When he heard about Eddie Lucco's desire for a big Mustang, Jerry took the cop round, opened the place up, and proudly showed him three beautifully restored cars, two soft tops and the coupe. Lucco agreed to take the coupe, said he would be paying cash, which does not in Miami receive the same surprised reaction it might in more conservative parts of America, and arranged to come around at ten-thirty next day to do the deal.

But here he was, staring at a notice on the huge armored-glass and chrome door, "Closed till 2 P.M."

Lucco had checked out of the hotel, having failed to sleep much because of the noise from the discotheque on the top floor, at ten before nine. Now he had time to kill.

He shrugged and drove at a leisurely pace out of the commercial district and found himself, almost by accident since he was not driving anyplace in particular, approaching a line of toll cabins, with the stunning, curving, climbing, concrete causeway to Key Biscayne stretching beyond.

The radio was playing and the sun was shining and

Eddie Lucco thought what the hell, so he paid his dollar and drove on along the causeway and descended onto Key Biscayne, the first of the Florida Keys, which stretched right down south, separating the Straits of Florida from the Gulf of Mexico.

On his right, he noticed a yacht harbor and a low, dusty blue set of wooden buildings, with a bar, right beside some moored marlin boats. Lucco spun the wheel, made a right, and parked in the yard behind the place, which a large sign announced was called Sundays on the Beach. Which was where David Jardine had eaten supper with John and Joni Consadine just a few weeks before.

He strolled along the moored, powerful deep-sea fishing boats where a few crews were cleaning and preparing for a day's fishing. At the couple of steps to the bar, a tall gray heron watched with mindless interest as a lithe and tanned waitress served coffee and waffles to a couple who were talking quietly and laughing gently. Lucco went into the bar and sat on a stool at the counter.

"How you doin'. . . ?" The waitress, who was about nineteen, smiled at him as she spoke.

"Pretty good. You got a large black coffee and some toast or something?" Even that early the sun was hot and strong on his back, for he was sitting near the veranda.

"We got waffles, would you like that? Amy's making waffles right now. I think it's the only thing she knows, but they're real good . . ." She laughed and as she turned around, her fair hair spun and lifted and her smiling, vital young face for a microsecond was exactly like the photo of the Jane Doe, standing in some square in Rome.

Eddie Lucco's blood went cold. He forced a relaxed smile and said waffles would be fine. But as the waitress sashayed off into the kitchen, from where giggles and friendly conversation could be heard, suddenly he was back there on that washroom floor in Grand Central, holding the waif's wrist and wiping flecks of vomit from his face, knowing it was too late for one more crack-OD'd kid.

And he had begun to treat the whole damn thing as some kinda game. Sure, take the Colombian's fuckin money, be a secret fuckin agent for the DEA. Yeah, go buy yourself a sports car, nobody said you couldn't enjoy yourself . . .

Enjoy yourself. Eddie Lucco felt a claw of guilt in his chest. For he had been enjoying himself. This Miami trip had been a welcome respite from all the shit going down in the 14th Precinct. Three crack-related killings the day before. Youngest victim nine. Oldest suspect, fourteen.

And the dead JD. She was not anonymous anymore. Siobhan Pearson. Daughter of Eugene Patrick Pearson. An Irish judge.

But Don Mather had sworn Lucco to secrecy. Judge Eugene Pearson was not to know his daughter was lying dead on a slab in Bellevue Hospital morgue. His knowledge of his daughter's death would compromise some "ongoing stuff."

Well, no cop on the force was straighter than Lieutenant Eddie Lucco. No cop understood better the need to keep the mouth shut, from time to time.

But it was tearing him apart, knowing that somewhere in Ireland this judge guy, and doubtless his wife, must be eating his heart out, wondering and praying for his missing daughter.

The hell with it, decided Lucco, and rising from his barstool asked the pretty waitress as she came out from the kitchen with his coffeepot and a white cup and saucer, "Do you have a pay phone . . . ?"

"Sure." She grinned, eyes friendly. "Go through the

inside restaurant and through the doors at the far side and the pay phones are there."

"Thanks."

"You want some quarters?"

"Its okay." A good detective was never short of quarters for the phone.

It took twenty-seven minutes for Eddie Lucco to find Judge Eugene Pearson's phone number. The young waitress brought his coffee to him from the outside bar. The phone companies' information services could not help. The girl on the switchboard at Police Plaza, Manhattan South, took eleven minutes to inform the homicide cop that Pearson's number was kept out of the Dublin information computer for security reasons.

Finally, Lucco phoned an Irish detective in the 14th Precinct who had three cousins in the Garda, the Irish police. He explained what he wanted and went back into the bar to tackle a big order of waffles and maple syrup.

Ten minutes later, a call came through to the bar and the girl let him take it right there. He scribbled down the number of Eugene Pearson's Dublin home.

The Homicide lieutenant thanked the waitress and left a fin beside his paid check. He went back to the pay phone in a lobby beside a beachwear- and Panama hat-boutique. A transatlantic call to Dublin was going to take more quarters than he had, and Lucco did not want to use one of his credit cards that would identify him to an interested party as the caller.

So he approached the plump, good-natured Cuban woman in the tiny boutique and asked if he could use her phone. He offered her $50 for the favor, plus whatever the call cost.

Having made the deal, Lucco squeezed into the cramped closet that was the "office," and sitting on a couple of boxes of beach shirts, put in his call to Eugene

Pearson's home in Dublin. It was Saturday and he figured the judge would not be at work, although five hours ahead of Eastern Standard Time made it about four in the afternoon.

The phone ringing tone was quaint. It conjured up an image of some cute Irish little people on the old movie channel.

It rang fourteen times before a woman's voice answered.

"Four seven one five . . ." it said, with a soft lilt.

"Uh, good morning, or should I say afternoon to you, may I—"

"Who's this?"

"May I speak with Judge Eugene Pearson, please?"

"Who's calling . . . ?"

Jesus Christ, what am I going to say to the man? Lucco took a deep breath. "I'm phoning from the United States on a personal matter."

Slight pause. The line was chillingly clear. Not a trace of interference.

"Will that be to do with the seminar . . . ?"

"Um, I wonder if I could just speak with him for a moment."

"Well, you're too late, Mr. . . . ?"

"Johnson. J.J. Johnson."

"He'll be landing in Miami at two-thirty. He left yesterday, it's a long flight, you know . . ."

"For the . . . seminar."

"For the legal seminar in Florida. Then he has some private business to attend to."

"Something pleasant, I hope." This was a seriously professional detective, not missing a beat.

"Our daughter, actually. He's meeting our daughter and they'll be flying back together . . ."

Meeting our daughter? Lucco's brain froze. Maybe

they had more than one daughter. But his instinct told him no.

"Hello?" asked the voice of Mhairaid Pearson.

"I'll, uh, thanks, Mrs. Pearson. Thank you." And sick in his heart, the expressionless New York cop put the receiver down. He paid for the call, leaving an extra fifty bucks, and walked out into the hot sun. Somewhere, an expensive sound system was playing the Bob Marley number, "No Woman No Cry". . .

Eddie Lucco leaned against the rented Dodge for a long time. The heron walked with a stiff, ridiculous elegance along the edge of the quay, inspecting those marlin boats that were loading bait. Sweat rolled down the cop's back. He had never in his life, since the day after the Tet Offensive was finally considered over, felt he *needed* a drink, but right then he would have taken a slug of bourbon if he had had a bottle in the car.

Okay, he mused, I phone the Jane's father, four thousand miles away, from Miami, a town I have visited only four times in my life, and what do I find? The guy, the bereaved, the unknowing bereaved guy, judge, bereaved judge, is due to land at Miami in a couple of hours' time.

Why?

To attend a legal seminar?

Gimme a break.

To attend to some personal business? To meet his daughter, says the wife, so that's what he told her. Why does the judge believe his daughter will be there? Is this an arrangement they made months ago?

Daddy, I'll just be snorting some ice around the USA. Meet me in Miami on such and such a date? Not likely. Not at all likely.

No, the cartel has been going crazy, look at Bellevue, Ricardo Santos, the five million they coughed up to buy Lucco himself to get him to cool the investigation. They needed to have some kind of leverage on the girl's father, this Judge Eugene Pearson, due in Miami at two-thirty.

And whatever reason the judge and his wife were giving out, there was no doubt in Lucco's mind that Pearson was on his way to Miami to deliver whatever the cartel needed from him. Or had delivered it, maybe, and believed he was coming to have his daughter handed over. In which case, he should not have bothered booking a return ticket.

As the sun beat down on Lucco and sweat ran down the sides of his face, the cop realized he was in possession of a couple, no, three good hands in this particular game.

There was no question the information he had just come by was important operational evidence in the investigation of the Bellevue killings. And he, as the primary law-enforcement investigating officer, was required to follow it up. Okay, that was one route to go.

He was also a sworn clandestine agent of the Drug Enforcement Agency, with Don Mather his case officer. So he was obliged to inform Don of the development. No problem.

And in addition, he was the Homicide officer on the original Jane Doe case. He could pursue that case just about anywhere it took him. NYPD would always get behind an officer on that score.

Eddie Lucco climbed into the Dodge and headed for Miami International Airport, a half hour's drive from Key Biscayne. He parked in F carpark and went into the air-conditioned arrivals hall.

From a pay phone, using his credit card, he phoned Don Mather's home on Long Island. Mrs. Mather, whom he had never met, said Don was playing golf and would be home about four. When she asked who she should say had called, Lucco said it was Gino Lucchese, calling from Miami, and he would phone back. Gino Lucchese was the work name Mather had given him.

The big detective was in part relieved that his DEA handler was out. That left him free to function as a straightforward Homicide cop with a legitimate reason for meeting Judge Eugene Pearson off the plane. But another part of him had come to respect the degree of backup and cooperation the DEA could rustle up at short notice. He had a feeling he might regret the absence of that.

He then phoned the 14th Precinct to inform them he was in Miami on a case. He did not mention Jane Doe or Bellevue because, as Captain Danny Molloy had pointed out, you could not trust everybody, even in the department, where the cartel was concerned.

However, Sergeant Sid Mercer, the precinct Detective in Charge that Saturday, asked no questions. Eddie Lucco was a reliable officer and a lieutenant, which gave him some muscle. If he chose to go to Miami on a case, no problem. The call was duly logged.

When Lucco replaced the receiver he felt better in himself, for he had hated the business of coming to Miami like some thief in the night. Now at least he had a reason to declare his presence. Which he would have to do, for he now required access to the flight lists, to find out which of the several flights due in from Europe Judge Pearson was on. And that would mean the use of a few favors and a lot of charm, for the Dade County Police Department did not take kindly to strangers on their territory.

By ten before two, Lieutenant Lucco of NYPD was standing inside the immigration control room, in the immigration lobby, awaiting the arrival of Air France Flight AF 108 from Paris, which had been delayed by a bomb scare at Charles de Gaulle Airport.

Sergeant Joe Bolo of Dade County Homicide Department had attended a course in New York City two years before, and Eddie and Nancy Lucco had taken him around and made his stay in New York a whole lot of fun. Lucco had also taken Bolo out, against all regulations, on a couple of antigang operations, and that was the sort of established trust and friendship a lone and unannounced detective from out of town needed like babies need warm milk.

"What's this guy look like?" asked Bolo.

Eddie Lucco shrugged.

"No problem . . ." The Miami cop turned to the Immigration senior agent. "Can we ID him on presentation?" He meant presentation of his passport.

"Sure thing," replied the agent, and they settled down to wait.

Lucco took the opportunity to phone Nancy and tell her he might not be home in time for Sunday brunch . . .

It would have been imprudent for Señor Armando Torres Tejada, Peruvian financier, to set foot in Colombia once Harry Ford's reliability had come into question, for Harry could identify Torres as the senior British intelligence officer David Arbuthnot Jardine, CMG.

Jardine felt a degree of annoyance about that; he had been comfortable as Armando Torres. And nobody could be certain that Ford had in fact gone bad. Perhaps he was just salting away a few millions for a rainy day. It was not unknown for black operators to make illicit provision for their future. Indeed, a number of the very best (and most reliable) had done just that, but in such a way that they had obeyed Ronnie Szabodo's eleventh commandment. They had not been found out, at least not while in government service. (There was a case where Her Majesty's government, in the shape of SIS, was dropping hundreds of thousands in gold Kruger-rands by parachute onto the desert somewhere in the Arabian Gulf, in order to buy warring tribal chiefs and princes. The black operator on the ground had success-fully bribed the Arab chieftains and just a few years later was able to purchase a luxury schooner for charter in the Mediterranean, from which he ran diving vacations to sunken Greek and Lebanese cities, in addition to running a few guns and a lot of hashish.)

But killing Alistair Reid. And withholding certain information about Pablo Envigado, of which he must have become aware, like Envigado's whereabouts im-mediately after his escape from the ambush—those factors suggested he had started on the slippery slope to becoming a renegade, or at least dangerous, agent.

So David Jardine was obliged to enter Colombia, via Bogotá, using another painstakingly constructed cover. This was not done while passing through the DAS checks at the airport, where he simply went through on a British diplomatic passport as Mr. George Patterson of the Foreign and Commonwealth Office, Financial Sec-tion, in Colombia to carry out an audit of embassy accounts.

Patterson was his regular work name when he en-tered Bogotá through their immigration and security systems and the DAS officer on duty smilingly welcomed him back to Colombia.

Once inside the arrivals hall he was met by a mem-ber of the embassy staff. Not the SIS head of station or his assistant, but the secretary to the head of Chancery and a driver-bodyguard.

The group drove away in the embassy car, a Honda that was suitably inconspicuous, and George Patterson would not be noticed again until his arrival back at the airport for a flight out of the country, protected by his diplomatic credentials. This sort of covert activity was known in espionage parlance as a gray, as opposed to black, operation. It was most wisely practiced in friendly or at least not seriously hostile environments.

By the time the Honda reached the British Embassy in north Bogotá, there were still three people inside, but none of them was David Jardine.

During the drive the SIS man had changed his pin-striped jacket for a sweater, removed his necktie, and traded his polished black shoes for a pair of scuffed but comfortable rubber-soled leather boots. They made the switch in a short deserted alley, where he crossed to a waiting motorcycle, its rider revving the engine, climbed onto the back, and sped off to a rendezvous with Colonel Xavier Ramón, who had all the necessary papers and clothing for Señor Miguel Heridia Gomez, a Bolivian security consultant in the private sector. Bogotá was full of such people.

The rendezvous was at an apartment near the Uni-centro in the north of the city. It was borrowed by Ramón from a former mistress who had become a successful nightclub owner and had moved in with a handsome young writer, twelve years her junior, whose father was a ceramics millionaire from Guatavita. Being a realist, she had kept her own apartment, and Ramón had whee-dled a key from her, saying he could use someplace to take his beautiful young ladies and he would make sure it was kept clean, tidy, and secure.

"So, buddy," said Ramón in English as he poured two generous tumblers of Scotch and passed a bottle of spring water to Jardine, "your young hero is giving us problems . . ."

Of the several things David Jardine liked about Xavier Ramón, one was his unblushing ability to become a solid member of whatever outfit he was working for at that particular moment. Thus, Carlos Nelson was giving "us" problems, which meant Ramón had settled quite comfortably into his persona as an agent of SIS. The man's demeanor, his thick-set frame and his part-Indian features (Ramón had Tierradentro and Tolima blood, mixed with Castilian, from hundreds of years back) with the hooded alligator's eyes, reminded Jardine of Ronnie Szabodo. And both men had that immovable integrity, combined with a chilling ruthlessness and a lifetime's experience of secret work at its most violent, that made him glad they were on the same team.

"I've devised a little test," Jardine replied in Spanish. "It involves another young man, with all Carlos's skills, and we should collect him, you and me, later today. Can we bring him back here?"

"He's in Bogotá?" asked Ramón.

"We'll meet him as he leaves the airport. His plane's due in at seven. I'll tell you his name later, Xavier."

Ramón nodded. He was used to Jardine being prudent. In fact, he often cited Jardine's professional technique in his lectures to young DAS officers, suitably disguising the source.

"This test, what do you need from me . . . ?" he inquired, watching the Englishman closely—*El Inglés*, as he usually referred to David Jardine with his customary economy.

And Jardine explained how he intended to lure Carlos Nelson away from his *grupo* friends and the precise and elegantly simple nature of the test.

"My God." Ramón nodded approvingly. "You should have been a Jesuit, Miguel Herida."

David Jardine smiled coldly. "I am . . ." he replied.

Eddie Lucco stood with the Senior Immigration Agent, watching the jet-lagged passengers from AF 108 decant into the serpentine queues, patiently shuffling first toward, then away from, then back toward the twelve functioning Immigration booths.

The Air France passengers had joined and mingled with others off a flight from Nassau, with colorfully dressed Rastafarians and lobster-pink tourists, and with a planeload just arrived from Germany, where a convention group was being marshaled and harangued by three brusquely efficient women of Teutonic origin.

"When he presents his passport and Immigration form, the computer will let us know," said Jack Lapointe, the Immigration agent. "This is gonna take some time . . ."

"We could page him, if you like," suggested Joe Bolo. "You said he's coming to a legal convention, we could page a Mr. Pearson for the convention."

"Uh-uh," said Lucco, "I don't want to do anything to alert him." For he was sure that someone from the cartel would be waiting for Eugene Pearson out there in the hall.

And they settled down to do what detectives do much of the time. They waited patiently, Eddie Lucco scanning the snaking queues, wondering if his intuition would inform him which of the three hundred travelers was the father of his Jane Doe . . .

———

Pablo Envigado and his closest accomplices were sitting on the roof terrace of a sprawling villa on the outskirts of Sabaneta, a town that had benefited from the cartel's largess.

The terrace was furnished with shrubs and small trees in big terra-cotta pots. There were solid wooden armchairs in Spanish colonial style, and a sun awning in pastel blue and yellow spread out from the rooftop library to provide some shelter from the sun for those who wanted it.

The man who called himself Restrepo sat at a table, using his laptop computer to bring himself up to date with the *grupo*'s administration.

Envigado stood at a corner of the roof terrace, deep in conversation with a man who had been identified to Harry as Juan Londono Rodriguez, a senior member of the Cali faction of the cartel, which was run by Gilberto Rodriguez Orejuela . . . .

Throughout 1988 and beyond, the Cali *grupo* had been suspected by Envigado of being behind relentlessly blatant attempts to kill him. Assassinate was the word used by *el padrino,* and he had entrusted Restrepo with the task of arranging talks with the Rodriguez Orejuela family in order to take the heat off so that he could prosecute his increasingly Wagnerian vendetta against the Colombian government more efficiently.

Restrepo had returned with protestations of innocence from Cali, but he warned Envigado that the other groups in the cartel, meaning the Cali and Bogotá groups, were certainly becoming hostile to Medellín, in cocaine-trafficking terms, because of the unwanted pressure Pablo Envigado's escalating violence was generating against all elements of the business.

Subsequent to this, Restrepo had suggested to Don Pablo that he could do worse than agree to clandestine meetings with the eighty-four-year old priest representing President Gaviria's Counselor for Medellín Affairs while at the same time making some statesmanlike gesture, like forbidding the murders of law officers above the rank of police captain, or circuit judge . . .

Now that those secret negotiations might result in Pablo Envigado surrendering to the authorities in return for the repeal of the hateful extradition treaty with the United States and all the other things Luís Restrepo had counseled, the other cartel leaders—themselves targets for extradition and lengthy sentences—had found the idea of two or three years in a Colombian prison quite tempting. For afterward, the slate would be wiped clean and they could get on with business, free from the present state of war with the elected government.

The hard fact of life was, Restrepo remarked to Harry, that in realpolitik the cocaine industry was, quite simply, the major factor in Colombia's economy. Why, in their fruitless negotiations contesting the extradition treaty the cartel had even offered to pay the Colombian national debt in cash.

No third world nation could ignore such natural wealth, and so long as the gringos, both American and European, spent hundreds of millions on the habit, cocaine was going to be a street commodity of staggering value.

"God forbid the day," Harry Ford remarked, strolling into the shade, Diablo by his side, "when the gringos have the common sense to legalize the stuff . . ."

"Don't even joke about it," replied Restrepo without looking up from his computer.

On the far side of the terrace they could see Pablo gesturing toward the mountain ridge above, which, in the startlingly clear light of that particular day, seemed almost to be overhanging the town.

"He's showing Londono where his prison is being built," said Restrepo, leaning back and stretching his arms.

Harry Ford went cold. *"Qué?"* he said. "What?"

"You'll see." Restrepo rose and crossed into the library, beckoning Harry to follow. Inside, he opened an icebox and took out a jug of iced tea and two tumblers. He poured the tea and handed one tumbler to Harry.

"Thanks." Harry Ford was wary. It was unlike Restrepo to give a man anything. Even a glass of iced tea.

"Sit down."

Harry sat on a comfortable armchair of old leather. The library was in perfect taste, with crammed wooden bookshelves, polished dark wood floor, Indian rugs of superior quality, and solid furniture in wood and hide. Something told him this was Restrepo's house, and yet . . . he could not imagine the *consejero* letting Pablo Envigado within a mile of his real home. Wherever that was.

"Carlos Nelson." Restrepo relaxed into a big couch and watched Harry over the rim of his glass. "I have a task of some delicacy for you."

"If I can do it, I will," replied Harry Ford courteously.

"Oh, it is what you do best . . ."

Harry watched Restrepo, his face betraying nothing.

"A man is arriving very soon in Bogotá. He will book into the Hotel La Fontana, I believe you are familiar with the layout."

"Yes." Somehow, Harry knew what was coming.

"He is bringing the access codes to some cassettes that belong to the *grupo*. I want you to—do you speak English? I should have asked before, but being a friend of Spencer Percy—"

"Of course I speak English. Luís, don't play games . . ." said Harry, in English.

"Forgive me." Restrepo inclined his head. "You are to take the codes, which he will give you, and send Murillo with them to me."

"Where will you be?"

"Nearby."

"And when you have . . . ascertained he's given you the correct codes?" Harry Ford could see where this was leading.

Restrepo smiled. "You don't have much to learn, Carlos. Murillo will contact you."

"And I pay him . . . ?"

Harry waited for Restrepo's reply.

"You kill him."

It was as if the whole valley, in the shadow of Pablo's possible future custom-built prison, had fallen silent.

"In the Fontana?"

"Certainly not. If it was a simple hit, Bobby Sonson or Murillo could do it. You are to make sure the body disappears forever. And check his hotel room and anyplace else he might have left evidence that he was ever in Colombia."

"Who is this man?"

From outside on the roof terrace, they could hear Pablo Envigado and the man from Cali laughing. Diablo, lying at Harry's feet, lifted his head up wondering, in vain, if maybe his former master, Jesus Garcia, was out there. Then his ears relaxed and he laid his head across Harry Ford's left foot, letting out a bored grunt.

"His name is Eugene Pearson. He is an Irish judge and a senior member of the Provisional IRA. We have conducted a little business with them."

"Luís Restrepo." Harry Ford laid his glass down. "Even the cartel should think twice about taking on the IRA . . ."

"Are you afraid of them?" Restrepo's eyes studied Ford's face.

"Actually, they leave me cold. But they could upset your European traffic . . ."

Luís Restrepo Osorio smiled. He sipped his iced tea, still smiling. "Carlos, relax," he said in English, "it's the IRA who want him dead . . ."

The last of the Air France passengers had passed through Immigration. Only three names on the flight manifest had not been recorded.

Eddie Lucco stared at the computer screen, then out through the mirrored, slatted glass window at the row of Immigration booths.

"Three names . . ." he said.

"Probably transit," said Jack Lapointe.

"Say what?" Lucco turned to stare with not a little menace at the Immigration agent.

"Jack means if they go directly onto another plane taking them out of the USA, they do not come through Immigration," Bolo said.

"Oh, shit . . ." Eddie Lucco's hands hung helplessly by his sides, like a boxer who has been stopped from fighting.

"You want me to check?" Lapointe was already hitting some keys on the computer terminal.

Lucco met Bolo's inquiring gaze. "What a mug. I believed he was coming into Miami because that's what he told his wife . . ."

"Man, there's eight flights stacked up right now . . ." The Immigration man punched another cluster of keys.

"Anything going to Colombia?" asked Lucco, his brain suddenly out of neutral.

"Let's see . . . Sure. Avianca Flight AV eighty-three to Bogotá. Hold it . . ." And the three men watched as the screen rearranged itself to inform them that AV eighty-three was right at that moment taking off.

Lapointe typed another instruction, a question. Who is on the plane . . . ? And back came the passenger manifest.

Silence as they scanned it.

"Row eighteen, seat C," read Bolo.

"Pearson, E.P. Now ain't that fuckin wonderful?" Eddie Lucco leaned his fingertips on the desk. Thinking hard.

"Tough break, *amigo*." Bolo glanced to the Immigration agent and raised his shoulders. Like, we've done all we can, was his message.

"One last favor."

"You name it, Lieutenant," said Lapointe. "Who knows, one day I might get posted to New York."

Lucco smiled ruefully. "Any more flights there today?"

Once more the computer was the focus of attention. There was an American Airlines flight at four ten, getting into Bogotá at seven-forty local time, Colombia being one hour behind Miami.

Lapointe picked up a phone and booked Eddie Lucco a seat on it. He put the phone down. "Well, Bogotá sure as hell is not where I would choose to spend Saturday night, but there's a seat if you want it."

"Jack, NYPD owes you. Next time you're up there, I'll take you out for the best spaghetti puttanesca you ever had."

They all shook hands and Bolo and Lucco left Immigration and, flashing their badges, strolled through Customs and out into MIA, Miami International Airport. They went directly to the American Airlines ticket desk, and the Homicide cop purchased a return ticket to Bogotá and confirmed his seat, choosing an aisle and not a window.

"Well, my friend, you got two hours, whadda you want to do, get laid or get drunk?"

Eddie Lucco said he would like to drive downtown and get some dollars.

"Hell man, there's a bank here . . ."

No, said Lucco, he needed to go to a particular bank downtown. He would drive himself, he said, thanking Bolo for everything.

"Any time, pal . . ."

"Just one last thing, if you don't mind."

"Name it."

And Lucco gave Bolo his gun to look after.

"What about your badge? That ain't gonna cut much ice in South America. Gringo cop's badge."

Eddie Lucco said he would prefer to keep his Homicide lieutenant's badge. So they parted, with a warning to Lucco—which was said in jest but meant in earnest—to come back in one piece.

It was so easy to withdraw thirty thousand dollars from the BCCI bank in the commercial district of Miami. Eddie Lucco was impressed till he realized Mafia dons and snow dealers probably used that kind of moolah two or three times a week.

He left his rented car back in Carpark F, and by the time American Airlines Flight 331 for Bogotá, a big DC-10, was thundering its enormous carcass upward over Key Biscayne and banking right over the bay, Lucco was fast asleep, with not the beginnings of a plan about how to locate Pearson or even really sure why he was doing such a cockamamie thing. But he knew that in some way there had been no option. Ever since the morning he had found the dead kid, it seemed every road had led to that moment, scoring through the sky like some ancient god on his chariot, toward Bogotá and, for better or for worse, the end of his quest.

It was his destiny, and as Lucco became aware of that, of a certain inevitability, an iron coldness caught his belly and he swallowed, putting the chill on the backs of his hands, the awareness of his heartbeat, down to maybe the onset of influenza. There was a lot of it about back in NYC, a town he could not wait to get home to. Back to the precinct, and Nancy.

The thought of her made him smile, and within seconds he was fast asleep.

Bill Jenkins, Operations Officer for West 8, was on weekend duty along with Ronnie Szabodo because David Jardine had phoned the office that Friday afternoon from Heathrow Airport. By coincidence, Kate Howard had picked up the phone in Heather's outer office while Heather was searching a filing cabinet for some admin memos relating to Personnel.

Kate had joked with Jardine about swanning off early, and immediately sensing the urgency in his voice leaned out of the door and called along the corridor after Szabodo, who was just leaving, Friday being Poets day.

Ronnie Szabodo had not been surprised to hear that Jardine was at Heathrow, about to board a British Airways flight direct to Bogotá. He had listened intently, nodding and scribbling on an internal letter Heather had just typed out neatly, a letter to Sir Steven McCrae about the next year's budget.

"Okay, David," he said, several times. "Yup. Yup. Okay . . . Yes. Don't worry. Bill Jenkins . . . Sure."

And Kate, leaning against the open doorway, had reached out an arm and held on to the sleeve of Bill Jenkins's old golfing anorak as he padded toward the main security door, head down, briefcase clutched to his left hand, escaping for the weekend.

Having been stopped abruptly, he turned to Kate, who maintained her hold on his sleeve. "What's up?"

Kate inclined her head toward Szabodo, who was listening, saying "Yup" and "Fine" a lot, and scribbling on the letter.

"That was my top copy . . ." complained Heather to Kate.

Then Ronnie Szabodo hung up and pulled the door closed.

"Okay. Bill, you and I are on duty till Tuesday. Heather, can you work this weekend?"

"I suppose so," said Heather. Such a request from the Hungarian did not carry the same promise of clandestine thrills as it did coming from her boss.

"Kate," said Szabodo, "this concerns Parcel and Baggage. You know as much about them as anyone, do you mind hanging on?"

"Okay . . ." Kate, by osmosis, had gradually become part of Corrida.

Ronnie Szabodo, studying the vandalized budget letter, trying to decipher his squiggles, went on. "We have to contact Baggage right now, in Venezuela. I hope to God he's not out sailing or off with some chicken for the weekend."

"I'll do that," said Jenkins, moving to a phone. "What's the instruction?"

"Move to Bogotá soonest. Do we have a safe place in the north of town?"

"Um . . ." Jenkins frowned. "Yes."

"Okay, David wants him there by tomorrow afternoon at latest. Full deep cover. Let's go." Szabodo rubbed his hands and strode through to Jardine's inner office, grabbing a chair and sitting at the spare desk.

―――――

"What is the purpose of your visit to Colombia?" The slender, sallow-skinned Immigration official sported a neat black mustache and wore a crisp white shirt under a light gray suit. In his lapel was the badge of the DAS, and Eddie Lucco could tell the official wore a revolver in a belt holster on his right abdomen, grip toward the front, under his gray jacket. A left-handed draw. The kind of thing the detective noticed automatically. The kind of thing that had kept him alive, thus far.

"Tourism," Lucco replied, and glanced ahead to the

Customs counters as if the question did not merit any qualms on his part.

The left-handed Immigration official studied Lucco's passport, checking every page and tapping out various entries and queries to his computer screen, which was impossible for the New York cop to read. Finally he stamped the passport and handed it back.

"Welcome to Bogotá," he murmured and turned his attention to the next in line.

It was already dark outside the safety of the airport arrivals hall, with its armed soldiers and police. Lucco strolled past the throng of locals waiting to greet their relatives, loved ones, or business colleagues and headed for the taxis, ignoring a couple that did not have radio aerials, for in a handbook on Colombia that he had purchased in the Miami airport, under a heading "Advice to Travelers" it said those were less safe than cars licensed by the *policia* and equipped with two-way radios to keep in touch with their taxi-company control rooms.

The dull red Fiat sedan had two aerials, one for communication and one for commercial radio, which he could hear was playing commentary on a bicycle race. Bicycle races were big in Colombia, he knew that from the talkative informer from the 110th Precinct.

The driver was aged anything between twenty-nine and forty. He had the round face and smiling eyes of a typical South American. Thick black hair and high cheekbones. His grin revealed one missing tooth, left of his two front teeth.

"Buenas noches." He got out and reached for Lucco's beat-up leather valise.

"You know the Hotel Tuparamanga?" asked Lucco in English. He had phoned from Miami and reserved a room.

"Sure thing," replied the driver, switching to English.

"No problems." And he put the valise in the trunk while Eddie Lucco climbed into the backseat, slamming the door behind him.

The interior smelled of tobacco and engine oil and peppermint. Nothing in "Advice To Travelers" had mentioned a Colombian predilection for peppermints. The bicycle-race commentary showed no signs of losing its laconic urgency and the driver—a stocky, well-built man of about five-seven—settled behind the wheel and started the engine.

As the Fiat made its way out from the airport environs, Lucco noticed a battered truck, painted blue and green and yellow, stopped by a junction, its driver wrestling with a wheel brace on the back wheel, which was jerked off the ground.

"Hey, asshole," called the taxi driver, pulling up alongside. "What's the problem?" All this in Spanish. The two men were laughing.

The truck driver, a younger man, straightened up and arched his aching back. "I need a new wheel, this one's from a different goddamn truck . . ." He looked pissed off. "How about giving me a ride, just to the garage? How about it?"

The driver shrugged. He turned and glanced at Lucco. *"Señor,* this is my wife's brother. You mind if we give him a ride for a couple of blocks? His truck is broke."

Lucco shrugged. A guy can get paranoid. "Sure," he said, "let's just get going." In English. No point in letting them know he spoke Spanish. And if it was a scam to roll him? Well, they picked the wrong damn guy. New York Homicide cops are not easy pickings.

But the young trucker was grinning as he climbed in. *"Muchas gracias, señor,"* he muttered, grateful, and smiled, his big brown Colombian eyes meeting the detective's casual gaze.

The taxi moved on, joining the crush of traffic, its radio still blaring the commentary on the bicycle race.

Eddie Lucco tried to see where the taxi's two-way radio was fixed, but the two men in the front blocked his view.

He moved, as if getting comfortable, and it became clear that while there was an aerial on the roof there sure as hell was no two-way radio inside the car.

Suckered.

Well, there was no way the cartel could have fixed for him to take that particular taxi, so if this was in any way sinister, it had to be a simple attempt at robbery. Lucco smiled at the thought of those two punks and the surprise that was coming to them if they tried anything. Goddamn, he thought, why can't life just be nice and simple?

———

It had taken some time to locate Malcolm Strong, who was riding on a ranch near Caracas with a Venezuelan bloodstock dealer and racehorse trainer, carrying out his operational task of quietly building up his cover. He had become, while still in Spain some months before, one Eduardo Cabezas Vega, a professional gambler, polo international, and suspected contract killer. He was now living in the home of a wealthy Venezuelan banker who was married to his "sister," both of them long-term and trusted assets of the British intelligence service.

The SIS staff at the Caracas embassy had contacted one of their operators working undercover as a doctor, and he had driven out to the ranch from where, with some story about Eduardo Cabezas's sister being ill, he had driven a slightly bewildered secret agent off toward Caracas.

Once in the car, the doctor, whom Strong knew socially, had astonished the former lawyer by identifying himself as an SIS man and conveying—in a coded form that allowed Malcolm Strong to understand, although the doctor was none the wiser—instructions to contact Century and to prepare to move to Bogotá by the afternoon of the next day.

Early on the Sunday morning, Ronnie Szabodo and Bill Jenkins were taking it in turns to man the Corrida room. Szabodo was dozing in the one comfortable chair when the weekend duty officer phoned up and said a top secret cipher Corrida Eyes Only had just been received in the main communications section from the Antioquia province of Colombia.

Szabodo sent Heather to collect the undeciphered message, and Eric, the cipher clerk on duty in West 8, soon had the floppy disc in his machine. The decrypting program buzzed and hummed, then it activated the printer and the VDU screen invited the operator to input the access codes necessary to persuade it to permit the printer to start work.

Eric typed in the access codes and the screen produced the message as the printer chattered out a copy of A-4 paper.

As each sheet came off, Eric passed it to Szabodo without reading it.

The deciphered message from Harry read:

Parcel. Sabaneta. 090114.

Am instructed by Keats to meet one—I spell: E.U.G.E.N.E.P.E.A.R.S.O.N.—endspell—who is judge. Dublin Appeal. location Bogota. Time Sunday 101200. E.P. in senior PIRA contact with CARTEL.

Keats Minor [this was Restrepo] has ordered PARCEL obtain from E.P. code for PIRA/CARTEL

632

Europe ongoing operation and Verify. Upon Verify comma PARCEL to Terminate E.P. quote no trace in Colombia unquote.

URGENT instruction requested from CONTROL. Maybe PARCEL deliver E.P. to FIRM Bogota query.

PARCEL moving will recontact for 2-way from location Bogota Sunday 0600 my local 7445

7445 meant the message ended there and Ford was not sending under duress.

Bill Jenkins arrived from the canteen. Szabodo handed him the signal. He read it three times, then handed it back. "Well, that's what I call serious intelligence. Did we know this Pearson chap was with the Brothers?"

The sewer children of Bogotá were not entirely without friends. Apart from church charities and older vagabonds—the one to minister to their spiritual needs and to give them shelter, the other to instruct them in the art of survival on the dangerous streets and alleys—there was a group of young people who worked in the traditional arts and crafts. Mostly from comfortable middle-class families. Somehow, they couldn't remember exactly when, they had taken to going down among the abandoned building sites, sewers, and urban wasteland, winning the confidence of the lost children and giving them food and clothing with a view to tempting some of them out of the sewers and into a home they had set up with their own money. There were three paid nurses, who themselves had once been orphans of the ditches, like little animals, with no understanding of the concept of hope.

That Sunday morning, instead of going to early Mass, three of those young people had taken some loaves of bread, some sausage, bottles of clean water, chocolate, fruit . . . and cigarettes.

They soon had a cluster of razor-toothed little humans, clad in filthy rags, surrounding them, all clamoring not for a share but for the lot. Laughing and calming them down, the three good Samaritans ensured that chocolate and cigarettes were evenly handed out.

After the initial feeding frenzy, one of the ruthless babes glanced at his fellows. By the shifty way they hung their heads and looked away, it was clear some kind of secret was being withheld from the visitors.

"What is it?" asked Maria de Lueva, a good-looking twenty-three-year-old with a master's degree in pre-Columbian Art. There was a muttered exchange between three of the leaders in a language that was barely intelligible as Spanish and finally one of them tugged at her sleeve.

Slightly apprehensive but with the courage of youth, which is immortal, the three followed the sewer children down into one of the main sewers, and after a stumbling, nauseating, ten-minute trek, they came out at the junction of three sewers in an excavated but abandoned construction site.

The man had been shot in the head, it seemed, for there was much blood encrusting his hair and his shoulders, but it was drying and the bleeding had stopped. His shirt had been ripped and a couple of slash marks from some kind of knife on his muscular stomach and side suggested he had been wearing a money belt, which had been cut away from his waist. His trouser pockets were turned inside out and one shoe was missing. The man had European rather than Spanish/Indian features. Some keys from Avis Miami lay nearby, and flapping open in a pool of rainwater, part of an airline ticket.

It was a depressing and familiar sight, in Bogotá.

Maria kneeled and crossed herself and laid a hand on the man's neck, feeling desolately empty that her beloved Colombia had not yet emerged into the light of the world.

———

David Jardine was having breakfast with Xavier Ramón when a coded copy of Harry Ford's signal was delivered to his Bogotá apartment, Ramón's ex-mistress's apartment, by the SIS junior from the British embassy, Steve Cunningham.

"I have to wait for a reply, Señor Herida," he said in excellent Spanish, with more than a hint of well-educated Colombian accent.

"Do you now," said Jardine, who had not shaved. Cunningham noticed a slight bruising around the legendary (to him) sphere controller's right upper cheek and eye. And the scar was quite livid.

"Xavier, excuse us for a few minutes." Jardine opened the envelope.

"Sure thing. I have to go around to the office. I'll be there when you're ready." Ramón rose and crossed to the door, picking up his jacket. His office was in a modern block in the banking quarter, maybe ten minutes' drive from the apartment.

David Jardine heard the elevator hum as the former DAS colonel descended to street level. He swiftly decoded the message and thought long and hard. For this was more like the old Harry Ford. Superb and timely intelligence.

Almost amazing. If anything could have amazed Jardine. Here was Judge Eugene Pearson, recently identified as the father of a teenage girl found dead of a crack OD in New York, himself the suspected object of pressure from Luís Restrepo Osorio and therefore the Medellín Cartel, in Bogotá.

That in itself was not amazing, for the man believed they were holding his daughter, what the hell was her name? Sian? Shona? But on a mission for the Provos? And destined to be murdered . . . Why?

What was so important to the cartel that they had gone to such homicidal lengths to entice Pearson, a senior, secret IRA person, doubtless of considerable influence in the Organization, from Dublin, where murder could be bought for a few bottles of stout, to Colombia and his death?

One answer and one answer only. Like the rest of the cartel's schemings, it had to do with vast sums of money. Jardine knew, from the anonymous informer who had sent him the Vigo discs, all about the cocaine link and the operational plans of the Lorca Group. The insistence of his informer that Lorca was a renegade faction cut no ice with David Jardine. He knew the Provos were already up to their elbows in heroin and marijuana dealing, which along with prostitution and extortion accounted for ten times more than the few hundred thousand from armchair terror junkies in the USA.

But Pearson's role was a mystery. He must be some kind of fixer, some kind of high-level emissary. Maybe the girl was being held to make him toe the line, for a judge would not, by the nature of his profession, be too keen to get involved with drugs. Jardine could see that. But why kill him out here? And leave no trace?

David Jardine's professional considering of those things could be likened to a top medical consultant looking at X-rays and the results of blood tests, along with notes on symptoms. Terrorist in-fighting, clandestine narcotics deals, international links between the two, and the Machiavellian scheming and exchange of murderous favors, they were the stuff of his particular experience and understanding.

Thus he considered that Eugene Pearson probably represented the more responsible element in the Provisional IRA who were against the Lorca Group's operation to receive and distribute cocaine from Colombia throughout Europe.

And the opposing element, the more cynical—perhaps practical, from their point of view—had somehow coerced Pearson into an involvement as go-between or whatever, and his daughter had been in the process of being lured to Colombia when she had slipped away in New York City, where she died in some seedy lavatory of an overdose of impure cocaine derivative.

How droll.

And as the wheel of fate turns on, Jardine's own deep penetration agent is tasked with carrying out the murder.

Well, strike me pink, thought Jardine.

He turned to the young SIS man, Cunningham.

"Tell London," he said, "we proceed as planned. Except we now know that Parcel will be here, in Bogotá. And my rendezvous with him must, repeat must, be effected before his meeting with Pearson. Can you remember that?"

Cunningham looked hurt. This was his absolute hero and Jardine doubted he could perform a simple task. He looked the senior man square in the eye and repeated the message verbatim. Including pauses.

Jardine smiled. "I'm sorry, Steve. This is a tricky one. You wouldn't be standing there if you were not the best."

And that made Steve Cunningham's day. Jardine could do these things with such ease. The young man smiled and shrugged. "Anything else, Miguel?"

Cheeky bastard, thought Jardine. He liked this guy. "Not right now," he said. And after Cunningham left, David Jardine sat down and thought as deeply as any experienced intelligence-agent runner and Jesuit convert could.

Finally he stretched, crossed to the bathroom, and ran a hot bath, pouring in some Original Badedas the owner or Xavier Ramón had put there.

And lolling in the bath, relaxing and breathing in the aroma, feeling it soak into his skin, David Arbuthnot Jardine actually did say, quite quietly, "Eureka . . ."

For if one followed the logic of his thinking on Pearson, cocaine, and the Provisional IRA, then it was not improbable (not improbable in Jardine-speak meant very likely) that Judge Eugene Pearson had sent the unsolicited intelligence denouncing the Lorca Group to Jardine's house, and his apartment, and his club.

For what was it Technical Section had noted in the forensic report on the writing paper posted from Dublin? From a batch supplied to the Irish legal service, something like that . . .

———

When Ramón arrived at his office that Sunday morning there were several messages on his answering machine. These reflected his wide range of contacts and informants.

One of the messages was from a nurse in the Hospitale de la Misericordia in the Eduardo Santos district, on Avenida Caracas and Avenida 1. A man had been brought in, robbed and shot. He was on a life-support machine and for a few moments had muttered incoherently, in English with an American accent. He had cuts on his side and stomach, where it appeared a money belt had been sliced away. And marks on his ankles indicated he had carried a gun holster taped to his left ankle and something else, less frequently, to his right.

A badge, thought Ramón. A cop. And since the nurse said it was touch and go for the *hombre*, he told his pretty young secretary, Francesca, to tell *el Inglés* when he called that he would be at the Misericordia Hospital, in downtown Bogotá.

Ramón went for two reasons, one because he was curious, and if the wounded man was some kind of U.S. government agent, say DEA or CIA, then there would be a good percentage in contacting the American embassy. The second was that he was slightly hurt that David Jardine had asked him to leave while the two SIS men discussed things he was, presumably, not trusted to hear. There was no one more trustworthy in Colombia than Xavier Ramón and he was justly proud of that fact.

So one factor that sent the ex-DAS colonel to the hospital was a half-admitted decision to remind Jardine that Ramón had other fish to fry and was not hanging on SIS's every whim.

As he walked along the corridor past open wards, with injured citizens being tended by nurses and harassed doctors, he nodded and exchanged clipped greetings with one or two staff and a couple of patients, for Ramón made it his business to know many different kinds of people.

He got to the emergency department and was directed to an intensive care unit behind a scene of some squalor, where a family of Indians were watching their father have a deep gash on his shoulder sutured.

There were three nurses clustered around the patient, efficiently disconnecting various tubes from the naked man on the gurney. His head was bandaged and the gashes on his side and stomach had been sutured.

"Well, this guy is sure getting a lot of attention," said Ramón gruffly, as he stood in the doorway. "I hope I get so many gorgeous nurses around me next time I'm wheeled in."

"You should pray you don't," replied one of the nurses, "this one's for the morgue . . ."

———

Harry Ford had no trouble slipping away for his clandestine meeting with whoever SIS had instructed to contact him in Bogotá. He first went with Murillo and Bobby Sonson to the Fontana Hotel and they identified Eugene Pearson, who was taking breakfast in the café off the elaborately paved courtyard surrounded by towering brick buttresses and neomedieval features.

He told the two *grupo* soldiers to keep the judge under observation, to note if he made any phone calls or spoke or glanced at anyone. He would be back in an hour. He then strolled out to his car, a nondescript-looking coupe that had been specially prepared for the *grupo* with armor plating, bulletproof windows, stiffened suspension, and a souped-up engine.

Harry gazed around, checking out the area. Apart from one or two obvious security men and a couple of bodyguards for one of the hotel guests, there was nothing. He climbed into the Toyota and drove out past the wrought-iron security gates and headed for his rendezvous. It was cool and blustery, with great dark clouds pushing each other across the sky.

Ramón stood alone in the hospital mortuary, gazing at the cadaver. Sounds of busy hospital life going on beyond the rubberized double swing doors of the white-tiled room only heightened the cold, absolute aloneness of death.

A fine-looking big fellow, this victim of what the airport police called "the Bogotá welcome." There were generally ten or twelve such killings every day. But this one had been some kind of law-enforcement officer. Ramón did not need forensic evidence, for he recognized it in the *hombre*'s face. Poor bastard. And an Avis rental-car key. He would check if Avis had rented a car to the dead man. No one had thought to mention the airline ticket, by now part of the rainwater pool where five sewers met.

The petite nurse who had informed him of the casualty poked her head around the doors. "Colonel, there is a man to see you."

And before Ramón could ask who, David Jardine had gently squeezed past the nurse and smiled ruefully to the Colombian standing by the mortuary table, on the far side of the corpse. Ramón nodded. The nurse left.

Jardine hardly noticed the dead body. "I didn't mean to be rude to you back there."

Ramón shrugged. "Forget it."

"Xavier, I need to secure an area pretty fast."

"What for?"

"Rendezvous. Other man, the main guy . . ." Jardine used the word "our" deliberately. He guessed his agent's pride had been wounded.

Ramón shrugged, his hooded eyes amused. "Why not?"

Jardine swiftly and quietly told him what he required, the lifeless thing on the table ignored. He wanted an area secured for a covert meeting and someone to watch for watchers. Also he would require a personal weapon. Ramón knew *el Inglés* favored a 9mm Uzi pistol, with three twenty-round magazines, fully loaded.

"Sure. No problem."

Finally the Englishman glanced at the corpus of

Eddie Lucco, sizing up the sutured wounds professionally. "Someone we know?"

"Just some John Doe," replied Ramón. "It's no big deal . . ."

And they strolled out of the morgue and headed for the elevators.

642

22

TORO

Meeting a deep-cover agent in a hostile environment was always risky, but no one was safer or more experienced a field operator than Jardine.

He had selected the rendezvous with regard to every parameter required to ensure privacy, ease of escape, and covering fire from his own wingers. He had arrived early and walked through the environment, checking for the tell-tale signs of a setup. The place was clean.

The SIS man had chosen a narrow artists' quarter in the foothills of the National Park, above the road that was used in the weekday rush hours to escape the city's monumental traffic jams. Having positioned himself, and with Ramón's men and women, twenty of them, covering the area, David Jardine settled himself into the doorway of a small, cramped store selling drawing and painting materials. It being Sunday, the place was closed.

They could hear the powerful, deep growl of the Toyota's exhausts quite a few seconds before it climbed into view.

He would never forget, *el Inglés,* how, further up the steep and narrow potholed road the profound clanging of church bells suddenly started, just as the Toyota drove past the rendezvous point and stopped.

The driver's door opened and Harry Ford climbed out. Jardine realized he was pleased to see his agent. The boy was gone. This was a tanned and hard-faced man, with quick, wary, hunter's eyes. He seemed to speak to someone in the car. Then, brushing his hand across his jacket instinctively to check his piece was exactly in the right place, he strolled down and stopped to gaze into the store window.

"Well, we are honored," he said, in English. "I somehow thought you were in London . . ."

"Who's in the car?" asked Jardine tensely.

"Just my dog. I've inherited, been adopted by, this bloody great dog. David, it's not very smart having this place crawling with Xavier's people. Christ, if they see me with you . . . You can bet at least one of them is on the take from Pablo."

My word, we are growing up, thought Jardine. Without looking at Harry, he said, "Further up this hill there is a small cemetery and a tiny chapel. You are to bring the judge to the cemetery, and you will tell—who's with you?"

"Murillo and Sonson."

"Well, nobody said this was going to be a cakewalk. Bring them to the cemetery, and tell them that's where you're going to do the business. Then you and I take out one each, just immediately you are all inside the place.

There's a huge black angel with spreading wings, like a fucking great hawk, ten o'clock as you go in. I'll be there, kneeling and praying, we do it instantly, *en seguida*. Then you and I take Pearson to a safe house where his debriefing will start at once. You know Señor Eduardo Cabezas, I think . . ." And Jardine indicated a man strolling past on the other side of the narrow street.

It was Malcolm Strong. Baggage. He paused to light a cheroot, then moved on. Passing out of sight.

Harry Ford experienced a moment's loss of grip on reality, reminded for some reason of *Alice in Wonderland*. "What the hell is he doing here? What is this Jardine, a fucking garden party?"

"After we kill Murillo and Sonson, you will not be going back to Pablo. You will be taken to an apartment in Bogotá, where you will be debriefed and where you will then spend a few days with Eduardo, telling him everything he will need to know in order to infiltrate the cartel."

Harry Ford stared at Jardine, trying to mask his sudden alarm. If he disappeared, leaving Murillo and Sonson dead in a bloody cemetery, Restrepo would find some way to get at his two million dollars, his and Elizabeth's, earning good interest in BCCI. No question. Play for time, he told himself. Think fast.

"David, there's something you don't know. Pearson thinks he's coming here to trade a code for his daughter. Listen, I don't know how much you people know about all this, what's going down here . . ."

Christ, thought Jardine, they really have taken you into their bosom. And suddenly SIS is "you people." "Go on," he said.

"Well, the girl is dead. I don't know how, but she's been dead for months. And Pearson is to be killed after they confirm his access codes are good. Apparently it's a favor for the Provisionals."

"That really changes nothing. Bring him to the cemetery. With the two hoods. End of story." Finally, he turned to look his agent in the eye. This was not going well.

Harry Ford seemed . . . thrown, as if he had plans of his own. "David, for God's sake don't throw it all away. Look, I can bring Pearson up here alone, tell the two bozos to wait someplace . . ."

"Don't be naive. The *grupo* will require confirmation of the hit. They won't let you waltz off on your own."

"Wrong! You have no idea how much Don Pablo trusts me."

Really . . . ?

"And once I hand Pearson over to you, I can go back to Medellín. Surely I'm doing a good job. Jesus Christ, Pablo thinks I saved his life, I could not be in tighter . . ."

"Just do what you're told, there's a good chap. Be at the cemetery between three and four." Jardine held Harry's outraged glare. "Look, Carlos, you're on a high. I've seen this kind of stuff. It's dangerous for all of us. But don't worry, we have lots of interesting work for you. And delivering a top Provo is a feather in your cap. I wouldn't be surprised if I can arrange a bonus . . ."

"Oh, great!" Harry Ford went to go, then turned back. "Just don't have the chorus line with you this afternoon, or I won't stop. I'll drive right on, understand? Good."

And clearly furious, the SIS operator strode back up the hill to his car.

Dear oh dear, thought David Jardine. The boy is doing himself no favors.

———

The suite in the Hotel La Fontana was spacious for one man, with its own kitchen and a sitting room with a study area separated by a dark wood bookcase.

Eugene Pearson was in excellent spirits as he glanced at his watch, sat down beside the phone with a glass of Coca-Cola, and tried to read his Mario Vargos Llosa book. But he couldn't concentrate and he got up, crossed to the window, gazed out over Bogotá. It did not seem so terrible, so violent as everyone made out.

He had sat down again, for the fourth time. He wondered if they would bring Siobhan with them. Surely to God he had suffered enough . . .

The door buzzer sounded.

His heart thumping, Pearson crossed to the door and peered through the spy hole. A man he had never seen before, a fit-looking bugger, aged about twenty-nine. It was Harry Ford.

"Who is it?" he called.

"It's Señor Diaz, about the theater tickets." It was the correct reply. And there was definitely somebody else there. Please Jesus let it be her.

Pearson's hands were trembling slightly as he undid the burglar chain and unlocked the door. He opened it cautiously, wondering if she would have changed. If his darling would look any older.

But it was just the man who called himself Diaz and that bastard bodyguard of Restrepo's, whatever his name was. (It was Murillo.) They strolled in, Harry glancing very professionally around the room. Murillo strode through to the bedroom and searched the bathroom and the closets without so much as a by your leave. Christ he would be glad to be rid of these people.

"Is she here?" he asked. "Is she in the hotel?"

"Your daughter's fine, Mr. Pearson." Diaz spoke good English, with just a trace of South American accent. "She asked me to give you this . . ." And he took a postcard from his pocket and handed it to Pearson, smiling. He was a decent enough fellow, this Diaz.

The postcard was of the interior of some Colombian

opera house with an arrow, in ink, pointing at the pianist, center-stage. "That'll be me one day!" said her unmistakable scrawl on the other side. "Love, Siobhan. XXXXX."

He swallowed as tears filled his eyes. Harry was looking at him with a certain sympathy. He patted Pearson on the arm.

"Won't be long now, *señor*. Do you have the codes?"

"Of course, but I would prefer to hand them over simultaneously."

Harry looked confused. "Simultaneous with what?"

"With the exchange of my daughter."

Harry blushed crimson. "My dear man. Señor. Your daughter has been our honored guest. Nothing more." Harry clapped a hand to his face. Murillo thought that was going a bit far. "You did not think we had kidnapped her?!" He laughed grimly. "Dear God, what a reputation us poor Colombians have."

Since when did you become a Colombian, you Chilean *gaucho*, thought Murillo, but he kept his mouth shut.

"Well, I would still prefer to have her with me. Shall we go?" Pearson could be quite a tough old bird, when he needed to.

Harry scratched his head. "Look, here are my orders, from Señor Envigado. You have had the pleasure of meeting him, he tells me."

"Get to the point, Diaz."

"Señor Pearson, I am to obtain the access codes from you. I understand they will be on a three-and-a-half inch disc. Then Señor Murillo here will take them to a colleague who is just in another room, right along the corridor." Harry flopped down on the leather couch and spread his arms. "It will take no more than a few minutes to verify that the access codes are—that they work. Then you and I will drive to the place where your daughter is waiting." Eugene Pearson did not like the tone in which Diaz had calmly said "I am to *obtain* the access codes." The meaning was clear.

"Well . . . If I have your word I will be with my daughter immediately after."

"Within the hour, I guarantee it," said Harry with honest sincerity. Behind Pearson, Murillo glanced at Harry Ford, expressionless.

Pearson considered for a long moment. Then he shrugged and went through to the bedroom. After a couple of seconds, he came back and handed a thick, manila envelope to Harry.

"Everything's there," he said. "Get on with it."

Harry threw the envelope to Murillo, who went out of the room.

"Make yourself comfortable, Señor Judge," said Harry.

"That's rich," replied Eugene Pearson. "This *is* my room."

Harry grinned his wolf's grin. "Ah, *sí*. But it's my town . . ."

In New York City, Captain Danny Molloy had made an unusual change to his routine. He went into the 14th Precinct on a Sunday. In the months to come, he could never explain why. After a few routine stops, on radio operators, on the cages, with the detectives who were working weekend shifts, he chanced upon the duty officer for the detective squads, Sergeant Sid Mercer. Mercer brought him up to date with the weekend occurrences, including a laconic mention that Eddie Lucco was down in Miami on a case.

"Miami? I'll fuckin Miami him. How do I contact him?"

"He did not leave a contact, Captain."

"Okay, next time he phones in, I want him on the first plane back. This is a busy city, Mercer, I need good detectives here. Not in fuckin Coconut Grove, all right?"

And Sid Mercer said, All right, Captain. And Danny Molloy left. But Eddie Lucco never did phone in.

———

Ramón listened unhappily to David Jardine, who had told him he would not require further assistance that day.

"David, you are crazy. I watched you talking with Carlos Nelson. Listen, I don't know much but I'm telling you, buddy, that guy has fallen in love with the life of a *narcotraficante*. He's a couple of million richer, buddy, you think he's going to come running back to the British government? *Ni pu'el putas!* No fuckin way, José . . ."

"Xavier, I've made other arrangements, that's all."

"You think SIS from the embassy can do something I can't? Me and my boys?"

"No, I don't. I just think you do different things, extremely well."

Ramón looked frustrated. He lifted his shoulders in a very South American gesture. "So tell me, I have to know. What should Carlos do to get off the hook? And do you think he knows he's being tested?"

Jardine stuck his hands in his pockets and leaned against the wall. They were standing beside Jardine's beat-up Nissan jeep, in a street beside the University de los Andes. Malcolm Strong was sitting in the jeep, dozing peacefully.

"What should he do . . . ? Ideally, Xavier, he should manage to deliver Pearson without Murillo and Sonson. He would then, as he rightly says, be in a position to return to the cartel. But he would also have to declare his personal wealth, from the *grupo*, and offer to bring my other agent"—Jardine indicated Strong, in the jeep—"into Pablo's acquaintance. Quite frankly I don't hold out much hope."

"He could also come to the cemetery with a bunch of hoods and blow you away. Or even capture you, buddy, and take you home to Medellín. That would be some fuckin trophy. That would get him in real tight with Pablo."

Jardine smiled. "Nothing is without risk."

Murillo was taking longer than Harry had expected. He glanced at his watch. Only ten minutes had passed.

"What's keeping them?" asked Pearson. "It's a simple enough process."

Harry shrugged. "Can I get you some more Coke, *señor?*"

"I think I'll explode if I have any more." This Diaz fellow seemed nice enough. A big improvement on that bastard Restrepo, whom Eugene Pearson had never encountered without some fresh horror. Pearson felt quite relaxed in the new man's company.

"There is one item of information you people should know," he suddenly confided in Harry. "I should really write it down, for your security people."

Harry smiled. *"Señor,* I am chief of security for Don Pablo's entire group."

Ah. That would explain the man's quiet confidence. "In that case, Mr. Diaz . . ." Pearson lowered his voice, ". . . you should be aware that my organization's Intelligence Department has learned the British MI-Six has infiltrated a man into your midst." He sat back, pleased to have delivered such a shot.

The *grupo*'s security chief stared at him. Then nodded gravely. "Tell me more . . ."

"Apparently he will have appeared, this snooper, quite recently. Excellent credentials. Fluent Spanish. Good background that will stand up to investigation. But he's a trained SIS operator."

Harry forced himself to relax into his armchair. "Do you have a name?"

"Sadly, no."

"Description . . . ?"

"No. Only that he is a yellow fellow."

"And how did you people acquire this information?"

Judge Eugene Pearson smiled. He leaned forward, confidential. "As a matter of fact, we have a priest in London who hears confession from one of the top brass in SIS."

"Que puteria!" exclaimed Harry Ford, not needing to pretend his astonishment.

"Well, apparently this fellow is running the agent and feels an access of guilt, because, you guess, *señor . . .*"

"I couldn't begin to." Harry smiled politely.

"Because he's fucking the young fellow's wife. Two or three times a day."

Harry Ford stood up and strode across to the window. His heart had stopped. He felt his chest was about to explode. He tried to concentrate on the mundane view from the window.

"In his place, in her place, apparently she's quite a beauty and the old fellow can't get enough of it."

"Really?" Harry found himself saying, and noticed he had dropped the South American accent.

"There are things she likes doing to tell you the truth I had never heard of."

Shut up shut up you doddering old fool. Harry looked at his watch. His wrist was trembling.

The door opened and Murillo entered with Bobby Sonson.

"It all checks out," said Murillo. "Time to go."

Pearson was out of his chair and moving to the door, picking up his jacket on the way. Rushing to meet his lost child. Harry stopped him. He spoke to the two *grupo* men with authority.

"Check the lobby. Sonson, take the stairs and meet us out front."

"*Sí,* Carlos." The two men went out.

Harry turned to Eugene Pearson. He felt a thousand years old. Sad, betrayed, and . . . bereaved. But cool now. He knew what had to be done.

"Thank you, *señor.* You must not breath a word of this information to anyone. You are in mortal danger."

Pearson nodded. These dagos tended to exaggerate. "Sure. Not another word. But you should take steps to root him out."

"Don't worry." Harry opened the door and glanced out. "Let's go."

———

The blackened stone angel was indeed like a bloody great hawk.

Its shadow fell across the broken iron gates as Murillo strolled into the cemetery, a bunch of flowers in one hand. Behind him, Harry Ford guided Pearson, holding on to his elbow. His face was cold and resolved.

Bobby Sonson locked the doors of the Toyota and followed.

There was one man, shabbily dressed in a cheap black suit, kneeling in prayer to the left of, and slightly beyond, the huge dark angel.

"Is this where the hand-over's to take place?" asked the judge in a hushed voice. He was so used to the IRA's habit of meeting in undertakers and at graveyards that he did not sense anything amiss. He glanced at Harry, who turned back to Sonson, who had just entered the cemetery.

"Is this—" Blood again, Jesus Christ the horror all over again, blood hot blood on his face the side of his face, and deafening noise of gunfire, and Sonson, ten feet behind them, was staggering, like a drunk puppet and BLAM! BLAM! BLAM! Señor Diaz was crouched, loosing off rapid bullets from his big black automatic, but the blood what was the blood? Pearson was on his hands and knees. He turned his head, the blood was still coming from out of the back of Murillo, who had dropped onto his knees and was spraying bright red blood from a severed artery.

Silence. Except for the screaming. It took a slap across the head from Diaz to make Eugene Pearson realize it was he who was screaming.

Trembling and shivering like a fallen horse, Pearson allowed Harry to haul him to his feet. The man in the black suit stepped forward, holding some kind of small submachine gun.

Murillo lay face up, his chest a soaking mess of dark blood. Sonson had fallen, crumpled, onto the ground.

"I don't understand . . ." Pearson heard himself say, lamely.

"Your daughter is dead, old man," Harry said, without a trace of a Spanish accent. "Siobhan Pearson died several months ago of an overdose of crack in a filthy lavatory in Grand Central Station. New York."

The hammer blow visibly rocked Pearson.

"My orders, from Luís Restrepo, are to kill you. This is part of a deal he made with Brendan Casey. You've been set up."

My baby my precious baby oh dear Christ. Pearson's glance fell on the man's pistol. His trouser leg became wet and warm. His senses aquiver, he could smell his own piss. And gun oil, from the man, and alcohol—rum, it was—on his tormentor's breath.

"By the Blessed Virgin, sir. Don't kill *me*. Please don't kill me." Judge Eugene Pearson fell on his knees and gripped Harry Ford's legs. "I beseech you."

The man in black stepped closer.

Harry took Pearson by the hair. "You must know a lot about the Provisional IRA."

"Jesus Christ, I am their policy man on the Army Council, I know everything. Don't shoot me, oh Hail Mary full of grace—"

"Be quiet."

David Jardine was amazed at the cold control Harry Ford was demonstrating. Whatever else, this was one hard *hombre*.

"I am the SIS officer you were informed about."

"Holy Mary."

"If spared, will you go directly with this man to a safe house where you will tell the British everything?"

"Yes. Yes . . ."

"Active Service Units . . . plans, targets, sleepers? The lot?"

"Everything, everything . . ." Pearson was sobbing uncontrollably.

Harry Ford turned to Jardine, his face flushed as if he was on some kind of high. "You hear that? You hear it? This man will open up the Provos' innermost treasures, their crown jewels, to SIS."

"Brilliant. Absolutely brilliant. Well done."

Harry smiled with some difficulty. His grip on his pistol was relaxed, Jardine noticed and knew that was a bad sign. "Help your career, David? Help your reputation . . . ?"

"Come on, let's get out of here. The man is a gem, okay?"

"That's what I wanted to hear, David."

"David . . . ?" Eugene Pearson frowned, lost in a fugue of grief and terror.

Then Harry Ford shouted, "You bastard! You treacherous, betraying bastard! You fucking whore!!"

Jardine went cold.

"Elizabeth! You wanton, desperate bastard! That was my wife! I loved her!!" And with a casual flick of the wrist, he shot Judge Eugene Pearson between the eyes. The judge looked quite surprised as his lifeless body toppled onto its side.

What happened next was something for which David Jardine would never be able to forgive himself or find forgiveness. No one on earth could blame him for firing first as Harry brought his Sig-Sauer P 226 in a sweeping curve toward his boss, the man he had trusted.

It was a short burst of five rounds that went straight through the heart of Captain Harry Ford, MC. But his heart had already been broken.

A - 17

10th up